I0763308

Mythras Roleplaying in Dark Ages Britain

ISBN: 978-0-9877259-5-0

CREDITS

Developed and Written By
Lawrence Whitaker
Additional Material by Pete Nash

Editing
Carol Johnson

Proof Reading
Lisa Tyler

Design and Layout
Alexandra James

Artists
Cover by Antonio Jose Manzanedo Luis

Pablo Castilla, Dan MacKinnon, Pascal Quidault, Michael Wolmarans
Alan Gallo and Eric Lofgren (Alan and Eric courtesy of Outland Entertainment)

Cartography
Colin Driver

Playtesters
John Bell, Colin Driver, Tim Evans, David Finch, Chris Gilmore, Jude Hornburg, John Hutchinson, Sebastian Jansson, Marcus Knapp, Adam Lundrgren, Brad Milburn, Pete Nash, Blain Neufeld, Michael O'Brien, Carl Pates, Sebastian Sandman, Erik Sharma and Howard Tytherleigh

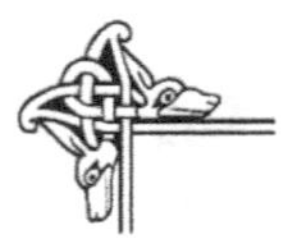

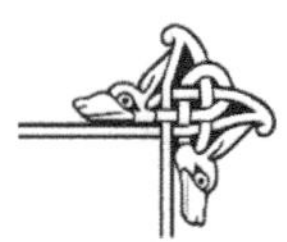

Dedication

This book is dedicated to the players and characters of the *Mythic Britain* playtests, conducted between 2011 and 2014 at the annual PeteCon summit held in Boden, northern Sweden, and at the fortnightly Toronto roleplaying sessions. The players are listed above. Their characters are:
Sweden: Ceinwyn, Culwch, Curwan, Dagrun, Efford, Eowald, Forni, Galahad, Glanwyr, Isca, Lanval, Nimue and Tristan
Toronto: Aed, Aild, Ayn, Cunnan, Cynan and Gwynneth
Mythic Britain is also dedicated to Bernard Cornwell, whose "Warlord Chronicles" were a huge inspiration and influence, and to Greg Stafford, who first trod the Mythic Island of Britain with "King Arthur Pendragon".
Without these friends, players, characters, writers and creators, this book would not exist.

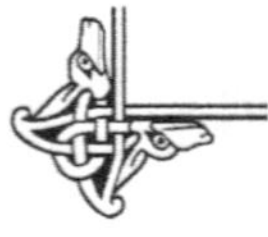

Contents

INTRODUCTION

This book concerns the British Isles during one of its most elusive and enigmatic periods: the so-called Dark Ages. It examines the culture and society of the post-Romanic era, speculating on life in the 5th and early 6th Centuries. It looks at the myths, beliefs, and magic of the Celts; it offers some views on legendary figures such as Vortigern, Uther, Arthur, and Merlin. Its intent is to provide a solid, gritty background for MYTHRAS adventures and campaigns, taking its cues from history, myth, and a few fictional sources such as Bernard Cornwell's Arthurian trilogy *The Warlord Chronicles*.

However, this is not necessarily an Arthurian book, although Arthur certainly figures in Mythic Britain, because he is intrinsically associated with the Dark Ages period. Rather, Mythic Britain is an exploration of the Dark Ages with as much focus on more general themes, including the Saxon invasion, as on the romance of the Arthurian story.

The book is divided into two distinct parts. The first part describes Britain and presents the games mechanics appropriate to the Mythic Britain era. The second part is a campaign consisting of seven scenarios that draw extensively on the previous chapters. The book's structure is as follows:

History

Britain's history up to, and including, the early 6th Century CE. This chapter forms the basis for the information in this book and the campaign scenarios.

Kingdoms

A description of Mythic Britain's kingdoms, ranging from the Pictish lands of the north, down to the lands of the south. The chapter also provides an overview of Logres - the Saxon lands.

Celtic Life and Society

The culture, daily lives, social conventions, and other background information essential to understanding the Celts of Mythic Britain and roleplaying a Celtic character.

Mythic Britain Characters

Full rules for creating Celt and Saxon characters, including new and modified cultural backgrounds, professions, skills, Passions, and so on.

Gods, Religion and Magic

Pagan and Christian beliefs and religions are examined, explained, and presented for play. This chapter supplies more detail on the druids and the Gods of Britain, along with rules for early Christian beliefs and worship. The nature and extent of magic is described here – how it works (or does not, according to belief), along with rules for using the different magic systems of MYTHRAS in a Dark Age world.

Britain At War

Rules concerning combat and battle in Dark Ages Britain. Armour, weapons, and equipment; Combat Styles; warbands; and strategy and tactics.

Mythic Britons

Descriptions and statistics for a wide range of Dark Age personalities, including Arthur, Merlin, Vortigern, and others.

The Mythic Britain Campaign

A set of scenarios forming a campaign arc, beginning in the year 495.

Rules for Mythic Britain

This is not a standalone game. Games Masters and players will need access to the MYTHRAS rules, but this is the only essential resource.

For an enhanced experience, we strongly advise some additional reading. The Bibliography on page 360 provides a list of books useful for learning more about this period and its myths. Reading some of the fiction and non-fiction suggested here will give players and Games Masters a great deal of inspiration and a real feeling for the period and its people.

Aside from the MYTHRAS rules and perhaps some additional reading, you need only this book, your imagination (and the imaginations of some friends), some dice, and a desire to travel back in time 1,500 years

Historical Accuracy

This book takes substantial liberties with Britain's history of the immediate post-Romanic period. Historical accounts of the time began a century after the period Mythic Britain covers, and continued for several centuries afterwards. They are incomplete, contradictory, and probably exercised their own liberties with historical truth. Indeed, even contemporary scholarly resources differ in their views and interpretation of Celtic society in the first half of the first millennium.

The simple facts are that little is known of the period, sources are unreliable in many places, and so what actually happened will never be known. The fun of a book such as this is that one can speculate and extrapolate. We have done just that. History provides the cues for imagination, and Mythic Britain mixes historical fact (where it is reliable enough), the wealth of Celtic and Saxon myth, and the MYTHRAS rules to create a believable setting for fantasy campaigns. So this book should be viewed as a work of fiction inspired by a mixture of history, historical fiction, necessary speculation and extrapolation, and even some deliberate twisting of the facts.

History and Overview

Britain and Ireland form Mythic Britain. These lands are the body of the Great Red Dragon who lives between the Mortal World and the World of the Gods. From its dreams is born the Spirit World, and within the Spirit World, but distinct from it, is the Other World, which is where mortals go upon death, to remain forever blessed and forever young.

Mortals cannot see the Great Red Dragon, but they can feel its presence in the wind, in the sun, and in the strength of the earth. The spirits, born of its dreams, are invisible but all around us, and can be seen by the druids, who are blessed by the Gods and the Dragon with such keen sight.

The Gods, who made All Things, are remote from mortals, but aware of them and needful of their belief. They live in their own land, also made of the body of the Dragon, and tell their own stories and do their own deeds, continually, living, dying, and being reborn. These actions perpetuate the cycle of Creation.

Side by side with the Great Red Dragon stands the Great White Dragon. It, too, forms the islands of Britain, but it is a baleful force that favours enemies and invaders. Normally it sleeps and the Great Red Dragon is all-powerful. But things have been changed with the coming of the Romans and the massacre of the druids. The Great White Dragon has awoken and the Great Red Dragon sleeps. Invader gods and invader peoples assail Britain. First, the Romans with their gods, then the Saxons with theirs, and now the One God of the Eastern Lands and his worshippers who call themselves Christians.

The Old Ways are dying. The Red Dragon is besieged. The Old Gods grow more distant; and the local spirits, overrun by spirits created by the White Dragon, have become evil and scheming.

If Britons do not challenge, if Britons do not fight, then the Red Dragon will die and all shall die with it, leaving a land welcoming of enemies and shadows, false gods, and evil ways. Celts shall become corpses and slaves. Parents shall mourn their children's souls, and the Bridges of Swords and Sighs will be sundered.

Now is the time to fight. For Britain! For the Red Dragon!

Britain and Magic

Britain was once a land rich in magic. In the Time of Heroes, long before anywhere else existed, everyone could work magic through cooperation with the spirits. When the Time of Heroes came to an end, and the Great Red Dragon separated the Spirit and Mortal Worlds, the druids were chosen as the sole custodians of the knowledge of magic and became its only practitioners. A druid is one who has etched on their bones the runes, carved there by the Great Red Dragon. Only with the runes so etched can magic be worked.

The druids were strong for uncounted years. Then the Romans came, in the reign of the Emperor Claudius, and enslaved Britain. They brought with them their invader gods, stolen from the Greeks, Egyptians, and others: Jupiter, Mars, Venus, Isis, and Mithras. They betrayed the druids and slaughtered them, almost completely, at the Holy Glade on Ynys Mon, above the very eye of the Great Red Dragon. From then on, magic faded in Britain. A few druids escaped the massacre, but they were forced to hide themselves and their powers. The Treasures of Britain, an inheritance from the Time of Heroes, were plundered and lost. Magic became weak, and it is only now that the Romans have gone, and the druids can emerge from their hiding places, that magic can regain its strength.

From the Anglo Saxon Chronicle

A.D. 449. This year Marcian and Valentinian assumed the empire and reigned seven winters. In their days Hengest and Horsa, invited by Vortigern, king of the Britons to his assistance, landed in Britain in a place that is called Ipwinesfleet; first of all to support the Britons, but they afterwards fought against them. The king directed them to fight against the Picts; and they did so; and obtained the victory wheresoever they came. They then sent to the Angles, and desired them to send more assistance. They described the worthlessness of the Britons, and the richness of the land. They then sent them greater support.

For those who believe in the Old Gods, magic is real and present. The druids can work simple charms and cantrips, as well as more powerful magic such as channelling the powers of the spirits and shape-shifting (again with spirit help). Non-druidic Britons never dabble in magic: they are not schooled in its ways and to do so is too dangerous. Magic is highly ritualised, secretive, and shrouded in lore. Without the depth of knowledge possessed by the druids, magic is impossible to work.

Those who believe in the Christian God reject magic entirely. Only God and His Son can work miracles, although occasionally they work through Saints to perform isolated acts of wonder. According to them, the magic of the druids is, in fact, the work of Satan; for it is clear in the Holy Scriptures that there is only One God and all other gods are false. Magic, then, is devilry. Spirits are demons who beguile and corrupt; charms and cantrips are direct blasphemies. Those who worship God and receive magic are sinners who must beg forgiveness or risk damnation.

The Saxons have their own gods and their own magic, although it is very similar, in practice and effect, to the magic of the druids. There is thus no practical difference between druidic magic and that of the Saxons.

Kings, Betrayers

Britain's history involves many important, legendary people. The key figures are Vortigern, Uther, Merlin, Arthur, Mark, and the Saxons Hengest and Horsa and, later, Aelle. It is a combination of ambition, treachery, and divided loyalties, resulting in war and chaos. The druids, and Merlin foremost among them, actually trace the roots of Britain's strife to the Roman conquest, the defeat of Boudicca, and the massacre of the druids at Ynys Mon. These events of the last 50 years caused the Red Dragon to sleep and for the White Dragon to wake.

So recent history — that which shapes Britain in this mythic time, begins with abandonment.

Abandonment and Vortigern.

The Roman Exodus and Vortigern's Rise

Rome abandoned Britain early in the 5th Century, in the reign of the Emperor Valentinian; its people steadily retreating to the heart of the empire and leaving the Celts to their own fate. In the first decades of this century, the Celtic tribes united under a loose confederation with a council headed by an agreed king. First of these kings was Vortigern, a successful warlord of Powys who brought about the unification with blood and iron, but created a culture of alliance that persisted for more than a century. The tribes frequently warred with each other even under this alliance, but the council helped provide settlement for disputes that might otherwise have escalated into all-out war between the tribes. This was Vortigern's success and his legacy. It was also his failure and downfall.

Vortigern was a clever and inspiring leader, but also ambitious and arrogant. Aided by omens and prophecies, he believed he was destined to rule the length of the island, south to north, succeeding where even the Romans had failed, establishing a kingdom beyond the Great Wall built by the Emperor Hadrian. Knowing that even with the tribes united he would never have the strength to conquer the lands of the Picts beyond the Wall, Vortigern sent emissaries to the tribes beyond the Northern Sea to find mercenaries. Many promises were made. Those who came to Vortigern's aid would be granted lands, rights to settle, cattle, and

Merlin and Vortigern

At that time, Merlin was a wandering druid, staying in no one place for very long. He was old, even then, and claimed to have witnessed the massacre at Ynys Mon. He came at last to Vortigern's hill fort for the Festival of Beltane and was made welcome in Vortigern's hall. Vortigern told Merlin of his plans to conquer the Picts and unite Britain as one kingdom. He introduced his mercenary allies. Some had said that his plans would fail: Vortigern asked Merlin for his insight.

Merlin reached into the Spirit World. He was quiet for a very long time. When Vortigern pressed for an answer, Merlin was grave and cryptic. "There are two dragons and they fight for supremacy. Only one can win. While two dragons are awake, there can be no peace, no stability, and no kings. You have awoken the White Dragon, Lord Vortigern. And it shall rock the world and bring much sadness to those blessed by the Red Dragon."

The druid would say no more, despite Vortigern's pleas. Outraged, Vortigern ordered Merlin from his hall, but Vortigern's greatest chieftain, Uther, had heard Merlin's words and understood what was meant. He gave Merlin a place in his own hall, and the two become friends and allies, while Vortigern made plans with the foreign warlords.

sheep; and be treated with the honour and respect the Celts were famed for. Mercenaries duly came — in small numbers at first, with only three ships making the journey to pledge themselves to Vortigern's cause. Vortigern, as High King of the Britons, made good on his promises and so more warriors, the Saxons (so-called for their knives, known as seax), came to the island.

Vortigern and his Saxon mercenaries, led by Hengest and Horsa, took his campaign to the lands beyond the Wall and failed. Repelled by the harsh landscape and overwhelmed by the ferocity of the Pictish tribes, his army had no option but to retreat. He blamed the Saxon mercenaries for this defeat, claiming poor organisation and even treachery — anything but admit that his own ambition lay at the heart of the failure. Vortigern reneged on his promises, demanding the Saxons leave Britain even though lands and rights had been granted. The Saxon leaders, Horsa and Hengest, demanded that the promises be kept. Furthermore, they warned that more of their people were coming, encouraged by all that Vortigern had offered. Vortigern refused and so began the war between the Celts and Saxons that would dominate the next one hundred years.

Some of the Celtic tribes sided with Vortigern. Others, such as the Dumnonii, led by Uther, would have no part in Vortigern's hubris and left the alliance. This divided the Celts into two separate regions (those loyal to Vortigern in the east and those loyal to Uther in the west) and greatly weakened both. Horsa and Hengest, strengthened by the mass of Saxons arriving in larger and more frequent numbers, made war against Vortigern. The East Celts and Saxons clashed in four battles waged across the southeast of Britain. Horsa was slain in 455. Hengest and his son, Esc, continued the war with Vortigern as subsequent waves of Saxons landed in the east and south of Britain. Vortigern managed to slow the Saxon advance and made continual pleas to Uther for help to drive the them completely from the shores. Uther refused. By now, invaders from Ireland plagued the western coast and all of Uther's energies were consumed with battling them, as well as dealing with several long-standing tribal feuds that had asserted themselves in the wake of the split from Vortigern. Thus, the eastern tribes found themselves alone.

Vortigern was defeated in the year 465, his army routed by Hengest and Esc's forces at the Battle of Wippedsfleot on the south coast. Vortigern survived the battle and offered a truce with the Saxons; Hengest and Esc accepted and a feast was arranged to seal the peace that Vortigern proposed (which gave the Saxons extensive lands between Londinium and the Wall). And here the Saxons executed their own betrayal.

The feast was held in a hall built especially for the truce. Many Saxon warlords and their retinues attended, outnumbering Vortigern and his loyal chiefs. Vortigern was untroubled by this, believing that the lands he was about to give Hengest and Esc would more than guarantee a lasting peace. Again, Vortigern was wrong. The food and drink was drugged. Saxon warriors defied the rules of hospitality and brought weapons into the feast hall. On a signal given by Esc, the warriors rose up for the kill. Vortigern's warlords were massacred: drunk, drugged, and unarmed, they had no ability to fight. Vortigern was seized by Hengest and Esc. He was made to watch as his wife and daughters were raped and then murdered. Vortigern was stripped, abused, humiliated, tortured, and finally beheaded publicly. Celtic rule in the east of Britain was brought to an abrupt and violent end. The Celts who managed to escape the massacre either fled east, seeking sanctuary in Dumnonia and the other regions, or were made slaves by the Saxons. A few fled across the southern sea to Armorica, joining the Celtic tribes there.

Hearing of this betrayal, Uther wept and swore that the Saxons would pay in blood for what they had done. Merlin, it is claimed, said: "The White Dragon is awake and we have heard its roar. Now it is time for me to awaken the Red Dragon and so restore the power of the Old Gods to this land. You, Uther, and your heirs, shall be my instrument."

Uther Pendragon

Before Uther, his brother, Ambrosius, ruled over the Dumnonii and was attributed the title of 'Dragon Head', or Pendragon, by his people. Ambrosius died during Vortigern's disastrous campaign against the Picts and Uther became king. He took the mantle of Pendragon for himself and was determined to distance himself from Vortigern's treachery. The eastern tribes rallied to Uther's banner at first, but quickly fell to squabbles and feuds that had simmered throughout Vortigern's years of alliance. The Silures made war against the kingdoms of Powys and Gwent, inviting the Irish tribes to land upon Britain's shores and raid deep into these territories. Other feuds followed. When news of Vortigern's death reached the west, it seemed to signal a growing chaos that even Merlin was hard-pressed to explain.

Yet the most serious of these feuds was instigated by Uther himself. Uther had battled with Kernow's king, Mark, for years, but eventually they came to a truce at around the same time Vortigern was battling Hengest and Esc. At the celebratory feast, Uther became infatuated with Mark's wife, Ygraine, and, while Mark led a campaign against the invading Irish, took Ygraine to his bed. Ygraine fell pregnant and, although Mark originally believed the child to be his, he was informed by his druids that Uther was the father. More war followed. Ygraine would have been slain by a vengeful Mark had she not been smuggled from Kernow by the resourceful Merlin.

Merlin brought Ygraine to Uther's hall, but Uther refused to acknowledge her because he had a wife of his own and legitimate children already: the twins, Morgana and Mordred. The baby, named Arthur, was placed by Merlin into foster care with a clan of the Brigantes and remained there until he became old enough to return to Dumnonia and serve under one of Uther's warlords.

During this time, the Saxons pressed ever further west, coming to dominate the lands almost as westerly as the old Roman city of Aquae Sulis. Uther and his warlords struggled to contain the Saxons, battle the Irish, and occasionally return to battling with Kernow, but somehow the Pendragon managed to prevent the Saxon advance. He did so through constant, short-lived alliances with other tribes, the counsel of Merlin, and his own cunning as a war leader. By 480 Dumnonia's borders were as secure as they could be – as were the borders of the tribes further to the north – but it was clear that the Saxons would never retreat and so the lands east of Sulis became known as *Logres*, 'The Lost Lands'.

The Coming of Aelle

In 477 a new wave of Saxon invaders arrived, led by the ruthless and ambitious Aelle. Hengest had died two years earlier and Aelle decided to take advantage by travelling to Britain, defeating Esc, and bringing the whole of the southern and eastern Saxons under the rule of one king.

Aelle brought many ships and many warriors. He defeated the small British tribes close to his landing place and then issued an ultimatum to Esc: serve and live, or die. Esc chose life and swore fealty to Aelle. In direct challenge to Uther, Aelle named himself the Bretwalda, or 'Britain Ruler'. Saxon raids into Celtic lands became more intense and demanded a heavy response from Uther and his sons, Mordred and Arthur, who were now of an age to fight.

The clashes across the centre of Britain were nothing less than a battle for the control of the entire island. Uther led the warbands of Dumnonia, while Mordred helped lead the warbands of Powys, Gwent, and southern Brigantia. Up and down the country, shield walls clashed and armies warred. These battles – too many to count – were short, vicious, and vital. The Celts adopted the cavalry tactics of the Brigantes warlords and led fast, brutal sorties against Esc's Saxons, who threatened to seize control of the very centre of the country. Uther held Aelle's forces along the southern coast, preventing the Bretwalda and his sons from advancing across the River Test. To Uther's north, Mordred fought along the marches, holding the Saxons at the fording of the River Wye.

It was here that Mordred died, leading an attack on the Saxon's flank. The Celts won that day, and the Saxon shield walls were broken; but Mordred sustained a ghastly wound to his stomach and died after several agonising days.

Uther was grief-stricken. Mordred was 24 years old and had not yet taken a wife and sired an heir. Mordred's twin, Morgana, was distraught with the loss, for they had been very close. Uther wanted to know why Mordred had died and yet Arthur, the bastard offspring of his night with Ygraine, lived. Merlin shrugged. "The Dragon takes many forms,' he said.

The war against Aelle continued for the next eight years, following a familiar pattern of raids and battles before and immediately after the harvest, and then peace through the winter. Uther grieved. Morgana sought Merlin's help in bringing Mordred back to life. When Merlin refused, the girl's anger grew and she vowed to find her own magic.

Meanwhile, Arthur became a fierce and seasoned warrior and horseman among the warbands of Elmet, and then in its cavalry where he built his own loyal following of warriors. Between 487 and 490, Arthur's reputation as a warrior and horseman grew considerably, as did his followers. Uther called for Arthur to bring his warband into Dumnonia, so that it could be tested against Aelle. Uther meant to have revenge against the Bretwalda for Mordred's death.

Caledfwlch or Excalibur?

Excalibur is a romantic name for Arthur's sword coined during the medieval French development of the Arthurian saga by (most likely) Chrétien de Troyes during the 12th Century. In the 5th and 6th Centuries, Britons call it *Caledfwlch* and the name Excalibur is unknown. Games Masters may, of course, call the sword Excalibur if they wish.

Caledfwlch is pronounced KAL-ud-FALK.

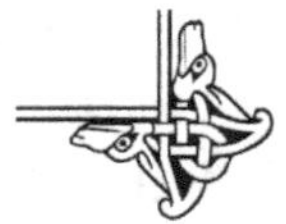

Aelle chose the autumn of 488 to once again press against Uther's borders. Saxon emissaries sailed to Kernow and brought gifts to King Mark. Among them were several beautiful daughters of Saxon warlords; King Mark, ever lustful and fond of young, blond wives, could take his pick. In return, Aelle wanted Mark's friendship and his warbands to cross the Tamar and attack Dumnonia from the west while Aelle attacked from the east.

Mark's treachery reached Uther's ears and so Uther massed his own warbands with a view to meeting both Mark and Aelle on two fronts, between the Tamar and Ex rivers. Arthur was part of the force to ride against Mark. The warbands of Kernow were known to be disorganised and easily broken, and Uther knew that Arthur's cavalry and spearmen would drive Mark's warriors into the river. He was not wrong. Arthur secured a decisive victory against the Kernow traitors.

Uther met Aelle at the Battle of Blackdown. The fighting was savage and both kings took to the field, driving their warbands against each other in many waves and over two days. Merlin led the druids of Britain and called upon mighty spirits to bring sickness to the Saxons. Saxon sorcerers countered with their own spirits and it is said the air turned black with the spells and curses hurled between the two.

Many died. Many fled. Uther fought like a demon of the Other World and, it is said, so did Aelle. It is not known if Uther and Aelle met in combat, but what is certain is that Uther was grievously wounded. The Pendragon fell, and the Britons had little option but to retreat, leaving the field to Aelle.

The Bretwalda's plan had failed, though. He had not managed to join with Mark's forces and seize Dumnonia. Together Uther and Arthur had inflicted two mighty blows against the Saxons, and Aelle had to content himself with the territories he had gained.

It took two years for Uther to die. Although his wound was treated, it suffered from continual infections. Nothing Merlin or Morgana did could bring healing. Uther wasted away, bitter at having lost Mordred, bitter at having been betrayed by Mark, and bitter that Aelle did not die.

Merlin and Arthur

Now that Arthur had returned to Dumnonia, he and Merlin became very close. Perhaps Merlin sensed Uther's imminent death, or perhaps he had always planned this mentorship, but the druid counselled Arthur in many things: the ways of the Old Gods, the history of the tribes, and the ways of politics and law. Merlin took Arthur to the most sacred places of Dumnonia and, so the bards sing, convinced the Gods to gift Arthur with *Caledfwlch*, the sword forged during the Time of Heroes, and one of the Treasures of Britain, hidden in the Spirit World so that the Romans could not seize it.

Although Arthur was not groomed for kingship, Merlin groomed him to lead. He groomed him to win the loyalty of others and give loyalty where it was needed.

With Uther's death, and with no heir to take the title of Pendragon, the time of the great kings has passed. This is the time of the Warlords. Arthur takes his place among them, and a new era, soaked in old blood, begins.

Key Events of 383 to 495

Note this time line differs slightly to that of the Anglo Saxon Chronicle. In the Chronicle Vortigern's invitation to the Saxons takes place, and is accepted, in 449. It is likely to have been a much longer process, begun several years earlier.

383	Roman rule over the north of Britain comes to an end.
409	Roman exodus from Britain begins; most likely complete by 412
419	Vortigern born
426	Ambrosius and Uther (twins) born
441	Vortigern unites Celtic tribes, becomes de-facto king
445	First Saxons invited to settle in Britain
446-448	First wave of Saxon settlement
448-451	Vortigern's campaign against the Picts. He spends two years before returning south.
450	Ambrosius dies. Uther becomes king of Dumnonia.
453	Vortigern reneges on promises to Horsa and Hengest
454	Eastern tribes, led by Uther, cede from Vortigern's alliance. Uther declares himself Pendragon.
454-465	Saxons and Vortigern at war. Horsa slain in 455 at Aylesford. Hengest and his son, Esc, maintain the feud with Vortigern claiming more and more land in the east and south.
465	Vortigern defeated in battle. Peace proposed, but Hengest and Esc lead a treacherous revolt resulting in Vortigern's capture. Vortigern is killed soon after.
464-466	Uther battles the Irish and Kernow.
467	Uther deceives King Mark and seduces Ygraine.
468	Arthur born.
469-480	Eastern tribes hold alliances. Uther battles Saxons and holds them east of Sulis.
475	Hengest dies.
477	Aelle lands on the south coast. Declares himself Bretwalda. Later that year, Guercha lands on the east coast.
488	Mordred (born 464) killed in battle.
489	Uther grievously wounded in battle.
490	Uther dies.
490-500	No male heir to succeed Uther. Dumnonia controlled by various warlords and a loose council. Arthur becomes prominent and, in time, is accorded title of Pendragon, although he never occupies Uther's standing of King of the Western tribes
495-onwards	The Present. Cerdic and Cynric land on the south coast of Britain and are engaged by several local warlords, including Natanleod, a warlord who had served Uther following the split from Vortigern. Saxons continue to press Celtic territories with more of their kinsmen arriving. Porta and his two sons, Beda and Mela, relations of Cerdic, lead this latest influx.

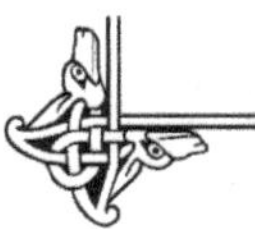
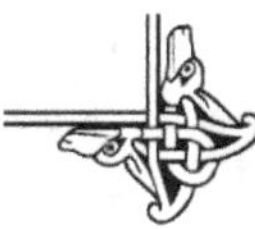

Rise of the Warlords

Uther died without a valid heir. He had two children, Morgana and Mordred, and is thought to have sired numerous illegitimate offspring although only one, Arthur, is known by name. Mordred was killed battling the Saxons several years before Uther's death and so, with no male heir, the title of Pendragon and kingship of the eastern tribes, fragments almost immediately.

Britain in this time is therefore called the era of the warlords. Some, like Natanleod, declare themselves kings but their claims are often suspect, frequently challenged, and their territories small. The last two Celtic kings of note were Vortigern and Uther, and their passing marks the passing of the rule of kings.

Britain is therefore leaderless. Its tribes are administered by the warlords – men with battle experience that have gained substantial followings of warriors to keep their positions secure. Battles for territory, for pride, and for long-forgotten slights are frequent. Warlords maintain their position only through strength of arms and the ability to prosecute battle effectively. While there is a duty to protect the weaker members of society, the aim of every warlord is to keep his own position secure, fight the Saxons and, when needed, other warlords.

Arthur begins his saga no differently to any other warlord of Dumnonia. Although exiled during his formative years, he returned to Dumnonia in his teens and joined the household of the warlord Cai. He served as a warrior, as most men do, displaying remarkable prowess in battle marking him as Uther's son. Under Cai, Arthur successfully built his own warband, including noted warriors such as Derec (Cai's son), Culhwch, and others. Arthur led his warband in many highly effective skirmishes against the Saxons and, after Cai's death, assumed leadership of Cai's followers and kin. Naturally Arthur swore allegiance to Uther, but following Uther's death, Arthur has no claim to the title of Pendragon and is just one of many warlords who come to control Dumnonia.

Arthur has one advantage over the other warlords: the patronage of Merlin. The old druid, having rescued Ygraine from Mark's fury and whisked Arthur away shortly after his birth, clearly feels something for the young warrior. Merlin has taught Arthur much about history, culture, druidism, and the Old Gods: and he continues to do so, offering his service to Arthur (amongst several other favoured warlords) after Uther's death. As a result, Arthur is instilled with an extremely strong set of ideals – especially that of the unity of the Celtic tribes. Merlin served both Vortigern and Uther, and saw the logic of unifying the warlords and petty kings into a coherent whole. Even though both attempts ultimately failed, Merlin believes that it can – and should – be done again, but this time with Arthur at the head.

To reinforce this ambition, Merlin has gifted Arthur with Caledfwlch, a weapon that was forged in the spirit realm for the great heroes of Celtic legend and which has been hidden in the Spirit World until one destined to wield it emerged. Both Vortigern and Uther demanded Caledfwlch and Merlin denied them; but Arthur, who has never asked for anything but the loyalty of his men and courage in battle, is gifted it readily. Merlin does not hide the significance of this gift, ensuring that every other warlord knows that Arthur carries a god-forged blade, one of Britain's Thirteen Treasures, and is the one who will unite the tribes once again to defeat the Saxons.

His legendary sword aside, Arthur is an experienced, capable, shrewd, pragmatic chieftain who sees the sense in uniting the warlords – but not necessarily through kingship. Kings have failed or been found wanting. A good warband has a good leader; if one considers the tribes of Britain as warbands, all it needs is a strong leader – not a king – to make it strong. Arthur eschews the title of Pendragon. Others may use it, sometimes disparagingly, but Arthur himself never does. He is simply Arthur-ap-Cynyr (he does not use Uther's lineage, even though he knows he is Uther's son), associating himself with the warlord who helped make him what he is.

In 495 Arthur is one of the main warlords of Dumnonia, but by no means foremost. He urges cooperation of all the eastern tribes but continually struggles with those who oppose the idea. He has yet to become a legendary figure and is just one of many warriors who continue to hold the Saxons at bay. His time will come, however, and parts of this book deal with Arthur's destiny in greater detail.

Morgana and Mordred

Uther's legitimate children, by his wife Ladwys, Morgana and Mordred are twins — or, at least were. Mordred died battling the Saxons on the borders of Dumnonia in 488 and the bards sing of his bravery and courage in the face of overwhelming odds.

Mordred was heir to the title of Pendragon and, had he lived, it is agreed that he would have had his father's astute political sense and ability to lead men with strength and conviction. His loss was mourned greatly by both his father and sister; but, while Uther accepted Mordred's death as part of the cycle of war, Morgana has become bitter and angry. She and Mordred were very close and she is unwilling to accept his loss.

Since Mordred's loss, Morgana has rejected all suitors. She has become an almost hermit-like figure, immersing herself in the ways of the Old Gods and begging the druids for tuition in the Spirit World. Her desire is to cross the Bridge of Sighs and seek out Mordred's soul in the Spirit World, bringing him back to rule the eastern tribes as was his birthright. Some say Morgana has a clear talent for magic and that the spirits are strong around her. Merlin refuses to favour her with his knowledge, fearing how she will use it. His favouring of Arthur angers Morgana still further, so that now she harbours a deep hatred for her half-brother, and a seething resentment of Merlin's rejection.

Merlin and the Druids

The druidic faith was almost wiped out by the Romans at the massacre of Ynys Mon around the year 61. Before this time, it was strong throughout Britain, Ireland, and Gaul, but afterwards it never recovered its former strength, even after the Romans left Britain in 409. Small druidic sects still existed though, with many druids becoming advisers to the various warlords and petty kings that sprang up in the wake of the Roman exodus.

Keepers of the Old Faith, Britain's druids venerate the pagan gods of the Celts, although they do not worship them directly. The Old Gods are considered to be deliberately distant from mortals although they rely on belief and faith to sustain their existence. Between the gods and mortals are the countless spirits of Britain; some are benevolent and some are malign. The magic of the druids comes through their ability to see, interact with, negotiate with, channel, and battle the spirits. They are therefore shamans — although they do not use that word to describe themselves — and their power is a direct result of interactions with the Spirit World.

Some druids, Merlin among them, are able to work Folk Magic, which is taught to them by the spirits. Druids do not teach either their animistic or folk magic to non-druids, but will work it on others' behalf if they believe the cause to be right and the recipient to be a believer in the Old Gods. The religions of the Romans, Saxons, and the new religion called Christianity are considered to be enemy religions. The Old Gods and the spirits must be rallied against these interlopers — or else Britain, and the Celts, will die completely.

From the Anglo Saxon Chronicle

This year (189 AD) Severus came to the empire; and went with his army into Britain, and subdued in battle a great part of the island. Then wrought he a mound of turf, with a broad wall thereupon, from sea to sea, for the defence of the Britons. He reigned seventeen years; and then ended his days at York. His son Bassianus succeeded him in the empire. His other son, who perished, was called Geta. This year Eleutherius undertook the bishopric of Rome, and held it honourably for fifteen winters. To him Lucius, king of the Britons, sent letters, and prayed that he might be made a Christian. He obtained his request; and they continued afterwards in the right belief until the reign of Diocletian.

In the time of Vortigern and Uther, Merlin is the foremost druid and becomes the High Druid when he sides completely with Uther in seceding from Vortigern's alliance. Merlin is already old by this time. He claims to have been a young man when the Romans controlled the whole of Britain and had to hide his true nature and faith to avoid death. Between 430 and 461 Merlin served Vortigern having prophesied first, Vortigern's union of the Celtic tribes, and then later, its sundering (the great battle between Red and White Dragons). He counselled against inviting the Saxons onto Britain's shores, but nevertheless remained loyal even when the Saxons brought their own gods – and some Roman ones – into Britain. Finally, when it became clear that Vortigern would never be able to resist the Saxon's strength, Merlin transferred his allegiance to Uther, who promised to maintain the strength of the Old Gods in the east and give Merlin free rein in resisting, and destroying, the intruder gods.

This alliance with Uther led to Merlin being regarded as chief of the druids. He is by far the longest-lived (he claims the spirits have made him semi-immortal) and certainly the most influential. As Uther's chief counsel, he was responsible for rescuing the pregnant Ygraine from King Mark and taking the infant Arthur into exile to spare Uther's embarrassment.

His foremost duty as a magician and druid is to restore the Old Gods completely to Britain by restoring the Thirteen Treasures of the island, driving out the Saxons, and destroying the Christian religion that gains credence throughout the land.

Christianity

Christianity has been present in Britain since the year 189, but in a highly rudimentary and simplistic form that was barely tolerated by the Romans. By the 5th Century, Christianity is a new, raw, fundamentalist religion reintroduced to the isles by a mixture of missionaries, artisans, and traders from Europe. The faith sees its earliest foundation more than a century before; Christianity had been tolerated by the Romans from around 313 under Emperor Constantine's rule – although it did not take hold as an organised and fervent faith until the Roman exodus.

Christianity challenges, and rejects, pantheistic faith – which is the dominating faith of the Celts, the Romans before them, and the Saxons. There is no room, in Christian eyes, for false gods, spirits, magic, or similar concepts. The word of Christ dictates that there is a single god and that those who do not believe in him are destined to suffer, whilst the faithful will find the glory of heaven. Any other belief is false and to be destroyed. Even though the Romans attempted to suppress Britain's old gods, replacing them with their own pantheon, they did not possess the same fervour as the nascent Christian religion and would tolerate the native, pagan beliefs.

The fundamentalist nature of Christianity in Britain is heightened by the belief that Jesus Christ came to its shores as a child, marking Britain as a place chosen by God. As a result Christians believe that Christ's spirit is alive in Britain and that a resurrection will take place here, disproving the 'false gods' and establishing Christ's reign absolute.

Naturally Christianity is opposed by the Celtic religion and growing antagonism between the two – driven by zealots on both sides – creates a conflict that mirrors the Saxon invasion: new ideals challenging entrenched beliefs.

The Dark Ages

When the Romans left, they took almost everything with them: their knowledge, their skills, their armies, their administrators, and their gods. They left behind a few remnants of their culture, their buildings and, in some scattered and isolated cases, their treasure. This almost complete exodus has left the island in a slightly more advanced state than it was found during the 1st Century, but one that rapidly collapsed into a tribal culture one could class as barbarianism.

Some vestiges of Roman Britain remain but are in a state of advanced decay. Buildings, towns, and cities have been plundered and dismantled for wealth and raw materials. With the exception of a few large settlements, Roman centres of civilisation have not been populated by the Celts and so have fallen prey the opportunistic and avaricious.

Both Celts and Saxons are organised along tribal lines with little in the way of central administration — the key feature of the Roman occupation. Things are decided locally, according to local traditions, laws, grievances, and superstitions. Quality of life has arguably declined: the dissipation of knowledge concerning crop cultivation, irrigation, building, medical care, and so on has reduced most of Britain's populace to a level of seasonal survival. If a harvest is poor or fails completely, then people starve. Reserves of food are small and designed to support local communities — not to act as a trade commodity. In fact, trade overall has declined. The Empire of Rome thrived on internal and external trade; but with no imperial presence in Britain any longer, trade has dried up to the point where little new comes to Britain's shores. Britain has had to become largely self-sufficient, but lacking the knowledge or Roman skill to exploit natural resources, the degree of self-sufficiency is low.

Ecology and Society

5th and 6th Century Britain was slightly warmer than in the current era, leading to longer, warmer summers, and relatively warmer winters. However, there were isolated pockets of severe cold, leading to long, desperate winters where rivers froze for weeks at a time. In general, though, Britain's climate, particularly in the south, is not prone to huge extremes or variations. It grows colder the further north one travels, and deep snows are a fact in the highlands north of the Great Wall. Britain can be a wet country, particularly during the spring and summer, with plentiful rain to help nourish crops. The autumn is a mellow time and ideal for harvesting. All the peoples of Britain, whether Celt or Saxon, live by the seasons, watching the changing of the weather carefully, and the lengthening and shortening of the days to gauge the timing and pace of key activities. Most people are able to read the weather with reasonable accuracy and, for farmers and herders, accuracy in this is crucial to successful crops.

Socially, Britain can best be described as a place of small communities huddling together for safety and security, and prepared to fight bitterly to defend their scraps. Without widespread administration, communities are insular, fragmented, superstitious, and selfish. Raiding neighbours for something they have that the other does not is common. Small amounts of wealth, whatever form they take, are hoarded and jealously protected. Cities, such as they are, are places to gather for trade — not for advancing self-sufficiency, community, or culture.

Life is short. One is considered an adult at the age of between 12 and 14. Child mortality is high. Life expectancy is low. Those who reach 40 are considered to have lived a full life; those who live longer than that are an exception, not a norm. Life expectancy is lowest amongst the peasants who scratch a living from the fields and streams. It is low amongst the warriors and warbands, who expect to die in battle or from battle's results. There are few expectations for long, comfortable lives. Disease is common, hunger and starvation a constant threat if a crop fails or a harvest is poor. All this is the fault of the gods, the spirits, the wrong sort of gods, or the lack of them. Faith is a means of attempting to control nature and so minimise its hardships. Even if that does not work, the faithful will, at least, be assured a better existence in the afterlife, be this the Other World of the Celts, the feasting halls of the Saxons, or the Kingdom of Heaven of the Christians. But existence pays no respect to religion, so Celts and Saxons, Pagans, and Christians suffer equally under Britain's skies.

Kingdoms of Mythic Britain

Britain consists of five major regions: *Middle Britain, Northern Britain, Southern Britain, Western Britain*, and *Logres*, or the 'Lost Lands'. Each of the major regions is home to several tribes of varying sizes and dispositions, with each tribe controlling lands that can be considered a kingdom, even if the ruler of the tribe does not accord him or herself with the title King or Queen. In all, there are some 12 major tribes. There were many more before the Romans came, and the current number is the result of destruction, displacement, and absorption. Some small tribes merged with larger ones; some left the island completely and others, such as the Icenii, were destroyed by the Romans if they proved to be too rebellious.

Tribal territories tend to be defined by obvious natural boundaries: rivers, hills, forests, and so forth, but this is not always the case, leading to border disputes, shifting kingdom sizes, and the inevitable feuds over land. Prime pasture, woodland, and cropland are highly prized, because these are the main sources of food and fuel for Celtic communities. Defensible positions, usually on hills, are also sought for tribal centres, where hillforts are built. Many hillforts have been in use for hundreds of years and were originally made by the pre-Celtic inhabitants of the island.

The south-eastern kingdoms are now home, largely, to the Saxons. The Celts who held these lands have been killed, enslaved, or displaced.

The Pictish kingdoms, north of the Great Wall, are still Celtic in culture, although the language spoken here, Goidelic, is different to the Brythonic of the southern Celts. The traditions and behaviours of these tribes are ostensibly Celtic in nature, but have developed along different lines shaped as much by the rugged landscape of northern Britain as by any cultural leanings. The word 'Pict' derives from the meaning 'painted one' and it is the distinct habit of the tribes north of the Great Wall to paint and tattoo their bodies with vegetable and mineral dyes, such as woad, or blood (usually for war but sometimes as part of day-to-day decoration). However, the Picts are no less cultured than their cousins to

BRITAIN 495 AD
NORTHERN BRITAIN
(PICTS)
Circind
Caledonii
Dal Raida
Gododdin
Caledonii
MIDDLE
BRITAIN
Carvetii
Brigantes
Parisii
IRELAND
Elmet
Gwynedd
Cornovia
WESTERN
BRITAIN
Powys
Mierce
Anglia
LOGRES
(SAXONS)
Gwent
Siluria
Ceint
Dumnonia
Kernow
SOUTHERN
BRITAIN
ARMORICA
KEY
Terrain above 660'
Terrain above 2000'
Forest
Bogs, Swamps &
Coastal Marsh
0
50
100 mi
0
50
100 km

Rheged and Elmet

Middle Britain encompasses the two kingdoms of Rheged and Elmet. Of the two, only Elmet is referenced in Mythic Britain, and is considered a region of Brigantes control, rather than a kingdom in its own right.

Rheged and Elmet's origins are tangled. Most sources agree that Rheged was founded by Urien Rheged at some point during the 6th Century, but a reasonably accurate date is difficult to pin-point; therefore, we have chosen not to define Middle Britain as Rheged. In Mythic Britain, the term is unknown and Rheged as a kingdom is likely have emerged from the mid-6th Century onwards.

Elmet is mentioned in a number of sources, but appears to be a regional distinction rather than a kingdom or political one. Elmet describes the region of West Yorkshire bounded by the Rivers Sheaf and Wharf. It certainly became a kingdom, but again, much later in the 6th Century

the south, and the term Pict has come to encompass all the Celtic tribes north of the Wall.

The Druids and the Picts

The vast bulk of the druids slaughtered by the Romans at Ynys Mons were from western, central, and southern Britain. The druids of the north were not amongst those murdered and so the druidic tradition — and hence magic — is far stronger amongst the Northern tribes than it is amongst those south of the Wall. The Great Wall served to keep the Northern tribes from invading Middle and Southern Britain, and it also served to strengthen the power and influence of the druids. Paganism amongst the Picts is militant and powerful. Druidic rites have never been forgotten and, in response to the Roman oppression, have subsequently grown in power. Vortigern knew this because Merlin, amongst others, warned him of it. When he decided upon conquering the Northern Britons, Vortigern did not want the Saxons simply for their spears: he also wanted their priests and magicians, believing that Saxon magic was as strong, if not stronger, than that of the Northern druids. Merlin warned him of that, too, but Vortigern did not listen, and it was his downfall.

The Northern tribes are still magically powerful. Their ways have not diminished. The Christian God has no influence beyond the Great Wall. This leads to the Northern tribes being feared by many in the centre and south, and even the Saxons respect the fearsome magic of the North and avoid it.

What follows is an overview of each region and the tribes it contains. The tribe's history and general character is presented, along with notable places, locations, personalities, and legends.

Middle Britain

Middle Britain covers the region, coast to coast, from the Great Wall all the way to The Wash, where it then abuts the lands now occupied by the Saxons: Logres, and in particular, the region of Logres known as Mierce. It encompasses the Pennine Hills, the Eastern Peaks, and the area of the Lakes, and reaches south towards the Cots Hills, which mark the border with Dumnonia and the region of Southern Britain.

This region therefore encompasses a wide range of terrains: from the steep hills and slopes of the Peaks and Pennines, through deep, dense forests that form the central spine of the region, and across to the flat swamplands around The Wash. Spanning the east and west coasts, and with excellent, deep, navigable rivers that flow east-west and north-south, the tribes of Middle Britain are raiders, traders, and merchants.

The ruling tribe is the Brigantes, which controls around half of the region, including almost all the lands immediately south of the Great Wall. Three other tribes, the Carvetii, Cornovii, and the Parisii, are much diminished in power and influence, but still have some independent presence, though they largely defer to the Brigantes.

Middle Britain supported Vortigern in his bid to become High King, accepting the vision he had for a united island from coast to coast. A number of favourable marriages of Brigantian sons and daughters into prestigious southern clans sealed the support and so Middle Britain was a prime supplier of warbands and supplies for Vortigern's

campaign against the Northern tribes. The Brigantes were, though, unprepared for the Saxon mercenaries who brought ships, warbands, wizards, and women to Britain's shores. When the campaign against the Picts failed, and Vortigern was busy laying the blame at the feet of Hengest and Horsa, the Brigantes sided with Uther and decided to play no part in the ensuing treachery.

But neither did the Brigantes want to submit to Uther's rule: they had had enough of High Kings and Uther was clearly bent on settling feuds with Kernow and the Irish marauders who continually harried the western coasts. Middle Britain had traded successfully with the Irish through the Isle of Mann, located between the two main islands, and could see no benefit it jeopardising their interests. Uther therefore united Western and Southern Britain, but the Brigantes, and so the whole of Middle Britain, went their own way.

Brigantes

The Brigantes tribe was created by the goddess Brigantia during the Time of Heroes. A warlike goddess, she fought with her sisters and needed a warband to lead into battle. She made warriors from clay and the water of the sea, and so the tribe was born. Brigantia fights still, in the Land of the Gods, and every member of the Brigantes who believes in the Old Ways knows that when he or she dies, they will ride to the Other Side on a chariot Brigantia will send and join her in the Shield Wall as she battles her sisters.

Yet the Brigantes are not completely pagan. The Christian God came to Middle Britain with the Romans and many traders found the religion across Europe and brought it back with them. The Christian priests amongst the Brigantes have learned that Brigantia was not a goddess, but was, instead, a Saint of Ireland, called Brighid, was enslaved by a druid, raped, and brought to Britain. On the voyage across the Irish Sea, the Mother of the Christ Child, Mary, appeared to her and told her she would be safe if she renounced the False Gods and embraced the One, True God. Brighid did so, and the druid who had captured her fell from the boat and was drowned. When Brighid reached shore, she was rescued by a local chieftain who had nineteen daughters and no sons. Brighid, blessed by the Virgin Mother, kissed the chieftain's wife and she then went on to bear nineteen sons. The nineteen daughters of the chieftain became the handmaidens of Brighid and, in time, took husbands and bore children. So was created the tribe known as the Brigantes.

With such strong matriarchal myths, both Pagan and Christian, it is unsurprising that the Brigantes have had many strong, capable queens to rule them as well as kings. When the Romans came, Queen Cartimandua recognised that fighting these invaders was pointless (as the warlord Caractacus discovered, when he opposed the legions) and instead accepted the authority of the Emperor Claudius. In return, the Brigantes became very rich, establishing good trading links with Rome. Cartimandua was betrayed by her second husband, Vellocatus, who took advantage of turmoil within the Roman administration and successfully seized power from the Queen (who fled to Armorica, it is said). Eventually Vellocatus was killed by the Romans when he tried to stage a revolt against them. He was an ineffective ruler who threatened the Brigantes' wealth and security, and ever since, the tribe has been suspicious of kings who try to command too much power.

The current ruler is Queen Elliw, who has been in power for fifteen years. Elliw is a Christian: her family can trace its lineage back to Goewyn, who was one of the Nineteen Handmaidens of Saint Brighid, and she has done a great deal to support the spread of Christianity throughout Middle Britain. She has created a large retinue of male and female priests, established refuges for women who wish to devote themselves to life of simple purity (the Daughters of Saint Brighid), and has reduced the influence of the druids within the tribe. Nevertheless, she has stopped short of driving out the druids completely or declaring the Old Gods as false, pagan demons, as others have done. She retains a druid as part of her counsel and allows all Brigantes to choose their own faith. There is no doubt that the number of Brigantes pagans is diminishing, and this is a source of huge consternation to the Old God worshippers and to the druids. The chief druid, and Queen Elliw's counsellor, is Glandwyr, and he is fearful that the Christian God will supplant the Old Gods within two or three generations if this rot is not stopped. Glandwyr is therefore an ally of Merlin and in favour of replacing Elliw with a strong, pagan queen – someone like Cartimandua – who will bring back the spirits and the Old Ways. Glandwyr plots in private and, in public, supports Queen Elliw, especially in her hatred of the Saxons who will, no doubt, try to press into Middle England once their strength is sufficient.

Notable Settlements of the Brigantes

The main settlement of the Brigantes, and the largest in Middle Britain, is Caer Ysc, the huge hillfort built by Queen Cartimandua's ancestors. Caer Ysc is an incredible sight: five miles of ditches and earthwork ramparts that surround several low hills and encompass woodland, hunting trails, streams, and grazing fields. The ramparts are topped with a tall, thick, wooden palisade strengthened with local limestone blocks. It has several entrances, each well positioned for defence and protected by ditches and walls enclosing the immediate entrance through the earthwork wall. Unless one circumnavigates Caer Ysc, its sheer size is difficult to appreciate. Within are several communities, each a Brigantes clan, said to trace their roots back to one of the Nineteen Handmaidens. Caer Ysc is largely self-sufficient. If besieged, it can last for years on its own resources, having access to clean, fresh water, livestock, and crops.

Caer Ysc has several Christian chapels. The Cross is not on prominent display within Caer Ysc's walls, but there is no doubting the Christian following that Queen Elliw cultivates. A House of the Daughters of Saint Brighid stands close to Elliw's own Great Hall and it is strongly rumoured that the Queen will, as she reaches old age (and she is not a young woman any longer) move permanently into the House of the Daughters and devote herself to Saint Brighid's example.

Caer Ysc is the largest of the settlements, but there are several other large centres of Brigantes population in the region. Most of these are towns established by Rome during its occupation, but some are ancient tribal holdings and hillforts, such as Isurium, not far from Caer Ysc, and Olicana, some thirty miles to the south.

Cambodunum, Eboracum, Epiacum, and Vinovium are legacy Roman towns. The Brigantes have small settlements living in, or near, each town, but like most Roman towns, the Celts have left them to nature, or plundered them for stone for their own communities. Eboracum is the only one of the Roman centres that retains its dignity. A small hillfort has been built on the hill at Eboracum's focus, and the buildings and streets created by the Romans are largely intact and some are inhabited by a mixture of Brigantes and other Middle Britain tribes.

Sixty miles south and west of Eboracum is the hillfort of Rigodunum, or Caer Rig, a much smaller settlement than Caer Ysc, and one that has, from time to time, been abandoned and then resettled, depending very much on the whim of the local chieftain. Currently, it is occupied again, and the chieftain is Gloedd, the eldest son of Queen Elliw, and the one expected to become the next King of the Brigantes. Gloedd is a pagan, much to his mother's chagrin, although he is well versed in the Christian ways and has apparently promised Queen Elliw that he will, on the day she moves into the House of the Daughters or the day she dies, whichever is first, be baptised into the Christian faith and accept Christ as his Saviour. Gloedd, ambitious and easily manipulated, is unlikely to do so. Glandwyr is a regular visitor to Caer Rig and he has, over several years, inculcated the necessity for the Brigantes to return to the worship of Brigantia and reject totally the Saint Brighid myth. Gloedd is fascinated by the possibilities of this deception and intends to do as Glandwyr advises, even though he would face huge opposition from the many Christian warbands within his own tribe. His belief is that a major defeat of the Saxons, performed in Brigantia's name, is essential to convert the tribe back to the Old Gods. Glandwyr is only too happy to foster Gloedd's desires to make war on the Saxons.

Sixty miles almost due south of Caer Ysc is the hillfort of Caer Wynd. This is the seat of Derec, Chieftain of the area known as Elmet and cousin to Queen Elliw. Caer Wynd is a large settlement (although not as large as Caer Ysc) occupying a pair of low hills almost at the edge of Brigantes lands and marking one of Middle Britain's borders. It is almost on the edge of Saxon territory and, when the Saxons eventually push north from their current lands in a bid to expand, Caer Wynd is likely to be the place for the attack. It is therefore strategically important, growing more so with each passing year.

It is also the stronghold where Merlin brought the infant Arthur, placing him in the safekeeping of the Chieftain at the time, Cai. Cai had another foster child in his care, Derec, and he and Arthur grew together, becoming life-long friends. That friendship remains, and so Derec, Arthur, and Caer Wynd share an important bond that Queen Elliw is fully aware of and keen to exploit in some way in the future. Derec is, like most Brigantes, pragmatic and careful. He rarely rushes to a decision and takes frequent council. He is much loved by those in the region of Elmet, and there are many who believe he should become King when

Tribal Divisions, Circa 480AD

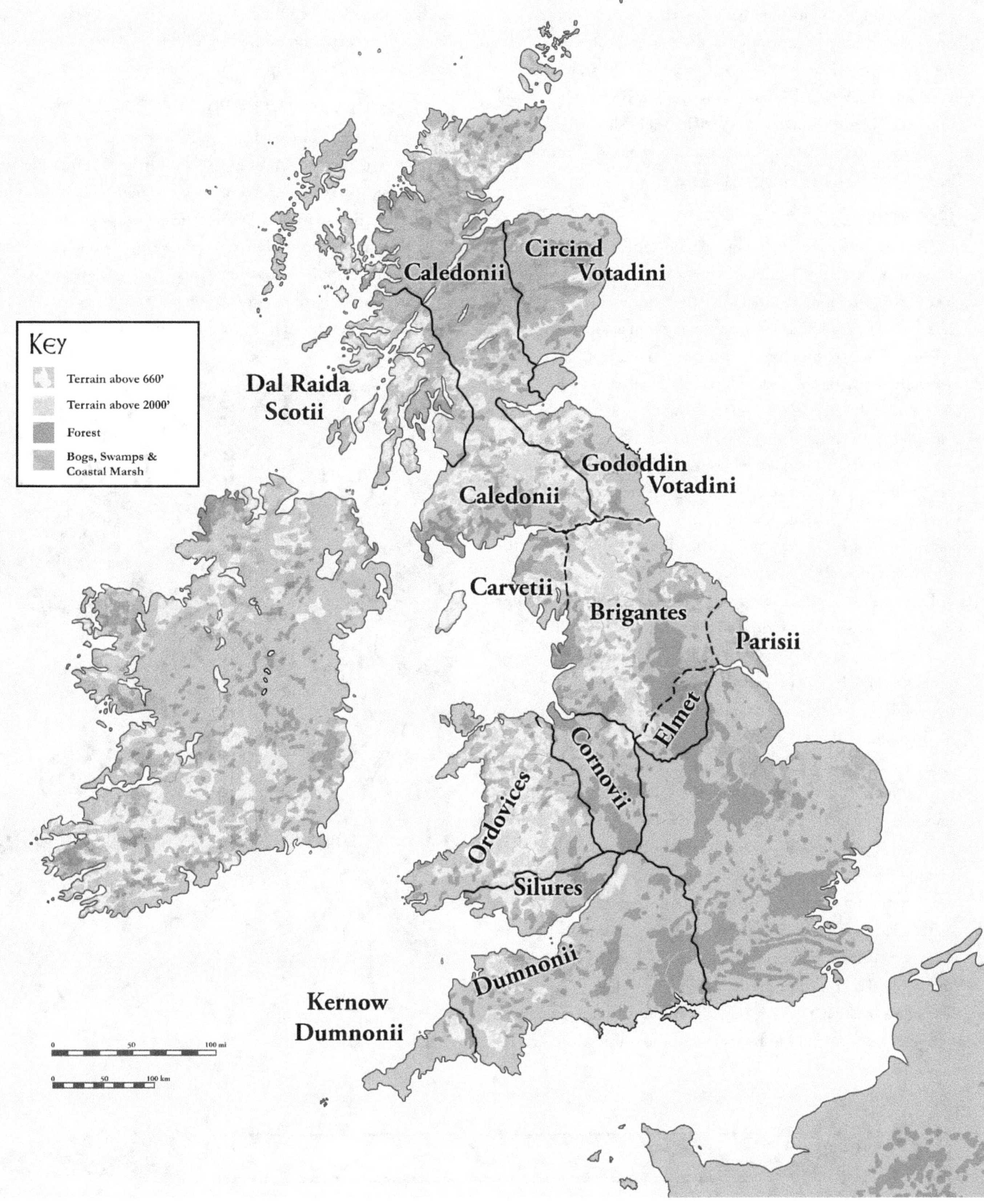

Queen Elliw either dies or goes into exile to become a Saint. Derec is both pagan and Christian, believing that both sets of the gods can coexist if they have a mind to. He maintains both Christian and pagan advisers, and loathes the druid Glandwyr, who he sees as a trouble maker. Derec has no love for Merlin, either, but welcomes the old druid out of the sake of his friendship with Arthur.

Caer Wynd is detailed in the opening scenario of the Mythic Britain campaign, beginning on page 217.

Brigantes Culture

The Brigantes are curious amongst the Celtic tribes in that they are a naturally accepting, reasonably tolerant culture. Although rich, ambitious, and domineering, they have never, culturally, seen a need to dominate absolutely, and often act in a pragmatic, cooperative way that successfully furthers the Brigantian interest, especially in matters of trade. The Brigantes, for example, did not seek to fully absorb or assimilate their smaller neighbouring tribes – instead they created strong, blood alliances, shared some of their own wealth; and recognised existing tribal statuses. Similarly, the Brigantes have Christianity and Paganism operating together within the tribe, although Christianity is clearly gaining dominance. Further back, Queen Cartimandua welcomed and allied with the Romans, helping the Brigantes to prosper.

This desire to prosper, to grow the tribe and protect its interests, is quintessentially Celtic. Where the Brigantes differ is in their desire to do so in ways that do not necessarily result in war and bloodshed. It is, perhaps, the pragmatic influence of so many strong and capable queens that has created such a culture amongst the Brigantes, but experience has also played a part. The Brigantes are well travelled and expert traders. They have spread across the seas in many directions, having links with Ireland, Armorica, Gaul, and even into territories still held by Rome. Warmongering is a sure way to meet a bigger and better armed enemy, and so the Brigantes have, with time and experience, learned to extend their interests through more careful, less violent ways.

But the Brigantes are still Celts. War comes naturally to them, and when their interests are threatened, they will fight, and fight ferociously. The Brigantes have not yet tested themselves against the Saxons because, thus far, there has been no need. They have, though, watched what has happened in the south and noted the Saxons' ambition. The Brigantes know the Saxons will come, eventually, to seize Middle Britain. When they do, the Brigantes Shield Walls will be ready and formed on Middle England's borders, supported by sharp, blood-dipped, Brigantian spears.

Particular Customs and Dress

The Brigantes mark their territory with a human face carved into wood or stone and positioned at a particular border or strategic point, to remind everyone of who rules. This is a druidic practice peculiar to Middle Britain; the carved face is asexual and actively connects the Spirit World and Mortal World at that particular point. A spirit that is friendly with a druid can see the Mortal World through the eyes of the carving and relay what is seen to the druid, even though the druid might be many miles distant from the carving.

In these days of the Christian God, the carvings are still made, but often they are fashioned to represent Saint Brighid and her Handmaidens, or other Saints of the Christian Faith. Whatever their source, a face carved into a tree, a rock, or a head-sized stone, placed just-so indicates that one is in Brigantes-controlled territory.

In terms of dress, the Brigantes favour heavy woollen cloaks dyed russet, red, mauve, or purple – a tradition started in the time of Queen Cartimandua to honour the Roman powers and demonstrate the strength of the alliance. The tradition has continued, and with it, many other Roman cultural traits pertaining to dress and clothing. Some Brigantes Celts wear their cloaks in the style of a toga, and chieftains have the right to fashion of wreath of leaves to be worn on the head as a sign of office. Many wear sandals and boots in the Roman military style, and other Romano-British clothing elements and styles linger, mixing and merging with traditional Celtic styles and patterns. There is also a habit for Brigantes men to shave, or wear their beards and moustaches trimmed and styled.

Allies and Enemies

The Brigantes share a certain alliance with the Dumnonii and there have been some strategic marriages in the past. When he was alive, Uther worked hard to bring the Brigantes into the united kingdoms he was establishing amongst the south and west of Britain, but by this time the Brigantes had had enough of High Kings and grand schemes.

In recent years, relations have mellowed and the Brigantes and the Dumnonii have traded very successfully – although calls for warbands by the Dumnonii have met with a muted response. This is more a case of Brigantes pragmatism than any desire not to help the south, but Queen Elliw knows that soon she will have to face the Saxons herself and so is beginning to warm to the idea of an alliance with Dumnonia: if the right overtures and assurances are made.

In terms of enemies, the only real enemy the Brigantes have faced is the Caledonii north of the Great Wall. Staunchly independent and with a burning hatred for all tribes who colluded with Rome, the Caledonii hate the Brigantes with a passion. In centuries past, raids across the border were impossible due to the Great Wall, but since the Roman exodus the Wall is no longer the barrier it was and the Caledonii have started to raid the northern fringes of Brigantes territory and, especially into Carvetii lands, where the raids have been vicious and punitive. The Brigantes chieftains have sent numerous warbands to the aid of the small Carvetii tribe and have driven the Caledonii back dozens of times – but they have never met this old foe in pitched battle. The Brigantes know that the Caledonii are probably preparing for much bolder strikes – possibly as far south as Caer Ysc – and with the help of the

Glandwyr's Treachery

Glandwyr the druid has secretly crossed the Great Wall and visited the Hall of the Caledonii, delivering news of Brigantes plans and defences, aiding the Caledonii to prepare for a major assault on key Middle Britain strongholds. Glandwyr believes he is acting in the Brigantes' best interests: the Caledonii lack the strength to defeat the Brigantes, but if the assaults are fierce enough, it may help check the spread of Christianity and so the Caledonii have agreed to direct attacks against symbols of the Christian God – Christian farmers, settlements with a chapel, and so on.

Curiously these assaults may work in favour of Southern Britain and Dumnonia, in particular. In return for Brigantes warbands joining the war against the Saxons, Queen Elliw could demand Dumnonia's help in defeating the Caledonii in a single, decisive battle.

The stage is set and the pieces moving

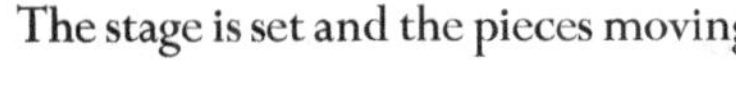

Votadini. The Pictish tribes hate not only those who paid tribute to Rome, but also Christians, and so the growing Christianity of the Brigantes is a sure way of angering the Caledonii.

Magic Amongst the Brigantes

Before Saint Brighid became the accepted legend amongst the Brigantes, the entire region was rich with spirits and sacred sites. The druids had many groves and sacred places, and the Ancestors – those who serve in Brigantia's warband – were frequently seen in the deep woods and on the lonely moorlands overlooking the coasts. As Brigantia's stories and myths have been replaced with those of Saint Brighid, the influence of the spirits has declined. The White Dragon's breath is strong in Middle Britain, and so the spirits of the region find it hard to commune with the druids and help work magic. But even though magic is failing amongst the Brigantes, it has some strength left, because there is still faith within the tribe: Queen Elliw has been sensible enough not to crush the Old Ways completely. Thus, the many forests and dales, but particularly the moorlands, of Brigantes territory, are sacred areas to the druids. The moorlands, with their stark, bleak beauty, cold, eerie winds, and vast skies, are the lands where Brigantia makes war on her sisters in the World of the Gods. In these windswept, wuthering places, the Ancestors can be contacted, and the spirits of the Wind and Water propitiated and channelled. It is here, on the moorlands of the west and east coasts, and in the centre of Brigantes lands, that the druids work their plans to beat the White Dragon and drive Christianity from the shores. In these remote places, amongst cairns made from limestone shards, sacrifices, both animals and human, are made to Brigantia and the local spirits. The rites are kept quiet: whilst not a secret, if their true nature came to be known, Glandwyr is certain that Queen Elliw would move against the pagans once and for all, instituting Christianity as the only religion in Middle Britain and driving Brigantia out of the tribal memory, replacing it with the false story of Brighid and her nineteen whores.

Notables of the Brigantes

Elliw, Queen of the Brigantes

Elliw-ap-Mellwr is the forty-five year old daughter of Queen Mellwr and her husband, Pol. Pol died battling the Caledonii and Mellwr never remarried, despite many suitors. A staunch Christian, her values were passed to Elliw who, as an only child, was destined to become Queen of the Brigantes. Elliw is married to Aneurin, the son of King Lend of the Cornovii, thereby maintaining the long alliance between these two Middle England tribes. Aneurin commands the Brigantes forces and heads the warbands of Caer Ysc. He is a stern, shrewd commander, but a poor Christian. He and Elliw share little love and are together purely through duty and oaths – a situation that suits them perfectly. Elliw has three children by Aneurin: Gloedd, who commands Caer Rig;

Enya, who took the vows of the Daughters of Saint Brighid as soon as she could, and Bronwyn, the youngest, who was born deaf and mute. Gloedd is, like his father, stern and obstinate and a very poor Christian. Elliw would have preferred to pass the rulership to one of her daughters, but Enya proved to be even more devout than her mother, and poor, afflicted Bronwyn is unfit for the role. This leaves only Gloedd, and Elliw is working hard to make him a fit King and a good Christian. In reality, Bronwyn, who is sorely

neglected, is bright and clever. She is gifted with Spirit Sight and Glandwyr knows she would make a fine druid.

Elliw is a shrewd and careful queen. She understands the needs of her people instinctively and is an arch politician. She lets nothing come in the way of the Brigantes' requirements and is a staunch defender of their rights, territories, and heritage. She is also a preservationist and wants to see power remain within her bloodline – after the security of the Brigantes, this is her chief goal in life. Despite her somewhat cold demeanour, Queen Elliw can be warm and charming. She has a natural way of discerning a person's character and motives: she is rarely wrong, and her one failing is her inability to spot the treachery lurking in Glandwyr, because he, too, is an arch politician.

Glandwyr, High Druid of the Brigantes

There are few druids left amongst the Brigantes and Glandwyr knows that, in a generation or so, the entire tribe will have given way to the Christian God, and so he is the one who must put the tribe on a course back to the Old Ways. Glandwyr is in his fiftieth year, with grey, cropped hair and deep, brown eyes. His voice is musical and he is charm personified. Like Elliw, he reads people accurately – a skill he learned from Merlin – and he knows how to position himself so that he is listened to and can listen. Although he is a pagan in a Christian court, Glandwyr ensures that his advice is secular, and sound, and matches with what Elliw wants and needs to hear. He will occasionally engineer a disagreement to sustain the pretence of reliability, but his ultimate goal is to drive Christianity from the Brigantes, and he has two plans for doing so. The first lies with Gloedd, Elliw's headstrong son. He will follow the Old Ways when he comes to power, and will be guided by Glandwyr totally. A major victory over the Saxons will make Gloedd a popular ruler and help staunch the conversions to the Christian God. The second plan is to destroy the Carvetii. This devoutly Christian tribe is hated by the neighbouring Caledonii; but they constantly place their faith in God to protect them. If Glandwyr can show that the Christian God cannot be trusted to protect even His most devout worshippers, it will help bring the Brigantes back to the Old Gods.

Gloedd, Chieftain of Caer Rig

Queen Elliw's son, Gloedd is a warrior, like his father, Aneurin. Like most Celts, he grew up away from the main household, and the druid Glandwyr ensured that Gloedd was raised in a community with strong, pagan traditions rather than the Christian devotion that dominates Caer Ysc. Tall, broad, and strong, Gloedd typifies the Celtic warrior male. He is happiest when fighting, enjoys the danger of the shield wall, and is easily bored when not training, hunting, or riding down enemies. He is desperate to take on the Saxons, but given his current location at Caer Rig, far from where the Saxons are most active, its has proved impossible to engineer reasons suitable enough to earn his parents' consent. He knows that his mother must make a decision soon, though. The Saxons grow bolder. Dumnonia's borders shrink, and it is only a matter of time before the Saxons come to claim the lands of the Brigantes. Glandwyr is a frequent visitor to Caer Rig, and he brings news of Queen Elliw's decisions to Gloedd's ears. He also ensures that Gloedd remains true to his pagan inclinations, whilst still displaying a semblance of devotion to the Christian God. The plan is for Gloedd to become King of the Brigantes as a Christian, but to revert to the Old Gods when it is shown that the Christian God is powerless and impotent. Gloedd wants only to make war on the Saxons: religion is for the priests, druids, his mother, and sister.

Derec, Chieftain of Caer Wynd

Derec-ap-Cai is the younger cousin of Queen Elliw. Derec was born and raised in Caer Wynd, where his father, Cai-ap-Cassi was the Chieftain of Elmet. Derec is a year older than his foster brother, Arthur, who was brought to live with Cai and his household by Merlin very soon after the child's birth. Cai, apparently, owed Merlin a service and took the infant grudgingly, wondering if it might provoke reprisals either from Uther or King Mark. Merlin told Cai that the Spirits of Britain protected the child and so would protect Caer Wynd. Sure enough, no one ever came looking for Arthur or paid any heed to the role Cai now played to Uther's bastard.

Cai raised Arthur as his own son. His natural inclination was always to Derec but his favours were more or less equal. Derec and Arthur grew up as closely as any true brothers could and Cai raised two strong, just, intelligent, and considerate warriors. Cai died following a hunting accident and Derec naturally became chieftain, having proven himself in the eyes of the people. Arthur swore

Key Locations

Places

1. Caer Ysc
2. Eboracum
3. Rigodurnum
4. Caer Wynd
5. Caer Luel
6. Caer Guracon
7. Caer Ffridd
8. Letocetum
9. Ard-Na-Said
10. Bannatia
11. Colanica
12. Devana
13. Inchtuthil
14. Orrea
15. Tamia
16. Tuesis
17. Vindogara
18. Dún Curia
19. Caer Cadbryg
20. Caer Dore
21. Ynys Wydryn
22. Lindinis
23. Isca
24. Caer Cradawc
25. Caer Went
26. Caer Leon
27. Caer Branog
28. Deheu
29. Anderida
30. Boede
31. Ratae & Caer Leonis
32. Caer Pedwyr

Circind
Caledonii
Dal Raida
Gododdin
Caledonii
The Great Wall
Carvetii
Brigantes
Parisii
Ynys Mon
Gwynedd
Elmet
Cornovia
Powys
Mierce
Anglia
Gwent
Siluria
Ceint
Dumnonia
Ynys Wyt
Kernow

0 50 100 mi
0 50 100 km

All the locations listed in the Places key are referenced in this chapter.

his loyalty to Derec and Elmet, but shortly afterwards Merlin returned with news that Uther, Arthur's father, wanted Arthur to return to Dumnonia bringing his horsemen and warband to fight the Saxons. Derec allowed Arthur to leave, but Arthur promised he would return and place himself at Derec's and Elmet's service in the future. Derec has since proved to be a capable chieftain. He has married Lynette, the raven-haired daughter of a local chief, and they have two healthy children. Derec has calmed feuds between several Brigantes clans, ensured peace with the Cornovii, and watched the way the Saxons have steadily pushed the Celts further and further west. He knows they will soon turn their eyes towards the north and Brigantes lands. Derec is therefore Queen Elliw's eyes and ears on the southern border: he will be her first line of spears too, and that is when he intends to summon Arthur.

Derec is naturally cautious and suspicious. He is a pagan, but is accepting of Christian ways in the fashion typical of the Brigantes. However, he fully trusts neither. The Christian priests advocate bloodshed against the pagans, and the druids, wily to the last, scheme and plot with their spirits and gods. Neither can be trusted, and Derec believes, deep down, that the gods, be they a single being, like the Christian God, or a multitude of them, like the Celtic Gods, care little for mortals. In the end, it will be man against man and no god will proffer aid, no matter what the druids and priests say.

So Derec works hard to strengthen Caer Wynd. He is welcoming to any Celt who arrives at the fort and offers service. He knows he must create and train more warbands in preparation for war with the Saxons. He will summon Arthur but cannot count on his support alone: Caer Wynd will, at first, have to stand alone and strong against the first wave of Saxon attacks.

Carvetii

Part of the Brigantes tribal confederation consists of the remains of the Carvetii tribe. These Celts inhabited the uplands and lowlands surrounding the region of large lakes in the north-west of Britain and, like the Brigantes, they did not resist the Romans when they forged north, instead preferring to offer tribute and cooperate. In recognition of their cooperation, the Carvetii gained the status of dediticii, a tribute-offering civitas that meant it enjoyed Rome's protection. It also meant that the Carvetii earned the hatred of the Caledonii, their neighbours to the north and, even now the Romans have left, the Carvetii, much dwindled in number, are still subject to raids by the Caledonii.

The lands of the Carvetii are hilly and rugged, characterised by many high, bleak, scree-covered hills and peaks, carved through by countless grassy valleys and woodlands. In the spring and summer, these are lands of great beauty and warmth. In the winter, when the winds drive rain and snow onshore, breaking against the great hills, Carvetii lands are sorrowful and bleak. This is ancient countryside and was once controlled almost entirely by the druids who named and knew the great spirits of each mighty hill and each long, deep lake.

This changed when most of Carvetii druids perished at Ynys Mon, slaughtered by the Romans. A handful of Carvetii druids returned, but their power was broken in this region. The Carvetii, being a relatively simple people, much given to superstitions and easily swayed, believed that the gods the Romans had brought with them were now meant to rule, and so the Great Spirits of the Lakes and Peaks were replaced with Jupiter, Juno, Apollo, Bubona, and Ceres. They did not erect temples to these gods, as the Romans did, but observed them with prayers and small images. The one old god the Carvetii continued to venerate was Belatucadros, the Bright Slayer, fierce god of battle who carved the lands occupied by the Carvetii with his spears and the wheels of his chariot, when he drove out the giants from this region. Even the Romans recognised Belatucadros' power, but their priests also showed that he had another name, Mars, and so the Carvetii began to use that name instead.

After the Great Wall had been built, the raids by the Caledonii stopped and the Carvetii prospered, able to enjoy crops and livestock without fearing Caledonii theft and murder. The Brigantes tribe was also growing in strength, and sent traders to buy — not steal — from the Carvetii. So began a trading relationship that grew into something much greater. Just as the Carvetii had queens, so did the Brigantes; the two tribes found they had much in common, and, when the Christian missionaries came this part of Britain, two hundred years ago, they showed that it was on the west coast, in Carvetii lands, that Saint Brighid came ashore, carried by the Virgin Mother of the Christ Child who had appeared in a vision and delivered the slave girl to safety and freedom. The Carvetii steadily

shrugged off their homage to the Roman Gods and began to learn about, and worship, the Christian God, Saint Brighid became their saint; and when missionaries from Ireland, also followers of Christ, came and showed the true light of the Holy Spirit, the Carvetii not only converted wholeheartedly, but allowed the Brigantes to all but subsume their tribe.

These days the Carvetii are a peaceful, client tribe, preferring trade to war. Settlements are chiefly farms and villages rather than hillforts. They are farmers, craftsmen, artisans, and traders more than warriors. Christianity is strongly established amongst the Carvetii and has been for well over two centuries. Many small chapels are scattered across Carvetii lands, and there is a strong missionary ethic amongst the Carvetii priests, who go south (and sometimes north) to spread the Word of the Saviour. Paganism is not tolerated in Carvetii country: the old shrines and groves of the northern druids have been defiled, razed, and destroyed, and it has been a long, long time since any druid was seen wandering through the dales and lakelands.

The Carvetii have no king or queen of their own, and recognise Queen Elliw of the Brigantes as their overall ruler. They do have several powerful chieftains though, and foremost of these, and married to a cousin of Queen Elliw, is Eanraig, a devout Christian, a reasonably effective warrior, but a leader of modest abilities. His wife, Muire, is related by blood to the royal line of the Brigantes and is a confidant of Queen Elliw and those close to her. It is Muire who makes most of the key decisions, after consulting with Raild, the stern Irish priest who has become the chief counsellor of the Carvetii. Eanraig is thus a puppet chieftain. His days are spent hunting, tending to his holdings, and working alongside the other men and women on the hills and in the fields of the valleys. Muire and Raild attend to the major affairs of the Carvetii people, ensuring that Eanraig is present when he needs to be, so that the right face and the right voice present news and decisions to the people.

Notable Settlements of the Carvetii

The Carvetii has only one, notable centre of settlement: Caer Luel, on the northern edge of the Carvetii lands. Once, it was a large and very prosperous community called Luguvalion and named for the sun god Lugh. When the Romans arrived and occupied the area, Luguvalion was fortified with a perimeter wall of stone and

Caer Luel

Named for the Lugh, the Sun God, Caer Luel is now a staunchly Christian settlement. The chapel design is typical of Christian churches in Middle Britain.

became known as Luguvalion. It formed an important outpost for the Roman administration and also continued to serve as the home of the Carvetii's rulers, who steadily ceded more and more power to the Roman administration. Luguvalion's fortunes rose and fell continually, according to which administrator was in power, what favour he had with the consul, and consequently, what favour he was held in by the emperor. The Romans abandoned Luguvalion before the general exodus when the administrator, Marcus Carausius, was assassinated. Its power as a settlement and centre for trade waned. The Carvetii rulers remained though, and renamed the place Caer Luel in a deliberate attempt to distance it from its associations with the pagan god of the sun.

Caer Luel is still a reasonably sized community located amongst the stones and crumbling remains of the Roman town. The perimeter wall is in sad state of repair and many of the villas and stone buildings have been raided for the roundhouses and Great House of the Carvetii ruling class. Eanraig and Muire have the Great House, a massive roundhouse, as their home, and it is surrounded by the Muire's relatives and those in Priest Raild's favour. Eanraig is frequently absent, spending most of his time in the hills and valleys in the company of his warband (although it has been some years since Eanraig commanded a shield wall).

Caer Luel effectively marks the western edge of Brigantes territory these days, even though the lands are still recognised as Carvetii. There are many Brigantes settlers, especially those who seek to convert to Christianity. Raild is a noted preacher of the faith and people come from all across Middle Britain to be baptised by him. Caer Luel is a small bastion of Christianity in the wild countryside of western Britain. Its pagan enemies are directly to the north and the people of Caer Luel have no interest in the Saxons who supposedly plague the south. Raild maintains that the Celts of the south have been chosen to suffer by God for not embracing Christ as the one, true Saviour. The Saxons, he claims (and claims loudly) are God's Scourge against the heathen. Caer Luel hangs on this belief, feeling safe in the knowledge that the Saxons are too far away, and that between Caer Luel and the Saxons are the warbands of the Brigantes, who will offer whatever protection God cannot.

Carvetii Culture

The Carvetii have always been highly changeable in their views and practices. They are primarily agrarian in nature and warlike only when faced with violent intruders and left with no other choice. They respect and fear Higher Powers: first the Old Gods, such as Lug and Belatucadros, then the Great Spirits of the Peaks and Lakes. Then they respected and feared the Romans and their gods, and now respect and love the Brigantes. It seems to be in the Carvetii nature to be accepting and accommodating, resigning themselves to inevitable fates or ignoring them altogether.

Nevertheless, the Carvetii are still Celts and espouse traditional Celtic values. They have, however, been shaped by the rugged, unforgiving, and insular nature of their environment. The lands of the Carvetii are incredibly beautiful and incredibly harsh; to survive, this must be accepted and endured. As a result, the Carvetii are a hardy, resilient people physically, but with a communal will that allows for easy dominance if a stronger will comes along. In the case of both the Romans and the Brigantes, that will has been largely beneficial to the Carvetii, and so whilst small (and it would be easy to be rid of such a small tribe), they have prevailed – and prevailed where many other tribes did not. The Icenii were broken; the Catuvellauni crushed and scattered. Yet the Carvetii still exist, and they believe that this survival is down to their accommodating and inclusive nature.

Particular Customs and Dress

The vast bulk of Carvetii are Christian and wear plain and simple clothes with little ostentation. Cloaks are in muted colours and jewelry, save amongst the High Women of the tribe (and those closest to Muire) discouraged. Hair is long and worn tied or bundled; men typically braid their beards or apply wax to keep them straight and discourage lice.

The Carvetii are fond of imagery. The symbol of the cross is common throughout Carvetii lands, displayed on doors, on cairns of rock, and carved into trees and stones. The complex, stylised artwork of the Celts has found its way into cruciform imagery, with stone crosses ornamented with complex, intricate knots that would once have been applied to pagan symbols.

The tribe is also deferential in its hospitality. Celts always share whatever they have with newcomers, but the Carvetii tradition is to give a guest the best and the most – even if this means others go without.

Allies and Enemies

The Caledonii are the sworn enemies of the Carvetii and would wipe them out given the chance. Before the Romans, the Caledonii saw the Carvetii simply as easy pickings for raids and sport. But when Rome arrived and the Carvetii welcomed them – and their gods – the Caledonii reacted with fury and swore blood vows to destroy them. That ire has not diminished with the years. Now that Christianity has been embraced, the Caledonii are more intent than ever on destroying the Carvetii. Some, like the Brigantes druid Glandwyr, would also like to see an example made of the Carvetii; after all, if their God protects, as they claim He does, there can be little to fear.

The tribe's greatest ally is the Brigantes, though, and the Carvetii live gratefully in their shadow, enjoying Brigantes protection and patronage. There are also strong links with the Christian tribes of Ireland who sail across the Irish Sea and use the Isle of Mann as a staging post before arriving in Britain. Many Irish missionaries come through Caer Luel, and they claim to have been tasked by God to go beyond the Great Wall and bring the Holy Word to the Picts. The Carvetii know better than to take such risks, and duly warn the Irish missionaries, but inevitably find themselves praying for their souls when they do not return (or their heads are reported, staked, atop the crumbling stones of the Wall).

Notables of the Carvetii

Eanraig, High Chief of the Carvetii

At first glance, Eanraig is an exemplary Celt. Dark haired, broad shouldered, strong, and scarred, he appears every inch the warrior and, indeed, he revels in warlike pursuits, physical work, and the company of warriors. Deep-down, he is insecure, indecisive, and wholly unsuited for the role of High Chieftain. He is a devout follower of the Christian faith and he compares himself constantly with the great Saints, knowing that he does not, and cannot, find measure with their piety. He feels himself undeserving of God's love and so toils physically as a way of earning it. His wife, Muire, is shrewish and continually reinforces his self-doubt; but she is also good at the business of understanding and running tribal affairs and so he is happy to defer to both her and Raild's council.

Muire, Wife of Eanraig

Muire is the spoilt only daughter of a Brigantes chieftain and is related to Queen Elliw. She loves comforts, nice things, and power. She has all these in her marriage to Eanraig, and the fact that she is brighter than her husband means she controls the affairs of the Carvetii in her husband's name. Like him, she is a devout believer in Christ, but unlike Eanraig she is entirely sure of her role in God's plan and entirely comfortable in using whatever means she can to secure her own position, drive paganism completely from Britain's shores, and worm her way deeper into the court of Queen Elliw so that her children (she has two daughters) will find power in the wider Brigantes tribe. As her husband is absent so much, Muire finds spiritual and physical solace with Raild, the stern, hard, passionate, devout, virile, alluring Irish missionary who has done so much for the Carvetii since arriving in Caer Luel a decade ago. Together they run the tribe, settle its affairs, advance its position, and tell Eanraig what he needs to know. For Muire, life is good. She is sure he knows nothing of her times with Raild, for the two of them are discreet and careful.

Raild, Preacher of Ireland

Raild is an Irish Celt from the land of Ulster. Expelled from his homeland for raping the daughter of a merchant, he underwent a miraculous conversion to God and decided to bring the word of the Saviour to the heathen Picts. He arrived in Caer Luel and never left: let others travel north of the Wall; God's work needs to be accomplished in Caer Luel first. He found a weak chieftain, a directionless people and a lonely wife. He has rectified all that. Eanraig knows he is worthless in God's eyes and so must atone through hard work abroad in the kingdom. The people of the Carvetii must know that there is only one God and abandon everything they knew of their old ways. They must atone for helping the heathen Romans and must do so through earning Christ's love. Muire, who is both radiant and wanting, is undeserving of that miserable sinner of a husband and must be fulfilled spiritually and physically. Raild is happy to provide all these services in return for a good roundhouse, a chapel, a Caledonii slave to cook his meals and mend his clothes, and ample time to minister to the affairs of the Carvetii. He is a devout and exemplary man.

Cornovii

The Cornovii tribe occupies the lozenge of land currently separating Western Britain from Middle Britain and Logres. The Brigantes rule the territories to the north; the Corieltauvi to the east, the Dumnonii to the south and the Ordovices to the west.

The Cornovii are not as large as the neighbouring Brigantes, but their territory is large enough, and they are certainly more populous than the dwindling Carvetii. Unlike the Christian-leaning Brigantes and Carvetii, the Cornovii remain staunchly pagan. The totem of the tribe is the stag, the animal of Cernunnos, the Horned God, and their name means 'People of the Horn'. The Cornovii lands encompass rich forests and woodlands and deep glades, alongside some of the best pasture anywhere in Britain. The Cornovii protect their lands fiercely and have, in the past, battled both the Brigantes and the Ordovices to prevent their territory from being eroded.

Like the Brigantes, the Cornovii accepted Rome's conquest and in return they were awarded the status of *civitas*, gaining Rome's recognition and protection. The Cornovii occupy many hillforts throughout their lands and the Romans established their base at one of the larger fortifications, Caer Guricon, which they named Viroconium Cornoviorum. Viroconium became a bustling place: timber, wool, ceramics, charcoal and, most crucially, salt were – and still are – traded there. The Cornovii became a wealthy tribe, just as did the Brigantes, and several other hillforts were developed into Roman-administered trade centres although none were as impressive as famed Viroconium. The Cornovii even supplied warriors for Cohors Primae Cornoviorum, such was the trust built-up between Romans and Britons, and in many respects, the Cornovii became some of the most 'civilised' Celts in the land. As well as salt, the Cornovii developed copper, lead and silver, further advancing their wealth, status, and position.

The fortunes of the Cornovii have changed somewhat since the Romans left. A reasonable number of the Cornovii who had adopted Roman ways and citizenship left the region, taking with them a lot of the region's wealth and a great deal of the knowledge crucial to mining. Factions within the Cornovii began to fight amongst themselves, making the tribe vulnerable to raids by the Ordovices and the Brigantes. It was only when Vortigern sought to unite Britain under one banner that the Cornovii halted a slide into destruction and turned around their fortunes. Vortigern's mother was Cornovii by birth, and Vortigern had spent much time there and knew many of the Cornovii chiefs and warlords. He reminded of them of Rome's legacy and showed them how strong they could be. The Cornovii were one of the first tribes to join Vortigern's confederation – and were also one of the first to abandon him when he committed his betrayal with the Saxons.

The Cornovii sided with Uther and were happy to submit to the Pendragon's rule. However, the old feuds re-emerged, with some chieftains believing that Vortigern deserved better and some believing he deserved worse. Matters came to a head when Uther betrayed King Mark of Kernow – the Cornovii have very strong links with Kernow, and many of their people dwell there. Caught between two so-called High Kings who turned out to be every bit as untrustworthy and petty as the feuding chiefs within the tribe, King Cereg declared that the Cornovii would be independent, following the lead set by the Brigantes. Some Cornovii who still sided with Uther moved into Dumnonia, but most stayed, and King Cereg and his heirs worked hard to rebuild the Cornovii as a force of Middle Britain.

The current ruler of the Cornovii is Lend-ap-Cereg. A fierce, intelligent leader, he is as staunchly independent as his father. King Lend knows that the Cornovii are important strategically to both the Dumnonii and the Brigantes. If the Dumnonii are driven out of their lands by the Saxons, the Cornovii will be pivotal in any move to stop them from dominating the west. King Lend therefore strengthens his warbands, trains them well, and waits patiently for Dumnonia to call for his help. In the meantime, he is still saddled with the feuding factions within his own tribe. The Cornovii chiefs have always been easy to take offence, and most have forgotten what caused the ructions in the first place, but several of his warlords continue to raid each other, refusing to listen to reason.

The one thing that unites the Cornovii is the pagan faith. Although Christian missionaries have made a few converts amongst the Cornovii, the Old Ways still prevail. Cernunnos is revered, and the game spirits of the forests and valleys are strong. The Cornovii druids are not as militant as some, but they are strong-willed and not about to let their tribe fall to any foreign god. The Romans did not try to subdue the old religion amongst the Cornovii, and it will not be permitted to happen now.

Notable Settlements of the Cornovii

Caer Guricon

Caer Guricon is the stronghold of King Lend and the spiritual centre of power for the Cornovii as a tribe. It consists of two separate areas: the old Roman town, much of which still stands and is in reasonable repair, and the Wrikon, which is the prominent hill about five miles east of the town where the hillfort that is Caer Guricon proper is located. Between the Roman town and the Wrikon are numerous small settlements where people work the land and go about their daily business. However, there is no mistaking Caer Guricon's size and importance. The hillfort is impressive, with double ditches, reinforced with stone; a solid wooden palisade hiding the hall from view, and, within, King Lend's superb stone and wooden Great Hall with additional buildings for accommodating guests, servants, stores, and so forth.

The Wrikon hillfort is only inhabited when there is some form of danger. Lend, his retinue, and other nobles retreat to the Wrikon and mastermind a defence from within its solid fortifications. The outlying people are given shelter either within the walls of the Wrikon or within the walls of the Old Town. The walls are still robust and kept in good repair, creating a second defensive area.

In peace time, the Old Town is a hive of activity. It is an important market and, because it is a Roman town in good repair, it attracts many visitors who marvel at the stone buildings, the organisation of the roads and alleys, and the sheer ambition of the place. King Lend and his family occupy a villa in the eastern quarter of the town, surrounded by his nobles.

Caer Guricon's Old Town contains several temples that were dedicated to Roman gods but are now dedicated to a mixture of Celtic gods and spirits. Cernunnos figures prominently. The largest temple is dedicated to the Horned God, with an immense pair of antlers fixed above the main entrance. Within, the walls are hung with many pelts and skins from the hunt, offerings to Cernunnos and the animal spirits of the nearby forests and woodlands. Cunomaglos, the God of Hunting and Healing, is also represented, in the form of a stylised wolf and wolf pelts. Elsewhere in the Old Town are smaller temples dedicated to Lug, Cicolluis the Battle God, and many ancestor spirits. For pagan Celts, Caer Guricon represents a centre of reverence and some travel from far away to make offerings and simply be near such a concentration of veneration.

The town is home to several druids. They conduct the standard feast-day ceremonies and ensure that offerings to the gods and spirits in the temples are replenished and kept fresh. Christians who come to Caer Guricon are treated with a certain degree of contempt, but then few Christians are drawn to such a centre of heathen devilry. There is also the matter of the rumours of shapeshifters, man-wolves who change at night and hunt Christians specifically. Thus, most Christians tend to shun Caer Guricon, or remain on its outskirts, fearing to venture within its walls, lest the druids take offence.

Caer Ffridd

A substantial hillfort and settlement in the north of the Cornovii lands, Caer Ffridd is close to the border with the Western kingdom of Powys. This was once an outpost of the Deceangli tribe, but the Romans defeated the Deceangli comprehensively and the tribe broke up, with the Cornovii subsuming some of its territory and holdings, with the rest being absorbed by the Ordovices. Caer Ffridd is a typical, reasonably sized hillfort with an enclosed settlement and great hall. It is the current seat of Llwyld, a powerful chieftain who has remained loyal to Uther and fiercely opposes the Cornovii's independent stance. Llwyld was always suspicious of Vortigern, but in Uther he found a strong, clever warrior that could lead and lead effectively. Uther and Llwyld were comrades, with Llwyld leading warbands against Kernow and also marching to Uther's aid against Aelle. Llwyld therefore has experience of fighting Saxons, but also has deep-seated grudges against several Cornovii families, especially those who still have sympathies for Vortigern. Llwyld is fast to anger, slow to calm, and never forgets a slight. There are several Cornovii clans he would happily see spitted on Saxon spears or gutted with their curious knives.

Because Llwyld is such an angry and vengeful man, it is rare for him to travel to meet with Lend at Caer Guricon, and he tends to remain within Caer Ffridd's environs. He has plenty of enemies and while he is unafraid of any of them, he is not going to risk the chance of a knife in his back, or poison in his mead just yet. He misses Uther. He detests the Saxons. He is ready to send warriors to Dumnonia's aid if it means defeating the bastard Saxons.

Man-Wolves of the Cornovii

High Druids of the Cornovii do have the ability to assume the form of a wolf. The wolf is the beast of Cunomaglos, a god who switches between human and wolf forms depending on whether or not he is healing or hunting. All the wolf spirits in the Spirit World close to Cornovii lands are kin to Cunomaglos and are manifestations of the god in the Spirit World. To attain recognition as a High Druid, the druid must enter the Spirit World, and find and tame a Wolf Spirit. If tamed (i.e., defeated in Spirit Combat), the Wolf Spirit becomes a constant, invisible companion to the High Druid on the Mortal World. On nights when the moon is full, the High Druid and his Wolf Spirit can merge, becoming a huge man-wolf, where the upper part of the body is that of a massive wolf and the lower part – the abdomen and legs – remain human. In this form the man-wolf hunts, often leading a pack of mortal wolves, with the kill being dedicated to both Cernunnos and Cunomaglos.

Do the druid man-wolves hunt Christians? Perhaps. One odious preacher from Powys came to Caer Guricon several years ago and set about defiling the temples to the Ancestors and Old Gods. He was driven out of the town and foolishly – because it was a night of a full moon – headed into the woodlands north of the Wrikon. He was found several days later, throat torn out, guts spilled, and with terrible wounds to his back and legs. His crucifix was found forced into an orifice not normally associated with proselytising.

Not all the druids of the Cornovii undertake the Spirit Quest to become a Son of Cunomaglos: it is a challenging rite and one reserved only for the most devout of druids. Naturally, Merlin has taken and passed the rite, and his Wolf Spirit is said to be Olcan, the Great Black Wolf and the pack leader of all the Wolf Spirits. Merlin neither confirms nor denies the claim.

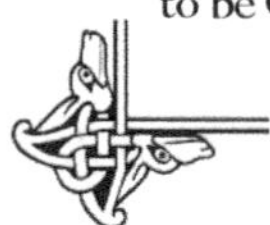

Letocetum/Caer Lwytgoed

Where the old Roman roads of Watling and Icknield cross is Letocetum. It was once a small, nondescript, Cornovii village, but the Romans built it into an important fortified staging post, which was used as a frontline for the wars against the Ordovices, Silures, and Dumnonii in the early years of their conquest. The seat of Governor Aulus Didius Gallus, it was as well appointed as Viroconium with temples, a bath house and several substantial garrison blocks.

The Cornovii were not displaced from the area and were gradually absorbed into the daily life and routine of Letocetum. Roman Governors allowed the local chiefs to strengthen their warbands and they acted as auxiliaries for the VIIth Legion stationed at Letocetum, eventually fighting against their people (and leading to many of the subsequent feuds that have plagued Cornovii history ever since). Around the year 390 Letocetum was the victim of a great fire, which destroyed many of the public buildings and led to the town being abandoned. It mattered little; Letocetum had served its purpose and so the remains of the once-prosperous garrison fell into a state of pure ruin. Caer Lwytgoed survives, though. A fortified settlement on the edge of Letocetum, the industrious locals have made use of the dressed stone from the Roman buildings to create stone roundhouses and a wooden and stone palisade around the main buildings. Caer Lwytgoed is the seat of Brochan, a cousin of King Lend, and an able warrior even though he is of advancing years. When Brochan's first wife died of disease, Brochan was heart-broken and actively sought companionship. His new wife, who has borne him two strong sons, is a Brigantes noblewoman from Elmet. She is hated by Brochan's sons by his first marriage, and they have disowned their father and young stepmother. Aiden, the older of the two, has moved to Caer Guricon and sworn his service to King Lend. The younger, Gwllyc, has moved to a neighbouring village, but has sworn to drive Brochan's new bride, Ella, out of Cornovii lands.

Brochan's remarriage has divided the people of Caer Lwytgoed into those who support Aiden and Gwllyc, and those who remain loyal to Brochan and Ella. To compound matters, Ella is a Christian

and, whilst nowhere near as devout as some Brigantes, her faith is the source of very deep unease and suspicion. Brochan shows no signs of converting, and he has made a show of welcoming the druids and propitiating the local nature spirits; but some believe it is only a matter of time. Ella intends to send her sons to Elmet to be brought up in a Christian fashion, and many, including Brochan's original heirs, are deeply troubled by the potential repercussions if these new sons are baptised.

Cornovii Culture

The Cornovii are one of the more warlike tribes of the Britons. Internally fractious, fast to anger, and very, very proud of their heritage and wealth, they enjoy battle and stirring up trouble. At least, that is the popular view. In most cases they are, like most Celts, keen to get on with their own lives but to defend what is theirs.

The high degree of interdependence between the Cornovii and Romans has led to a certain amount of Roman culture remaining in the current tribe. Roman clothing styles are favoured, and the Cornovii warriors still retain arms, armour, and shields inherited from the Roman army, or manufactured in a similar style. It is common, therefore, for the Cornovii to be armed with short-bladed stabbing swords, throwing spears akin to the pilum, and large, curved shields similar in style to the scutum. The tactics they use, though, are thoroughly Celtic. The Roman martial disciplines have not rubbed-off on the Cornovii and, once a shield wall is broken, Cornovii warriors revert to hack-and-slash tactics designed more for self-preservation than the preservation of a fighting unit.

On more peaceful notes, the Cornovii tend to favour leather goods over pottery and clay. Harder-wearing and easier to make, and lighter to carry when marching, the Cornovii are noted for their leather tankards, goblets and cups, closely stitched and often waxed to make them leak-proof.

Specific Customs and Dress

Being diehard pagans, Cornovii see the presence of the spirits everywhere, and constantly look for both good and ill omens. Any bad or poor omen results in the need to touch a piece of iron or flint to deter potentially evil spirits or poor luck. The many, many complex rites relating to hospitality, courtesy, and etiquette are acute in the Cornovii, because ignoring them incurs the wrath of the spirits who watch over such things. Every Cornovii has an Ancestor spirit, earned at birth, who watches over them — and although only the druids can commune with the spirits, this does not prevent the Cornovii from invoking the name of their ancestor frequently, and making regular offerings. At meal times, for instance, it is customary for a portion of meat, bread and either mead, wine or water to be left aside for the Ancestor.

Allies and Enemies

The Cornovii have feuded with most of the surrounding tribes. The Brigantes are their closest allies, although relations between them are not especially strong: there is merely an absence of feuding. Relations with the Dumnonii are similar; not strong, but neither are they strained. The closest, in terms of alliance, are the people of Kernow, which boasts an old and strong Cornovii presence within its borders (although the indigenous tribe is an offshoot of the Dumnonii). Kernow and Cornovii do support each other through blood-ties, and there are many, many intermarriages sealing this somewhat unlikely alliance.

Where enemies are concerned, the Cornovii have fought bitterly with the Ordovices — especially the kingdoms of Powys and Gwent — and the Silures. The Cornovii readily allied with the Romans, whilst the Ordovices, Deceangli, Dumnonii, and Silures resisted occupation. The Dumnonii capitulated eventually, but the remaining tribes of the west fought long and hard against Roman rule. The Cornovii assisted: long before the Romans arrived the Cornovii had fought against the western tribes for territory and here, now, was an attempt to settle some very old scores. The Deceangli were destroyed, and the Cornovii played a large part in the tribe's demise. The Silures and Ordovices united to oppose the Romans and were successful for a long time, but also found they had to surrender territory (which was granted to the Cornovii) in order to avoid complete destruction.

In the wake of Rome's exodus, the hatred between the Silures, Ordovices, and Cornovii has flared once more. The battles are over territory along the Cornovii border, but also over faith. Gwent and Powys have embraced Christianity to some extent, and this creates new tensions with the devoutly pagan Cornovii. These long-standing, destructive feuds continue to take lives year after year and only serve to weaken Western Britain.

Notables of the Cornovii

King Lend

King Lend rules over the Cornovii and has his seat at Caer Guricon. A sour, brooding man, he directs his hatred at Powys and makes no secret of his desire to conquer this Ordovician kingdom and bring it back under Cornovii rule. Lend affects the dress and manners of a Roman commander. His armour is authentic and has been in his family for two centuries. Lend is easily identified by the scarlet horsehair crest of his helmet and crimson cape. He is arrogant and disdainful, believing the Cornovii to be the inheritors of Britain, to have been betrayed by both Vortigern and Uther, and probably, soon, by the Brigantes. He has nothing but hatred for the Saxons – yet, until they threaten him directly, his full hatred is reserved for Powys. Lend is further soured by progeny that consists entirely of daughters. The three children by his wife, Ygrif, and several bastards produced by women of different clans, have all been female. Lend wants sons. The High Druid, Askrigg, tells him that the Ancestors are angry that Powys has not yet fallen, and that Lend will never have a son until it does. Lend believes this, and it fuels his hatred of Powys even more.

Askrigg, the High Druid

The Cornovii High Druid is the small, cadaverous Askrigg. Afflicted by alopecia leaving unpleasant tufts of grey-black hair and a scalp pocked with scabs, Askrigg is a grimy, intense, very clever, and very dangerous individual. A militant disciple of Merlin, Askrigg is a Wolf-Son, and capable of transforming into a man-wolf on nights of a full moon, and at each major ceremony. He does hunt Christians and is happy to rip out their throats when in wolf-form or slit them when purely human. Sacrifice is natural to him: the only means of appeasing the spirits and the Gods. Much of his time is spent in a cave in the woods north of Caer Guricon, but he has a small retinue of lesser druids who attend the crucial business that bores Askrigg rigid.

Askrigg is one of King Lend's chief counsellors. He has spun the king the tale that the Ancestors have cursed him merely to maintain power over the man – something Askrigg enjoys, but which is against Druidic tradition. Askrigg knows that Lend's daughters are the result of nothing more than chance, but it delights him to see the king brood and plot war against the old enemy of Powys, believing that the Ancestors want it more than anything. In fact, the Ancestors do advocate war against Powys: but only because they are as vengeful as any Celt, alive or dead. Lend is not held responsible and, when he reaches the Other World, it will be interesting to see what Lend's spirit makes of the truth.

Brochan of Caer Lwytgoed

If King Lend is sour and tormented, Brochan is tormented by grief and sour sons. He took the death of his beloved wife hard, and never thought he would find another woman who could give him the strength and support he craved. With Ella, the spirits and Ancestors smiled upon him. She has been everything he could have wished for: intelligent, witty, and pretty, and she has already borne him two more sons. Brochan should be a contented chieftain.

He never counted on his existing sons taking the offence they have. It was never Brochan's intention to insult them or their mother's memory, or drive them away. He has tried everything to be equitable, but in the end, they have chosen to become his enemies. So be it. They are grown now and make their own choices. If they choose to fight, they will find their father a mean and angry warrior who is not without support amongst the clan at Caer Lwytgoed. Brochan is keen to foster more support and those who visit him are carefully scrutinised for signs of sympathy and potential alliance.

Parisii

A tribe smaller than the Cornovii, but larger than the Carvetii, the Parisii occupy the lands immediately to the east of Elmet and running to the eastern coast of Middle Britain. The Parisii's origins are different to those of the other Celtic tribes: they came to Britain via Gaul, during the Time of Heroes, riding their chariots across the waves of the Northern Sea, or so their stories declare. Before the Romans came, the Parisii warred constantly with the Icenii, directly to their south, and forged alliances with the Brigantes of Elmet to do so. The Parisii always considered the Icenii untrustworthy, and that was to be proved when their Queen, Boudicca, turned against Rome. The Icenii were brutally punished for their efforts, and the Parisii were grateful to be rid of an old enemy.

Now the Romans have gone, there is a new threat. The Saxons wash up in their ships along the eastern coast and draw ever closer to Parisii borders. So far their main focus has been in the south,

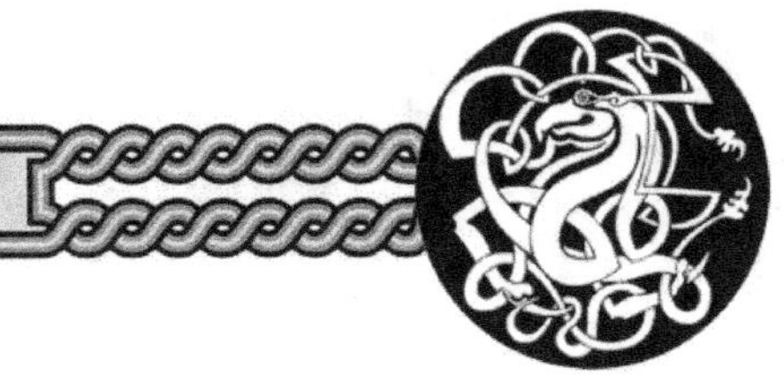

driving the Dumnonii further and further west, and probably into the sea to drown them. This is of no concern to the Parisii: in fact, the longer the Saxons are concerned with the Dumnonii, the less they will be concerned with moving north. But, as with the Brigantes, the Parisii know it is merely a matter of time.

The Parisii certainly do not have the strength to drive off the Saxons alone, and will need to unite with the Brigantes if they are to survive. It is not something they relish doing. Trade relations with the Brigantes are good: they have plenty of silver, and the Parisii have much that the Brigantes want to buy. Culturally though, the two tribes are very different. The Parisii are pagan, like the Cornovii, and the Brigantes' embracing of Christianity is troubling to them. The Parisii venerate the Spirits of the Wind and the Northern Sea. They venerate the Sky God Lugh and the Fertility Goddess Brigg. The Brigantes want the Parisii to reject these gods and accept the New God. Priests of the Brigantes say that the Son of the New God came to Britain once – a sign that Britain is beloved by the New God. But the Parisii are sceptical: why did this New God not come himself? Was he busy? Was he making war on other gods? Why send a child? None of it makes any sense.

The Parisii have only one settlement of note. Caer Pedwyr is thirty miles due east of Eboracum, the Brigantian settlement, and overlooks the whole sweep of the Brigantes territories from its position on the escarpment. Reaching Caer Pedwyr from the east means traipsing up the steep, narrow trails cut into the sharp face of the escarpment. From the west, the fort is protected by several ditches and palisades, but the broad view out over the plain makes it tough to assault the settlement without being seen a long time in advance.

The ruler is King Achaius, a king who is only fifteen years old, having been appointed the title by his peers following the death of his uncle, the previous king. Achaius could be the one to break the mould that has kept the Parisii insular for all this time. He is a good horseman, a keen hunter, and even more keen to take the war to the Saxons rather than wait for them to come to the Parisii. Achaius believes in strengthening the ties with both Elmet and the wider Brigantes, and even reaching out to Dumnonia. He is stirred by the stories of Uther's battles against Aelle, but is even more stirred by the stories emerging of Arthur – a young, fearless warrior and horseman who is determined to drive the Saxons off Britain's shores for good. Every visitor to Caer Pedwyr is asked if they have news of Arthur. Dumnonians, especially, are made incredibly welcome and the young king delights in even the slightest, most dubious tales of Arthur's exploits. When Achaius heard rumours that Merlin was somewhere in Elmet, he rode out personally in search of him, hoping to meet Arthur too.

Of course, the fact that Arthur's home for a long time was Caer Wynd has a great deal to do with Achaius' desires to formally strengthen ties, but the young king is no fool, either. He knows the Parisii cannot stand alone and alliances made now are more sensible than last-minute, desperate-seeming affairs that hold as much water as a bucket of twigs.

To start the alliance process, Achaius believes it prudent to marry a suitable woman of Elmet. He has sent emissaries to find a potential bride, instructing them that a Christian bride is just as desirable as a pagan one (if such can be found). Naturally, this troubles the King's Council: a Christian bride can bring only trouble, because it would mean inviting more of the Brigantian priests (troublemakers, the lot) into Parisii settlements. So they try to caution young Achaius away from being too accepting of an Elmetian bride and have been trying to find suitable alternatives from amongst the Cornovii instead.

Notable Places of the Parisii

Caer Pedwyr

The only large settlement of note, Caer Pedwyr is a fortified community positioned on the escarpment overlooking the vale leading west to Eboracum and sloping gradually east to the Northern Sea. It is an uninspiring place: the buildings are low, turf-roofed affairs, constructed of local stone and timber felled from the woodlands in the vale below the sharp face of the escarpment. Sheep are allowed to roam and graze within the palisade, and perhaps the most impressive parts of Caer Pedwyr are the semi-circular rows of deep ditches that flow out beyond the palisade like ripples on a pond. There are four of them in total, carved from the earth long before the Parisii took up residence in the area.

Caer Pedwyr is home to young King Achaius. Most of the community have direct relations with Achaius's family, making Caer Pedwyr a single, very large clan. There has been much inbreeding over the years and the elders of the family know that new blood is

needed. Caer Pedwyr's menfolk are therefore encouraged to find wives from outside Parisii lands. This is difficult to do though: Caer Pedwyr has little anyone else wants, and the prospect of a life in the draughty fort is quite a deterrent to marriage prospects.

Henges, Barrows, and Monoliths

The Parisii lands are peppered with a great number of ancient structures: stone circles, burial barrows, and mounds, and massive, single stones carved into a distinctive, tapering shape. The Parisii druids have counted over fifty such monuments, and have found that each is controlled by a Great Spirit and is home to many lesser spirits of related types and functions.

In the Time of Heroes, these lands were the scene of a mighty battle between the Spirits of Britain and the Giants. The Giants were driven back into the frozen seas and the Spirits prevailed, creating the island of Britain from the Great Dragon's scales. To ward against the Giants' return and commemorate the fallen heroes of the battles, the Spirits showed the mortals who lived here how to make stone monuments that acted as wards, temples, guards, and means of plotting the path of the stars across the heavens (which are the souls of heroes, passing into the Other World). The people who built these monuments are long dead, but the Great Spirits are still vibrant and vital, protecting this part of Britain's coast from invasion. Such is the presence of the Great Spirits, not even the Christian God can gain influence in Parisii lands: the Great Spirits will not allow foreign deities to enter their lands and bring doom to the people.

Every henge, barrow, and monolith, no matter how small or how windswept, is sacred and powerful. Every druid of Britain must, as part of their training, come to the Parisii lands and tour the old monuments, opening themselves to the spirits, learning their names, understanding their role in Britain's protection, and their importance for its future. Although the Parisii have little in the way of material commodities (save for good wool and peat), their land is very close to the Spirit World and a powerful source of magic.

The two most potent sites are Maiden's Ring and the Wyl Barrow. The Maiden's Ring is a henge of stones located close to the Gwyr River that flows from the northern edge of Parisii territory and then down to meet the sea. The Ring consists of thirty stones,

none of them more than four feet high, formed into a circle 300 feet in diameter. The stones form the torque of the Maiden, a fertility spirit who was pursued by the giants and almost ravaged at this place. The Maiden is a part of the torque now, and she watches over the lands and ensures the good health and fertility of both people and animals. Her saviour was the great hero Dair, who slew the giant, Alchendic, who was preparing to rape the Maiden, but was also mortally wounded in the process. The Maiden could not save Dair's life, but in those final hours as she cradled him, they were deeply in love and the Maiden pledged to remain close to his burial site for eternity. The Maiden then placed Dair in the Wyl Barrow, along with his spears, shield, and helmet. She placed her own torque nearby and then went to sleep, waiting for the Spirit World to embrace both of them as the Time of Heroes came to an end.

Both the Ring and the Barrow are of huge importance to the druids. As well as being able to communicate with two major spirits at these locations (the Maiden is an Intensity 8 Nature Spirit, and Dair is an Intensity 6 Ancestor Spirit), the Barrow is the site of

one of the lost Treasures of Britain. When trying to save Dair's ebbing life, the Maiden caught his blood in her drinking bowl. When Dair finally walked to the Spirit World, she placed the bowl on Dair's burial mound. The bowl was stolen, but the depression it left is still visible. The bowl, or cauldron, has powerful healing properties. It is not known who stole the bowl; some claim the Romans took it with the intention of sending it to the Emperor Claudius, whilst others claim it was hidden by the Maiden herself to prevent the Romans from finding it. The Maiden spirit cannot recall what happened to the bowl, but Merlin has spoken with her and it is clear the bowl is somewhere in Britain and of great importance in the struggle against the Saxons. One of Merlin's tasks, therefore, is to find the Maiden's Bowl and return it to druidic safe keeping.

Parisii Culture

People are shaped by their landscape. The landscape of the Parisii is ancient, wind-swept, and frequently Spartan: these same characteristics seem to apply to the Parisii. The word 'dour' might be used to describe a typical Parisii, and they can certainly come across as being taciturn and humourless. In reality, they are warm in their own company, but economical with their words and how they show their feelings to outsiders. Parisii are acutely aware of being part of a very, very old, very significant landscape. They consider themselves the custodians of a very ancient, raw tradition that is embodied by the monoliths, barrows, and henges of their land. They have to eke a living; and although the rivers and the sea produces much of what they need, they know that they are relatively poor when it comes to materials and tradable commodities. The Parisii therefore compensate with the richness that proximity to the Spirit World brings. They are skilled bards, extremely knowledgeable in the lore of the Celtic tribes, close to the ways of the spirits, and conscious of the mortal place in the great scales and folds of the Red Dragon.

Specific Customs and Dress

There is an abundance of flint in Parisii lands, and the Parisii are expert flint knappers. Although iron is the predominant material for weapons, Parisii still make flint knives, spears, and arrowheads, setting the stone blades into elaborate wooden and metal hafts and handles.

The Parisii are also experts in the making of wool. Their clothes are almost all woollen, from shirts to trousers to shifts to cloaks. This is not the rough homespun of many Celts, but finely crafted, soft, warm, breathable fabrics that are as different from the rough, scratchy, woollen cloths of other tribes as silver is from iron, or gold from bronze. Parisii wool is sought-after. The colours favoured by the Parisii are naturally muted: russets, browns, and greens – but traders from the Brigantes and Dumnonii like to buy undyed fabric and then apply their own colours. There is therefore a good market for Parisii cloth, and it is renowned for being hard-wearing and hugely practical.

Given the sacred nature and history of the Parisii lands, the people themselves are immersed in the superstitions typical amongst most Celts, but particularly strong with the pagans. Parisii look for omens and signs everywhere. Numbers of things are important – birds, groups of trees, calls of animals, and so on. The spirits, the Parisii know, express themselves through numbers, as is proved by the positioning of the stones in their ancient monuments, all of which conform to several different and important patterns. This expression through numerical patterns is the way for the spirits to communicate with the Mortal World without needing to go through druids.

Parisii Animal Omens

Good Animals	Good/Bad Depending on Number	Bad
Swan	Owl	Wolf
Squirrel	Fox	Black cat
Sheep	Crow	Raven
Light-coloured cat	Badger	Adder
Rabbit	Stoat	Bat
Hare	Grey cat	
Heron	Seal	
Deer	Hawk	
Boar	Bear	

To the Parisii, the multiples of 3 and 9 signify good, positive omens. Bad and negative omens are symbolised through multiples of 4 and 13. Animals – whether observed outright, heard, or their tracks found – also have the capacity to be good or bad omens, depending on their type and number.

Notables of the Parisii

King Achaius

Achaius-ap-Coell never expected to be appointed king of his tribe. His uncle, Cerrig, was a strong and confident leader and was expected to name his successor as his son or daughter. Disease took Cerrig two years ago, swiftly and before he could suggest an heir. The tribe turned to their chief druid, Hywel, and he toured the ancient sites, consulting with the Great Spirits and making many divinations. When he returned he announced that the Spirits chose Achaius above Cerrig's own offspring. This was a surprise to everyone, but Hywel insisted that the Spirits had chosen a 'Man of Destiny and Purpose'. Not a people to question the will of the Spirits, the council of the tribe acclaimed Achaius king at the Wyl Barrow, and the divination omens, taken by Hywel, were most favourable. The slave did not cry when his throat was cut, and his entrails spilled easily on the sacrificial stone. Three swans were seen flying south, and the day was calm and clear. Achaius would make a Good King.

And so he has proved. His youth belies a keen intelligence and a willingness to rule well and in the interests of the tribe. He listens to his councillors and is keen to help drive the Saxons from the shores of Britain. Achaius is enamoured of the great warlords of Britain – both historical and current. Arthur's reputation is something Achaius wants to emulate and he goes to great lengths to study and learn what he can from reports of Arthur's exploits.

As a young man who has not yet experienced a proper battle, Achaius has much to learn, but there is much trust placed in the Spirits' choice of a leader. Confidence in Achaius is high, and with it a hope for the Parisii's longer-term prosperity.

Hywel, High Druid

As the high druid of the Parisii, Hywel is extremely well versed in both the lore of the Parisii lands and the many spirits attached to the many monuments. He believes that he has achieved a special relationship with each and every spirit, and it is his duty to minister to their needs and reflect those needs within Parisii society. Hywel divides his time between touring the monuments, entering a trance to communicate with the spirits at each one, and performing duties at the settlements of the Parisii. In fact, Hywel is spending more and more time amongst the spirits and less and less time with mortals. It may be fair to say that Hywel is losing touch with the real world.

He is also becoming very possessive of his relationships. No other druid is permitted to communicate with the spirits of the Parisii monuments without Hywel's permission. There is no druidic precedent for permission being needed, and those who ignore Hywel have every right to do so. They also earn Hywel's enmity, and his increasing distance from the Mortal World is isolating him from the wider druid community. Merlin, a much more experienced and rational animist than Hywel, regularly ignores Hywel's demands to seek permission and, as a result, is loathed by the High Druid of the Parisii. The fact that the Great Spirits seem to reveal to Merlin (and several other druids) knowledge they have never revealed to Hywel only fuels his resentment. It is therefore Hywel's agenda to disrupt and undermine Merlin's efforts, and those who follow him, through fair means and foul. One such way is to sponsor Morgana. Hywel knows that Morgana is Merlin's greatest threat and so he has reached out to her with promises of helping restore Mordred to life. His plans are obscene and potent: driven by jealousy and hatred, they are every bit as injurious to Britain as the Saxons and Christians.

Northern Britain

The Great Wall built by the Emperor Hadrian defines the boundary of the Northern Kingdoms of Britain. The Romans tried numerous times to conquer these hardy, rebellious Celts: legion after legion of the Roman army ventured into the rugged, hilly, heavily forested landscape of the north and each time they came away battered and bloody. The terrain is tough: steep, with dense vegetation in the lowlands and sparse in the highlands where the winds bite and the temperature drops low enough to freeze swords in scabbards. The people, intimate with their landscape, move like shadows, suspicious of outsiders and hostile to the organised troops of the Roman army. Their magic is powerful too, with the druids shape-shifting into wolves and bears, marshalling the local spirits and peppering the land with impassable Ghost Fences. Too many Romans perished. The legendary Ninth Legion was lost in its entirety. These painted Celts – these 'Picts' – could not be conquered and so, under the instruction of the Emperor Hadrian, a Great Wall was constructed, sealing in the Picts and confining them to their brutal lands.

The tribes beyond the Wall cared very little. Their relations with the south had consisted mostly of raids anyway, and in their own country, they had everything they needed. That Rome chose to hide behind a wall of stone, earth, and wood proved them to be cowards, and so the Northern Celts went about their business unmolested.

Two tribes dominate Northern Britain: the Caledonii, who rule the west of the region, including the many small islands of the rugged west coast; and the Votadini, who control the east, being one of the tribes for whom the slur 'Pict' was coined. Before the building of the wall there were many smaller tribes, such as the Edini, the Novantae, the Damnonii, and Selgovae, but these have been subsumed into the Caledonii and the Votadini – although some clans still relate to their origins and identify themselves as such.

A third tribe has, over the past two or three generations, begun to encroach on the Caledonii's sparsely populated western quarter. The Scotii, from the north of Ireland, have been mounting steady migrations across the narrow seas, occupying the hilly, blustery, starkly beautiful coastal areas where few Caledonii live. As their numbers have grown, so have their ambitions and, in a mirroring of what is happening south of the Great Wall, these invading Celts are seeking more and more territory for themselves, pushing the Caledonii slowly and steadily into the centre of the region, which, of course, impinges on Votadini territory.

These three tribes are antagonistic to each other. Highly territorial, highly belligerent, and highly warlike, the Caledonii, Votadini, and Scotii ignore largely what happens south of the Wall and fight each other. The Caledonii, although the most numerous, are squeezed on the eastern and western fronts. The Scotii are ambitious and bring with them a raw fervour that is the antithesis of the strictly pagan Caledonii and Votadini beliefs (even though the Scotii mix pagan and Christian practices).

The Great Wall

Seventy miles long, stretching from coast to coast, the Great Wall divided Britain into Pictland and Albion. It was one of the Roman Empire's greatest engineering feats, a wall of dressed stone, layered turf, thick, wooden palisades, deep ditches, and high – sheer, in some places – ramparts; the Great Wall was an ingenious mix of fortification, barrier, and garrison. The wall itself was an almost uniform 10 feet in width and varied between 16 and 20 feet in height. A total of fifteen forts, located at strategic intervals along its length, provided a permanent garrison for around 8,000 troops and auxiliaries, both infantry and cavalry. With the exception of a brief period under the rule of the Emperor Pius, the Great Wall was permanently garrisoned from the time of its building until the time of the Roman retreat from Britain. It suffered countless assaults by the Northern Celts – some severe enough to overrun some of the forts and the breach the wall itself, but essentially the Great Wall prevailed, and it had the effect of creating separate cultural identities and developments between Northern and Southern Celts.

When Rome left, the Great Wall was abandoned. The forts were over-run by the Caledonii and Votadini, ruined and razed. The wooden palisades were ripped down or placed to the torch, and the stones plundered for other uses. By the time of Vortigern's campaign against the Picts, the entire length of the Great Wall was a ruin – but still an impressive one, for all that. The northern tribes were selective in their destruction, and large stretches of the Great

Wall remain intact, or at least capable of offering a limited defensive barrier, depending on the hostility of the terrain.

The Great Wall therefore remains as a symbolic division. For the Southern tribes, it represents the strength and capabilities of the Roman conquerors. For the Northern tribes, it symbolises the demarcation line between those who continually resisted the Roman invaders and those who capitulated. It represents the separation of the strong from the weak: the truth and its denial. The Northern tribes view almost everything south of the Great Wall with derision and contempt – even almost a century after the Romans' departure. The Great Wall might have sealed the Northern tribes into one area, but it also preserved the purity of their culture. Their druids were not murdered en-masse, and, until the Scotii began to land in the west, Christianity was unheard of. The Northern tribes therefore believe themselves to be the true Celts, the pure Celts. They did not surrender to Rome's might, did not take its gold, and did not make themselves slaves to a far-flung emperor's demands.

The Great Wall was, perhaps, the best thing the Romans ever did for the North.

Caledonii

The Caledonii occupy the central stretch of the northern lands. The Caledonii is actually an amalgam of several smaller tribes: the Caledonii, Caereni, Carnonacae, Taexali, and the Vacomagi. Before Rome occupied Britain, each was a separate tribe, but they unified around 84 AD under the leadership of Calgacus to repel the Romans. Calgacus and the Caledonii met the Roman army, under the command of Gnaeus Julius Agricola, at Mons Graupius. The Caledonii had far superior numbers and occupied the high ground, but Agricola, an experienced commander leading seasoned, well-organised troops, proved to be more than a match for the undisciplined Celtic warriors and successfully routed the Caledonii. Despite this defeat, the Romans were deterred from attempting to conquer the highlands of Britain and retreated south, allowing Calgacus to retain his lands and the Caledonii its identity.

Calgacus' efforts allowed the Caledonii to dominate the smaller tribes and absorb them. By the time the Great Wall was nearing completion, the smaller tribes had ceased to exist as cultural entities, and the Caledonii were prevalent. Only the Votadini, numerous and magically powerful, did not integrate with the Caledonii confederation and maintained their own kingdoms in the east.

Language North of the Wall

The Northern Celts speak the Goidelic version of the Celtic language, belying their Irish roots. There are some Brythonic roots in the Northern version of Goidelic, but it has far more in common with the language of Eire than it has with the language of Southern Britain.

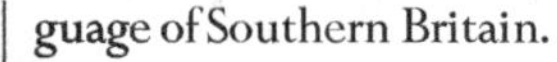

After Calgacus's death, the Caledonii continued in their defiance of Rome. In 180 AD the tribe assaulted the Great Wall, breaching it at several forts and launching raids into Roman-held lands of northern Britain. These assaults were frequent and aimed at defying Rome more than raiding beyond the wall. The raids only ceased when Governor Ulpius Marcellus agreed peace treaties with the Caledonii warlords, guaranteeing them lands in the shadow of the wall and giving his assurance not to interfere in the politics of the north. These treaties did not last. Seventeen years later, the Caledonii staged further assaults as various garrisons were weakened by Clodius Albinus. This state of affairs continued until, in 209, the Emperor Severus led an invasion of Caledonii lands to quell the continued rebellions once and for all. Severus was unsuccessful – as was his son, Caracalla, after him. The Caledonii waged long bouts of guerrilla war against the Romans, drawing them deep into the 'Pictish' kingdoms where the wild land and harsh conditions wore down the soldiery and made for easy pickings.

Since the Romans left Britain, the Caledonii have maintained their lifestyles and reputations as fierce, xenophobic warriors who are seemingly immune to the elements. Even though it is over 100 years since the Caledonii last fought the Romans, they are still highly insular, preferring the high hills and deep glens of their home to anywhere else. They do venture south to trade, but it is rare. The Saxons have not managed to reach Caledonia and, if they ever do, will find a violent welcome, for the Caledonii do not

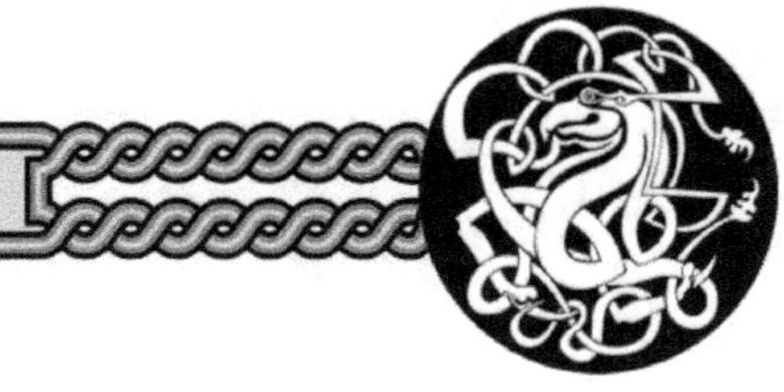

Calgus Speaks

"Whenever I consider the origin of this war and the necessities of our position, I have a sure confidence that this day, and this union of yours, will be the beginning of freedom to the whole of Britain. To all of us slavery is a thing unknown; there are no lands beyond us, and even the sea is not safe, menaced as we are by a Roman fleet. And thus in war and battle, in which the brave find glory, even the coward will find safety. Former contests, in which, with varying fortune, the Romans were resisted, still left in us a last hope of succour, inasmuch as being the most renowned nation of Britain, dwelling in the very heart of the country, and out of sight of the shores of the conquered, we could keep even our eyes unpolluted by the contagion of slavery. To us who dwell on the uttermost confines of the earth and of freedom, this remote sanctuary of Britain's glory has up to this time been a defence. Now, however, the furthest limits of Britain are thrown open, and the unknown always passes for the marvellous. But there are no tribes beyond us, nothing indeed but waves and rocks, and the yet more terrible Romans, from whose oppression escape is vainly sought by obedience and submission.

Continued...

welcome strangers, even other Celts. For the most part though, the Caledonii are unconcerned with the Saxons, who they consider to be a problem for the Southern tribes to deal with: they have problems of their own with the Scotii and Votadini.

However, being warlike, Caledonii mercenaries are not uncommon amongst the southern tribes, seeking the silver of other tribes in return for the opportunity to fight the Saxons. There are rumours too, of certain Caledonii mercenaries, such as the remnants of the Vacomagi, joining with the Saxons — such is their love of war and money.

The Caledonii are noted for their physical hardiness, being able to deal with cold, hunger, and environmental hardships that would quell most others: indeed, the very name Caledones derives from Brythonic and Goidelic terms for 'great' and 'hardy'. The Caledonii tend to be thick-set and large-limbed, giving them a formidable physical presence and reputation. Red hair is very common amongst the Caledonii, although all hair colourings are found within the tribe. Although unfair to characterise all Caledonii in the same way, it is true to say that they are culturally a very violent, warlike tribe with an immense enjoyment of feuds, raids, battles, and vendettas — many of which run through bloodlines and are based on ancient slights, disagreements, or injuries. A good example of this is the Caledonii persecution of the Carvetii. Before the Great Wall the Carvetii were disdained as farmers and shepherds, good only to be raided and plundered. Later, when they capitulated to Rome, the Caledonii had an even greater reason to hate the Carvetii: and, when Christianity took hold, that hatred took on an even deeper meaning. The Caledonii will not be happy until the weak, fawning, cross-worshipping, Roman slaves are wiped out. The protection of the Brigantes only gives the Caledonii greater reason to make war on the Carvetii: it may result in the kind of battle that the Caledonii adore.

Brochs

One feature of the kingdoms north of the Great Wall is the brochs. These tower-like structures vary between 16 and 50 feet in diameter, with walls in the region of 10 feet in thickness. Made of stacked, linked, stone slabs, the walls are often galleried, with the outer and inner walls separated by an open space and linking stone slabs set at intervals in the vertical structure of the broch. The roof is usually timber and thatch, and doorways are covered by doors with a wicker frame and then layers of moss, straw, and hide to preserve warmth.

Brochs are cultural buildings: that is, they are common to those Celtic cultures that originally colonised the coastal regions of north, especially the west and northern coasts. Brochs are similar to many Irish round towers, belying the ancestry. However, for Mythic Britain's purposes, brochs are far more widespread and form part of the structure of the dún. Brochs are another cultural differentiator between the Picts and Celts of the south: brochs are structurally ambitious and every bit as impressive as the largest halls and roundhouses of the south. Perched atop the craggy hills of the Caledonian highlands, brochs are an impressive testament to a local chieftain's power and wealth. Consider each of the fifteen dún on page 48 to have at least one broch.

The Righ

The High King of the Caledonii is known as the *Righ*. The lineage of the Righ can be traced to Cruithne, first of the kings, who ruled for one hundred years, and includes several kings who exhibited similarly impressive lifespans (Oenbecan, Gilgidi, Tharain, and Ru, to name four of the most famous and long-lived). The Caledonii — and the Votadini — believe that the Great Spirits of the Northlands, those who inhabit the high

peaks, steep glens, and deep lochs, favour the Righ and grant them lifespans far longer than most men, although such a gift can be rescinded at any time. The druids of the north are, of course, always blessed in this way, and most, like Merlin, claim lifespans of over a century (although none claim to have been alive, as Merlin does, at the Ynys Mon massacre).

The current Righ of the Caledonii, the High King, and chieftain of Àrd-na-Said is Drust Guorthinmoc. He has ruled for 20 years and is a grizzled, hard-bitten, brutal chieftain who has quelled several rebellions and challenges over the long years, most notably defeating the uprising led by the Munaith brothers of Dun Orrea. These ambitious brothers came with support from the Votadini, including druids and powerful magic, and were angry that Drust had not destroyed the Great Wall, as had frequently been promised, and raided deep into the lands of the Brigantes. Irritated by their impatience and impudence, Drust Guorthinmoc assembled an army of three hundred warbands and met the Munaiths at the Battle of Talorg Glen, where the fighting lasted three days and three nights, and involved the battling of local spirits as much as the battling of shield

Robbers of the world, having by their universal plunder exhausted the land, they rifle the deep. If the enemy be rich, they are rapacious; if he be poor, they lust for dominion; neither the east nor the west has been able to satisfy them. Alone among men they covet with equal eagerness poverty and riches. To robbery, slaughter, plunder, they give the lying name of empire; they make a solitude and call it peace."

Calgacus, 84AD
(After Tacitus)

Drust Mac Erp and the War with Vortigern

Drust Mac Erp, Righ of the Caledonii between 413 and 453, was responsible, along with Votadini allies, for launching many sustained, brutal raids into the lands south of the Great Wall. His fury was levelled at the Brigantes, but his raiding parties reached deep into the heartlands of southern Britain and antagonised the Celts to such an extent that Vortigern was able to unite them into a coherent force to take the war back to the Picts.

Drust Mac Erp had no desire for conquest of the southern lands: he was driven merely by spite and the need to punish those who had once colluded with the Romans. The Brigantes, as the nearest collaborators, felt Mac Erp's wrath the most, but he considered everyone south of the Great Wall to be a traitor and so worthy of his vengeance. In contravention of typical Celtic custom, Mac Erp took slaves from the south, deliberately destroyed property, and delighted in inflicting misery upon his foes. He encouraged his warbands to inflict atrocities that are still remembered: death pits, frequent sacrifice, enforced bestiality, rape, torture, disfigurement, and cannibalism.

Vortigern's desire to defeat the Caledonii and Votadini was born of a genuine desire to rid Britain of this terrible scourge. Every Celtic king must contemplate dreadful acts, but it was evident that Drust Mac Erp was something far, far more, and his campaign of merciless terror was enough to bring the southern tribes together under one leader – something that had never happened before.

Vortigern knew he would need more than the Celtic warbands to defeat Mac Erp and his powerful druids. He would need different magic and different warriors. This was why he turned to the Saxons for help. He thought he could replicate Mac Erp's tactics in the Pictish lands, but, like the Romans beforehand, Vortigern underestimated the harshness of the countryside and the intimacy with which the Caledonii and Votadini knew it. Like the Roman legions who venture north, Vortigern's forces were separated and butchered. Eventually, Vortigern was forced to return south leaving his enemy, Mac Erp, triumphant and gloating.

After a reign of forty years as High King of the Caledonii, Drust Mac Erp met what Vortigern would have considered a fitting death. He married a druidess of the Votadini – Aeryth, a member of the old Venicones clan – and she lusted for power. When he refused to name her Queen of the Highlands, Aeryth poisoned him with mushrooms bound with a Sickness Spirit. Mac Erp literally wasted away over the course of a year and a day, turning into a living corpse that filled the broch with the stench of decay to such an extent that his own warriors walled the dying king into the tower. Aeryth tried to assume the rulership of the north, but was slain by Talorg Mac Aniel, Drust Mac Erp's champion, who held the throne at Àrd-na-Said until Nectan Morbet Mac Erp, Drust's younger brother, was able to return from exile in Ireland to become the rightful Righ.

Some wonder if Drust Mac Erp is truly dead. After he was walled into the broch at Dun Gyll, he moaned and screamed for several weeks while he died and then all fell silent. Since then, usually in the time approaching Samhain, the moaning and scratching at the Dun Gyll broch begin again. The druids forbid the broch to be opened, afraid that the Sickness Spirit that killed Mac Erp will be released and exact horrific vengeance.

walls. Eventually Drust broke the walls protecting the Munaiths and warriors who had circled round the high points of the glen fell upon the brothers from the rear. The Munaiths were slain most brutally, torn limb-from-limb by the loyal warbands of Drust, and Drust Guorthinmoc followed this massacre by slaughtering every last member of the rebellion, and then directing his wrath against the relatives of those who had dared raise their spears against him. Every settlement loyal to the Munaiths was raided, razed, and every woman and female child enslaved: the males, regardless of age, were killed and piled into parodies of brochs as a warning to others.

This was the last time any chieftain raised an army against Drust Guorthinmoc, and he is the most feared Righ since Drust Mac Erp.

Caledonii Culture

The Caledonii have a well-earned, well-deserved reputation for hardiness, ruthlessness, and vengefulness. Grudges are held and held bitterly; slights are taken easily and appeasing an angered Caledonian is a difficult task to undertake. Weakness is scorned and treachery treated with death. There is little compassion in the Caledonii heart: these people are survivors, and one does not survive through demonstrations of regret or remorse. One cannot take back the past, so when something is done it is done. Caledonians rarely grieve and have the ability to easily shrug off their actions.

As the Caledonii is a complex amalgam of much older and smaller tribes, each with their own customs, there is considerable cultural diversity across the kingdom in terms of generally held beliefs, stories, songs and tales. Some Caledonii clans cling to their Irish past more than others. Some loathe the southerners more than others. Some consider themselves more Votadini than Caledonii, but recognise it would be stupid to act otherwise. The Caledonii identity is merely a convenient label for the central geographic area and broad cultural group of these people: loyalty to Dún Àrd-na-Said is assured, but true loyalty is far more localised and granted to the ancient clan ties, as told in the songs and lays.

Specific Customs and Dress

The Caledonii have developed a form of patterned weaving that identifies their clan in the same way that warlords of the south have adopted animal and nature totems as their standard. This chequered pattern, known as tartan, is found throughout the Goidelic-speaking Celts and especially so in the clans north of the Great Wall. The chequered pattern is ubiquitous, but the differentiation comes in the colours, the strands used in the weave, the closeness of the bands creating the chequering, and so forth. Many different pigments are used to colour the tartan and each clan has a specific, closely guarded recipe for its dyes.

The garments made from the tartan are traditionally a long length of wool that is wrapped and folded around the body, over undergarments of linen trews or skirts, and shirts or tunics. This provides warmth as well as acting as an identifier, and the whole assembly is held in place with a series of pins and brooches. In battle, many Caledonians strip themselves of their day-to-day clothes and wear just their tartan robing. Coupled with the fondness for woad tattoos and body paintings, and the spiking of the hair using lime, it is easy to see how the word 'Pict' came to be applied to the Caledonii by the Romans.

Indeed, Caledonii warriors tend to shun the use of armour, seeking proactive magic from their druids, or simply relying on their wits, woad, and kilts. Armour can be restrictive, and the Caledonii do not have a tradition of wearing it. Some Caledonii mercenaries, operating south of the Great Wall, do not cling to such traditions and many can be found wearing leather armour, but when operating as a Caledonii warband, armour is a great rarity and those who use it habitually are often treated with disdain.

Allies and Enemies

The Caledonii have no allies. In the past, they have briefly found common cause with the Votadini, but that has always been short-lived. In general, the Caledonii see everyone outside their borders as the enemy.

Special hatred is reserved for the Carvetii, the tribe that once was part of the Caledonii, but committed the dual crimes of capitulating to the Romans and then embracing the Christ-God. Their betrayal is compounded by their seeking the protection of the

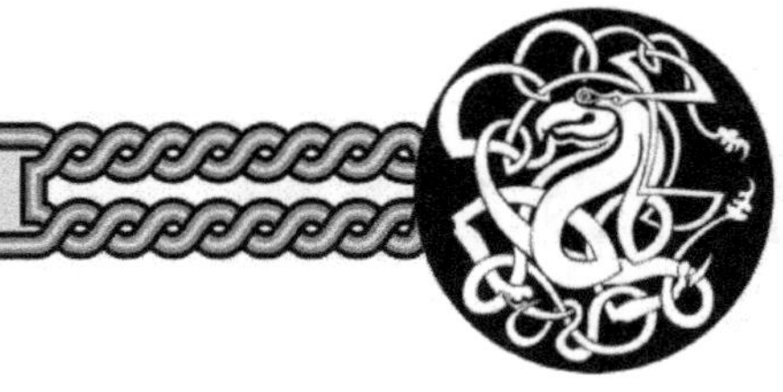

Brigantes, who are also traitors and Christ-Worshippers, and so the Carvetii deserve to be wiped out.

The Brigantes are enemies also, for similar reasons to the Carvetii, although the hatred towards them is tempered only in that the Brigantes have always been their own people and were never part of the Caledonii to begin with.

Drust Guorthinmoc, King of the Caledonii, loathes the legacy of Vortigern and, although he dislikes the Saxons, their efforts to crush the southerners fill him with a certain amount of admiration. He has therefore had no hesitation in sending Caledonii mercenaries into the Saxon lands to try, sometimes, to aid the invaders. Guorthinmoc has received Saxon emissaries from time to time, but he finds their ways and customs brutish and coarse, and so gives them as little time as possible. However, he is certain that, as long as the Southern Celts remain divided, and remember the betrayals of Vortigern and Uther, the Saxons will succeed in wiping out all those who dared collude with Rome over the centuries, this saving him time and effort.

And this is important. The Votadini are constantly seizing Caledonii territory in a bid to extend their own lands and, in recent years, the Scotii from Ireland have also arrived on the western shore and started to take lands for themselves. It has been a long time since the Caledonii were forced to make war on their neighbours, but it just might be the right time for Drust Guorthinmoc to flex his muscles and reinforce the old boundaries that the Scotii and Votadini now seem to be ignoring.

Notable Settlements

As is traditional amongst Celtic tribes, the Caledonii build and occupy hillforts. The undulating, hilly landscape forming the bulk of the Caledonian kingdom is ideal. Each major hillfort, or dún, marks the territory controlled by one of the ancient clans absorbed into the Caledonii whole. Hence, there is considerable regional identity, clan pride, and familial competition. The centre of the Caledonian kingdom, its ruling seat, is Dún Àrd-na-Said – Fortress of the High Arrows – on the Forth estuary, where the Strath River flows into the Northern Sea. Àrd-na-Said is hugely impressive: occupying the entire summit of an extinct volcano, the fortress dominates the local landscape and overlooks many miles of open landscape in every direction. Ascending to Àrd-na-Said is possible from any direction, but only if one can negotiate the numerous switchback paths with their concealed death-pits, sheer ramparts, deep ditches, and the unbroken double palisade of wood, stone, turf, and rubble that forms a double-defensive ring around the buildings within.

Other forts are similar, and there are nine important or major fortresses (including Àrd-na-Said) stretching Caledonia's length and breadth, each the stronghold of a chieftain.

Caledonii Duns

Dun	Chieftain
Alauna	Aroic the Bear
Àrd-na-Said	Drust Guorthinmoc
Bannatia	Gara Mac Aban
Colanica	Oengus Mac Kay
Devana	Fiach Fib
Inchtutill	Gede Mac Nairn
Orrea	Paraig Mac Necht
Tamia	Naish Mac Brude
Tuesis	Nara Mac Ana (Chieftainess)
Vindogara	Hamich Mac Esc

Notables of the Caledonii

Drust Guorthinmoc

Drust Guorthinmoc, as already noted, is a hard, brutal, no-nonsense ruler. He is, however, a complex man and not without subtlety and learning. He is a devout believer in the Old Gods and has studied the legends of his people intently, convinced that the great, long-lived rulers of the past shared a similar passion for the ways of the Spirit World and God's World. Drust relies upon two councils: one of his own chieftains and the other a circle of five druids who act as his spiritual mentors. Drust is fluent in Goidelic and Brythonic: he can also read and write some Latin and appreciates fine poems and songs (bards are always welcome in his hall – even bards from south of the Great Wall). He can play the flute and the

harp and although he stops short of creating his own music, he can accompany others and does so at feasts and celebrations.

But Drust's reputation has been made as a warrior first and foremost. A huge, broad-shouldered man, his favoured weapon is his long spear, which is twice his own height. He carries a sword and is skilled with it, but it his spear that marks him. When the Munaith brothers were captured, and before they were ripped to pieces, they were forced to stand in front of an old elm tree: Drust rammed his spear so hard that it cleanly impaled both men and split the trunk of the tree in two. The spear is therefore known as Tree Splitter, and it is as famous and feared as its owner.

Drust, having killed everyone that could be considered an enemy, has several wives and at least twelve children. This extended family is housed in a specially built wing of Àrd-na-Said, and only he and his advisers are allowed in there. Much of his time is spent travelling up and down the kingdom visiting the various chieftains to ensure they are kept in line and understand, at all times, who is in charge. He travels with his druidic council, his warband, and his champion, Wurgest, an equally large and brutal Caledonian of Maetae stock and descent. Wurgest is known as The Smiling Killer, because he always has a welcoming grin on his innocent-looking face. The grin is a facade: the only life Wurgest respects is Drust's. Wurgest has, at one time or another, killed every permutation of human being and in some of the most brutal ways. His presence at Drust's side is yet another reminder to the chieftains that Guorthinmoc commands and rules: any who want to challenge him must face The Smiling Killer and then suffer Drust's wrath with Tree Splitter.

Nara Mac Ana, Chieftainess of Tuesis

One of the more northerly clans, the Ana occupy the hillfort of Dún Tuesis, and their leader is Nara, the sole female chieftain of a Caledonian stronghold. Nara seized control after the previous chieftain, Usc, lost his mind and took it into his head that every child was a changeling, a plan by the druids of the Votadini to seize Tuesis. In his madness, he decided to kill every child younger than

five summers and would have succeeded had Nara, the widowed wife of Usc's dead champion, not stopped him.

With her dead husband's sword and shield, Nara challenged Usc in the Court of Swords, where justice is granted to the one who emerges victorious. Usc was a potent warrior, but Nara had visited the druids and they had seen the madness in Usc's mind and so helped her. The spirits of forest came to Nara's aid and gave her incredible strength and speed. She fought Usc and defeated him. The druids declared that the Great Ancestor Spirits of the clan wanted Nara as the new chieftain of the clan, and her people accepted her. So has Tuesis been for the last ten years, and the Clan Ana has strengthened and prospered in that time.

Drust Guorthinmoc views Nara with grudging respect. Usc was a friend, but even Drust could see the man had gone insane, which happens from time to time and is usually the Will of the Spirits and Gods. Nara is loyal to the throne, pays tribute to Àrd-na-Said, and sends warbands and warriors when told to. Over the course of the past decade, they have been lovers, but it was never a serious relationship. Both have been counselled by their druids to remain apart, and so Nara and the High King of the Caledonii treat each other with measured respect.

Nara has had to contend with prejudice and hatred during her rule. She has met this as any other Caledonii chieftain does: by challenging and defeating her enemies. She is skilled with a sword and has the added advantage of being able to call on the spirits of her dead husband and several other warrior-ancestors to aid her as needed.

Votadini

While the Caledonii occupy the central, north-south stretch of the lands beyond the Great Wall, the Votadini occupy the neighbouring lands to the east, controlling the coastline almost to the Orkneys. When the Romans arrived this whole area consisted of many, much smaller tribes (mostly extended families), with the largest clan being the Venicones. The Venicones suffered several Roman incursions but successfully resisted occupation and defeat. Unlike the Carvetii, the Venicones did not become a civitas and, unlike the Caledonii, they were not routed and dispersed by Agricola's forces. The Venicones, and their close neighbours, the Taexali, explained this good fortune through their strong relationship with the spirits and gods of their lands, particularly the ancestor spirits, who guard the Venicone lands from invaders and aggressors.

The Votadini lands are divided into two sub-kingdoms: Gododdin is the kingdom between the Great Wall and the Forth estuary. Circind is the remote, inhospitable land north of there. The clans of these regions were united by the druid Vot the Grey during his Spirit Walk of the late Third Century. Vot the Grey wandered between the clans accompanied by many spirits and many ancestors. At each chieftain's hall, Vot demonstrated how the lands were united and how the people should accept one tribal ancestry; through magic and persuasion, gifts, and (sometimes) threat, Vot the Grey created the Votadini tribe over the course of twenty years of wandering.

Of course, there was political purpose to this. The Caledonii threatened to swamp all lands in the east and they had old scores to settle with the Venicones and Taexali, both of which had accepted some gifts and emissaries of Rome. Vot the Grey set the new Votadini tribe firmly against Roman rule, and encouraged raiding against the Roman outposts along the Great Wall's edge: but he also set the Votadini against the Caledonii and in sufficient numbers to resist the assaults launched by Gartnaith Loc and Breth Mac Buthut – brutal leaders of the Caledonii during Vot's lifetime.

When Vot crossed into the Other World, aged 133 years, the Votadini alliance continued, much to the surprise of the Caledonii who thought that Vot's passing would lead to civil war and easy pickings. It did not. The druidic tradition Vot the Grey created from the eastern people ensured that the Votadini prevailed as a tribe, even if it occupied two very different geographical areas.

In 460 the southern Votadini elected a new king, Lot, and this ambitious warrior had ideas that did not include the wider concept of the Votadini tribe. He declared the lands between the Tweed and Tyne rivers his own kingdom, known as Gododdin. Lot, like the Caledonii, loathes the kingdoms to the south and would see an empire built. When Vortigern came to mount his futile war against the Caledonii, Votadini settlements were attacked and many destroyed. Lot was one of the warlords who led the resistance against Vortigern and his Saxon mercenaries, and even after Vortigern's defeat he believes that the Caledonii and Votadini should take the fight back to the southerners, smashing

them against the Saxon wall in the very south of the country. That the Caledonii seems somewhat reluctant angers Lot, and so he directs the wrath of his Votadini warbands against the Caledonii south-eastern flank as a punishment for deserting the Pictish way that has held these lands for centuries. Lot also wants to see Christianity, which the Brigantes propagate, wiped from the island. It creeps steadily north and will, like a disease, surely cross the Wall at some stage.

Votadini Paganism

Paganism is very strong amongst the Votadini and, despite the strengthening presence of Christianity to the immediate south, the Votadini still have a druidic tradition and an unshakeable belief in the Old Ways supported by some unique traditions that keep their relationship with the spirits strong and potent.

The Votadini venerate and revere their dead. Bodies are buried in stone-lined graves and tombs, along with all the accoutrements needed for a prosperous existence in the Other World. The rites performed by the druids ensure that the spirit does not wither into non-existence but safely makes the journey to the Lands of the Ancestors, thereby continuing to live and watch over the people of the Mortal World. This creates a very strong mortal/ancestor relationship, with the druids of the Votadini able to work potent magic through ancestor and other spirits.

Every Votadini settlement has at least one druid and apprentice. Druids are both male and female, and selected by the druid ancestors who, unlike the general Venicone ancestors, are sent to the Other World through cremation rather than burial. Votadini lands are filled with sacred groves, shrines, and magical links to the Spirit World, such as bogs, lakes, and ponds, each of which is tended by its own nature spirit. These places are deeply sacred to the Votadini and offerings — of precious goods and human lives — are frequently made. But for all their insularity, the Votadini are not unsophisticated. Their skills in metalworking, particularly bronze, are well known, and the huge bronze torques Votadini warriors wear about their upper arms are beautiful, complex, and highly sought-after by many.

The strength of the spirits and the presence of so many druids keeps Christianity at bay. Missionaries from the Brigantes refuse to enter Gododdin lands, and the scant few who have, have become sacrifices to the spirits and ancestors of the Votadini. This protection extends beyond Christianity: the Roman gods have no power in Votadini lands, meaning that the Roman army soon became demoralised and disoriented when campaigning in this region. Aided by their spirits, the Votadini were able to stealthily pick-off the invaders with spears and slings, their spirit guardians guiding their arms and eyes, but also seizing fearful, isolated Roman soldiers to drag them into marshes and bogs or send them tumbling down concealed ravines.

The reputation of the Votadini has spread across Britain. Christians view them as demons. The southern kingdoms of the Celts know them as shadowy killers aided by kinds of magic that has been long-forgotten across the rest of the land. The Votadini are respected, feared, and hated in equal measure. Their lands are a heart of darkness where outsiders fear to tread: a land of spirits and sacrifice, sacred and unforgiving.

Ancestor Spirits of the Votadini

The powerful ancestor spirits venerated by the Votadini are those chieftains, warlords, and kings who founded the tribes of the northern lands, and many of them are Irish by origin. Each ancestor resides in the Other World, accompanied by his warband. There are 21 in all, and of varying Intensities (see MYTHRAS page 145) as listed in the table on page 52.

The ancestral chieftains and kings recognise the blood and veneration found in all Votadini and can therefore be persuaded, using the usual Animism rules, to inhabit heirlooms; manifest in a suitable body; offer information, knowledge and insight; and so on. Their Intensity means that, usually, only the most powerful druids would attempt to channel one of the major ancestors directly, but it is often the case that an ancestor will send a lesser ancestor (generally one of his spectral warband) in his place to fulfil any bargains struck with druids of lower power or lesser experience.

Every ancestor listed in the Votadini Ancestor table is an enemy of Christianity and also the direct enemies of those who lack Pictish blood. This means anyone born south of the Great Wall or who is not of Pictish descent. However, it does not automatically mean that an ancestor summoned by a Votadini druid would treat a Caledonian as an enemy, or even someone south of

Votadini Ancestor Spirits				
Ancestor (Intensity)	INT, POW, CHA	Customs & Lore	Spectral Combat & Willpower	Abilities
Cing (5)	10, 31, 14	120%	95%, 111%	Folk Magic 124% (Bladesharp, Demoralise, Fanaticism)
Cruithne (5)	12, 33, 8	124%	70%, 116%	Insight 120%, Discorporate 70%
Got (5)	10, 34, 13	120%	73%, 118%	Influence 126%, Folk Magic 73% (Find Enemies, Glamour)
Fidach (6)	10, 40, 14	120%	74%, 130%	Folk Magic 124% (Curse, Repugnance, Shove)
Ce (6)	16, 41, 16	132%	82%, 132%	Lore (Strategy and Tactics) 132%, Discorporate 82%
Fotlaig (6)	13, 40, 13	126%	76%, 130%	Perception 126%, Survival 126%
Cirech (4)	15, 28, 17	130%	82%, 106%	Folk Magic 82% (Avert, Befuddle, Calm)
Fortriu (4)	12, 30, 10	124%	72%, 110%	Discorporate 122%
Fibald (5)	15, 35, 11	130%	76%, 120%	Athletics 126%, Brawn 126%
Olgudh (4)	11, 29, 17	122%	78%, 108%	First Aid 128%, Healing 128%
Oenbach (6)	13, 38, 15	126%	78%, 128%	Folk Magic 68% (Bladesharp, Bludgeon, Coordination), Discorporate 68%
Guidid (4)	13, 30, 16	126%	79%, 110%	Deceit 129%
Bront (4)	14, 27, 12	128%	76%, 104%	Survival 126%
Gilgidi (5)	11, 36, 11	122%	72%, 122%	Folk Magic 72% (Find Lies, Protection, Slow)
Tharain (4)	13, 26, 9	126%	72%, 102%	Lore (Strategy & Tactics) 122%
Morleo (5)	13, 34, 9	126%	72%, 118%	Discorporate 72%
Declan (6)	10, 37, 9	120%	69%, 124%	Influence 119%, Oratory 119%, Insight 119%
Cimoiod (4)	13, 29, 12	126%	75%, 118%	Folk Magic 75% (Darkness, Fanaticism)
Arcois (5)	15, 36, 17	130%	82%, 122%	Discorporate 132%
Beli-Mawr (6)	13, 42, 11	126%	74%, 134%	Folk Magic 124% (Bladesharp, Bludgeon, Fanaticism), Discorporate 74%, Lore (Pagan) 124%
Diu (4)	17, 28, 12	134%	79%, 116%	Insight 129%

the Wall. If there is northern blood flowing in someone's veins, the ancestor knows it and weighs carefully how it will act.

As can be seen from the list of ancestors, these are very powerful, potent spirits. Calling for their aid always comes with obligations and, for those of Intensity 6, a blood sacrifice. None of these ancestors can be bound (one can always try, of course, but no true druid, even Merlin, would dare), so calling upon one of these ancestors is for the purposes of a one-off favour, power, or spell. The Votadini druids know the names of each ancestor and the powers they are said to command, and so can always make informed petitions.

The Two Kingdoms

The Votadini are divided into the two kingdoms of Gododdin and Circind. Gododdin is the smaller sub-kingdom, but the more populous; Circind is largely wild, untamed country, where the Votadini live in small, very insular, hostile communities that can be antagonistic to each other, despite the tribal connection. Even some Gododdini are fearful of their Circind cousins (and the spirits commanded by their druids). Rumours of cannibalism and frequent human sacrifice are well founded, especially in the more isolated communities. In fact, Circind has no notable hillforts: the nature of the landscape is ideal for them, but the Picts of Circind have never needed such fortifications, and have always been content with stockaded villages and the natural defences offered by the landscape.

Gododdin and King Lot

In Gododdin, things are more akin to traditional Celtic life. The Gododdini inhabit small farms and the traditional dún and brochs found across the northern lands. Largest of the Gododdin hillforts is Dún Curia, which looks out across the Forth estuary, and covers around 40 acres of the hill's summit. The hill was occupied long before the Celts arrived and was a burial centre for the prehistoric peoples of these lands. Their spirits are still strong around Dún Curia, manifesting as a strange mixture of ancestor, Curse, Death, Guardian, and Nature Spirits. In fact the hill's substance holds every form of spirit available (see the Animism section of MYTHRAS): it is simply a question of the druid's ability and willingness to look for a particular type.

The kings of the region, Gododd and his direct ancestors have always been materially wealthy. Silver, in particular, has been

hoarded for a long time; payment from Rome for various deals; money taken through theft and murder; silver gained through legitimate trading deals; and money obtained from raids. Beneath the King's Broch, which is the central hub of the Curia fort, are a series of passages and tunnels that burrow deep into Curia's heart and even penetrate the many ancient tombs. The wealth of the Gododdin Kings is stored in these passages — bags, boxes, and chests of silver, gold, precious stones, and other artefacts. The wealth is used generally to trade, but most is held in trust for the Votadini tribe, a symbol of its power and cunning.

Gododdin's ruler is King Lot. Lot is in his middle years but forged his reputation raiding south of the Great Wall (where he added to the Curian coffers) and battling Vortigern's invasion force. He is an ambitious, impatient, avaricious man, prone to murderous, jealous rages, such as the one that led to the death of his daughter, Teneu, when it was discovered she was pregnant by a warlord, Owain ap Urien, who had incurred Lot's wrath. Lot dragged the girl to the sheerest edge of Curia and threw her from it. Teneu would have been dashed to her death on the jagged rocks below, had not the guardian spirits of Curia saved her. Lot's

youngest son, Gawain, was called by the spirits and went in search of his sister, finding her unconscious body at the foot of the hill. He took Teneu south, beyond the Great Wall, and into the lands of the Brigantes where he knew she would be safe. He also renounced his heritage, declaring Lot of the Votadini to be his enemy. Gawain now serves as a mercenary, moving between Elmet, Dumnonia, Powys, and Gwent, where he has gained a fearsome reputation as a warrior and leader.

Lot's fury has not abated. Gawain has committed the ultimate treachery, and King Lot has offered a substantial payment of silver from the Curia Hoard for anyone who brings to him Gawain's head. He knows that Teneu survived, has taken to the Christian religion, and now has a son, Kentigern.

Circind and the Druid Kings

The tradition amongst the Votadini of Circind is to be ruled by their druids. Although this has not been an unbroken tradition, it is a common one, and over the centuries there have been many Druid-Kings, ruling the remote and wild lands of Circind through both magic and battle. Most famous of the Druid-Kings, and now one of the most potent ancestor spirits, was Beli Mawr, a founder of the Votadini tribe and a demigod in his own right. Beli Mawr called upon the spirits to drive the Giants out of Britain before forming the Votadini. After that, it became commonplace for a druid to rule the Votadini, channelling the power and wisdom of the ancestors for the greater good of the tribe. In time, views on this practice changed, with Gododdin following the more typical Celtic path, and Circind retaining the Druid-King pattern.

The druids of the many clans of Circind meet when the old ruler dies, to assess the strength of their number and identify likely Druid-King candidates. Competition is fierce with druids seeking the position for themselves or wanting to secure it for a protégé. Many rituals are conducted, many ancestors questioned, and, if no consensus is reached, then Beli Mawr himself is consulted. Whoever is identified becomes the next King, be it druid or non-druid. This conclave is an elaborate, secretive affair, closed to non-druids, and held, whenever possible, at either Imbolc or Samhain.

Votadini Customs and Culture

The Votadini, both Gododdini and Circind, revel in tattoos, piercings, and ritual scarifications. The designs are traditionally Celtic in many cases, but further supplemented by bizarre totemic designs, harsh patterns, and runes and sigils devised either by their druids or the wearer. The first tattoos are gained at puberty, marking the passing into adulthood. From then on, every individual adds at least one tattoo each year marking one or more special events — be these killings, hunting trophies, children sired, or other events the individual considers notable. Because such body art is a source of great pride, the men keep themselves clean-shaven, and

many shave their heads too, allowing for the whole body to accommodate tattoos.

The Votadini are expert hunters and trackers, intimately familiar with the terrain for many miles surrounding their settlements. They are masters of moor and forest, ridge and dell, able to move silently and blend with the shadows and natural cover effortlessly. The Romans understood the importance of such skills and employed Votadini trackers to help their own legions. The Votadini were happy to help at first, until it became obvious that Rome simply wanted to conquer the north: then the Votadini turned on their former allies and slaughtered them in cunning and terrible ways. The infamous Ninth Legion was one of the Votadini conquests: scattered, harassed, hunted, and then slaughtered to a man in the labyrinthine forests and vales of Circind.

A further cultural trait of the Votadini is isolation and circumspection. Votadini are uncomfortable outside their own lands – which they know and understand intimately – and in the company of other tribes, even if these are considered allies. It is almost as though the Votadini are 'pure' Picts: naturally aggressive, naturally isolationist, and culturally xenophobic. Although the Votadini can and do travel beyond their borders, it is rare to find a member of the tribe who comfortably socialises with others beyond cursory reciprocations of hospitality. Gawain is an exception – a Votadini who has shunned his homeland in order to protect his sister and himself.

Allies and Enemies

In the past, the Votadini, particularly the Gododdin clans, have allied themselves with the Caledonii, but such alliances have been generally short-lived, designed to achieve a specific goal or purpose. Usually, they are enemies, and this is the current state of affairs. The Druid-King Mawgaus accuses the Caledonii of becoming soft and weak and King Lot follows this lead, encouraging his warbands to raid Caledonii settlements close to the Votadini borders. King Lot had intended to marry his youngest daughter to a Caledonian chieftain, but her betrayal meant that could never happen and so Lot has reverted to a state of antagonism towards the neighbouring tribe.

The Votadini are aware of the encroaching Scotii but could not care less about them: the Scotii are taking Caledonii lands, not Votadini territory, and so further punish the arrogant Caledonians. Of course, the Brigantes will always be an enemy as will any Southern tribe. The Saxons, though, are a curious people. They turned on Vortigern after being his ally and have effectively divided Britain into three. The Votadini do not, for now, consider the Saxons a direct threat: neither do they believe that they will, on their own, wipe out the enemy tribes south of the Great Wall, and so the Votadini must maintain their hatred of the Southern Celts, continue their raids, and make life as miserable as possible for those who aided Rome for close to five centuries.

Notable Votadini

King Lot

Lot ap Lein forged a reputation as a fearsome and fearless reiver, raider, and war chief, leading daring missions across the Great Wall to steal and harry the Brigantes and others. When Vortigern came north with his Saxon allies, Lot was amongst those who lured the invaders deeper and deeper into Pictish lands before picking-off Vortigern's warbands steadily and methodically, until Vortigern was forced to retreat. It was a tactic that served the Picts well against the Romans, and it remains effective.

Later, Lot became the King of Gododdin, taking the rulership at Dún Curia from King Culdh and swearing an oath to honour the great traditions of Curia's kings to safeguard its wealth and extend it.

Lot already had several children who had grown into fine adults. His favourites were Teneu and Gawain, his youngest daughter and son, respectively. Lot had in mind marriage with a powerful Caledonian chieftain for Teneu and so, when he discovered that his beloved daughter was pregnant with the child of Owain ap Urien, a warrior who had defied Lot several times, he was furious to the point of insanity. That Teneu cheated death, and Gawain, also beloved, defected to the south, were two betrayals Lot could not bear. His mind, bent with grief and jealousy, is broken, and he is now beyond hope. Crazed and vengeful, Lot is prepared to squander every last coin of the Curian Hoard to have Gawain punished – and only death will do. Lot has sent several formidable warriors south to hunt for Gawain and bring back his

head. Foremost of these hunters is Uidre, a man of prodigious size known by some as the Warrior in Green because of his emerald cloak. Uidre has a reputation as an excellent hunter but also the reputation for being a blood-thirsty murderer and almost as mad as King Lot has become.

Gawain

The youngest of Lot's children, Gawain is extremely close to his siblings but especially so to Teneu, his sister. When his father threw Teneu to her death, the spirits of Curia saved her and brought that news to Gawain in a dream. The young warrior knew he must get Teneu to safety and, although he had been a loyal Votadini warrior, serving in Curia's warbands, he was certain Teneu would never be safe while in the Pictish lands. He therefore brought her south, to the land of the Brigantes, and foreswore his oath to his father and Curia, becoming a wandering Pictish mercenary, prepared to fight for whichever chieftain might need his spear and sword. In the ten years since he fled Gododdin, Gawain has never remained in the same community for very long, flitting between Powys, Gwent, Elmet, Dumnonia, and even Kernow. He knows he is hunted, and he knows Uidre the Warrior in Green hunts him. Soon there must be a reckoning, but for now he has been able to keep himself several steps ahead of Uidre, using a variety of names (Gwalchmei, Gualguanus, and Gauvain, for instance) and invented histories.

The bounty on Gawain's head is substantial: a man's weight in silver, so it is said, or half his weight in gold.

Mawgaus, Druid-King of Circind

Mawgaus is the current Circind Druid-King. A terrifying figure, his entire body is covered in tattoos of red and blue, his hair bleached white and worn in stiff spikes, his eyes devoid of pupils having stared for too long into the Spirit World.

He is a potent druid – some say he rivals Merlin in his power – and he derives much of that power through the sacrificed souls of enemies and prisoners. The blood drained from these sacrifices is used in the ink that goes into the tattoos covering Mawgaus' body, and, in this way, he retains a little part of the spirit of the victim, accessing their knowledge and memories even after death.

Mawgaus surrounds himself with strong, vicious warriors who style themselves after the Druid-King, with blood tattoos and bleached, spiked hair. The initiation rite to join Mawgaus's warband is to consume human flesh following a sacrifice, and those willing to eat of the brains, heart, or genitals are considered the most special and important warriors. Mawgaus is protected by fifty or so of these warriors, and always travels in their company. Usually though, his home is Broch Dubh – the Black Tower

— deep in the centre of Circind, close to a small, black pool that is a gateway to the Other World.

Although insular and rarely seen, Mawgaus's influence is felt across Circind. His warbands travel between the scattered communities exacting tribute and sacrificial victims, ensuring that Mawgaus continues to be to respected and feared. In return, Mawgaus petitions local spirits to help protect the communities and, from time to time, offers personal divinations to reassure his subjects and assure their continued loyalty.

Scotii - Dál Riada

Just as the Saxons have steadily migrated from the east, so the Scotii steadily migrate from the west. These Irish Celts are a mixture of warriors, farmers, and general settlers looking for their own lands and territories beyond Ireland's shores. Many are refugees from persecution by Irish warlords. Others are religious refugees, unwilling to accept the tide of Christianity sweeping through Ireland. Still others are Christians looking to bring the word of God into the heathen north of pagan Britain.

The migration began before Rome departed the island. In reality, it had been going on for decades, with the Irish raiding the coastal settlements and a few making homes for themselves; but it wasn't until the first years of the 5th Century that the migration become truly numerous, and these Irish migrants began to form cohesive clans and claim a viable cultural identity. Scotii is a Roman term for these people, but it has taken hold to the extent that even the migrants use it to refer to themselves as a people.

The Scotii occupy the rugged, complex west coast of the north, including the many islands that pepper the sea separating Britain and Ireland. They call their lands Dál Riada and it comprises three large clans that collect together under the Scotii tribal name. These clans, or Cenél, are Cenél Loairn, Cenél Oengusa, and Cenél Gabrain. Like the other Pictish inhabitants, they speak Goidelic, but they do not trade with the Caledonii to their immediate east. The Caledonii have, for the most part, tolerated the Scotii presence: the lands they occupy are remote, tough to farm, and tough to reach. However, the Scotii have started to extend their territory as more people come across the sea. The Scotii now raid Caledonii lands and sequester unoccupied regions, challenging local warlords to drive them out. In recent years, the antagonism has increased, more so with the accession of Domangart Réti as King of Dál Riada. Domangart has promised to extend Scotii lands and establish not just a territory, but an entire nation separate from both the Irish and Pictish Celts. This ambition has galvanised the Scotii, and Domangart is attracting the support of warlords from all across Dál Riada, keen to gain more lands and more glory.

Domangart is driven by more than just territorial ambition: he knows that beyond the Caledonii are the Votadini, and that Dún Curia is filled with ancient treasures and burial goods — enough silver and gold to buy the world twice over. His sights are set firmly on conquering the whole of the north, turning the Pictish Lands into Scotii Lands from coast to coast and the highlands to the Great Wall.

This ambition is tempered somewhat by Irish pragmatism: Domangart does not believe that the whole of the country will become Scotii in his lifetime; he knows it may take several generations for conquest to be complete. But Domangart wants to be remembered as the instigator of the full colonisation of the Pictish territories — the father of a new empire that will rival that of the Roman conquest to the south.

Meanwhile, the Scotii continue their daily lives, growing oats and barley, herding their livestock, and tending to their personal affairs. The Scotii lands do not support enough surplus food for trade, and so the Scotii follow a subsistence economy, supplementing what they eke with raids into Caledonii lands. The quality of the land for crops is variable. In many regions, the soil is thin and requires careful management; it is commonplace for communities to move with their cattle and sheep herds between summer and winter pastures in a semi-nomadic style. Yet on some of the islands, such as Islay, the soil is rich and fertile giving year-round pasture and good cereal crops.

Religion Amongst the Scotii

There is a curious mix of pagan and Christian faiths amongst the Scotii. On the Irish mainland, the Christian religion has gained considerable strength through the work of the preacher Pádraig: but the Irish Christians have retained a healthy respect for the Old Teachings, meaning that the antagonism between the two religions found south of the Wall is somewhat absent amongst the

Scotii. Many still venerate the Old Gods, the spirits, and ancestors, while accepting that a new god, with his own spirits, now exists.

Christianity and paganism therefore find a certain level of peaceful co-existence amongst the Scotii – although the Scotii regard other forms of both Christianity and pagan belief to be inferior to those practised by the Irish and, especially, amongst the Scotii. Indeed, the Scotii cleave to the inherent belief that the inhabitants of Britain are diluted descendants of the true Celts (the Irish). The Britons may have become more numerous, but they will always be the inferior cousins. The Irish were never invaded (and they would have repelled the Romans even had they tried); the Britons' stories are pale copies of the original Irish legends; the language the southern Britons speak is a pale copy of Goidelic; their artwork is uninspired; and so on..

Key Settlements of the Scotii

The Scotii have four major hillforts: Dun Add, Dunaverty, Dun Dal and Tarbert. Dún Add is the foremost of the dúns –although not the largest. Occupying a rocky crag that was once a island in the River Add, this is where every Scotii king has been acclaimed, beginning with Fergus Mór, and the stones of the broch, walls, and buildings are thick with carvings that recount of the glory of each acclaimed king, his deeds done, and deeds to come. Of significant importance, but a recent additional to Dún Add, is the Stone of Scone, a magical relic brought by Fergus from Ireland and placed in the fortress to act as the Proclamation Altar for all Dál Riada's kings to come.

Dun Add

Dún Add is considered to belong to the Scotii King, but is not considered to be the home or main residence: it is largely ceremonial, although a small contingent of local farmers and a warband or two maintain and protect the place. Dún Add is also a place of religious significance. The fort and nearby lands are ostensibly Christian: the priest Faoin has built a substantial chapel at the base of Dún Add and this stone, wood, and turf church is a focal point for local Christians. It is dedicated to a number of Saints whom Faoin claims have visited him in visions in dreams, continually guiding his Mission to spread Christ's word far and wide across the northern lands of Britain. Faoin is pious to the point of violence, voluble to the point of hysteria, and sly to the point of criminality. In Ireland's south, many years ago, he claimed to be a druid guided by the spirit of Cú Chulainn himself. Later, fleeing up the west coast of Ireland, he claimed to be a Roman missionary, a dispossessed noble of a Connacht family, and a robbery victim suffering from amnesia. His past crimes include rape, robbery, murder, livestock slaughter, and desecration of holy sites, both Christian and pagan. Here, amongst the Scotii, where none know of his abhorrent, duplicitous past, he is Father Faoin, servant of Jesus and four Saints of his own invention.

Faoin surrounds himself with as much luxury as possible (and that is precious little, in this cold, damp, windswept country), exacting tribute from the devout locals in the name of Christ, Saints Erimius, Euripheny, Lodus, and Maiore the Pure – and, of course, the King. In return, Faoin harangues the congregation with screeching sermons; frequent admonishments for their many, many sins; and reminders of the torments of Hell awaiting all but the most humble, just, and diligent contributors of tribute.

Faoin enforces all of this with a small gang of toughs who benefit from his generosity (sourced, naturally, from the tribute collected in Christ's, the Saint's, and King's names) and both spy and beat upon the surrounding community to ensure Faoin and his chapel remain the prevailing power in the vicinity of Dun Add. This life has suited Faoin very well for many years, and will continue to serve him until someone stronger, more cunning, or better versed in the true scriptures of the Christian faith happens to challenge his spurious teachings and claims. At that point, Faoin, the master of self-preservation, will disappear (with as much silver and gold as he can carry), lapsing into one of many well-rehearsed aliases as he places distance between himself and Dun Add.

Tarbert

Located on the isthmus connecting Kintyre with the mainland, the settlement of Tarbert (which means 'Place of Carrying Across', in Goidelic) is a large, prosperous, flourishing port settlement where the Scotii kings make their home and which is the administrative hub of Dál Riada. The three clans – Cenél Loairn, Cenél Oengusa, and Cenél Gabrain – dominate Tarbert with Cenél Loairn having the largest concentration of inhabitants. The settlement is divided into three areas. Lower Tarbert is the port and boasts a fishing community that sprawls along the coast. To

the east of the coastal town is the small hillfort belonging to Cenél Oengusa and is the home of the warlord Ardal mac Áedán and his warbands, who protect Tarbert and the surrounding farmlands. To the north east is Dún Dal, the larger of the two hillforts and home to Domangart, his extended family, and his own warbands. Domangart has secured the support of the three founding Cenéls, mainly due to his ambitious but level-headed approach to rule.

Domangart is a fair man, with a reputation for intelligence and a shrewd eye on the long game. He does not, for instance, waste time brokering with the Caledonii, whose lands and territories the Scotii impinge upon. Instead, he maintains strong links with the clans of his native Ireland and has, in recent years, extended relations with the tribes south of the Great Wall, especially the Brigantes and the kingdom of Gwent, which has suffered raids from certain Irish warlords. Domangart's connections in Ireland, and his strong position in Dál Riada, are powerful tools for gaining what he wants without resorting to raids and threats. Instead, he progresses through trade, clever alliances, and persuading some of the more belligerent Irish clans to lessen their raids in return for favours and political support.

In this way Domangart separates and distinguishes the Scotii from the rest of the northern tribes, particularly in the eyes of the southern Celts of Britain. They see everyone north of the Wall as Picts: an old, untrustworthy, brutal enemy. Domangart shows the Scotii are different: civilised, rational, able to trade, able to barter, and able to reach agreement. Domangart watches the affairs of the south closely and keenly, and notes the rise of the Dumnonian warlord Arthur ap Uther. There could be a useful alliance here: Domangart senses it and so sends emissaries (all members of Cenél Gabrain, the clan noted for their diplomatic touch) to meet with this young, successful warrior to see what mutual benefit can be gleaned.

Scotii Customs and Culture

The Scotii are forging their own cultural identity — a successful mix of traditional, pagan Irish values and more recent Christian ones — but are still culturally and resolutely Irish. Their songs and stories are of Nuada of the Silver Hand, Cú-Chulainn, Cormac, and the Old Irish Gods. Their music is based on the pipes and drums of the Irish mainland, and their accent the soft lilt of the Western Irish coast rather than the heavier brogue of the Pictish highlands. Their rules of hospitality and ritual are well known, and a welcome contrast to the insular, suspicious nature of the Caledonii and Votadini. Scotii feel obliged to share hearth, home, food, and drink. In return, they like news, stories, and songs, regardless of whether they are pagan or Christian in nature.

Dress is a mixture of practical Pictish (heavy wools fashioned into kilts and robes) and Irish (softer, more colourful fabrics woven in the Cenél patterns). Gold and silver jewelry is popular and displayed whenever possible. Amber is a popular adornment, but all Scotii love precious stones and metals; intricate, geometric designs; and all things that shine. In contrast to the Picts, the Scotii do not tattoo their bodies, paint their faces, spike their hair, or display the bones of the enemies as battle trophies. They combine restraint with a genuine good-natured view of the world, making them an easy people to like (something the southern Celts of the Britain appreciate, given how some of the Irish like to raid, steal, and slaughter their way up and down the western coast).

Allies and Enemies

Naturally, the Scotii are enemies with the Caledonii. The Scotii are surreptitiously expanding their influence, taking a little more Caledonian territory every year, but doing it in such a way that the Caledonii have failed to properly react. In the Caledonii's minds, the Scotii are a nuisance that will be stamped out when the time is right (and that time is not now). The Scotii would also be enemies of the Votadini if the squabbling tribe knew much about what the Scotii are doing, and the threat Dál Riada really represents in the long term. But they do not, and so the Scotii and Votadini remain blissfully separate.

The Scotii have many solid alliances with Irish clans in the north, west, and east of Ireland. Every Scotii can trace his or her lineage to a particular Irish Cenél and these family bonds are still strong, despite the Scotii's new way of life amongst the Picts. Of course, some Cenél dislike the Scotii, but they are too far north and too hard to reach for anyone to truly care, which simply reinforces the unique position the Scotii are carving for themselves and Dál Riada as a kingdom of Britain.

Gwent is becoming an ally. Domangart's emissaries and efforts with the Irish raiders have done more for beleaguered Gwent in recent years than many of the tribes of Britain. The Scotii have a strong Christian presence, and this reassures Gwent, particularly

King Meurig, who is a very devout and pious ruler. Relations between the Scotii and Gwent flourish, and this helps pave the way for Dál Riada's influence to extend into Powys and Dumnonia, if King Domangart continues to promote the Scotii as civil and willing allies of the south.

Notable Scotii

Domangart Reti

King of the Scotii, Domangart mac Fergus is a second-generation Dál Riadan born into the powerful Cenél Loairn clan, and rightful king of the tribe following the death of his father, Fergus mac Eirc. Fergus was a strict, warlike king who left much of the administration of Dál Riada to his Cenél chiefs and spent much time travelling between Dál Riada and Ireland. Despite being absent for long periods, Fergus did much to forge Dál Riada's identity, and imported many Irish traditions and cultural practices into the region to maintain the Irish heritage of the new tribe. In one of his infamous raids, he stole the Stone of Scone, a powerful magical stone, said to give powers of wisdom and insight, from an Irish burial chamber, and brought it to Dún Add. Although Fergus was not proclaimed king over the stone, Domangart was, and many believe his wisdom and guile is a result of the stone's power.

Domangart is certainly clever. In terms of looks and presence, he is nothing out of the ordinary: dark haired and dark browed, handsome, but not overly so, his eyes nevertheless sparkle and his wit is fast and dagger sharp. He and his wife, Saorise, are known to spar intellectually and frequently in public, leading many to think the two have a poor relationship. In reality, they love each dearly and Domangart treats his queen as his equal, enjoying her own, fierce intellect.

Domangart is focused on making the Scotii a tribe that history and the bards will remember for eternity. He sees the whole of the north as an empire in the making, the crude and vicious Picts an anachronism that both time and the Scotii will erase. He sees the lands south of the Great Wall as ripe with possibilities and, in time, part of a much greater Scotii empire. He hopes that, one day, perhaps a thousand years or more in the future, the Scotii will command an empire as great as Rome's. All empires start small though, and Domangart understands his limited place in history. He sees himself as fostering a culture of prudent ambition that will lead to a lasting base of power.

This King of the Scotii enjoys the arts — poetry, song, and story — and considers them important tools of diplomacy. He always welcomes bards to his hall, wherever they hail from, and those bards who entertain him well are richly rewarded. Domangart is a good and shrewd warrior, having learned much from his father. His men are loyal and well trained, and he ensures that the Cenél chiefs and their warbands remain that way with training and raids into Caledonii territory — although never as far as to provoke open war with the Caledonii Picts.

Domangart's current plan is to secure alliances with Gwent, Powys, the Brigantes, and Dumnonia. He stops short of supporting these kingdoms against the Saxons, but he seeks strong alliances through trade and, when necessary, a certain amount of more direct aid if it can be spared. He is keen to marry Scotii men and women into these kingdoms, securing relationships and children that will spread Scotii influence further and further with each generation. It is a subtle and long-sighted plan; if anyone can do it, it is Domangart.

A typical Pictish design depicting a pair of swans - a delicacy among all Pictish tribes.

Conor mac Mahon

Of Cenél Gabrain, Conor mac Mahon is King Domangart's chief emissary to the Celts of Southern Britain. He leads a warband retinue of forty warriors, all of Cenél Gabrain, and acts as Domangart's representative, active in Gwent, Powys, Dumnonia, and the Cornovii lands. A Christian, but one who is also sympathetic to the Old Ways, Conor is able to move easily with his Dál Riada entourage, acting in Domangart's name, gathering intelligence for the Scotii, and forging alliances with the southern tribes. Conor is charismatic and easy to like: a cousin of the king, he is clever and subtle, able to engineer friendships easily. He is also skilled with understanding and adopting customs and social conventions. This makes him a man that many diverse people, from kings to fierce warlords, easily trust.

Conor's mission is simple: to spread Scotii influence as far as he can. Conor locates ideal matrimonial matches for Scotii men and women, and sows the seeds of such unions. He can advise on Irish matters, helping prepare those kingdoms suffering Irish raids to deal with them. In short, Conor is an ambassador, a spy, and a power broker. He returns to Tarbert regularly to make personal reports, but otherwise relies on messengers to deliver news and gain new orders. He travels widely, he and his entourage rarely remaining in one hall for more a month at the most. And he always pays his way: Conor trades openly, pays in good coin, and always has valuable news.

Southern Britain

Southern Britain is the broad foot of the island that begins with Kernow in the west and ends with lands now called Kent. Its northern border is the Tamesas River, the second longest of Britain's rivers; a body of water sacred to the druids who recognise it as the artery of the Great Red Dragon.

Southern Britain was once home to over a dozen tribes of Celts, including the Durotriges and the Atribati, but most were either destroyed by the Romans or later destroyed by the Saxons. Now, the dominant tribe and dominant kingdom are the Dumnonii and Dumnonia, which holds the south against the ceaseless incursion of the Saxons. In the west, Kernow dozes, protected by Dumnonia, and culturally separate from this staunch Celtic heartland.

The south is physically divided. The Saxons have taken all lands to the east of the River Itchen (a river sacred to Ancasta, a Great Spirit of the region) and even north of the Tamesis. Each year more of their ships land on the east and south coasts, bringing settlers and warriors, and each year the Saxons press even more on Celtic lands, displacing, killing, and enslaving those who have made Southern Britain home for hundreds of years.

Each year then, Southern Britain shrinks a little more. Dumnonia is all that stands between the Saxons and the Severn Sea and, if the Saxons reach the west, Britain will be divided completely, allowing the Saxons to make their assault against the Western and Middle Britain tribes.

Southern Britain is therefore of crucial important to the Celtic tribes. If it falls, Britain falls. If the south becomes Saxon, then the Celts are doomed. The Red Dragon's heart will be sliced through, its arteries opened, its lifeblood spilling into the Irish and Northern seas through two massive untreatable wounds.

The Countryside of Southern Britain

The south is precious, fertile land. It is a patchwork mixture of woods, forests, wide rivers, rolling downs, and miles and miles of good, workable soil and verdant meadows that have been watched over and blessed by countless local spirits ever since the island was created by the Great Red Dragon. This is prime land for raising crops or cattle, quarrying stone, mining metals, and building settlements. Rome saw its importance and quickly secured the south, either absorbing or breaking the indigenous tribes according to whether Rome was supported or opposed. It created civitates from many smaller tribes who saw the sense of alliance, and just as easily destroyed those who resisted. Southern Britain became the garden of the Roman presence in Britain and fundamental to its operations. The quality of its soil, and therefore the quality of goods produced, was unsurpassed and so the Romans worked hard to keep Southern Britain secure, building some of their most important cities here, and being cognisant of the importance of the local spirits to the health and wealth of the countryside.

The Spirits of the South

Britain is home to hundreds of thousands of spirits: they can be found in every corner of the island, but some of the most important and revered are the Spirits of the South. Two of the foremost spirits are Tamesis and Ancasta, the Great River Spirits. Tamesis flows across Britain, west to east as the River Tamesas, and Ancasta, known as Itchen, flows north to south. They are daughters of Rosmerta and the Great Red Dragon. Rosmerta, a fertility goddess who is mother of all things green and growing, mated with the Great Red Dragon so that the plants of the Mortal World might be fed with the magical blood of the Dragon, making the island strong. She gave birth to many silvery, slithering daughters who were the Rivers of Britain, and they went out to sustain the plants and forests. In the south, Tamesis, Ancasta, and Sabrinna (Spirit of the River Severn), were, and still are, the most powerful. The Romans recognised this power and erected temples to all three sister spirits. Such was the Roman reverence for Ancasta, their god Mercury took her as his consort for a time, but left her when the Romans left Britain.

All three River Spirits are revered by pagan Dumnonia, and the druids of the region, Merlin in particular, maintain that they are the most powerful and important of all Britain's spirits. This further reinforces Southern Britain's importance amongst the pagan Celts, and Merlin is actively taking great steps to ensure the Sisters are placated and happy: they may be key to Britain's defence against the Saxons.

Yet there are two more important and deeply sacred places in the south: Ynys Wydryn, where Merlin makes his home on occasion, and The Stones

Ynys Wydryn

Ynys Wydryn is the sandstone tor that rises 500 feet above the marshes and watercourses of the Summerlands, south of the Severn estuary. It was raised by Sabrinna, the Great Spirit of the Summerlands, and given to the druids in recognition of their devotion to her. Ynys Wydryn has traditionally been the stronghold of the High Druid of Britain, and it has been claimed by Merlin ever since most of the druids died in the Ynys Mon massacre. It is the centre of Merlin's ritual magic; here, he has built his Tower of Dreams where he can sleep – sometimes for decades at a time – and easily enter Annwn, the Other World. Ynys Wydryn is protected by the marshes and bogs of the Summerland – a complex series of water courses filled with water and nature spirits who, being children of Sabrinna, ensure that only those Merlin favours can approach the tor and make their way up the Dream Tower. Attempting to navigate the Summerlands is a risky business: the spirits cause abrupt, dense fogs that cause even the best navigators to lose their way and stumble into the deep, dark pools where the waiting spirits drag souls into the Spirit World. Other spirits cause noxious gases to rise that poison the senses, and the earth spirits make solid ground turn to sucking slime that devours the unwary and cuts off their life. Of course, all these horrors cease if Merlin commands it, and the old druid can make the Summerlands a beautiful, calm haven of reflections and birdsong, giving true meaning to Ynys Wydryn: the Isle of Glass.

Merlin is not the only inhabitant of the Isle of Glass. Many others – druids, warriors, renegades, and exiles – come to Ynys Wydryn seeking sanctuary. If they intrigue Merlin, and he senses a use for them, they can stay, inhabiting the seven deep and broad terraces cut into the tor. The newest arrivals must make for shelters on the lower terraces where the food is scarce, the inhabitants less than reputable, and Merlin's power less acute. But in time, through

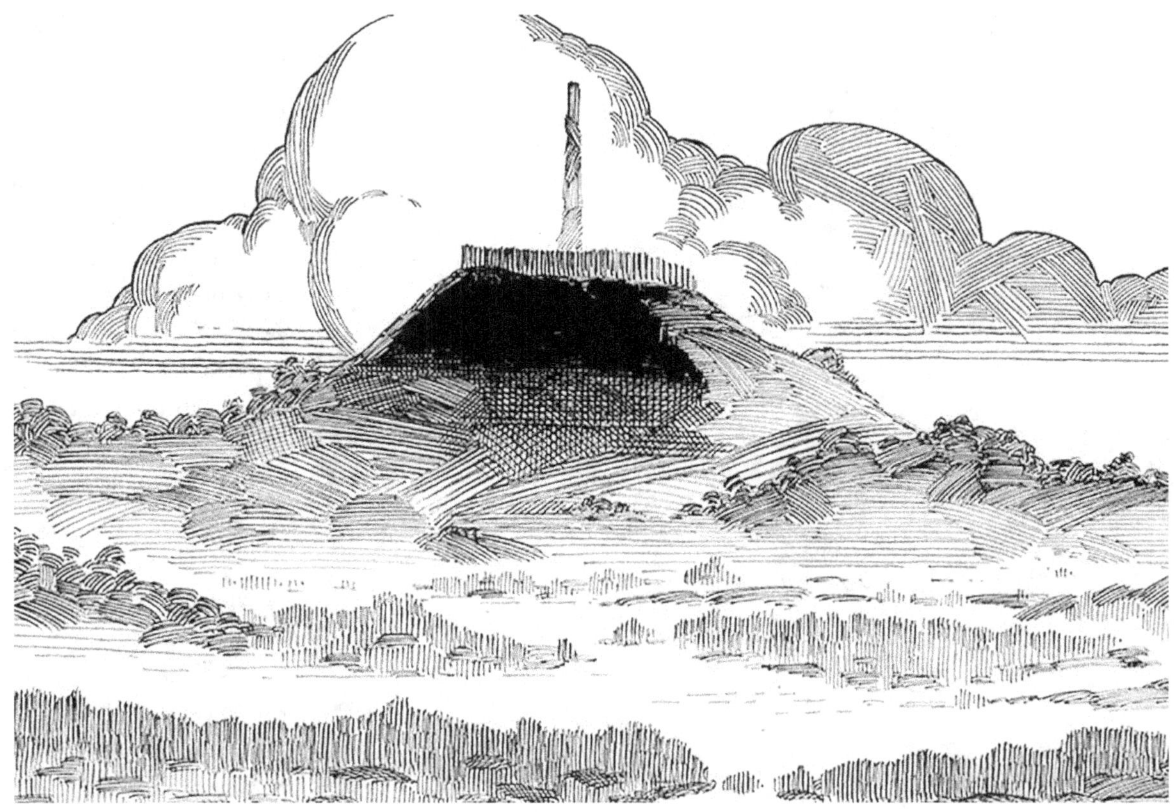

ambition and, mostly, Merlin's favour, one can climb the terraces, benefitting from better shelter, better food, and better company, until the terrace directly below the Dream Tower is reached. This is where Merlin's most trusted followers live, a mixture of warriors, druids, bards, schemers, and the exiles who have pledged their lives to Merlin and their souls to the Great Red Dragon. These disciples are initiated into Sabrinna's cult and pledge oaths to the Dragon, Merlin, Sabrinna, and greatest of her daughters, the Lady of the Lake, who is the foremost of the Summerland spirits.

Most favoured of Merlin's followers, and Priestess of Sabrinna, is Yneera, Merlin's most trusted disciple. This calm, deep-eyed woman is blessed by both Sabrinna and the Lady of the Lake. Merlin rescued her from the marshes when Sabrinna called him to do so. Yneera had wandered into the Summerland, perhaps intentionally, and been swallowed by the marsh spirits. She crawled free from the quagmire and was then dragged into a bottomless pool where the Lady of the Lake questioned her for a year and a day. When Yneera answered each question correctly, it was known that she was destined to serve Ynys Wydryn and so Merlin was called to her rescue. Since then, twenty years ago, he has nurtured Yneera, taught her the secrets of the druidic order, and created a potent shaman and magician. Yneera controls Ynys Wydryn in Merlin's absence, commands the Initiates of the Cult of Sabrinna, and keeps in order the lower tiers of the tor. When Merlin is absent, Yneera rules, and she is a woman to be feared.

Glestinga and The Thorn

The small settlement of Glestinga, not far from Merlin's tor, is home to a substantial chapel that attracts Christian pilgrims from across Britain and mainland Europe. Here, it is said, Joseph of Arimathea and his entourage, fleeing the Romans, sought refuge. At that time, the Romans had not colonised the region, and these refugees brought with them a substantial amount of gold and silver. They paid due tribute to the local kings and druids, and were granted the lands in the shadow of Ynys Wydryn, so that the druids could watch over them.

The druids, of course, knew that Joseph and his followers did not worship the Old Gods, but some single god popular in the warmer lands of the east. This did not trouble the druids; the spirits of Dumnonia were uncaring what these refugees believed, and they made no trouble. Joseph built a small temple of wood and stone. He had, his followers said, allowed his own tomb be used by a priest they called Christ, or Jesus, to be buried. This Christ was a teacher, a healer, and a prophet: a great man, persecuted and murdered by the Romans, but who rose from the dead and returned to the Spirit World to be with the god who lived there. Joseph had with him some relics of this persecution: a staff, said to be carved with the wood of the tree where this Jesus was crucified, and one of the nails that was hammered into his feet.

This small, inconsequential group of refugees, members of the Tribe of Abraham, lived in the shadow of the Celts and kept to themselves. In time they left or died, but their temple remained, and close to it a gnarled, thorny tree grew. The descendants of the Arimathean settlers claimed it was the wood of the crucifixion tree that had miraculously taken root, sustained by the blood of the Christ that had seeped into its fabric. These Christ worshippers, supplemented now by others who venerated the One God and his prophet, Jesus, grew and their religion spread. From humble beginnings, Christianity began to flourish in that most unlikely of places in the shadow of Merlin's Dream Tower.

Given the importance of the Chapel of the Thorn to Christians, it is no wonder that a reasonable number of Dumnonians have embraced and converted to Christianity. The Chapel of the Thorn has had a succession of strong, capable priests who have helped the Christian religion grow, despite the proximity of Ynys Wydryn. Many have become advisers: Bedwin, the Bishop of the Chapel during Uther's reign, was part of the Pendragon's council. Yet, for all its long history, the pagans of Dumnonia, and especially those chosen to live on the terraces of Ynys Wydryn, despise and fear the Chapel of the Thorn's power. More and more Christians make the chapel the focus of pilgrimage, bringing riches to the church that would be the envy of many chieftains or warlords. Each year it grows a little larger, as does the pious community of Glestinga, with pilgrims choosing to remain close to the church and its charismatic priest, Bishop Geraint, a man who has ventured to Rome and gained audience with Pope Gelasius. With each year, the Christians become more vocal in their denunciation of the pagan gods, the druids and even Merlin. Tensions between pagans and Christians grow — a further threat, if any were needed.

The Stones

Even Merlin does not know who built The Stones. It was not the Druids, certainly; and not the race of Giants who were driven from Britain before mortals came. The druids believe that The Stones, which align perfectly with the stars, sun, and moon, allowing the solstices and equinox to be predicted, is one of the eyes of the Great Dragon, allowing them to observe the universe. It is close to a further ring of stones, and so the druids know that the lands around the plain are of great magical importance, and The Stones are thick with spirits — many of them Ancestors, some malevolent predators and curses, and some mere haunts — the sad remains of ancient sacrifices.

In general, the druids do not use The Stones as a place of worship, because they did not create the place. However, they do conduct some rituals there. It is useful for seeking Spirit Allies, Spirit Knowledge, or simply to replenish magical energy. Merlin visits The Stones infrequently: he has little need to commune with the local spirits, because his Dream Tower and relationship with Sabrinna, Tamesis, and Ancasta suffices; but many other druids feel a need to visit The Stones when it is necessary to negotiate or commune with powerful spirits of a sinister nature. The Stones do not hold peaceful or benign spirits: the spirits who congregate here have a sinister purpose, a tendency towards mischief, malevolence and harm, or seek some form of callous revenge on the Mortal World. This henge, then, is a dark and fearful place: frequented by only the strongest-willed mortals, and druids with specific needs, it broods on its wide, flat, desolate plain, alone and pitiless.

Dumnonia

Largest of the two kingdoms, Dumnonia is the ancestral home of the Dumnonii tribe and, after the Brigantes, the largest of the tribes south of the Great Wall.

Dumnonia stretches from the River Tamar (which, like all the rivers of the island is a spirit goddess, born of Rosmerta and the Dragon, but minor when compared with Ancasta and Tamesis) to the River Itchen. It is bordered by the Severn estuary to the north, and faces the kingdoms of Gwent and Siluria. Ynys Wydryn and the Summerlands are contained within its borders, as are The Stones, meaning that Dumnonia holds special significance for most Celts and, particularly, the druids. However, the quality and diversity of its landscape reinforces its importance as a kingdom: good soil, pastures, croplands, forests, and, along the south coast, tin, copper, iron, and other metals easily mined from the earth. Dumnonia is rich and blessed. It is also fragmented, besieged, and envied.

The last king of the Dumnonii was Uther. A formidable warrior, leader, and politician, Uther was, nevertheless, rash, lustful, and prone to folly. Before becoming Dumnonia's king, and gaining the title Pendragon, which was accorded to the High King of the western and southern tribes, Uther was Vortigern's staunchest

supporter and foremost warlord. He helped unite the whole of Britain, leading campaigns to bring to reason the Cornovii, Silures, Ordovices, Brigantes, and, of course, his own tribe. Only the Pictish tribes eluded them: the Caledonii and Votadini. Uther was happy to let the Great Wall maintain that division: a united Britain directly south of the Great Wall was enough. But Vortigern sought vengeance for old scores and brutal raids, and believed he could succeed where even the Legions of Rome failed.

Vortigern failed too. He then compounded that failure further by enraging the Saxon mercenaries who had assisted his campaign against the Picts. Uther would have none of this. Merlin, once Vortigern's adviser, became Uther's counsel, and so the alliance split. Uther commanded the west, was granted the title of Pendragon, and went his separate way. Vortigern was doomed.

Uther died after battling the Saxons, as did his heir, Mordred. With the Pendragon gone, the alliance of the south-west and west broke and the kingdoms went their separate ways. Old feuds reignited, fanned by the Cornovii and Silures. Dumnonia also fragmented into separate territories controlled by warlords. Dumnonia's eastern quarter is controlled by Natanleod, a proud chieftain who has tirelessly battled the Saxons and would, many believe, be a natural candidate for the title of Pendragon. In the west, close to the Kernow border, Havgan controls the rugged landscape: one of Uther's trusted warlords, he is a close ally of Arthur now, and distrusts Natanleod's ambitions. In central Dumnonia, based at Caer Cadbryg, Arthur has taken Uther's old seat and, although not a king (and seemingly unwilling to assume that mantle), he has built a substantial following of warlords and warbands in the region. Further to the north, bordering Gwent, Uther's younger brother, the ageing Custennin, holds power: Custennin is bitter, hating Natanleod, Havgan, and Arthur equally, and refusing to acknowledge the authority of any of these leaders. In recent years Custennin has converted to Christianity, thanks to his relations with King Meurig of Gwent, and views the Saxon invasion as God's retribution for Britain's pagan associations.

Dumnonia then, is a kingdom as divided as anywhere else in Britain. Jealousy and ambition plague Arthur's attempts to unify the kingdom in preparation for the massed attack the Saxons will surely launch in the near future. A king might unify Dumnonia, but with Custennin, Natanleod, and Havgan all vying for the position (and no clear support for any of them), it appears to be an impossible task. Arthur could claim the popular support — and he has Merlin's counsel — but for reasons no one understands, he refuses the responsibility.

Kernow, Mark, and Uther

Kernow is a separate kingdom to Dumnonia, although its people are Dumnonii in tribal ancestry. Kernow is the bleak and rugged peninsula west of the River Tamar and is ruled by the ageing King Mark, a vast man with vast appetites. Mark and his predecessors have always distanced themselves from Dumnonia. They have raided western Dumnonia constantly and frequently over the years, and Uther and Mark were always bitter enemies. Their own attempt at conciliation, when Uther united eastern Britain under the Pendragon banner, turned into tragic war when Uther betrayed the tentative alliance and slept with Ygraine, Mark's wife and queen.

Why did Uther do such a stupid, treacherous thing? Kernow and Dumnonia were finally at peace and ready to ally against the Saxons, only for Uther to wreck the alliance utterly. There are many stories and explanations. Some claim Ygraine tempted Uther because she hated Mark. Some claim Uther raped Ygraine. Others claim Merlin used magic to fool Ygraine into believing Uther was Mark. Others still believed that the two simply fell in love and, had Uther not already been married, he would have carried Ygraine away and made her queen of Dumnonia. Only Uther and, most likely, Merlin, know the truth. Uther is dead and Merlin will not speak of it. However, the affair between the two is well known and Arthur the result of that union.

The betrayal broke Mark. Always a belligerent man, he was, at the time of his marriage to Ygraine, fit and hardy. Afterwards, he changed completely. His marriage to Ygraine over, he took a succession of wives — all of them young, all of them beautiful — and began to drink and eat to excess. Ygraine was Mark's second wife and he had several sons by his previous spouse, Elise, including Tristan. Tristan and his brothers became the de-facto rulers of Kernow while Mark ate, drank, and whored. Each of his wives met untimely ends: one died in child birth (the child, a daughter, died too); another succumbed to a plague; a third died in a riding accident. Mark's sixth wife is the very young daughter of an

Irish warlord, a gift in return for trade and information helping Irish raids further north. Iseult is barely a woman: pretty, fragile, and frightened. Worse, she resembles Ygraine and, for this reason, Mark is tremendously possessive of his young bride. Tales from Mark's court have it that Iseult is subjected to terrible abuse and torments. When drunk – which is most days – Mark mistakes her for Ygraine and punishes her. Mark is surrounded by a loyal warband and no one dares challenge his fitness to rule. Of his sons, only Tristan remains: the others have left (one to Armorica, one to Ireland) and so Tristan must weather his father's inadequacies, rages, and atrocities.

Kernow is therefore a kingdom in turmoil. It was never very rich, but Mark's neglect (and raids by the Irish) compounds its poverty. Its settlements are small and widely spread, its warriors centred on Mark's fortress at Caer Dore. It is a lawless place: somewhere for renegades to hide and where few questions are asked. Its rough, hilly countryside is bleak, rain- and windswept year-round. Although there are peaceful, sheltered areas, they are few and far between and often occupied by unwelcoming, insular people whom the Dumnonians liken to the Picts in their customs, habits, and brutish natures.

The Dumnonii

The Dumnonii are a large and strong tribe with a cultural identity as strong and well developed as that of the Brigantes. Unlike the Brigantes they did not initially cooperate with the Romans, and in the early days the Dumnonii fought hard to keep the Romans out of their old territories. In time, and particularly after the destruction of the druids, the Icenii, and Queen Boudicca, the Dumnonii became less quarrelsome and entered into a series of agreements with the Romans that allows the Dumnonii to retain much of their land and heritage, in exchange for free passage, a small tribute, and general acknowledgement that Rome was now the ruling power. Over the course of two centuries, the Dumnonii allowed several large Roman settlements to be built in Dumnonia, including Aquae Sulis, Lindinis, and the prosperous port of Isca. The Romans took to worshipping some of the local spirits, particularly the three River Spirits of Sabrinna, Tamesis, and Ancasta. Roman priests so revered Ancasta that they called upon their own god, Mercury, to become her consort: she and Mercury agreed to the union, and so Rome and Dumnonia became united on the Spirit Plane, if not necessarily on the mortal one.

This reverence for the local gods and spirits meant the Romans took a more lenient attitude towards to Dumnonia's druids, especially a young druid known to them as Myrddin , who helped broker the betrothal of Ancasta with Mercury. The druids, therefore, remained a solid presence in Dumnonia and remain strong still – especially as Merlin, foremost of Britain's druids, has long made Dumnonia his home.

The Dumnonii are typical of most Celts: communal, boastful, fractious, and warlike. They are also pragmatists and, in this sense, have much in common with the Cornovii and the Brigantes. The Dumnonii were staunch pagans, but even before the Romans left, Christianity had begun to take root in the area, and not far from that shrine of paganism, Ynys Wydryn, Merlin's home.

The Four Chieftains

Dumnonia is divided into four holdings, each controlled by a chieftain: Arthur, Custennin, Natanleod, and Havgan. Each chieftain, Arthur included, served Uther and is experienced in battling the Saxons. Each is, in his own way, loyal to Dumnonia and the Celtic way of life, but each holds grudges against one, some, or all of the other warlords, which prevents a single Dumnonian king from emerging. The traditions of the Dumnonii stipulate that all warlords of the kingdom must agree on Dumnonia's rightful king: without that agreement, it remains kingless and is governed by its war council. As the war council only meets when there is an external threat, Dumnonia is, essentially, four smaller kingdoms and not the united the power and tribe it ought to be.

Custennin and Caer Sulis

Younger brother of Ambrosius and Uther, Custennin is a thwarted and bitter chieftain who carries a chip the size of the Stone Henge. Both his brothers were fine warriors and charismatic leaders, and became kings. Custennin, forever in their shadow, lacked the subtleties and wit of his elder siblings and achieved his position through their benefaction and grace. He knows it; the people he lords over know it. Custennin is, and shall ever be, 'The Other Brother'.

When Uther's beloved son Mordred died, Custennin expected to be named heir and assume the title of Pendragon on Uther's own death. Uther, who always hated the entitlement and simmering rage of his younger brother, did no such thing. He named no heir. When he died, the Dumnonii found themselves kingless for the first time in living memory. The warlords could not agree on who should follow Uther and so, from that day to this, Custennin, who believes the title of Pendragon is his birthright, sits on the sideline and glowers at Havgan, Natanleod, and Arthur. Of all of them, he loathes Arthur the most.

Uther's bastard has become as fine a warrior and leader as ever Uther was. Custennin knows it; the people he lords over know it. Arthur's very existence taunts and tortures the Other Brother – a constant reminder of all that Custennin has failed to be. Arthur tries to make peace with his uncle, but Custennin rejects all attempts at kinship: Arthur is not of his blood. Never shall be. Unless Arthur gets down on one knee and offers his spears in honour of Custennin's claim to the title of Pendragon, hatred shall ever remain between them.

Sour-souled Custennin has found something approaching identity and purpose by embracing Christianity. One of his only friends is King Meurig of Gwent, a pious Christian Celt who has shown that a Christian King can be acceptable to the tribes and espouse the old traditions. Meurig took Custennin to the Chapel at Glestinga and there Custennin found God, Christ, the Virgin, the Saints, and the Holy Ghost in one rapturous revelation that led to an immediate conversion to the new faith. Not only does Custennin believe it is his right to become the next Pendragon of Britain, he believes it is his destiny to become Britain's first Christian King.

To this end, Custennin is steadily outlawing the Old Gods amongst his people. Pagans have been hounded from their homes and the druids along with them. Many loyal to Custennin have embraced Christianity with the same enthusiasm as their lord, but an equal number are reluctant converts who have done so only out of duty and oaths. Those who refused to bend to the cross left and went to Arthur and Natanleod. Custennin has filled the gap by ensuring marriages between his nobles and those of Gwent, bringing himself and Meurig closer and closer together, forming a Christian alliance on the borders of pagan Dumnonia and in the face of the heathen Saxons.

Custennin is in his fifties now, and frailty begins to take its toll. He is of the firm belief that God will not let him die until he has become Pendragon and established Jesus Christ as the Saviour of Britain and led the defeat of the Saxons with Gwent spearman before him and King Meurig at his side. Custennin believes he will see Arthur baptised and swear oaths of allegiance to a Christian Pendragon. Havgan and Natanleod he intends to simply sacrifice to the Saxons in some battle or another. Custennin schemes towards this, anticipating the day.

Of course, if Arthur, Natanleod, and Havgan ever discovered Custennin's true schemes, they would move against him without hesitation. He poses a severe risk and all three know that he is not competent to lead. King Meurig of Gwent has made no secret of his desire to have control over the west of Britain and, in all actuality,

Custennin would become Meurig's puppet; Meurig is not the Christian ally Custennin believes he would be. Custennin's biggest flaw is his naivety; his second his jealous ambition. As things stand, he is trouble for Dumnonia.

Caer Sulis

Caer Sulis is a well-appointed and ancient hillfort that is the ancestral home of Ambrosius, Uther, and Custennin. It is not the largest of Dumnonia's forts, but it is important, overlooking the old city of Aquae Sulis, ruined now, but once an important place for trade and a significant Roman outpost. The goddess Sulevia held this small region sacred, and the natural hot pools are gateways to her realm in the Land of the Gods where she dwells. Her breath makes the waters hot and her love for the land grants the waters potent powers of healing and vitality. The Romans recognised this and honoured Sulevia, building a temple in her honour and bathing in the hot springs bubbling up through the rocks. She has always had a powerful and sacred presence in Dumnonia – that is, until Custennin converted to Christianity and now denounces this most ancient and benevolent of goddesses as a hag born of Satan. The springs of Aquae Sulis are forbidden to those who have sworn oaths to Custennin and those who dwell in Caer Sulis. Small chapels have been built amongst the ruins of the old city, so that the love and mercy of God will keep Sulevia away from corrupting the people further.

Not all in Caer Sulis appreciate this abjuration of Sulevia: once, the Caer and Sulevia were inextricably linked, and the druids, Merlin among them, maintain that it was her will that Ambrosius and Uther would be Britain's leaders. Many see Custennin's actions as harmful and likely to weaken Dumnonia further. Should Sulevia abandon Britain, then Britain's enemies, the Saxons, will find it easier to conquer and ravage. Indeed, the Saxons push closer and closer to Aquae Sulis with each passing year, and their ability to do this is viewed, by some, as proof-positive that Christianity makes Dumnonia weaker, not stronger.

Havgan and Caer Uisc

Havgan controls the western quarter of Dumnonia with his base at the fortress of Caer Uisc, overlooking the old Roman port of Isca. Isca was abandoned with the Roman exodus and successive chieftains have let this once vibrant town fall into wrack and ruin. Caer Uisc itself as a large and impressive fortress built in the traditional style with successive rings of mounds and ditches forming a formidable earthworks before levelling into the wide, flat, palisade-circled settlement. Surrounding Uisc's base are smaller gatherings of buildings and farms: groups of families loyal to Havgan and allowed to live under Uisc's protection.

Havgan is a grizzled, one-eyed, one-eared warrior who was rewarded with Caer Uisc by Uther Pendragon in return for loyal service against both Kernow and the Saxons. Havgan lost his eye to a Kernow spear and his ear to a Saxon seax : the wily old general says he sees and hears far better as a result. A ruthless but not unkindly chieftain, Havgan maintains patrols along the border with Kernow and has established several outposts and small forts there to guard against possible sneak attacks by King Mark's warbands. Havgan does not trust Mark, even though the fat old king seems to spend much of his days in a drunken stupor; but then, there are very few Havgan does trust. He has seen plenty of battles and schemes in his time to know that chieftains like him are schemers and only remain that way by playing dirty. As a result, he does not trust Natanleod (although he likes him) or Arthur (whom he also likes). Havgan does, however, hate Custennin, Uther's only surviving brother. When Uther called for Custennin's help against Aelle, it was refused. Uther was wounded in those battles, and those wounds killed him. Custennin is, in Havgan's eye, a treacherous, selfish, greedy fool who wants only to be Pendragon at any cost. He's also a Christian, and Havgan hates Christians.

Despite not trusting the other three warlords of Dumnonia, Havgan never misses the opportunity to take the fight to the Saxons, and his warbands are enthusiastic and consistent members of Dumnonia's forces when the time comes to defend their lands. Havgan used to lead from the front, fighting in the shield wall and revelling in the slaughter, but these days, cursed by a racking cough (he knows he is dying: so be it – he's had a good life), he remains behind the lines and relays his orders through his trusted warlords, all of them excellent Saxon killers.

Havgan loves hunting – especially boar – and he employs farmers to ensure that the forests and woodlands surrounding Caer Uisc are managed well so that, come the season, there is plenty of boar to hunt. A boar's head with bloody tusks is Havgan's battle

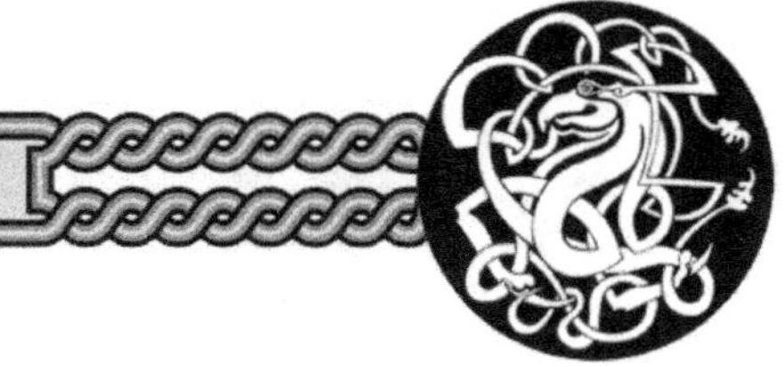

standard and, with his fearsome, scarred face, many reckon Havgan comes to resemble the standard more and more each year.

Havgan's druid, Oelias, knows that the warlord is dying. He has spoken with the spirits, and the Ancestors are looking to welcome Havgan to their hall in three years or so. The cough that causes Havgan to spit blood cannot be cured and is the result of too many years punishing his body through fighting, feasting, and drinking. It is their secret though; Oelias is sworn to secrecy and Havgan has no intention of letting his Dumnonian rivals know of his impending death. He intends to fight in the shield wall one last time and hopefully die with a spear in his hand rather than cough out his lungs in the middle of the night. On his death, he will let his warlords choose their next leader. Havgan has six fine sons and he would not insult any of them by naming a successor.

Isca

For four hundred years, Isca was a primary port for Roman Britain. Large and vibrant, it had many homes, shops, temples, stores, and a good, deep-water harbour with sturdy wooden and stone docks. When the Romans left, many did so from Isca's quayside. In the subsequent decades, the Celts have drifted away from Isca and used the stones of its buildings for settlements elsewhere, steadily repurposing the masonry until all that is left of the port city are the shells of buildings, mosaics, and memories. Its quayside is still in good repair – local fishermen have seen to that – and so it remains a busy place for the small fishing vessels that ply the south shore. Havgan keeps warbands on patrol around Isca because he knows that it would make a good landing ground for Saxons, once they grow balls hairy enough to push this far west along the coast. At present, Isca is not a target for the Saxons – but it is only a matter of time before it is. Isca offers a way to outflank Arthur and Natanleod, plus an excellent staging post for sallies into Kernow. It comforts Havgan to know that, in his final years, he is responsible, as he puts it, "for covering Dumnonia's arsehole."

Natanleod and Caer Gradawc

The warlord Natanleod controls the eastern boundary of Dumnonia and is the buffer between the west and the Saxon territories. A gruff, shrewd, careful, cunning man, Natanleod was oath-sworn to Vortigern as a young warrior and served the old king well until it was clear that Saxons would defeat him. Natanleod broke his oath and swore allegiance instead to Uther, vowing to prevent the Saxons from passing the fortress given to him, Caer Gradawc, close to the old city of Sarum, which the Romans called Sorviodunum.

He has been true to that oath. Natanleod has spent years surrounding himself and his lands with strong, loyal, well-trained, well-disciplined warbands who have been blooded against Saxon shield walls and know the enemy perhaps better than any warriors in Britain. Every year his warbands sally east, engaging Saxon scouting parties, raiding Saxon settlements encroaching on Dumnonian land, resettling displaced Celts from further east and north; and continually harry and harass the questing Saxon forces, showing them that Dumnonia is strong and ready to fight.

In truth, Natanleod is weary of this role. Year after year it is the same routine – almost like tending crops, save it is spears, rather than ploughs, that ready the earth. Natanleod wants, and is ready for, that decisive battle that breaks either the Saxons or Dumnonia: that single reckoning that will end decades of attrition. Since Uther died, Natanleod has been grateful for Arthur's rise as a warlord; the young commander has sent well-trained warriors to supplement Caer Gradawc's spearmen and he has done so for exactly the same reasons as Natanleod: to have them know their enemy: their ways, their patterns, and their plans. In Arthur, Natanleod sees much of himself: careful, prudent, prepared. He likes the man.

But Natanleod still has ambitions. If the Saxons can be forced into a single, decisive, battle, and if Dumnonia wins, it will be because of him. As his reward, for years of diligence, patience, and sacrifice, Natanleod wants the title of Pendragon. Havgan does not care for it, Arthur has a lesser claim, and Custennin is a dangerous idiot. Only Natanleod has the skill, foresight, expertise, and claim to rule Britain. Once the Saxons are defeated, he will deal with the Irish who maraud along the western coast. He will force Kernow into submission, replacing Mark with a competent king who will pay allegiance to the Pendragon banner. Then, with the help of Dál Riada (because Domangart's emissaries have reached Caer Gradawc), he will tame the Picts, succeeding where Vortigern failed. If he can succeed in these trials, Britain will be his. He will restore its unity. No one – not the Brigantes, not the Cornovii, not the Ordovices – will be able to deny him.

Or, he will die trying.

Caer Gradawc

The fortress of Caer Gradawc overlooks the conjunction of five important Roman trade routes and the river Ayvon. Broadly oval in shape, it is protected by a steep double-bank of earthworks and an intermediate ditch between the two. It has only one entrance in its eastern slope. The walls are 1,300 feet in length and 1,180 feet in width; built of wood, slate, and local stone, it is a formidable fortification reflecting the serious-minded nature of Natanleod, who has added to the defences year on year.

The protection Caer Gradawc offers, and the importance of Natanleod's presence here, can be measured in the other hillforts in the direct vicinity: at least eight hillforts spread out from Caer Gradawc, forming a defensive cluster facing out towards Saxon territories. Every hillfort is operational and commanded by a trusted warlord placed there by Natanleod. Every warband within a 20-mile radius is oath-sworn to Natanleod and Caer Gradawc, and this makes them both hugely important and influential in Dumnonia's well-being.

There is also the matter of the Stones. A mere day's walk or quarter-day ride due north from Caer Gradawc brings one to the Stone Henge and, close by, the larger stone circle of Tartadun . The Stones are under Natanleod's protection and Merlin is an occasional visitor to Caer Gradawc when he pays his ritual visit to the Henge. Natanleod is suspicious of Merlin and his motives, but respects the old druid and is a reasonably devout pagan. He has both a druid serving him and a druid serving the extended community around Caer Gradawc, a brother and sister who have roots in the Brigantes and who have come south to practice their faith and be closer to the Stones and the Sister Rivers. Ceidmon is Natanleod's druidic adviser: his name means 'Wise Warrior' and he is as skilled with spear and shield as he is with the spirits and lore of the Old Ways. Ceidmon is therefore a rare thing: a priest and a military adviser to Natanleod. Ceidmon has spirit allies who can make spearheads and sword blades sharp for a time, and induce confusion in the minds of the enemy. Ceidmon can work this magic when he really feels the need, and this is generally reserved for fights with the Saxons.

Ceidmon's sister is Birkita. A tall, broad-shouldered woman, she cuts an imposing physical presence but is tender-hearted and warm to most. She tends to the extended female community of the region and is a very skilled midwife, having a special fertility spirit ally who has helped ensure that not one woman or child has died in childbirth since the brother and sister druids arrived at Caer Gradawc. Birkita is also the priestess of Ayvon, the local river spirit, and Ayvon is Birkita's allied fertility spirit. The two have an uncommonly strong bond — a passion and love for each other that is peculiar even amongst druids. If she were to call for it, Birkita could have Ayvon take the soul of a mortal person into her grove in the Spirit World and either prolong life or restore it, such is the love and trust between them. When she dies, Birkita knows that she will not pass into the Other World, Annwn, but will instead go to live with Ayvon, where their love will be consummated and eternal.

Arthur and Caer Cadbryg

Arthur controls central Dumnonia, which was Uther's domain. His seat is Caer Cadbryg, which was also Uther's fortress, and is the largest of the Dumnonian hillforts. But Arthur had to fight for what he currently controls. Uther's younger brother, Custennin, challenged Arthur for Caer Cadbryg, believing himself entitled to all that had been Uther's. Arthur would have relented to Custennin's claims, but his councillors, who include Merlin and several of Uther's old commanders, told Arthur to stand his ground and take control of both Caer Cadbryg and central Dumnonia.

Arthur had, after all, proved himself a worthy warlord in many battles against the Saxons. When Mordred died, Uther turned to his bastard son by Ygraine to lead the warbands against Aelle and the Saxon hordes threatening to cut through Dumnonia and reach Kernow. Arthur and Uther, and then Arthur, Havgan, and Natanleod, drove Aelle back, barred his way, and secured Dumnonia's borders for a time. Caer Cadbryg was Arthur's reward: it was earned with sweat, blood, and fury. It also sealed Arthur's reputation as a leader. Beforehand, he was known as an excellent warrior, but in the campaigns against Aelle, he became a warlord. Warbands came willingly to Arthur's service, swearing oaths to his standard of the Bear, and strengthening Caer Cadbryg and its satellite communities. Merlin played no small part in this. By associating himself with Arthur, Merlin knew he would be creating a potent figurehead; young, clever, brutal in war, and good at it. Many see Uther, the flawed but brilliant leader of the west,

reflected in Arthur. When Merlin brought to him Caledfwlch, the Sword of the Other World, and one of the Thirteen Treasures of Britain, he started to create a legend. The warriors of Dumnonia saw a leader trusted by the Old Gods, which strengthened their faith in the spirits and gods of Britain, even as Christianity grew stronger in Dumnonia. The Kings of the tribes saw that Dumnonia might be kingless, but was far from leaderless. The Saxons saw resistance galvanised. If Aelle and his allies had thought Dumnonia would be easily crushed with Uther dead, they had not reckoned on this Arthur.

In Dumnonia then, and certainly in the lands under Caer Cadbryg's control, Arthur is popular and loved. Elsewhere in Britain, his popularity is viewed with suspicion and, in some parts, derision. Celts like strong leaders, but when a leader grows too popular too quickly, those with life experience always approach the rising star with a certain, weary cynicism. Such is the case with Arthur outside Dumnonia. His triumphs are noted, certainly, but many do not believe that Arthur has the maturity of, say, Natanleod or King Lend of the Cornovii. He has had some luck – not least in having Merlin at his right hand and some good advisers – but he has yet to be truly tested.

Caer Cadbryg

The fortress of Caer Cadbryg is an ancient and isolated hill of limestone and sandstone that has supported fortifications for almost eight hundred years. From the summit and over the considerable ramparts, Celts have a wide view of central Dumnonia, including the Tor at Ynys Wydryn 12 miles away, and, in clear weather, Brynt Tor beyond. It has four lines of earthworks and is surrounded, at the base, by thick woodland. This is a deliberate part of Caer Cadbryg's defence and is host to several small garrisons who provide protection before one even reaches the ditches and ramparts of the earthworks. The main gateway is on the southwest side of the hill, overlooking the village of Montyd, where another garrison is positioned.

Uther's line has occupied Caer Cadbryg for as long as anyone can recall. It is a town in its own right within the wood and stone palisade; halls, houses, workshops, smithies, yards, and pens for livestock. It is fed by several wells and springs with good, clear water. The hill is named for the great spirit Cadbryg – the warrior of the Old People who built the rings of stones throughout Dumnonia, carved the White Horse, and were the ancestors of the Celts. The bards tell that Cadbryg fell to the poison of a shehag that was attempting to kill the Great Red Dragon. The Gods took Cadbryg into the Other World but left behind his helmet, and this became Cadbryg hill. The ancestors then built the fortress to watch out for the hag's return. Cadbryg's spirit rests within the hill and it is his skill and bravery that has blessed Uther's line. This is why the Kings of Uther's line bear the name Pendragon, which means 'Head of the Dragon': Cadbryg fell protecting the Great Red Dragon, and his successors maintain that duty.

At the centre of the Cadbryg community is the Great Hall of Emrys, great, great grandfather of Uther and a warlord who fought against the Romans. Even the Romans recognised his bravery and gave him the name Aurelianus, such was his renown as a warrior. The Great Hall of Emrys is actually three separate halls that have been joined together and now form an 'H' shaped residence unique in Britain. It has many rooms, and the building that connects the two outer halls is a huge feasting hall that can hold hundreds. The nobles of the region have rooms and servants in Emrys' Hall, and it forms the administrative hub of this part of Dumnonia. In Uther's time, it was the seat of administration for all the kingdoms of the west.

Uther's rooms are still occupied by Ladwys, Uther's widow, and Morgana, Uther's daughter and Mordred's surviving twin. Arthur has a couple of modest rooms on the other side of the hall and he deliberately does not presume to take over Uther's old accommodation. He does not believe it is his right, and, besides, relations between himself, Ladwys, and Morgana are strained. Both women blame Arthur for Mordred's death – Morgana especially, who was extremely close to her twin brother. They keep out of each other's way, save when ceremony and ritual dictate they must come together, when they are as civil as needed. Arthur has tried several times for a reconciliation, but knows that nothing he does or says will bring him into Ladwys and Morgana's favour.

Notables of Central Dumnonia

Merlin, Arthur, and Morgana are discussed in greater detail in the Mythic Britons chapter.

Ladwys

Uther's widow, mother to Mordred and Morgana, Ladwys is bitter about the death of her husband and son, even though she hated Uther for his betrayal with Ygraine of Kernow. Arthur is a constant reminder of that betrayal and so she hates him too. Small, ageing, and seemingly frail, she has turned to Christianity and frequently visits Custennin at Caer Sulis where they pray together and, most likely, scheme against Arthur. Ladwys is saddened that Morgana, once an obedient girl, has not turned to Christ as she should, and instead pursues the pagan ways and even continues to court Merlin's attentions – the sorcerer who brought Ygraine and Uther together and is an abomination in the sight of god. Given so much bile and hatred, Ladwys rarely makes herself seen around Caer Cadbryg and, when she does so, is always accompanied by her favourite priest, the unctuous Father Samsun, a Gwent missionary priest sent by Bishop Dyfrig to spread the word of Christ in Dumnonia.

As the widow of a High King, Ladwys is accorded special privilege in Caer Cadbryg. She has no real authority since that has passed to the Council which is headed by Arthur, but the Council recognises her special role and therefore indulges her in most things. To her credit, Ladwys could exploit this indulgence far more than she does (Morgana and Samsun take full advantage) but prefers simply to remain aloof, hating Arthur with every look and glare, and confiding in Custennin and Samsun more and more.

Father Samsun

Originally of Gwent, Bishop Dyfrig sent Samsun into Dumnonia to spread the gospels far and wide. Samsun is a small, timid, pock-faced man who is as pious and devout as he is ugly and snide. Samsun likes comfort, hates pagans, and has a knack for attaching himself to powerful and influential people whom he can milk for sympathy and comforts as his needs arise. His latest host is Lady Ladwys, an enthusiastic but sorrowing convert to Christ who clearly suffered much at the hands of her pagan husband, his pagan mistress, the pagan sorcerer who brought them together, and the pagan bastard whelped to the world that now commands Caer Cadbryg. Samsun sees himself as the personal saviour of Uther's surviving family. Already a confidant of Custennin, Uther's brother, Samsun is managing to inveigle his ways into Dumnonian affairs, exerting a subtle (but noticeable) influence designed to advance his own position (and then that of the church). He has already persuaded the council to build two chapels within Caer Cadbryg's confines and, so that they can properly tended, a decent roundhouse for himself and two attendant priests who answer only to him. Samsun has his eyes on the Church of the Thorn at Glestinga, believing it to be his ultimate calling. While he schemes towards that prize, Samsun also schemes against Morgana, Ladwys' daughter and as confirmed a pagan as he is a Christian. They both hate Arthur but also hate each other; Samsun sees in Morgana a corrupting influence that challenges Ladwys' happiness and one that must be driven from Dumnonia just as Christ drove the moneylenders from the Temple.

Bors

Bors is a Gaulish Celt, brother of King Ban of Armorica, and a relative of Uther. In his fifty-eighth year Bors is still fit and hale, and a formidable warrior, as his is son, also named Bors, who serves in Arthur's warband. Bors the Elder came to Dumnonia at Uther's request more than twenty years ago and has made Caer Cadbryg his home. He was a close adviser to the Pendragon, made Caer Cadbryg's commander, and now serves as its Chief Steward and head of the Council, advising Arthur and the other members of Dumnonia's High Council. Bors is a Christian, but accepting of paganism and certainly in no mood to see it squashed, as Father Samsun (and Lady Ladwys) continually petition for. His focus is on defeating the Saxons: he fought against Horsa when he came across the see from Benoic in Armorica, and has vowed not to return until every last Saxon has sworn allegiance to the Celts, been driven out of Britain, or killed in battle. He is a hard, practical man, and he ensures the smooth running of Caer Cadbryg, as well as fulfilling his more strategic role. It had been hoped that Bors would marry Ladwys, but Bors has shown no interest in marriage since the death of his wife, Dahut, mother of Bors the Younger. Dahut was a beauty and love of Bors' life: he prays for her soul each evening in one of the Caer Cadbryg chapels built by Father Samsun and will not betray that love, or her memory, by taking another wife.

Kernow

Kernow was never conquered by the Romans, something of which the independent Kernovians are very proud, but also in which they find some resentment. Although many tribes succumbed to Roman rule, it is clear that that rule brought wealth and power. Kernow missed out on all of this. The people of Kernow are Dumnonii by heritage, and it hurt them to see the heartlands of their tribe grow and become prosperous even though Rome was a hated enemy.

Kernow certainly has resources: tin, timber, some silver, iron, and so on, but these things are available throughout Britain; the other Kingdoms seem to view Kernow as an irrelevance, and this has made Kernow belligerent and resentful, resulting in antagonism and raids — not least because its current ruler, King Mark, is, by disposition, bad-tempered, vindictive, and antagonistic. Kernow reflects its ruler — and this makes the other kingdoms of Britain, especially Dumnonia and the Western kingdoms, suspicious.

The kingdom of Kernow is tough countryside. The moorland that separates it from Dumnonia is bleak and harsh, subject to mists, driven rain, bogs, uncertain footing, and with few navigable trails. The Romans built no roads here, as there was no basis for easy movement. The interior of Kernow varies between pretty, peaceful glades and the rugged, wave-beaten coastline where the massive western ocean brings huge waves to break against the dark cliffs and long strands. Settlements are highly scattered and ruled by local warlords who, while loyal to Mark, are allowed to rule as they see fit, creating their own laws — or breaking them. Kernow is a haven for misfits, outcasts, fugitives, criminals, and lowlifes. It represents the very edge of Britain — the very edge of the world — and the very edge of civilisation. Common laws can be ignored here; only strength truly rules, and so Kernow is dominated by countless petty factions that are little more than capricious rabble. Feuds are frequent, bitter, and bloody. It amuses Mark to see his chieftains battle this way — Mark is tolerant of chaos and even seems to revel in it. This is no land for children.

The various chieftains are all sworn to King Mark but, in reality, place little value on their oaths. Mark is old and neglectful, and it is only the inertia that a lack of central authority brings that prevents one of the warlords from seizing control of Caer Dore from Mark and Tristan and bringing in a new ruling dynasty. Occasionally, a few chieftains gather to discuss the opportunity, but petty squabbles put paid to serious rebellion and so Mark's reign prevails — although how long that will continue is anyone's guess. The Kernovians know that Dumnonia acts as a stout shield against the Saxons, but if that shield fails, then Kernow may be fighting for its very existence and few believe that the country would be able to resist a Saxon invasion. Some warlords think that the Saxons, like the Romans, are uninterested in Kernow. If they were, surely they would have invaded by sea already. So the inertia continues, and all the while Mark broods and simmers in Caer Dore.

Yet there are a handful of warriors in Kernow who have not succumbed to complacency. Tristan tries to strengthen relations with Dumnonia and Gwent, but has limited opportunity to reach out to either kingdom because of Mark's hatred for both Arthur and the Christian kingdoms of the west. Tristan leads a warband

of reasonably competent warriors and is frustrated at Mark's indolence. Another Kernovian warlord who has actively broken from Mark's shackles is Outigirn, once a champion of the kingdom, but now a mercenary warrior who has taken his spears and shield across the Tamar and intends to fight the Saxons. Outigirn believes that it is only a matter of time before the Saxons break Dumnonia and send their ships west to sack the coastal communities of Kernow. His aim is to move quickly through Saxon-held lands, striking hard and joining with other Britons when necessary. Outigirn fights under his own standard of the Oak Tree, and although loyal to Kernow as a kingdom, he despises Mark as a leader.

King Mark's Rule

Mark rules from Caer Dore, in the north of the country and west of the Fow River estuary. Caer Dore is not a hillfort like Caer Wynd or Caer Cadbryg, but a much lower, less impressive earthwork where Mark has built his Great Hall. It does not require the ramparts and earthworks of other fortifications because no one threatens Mark directly any longer. His last war was with Uther — and that was fought further east and was one that Mark lost. Now that Uther is dead, there is no need to continue fighting. Caer Dore is therefore a hall on a hill surrounded by a community of wood and stone huts, barns, corrals, and muddy lanes that form the town of Dore, the largest of Kernow's towns. Dore sprawls across the landscape with a thick cluster of buildings close to Mark's Hall, but gradually thinning as it radiates away from the meagre earthworks. The roundhouses of Mark's closest allies are nearest to the Hall, including that of Tristan, Mark's son and the closest thing to an effective ruler in Kernow.

Caer Dore

Caer Dore is Kernow in microcosm: neglected, lawless, and complacent, but filled with potential if only a strong hand brought leadership. Tristan, the only one of Mark's three sons to remain, struggles to keep the chieftains in line and drag Kernow out of its malaise, but his father's shadow is too large, too strong, too bitter and too long. Kernow is a kingdom waiting for death —Mark's — but too indolent to hasten the inevitable or prepare for an uncertain future.

And then there is Iseult: and to understand Iseult, one must understand what happened with Ygraine — the woman who broke a kingdom.

King Mark is old now and grossly obese. It is remarkable he has survived as long as he has, given Uther's attempts to kill him, and given his vast appetite for food and alcohol. In his youth, Mark was a fit, athletic, good-looking man who squandered such fortunes on transient pleasures — usually of the sexual kind. He was always a womaniser and it is claimed he seduced his own mother. He married late when he was already King — he was twenty-three when Ygraine was brought to Caer Dore, the beautiful and sensual daughter of a chieftain from the very edge of Kernow who owed Mark a favour. Tall, slender, dark-haired, confident, Ygraine was said to be the most desirable woman in the whole of Britain, a Daughter of Danu, the Irish Goddess (for her mother was an Irish sorceress, so her father claimed). Mark fell in love with her immediately and, many claim, the love was shared and stabilising: Mark became a mellower, more attentive man, less governed by his base desires and more prepared to rule Kernow as it deserved to be ruled.

Kernow and Dumnonia had always fought. The scattered warlords enjoyed raiding across the Tamar, taking whatever they could from Dumnonia's settlements. Uther fought back, with raids of his own into Kernow, but always stopping short of an assault on Caer Dore. As the war with the Saxons intensified, Uther decided that he needed Mark's spears and so offered a truce, backed by gifts, designed to bring Mark into the greater alliance Uther had formed following Vortigern's death. Mark agreed and so the two kings met at Caer Dore and agreed to cease their raids and concentrate on fighting the Saxons instead. Uther brought Merlin as one of his counsellors, and Mark had his own druid, Wella, present at the talks. Agreement was reached; a peace to be celebrated. Mark, eager to show-off his beautiful, enigmatic wife, paraded Ygraine before Uther and his delegation. She danced a dance of the gods — a dance so erotic that even Merlin was entranced, the bards say. Uther desired her more than any woman he had ever seen and conspired to have her. What really happened, no one can say for certain: even Merlin refuses to be drawn on the specifics, but while Mark was away — a voyage to Ireland, perhaps — Uther and Ygraine lay together and Ygraine fell pregnant.

Merlin knew that Mark's rage would be fierce and he helped Ygraine escape Kernow, taking her north. When Arthur was born, he was taken into care in Elmet, but Ygraine could never return to Kernow and Mark's rage was as bitter as Merlin had sensed. Mark waged war against Dumnonia, aided the Saxons with spies and information, and did all he could to punish Uther and Ygraine for their infidelity. He has never forgotten and can never forgive. Since Ygraine, he has had other wives, each chosen for their dark and Other Worldly beauty. None has survived, and Mark's frustrations have deepened with each bride.

Iseult came to him as a gift from an Irish warlord Mark had aided in the past. Dark haired and ethereal in her beauty, she is so like Ygraine that many in Kernow believe she is Ygraine reborn, or another Daughter of Danu. But she is still a child – and a terrified one at that. Mark's paranoia has grown so deep that he is convinced someone will come again to steal her away, just as Uther stole Ygraine. Mark suspects Arthur – a replaying of the father's crimes by the bastard son. And because he never got to punish Ygraine, Iseult becomes a focus for both Mark's lust and his rage. The abuse is known to all – especially Tristan – yet people are so afraid of Mark – and that Ygraine's story will be replayed – that none will act.

A key instrument in all of this is Mark's druid, Wella. Wella has never forgiven himself for not countering the magic Merlin undoubtedly used to bring Uther and Ygraine together. Over the years, this guilt has gnawed at him, driving him mad. Wella seeks revenge on Merlin just as Mark seeks revenge on Uther and Arthur. When Wella sees Iseult, he sees Ygraine, and Ygraine was always too clever to be controlled by Wella. Ygraine was smart and cunning; she taunted Wella with her body, just as she taunted Uther and toyed with Mark. Wella sees her still and lusts for her. He lusts also for poor, terrified Iseult, but his body is withered now, and there is little he can do. So his lust turns to spite, and his spite fuels Mark's rage, and Iseult becomes the target.

Kernow. This is no land for children.

Western Britain

The west of the island is divided into four kingdoms split between two tribes. The kingdoms are Gwent, Gwynedd, Powys, and Siluria, and the tribes are the Ordovices and the Silures.

The whole region has undergone much political and cultural change since the arrival of the Romans. Once, four tribes controlled the west, but the Deceangli and Demetae ceased to exist – a mixture of both steady destruction and absorption into the Ordovices and Silures. The kingdoms of Powys and Gwent are relative newcomers to the political landscape, coming into being during Roman rule as an act of defiance against the invaders. Both the Ordovices and Silures actively rebelled against the Romans, with King Caractacus leading that rebellion around the year 50 and beyond. The Romans came close to wiping out the Ordovices, but failed to do so because, quite simply, the Ordovices, being masters of the tough terrain of the west, were able to hide and survive. The tribe began to rebuild from the year 100 onwards and regained much of its old strength by the time the Romans departed Britain. Before that, Rome adopted a policy of containment, preventing the rebellious Ordovices and Silures from spreading east, using its own legions and the allied Cornovii to keep both tribes where they belonged.

Even though the Ordovices and Silures fought against the Romans, they also fought each other. Caractacus achieved a loose alliance in the early stages of Roman occupation, but it couldn't be maintained after his death. The Silures lacked a great deal of what the Ordovician territories had in abundance, leading to constant raids and territorial disputes. When the Ordovices were forced into hiding by the Roman and Cornovii forces, the Silures took advantage and occupied lands they had no right to hold. When the Ordovices started to rebuild, they retaliated hard, pushing the Silures back towards the south of the region.

Things have not changed. Indeed, they have grown worse. The Silures have made alliances with tribes from the east coast of Ireland and allow them to raid into Gwent and Powys, using Siluria as a staging post. The Silures mount their own raids – constant, punitive actions – in a bid to seize control of the west once and for all. Tensions are compounded by the fact that Gwent and Powys have

embraced Christianity while the Silures remain pagan: a further reason for sustained enmity between the two tribes.

Ordovices

The name means 'hammer'. Quite how the tribe came by this name is lost to time, and the Ordovices are a very old tribe of Britain, claiming to be amongst the first to come to the island. Generations ago, when the tribe was pagan, the Ordovician myths claimed that the gods brought them to Britain; these days, the priests merely say that it was God's Will that the Ordovices came.

The tribe is fiercely proud and defensive of everything it has and owns. Warlike and clever, the Ordovices have made sure they have an intimate knowledge of, and relationship with, their landscape – essential when your southern neighbour is as fierce and hungry as the Silures, and the enemy to the east is the well organised and tenacious Roman army. The Ordovices have never trembled in the face of overwhelming odds; instead they adapt, changing their tactics and dispersing before they can be forcibly dispersed or overwhelmed. Then, they adopt guerrilla tactics, working in small clan groups, never remaining in one place, hitting and running, melting into the terrain. The Ordovices are excellent with ranged weapons: spears, slings and bows, which immediately differentiate them from the other Celts. They are fleet of foot and prefer skirmishing to the resolute brutality of the shield wall.

Nevertheless, they still suffered at the hands of the Romans and Cornovii auxiliaries. Although King Caractacus successfully rebelled, the Ordovices suffered two major defeats and were forced to disperse to preserve their numbers. This lack of cohesion almost destroyed the tribe, and they found themselves fighting in small groups against Silures, Romans, Cornovii, and even the first Irish raiders, taking advantage of the west's chaos.

That the Ordovices survived is, perhaps, miraculous. The Ordovices certainly think so, and their bards and priests tell of how, in those dark days, after the massacre of the druids, the tribe learned of the Will of God and how this separation and suffering was one of many tests. Missionaries from across the seas managed to spread their word amongst the Ordovician clans, and many parallels were found in the testaments of the One God. Clan by clan, the tribe converted to Christianity. This was God's Will. God wanted them to survive, but only if they could pass this crucial test of faith. They did, and they have.

As a consequence, the Ordovices are full Christian converts. Some still pay lip service to the Old Ways, but essentially they are Christians. Most of their druids were lost in the Ynys Mon massacre, leaving a huge gap to be filled by those missionaries preaching Christ's Gospel. As the tribe adopted this new religion, the stronger it became. The stronger it became, the more God revealed. When Pádraig – a Roman slave who escaped to Ireland – returned to the west with Christ's word, it was obvious (if it had not already been so) that Jesus Christ had saved the tribe and led them to inherit the lands the Romans sought to take. He had delivered Britain from the Romans by casting them out, just as Pádraig cast out the snakes from Ireland.

As the Ordovician identity changed, so the tribe split into two kingdoms. During the lean years of isolation and near-destruction, two centres of control had emerged, and these became the centres of two kingdoms: Powys and Gwent. Powys is the larger of the two, in terms of both area and population. What Gwent lacks in size and people, it compensates for in terms of piety and suffering: Gwent is as devotedly Christian as the Brigantes and bears the full brunt of Siluria's attacks (and those of its Irish mercenary allies).

The Silures

If the Silures were moved wholesale to the lands of the Picts, they would feel very much at home. Sullen, insular, violent, resentful, the Silures have far more in common with the Caledonii and Votadini than they do their Brythonic-speaking neighbours. The country is heavily wooded, filled with steep, dark valleys, and is difficult to farm and cultivate. As a result, the Silures have developed a culture of perpetual raiding, taking from others what they cannot create for themselves. Their druids have been largely to blame for this; the spirits of Siluria are dark, malevolent beings that whisper malignant secrets to the Silurian druids who, in turn, beseech the warlords to greater atrocities. It was ever thus, and neither the Silures nor Ordovices can a recall a time of peace between them. When the Ordovices converted to Christianity, this was the signal for the Silures to wipe them out, once and for all.

Few Silures venture from the valleys unless it is to raid or march to war. A hard, insular people, they are unwelcoming of strangers

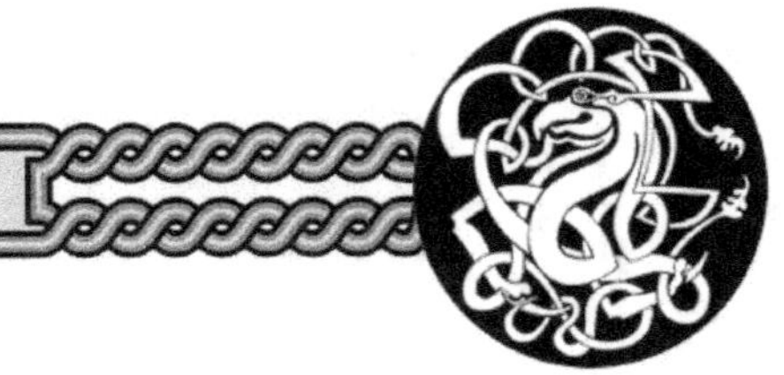

(many are sacrificed) and intolerant of change. Silurian chieftains rule through right of arms; anyone can be chief if they can kill the current incumbent and then kill any subsequent challengers. The Silures despise weakness, sneer at mercy, and delight in the nature of killing and bloodshed. Of course, there are a few isolated Silurian villages where life is a little more peaceful and balanced, but they are a rare exception. The Silures are survivors, and brutality is an efficient means to an end.

Gwent

Bordered by the Rivers Uisc and Wye, and the Severn Sea in the south, and centred on Caer Went, the small kingdom of Gwent is formed from territory the Silures never occupied to any great degree, but consider to be theirs. Located close to the Dumnonian border, Gwent is a land of rolling valleys, thick woodland, and fertile rivers. It was once Dumnonian territory, and later ceded to the Romans who established the town of Venta (now known as Caer Went), driving out the Silures. The Romans established other settlements in this region, including Caerleon, which, like Venta/ Caer Went, is an important town.

Gwent's ruler is King Meurig, son of Rhys. Meurig, like his father, is a highly devout Christian who surrounds himself with priestly advisers, including the pious and clever evangelist, Dyfrig (who history will remember as Saint Dubricius), a priest who has done much in his thirty-five years to spread the word of Christ far and wide across the Celtic kingdoms. Meurig is a sickly, frail man, and his priests pray daily and nightly for the Lord to deliver him from his ailments. At times Meurig is too weak to walk and must be carried in an old Roman palanquin by a retinue of young monks from the abbey at Uisc. Meurig is very fond of the abbey and its young monks; it is believed that, when the trials of kingship grow too wearisome, he will retire to the abbey to devote his life to God and the welfare of the Novices. Indeed, Meurig is so dedicated to God and Christ that he has forsaken his wife, Agnes, and son, Pyrigg. Agnes has been sent to join the convent at Caer Leon and Pyrigg has become a Novice at the newest monastery to be built on the banks of the Wye river. Many admire this show of utmost piety, but some, mostly the warlords of Gwent who are constantly beset by Silurian raids, wonder if it is not simply negligence.

Meurig and the Gwentish priests, particularly Dyfrig, are certain that God will deliver Gwent from the ravages of Siluria and grant Britain victory over the pagan Saxons. Much of that victory will come in the form of conversion: the more who accept Christ's love, the fewer there will be willing to fight. Indeed, Meurig and Dyfrig see a Kingdom of Britain united under Christ — a view shared by the Brigantes. Where the Gwentish Ordovices and Brigantes differ is in where the capital of this new Christian Kingdom should be located: Gwent or Brigantia. There has been much debate and much argument. The warlords of Gwent have agreed that they would rather face a rabid, druid-driven Silurian shield wall than endure a hall full of Gwentish and Brigantian priests arguing over which kingdom will rule Christian Britain.

Meurig and Dyfrig are steadily increasing the power of the church in Gwent. Meurig has granted a great deal of land to Bishop Dyfrig for the building of churches and monasteries, and with these lands come simple Celtic homes. The dues they pay, once given to the King for the common good, are now given to the church for the glory of God. The church in Gwent is growing wealthier, while the freemen of the kingdom grow poorer, as does the royal household. To maintain the ambitious programme of building and evangelism Bishop Dyfrig demands, dues have increased substantially, with those living on church lands being forced to pay up to a third of their income and produce. Those who pay less or pay late are fined, increasing their debt. Those who are deemed to have broken the King's or the church's laws are also fined, further swelling the holy coffers. The traditional Celtic values, found in most Celtic communities, are diminishing in Gwent, being replaced by a church-driven economy where wealth is concentrated in the hands of the clergy and used for ends they dictate, rather than for the all that is the traditional Celtic way.

Of course, this is God's will. Christ and the apostles donated all their wealth to God's estate and this is the only way to prove one's devotion: through obedience and austerity. And if Bishop Dyfrig and his senior priests drape themselves in silver and silk, it is merely to demonstrate that they have been chosen as God's representatives. Such riches belong to God, not to them, and God is all wise and all merciful.

Caer Went

Once a Silurian trading post, the Romans drove out the tribe and turned the little-used market area into a proper, Roman, town — Venta Silurum or, simply, Venta. It remained a garrison and trade hub for the south of the region up until the exodus and survived beyond that. The Ordovices returned to claim Venta and renamed it Caer Went, making the Roman name appear more Celtic.

Caer Went became the centre of the new kingdom of Gwent. The Christian kings swiftly added churches and chapels, and the Silures quickly moved to attack the settlement, wanting back territory that was, originally, theirs. Around the year 450, the Gwentians built a formidable stone wall around the town with the precise purpose of keeping the Silures out. The building work was funded by the church and so the wall ensures that every church and chapel is safe, although several housing groups were left outside the stone wall and forced to build their own ditches and palisades. And so Caer Went is today: a mostly intact Roman city, protected by earthworks, log palisades, and a fine, strong wall of good Silurian stone. Caer Went is well protected and the Silures have stopped bothering to raid the place.

King Meurig believes that Caer Went is protected by God. The symbol of the cross is everywhere, and the town's garrison wear the cross as the device on their shields. Meurig's hall is a converted Roman villa close to the centre and close to the largest church, which is dedicated to the Virgin Mother, Mary. Despite Meurig's devotion to property, his hall is a grand affair and he is attended by several Silurian slaves who have converted (forcibly, no doubt) to Christianity. The hall is built around a sumptuous courtyard, which has a fountain and a striking mosaic depicting many types of fish. Many say that the mosaic was made by pagan Romans who worshipped a god who was part man and part fish, but Meurig maintains that it commemorates the importance of fish to Christ and the apostles, and the attendant priests agree.

Close to Meurig's hall is Bishop Dyfrig's house, another grand villa from the Roman era that is larger than King Meurig's. From here, Dyfrig runs Christianity throughout the west and across a reasonable part of Celtic Britain. He controls the many itinerant, evangelical preachers who take God's word to the heathens, and he employs a room full of scribes to keep meticulous records of which settlements have converted, their priests, the lands around, estimates of holdings, revenue, and so on. Amongst the scrolls, parchments, and books is the largest, most complete, record of Celtic Britain's wealth, as possessed by the church. Dyfrig's administration also acts as a counting and clearing house for tithe and tribute, most of which is kept safely buried with Caer Went; but a decent amount goes to the Pope in Rome, sent in ships that sail down the River Wye and into the Severn Sea, making towards Armorica. Considerable wealth flows through Dyfrig's hands, and he ensures that the churches of Gwent want for little, that the itinerant preachers have coin to help gain converts, and that God's work is done as well as it possibly can be.

The Church of the Virgin Mary, next to Bishop Dyfrig's house, is made fully of stone — a rarity for churches. It has a slate roof, an impressive bell tower, and can accommodate several hundred worshippers before its great, marble altar. Beneath that altar are stairs leading to the narrow crypt (former wine cellars for the house that occupied where the church now stands) and this is where much of Gwent's wealth is hidden. The church has a full time complement of priests to run the place, supplemented by novices from the monastery at Caer Leon. When not involved in administrative duties, Dyfrig can be found here, as can King Meurig — when his health permits or when Dyfrig commands his presence.

Of course, Meurig is king in name only. Real power lies with Dyfrig. He controls Gwent's wealth, commands its clergy, and has a keen and clever mind. Meurig consults him on everything, much to the consternation of the Gwentish Ordovician chieftains who form the official council, yet find themselves sidelined.

Caer Leon

West of Caer Went, Caer Leon is the Brythonic name for Isca, the fortified settlement and hillfort built next to the Uisc River. The Romans created a large, important and impressive administrative centre here, with an amphitheatre, baths, grand buildings and a substantial garrison. It protected river-borne traffic and kept the Silures and Ordovices separate during the occupation. From here, the Romans were able to control the northern coast of the Severn Sea and easily patrol the whole of the region, ensuring the rebellious tribes stayed in hiding.

The Christian Ordovices moved quickly to secure Isca from returning to Silurian rule, placing a garrison on the hillfort and fortifying the Roman settlement. Stone from old Isca helped build the wall at Caer Leon, but otherwise the Roman town is largely intact and home, like Caer Went, to priests, monks from the nearby monastery, traders and crafters. It has suffered raids from the Silures in the past, and, more recently, raids by the Irish warbands the Silures allow to use the Severn and their lands to plunder Gwent's riches, As a result, Caer Leon remains in a state of readiness, commanded by Tewdric, one of Meurig's trusted warlords, and a staunch enemy of all things Silurian, Irish, and Saxon in that order.

Tewdric is a Christian – as are all the warlords of Gwent – and is also highly practical. He is well aware of the control the church has over Gwent, but he has also seen Gwent prosper as a result. As Caer Leon protects Caer Went and Gwent's interior, Tewdric wants for little in terms of resources. His warbands are small, but well armed, well trained, and loyal to King and Church. Bishop Dyfrig ensures that Tewdric can maintain Caer Leon's defences and has built him a decent hall on the summit of the hillfort overlooking the old Iscan settlement. The church might rule Gwent, but Tewdric rules Caerleon, and he does so with traditional Celtic hard-headedness. If this means kneeling to a Bishop whenever Dyfrig visits, so be it. Everyone bows to someone else eventually.

Notables of Gwent

King Meurig

Meurig ap Rhyddfedd suffers from a weak heart. He was a pale and sickly child, raised by monks, and denied any parental care. Frequently beaten and frequently abused, he has grown into a pale and sickly king who has been beaten into obedience of the church and fully believes that his ailments are a punishment from God. He hates kingship. He is, first and foremost, a servant of Christ, and then a leader of Gwent as a distant second. His marriage to Agnes is a mere expedience to produce an heir, which they were lucky enough to do on their wedding night. They have not shared a bed since and Agnes, distraught at her husband's negligence, found easy comfort in the arms of others. When her indiscretions were discovered, Bishop Dyfrig suggested that she should take Holy Orders as penitence – hence her unwilling entry into the nearest convent. Their son, Pyrigg, is a robust and ruddy boy of seven, but has been entrusted into the care of monks where, no doubt, the same trials visited on his father are being visited on him.

Although weak in body and will, Meurig is not stupid. He does not want to be king and, indeed, he will abdicate in favour of Pyrigg once the boy is of age. Until then, he knows that the church is making Gwent wealthy, and that wealth is attracting more Christians who are willing to pledge loyalty to the King of Gwent. Gwent will grow – as long as the Silures are kept at bay and the Saxons defeated. It will grow to shadow the Brigantes, Powys, and Dumnonia. Meurig believes paganism is doomed and this is now the era of Christianity: the Saxons are merely a test. With Dyfrig as his ally, Meurig believes that the kingdoms of Gwent and God are destined to grow together and make Britain whole once more, but under the holy light of Christ. He is determined to let nothing interrupt that vision.

Bishop Dyfrig

Dyfrig's life has been spent bringing Christ to the masses, converting as many pagans as he can, and building both God's and his own missions spiritually, politically, and financially. He is an astute and clever man, fluent in Goidelic, Latin, and even some of the Jutish tongue, and very, very good with numbers. His piety is without question, and he makes converts through subtle manipulation, steady exposure of character weaknesses and foibles, and then an ardent demonstration of how turning to Christ will absolve sin, build strength, bring riches of the soul, and ensure salvation. A compelling and skilful orator, it is little wonder he has risen to the rank of bishop and come to rule Gwent through the proxy that is King Meurig.

They have an excellent relationship. Meurig knows that Dyfrig governs, and Dyfrig knows precisely how to play and manipulate Meurig – a man riddled with guilt, saddled with sexual predilections that must be kept secret, and a deep desire to be saved by God. Dyfrig is adept at spotting the weakness in all men and exploiting it by adapting his attitudes to gain their confidence and trust, before carefully exposing them to the potential repercussions of their sins.

Gwynedd

Sorrowing Gwynedd is a fraught, contested kingdom that is currently without a monarch. Irish settlers and raiders, the Gangani, migrated across the sea and settled the island of Ynys Mon long before the Romans arrived in Britain. They held the land during the Roman occupation and formed two tribes: the Gangani and the Deceangli, but when Rome marched west, ostensibly to deal with the troublesome druids at Ynys Mon, they also dealt with the rebellious Irish descendants, dispersing and then destroying both tribes. The lands around Ynys Mon, known at that time as Llyn, remained wild and sparsely occupied. The Celts believed that the furious spirits of the murdered druids drove anyone attempting settlement of the region mad, and perhaps they did.

When Rome left, the Irish and Manx raiders began to return, this time supplemented by Silurian warbands. Around the year 445, Cunedda, a warlord of the Votadini, learned of rich pickings in this area of the west, and led his army to defend it against the Irish incursion. Vicious fighting over the next five years saw Cunedda vanquish the Irish and forge a kingdom of his own, which was named Gwynedd. Cunedda ruled for a decade; afterwards, Einion,

the elder of Cunedda's two sons, became the warlord of Gwynedd, but never assumed the title of King, probably because his brother, Ceredig, contested the right to rule. Indeed, Gwynedd has plunged into a ragged civil war, with Einion and Ceredig's clans battling for supremacy. Both Einion and Ceredig are dead, but their sons maintain the blood feud. The Einion clan is led by Einion's sons, Cadwallon and Owain, and is supported by Christian Powys. The Ceredigion clan is led by Meirion, Ceredig's nephew, and supported by the pagan Silures.

The civil war has left Gwynedd vulnerable. Encouraged by the Silures, Irish raiders have returned to the region, seizing Ynys Mon and long stretches of coastline between the Ceredigion and Einion territories. As the Ceredigion clan is allied with the Silures, and the Silures have strong ties with the Irish, it is the Einion clan that is currently losing the war for the control of Gwynedd. The constant raids and skirmishes have taken their toll on the populace with many fleeing over the hills to Powys, Gwent, and even as far as Cornovii and Dumnonii lands. The harvests have suffered, Irish raiding goes unchecked (with many shipped back to Ireland as slaves), and each year seeing the bodies pile up in the bleak, wind-torn hills and valleys. The kingdom Cunedda created by driving the Irish out has reverted to the lawless wasteland it was before he arrived. King-less (and it will remain so for at least twenty years), Gwynedd has almost become an irrelevance to the rest of Western Britain.

The Einion Clan

When Cunedda died, it was both his wish, and that of his council, that Einion be named King of Gwynedd. Einion, unfortunately, was never a universally popular choice. Although a good and fierce warrior, he was also a confirmed Christian in a largely pagan community. Before his conversion, he had been a womanising drunk and had, allegedly, raped the wife of his younger brother, Ceredig. Ceredig and Einion certainly loathed each other, and when it was announced that Einion would succeed Cunedda, Ceredig violently opposed the idea and had enough warband support to challenge the tribal council. Einion had his own followers, mostly Christian converts, and they turned to Powys for help and assistance, which was readily provided by King Rhyddfedd, father of the current Powysian king, Cyngen. The Einion clan has, over the years, become even more fervently Christian, and under the leadership of Cadwallon and Owain, Einion's sons, it views the war against the Ceredigions as a Holy War – one to make most of the west into a Christian region as large and influential as that of the Brigantes.

The Einions are struggling to hold their territory against the massing of the Ceredigion, Irish, and Silurian warbands. Much faith is placed in God and the Saints to deliver them to victory, but Owain, the more pragmatic of the two brothers, has travelled to Powys, Gwent, and Brigantia seeking more help for the struggle against the enemy. Owain is finding it difficult to convince the Powysians and Brigantes to send more help given the growing threat of the Saxons. Gwent, beset by the Silures along its own borders, is stretched far enough as it is.

As things stand, the Einions are losing the war for Gwynedd, and it does not appear that God and the Saints are that interested in the kingdom's fate.

The Ceredigion Clan

Ceredig was not Cunedda's choice to succeed him as King of Gwynedd: Ceredig was young, impetuous, and, although remaining pagan, never his father's favourite. Ceredig maintained that his wife, Aula, was raped by Einion following a night of drunken feasting, but Cunedda never believed the charge. Aula had a certain reputation, and so it was felt that Ceredig was simply trying to make trouble. Ceredig was, though, popular with many of Gwynedd's warbands and their lords. When he decided to challenge Einion's accession to the throne of Gwynedd, he had close to 800 spears to support his position. The Silures added their own support, and brought with them the Irish who had been arriving in greater numbers along the coast of the Severn Sea. Some of these Irish were Christians, and Ceredig was a confirmed pagan, but that did not matter; the Irish wanted to reclaim the old prize of Ynys Mon and the coastal regions of Gwynedd, and Ceredig promised them such territories if the Einion clan was defeated.

So the brothers went to war, and their clans have warred for the past thirty years.

With Irish and Silurian support, the Ceredigion clan is winning. However, it is facing crisis. Ceredig never had any sons and so leadership of the clan passed to his nephew, Meirion. Meirion

began as a strong and controlled leader, but as he has aged, his grip has become shaky. He has allowed his Irish and Silurian allies too much power in Gwynedd, and there is now a real danger that the ageing and ailing chief will be supplanted by someone of King Iuchar of Siluria's choosing — or, as is more likely — an Irish chieftain. Like Ceredig, Meirion has no male offspring and his line of the family seems to display a form of congenital madness. Meirion's brothers and nephews demonstrate a distinct unreliability and, although the Ceredigions are winning the war for Gwynedd, there is a growing belief that no one in Meirion's line will be fit to inherit the throne once the Einions are defeated.

In truth, the Silures are more interested in eradicating Gwent than they are in defeating the Einion clan: this means that the Irish, under the command of Connor mac Eird (The Blackshield) will seize power and turn Gwynedd into an Irish province, displacing all the Britons who fought to establish Gwynedd in Cunedda's name. More boats from Ireland arrive each year, bringing more warbands, more settlers, and more claimants to Gwynedd's heritage.

Powys

An old kingdom, Powys is the home of Vortigern, first of the High Kings of the Britain and the man who divided the island so brutally. It is the largest of the Ordovician kingdoms and has been a Christian hub since the rule of King Catigern, second of Vortigern's sons (which are Vortimer, Catigern, Pascent, and Faustus). Catigern was a late convert to Christianity, being baptised (under the name of Cadeyern) a year or two before his death. His son, Cadell, had been baptised several years earlier and it is said that Cadell was a favourite of Saint Germanus, a Christian priest of Gaul who visited Britain to bring the Word of God to the pagans. Germanus helped Cadell defeat the Irish that threatened Powys's borders (allowed through by the Silures) and bring him to the throne when his father died.

By the time of the current king, Cyngen, Powys has been Christian for four generations. The largest Ordovician kingdom, its traditional ally is the Dumnonii tribe and its traditional enemy the Cornovii — even though Vortigern himself had roots in the Cornovii. As Christianity has become the dominant religion in Powys, this old enmity has increased — although Christianity in Powys is less fervent than it is Gwent, where it has come to rule the kingdom, rather simply be its belief system.

Due to its size, Powys is rich in many natural resources: excellent timber, pasture for livestock, minerals, ores, precious metals and gems — an attraction for traders and raiders. Rome began a lot of the work, exploiting those areas they seized from the Ordovices in the eastern part of the region, but the Celts have learned from what the Romans did and continued the work under subsequent kings, making Powys a rich and desirable kingdom.

The capital of Powys is the town and nearby hillfort of Branogenium/Caer Branog. Vortigern was born here, and it has been the residence of each king of Powys since the Romans left the country. The Powysians have retained the old Roman name because it is synonymous with trade in the region. The town has no wall, although Caer Branog is the usual ditch and earthwork construction familiar throughout Celtic Britain. Powys has many smaller towns and hillforts, each the seat of a local chieftain or warlord sworn to King Cyngen's service. The communities and warlords close to the Gwynedd border help strengthen the Einion clan in its war against the Ceredigion clan; and the settlements close to Gwent help keep the Silures and Irish away from Powys by supporting King Meurig.

Although Christianity dominates, there are still pagans in Powys. They have been forced to follow their religious practices discreetly and druids are unwelcome in the villages and towns where Christian churches flourish, making the old Celtic religion very much a countryside activity. Ever since Saint Germanus visited the kingdom, back in Cadell's time, Powys has become a place where miracles seem to take place (if the priests are to be believed) on a regular basis, and where holy relics seem to gravitate. Much of this activity is a propaganda campaign mounted by Bishop Frych, the head of the church in Powys, to counter the inherent countryside power of the pagan spirits. But despite being surrounded by miracles and saintly relics, the Powysian pagans are able to go about their business more or less unmolested — if one discounts the constant attempts to convert as molestation.

King Cyngen is, like Vortigern before him, a man with ambition. That ambition is to see a united west, and one that is shared with Gwent's Meurig. He does not care if Western Britain is Christian, pagan or a mixture, just as long as it is under Ordovician

control, that the Irish are driven out, and the Saxons stopped before they overrun the whole of Britain. This means Cyngen is constantly watching his borders and prepared to maintain alliances with Dumnonia and, wherever possible, Cornovia. There is a sense of duty in all of this; Vortigern is considered a traitor across much of Britain, and although there is distance between Cyngen and his great, great grandfather, Cyngen feels responsible for checking the Saxon advance. Powys can afford to train, equip, and support good armies, so Cyngen makes sure that happens. He talks frequently with the Dumnonian leaders and, in particular, Arthur and Natanleod, and is keen for Powys and Dumnonia to act together. Cyngen would like his daughter, Einwyn, to marry Arthur, sealing a Dumnonia/Powys alliance, but that is a move he is yet to suggest. Bishop Frych would prefer Einwyn to marry a Christian, which Arthur is not, and the relationship Arthur has with Merlin troubles the Bishop. But, like Cyngen, Bishop Frych is a practical man and he understands the importance of strength in these times. Both men have a long-term and quite strategic view of Powys's future: deal with the Saxons first, and then turn to deal with Irish, Silurians, and the upstart Ceredigions.

Notable Settlements of Powys

Branogenium/Caer Branog

Branogenium is close to the River Lent and was established by the Romans first as a garrison and then as a trading and staging post. Like Viroconium, which is not far away, it became rich and prosperous, attracting trade from across Europe. The garrison was moved to the hillfort, Caer Branog, around 170 when the fortifications were strengthened, but as the Ordovices were scattered across the west, the need to maintain a garrison at Caer Branog lessened and so it was abandoned after about 50 years.

Vortigern was born at Caer Branog but spent more time in Viroconium amongst the Cornovii. When he became king of Powys he returned briefly to Caer Branog and began to establish his plans for uniting Britain. He did this by establishing solid relations with the Dumnonii and the Cornovii; a capable leader and a good politician, others saw that Vortigern was worth following. By 441, at the tender age of 22, Vortigern had a substantial following behind him. Supported by Uther, King of the Dumnonii, and counselled by Merlin, Vortigern moved his power base away from Powys, to Durocobrivis, which was a more central and politically strategic location for Britain's first High King.

Branogenium still flourished, even without Vortigern, although its garrison needed to be continually vigilant to guard against Silurian and Irish raids. Uther eventually put a stop to these by leading an army against the Silurian raiders in the hills due south of Branogenium, slaughtering those who would have plundered Vortigern's birth place. From then on, Branogenium has been unsullied by raids and a great deal of its original Roman architecture and structure is left intact.

The market of Branogenium takes place in the wide meadows beside the Lent River and is held three times a year (spring, summer and autumn), attracting traders from across Celtic Britain. The town is also home to the Church of the Magdalene, also Bishop Frych's residence, which was blessed by Saint Germanus. The church has several Magdalene-related relics in its possession: a lock of Mary Magdalene's hair (used to wipe clean the feet of Jesus), a glass vial of her tears (collected as she wept at the foot of the crucifixion), and a shred of her gown (worn when Christ rose from the dead). Those lucky enough to be granted a view – and, on occasion, an actual touch – of these relics report miracles. Ailments are lifted, diseases cured, and pagans converted. Both King Cyngen and Bishop Frych are incredibly proud of these relics and, naturally, protective of them. A warband protects the church at all times, drawn from the most devout Christian warriors, and it is a great honour to serve in the Warriors of the Magdalene, protecting her treasures from those who would steal or destroy them. And there have been several attempts – by pagans and those from other churches jealous of Powys's wealth.

Magnis

If Branogenium is important to the Christians, Magnis is important to the pagans of Powys. South of Branogenium, it has been a settlement for far longer than the capital and its importance was recognised by the Romans who established a major temple of their own here, thereby showing respect for the local spirits. After the Romans left, and before King Catigern became a Christian, Magnis was an important hub for Powysian pagans: a trading place and a place sacred to the spirits. Magh is the local water spirit, manifesting through the natural spring that bubbles through the ground

close to the Wye River. Magh had powers of healing and fertility, and the Romans embraced those powers, building an octagonal shrine for her. Over the years, and with the rise of the Christian religion, Magh's powers have diminished and she rarely manifests (save for those occasions where the druids make a concerted effort to call for her aid and make appropriate sacrifices). The Christians have established a chapel not far from the shrine and they attempt to keep the pagans away from Magh's spring, but the followers of the Old Gods still find ways to leave Magh tokens and gifts: posies of flowers, hunks of cheese wrapped in leaves, cobs of fresh-baked bread, and so on. The local priest, Father Herydd, sends his faithful to steal these offerings which then grace his own table, and he claims that the spring is a miracle sent by God; but the pagans of the hills and valleys surrounding Magnis know the truth and ignore Herydd's violent proselytising.

Notable Powysians

King Cyngen

Cyngen ap Rhyddfedd carries the weight of Vortigern's legacy on his shoulders. Had it not been for his illustrious ancestor, there would be no Saxons in Britain and all Powys would need to worry about would be Siluria and the spiteful war in Gwynedd. As it is, Cyngen feels a duty to set to rights the wrongs of his great, great grandfather and ensure that the Saxons do not finish what Vortigern allowed them to start.

He is a solemn, dutiful, Christian, Cyngen; he prays regularly, observes the Saints' Days, reads the scriptures and prays for sinners. But he is also a practical, pragmatic man who understands that kings lead, and lead in battle. So, Cyngen is a decent (although not exemplary) warlord who is not averse to drawing a sword or levelling a spear when it comes to defending Powys. He ensures his counsel consists of hard, level-headed, practical men, be they pagan or Christian, and he looks to the long-term survival of Powys rather than the loftier spiritual goals Gwent's King Meurig holds dear.

Cyngen has three daughters and two sons. Einwyn is the oldest of his children and the apple of his eye. A dark haired, brown-eyed beauty she is, at 14, ready for betrothal and there are many men who would commit murder to have her as their wife. Cyngen loves her dearly but also knows she is an asset who must be married wisely. Arthur is Cyngen's personal choice, but he already has a solid friendship with Dumnonia, and it might be wiser to marry Einwyn into a Cornovii clan, thereby sealing an alliance with an old foe.

Of his sons, Cuneglas, the eldest boy, is shaping-up to be the kind of leader Powys needs. A good Christian, a sensible head, and an easy gift that makes him popular with his fellows. A marriage with a Cornovii girl could be the way to bring Powys and Cornovia together as they should be, and Cyngen knows that soon he must make his choice for Powys's future.

Where other matters are concerned, Cyngen delegates to his warlords. He has some fine men, battle-hardened, who can look after the situations in Gwent and Gwynedd while he focuses on the greater threat of the Saxons. This is one of Cyngen's strengths: he trusts the right people and is trusted in return. It is trait that faltered and failed in both Vortigern and Uther. Some see Cyngen as

a possible High King, a possible Pendragon, if the Saxons can be defeated.

Bishop Frych

The portly, jovial Bishop Frych is very much a complement to King Cyngen. Where Cyngen is serious, Frych is light-hearted; where Cyngen examines details, Frych looks to the Big Picture. Big, loud, bearded, bald, Frych is an awesome sight, his gowns barely covering his massive, lumbering frame. He is also a devout, insightful man who understands Cyngen very well, and knows how to play the political game well. Frych was also a warrior in youth, serving in the warband of Cyngen's father. Injury put paid to his military career, and he still walks with the limp caused by a seax (knife) wound to his right calf. He maintains a warrior's soul though, and is highly sympathetic to the warrior ethos, understanding the mind-set needed by a soldier to survive the horrors of battle. He became a priest once his leg healed: an angel appeared to him as he lay, wrapped in fever, and commanded him to become God's Soldier. The vision was so profound, Frych hung up his sword, took up the bible, and studied to become a priest with the old bishop, Meddyn, as his tutor. Over the years, he has proved to be a valuable and trusted adviser with a keen brain and an eye for human character. That said, he is undoubtedly pious and has sworn to protect the relics of Branogenium. The Warriors of the Magdalene — the warband protecting the relics — is hand-picked by Bishop Frych and, as an old warrior himself, he knows how to choose hardened, competent fighters. He has also come to pity pagans. He does not hate them nor does he despise them, but he considers them wayward in nature and capable of understanding the nature of the True God. He delights in trying to convert hardened, confirmed pagans, believing that they bring more to the church than those who convert willingly.

Siluria

The Silures are distinct from other Celts of Britain largely due to their colouring: swarthy skin and very dark/black hair, frequently curly, hints at a relationship with the Celts of the Iberian Peninsula, although the Silures possess few myths or stories supporting such an ancestry. What they do possess is a reputation for brutality that rivals the Picts and a strong survival streak that has preserved the tribe even though their neighbours, the Demetae, were crushed by Rome and the Ordovices scattered.

Like the other tribes of Western Britain, the Silures resisted Roman occupation. Their territory is heavily forested and a maze of steep-sided valleys, gloomy glades, and half-hidden trails that proved a nightmare for Roman forces to penetrate. Those that did found themselves facing an almost invisible foe that used the terrain to its utmost, waging a guerrilla campaign against the legions. Rome captured the eastern edges of Silurian territory, and pushed the tribe into the interior, but never conquered their lands fully or managed to subjugate the Silures. The Silures fought with everything they had and still do: for them, nothing has changed. They dislike the other Celts and are disliked in return.

Particular hatred is reserved for the Ordovices. Always enemies, the hated Ordovices have, since Rome left, taken over territories that once belonged to Siluria, creating the Christian kingdom of Gwent. Siluria would see Gwent wiped out, its Christians murdered and its settlements burnt. But the Silures have never been numerous enough, and no king of the tribe has successfully united the different factions that make war upon each other as much as they make war on Gwent. For these reasons alone, the Silures, while vicious and tenacious, do not pose the kind of threat that would worry Powys and Dumnonia.

Siluria is rich in wood and game, but little else. Many communities live a subsistence existence, necessitating raids into Gwent to supplement meagre supplies. Others survive through making charcoal which is traded (sometimes) with the Cornovii, Dumnonii, and Kernovians, but more often than not with the Irish. Siluria has strong links with the Irish tribes on that island's east coast. At first, Ireland raided Siluria, but when the Silures sent a boatful of Irish heads back to the king of Uí Garrchon, the Irish tribes realised that the Silures might be better used as allies. The kings of the Uí Garrchon, Uí Mail, and Uí Cennselig tribes met with the Silures and it was agreed that the Irish would trade valued commodities with the Silures in return for the right to pass through their lands to raid Powys and Gwent. The Silures don't care that Ireland is becoming Christian; the Irish can worship whoever they want — but they never stole land from the Silures that had been stolen first by the Romans.

Siluria does not include any hillforts of note; those it once possessed are now part of Gwent and have not belonged to the Silures for several centuries. The heavily wooded terrain of Siluria makes building hillforts difficult without a great deal of land clearance and so the Silures have adapted, building roundhouses and halls, protected by steep-sided valleys and the natural woodlands. Communities are small, scattered, insular, and xenophobic. Stepping into Siluria's grim, rain-soaked woodlands is to step beyond Britain and into a shadow kingdom ruled by suspicion and fear. The Silures are primitive, defensive, and automatically hateful towards outsiders. Their druids command powerful nature and predator spirits, appeasing and controlling them with frequent blood sacrifices. Indeed, the Silures worship the Celtic death god, Crom Cruach, and his spirits of death and violence are rife in the dense, dark, woodlands of the Silures, attracted by the opportunities for prey and the sacrificial souls the Silures delight in offering.

Notable Silurians

Iuchar the Boar

King of the Silures is Iuchar the Boar, so-called because he slew the Great Black Boar, Haed, with his bare hands. He wears the boar skin, replete with its head and tusks, as a cloak, and his chief druid, Tadhg, imprisoned the spirit of Haed within the skin's tusks, and so Iuchar now controls it. In battle, he almost becomes Haed: a vast boar in human form, raging and terrible, in his desire for death. Iuchar embodies the fierce, unforgiving nature of the Silures. He is a man of primal passions, as are the Silures; he is driven by the lust for battle, death, and revenge, as is his tribe. What he wants, he takes, just as the Silures do, and he cares nothing for human life. The Silures have to be strong, and so the leaders they make, like Iuchar, are the strongest of the strong: battle-hardened, blood-soaked, bile-dripping killers with souls as dark as the forest shadows at mid-winter's eve.

Iuchar has paid a blood-price for his rulership of the Silures. Tadhg told him that if he was prepared to sacrifice his eldest son and youngest daughter to Crom Cruach and Haed, the kingship would be his and no mortal man would ever beat him in a challenge. Iuchar had little hesitation in sacrificing both children, and when his wife attacked him with a boar spear for killing two of their three offspring, he spitted her on it and had her roasted at his proclamation feast. From that day on, every Silurian knew that Iuchar was capable of anything and most live in fear of him. He is a generous king though, rewarding those loyal to him with silver and slaves (Christians, he finds, make good slaves) and keeping the Silures true to their pagan roots. Otherwise Iuchar rules through fear and magic. With the spirit of Haed in his boar skin, and Crom Cruach's protection from challenge, Iuchar is considered invincible.

Tadhg, High Druid of the Silures

Tadhg, of course, is behind much of Iuchar's power and ambition. He is an accomplished druid, but an even more accomplished manipulator of image and presence. He ensures that news of Iuchar's bloody deeds are exaggerated and spread far and wide: he carefully orchestrates the way Iuchar appears and conducts himself, so that the Silures continue to respect and fear him. The two are a brutally effective team – not that the Silures have ever lacked brutality, but Tadhg has a knack for promoting it. He himself

cultivates a careful image. Naturally thin, he paints his face white so he appears almost skeletal and knots human bones into his hair and beard. Around his waist is a belt of children's skulls and he cloaks himself in a cape of flayed human hides. He secretly practices cannibalism – a compulsion that is the direct result of him binding his fetish spirit, Fegg, into the bones worn in his beard. Fegg is a predator spirit and a powerful one: it agreed to ally itself with Tadgh in return for being fed, via the druid, with human flesh. Tadgh was initially repulsed by the idea but has come to savour human meat. He feeds in privacy, although Iuchar knows of the compulsion and understands why Tadhg must indulge it.

Notable Settlements

Iuchar's seat is the settlement of Deheu, a sprawling collection of huts and halls surrounded by a bank of mud brick, wattle, and a crude palisade set atop. Deheu is arranged in a steep valley close to the Llynf River. The steep sided valley is heavily wooded, making any massed approach difficult and treacherous, and has only one gate, facing to the north end of the valley, which is protected by ditches, pits, and tree-trunk barricades. Only those native to the area know the safest route through the traps placed before Deheu and many warbands have fallen foul of the Death Pits (15-feet deep pits lined with sharpened stakes) when trying to raid Iuchar's home. To add to the protection, Iuchar's fierce warbands are housed in several smaller settlements ranging out from Deheu proper, extending its early warning system. From Deheu, Iuchar plans and schemes the downfall of both Powys and Gwent, aided by Tadhg and his sister-wife, Brygg.

Brygg is two years older than Iuchar, her brother, and a dark beauty. She took him as husband, rather than he taking her as his wife, but the arrangement suits both. She is as brutal and scheming as Iuchar, and is also Tadhg's occasional lover, but prefers to keep her power and influence neatly hidden away, letting Iuchar take charge, retaining the confidence and loyalty of the Silurian warbands. Iuchar has promised to make Brygg queen of the Gwentish lands while he marches on Powys and brings that kingdom to its knees also. Then the two of them will rule together, with every Christian made into a slave or sacrifice, as needs see fit.

Logres: Kingdoms of the Saxons

Logres means 'Lost Lands' and refers to those regions of Britain that are now firmly under Saxon control. Roughly, Logres can be divided into three regions: the kingdom of the South Saxons, known as Ceint, ruled by Aelle; the kingdom of Anglia, ruled by Guercha; and the north, which is not controlled by any one ruler and is currently where various rival Saxons struggle for supremacy, fighting each other as much as they fight the Celts

South Saxons and Ceint

Aelle came in the wake of Hengest and Horsa: a Jutish warlord exiled from his homelands who came across the sea in a fleet of three ships, but was soon joined by others loyal to him from Jutland. Aelle and his sons, Cymen, Wlencing, and Cissa, came with the express purpose of creating a kingdom. Aelle was forced out of Jutland when his family's war against that land's ruler turned sour, and he was forced to seek somewhere else to fulfil his ambitions. Aelle landed on Britain's south shore in territories already conquered by Saxons, but under no firm leadership. Aelle sent his three sons – all bloodied warriors – to kill any local chieftains who refused to swear to serve him, and they quickly brought the region to heel. Since then, Aelle and his sons, strengthened by more and more Jutes, have taken control of all the land south of the River Tamesis – which they call Thames – and as far west as Natanleod's territories controlled from Caer Gradawc. Aelle has raided deep into Dumnonia many times, attempting to capture the whole of the south for his growing empire, but has always been thwarted by the likes of Uther, Mordred, Natanleod, and, more recently, Arthur. This makes Aelle more, not less, determined to seize control of all lands between the Thames and Severn – and, when the time is right, Kernow too.

Aelle's kingdom of Ceint is rich, prosperous land, filled with good pasture (and plenty of it), fine forests, good game and plump fish in the rivers. He has capitalised on what Hengest and Horsa began, and has done it through a mixture of ruthlessness and pragmatism. When Hengest and Horsa fought Vortigern, it was as much a matter of pride and vengeance as it was a land-claim.

Aelle grinds no such axe; his sole ambition is to rule, and to rule as much territory as he and his sons can claim. Aelle knows that this requires pushing the Celts out, but only the Celts who mount effective opposition. Those who fight and lose become slaves (if they do not die); but those who agree to be ruled are allowed to keep their lands and pay their tributes to Aelle's halls rather to than Celtic chieftains. The Celts can keep their gods, their language and anything else they like – as long as they swear to serve Aelle and to live peacefully in the South Saxon kingdom.

Many have chosen to do just that. There are many villages that still belong to Celts but recognise Aelle as their King. They exist side-by-side with new settlements that are wholly Saxon worshipping the Saxon gods of Woden, Thunor, Tiw, and Frey. They trade and, with time, grow together. So, Aelle's kingdom grows, and his ambitions are still concerned with capturing the lands of the Welsh – the foreigners of Dumnonia, Powys, Gwent, and Kernow.

His kingdom is split into three, with two of his surviving sons governing a region each, controlling the chieftains and strengthening the Saxon forces. Aelle's seat is at Anderida, an old Roman fortress that Aelle captured from the Britons, close to the region known as Ceint. Anderida had been the stronghold of Glaes, a Celtic warlord who had served Vortigern, and Aelle placed the fortress under a siege that lasted for three months. Aelle sent Cymen, his eldest son, to discuss a surrender, but Glaes broke the truce, murdered Cymen, and so provoked Aelle to vengeance. Aelle summoned his remaining sons and all their warbands to Anderida and launched an assault of such ferocity that Glaes, unprepared, could not resist. His men within were starving and, when they saw the size and viciousness of Aelle's army, lost the will to fight. Aelle avenged Cymen's murder by slaughtering everyone in Anderida – men, women, and children. When news of this spread across the south, many Britons simply surrendered to Aelle's authority rather than be wiped out.

Anderida is a well-protected combination of stone walls, wooden palisades, and earthworks occupying a peninsula of dry land surrounded by marshes to the north, east, and west, and the open sea to the south. It is close to an excellent harbour, and has navigable roads, strengthened by Aelle, that lead out into his kingdom. The community at Anderida is strong, prosperous and growing. All tribute comes here, and the community outside Anderida's walls gets a little bigger each year.

Although Dumnonia is the prize, Aelle and his sons have other concerns. Aelle knows that other warlords are making preparations to challenge him. Aelle calls himself the *Bretwalda* – King of the Britons – and warriors such as Guercha, the Angle who rules in Anglia, the kingdom north of the Thames, and Cerdic, a Saxon with a fearsome reputation – also seek that title. Aelle may therefore find himself surrounded by enemies: Dumnonia to the west, Guercha to the north and Cerdic to his south. Making a kingdom is easy; holding it — *that* is the challenge.

Anglia

The lands north east of the Thames are ruled by Guercha, an Angle who claims descent directly from Woden. Like Woden, Guercha gave one of his eyes for wisdom, and so is known as Guercha One-Eye, and that wisdom helped him conquer the low-lying region that is now firmly in his grip and named for his tribe, Anglia.

The land is very flat, very wet, very marshy, and very old. Few Celts lived here so it proved easy to conquer, but Guercha found that Anglia is an intensely magical place, controlled more by the Ancestor Spirits of the people who lived here long before the Celts. The ancient marshes and waterways, the fenlands, whisper with the voices of the ancestor spirits and the songs of long-dead warriors who swim between the reeds and rushes. Guercha has invested heavily in shaman of his own, bringing them from his homeland to drive out the local spirits, placate the ones that are not so hostile, and bring new spirits from the old country that are allies of the Saxons, Angles, and Jutes.

The drier lands of Anglia are fertile and yield good crops, but Guercha would have more. He wants the region of Ceint, south of the Thames, which is controlled by Aelle and his sons; and he would control the lands north of Anglia – the central lands of Britain that border with Elmet and the regions controlled by the Brigantes. Aelle wants these lands too, and has sent his middle son, Wlencing, to claim as much of the uncontrolled northern territories as he can. In response, Guercha has sent his own warlords, Hengwulf and Wiglaf, to do the same. Hengwulf and Wiglaf have met with some success, capturing Ratae, a Celtic city in the heart of Britain. Their orders are to extend Anglia's boundaries, but reports have it that Hengwulf and Wiglaf have become enemies, falling out over some treasure found in one of Ratae's temples.

Guercha's seat is Boede, a town established by the Romans, ceded to the Celts, and now conquered by the Saxons. Boede is located between the River Laek, which flows from the north, and the River Lyn, which flows from the west. Guercha's halls are, much like Anderida, built within the old Roman walls and use much of that ancient stone for Boede's fortifications. The rest of the town follows a distinctive, grid-like pattern favoured by the Angles, creating a lattice of avenues and streets between the houses, tanneries, grain stores, and so forth. Boede is prosperous: a market for the outlying Saxon communities of the marshlands to east and south, and the drier regions to the west and northwest. When Guercha arrived, there were few Celts here, and those who the Saxons found surrendered rather than be put to the sword. These Celts are Christians, missionaries from the Brigantes and Carvetii who came south east to form a new community within Boede's walls, only to have the Saxons arrive soon after. The Celts did not need to be made into slaves: they serve willingly enough, although a few Celts to the west put up a token resistance and had to be broken by Wiglaf and Hengwulf's warbands.

Guercha is, like Aelle, ageing. His son Uffa will be king after him although Guercha is beginning to sense a challenge from either Wiglaf or Hengwulf (perhaps both) because they are proving to be as ambitious as Guercha is. Guercha wants to secure territory for his immediate family, and that means defeating Aelle's intention of occupying more and more land north of the Themes. King Guercha has sent word to his homeland, telling more Angles to migrate, bringing spears and horses, so that Aelle's ambitions can be countered. It is this countering of Aelle that prevents Guercha from sending warbands into Elmet and the Brigantes kingdom. Once more ships arrive, he intends to push further north – hopefully with Wiglaf and Hengwulf – once Aelle has agreed

to keep south of the Themes and leave Anglia to its own, natural expansion.

Mierce

Mierce means 'Border' or 'Border people' and refers to the lands west of Anglia and north of the Thames that, while under weak Saxon control, have yet to become a kingdom. These lands border Celt-held territories directly, and so are a ripe battleground. Whoever wins Mierce will win northern Britain.

The Saxon efforts have been thwarted so far by the Cornovii, Brigantes, Dumnonians, and Powysians, each of which have borders with Mierce and understand the importance of holding this land. Much of Mierce is forested, making it a difficult terrain for decisive battles, and much of the fighting has been skirmishing and raids, advancing borders backwards and forwards from one year to the next, but with no outright victories.

From the Saxon point of view there are four major players struggling for Mierce.: Wiglaf and Hengwulf, fighting for Guercha; and Wlencing and Cissa, fighting for Aelle. All four command substantial warbands with more warriors coming on ships that land on the Ceintish and Anglian coasts. Wlencing and Cissa are closely united and currently hold Lunden, the old Roman city; the Ox Vale; and territories bordering Dumnonia and Cornovii lands. Wiglaf holds Ratae and is rapidly expanding his influence to cover the lands bordering Powys, while Hengwulf has moved north of Ratae, capturing the heavily forested areas that eventually reach Elmet.

Progress for all four warlords is slow. Wlencing and Cissa have large territories to control but are better organised and benefit from more warriors. Wiglaf and Hengwulf were once good friends but have since fallen out – a strife that is discussed in the scenario 'Bran Galed's Horn', beginning on page 234. Nevertheless, Mierce is thick with Saxons and the isolated Celtic settlements have been forced to cede to Saxon warbands and both Angle and Jutish colonists eager for this new, fertile country known as Britain.

So these are now Logres: the Lost Lands. In time, they will become Wessex, Mercia, East Anglia, and Northumbria – and even later still, will become England. Other invaders – the Danes, Norse, and Swedes – will put pressure on the Saxons just as the Saxons pressure the Celts.

ᚠᛒᚳᚻᛖᚩᚷᚻᛁᛄᛣ
ᛚᛞᚾᚫᛈᛉᚱᛋᛏᚢ
ᚹᛠᚣ

The runes of the futhorc, the Saxon alphabet.

Celtic Life and Society

This chapter discusses the daily life and social structure of the Celts of Mythic Britain.

Much of this chapter takes a broad-strokes approach. Different tribes and different clans within the same tribe will have variations of the information provided here. But, by and large, what is presented is true for most Celts, whether they come from north of the Great Wall, the West, or the very edge of Kernow.

Who Are the Celts?

The word 'Celt' derives from the Greek Keltoi. The Celtic civilisation is an ancient and expansive one. Originating in eastern Europe, the Celts came to occupy a wide band of land ranging from Gallatia in the east to Ireland in the west, and as far south as the Iberian peninsula. The Celtic tribes share a set of common languages and customs that marked them as separate from the Greek, Roman, and Germanic peoples of pre-Christian Europe. The Romans first encountered the Celts circa 450 BC when a tribe of hitherto unknown barbarians displaced the Etruscans from the Po valley of Italy. The Roman Empire, then in its infancy, sent envoys to these new settlers, whom the Romans named *Galli*. The meeting, so Livy records, was educational:

"The Celts told the Roman envoys that this was indeed the first time they had heard of them, but they assumed the Romans must be a courageous people because it was to them that the Etruscans had turned to in their hour of need. And since the Romans had tried to help with an embassy and not with arms, they themselves would not reject the offer of peace, provided the Etruscans ceded part of their superfluous agricultural land; that was what they, the Celts, wanted.... If it were not given, they would launch an attack before the Romans' eyes, so that the Romans could report back how superior the Gauls were in battle to all others. The Romans then asked whether it was right to demand land from its owners on pain of war, indeed what were the Celts doing in Etruria in the first place? The latter defiantly retorted that their right lay in their arms: To the brave belong all things."

Livy, The Early History of Rome

Rome reneged on the good faith its envoys had initially shown and provided martial aid to the Etruscans. This, in turn, led to the Celts marching on Rome and laying siege to the city for seven months. The Celts eventually agreed to leave if a tribute of one thousand pounds of gold was made. The Romans agreed to the terms, despite the sheer difficulty of finding such a sum, but this did not prevent them from accusing the Celt leader, Brennus, of attempting to cheat the tribute by using faulty measures. Settlement was eventually reached and the Celts departed, leaving Rome humiliated in defeat. They had never encountered such a people before, although this was far from their last meeting.

By 275 BC the Celts had established a presence across most of central and western Europe, including Britain and Ireland where they displaced and absorbed the indigenous Iron Age tribes. Even though the Celts shared many customs and tongues, the Irish and British Celts diverged in terms of their myths and beliefs. The southern tribes of Britain retained strong relations with the Gauls of northern France, especially in the Gaulish territory known as Armorica. The Irish Celts similarly maintained strong relations with the tribes of Scotland and the Hebrides, but essentially the tribes of the Britain and Ireland progressed along different paths whilst maintaining their distinctive Celtic culture.

Throughout its expansion across Europe, the Celts left a distinctive legacy in terms of their arts, crafts, and beliefs. Although they were fierce conquerors who believed in the right and supremacy of battle, they were also sophisticated in terms of their arts and crafts, especially in metal and gem work. Expert traders, the Celts ventured far and wide, and commodities traded from the eastern edge of Celtic civilisation found their way west to Britain and Ireland. Indeed, across Europe, the Celts developed a reputation for a certain grandeur and style. Their settlements were established in areas of natural beauty but also with a mind to practical necessities. Their skill in farming and crafting was much admired and, in places, imitated, and their love of both treasure and battle marked the Celtic tribes socially, economically, and militarily. In the days prior to the Roman conquest of Britain, the Celts were considered

to be one of the wealthiest peoples in Europe — a fact the Romans had learned from their first meeting with the Celts and one they were keen to exploit through their own conquests.

Julius Caesar's campaign to bring western Europe into the empire was based around dominating the Celts, either peacefully or through arms. The Celts' pan-European migration was unsettling to the equally ambitious Romans and so Caesar's strategy was to halt further expansion, control the dispersed Celtic tribes, and supplant their culture with the Roman ways of administration. Resistance, which was inevitable, was met with force. Caesar attacked and defeated the Helvetii tribe that had migrated into northern Switzerland. He forced war with the Aedui of southern Gaul and thoroughly routed the Belgae of northern Gaul. Facing the substantial Belgae with eight legions of soldiers, the Belgic tribes effectively disintegrated in the face of sure defeat and capitulated their lands to the Empire.

The way in which the Romans dealt with the Celts across Europe points to a failing in Celtic society as a whole. Although related through common languages and beliefs, there is an underlying lack of unity between the tribes. Celtic tribes are frequently hostile to one another and find it difficult to make common cause. This makes a strategy of 'divide and conquer' that much easier, and the Romans exploited this flaw in Celtic culture to full advantage, replicating the process when Caesar invaded Britain in the 1st Century BC. Indeed, the fractious and fragmented nature of the Celts is a defining factor in Britain's history, as evidenced by the post-Roman events and the ease with which the Saxons mounted their own invasion and occupation.

When Caesar reached British shores his disciplined and well-ordered legions found it easy to dominate the tribes of Britain. Some, like the Silures, mounted continued resistance and refused to be dominated. Others, like the Icenii, became clients of Rome. In Britain, Caesar adopted a slightly different tactic to those he had used in Gaul. He allowed many of the tribes to remain independent, but accept local rule under a consular system. He was not afraid to use force against those who rejected the inevitable, but those tribes who accepted Rome were treated well, offered splendid concessions, and allowed to flourish. Prasutagus, King of Icenii, for example, left half his wealth to his two daughters and the other half to the Emperor Nero and the Roman Empire. The client-king relationship served many tribes very well, although it must be noted that the arrogance with which Rome prosecuted King Prasutagus's legacy led to Queen Boudicca's rebellion and the destruction of the key Roman garrisons of Camulodunum, Verulamium, and Londinium. The Celts, when angered, react with substantial force and violence. At the same time as Boudicca's revolt, in 60 AD, Gaius Suetonius Paulinus set out to subdue and destroy the druids of Britain. Rome had long tolerated the druids, but in Britain they were viewed as dangerous and subversive, encouraging rebellion and rejecting Roman authority. Paulinus' assault on Ynys Mon, the island sacred to Britain's druids, resulted in a massacre that reduced the druid's power throughout Britain considerably. They might have been destroyed completely had news of Boudicca's rebellion not reached Paulinus, forcing him to return east to deal with the troublesome queen.

The Icenii were isolated and defeated by Rome at the Battle of Watling Street. Despite Boudicca's rebellion, Rome did not punish the entirety of the Celtic tribes and continued to deal with them on a one-by-one basis, respecting the client-kings and subduing the troublesome tribes. An example had been made of Boudicca and the druids had been subdued to the point that their considerable influence was broken: Rome's authority, although challenged, prevailed. Examples continued to be made; in 77 AD, Gnaeus Agricola destroyed the Ordovices tribe and drove the Brigantes into submission, all within a year of his arrival. Others though, such as the Dumnonii, flourished and prospered, with the Romans establishing substantial settlements across the south of Britain. The Empire exploited and manipulated the fractured nature of the Celts to its own advantage, but also brought advantages to those tribes who fell into line and accepted the client-king relationship. Rome could be tolerant, generous, and merciful, as long as the Celts remained obedient.

With Rome firmly in charge of Britain, the Celts — aside from those few tribes that delighted in rebellious defiance — achieved a distinct measure of peaceful co-existence and cultural symbiosis with Rome's citizens. Roman men married Celtic women and vice-versa. Some tribes adopted Roman customs wholeheartedly whilst still retaining their original identity and gods.

Romano-Celtic Britain prospered for the next three centuries. Although a far-flung outpost its resources were important to

Rome. Tin, iron, and timber were key exports. Rome developed towns and cities and built new ones. It brought its knowledge and expertise as well as its language and gods. Eventually though, stretched to its limits, the Roman Empire found itself under considerable strain. Internal political strife and rebellion, growing trouble with the Germanic tribes, and the sheer cost of maintaining such a vast empire became too much. From 383 AD Rome started to withdraw its legions from the north and west of Britain. By 409 its legions were withdrawn from the south. Emperor Constantine's grip on the empire was crumbling significantly and letters, sent by Honorius to every major city in Britain, informed the Romano-Britons that they were now responsible for their own defence: Rome would no longer help them. Roman magistrates and other officials were expelled from many cities across Britain, and this marks the end of Rome's rule over Britain. It also marks the end of reliable histories. Despite the learning Rome brought to Britain, the Celts maintained an oral tradition and so little of the Celt's history from 410 onwards was written down, ushering-in both the 'dark age', and the reclamation by the Celtic tribes of their island.

Language

Two versions of the Celtic language are spoken in Britain: Brythonic, which is the language spoken by the tribes south of the Great Wall and in Kernow and Armorica; and Goidelic, which is spoken north of the Great Wall (and in Ireland) by the Caledonii and Picts. The Picts speak a distinct dialect of Goidelic, which helps differentiate them from the Caledonii. Similarly, there are distinct Brythonic dialects differentiating the northern Britons, the Welsh Kingdoms, and Kernow.

Although Brythonic and Goidelic are separate languages they maintain a common root, meaning that grammatical structure and many words share pronunciation and meaning. Brythonic speakers can understand and make themselves understood in Goidelic (with all Language rolls at the Hard difficulty grade) and vice-versa. There is no penalty for understanding a different dialect.

The Saxons have a variety of languages reflecting the Germanic tribes of their origin. The Germanic tongue is substantially different to the two Celtic languages, meaning that there is no common understanding between native speakers. For the sake of simplicity, *Mythic Britain* does not break the Saxon languages down any further: it is simply known as Germanic.

Tribes and Social Structure

Celts are tribal by nature: that is, the formation of large, extended communities controlling one or more territories and defined by certain cultural traits and behaviours. Tribes are therefore distinct social units and some tribes may be overtly hostile to others, even though they share the Celtic heritage. The word 'tribe' derives from the Celtic word meaning 'boundary', 'trench', or 'ditch'.

In general, a single tribe occupies a single region, although some tribes have extended their sphere of influence through marriage, trade, or conquest. Each tribe has its own social structure with a king or queen at the head. The monarch is aided by a council drawn from loyal supporters and has the powers to dispense wealth, land, and patronage as he or she wishes (although usually in line with advice from the council). Celts have a highly developed sense of social justice, sharing of responsibility, and the development of common wealth; this means that monarchs who seek to abuse their position are likely to be challenged and replaced. The monarch rules by common consent and not through any divine ordination – although Celts do believe that the gods have some distant influence over who becomes ruler.

Land Ownership

Tribal land is owned by the tribe and not by individuals – although rulers can, and do, allot territories to individuals and families to be settled, farmed, or worked in their own name. These allocations still belong to the tribe and can be reallocated if necessary; they are also subject to tax – a tenth of the income generated by whatever use the land is put to. However, tax is limited to an individual life and relatives are not responsible for unpaid taxes on

the death of a family member. Celtic custom dictates that "every dead man kills his own liabilities."

Ultimately, there is no absolute ownership of land in Celtic society. The land held by chieftains, kings, and nobles is still held in the public name and every member of the tribe, regardless of class, is able to keep and work allocated land, but cannot not sell it, conceal it, or use it to pay for any crime or debt. This is also true of livestock: all livestock, especially cattle, are considered the property of the whole tribe, and the whole tribe is responsible for its defence and its growth. Individuals may breed and rear their own stock, slaughtering it and selling it as they need, but they do not, ultimately, own it. The herd belongs to All.

Essential land management chores, such as ploughing, sowing, and reaping, are performed communally. With the exception of certain classes, everyone is involved in preparing and sowing the land, and then harvesting the crop. Warriors work the land side by side with crafters and farmers. It is an expected duty and very few Celts attempt to shirk this responsibility. Those who do not work cannot expect to be fed from the stores. This makes harvest time, especially, an important part of the year. All feuds and battles cease while the fields are reaped. Without the harvest, and the labour needed to reap its rewards, the long, hard winters are unbearable. All Celts know this, and work together to avoid hunger through the lean months to come.

Appearance, Personality and Customs

The Celts have a distinctive physiology. They are typically taller than the average for the European body type, with Heavy body frames and well-muscled physiques, making for the physically imposing people the Romans encountered in their invasion of the island. Skin is pale and clear, and although hair colours run the full gamut, there is a preponderance of red, blond, and auburn, rather than brown or black. Some of the resolutely pagan kingdoms maintain an old druidic practice of bleaching the hair with lime, either combing it back from the forehead or drawing it into spikes. This practice faded during the Roman occupation, and it is more common for Celts to wear their hair long in plaits and braids, although bleaching and spiking is still found amongst some tribes.

It is common for Celt warriors to shave their bodies, but beards and moustaches are almost ubiquitous. Maintaining a clean-shaven appearance was a very Roman characteristic and although some Celts adopted it, the vast majority shave only their bodies – an old pagan practice symbolic of cleanliness, but also making it easier for painted designs, such as woad, or even permanent tattoos, to be applied and displayed. Nobles sometimes display their rank by shaving their chin to leave only a moustache, but being clean shaven is associated with a lack of maturity and experience.

Celtic dress varies considerably from region to region in terms of cuts, dyes used, patterns employed, and so forth, but there are some constants. Men wear trousers (usually of wool) called bracae: calf-length trews secured with a drawstring at the waist and, sometimes, drawstrings at the hem of each leg. Shirts and jerkins of wool and linen are worn on the upper body, and the ensemble is topped with a light or heavy cloak (depending on the season), secured at the shoulder with a heavy brooch. The cut, colour, and length of the cloak and the style, metal, and ornamentation of the brooch symbolises social rank. The finer the weave of the wool, the deeper the colour, and the finer the craftsmanship (and metal) of the brooch, the higher the social standing. Chieftains gift brooches to show appreciation, and a good, finely crafted brooch is a prize possession for most Celts.

Women sometimes wear similar ensembles to men, but tend to favour simple woollen (and, for higher ranks, linen) gowns and shift dresses, falling to the calf or ankle. The cloak and brooch is ubiquitous, and Celtic women adore jewelry – indeed, both sexes do – and Celtic jewelry can be of the most exquisite forms: delicate and intricate knots; fluid geometrical designs; stylised mixtures of plants, animals, and mythical creatures; or simple yet elegant inscriptions.

Jewelry is fashioned from most metals, with bronze being ubiquitous. Silver is the metal of station for the Aes and Nobles, and gold for those who can afford it, since gold is very rare across Britain and thus both highly treasured and jealously guarded.

Personality

If dress is distinctive, then the Celtic personality is more so. Celts are proud, generous, hot-headed, socially minded, and free-spirited. Celts love freedom, view each other as equals (more or less), and believe in the generosity of the tribe. Indeed, generosity is essential to Celtic belief and society. If one is generous, others are generous back. In the afterlife, the rewards one can expect are based on the generosity of the first life. Frugality is often necessary in lean times, but one can still be frugal and generous, by ensuring that everyone shares equally in what is available.

As hosts, there are none more hospitable than the Celts. The rules surrounding hospitality are quite simple, but come with a certain degree of complexity.

Foremost, strangers are always given food, drink, and a place to sleep without questions being asked — even if the guest may be from an enemy tribe or territory. Once eating and drinking is done, questions may be asked and honesty is expected in the answers. If a lord guarantees the safety of a guest, then anyone who threatens the guest's safety is subject to punishment. Failing to show courtesy and respect for offered hospitality is considered a grave insult and may result in rejection from the hearth. Therefore, the easiest way for anyone visiting an unfamiliar Celtic settlement is to accept the offer of hospitality made, be truthful when questioned, and respect the generosity on offer. In that way, safety is guaranteed.

It is also customary for a newcomer to provide news and information. This can be as serious or trivial as the guest desires, but news of some kind is expected. Failing that, a song, tune, or story is likely to be expected — something entertaining, no matter how brief or how inexpert, to show gratitude for hospitality. It is not an insult to offer neither news nor a performance, but one is likely to encounter disappointment and a cooling of hospitality otherwise.

Celts are fond of declaiming their lineage when introducing themselves, and, indeed, are masters of it. It is expected for any Celt, making a new introduction, to list his forebears for several generations, including in the declamation exaggerated details of their great deeds, victories, generosity, bravery, and so forth. Equally, foes are to be vocally disparaged — but only foes in common.

"I am Owain-ap-Gerhaint-ap-Gryffyd-ap-Owain: the same Gerhaint who slew the great black boar of Elmet and the same Gryffyd who defeated twenty foes, sky-clad, single-handed, and armed with only the thigh bone of a swan. I spit on the Saxon scum and am delighted to bring courage to this hall!"

There is no question that the Celts are warlike and eager to spill blood. Personal insults, when they are clearly not offered in good natured jest, cut deep, as will a Celt's knife if the opportunity arises. Slights against personal integrity, and the integrity of the clan and tribe, easily escalate into full-blown feuds, if mediation is not quickly brought to bear.

This swiftness to violence is a result of the Celtic tribal mind-set. Celts view the world in terms of distinct social units that must be defended to the death if honour is to be maintained. Violence as a means of resolving disputes and punishing those who would assail the tribe, or the units composing it, is wholly and irrefutably acceptable. It demonstrates personal and community strength, and sends out a clear message to others.

There is also the sheer joy of conflict and battle. Celtic war-songs tell of the excitement of the lead-up to battle, of the thrill of the charge, of the sheer ecstasy of killing one's foes. Fighting, maiming, killing, and, crucially, surviving the same is considered just, honourable, and essential to developing personal integrity. It also demonstrates one's desire to defend and protect the tribe and the tribe's territories. A good Celtic warrior is not afraid of death and, indeed, may seek it out willingly on the battlefield because it is the ultimate way of repaying the tribe for all it has done.

Thus, while Celts grieve for their dead, it is never for long and never without celebration. One who dies in battle, and one who dies honourably, is already being rewarded in the Other World, where they are assured glory and the kind of immortal life they strived to achieve while alive.

The Five Aspects of Character

Although Celtic culture is wide-ranging and subtle, its core comes down five key facets: Devotion to Tribe, Conformity to Tradition, Honour and Prowess, Blood Vengeance, and a Clean and Honest Death. These facets mean different things to different people and what one tribe considers honest another may consider deceitful; but, on the whole, most Celts subscribe to these five facets for most of the time.

Devotion to Tribe

The tribe is everything to Celts. The extended family nurtures and supports, creates a fabric of social values, educates, and perpetuates the British warrior spirit. It is for the tribe's honour that a Celt makes war on his enemies; for the tribe's prosperity that he works and raids his neighbours; and for its continued existence that he ultimately lays down his life.

Most Celts are indivisible from their tribes. Children are raised communally, by both the women and men, and schooled from the earliest possible age in the tribe's ways, duties, allies, and enemies. Irrespective of its true position in Celtic society, the tribe is the most noble, most hard-working, most potent in battle, and most blessed of all the tribes scattered across Britain's hills, valleys, and forests. As he grows, the young Briton usually learns that his tribe's position is not necessarily as illustrious as his peers have described it, but by that point, the tribe's spirit flows through his blood and the young Briton perpetuates the tribe's strength to others despite knowing and understanding its flaws.

For every Briton, the crowning moment is the tribe adulthood ritual, the point where the youth becomes an adult. For females, this means the onset of menstruation, indicating the beginning of fertility. For males, the rituals vary, but the rite of passage usually signals that the youth is now capable of killing enemies in the tribe's defence, laying down his life for the tribe, and siring children. Although every Briton upholds the tribe's values and traditions from the moment he begins to understand them, it is the adulthood ritual that demands he do so. Passing from youth to adult confers on every Celt the duty of protecting the community and upholding its ways in the face of any adversity. Every adult in a tribe is expected to be prepared to lay down his or her life for the tribe and take the life of its enemies without question.

While the rite of passage varies from tribe to tribe, there are many common elements and similarities. The rite of passage usually involves several tests involving bravery, cunning, martial prowess, mental fortitude, physical fortitude, and a measure of the individual's devotion to the tribe and understanding of its nature and purpose. In some tribes, there is a religious element, presided over by a druid, indicating the individual's acceptance and recognition by the spirits and gods. In other tribes, there are few, or no, religious elements, and the rite of passage is simply an expedient way of acknowledging adulthood and its key responsibilities.

Conformity to Tradition

Celts generally dislike change: some hate it and some positively fear it. The British outlook is founded on things that work and continue to work with as little interruption as possible. This means that Celts act and think in the ways they do because it has always been done that way. Change is destructive; Tradition preserves and endures. Change alters everything; Tradition ensures predictability – and, in a landscape as harsh as Britain can be, predictability is fundamental to survival. Even the gods work in predictable ways. Their myths and legends define how they work, how they think, what they do, and how they do it. Predictability reflects nature: patterns, cycles, and seasons. If these are interrupted or disrupted, misfortune usually follows.

Celts have countless traditions: efficient routines, tribe-focused beliefs and rites, and modes of thought and action that have developed over hundreds and hundreds of years and are proved to be effective. Few traditions are maintained for sentimental reasons; almost all of them are developments for practical necessity. Some traditions are based on superstition and folklore, but few are designed to appease the gods outright.

Celts who deny the traditions or actively baulk at them are viewed with deep suspicion and hostility because, inevitably, such people are troublemakers. Traditions underlie the key laws Celts follow and, if the traditions are challenged, then so is the fragile rule of law. Respect for the tradition and the 'old ways, the right ways' is inculcated from birth and therefore any adult who wilfully

takes a stand against a tradition is rejecting the years of teaching and wisdom the tribe has tried to instil. The honourable option is to leave the tribe; any who attempt to stay and create or impose change are likely to face ostracism.

Honour and Prowess

Celts live by a rough code of honour. Irrespective of the tribe one comes from, Honour can be defined in the following terms:

- Accept hospitality gracefully when it is offered, but always be wary.
- Accept no imprisonment.
- Accept no insult.
- Defend the honour of kith and kin.
- Defend those who need defending; attack those who need attacking.
- Listen to those who seek your aid, but always be wary.
- Never harm a druid.
- Offer foes a clean and swift death, if they are deserving of it.
- Remain true to one's tribe (and by extension the tribe's traditions and customs).
- Remain true to one's word.
- Show no fear.
- Sometimes, even theft is necessary.
- Speak only the truth; punish liars and expose falsehoods.
- Take no woman by force. Allow no man to take a woman by force.
- Take only what is necessary; taking more than is necessary is theft.
- Violence is an acceptable option.

Celts, then, have a very simple view of what constitutes 'honour': speaking and acting truthfully, and decisively, whilst maintaining respect for those who do likewise. To Celts, honour does not need to be any more complex and should always be a straightforward business. Celts do not make the mistake of confusing honour, honesty, and tact; neither do they believe that politeness and gratitude need to be dressed in false sincerity or fawning courtesy. When a Celt offers his thanks, he means it. When he wants something, he asks for or demands it, depending on urgency. Most Celts speak and act plainly, clearly, and bluntly — but always honourably.

Prowess — personal excellence in a given area — is a matter of deep personal honour for all Celts. Generally, most Celts place import on their prowess as hunters and warriors although, for some, prowess in other fields is held in higher regard. It is the desire of most male youths to be considered fine fighters first and foremost, but not all; some are destined to be better craftsmen or herders and, whilst the hunter-warrior creed is expected of all Celts, it is understood at a cultural level that a range of skills and talents are essential for the tribe's survival. What is most important is the honesty and honour of understanding where one's talents lie and achieving excellence in that field, whilst still cultivating the ability to both hunt and fight well.

Thus, all Celts are geared towards being the best at what they do, because prowess yields success for both the individual and the tribe. Every tribe sincerely believes it produces the best fighters, hunters, crafters, herders, and so forth in Britain. Each tribe's traditions are bent towards this goal even though every tribe exhibits different areas of excellence.

Yet Celts are not innately boastful. Great pride is taken in every endeavour that proves personal excellence, but few Celts use their expertise as the basis for boastful declamations. Such actions always invite challenge and, although Celts never baulk at a challenge, it is always better to err on the side of caution and reserve because each and every Briton knows that life is harsh and unforgiving. No Briton believes himself singled out by fate above his kith, kin, or comrades; whatever success one achieves is the result of hard work, training, listening, watching, and learning. Boastfulness is foolhardy and most likely displays a lack of personal confidence. And that — confidence — is the key to both honour and prowess in Britain. Every Briton is confident in his abilities and confident that he can be the best of the best; but displays of arrogance and misjudged pride always attract a fall. Celts know this and simply work towards developing their prowess through deeds, not words. The truly excellent swordsman or crafter knows that his work will speak for him; if he is as good as he believes himself to be, it will be evident to others without the need for rash and arrogant boasts.

Blood Vengeance

Celts are passionate and proud. Slights can be weathered from time to time, but insults and assaults against the family or tribe are taken seriously and never allowed to rest. The desire for vengeance runs through every Briton as freely as their blood. Insults and assaults must always be paid for and usually in blood.

Because community ties and personal honour are closely bound together, injury to an individual becomes the responsibility of the entire family or tribe to avenge. Refusal or unwillingness to seek revenge is seen as a sign of weakness and likely to attract further attacks. Thus, any Briton who feels his honour, or that of his tribe, has been challenged, always seeks vengeance against the perpetrator; the matter cannot be allowed to rest until vengeance has been satisfied.

Tribes therefore can, and do, engage in feuds and war between themselves. Individuals may even accept the burden of extracting blood vengeance as a perfectly acceptable means of proving both their honour and prowess. It is commonplace for Celts to brood upon an insult or attack for days, weeks, months, or years before taking action, but action is always taken. Anything that challenges, insults, or harms the honour of a person or the honour of the tribe attracts a furious response. And, naturally enough, vengeance begets further revenge, resulting in long-running and bloody feuds that persist long after the initial provocation has been forgotten. Grandsons seek vengeance for long-dead grandfathers; tribes battle tribes for decades, becoming ignorant as to why, but retaining the certainty that they must. A Celt who has been wronged becomes a life-long enemy and, given the insular and sullen nature of each and every tribe, it is impossible to gauge what is likely to provoke vengeance.

This uncertainty leads tribes and individuals to act cautiously whenever they encounter an unfamiliar tribe or individual. Celts do not like to give offence; not because they believe in being deferential (far from it: deference is for slaves – no Celts will ever allow himself to be a slave), but because one can never be certain what will provoke a violent response. Once a certain level of trust and understanding has been developed, Celts relax, but always take care not to overstep perceived boundaries. Known enemies, of course, never receive such caution, but no tribe wants to make more enemies if it can help it. Many tribes have been wiped out through a constant willingness to attack and insult their neighbours, and making an enemy of one tribe usually results in making enemies of all the tribes the injured party is allied with. A single insult can, and does, result in attracting a fierce and disproportionate response.

A Clean and Honest Death

Celts do not place any faith in their gods to provide them with a happy afterlife. Death is part of the natural cycle of things, and every Briton knows that death is never far away. Death is not spoken of in hushed tones; it is discussed matter of factly and without sentiment. Every Briton wants a death that is both clean and honest. That is, a death that would not bring shame on the tribe or the individual. Dying in battle, sword in hand, surrounded by the bodies of the enemy, is a good and honest death. Being executed after capture, pleading for one's life, is exactly the opposite. Dying whilst behaving with honour is the way every Briton wants to die and they have no fear of it; but dying pitifully, weakly, and either denying honour or having it denied to them, shames the soul and tribe.

Similarly, when dealing death, Celts tend towards offering it cleanly and honestly. If a foe fights well and honourably, a fast, cleanly delivered death is an honourable thing to offer. A clean death is delivered without cruelty and without resort to unclean methods such as poisons or venoms, which are the weapons of cowards who lack the prowess to slay their foes cleanly. When facing death from other Celts, every Briton expects a fast and clean death (assuming he has, himself, behaved honourably); but when dealing with outsiders, Celts know that they cannot be guaranteed such a death. Plenty of outsiders do not understand the concepts of honour and an honourable death, and resort to tactics and weapons that deny such honesty. Foes who do not offer clean and honest deaths will always incur the enmity of a tribe; foes who take lives as Celts expect are simply acting with honour and will be recognised for it.

Those who die with honour are always highly regarded in the tribe, but, again, never with undue sentimentality. Death comes to everyone and one cannot choose when they will die or by what

method, but how one dies is important. Those who die bravely are honoured in song and reputation. Those who die weakly or with cowardice are erased from the memory of the tribe.

Children

Very young children have very low status in Celtic society, counting, to begin with, as mere extensions of the family. Individual identity is only recognised and accorded as the child grows and natural character, traits, and behaviours start to develop. There is both a practical and cultural side to this approach. Infant mortality is high, and it helps to keep emotional attachments as tenuous as possible until the child's survival is assured. Secondly, the Celts, believing in freedom of expression, firmly believe that personal character and identity take time to form in the way that the gods and spirits believe it should. Therefore, there is as little parental interference as possible until the child can articulate its thoughts and begin to make its own judgments.

Fostering is also a widespread practice, especially amongst the nobles, with children being sent to another family – and often another clan or tribe – to be raised. Again, there are certain practical necessities. Fostering encourages cooperation between clans and tribes, and fostering forms part of a hostage arrangement, ensuring that there will be no wide-scale feuding. Secondly, fostering creates new kinship groups and helps spread customs and practices that, ultimately, help create a cohesive Celtic identity.

A child who is fostered can expect to leave his or her home at the age of six or seven, and not return until it is time for the rites of passage that signify the transition to adulthood. A fostered child is never encouraged to forget or deny its roots, but instead to learn the ways and whys of the fostering environment and return home with this knowledge and experience as a distinct quality. Fostering also ensures that a child's talents are properly nurtured; Celts do not believe in stifling natural aptitudes unnecessarily. The exchange ensures that the tribe's resources are not depleted and that it continues to benefit. As the parent/child relationship in British tribes is nowhere near as sentimental and strong as elsewhere, most children are unaffected by such a transition. With their typically brutal honesty, exchanged children are told why they were placed with a new tribe and the benefits to both tribe and child explained.

But, for the most part, children are born, raised and die within the tribe. As children they live relatively carefree lives but, once they reach the age of 13 or 14, they undergo the rites signalling

Infant Mortality

Many children do not survive beyond their first year. Britain's damp climate is hard on young lungs and many succumb to illness and disease before they have been weaned.

It is customary for many tribes to present a newborn child to the chieftain who inspects it for physical deformities. Whilst this is quite often a formality, some chieftains decide that any child who carries some form of defect should be taken out into the wilds and disposed of. Anyone who may come to be a burden on the tribe cannot contribute to its long-term welfare and it is considered better to get rid of such burdens before they become troublesome.

Where a newborn is condemned to such a fate, it is customary for the child to be taken deep into the forests and abandoned to either the elements or predators. In some tribes, the child is either drowned or swiftly strangled. The parents are usually compensated by the chieftain in some way, perhaps with a precious token or with better than average food for a short period. This is not some form of sentimentality; however, Celts believe that parents who have brought a less than healthy child into the world stand a better chance of producing a healthy child swiftly if their loss is rapidly compensated for. The act has no deeper emotional connotations.

the transition from child to adult. For males, this symbolises the youth's readiness to fight for the tribe and perhaps die for it. For females, it signals their readiness for marriage and child rearing.

Women

Women are naturally expected to be hearth-makers and mothers, but they are not denied the occupations traditionally occupied by men. Celts are practical people and if a woman shows an aptitude with spear, sword, or bow, then it is quite acceptable for her to fight alongside the menfolk and, in some tribes, even expected as a duty. Women are not perceived as being weak or inferior and, typically, they are anything but. Because strength survives and because British life is about survival, British women are strong in body, spirit, and purpose. Strong British men can only be born of strong, British women, as the old claim goes.

Women and men usually share equal status in terms of tribe rights. Tribe tasks and chores are shared; women chop wood and hunt, and men fix the hearth and cook. A wife is not a husband's property or chattel, but she is expected to be faithful to her man (and vice-versa). This independence of female spirit may account for the way that many British men who travel outside their borders view the women of other cultures. In cultures where women take a more subordinate role, British men naturally assume this is an inherent weakness and therefore have a propensity to treat women as chattels rather than equals, to be taken as and when the man decides. Strong women of other cultures are admired, and Celts tend to appreciate foreign females who display similar characteristics and personalities to British women far more than do the menfolk of the culture concerned.

One role that women cannot escape, though, is child birth. Some British women are quite content to do little else but raise large families; others are content with raising only a few. Every woman is expected to bear at least one child, and usually within a few years of the adulthood rite. It is therefore very common for British women to be married as soon as puberty begins and to have birthed their first child within the year. Marriages are quite often completely arranged affairs, usually by the parents, either because the match is considered to be one that will produce plenty of good, strong, handsome children, or because the union cements an alliance between two tribes. Marriage is very rarely for love, and it is considered against tradition for a woman to disagree with an arranged union because she does not love (or even like) the intended husband.

Whilst most women marry, some do not, and will lie with whoever they wish. If a woman tempts a married man (even if she did not actually do the tempting), it is generally considered grounds for expulsion from the tribe although the child, if one results from the union, is usually kept within the tribe and raised as part of the father's household. Unmarried women and men may sleep together and have as many children as they want; there are very few taboos surrounding illegitimacy because, once again, the overall welfare of the tribe is strengthened by the presence of children.

Men

The expectation is that every man will be a warrior or hunter. Indeed, every British man is considered to be a warrior and/or hunter unless, quite clearly, they are incapable of fighting or stalking. Very few male British children ever express the desire to grow up to be a farmer or weaver; those that do are usually frowned upon and considered for exchange. From the earliest years, British boys are taught to fight — to fight hard, skilfully, and cleanly.

Whilst British tribes display a great deal of sexual equality, the tasks of hunting and protection fall naturally to the menfolk. Adopted into hunting and warbands from an early age, British men form strong masculine alliances, learning to rely upon and trust their comrades. This is less concerned with machismo and far more concerned with survival. The tough terrain of Britain means that even the task of hunting is a risky business, and teamwork and trust are essential to avoid injury and death. With so many warlike tribes vying for territory, British men know there is strength in numbers and greater strength in trust. An enemy is more easily bested or outwitted if you can trust another to watch your back.

British men therefore enjoy male company and are capable of making male friends easily. They enjoy the competitiveness that inevitably arises in male groupings: drinking contests, friendly boasting, and tall stories, games of chance, do or dare, and so forth. Raucous behaviour offsets the hardships of life in Britain and helps form strong bonds that can be relied upon in adversity. To outsiders, groups of British men are intimidating; brooding, invariably toned and muscled, and usually exuding aggression. However, if trust is gained, such groups prove to be boisterous, loyal company. If a Celt gives his word, then it is binding; if a group offers its trust and friendship, then it is far-reaching — as long as the same courtesies are returned.

When there is no hunting or fighting to be done, men get on with the mundanities of communal life, completing the common tasks, whatever they might be, without any real complaint. Thus, British men are remarkably capable where home-making tasks are concerned. All good British men can look after themselves and any dependents, cooking, cleaning, stitching, and so forth. Of course, no great honour is accorded to such mundane tasks; true honour and prowess is found in hunting and battle, but British men rarely scorn mundane activities as being 'women's' work. Instead, they just get on with the job.

Clothing

For everyday life, Celts shun finery and ostentation in their clothing, as it is simply impractical. Typically, clothing for men and women consists of simple tunics or shirts of coarse wool and linen worn either with kilts or woollen trousers, dyed with simple, natural dyes derived from minerals or vegetables. This is everyday garb worn to protect against the seemingly incessant rain and cold, chilly nights. When visiting, feasting, or attending important events, jewelry — and plenty of it — along with fine clothes, leather belts, glittering brooches, arm rings, finger rings, and torques are donned and shown off. Celts love and appreciate fine crafts and jewelry. Often it represents the total of their worth, but more importantly it marks accomplishments — either through service, loyalty, or battlefield prowess. When not being worn, jewelry is hidden away (often buried) in a simple sack or wooden box.

Footwear, when worn (often it is not — many Celts go barefoot), is a pair of simple leather sandals laced around the ankle and calf.

Every tribe adopts specific colours that are displayed in the patterns woven into kilts, tunics, or trousers. These colours are often plaids or crude tartans — regular, geometric patterns that are simple to weave but intricate enough to promote tribe identity.

In cold weather cloaks are very common, being of wool, sheepskin or goatskin, or, occasionally, leather. Hats and other forms of headwear, with the exception of helmets for battle, are extremely rare amongst Celts, although a cloak might have a hood stitched to it if lengthy travel in inclement weather must be undertaken. Celts generally consider headwear to be a form of disguise as it shadows the eyes or masks the hair. Every Briton is proud to be a Celt; disguises, or attempts at them, are for cowards and thieves.

However, when it comes to hunting and warfare, dress changes radically. Loincloths of soft leather, sometimes accompanied by leather jerkins, replace the woollen shirt and kilt. Such woven garb would easily snag when out in the wilds and, although it protects against the cold, Celts would far rather shiver than be impeded when it comes to a high-speed chase through forest and briar or

Typical Clothing of the Britons

Léine — a shirt of soft linen, usually worn under a woollen tunic or robe. The léine has no collar and is often slit in a V from the throat to the top of the chest. For men, the léine is calf-length and for women, ankle length. It is usually dyed a deep saffron colour although bleached linen (a creamy-white) is also common.

Braecci — linen or woollen trousers worn under the léine, belted at the waist and, sometimes, gathered at the ankle.

Inar — a woollen, collarless jacket worn over a léine and cut in the style of a robe. Designed to be worn open, but sometimes secured with a belt.

Trius — woollen or coarse linen pants formed from two rectangular leg tubes and a centre flap of rectangular cloth that folds from the belly to down between the legs, and then back up to cover the rear.

Mantle — woollen rectangular cloak with length indicating status within the tribe. Fringing is common and many are decorated with tribe symbols. The mantle is held in place by a clasp of horn, antler, or bone, although chieftains and other high-status individuals may have claps of bronze, iron, silver, or gold.

across bleak moorland. When going into battle, those Celts who have armour, either taken from slain enemies, gifted by fathers or tribe elders, or bought (although this is rare), wear it — especially helmets. Celts, whilst proud of their prowess in battle and eager to display their strength and tenacity, are not fools and value good, solid protection.

Tattoos

Tattoos are common. Using vegetable and mineral pigments, tattoos are intricate and symbolic. Animal designs and geometric patterns are favoured designs, and a youth's first tattoo is part of the transition to manhood. The arms, chest and back are the most popular canvases but some Celts tattoo their entire bodies - although this is more commonly a Pictish practice. Tattoos are added to and embellished to celebrate life events: battles, great deeds, marriage, parenthood and so on.

And, having gone to great pains to permenantly paint the body, many Celts like to display their tattoos especially when going into battle. Tattoos tell stories, exhibit prowess and mark the strong from the weak. Celts are loathe to cover their designs with armour and so arms are frequently left bare so that tattoos can be seen by all.

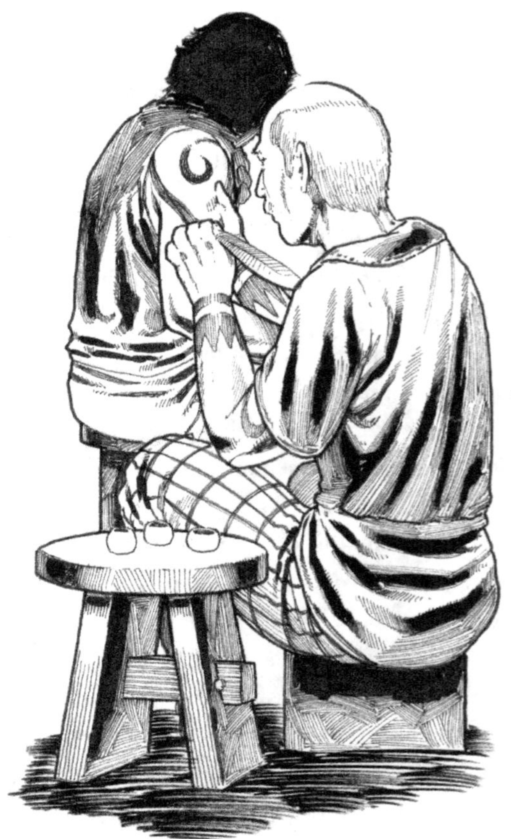

Warriors

The warrior is the lynchpin of the British tribe. Every man is expected to become a warrior, and many women join them. Warriors are expected to defend the tribe from its enemies, make war on the same enemies, raid when raiding is necessary, and promote the tribe's strength and pride at every opportunity.

Good, strong, fast, brave warriors are the most prized commodity of Britain. The ideal warrior fights without regard for his own safety, offers no mercy, does not shirk from slaughter, and is unafraid to die. At the same time, the ideal warrior is expected to obey orders and to fight with honour and dignity. Britain's history is one of countless tribal wars stretching back into the mists of time, and Celts have learned their lessons in warfare the hard way. Some Celts – the foolish ones – do charge headlong into battle at the first opportunity with absolutely no regard for themselves or others, but these are the ones who quickly die and are, ultimately, a waste. A good warrior listens to his chieftain or commander, thinks a little before he strikes, uses cunning (but not deceit) to gain an edge over his opponent, but still becomes a merchant of death feared by all before him.

War-making seems to be a natural aptitude for most Celts. They have an uncanny ability to appear fearless in battle and openly relish the opportunity to engage in bloodletting, even if the odds almost guarantee their own death. Celts rarely offer surrender to a foe and never expect it to be offered in return. But they are not, by and large, reckless berserks. Certainly some, the most feared, enter a berserk killing rage in the middle of battle, gripped by an insatiable bloodlust that has them howling with glee at the carnage, but this tends to be a result of hard experience rather than reckless abandon.

Britons train with a variety of weapons and across a variety of different techniques: close combat against single and multiple foes; battlefield combat; ambush, and so forth. Favoured weapons are the longspear, sword, and shield. Every Briton is schooled in the use of the dagger and knife, and this is usually the first weapon a Celt learns to handle.

For many warriors amongst the barbarian cultures of Hyboria, a combat or battle begins with drinking and taunting of the enemy; this is not so for the British. Celts spend the moments before a battle in steely concentration, focusing on their enemies, their weapons, and likely weaknesses or points of vulnerability. Ranks of British warriors preparing to clash are a line of sullen concentration, with dark eyes narrowed, brows furrowed, and fingers tensing and relaxing around the hilts and hafts of their weapons. When concentrating thus, British warriors are oblivious to everything save their enemy and their nearby comrades, and are ready for the first orders commanding them into engagement.

Slaves

Celts have a nonchalant attitude towards slavery. Some tribes abhor the practice whilst others make ready slaves of captured enemies. Slaves are most frequently taken whenever an enemy tribe is vanquished in order to prove mastery, and the treatment slaves receive depends purely on the outlook of the owner. By and large, slaves are considered to be chattels and receive the most basic level of care but are often abused, depending on the will of the owner. Slaves are expected to do the drudge-work of the tribe and wait on the chieftain or owner, and have no rights within the tribe other than food, somewhere to sleep, and a few exceedingly modest possessions. Slaves might be traded between allied tribes, much as any other goods might be traded and, if a slave is especially fit, diligent, and obeisant, he or she is valued as highly as gold or silver. However, the British tribes do not, as a rule, deliberately go in search of slaves and make a practice of trading them to further the tribe's position. Slaves are an occasional necessity and a right of victory, but not a commodity to be farmed and bartered.

Of course, Celtic pride makes them poor slaves. To be taken into slavery is considered shameful and no Briton worth his salt accepts slavery as an option of defeat. Acceptance of slavery automatically confers a position of weakness and almost all Celts prefer death to a life of enforced servitude. It is therefore rare to find strong warriors amongst slaves. It is more common to find the old and those less capable of fighting amongst the slave ranks, and invariably these slaves have a subdued, morose attitude because they are abundantly aware that, in being captured and enslaved, they have effectively failed to be good, proud Celts.

Love and Marriage

Celts are a passionate people. Although many marriages are arranged, Celts do love, and love deeply. They love their tribes, their families, their hunting bands, their war comrades, and, of course, romantically. Where they differ from other cultures is in the way love is expressed. There is little time, motivation, or appetite for idealised expressions of love; instead, Celts simply get on with their lives personally confident that those who are loved know it because they are not considered to be enemies and are treated with respect and kindness. Occasionally, a couple might be so stricken with each other that they hold hands and adorn each other's hair with flowers, but such practices are quickly subjected to scorn and ridicule because they serve little practical purpose beyond mawkish sentimentality. When a Celt loves someone, he tells them, bluntly and matter of factly, but usually he does not feel the need to do so.

One exception is the feast of Lughnasa, which marks the harvest season. One of the rituals is for lovers to build a byre and share a bed together. This fertility rite helps ensure the continuity of the tribe, of course, but it also ensure that children born of a Lughnasa conception are born in the spring, rather than in the winter or at the start of the next harvest. Lughnasa Eve is therefore a time for tenderness and lovers, when love play, and even sentimentality, is expected.

Marriage is almost always a political union, designed to forge new alliances, bring to an end old enmities, or advance the standing of the families involved. Couples do marry for love, but it is the exception rather than the rule, and a union that would benefit the tribe is far more likely to be approved by the chief than a union that is being made out of love.

Before marriage takes place, the couple must gain the consent of the heads of each family; if one family refuses permission, then the couple can ask the relevant chieftain to overturn the decision if he approves the union. Once the families have consented, then the couple are presented to the chieftain of the bride who must also consent. If the chieftain refuses his consent, then the marriage is not permitted to take place — even if the chieftain of the groom approves the marriage.

Once consent has been given, the couple must marry within ninety days. This period varies from tribe to tribe sometimes, but is a widespread and accepted tradition. In this time, the couple must have minimal contact with other — something that is not difficult if the bride and groom are from separate tribes — and when they do come into contact they must be chaperoned by a relative or close tribe member. This particular tradition is designed to prevent the bride and groom from either eloping or having enough time to decide that they dislike each other before the marriage ceremony. It is not designed to ensure that sexual relations do not take place.

The marriage ceremony itself is a nine-step process that involves the entire tribe or tribes. The groom's tribe acts as host and both tribes are forbidden to carry weapons for the duration of the ceremony — which generally lasts from dawn until dawn of the next day (or whenever the drinking stops).

First Step: Casting and Consecration of the Circle

The women of the tribe prepare a circle for the bride and groom to be married within. This might be a circular area in the centre of the tribe's seat, or it might be a sacred or special place in a nearby forest or on a moorland. The circle is clearly marked with either stones, flowers, petals, or some other marker and is always with a nine-yard radius. Only the bride, groom, and the community elder, who performs the ceremony, may enter the circle; anyone else who does so is considered to be cursed with bad luck for nine years.

The circle is consecrated with the urine from nine virgins, which is sprinkled around the perimeter. This wards against evil spirits and is considered to be a powerful charm aiding fertility.

Second Step: Presentation of the Bride and Groom

The bride and groom are brought from respective ends of the tribe settlement where they have remained in seclusion from the previous night. The chieftains and elders of the respective tribes and families receive the couple and offer a formal blessing, usually requesting the tribes' ancestors to look favourably on the union. It is at this stage that the bride's family presents her dowry to the groom's family. The dowry is usually an agreed amount of some commodity that has been negotiated before the ceremony.

It might be gold or coin, slaves, food, or even armour or weaponry. If the bride and groom separate for any reason within nine years of the marriage, then the groom's family forfeits the dowry.

Following the exchange of the dowry, the bride and groom are presented to the gathered tribes in preparation for the third step of the ceremony.

Third Step: Statement of the Bard

It is the bard's duty to explain, simply and concisely, why the couple are to be married, and to call upon those gathered to either bless the marriage or speak against it. It is accepted tradition for the marriage to be blessed; any opposition is expected to have been voiced in private with the relevant chiefs before the ceremony takes place. However, it is still an opportunity for people to protest.

Anyone who challenges the marriage must step forward and justify the opposition. It is then the duty of the groom's chief to either accept or deny the challenge. If he accepts it, the marriage is denied and tradition dictates that each party must go their separate ways without bloodshed or rancour. In practice, when this unfortunate state of affairs has arisen, it has invariably led to the creation of a feud or the intensification of one.

If the chieftain denies the opposition, he may call the challenger out. This always signals a duel of honour between the challenger and whoever the chieftain nominates as his champion. Usually this is the tribe's foremost warrior, but may be anyone the chief decides to nominate, including the groom. The stakes for the duel depend purely on the severity of the opposition. Where considerable tribe or personal honour is at stake a duel to the death is not uncommon. If the charge levelled is less serious, then the duel might be to first blood or even disarmament; if they duel is simply being fought to prove a point or make one, then a physical contest, such as wrestling, might be used instead of a duel with weapons.

If the challenger wins the duel, then the charge made stands and the marriage ceremony is either suspended or called off completely, until a resolution (if there is a resolution) can be found. If the chief's champion wins, then the marriage continues – although British superstition holds that any marriage challenged in this way is always doomed to failure in some form or another.

Step Four: Declarations of the Husband and Wife

Once the bard's statement has been made, the bride and groom, followed by the congregation, proceed to the circle. Here, the person conducting the marriage calls upon the bride and groom to declare their vows. There is no specific form of words, but essentially the groom must declare that he will:

Protect and honour his wife
Provide for her and his family
Place her needs above those of any other woman
Remain faithful to her

And the bride must declare to:

Honour and obey her husband
Ensure his needs are well-met
Raise his children in the traditions and ways of the tribe
Remain faithful to him

Step Five: Exchange of Rings

The rings exchanged between husband and wife need not be finger rings of metal; they can be of any circular object – torques of bone or antler; warrior rings forged from the weapons of defeated

enemies; necklaces of flowers or beads — anything, as long as it is symbolic of the circle.

The bride presents the groom with her ring and then the groom returns the action.

Step Six: Fasting of Hands

The couple clasp hands and present them to the elder conducting the ceremony. Their hands or wrists are then bound together in a loosely tied length of soft linen or silk. This signifies the completion of the union.

Step Seven: Passing of Light

The elder performing the ceremony takes either a lit candle or burning brand and encircles the couple nine times, chanting their names. The light source is then passed to the couple who, holding it together in their fasted hands, must proceed nine times, anticlockwise, around the inner perimeter of the circle. This act represents the spirit of the union and everyone watches the light source carefully to see if it will be extinguished. If it goes out at any point, then it is relit by the elder of the ceremony, but the rotation in which the light goes out signals the year or years in which troubles might be encountered by the couple. The more times the light source is extinguished, the more troubled the union will be and if the light source goes out more than once in any rotation, or is extinguished in every rotation, then the marriage is considered to be cursed from the start.

Step Eight: Thanksgiving and Oath

Once the Passing of the Light is completed the couple kneel in the centre of the circle and jointly utter a simple prayer of thanks to the ancestors, spirits and the appropriate deity and pledge to serve the clan that will be their home as a married couple.

Step Nine: Blessing and Opening of the Circle

The elder of the ceremony blesses the married couple by offering them a sip of either wine or mead. This done, the circle is opened by the married couple each taking one of the markers of the circle and stepping out of the perimeter. They emerge from the ceremony as husband and wife, and the opening of the circle is the signal for the feasting to begin. The couple can remove the tem used in the Fasting of Hands and tradition demands that it is tossed by the bride into the throng of the congregation; whoever catches it will be the next to marry.

Officially, the marriage ceremony lasts for one full day, but celebrations might continue for several days depending on the status of the married couple, and how much eating and drinking is available. It is the mark of a good chieftain to sustain the feasting for as long as he can; and, although no chieftain has any obligation to continue the feast any longer than dawn the next day, it is considered poor form for the celebrations to end at the appointed time.

Housing and Property

The two most common housing structures are the roundhouse and the Great Hall, which are described below. The elements common to all abodes are as follows:

Bedding is made from clean bracken, rushes, straw, or reeds, topped with a length of cloth to be wrapped around the body at night. Even the cleanest bed soon becomes riddled with fleas, lice, and other fauna and so regular changes of bedding and sweeping out of the bothy is essential. In cold weather, it is common for livestock to be brought into the dwelling at night to offer yet more warmth and protect against predators.

Celts rarely use tables, chairs, or other furniture. When sitting, it is cross-legged on the floor, with perhaps an animal skin for comfort. Meals are eaten from carved wooden bowls and trenchers of thick, unleavened bread, which are held in the hand. Cutlery is either a personal knife/dagger or a spoon carved from wood or antler.

The only concession to furniture is likely to be a possessions chest, made from stout wood and secured by iron or steel fittings. The chest contains items of value or things that need to be kept dry, such as spare clothing and flint and tinder. The chest may or may not be lockable, depending on what the owner has been able to afford.

The Roundhouse

The roundhouse is the building occupied by the vast majority of Celts and its design varies little from region to region. As the name suggests, the roundhouse is circular in design and varies from about 9 feet to 30 feet in diameter. A number of posts, planted firmly in the ground, provide support for a conical roof made of thatch. Walls are of woven reeds, covered with wattle and daub. Larger and wealthier roundhouses may have a stone perimeter base on which the reed walls are built, but most do not. Openings in the walls serve as windows, with hide coverings to afford privacy. Doors are made from more woven reeds, or, sometimes, planks of wood, and attached to a wooden frame with leather hinges.

The entire family lives in one room. A central, circular hearth maintains a fire that burns constantly, for both heat and cooking. Fumes find their way out through a hole in the roof directly above the hearth. The living area can be sectioned by stringing drapes (cloth or hide, sometimes reed and thatch) between the supporting posts, thereby creating a remarkable number of interior configurations according to family needs. A well-built roundhouse is sturdy, warm, and weather-proof. The chief danger comes from fire, and so every Celt is disciplined about how fire is used and treated inside the roundhouse. Care is taken to extinguish errant sparks and materials likely to spit or flare are cooked outside in dedicated fire pits, well away from the flammable thatch and reeds.

If a family keeps livestock, it is not uncommon for the animals to be brought into the roundhouse, especially in the colder months. This guards against predators and the cold, but also creates additional warmth.

Water is drawn from nearby streams and rivers using wooden buckets. The daily ritual is to stoke the fire, fetch fresh water, and prepare food for the day ahead.

The Great Hall

The Great Hall is rectangular structure of stone, wooden posts, beams, reed, wattle and daub walls, and thatched roofs. The hall is a multi-purpose building with the following functions:

- The abode for the chieftain, his family and immediate retinue (usually his warband)
- The council hall for clan/tribe business
- The feasting hall for honoured guests and Holy Days
- A meeting place for news, announcements, and local judicial matters.

The Great Hall may even be a large (10 metre or more) roundhouse, but the rectangular design reinforces status, station, and practicality for large gatherings. A typical chieftain's Great Hall is between 10 and 45 feet long, and between 15 and 24 feet wide. The Great Hall for a king, such as the hall at Caer Cadbryg , might be up to 60 feet long.

The roof has a steep pitch and is made of thatch and, sometimes, turf. The walls are a mixture of stone, wooden beams, woven reeds, and the ubiquitous wattle and daub. The doorways are of stout timbers, usually with an oak or ash lintel, and with heavy doors made from wooden planks and secured on metal and leather hinges.

The Great Hall is built to impress, but also built for practicality. In times of dire need, a large hall can accommodate well over two hundred people, and its purpose as a meeting and feasting area means that it is designed for regularly housing large numbers in relative comfort. As with the roundhouse, the posts used to support the roof and define the shape allow for different configurations, using wicker screens, drapes, and so on to provide private subdivisions according to need.

For normal daily use, the chieftain and his family occupies two or three rooms at the rear of the hall. A further area might be set aside for private meetings and councils. The main area is left open and plays host to the chieftain's warband or important retinue, offering them a place to sleep at night and to convene during the day. It is a great honour to be offered floorspace in the Great Hall, and the closer to the hearth, and closer to the chieftain's quarters, the greater the honour and status.

Although the Great Hall usually has several hearths, food is rarely prepared here. Smaller, satellite roundhouses are used for that purpose, along with outdoor fire pits for the huge carcasses roasted for feasts. Food, when ready, is brought into the Great Hall on large platters with serving staff or slaves ensuring that everyone receives a share according to rank and honour (the chieftain, then guests, followed by family and then retinue, in order of rank or service).

Feasts

Feasts are large – sometimes huge – communal banquets designed to celebrate a sacred event (such as harvest, a great victory, marriage, and so forth) or simply to celebrate life and raise morale. Celts love feasts: they are a vibrant, boisterous affair that mixes as much food as can be spared (typically bread, barley, oats, roots vegetables, and roast or boiled meat) with ale, mead, and, if available, wine. Bards play music, sing, and recite poems and stories while people eat, and then afterwards there is more drinking, dancing, drinking, and carousing until no one can continue, falling asleep or lapsing into reverie.

Food is served on long wooden tables with the feasters seated on hay or straw bales to either side. Several rows of tables are positioned to run at right angles to the chieftain or lord's table, which is on a raised platform at the closed end of the Great Hall.

Fights are common during feasts. Although weapons such as swords and spears are forbidden in the feasting hall, knives and daggers are used for cutting food and these rapidly become weapons when drunken men take offence at some slight and decide to retaliate. Most fights are over quickly with one combatant being knocked unconscious or surrendering following a wound, but sometimes they can escalate into full-on, to-the-death duels. These fights are, surprisingly, tolerated in most feasting halls. They help release aggression, settle long-simmering feuds, and also help weed the sober and level-headed warriors from the drunken, impetuous, rash fools that cause trouble rather than deal with it.

Fortified Settlements and Hillforts

People gather into communities for safety, protection, and common advancement. A typical Celtic settlement comprises of

about 10-30 roundhouses, with each roundhouse representing a single family of between two and eight people. Larger communities cluster around the Great Hall of the chieftain or king, and every community has communal outbuildings for storing food, tools, and other shared commodities.

Fortification is common. At its most basic, a wooden stockade surrounds the immediate cluster of roundhouses with two gates, positioned opposite each other, made of stout timber. The palisade is usually sharpened at the top of each post to deter climbers and may even be equipped with a platform (or several small platforms) to provide further defensive capabilities.

The most sophisticated fortification is the hillfort. The settlement is built at the summit of a cleared hill, and carved into the hill, sometimes in multiples, are ditches and ramparts designed to slow enemies and provide a continuing height advantage for defenders. Hillforts of this kind are a common sight throughout Britain and mark the steads of chieftains and kings. The community within the palisade of the hillfort can be very large: forty or fifty huts, plus livestock, food reserves and perhaps a well or some form of water course or cistern.

The largest hillforts have several enclosures and earth-work circuits, with the Great Hall at the centre of the enclosure network. This increases the defensive capabilities of the occupants, slowing enemies considerably and providing several avenues of retreat with the sturdy Great Hall acting as the epicentre. Forts such as Caer Cadbryg, Caer Ysc, and Caer Gradawc are huge complexes with several inner and outer palisades, multiple ditches and ramparts, deep killing pits, and steep, almost vertical, faces designed to slow and confound enemies.

Although many hillforts are self-contained settlements, there are plenty that are surrounded by a number of smaller, satellite communities. It can be hard — if not impossible — for the hillfort alone to defend these satellites, and so they are most commonly found in geographical regions that afford lines of natural defence,

such as two or more deep rivers flowing around the entire community, narrow valleys, or steep-sided hills. The hillfort is designed, of course, to provide the advantage of elevation and therefore spot enemy approaches, but much depends on the height of the hill and the lay of the land. There are many regions in Britain where the area of observation is obscured by the geography, or where the rise of the hill provides only a limited vantage point. For this reason patrols, mounted by the chieftain, are not uncommon, ensuring that the borders of the territory are policed, especially during key raiding times.

Personal Possessions and Tools

Most Britons have an ambivalent attitude to property, needing only the tools of their trade (weapons, mostly), somewhere to live, and clothing to keep warm. Many Celts own only what they wear and can carry, considering all other non-essential property as just so much excess baggage. But Celts do appreciate and admire quality and craftsmanship; they also understand the value of precious metals, both for use in trade and in creating items of outstanding value.

A typical Briton can be expected to own the following range of possessions:

- Spear
- Sling
- Sword (usually handed down from his father, or taken from a fallen foe)
- A dagger or broad-bladed knife
- Ordinary day-wear (see Clothing, above)
- War gear (a few pieces of armour, a helmet or cap)
- Léine, braecci, inar, trius and mantle (see page 104)
- Leather sandals
- Cloak and bone brooch or clasp
- Hunting tools (snares, bone or antler fishing hooks, fishing line)
- Flint, steel and tinder
- Wine/water skin
- A few items of jewelry – a torque, some warrior rings made from the spear tips of defeated enemies, and perhaps a necklace

Additional items depend on status, experience, and so forth, but most British warriors consider the above to be the essentials.

Property within a community is divided into three types. Personal property – that which is a hunted, made, bought, or traded by an individual (and summarised in the list above). That property is an individual's by right and taking it away from him is an act of theft and punishable under whatever laws a tribe enforces for theft. Communal property – that which belongs to the tribe and is administered on behalf of the tribe by the chieftain and his council. This is essentially land and territory, but also extends to treasures and items that are known to symbolise the tribe and its heritage; it also includes specific gifts made to the tribe by other tribes, whatever form these take. Communal property therefore expresses the tribe's wealth, heritage, and standing. Chief wealth is the third kind of property; this is property owned by the chief's position and which can be freely gifted by the chief either as rewards to other tribe members or to other tribes as an expression of gratitude or alliance. When emissaries come to a tribe it is typical for them to bring two gifts; one for the tribe and one for the chief. The tribe

gift becomes communal property whereas the chief gift enters the chief's wealth and can be used by him in whatever way he decides.

Laws Regarding Personal Property

Theft is regarded as a grave offence within a tribe. Mutual trust and respect plays such a strong part in tribe life that stealing from another tribe member is considered a critical breach of trust. If caught stealing from another tribe member, the thief can expect to, at the very least, lose his left hand. If the item stolen is particularly valuable, or is either tribe or chief wealth, he might pay with his life, and the chief is always called upon to make the final decision in some circumstances. Even if the thief loses just a hand, he will be expelled from the tribe and, bearing the mark of his crime, will find it difficult to gain sanctuary in another community.

The only circumstances where theft is deemed acceptable are the following:

- Looting the body of a defeated enemy. Tradition always gives the victor the right to the spoils.
- Seizing livestock in a sanctioned raid when there is no other option.
- Sacking a village that has been defeated in battle, if the residents have offered resistance. In these circumstances, only tribe property and chief wealth should be looted; personal property, with the exception of weapons and armour, should be left untouched.

In resolving a dispute between two tribe members, a chief might levy a confiscation of personal property as a punishment for the guilty party, but this tends to be a rare occurrence. Most disputes tend to be settled through tests of honour in some form of challenge.

Money

Despite not minting their own, Celts have a love of coin, especially gold and silver. Day-to-day transactions are conducted using the barter of goods and services rather than payment in coinage, but whenever Celts receive coins somehow, they hoard them for use elsewhere; and if a chieftain or tribe needs to make a particularly impressive gift, either within a tribe or outside of it, coins are often the means for doing so.

However, for most Celts, there is little use for coins in their daily lives. The British economy has no centralised mechanisms, no exchequer, and moves fluidly on the straightforward transfer of goods and favours.

Lords though — chieftains and leaders — are expected to be givers of silver to their followers. This usually takes the form of jewelry which may cut up or melted down so it can be evenly distributed. Currency, when Britons have it, may often be lumps and scraps of silver as often as recognisable coinage.

Food and Drink

Celts are farmers and hunters. Meat is highly prized: beef, mutton, pork, deer, boar, rabbit, wildfowl, pigeon, and so forth. Celts will eat anything they can trap or stalk and have a use for just about every part of an animal. The highest prized meats are deer and boar, due to the whole effort and ritual of the hunt. Both require stealth, skill, and cunning to be successfully hunted and their skins, antlers, and tusks are prized for all manner of crafts. Hunts takes place every week with a full hunting band of twenty-seven individuals, men and women, spending one or two days ranging through the territory checking snares, stalking the hunting trails, and bringing down prey. This extended hunt brings back meat for the whole community: several deer, boar, and rabbits being the most common catches. This weekly food supply is supplemented by individual hunting expeditions where smaller game is targeted and the yield is not expected to be shared with the rest of the tribe.

Cooking is simple: spit-roasted meat served on the bone, with left-overs being used to make broths. A portion of any large catch is reserved to be air-cured for the lean, winter months when hunting might be scarce, and Celts are experts in such techniques of meat preservation.

Vegetables and herbs figure in the diet, but are not high on the agenda. Whatever is seasonal is gathered in the wild: nettles, wild garlic, berries, nuts, edible weeds, and edible fungi. Cereal crops such as wheat and barley are cultivated where the land is available, and fertile enough, to support successful harvest, but cereals are by

no means widespread and bread is not a staple of the diet. Agricultural methods are simplistic; Celts have not developed crop rotation to optimise soil fertility and many crops are prone to disease and blight.

When the hunting is lean and food scarce, communities turn to raiding others, usually those that maintain sizeable herds of livestock that are worth the risk. The hunting bands turn their skills to reconnoitring a rival community's territory, sizing the livestock, understanding the defences, and then using the cover of night and inclement weather to steal into the compounds and take as much as they can carry. Naturally enough, any tribe with livestock understands it is prone to plunder and uses its own warbands to form defences against raiders. Clashes over livestock are fiercely fought affairs – as much a way of settling territorial and other disputes as for obtaining and protecting food. A raiding community may disguise its identity by dressing and acting like another tribe in a bid to minimise the likely retribution that will follow a raid, and, in this way, feuds develop, fester, and spill over into long-term bloodshed.

A raid is usually the first taste of combat a young warrior will experience. Raids are considered part of the training and initiation of all new warriors – a chance for a young man to prove himself in conditions that are dangerous, but less so than a full-scale battle. Hot-headed warriors, keen to prove their mettle, are therefore at the heart of many raids and receive their first battle scars from the defenders. Particularly ambitious, fierce, and successful raids are lauded as reverentially as any major battle, with those who distinguish themselves (especially young, newly blooded warriors) being feted for their deeds. Raiding season is thus an eagerly anticipated time as it relieves some of the grim monotony of the cold, dark, long British winter.

Trade

Most tribes produce everything they need internally but, sometimes, trade is necessary – either with neighbours or further afield. Celts have an active merchant tradition, with some very widely travelled across Britain and overseas (especially Ireland, Armorica and even into the Saxon homelands). Of particular interest as tradable commodities are meat (fresh and cured), metals, weapons, and armour.

Lacking a currency of their own, Celts are prepared to deal in whatever communal treasure the community possesses. Coins, when a tribe has them, are always valuable, especially when silver and gold, but usually they must deal in whatever items they have available.

Merchants from outside Britain are, at once, both admired and distrusted. Celts admire those who, through the gift of the gab and slick negotiation, can obtain a superb deal for minimum outlay; however, they are deeply suspicious and even contemptuous of certain mercantile skills. Slick negotiation is one step up from lying, and lying is not in the Celtic character. Few merchants speak plainly and say precisely what they mean; many bend the truth to unacceptable lengths to get what they want and at the lowest price.

Culture and Art

The need of Britons to hone prowess extends as far into the creative arts as it does into the arts of war and battle. Metalwork, bone work, and textiles exhibit incredible subtlety, grace, skill, and craftsmanship. One might expect the rough, crude, and slipshod, and amongst many Celts such things will be found, with the functional being placed over the aesthetic – but no more than in any other culture. Celts are highly capable of producing stunning works of art fitting enough for the finest halls of Constantinople. Textiles are filled with vibrant colours and rich patterns, the quality of the fabric second to none in quality and durability. Celts do not paint, but the designs they tease in their metalwork and knot work (used in belts, sashes and as fringes for robes and cloaks) are abstract and beautiful.

Celtic artists prefer natural subjects, reducing the image to its raw essentials, creating highly stylised depictions of every day plants, trees, and animals. The aim is to simplify and draw attention to the raw qualities of the subject or to specific characteristics. Carvings and etchings are done with great care and precision, without necessarily producing a realistic representation of the subject. The same is true for Celtic bronzes – statues, brooches, and

the like — feature highly stylised, delicate, intricate, rhythmic, and fluid representations.

Celtic imagery frequently mixes elements to arrive at some bizarre combinations: a god with serpents for limbs; or combinations of plants and animals, humans, and trees. Some of these representations come from the myths and legends of the Britons. Others come from dreams sent by the Spirit World or from things druids have seen when present in the Spirit World themselves. Such stylised, chimeric artworks are therefore considered to have magical or powerful significance, since something of the Spirit World is always captured when such a work is produced.

The Celts work in any number of materials. Bronze, wood, bone, and antler are very common. More precious metals are silver, jet, occasionally amber, and sparingly gold. Britain does not have much gold of its own, and what little it once had was imported during Roman rule and much of it taken back again when the Romans left. But there is a small amount in circulation, and so it is highly prized, highly sought-after, and highly protected. Craftsmen able to come by gold in very small quantities hammer it into extremely thin sheets so that it goes as far as possible but always with the same lustrous effect.

Metalwork

Celts are skilled metalworkers, particularly in copper, bronze, and iron. Gold and silver, whilst scarce, are merged sparingly and skilfully into the mix to create precious items such as bowls, plates, goblets, jewelry, and weaponry that are highly prized in the British community. A good metalworker is an asset to any tribe, and so the profession is considered honourable and necessary to tribe fortunes.

British metalwork shuns straight lines and rigid patterns. It favours flowing, intricate, interconnected patterns of curves, waves, concentric circles, and complex knot formations. Such intricacy is always sparingly applied, but highly detailed and finely wrought. British metalwork is, at first glance, quite simple to look at but, as the detail is studied, the intricacy and beauty of the design becomes apparent. Ostentation is deliberately avoided; quite simply, for Celts, less is more.

The patterns and motifs used in British design, especially their metalwork, avoid direct representations of nature and focus instead on symbolism. The main symbolic areas are: the tribe, the ancestors, and the sacred numbers. Each tribe has its own designs, expressed in the patterns and colours used in fabrics, but also in the knots and circular patterns used to decorate metalwork. The patterns followed allow Celts to identify the tribe producing the item.

Ancestors have their own combinations of nonlinear patterns, typically swirls and whorls reflecting the turbulent nature of life. These tend to be etched into the surface of an item, expressing how deeply ingrained the memory and influence of the ancestors is to a tribe.

The Sacred Numbers

Certain numbers are highly sacred to the Celts. Three is a sacred number in ancient Celtic mythology and religion. Riddles and triadic phraseology appear frequently in myths, stories, and songs. The triskel, a figure composed of three spirals, signifies the three-layered nature of a human soul and is itself a central figure in ancient Celtic symbolism. The earth, sea, and sky were thought to share a threefold marriage in oaths and as witness to deeds, and represent the sacred elements. The number nine is three times three — the tripling of the basic sacred number.

Seventeen is the number associated with the cycles of the visible moon, particularly the new moon. On the seventeenth day of the moon's cycle, many influential and monumental events are thought to take place, and the barriers between the Spirit and Mortal Worlds are at their weakest. The seventeenth generation is considered to be at the farthest reaches of ancestral memory,

putting the longevity of memories within a tribe at approximately 400 years.

Twenty-seven represents the sacred number nine tripled, which therefore triples its potency. Twenty-seven also signifies the minimum number of warriors comprising a warband, and the number of the members of a Celtic chieftain's court of counsel.

Thirty-three represents the royal or judiciary number, signifying great honour. The courts of great gods and heroes number thirty-two, with the king of the gods making the tally thirty-three.

Standards and Symbols

Every chieftain has a symbol, or device, which is painted or etched onto the shields of his warriors. A banner is occasionally carried, but more often than not a device on a shield suffices.

Most chieftains choose symbols from nature: animals (often predators, but not always), trees and plants, or a combination of the two. Designs are simple and stylised, allowing for easy recognition and differentiation – both on the battle field and where two rival chieftains use the same device.

The one exception is the Dragon device. This is reserved for the Pendragon – the high king of the tribes of Briton. No chieftain would dare to appropriate it.

Literacy and Numeracy

The Celtic tradition is largely oral. This does not mean that Celts cannot read and write – many can, both their own tongue and Latin, the language of the Romans – but the truth is simply that things, especially important things, are not written down. There are, like most Celtic practices, practical and socio-religious reasons for not committing things to writing. First, the druids believe that written records can be preserved and communicate great secrets that enemies can use. The druids themselves are a literate class, but the tradition of self-preservation means that nothing of their ways, beliefs, rituals, and, especially, magic is ever committed to text.

The second is that an oral tradition means that one must commit things to memory if they are to be communicated consistently and accurately. A good memory can be trained, and learning things word-for-word, be it in prose, poetry or song, ensures a strong, vibrant, accurate, and truthful memory.

Generally, freemen learn to read and write only if there is seen to be a need for it: if they are to become officers or counsellors, say. Nobles are taught to read and write because the mark of a good leader is good communication, and because one might need to entreat with others from beyond Britain's shores in a written form. So although Britons are not an illiterate race, literacy is not the norm. Numeracy, however, is. Counting, and the basic mathematical functions, is essential in every walk of life – from counting cattle and managing crops, through to counting and ordering warbands into an army. Just about every Celtic child is taught the importance and function of numbers (especially the sacred numbers and the numbers defining the seasons, solstices, and the equinox).

Games and Sports

Celts love games and sports. Athletics contests involving foot races, wrestling, swimming, and jumping (through fire, over spears, etc.) are a frequent part of festivals and feast times with the winners receiving a reward of silver: coins or jewelry. Sport is a vital part of training, designed to improve fitness, encourage teamwork, and develop the discipline of warbands; however, it also encourages individual pride and prowess, something dear to the heart of every Celt.

Board games too are popular; one, *Gwyddbwyll*, is played on a wooden board, half a metre square, with 12 black and 12 white pieces (wood or stone), with the objective being to blockade the opponent's pieces and capture the 'King' piece. A development of a Roman board game, it is similar to the Saxon board game known as 'tafl' and is an important way of teaching and learning strategy and tactics. Another popular game is played with dice and is known as Throw-Board. The dice are rolled on a wooden board, about the length of an arm, with different combinations marked down each side. Wagers are made on particular combinations of dice and scores achieved, with some wagers accumulating depending on the numbers of dice used or scoring combinations agreed upon. Wherever people gather, Throw-Board and Gwyddbwyll

will be played: in huts, halls, taverns, roadsides, fields, and, even, at camps the night before a battle. Board games develop cunning and guile, demonstrate luck, teach probability, and can also be played in doors when the weather is too inclement for outdoor activities.

Drinking contests are also popular and frequent – especially at feasts. Most contests are based on personal capacity but often with the added complications of having to recite a poem, sing a song, answer a riddle, or some other feat of mental agility, which naturally diminishes with the amount of ale or mead downed. Contests involving speed drinking – usually from an oversized goblet or horn – are as popular as those involving how much can be drunk. For the ultimate in competitiveness, drinking games are mixed with board games, a drink needing to be taken each time a piece or wager is lost.

Law, Order and Crime

Celts are not governed by written laws: instead they are governed by traditions and customs that determine appropriate behaviour and what can be expected as punishment if one misbehaves or commits harm against someone else. There are some common sense rules in place, and many punishments are scaled to fit the severity of the crime. Punishments are also different for men and women, with some acts being viewed very differently depending on the gender of the perpetrator. For example, it is expected that a man will, at some point, be unfaithful to his wife. It might be frowned upon, but is not considered to be that great a transgression. However, if a wife is unfaithful to her husband, it is considered a betrayal that can, if the husband wishes it, result in shame and exile for the wife.

The chief or lord in charge of the community is responsible for deciding if a crime has been committed, a law broken (or merely bent), and the appropriate punishment. He might allow appeal, but usually his word is final and punishment – usually a fine or sentence involving labour – is carried out at once. For crimes such as theft, the punishment is far more serious: removal of the offending hand is common, or sometimes it might be an eye or ear, depending on the severity of the theft. Amputating someone's hand reduces their ability to work or fight, and so could be counterproductive; therefore, a physical punishment that maintains that capacity is often the better choice.

Reduction in social status – shame – is also a common punishment for serious crimes, usually involving loyalty, dishonesty, or oath-breaking. Great store is placed on status and for it to be taken away is often a greater punishment than something physical or a monetary fine. A list of typical crimes and expected punishments are listed on page 118.

The Nine Witnesses in Law

When someone makes an accusation of a crime, the strength of the accusation is dependent on the status of the witness. There are nine levels of Witness:

A Lord
A Druid
A Priest
A Father speaking for his children
A Magistrate
A Gift Giver speaking of, or for, the gift he has made
A Maiden speaking of, or for, her purity
A Herder speaking of, or for, his animals
A Condemned man speaking his last words

Thus, the accusation made by a Lord carries more weight than that of a Druid. In turn, a Druid's accusation carries more weight than that of a Priest, and so on. Anyone not in this list can make an accusation, but it carries no weight and can therefore be discounted unless a valid Witness makes the accusation on behalf of someone who has no Witness status. The ranking one has amongst the Nine Witnesses is therefore of great importance if an accusation is being made, or one must defend against an accusation.

Blood Price

Blood Price is the price that can be demanded by the family of someone who is killed not as an act of battle (be the death accidental or deliberate). Thus, the wife of a warrior killed in a drunken fight at a feast can demand her husband's Blood Price in recompense, and the law will support her claim. Blood Price is measured

either in silver (nobles and Aes) or in property (freemen and churls). Outcasts and slaves command no Blood Price.

The typical Blood Prices are:

- Noble: 1000 - 10,000 Silver Pieces (depending on reputation, holdings, importance and so forth)
- Aes: 500 - 5,000 Silver Pieces (again, depending on age, experience, and so on)
- Freemen: 1-20 Cows (again, depending on age, experience, and so on)
- Churl: 1-10 Chickens, 1-3 pigs or 1 Cow - (again, depending on age, experience, and so on)

(See page 124 for a detailed explanation of the social ranks.)

In the case of freeman and churls, if the livestock is not available, then property or coinage to the equivalent is acceptable. A lord might demand that the Blood Price is paid as labour for a specific term: a season, a year, two years, and so on, if the perpetrator cannot pay or if an example needs to be made. The Blood Price may even be a combination of different repayment methods – but in each case, the determination of the Blood Price is based on the person's status and worth, as indicated above.

Typical Crimes and Punishments

- Adultery: Exile or a period of shamed penance
- Arson: Exile
- Assault: Fine equal to One Tenth of the victim's Blood Price
- Burglary/Theft: Exile for nobles and Aes Dana: Loss of an eye, ear or hand for freemen and churls; death for outcasts and slaves
- Manslaughter: Payment of Blood Price
- Murder: Exile and payment of Blood Price for nobles, Aes and freemen; death for churls and outcasts
- Rape: Payment of the half the Blood Price
- Treason: Exile (nobles, Aes) or death (everyone else)
- Breaking an Oath: Reduction in Social Status by one level (or Exile – depending on the oath and severity)
- General Misdemeanours: Fine of between 1 and 100 Silver Pieces, depending on severity – or equivalent in property, livestock, or forced labour.

Trial by Combat

Anyone accused of a crime can choose to have their case heard by the lord and accept the punishment given, or, if the crime is severe enough, claim justice in Trial by Combat. This is, quite simply, a duel between the accused and either his accuser or someone appointed to fight in the accuser's place (such as a clan champion or someone else willing to take up arms). If the accused kills his opponent, he is innocent and walks free. If he dies, he was clearly guilty.

The lord presiding over the community always decides if Trial by Combat is applicable or not, and it may be declined if he decides the crime does not warrant the duel. He can also decide if it should be to the death or merely to first blood – it is, though, considered a sign of weakness if the latter is decided. Demanding, and being granted, Trial by Combat, means that the accused is willing to stake his life on his innocence, and so nothing less than a fight to the death is considered honourable.

The combatants meet at an appointed time and place: the accused is allowed to choose the place, the lord the time. The

combatants are allowed only a sword and shield: armour is forbidden. The fight takes place in a circle 42 feet in diameter, marked by spectators, hay bales, sticks, stones, or some other method. Stepping outside the circle is forbidden, and there will always be someone placed to push the combatant back into the fray if the perimeter is crossed.

The fight continues until a victor is established. All tactics are permitted: it is important only that both combatants fight well and die well. A lord can intervene to end the Trial by Combat, but it is rare for it to happen. Mercy can be offered by one or the other combatant, but is, again, very rare. Every Celt knows that to enter Trial by Combat, or the Court of Swords as it is sometimes known, justice is only attained through death.

Calendar and Festivals

Celts treat days as starting at sundown, and months are moons, based on the lunar cycle. A two-week period is a fortnight, a contraction of 'fourteen nights' with one week known as a sennight (seven nights).

Festivals are held on the nearest moon, new or full depending on the festival. The length of the lunar cycle is just over 28 days, giving 12 moons in a normal solar year. Every 21 years, there are 13 moons in the year and this is called a Great Lunar Year; Celts mark the passage of the solar and lunar years and hold a Great Lunar Year as a period of unusually powerful foreboding.

The British year is divided into four main parts based on the farming and hunting cycle, each marked by festivals symbolising the transition of the world.

Samhain begins the New Year, when the world starts to darken into winter. The veil between the human world and the world of the dead becomes very thin. Feasts are held and the ancestors of the tribe honoured. The following day in the calendar has no name to prevent the ancestors from being trapped in the Mortal World and to make the journey back over the veil of death much easier.

The end of winter and the start of the awakening of the world is marked by Imbolc, which translates to 'the lactation of the ewes'. The birth of the first lamb means that there is once again fresh milk available and is proof of new life returning.

Beltain is the liveliest festival of this gloomy realm, as it marks the first day of summer. It is evidenced by the appearance of the first May blossoms amongst the twisted branches and shoots of British tress. A time of partnerships and fertility, this is the time for declaring alliances of politics and marriage. New couples proclaim their love for each other on this day, and tribe chieftains take stock of what prosper or problem alliances and enmities will bring for the year ahead. Animals are transferred from winter to summer pastures, and are driven between the Beltain fires to cleanse them of evil spirits.

The last major festival of the year is the bringing in of the harvest, starting on the feast of Lughnasa. The festival is a celebration of the tribe coming through another year and entering the darkening days with plenty in store for the winter. In those tribes where agriculture is practised, the culmination of the festival is Harvest Home, marking the last load coming in from the fields.

Minor festivals and feasts are held traditionally on the ninth day of the third, sixth, ninth, or twenty-seventh month.

Celtic Festivals		
	Contemporary Date	Festival
Samhain	31st October	New Year
Imbolc	31st January	Awakening of the world
Beltain	1st May	1st day of summer
Lughnasa	31st July	Harvest

Mythic Britain Characters

Mythic Britain characters follow a very similar creation process to normal MYTHRAS characters. When creating your character, you will need to follow most of the Characters, Culture & Community, and Careers chapters of the MYTHRAS rules, but note the changes introduced by this chapter. A Mythic Britain Character Sheet can be downloaded from the Design Mechanism website.

Characteristics and Attributes

These follow the same steps described in the Characters chapter of the MYTHRAS rules. The only slight change is the introduction of a new Standard Skill, Superstition. What Superstition represents and how it works is described on page 136.

Culture and Community

Certain decisions need to be set by the Games Master or agreed on with the players:

Character Culture

Either Celt or Saxon

Homeland/Tribe

Either chosen by the players, determined by the Games Master or randomly rolled. Do the characters all come from the same Homeland and settlement or are they a disparate mix?

Religion

Either Christian or Pagan. This can be rolled randomly, and the chance of being one or the other is determined largely by Homeland and Tribe.

Cultural Skills

Every character assigns cultural skill points as per page 13, of the MYTHRAS rules. The skills are dependent on whether the character is Celt or Saxon.

Passions

Every character has five Passions, with slightly different values to the MYTHRAS standard. See the appropriate Culture for details.

Background Events

Mythic Britain has its own Background Events table, found on page 128. Every character gains one roll on the table.

Social Class

This is best decided in conjunction with the Games Master, and with characters being of the same Social Class (typically Freeman, Aes, or Noble). See the Social Class table on page 126.

Families, Allies, Contacts, Rivals, and Enemies

These are all determined as per pages 21 to 22 of the MYTHRAS rules.

Careers

The careers open to characters are culture and class dependent. These are explained on pages 135 to 136.

The Celtic Culture

It is worth reading the previous chapter, Celtic Life and Society, beginning on page 92, to learn more about the Celtic culture and way of life. Generally, Celts tend more towards the Barbarian culture than the Civilised one, although they cannot be satisfactorily classified as 'classic' Barbarians. The skills for Celts are listed below. Distribute 100 Skill Points as per page 13 of the MYTHRAS rules unless noted otherwise.

Customs, Lore and Language

Customs (Celt) +40% (does not count towards the 100 Skill Points available)

Lore (Celt) +40% (does not count towards the 100 Skill Points available)

Native Tongue (either Brythonic or Goidelic - see page 124): +40% (does not count towards the 100 Skill Points available)

Standard Skills

Athletics, Brawn, Endurance, First Aid, Locale, Perception, and one of the following: Boating, Sing, or Ride

Professional Skills (Choose 3)

Art (Poetry), Craft (any), Healing, Lore (Christian), Lore (Pagan), Musicianship, Navigate, Seamanship, Survival, Track

The choice of Lore should be determined by the character's religion.

Combat Styles (Choose 1)

- Hunter (Dagger, Sling, and Bow. Trait, Skirmishing)
- Warrior (Spear, Sword, and Shield. Trait, Formation Fighting)
- Noble (Spear, Sword, and Shield. Trait, Mounted Combat or Trained Beast)
- Shield Wall (Spear, Sword, and Shield. Trait, Shield Wall)
- Self Defence (Dagger, Unarmed. Trait, Unarmed prowess)

Passions

Every Celt has five passions:

- Loyalty to Lord: 45%+POW
- Loyalty to Community: 40%+POW
- Love (Person, Ideal, Concept, or Thing): 30%+ POWx2
- Hate (Person, Ideal, Concept, or Thing): 30%+POWx2
- *Either* Christianity: 45%+POW *or* Pagan: 45%+POW

The Saxon Culture

Like Celts, Saxons are tribal and clannish, and veer more towards the Barbarian than Civilised end of the cultural spectrum. All Saxons are pagan and worship different gods to the Celts, but are in many respects very similar.

The skills for Saxons are listed below. Distribute 100 Skill Points as per page 13 of the MYTHRAS rules unless noted otherwise.

Customs, Lore and Language

Customs (Saxon) +40% (does not count towards the 100 Skill Points available)

Lore (Saxon) +40% (does not count towards the 100 Skill Points available)

Native Tongue (Jutish, Angle, or Saxon - see page 124): +40% (does not count towards the 100 Skill Points available). The three Saxon languages are closely related although with different dialects. Treat the differences in language as per the notes in Language found on page 124.

Standard Skills

Athletics, Brawn, Endurance, First Aid, Locale, Perception, and either Boating or Ride

Professional Skills (Choose 3)

Art (Poetry), Craft (any), Healing, Lore (Norse Gods), Musicianship, Navigate, Seamanship, Survival, Track

Combat Styles (Choose 1)

- Hunter (Dagger, Sling, and Bow. Trait, Skirmishing)
- Fyrdman (Battleaxe, Seax, and Shield. Trait, Formation Fighting)
- Ealdorman (Battleaxe, Seax, and Shield. Trait, Mounted Combat or Trained Beast)
- Shield Wall (Spear, Seax, and Shield. Trait, Shield Wall)
- Berserker (Battleaxe, Greataxe. Trait, Intimidating Scream)

Passions

Every Saxon has five passions; four social and one religious:

- Loyalty to Lord: 45%+POW
- Loyalty to Community: 40%+POW
- Love (Person, Ideal, Concept, or Thing): 30%+ POWx2
- Hate (Person, Ideal, Concept, or Thing): 30%+POWx2
- Norse Gods: 45%+POW

A Saxon Amongst the Celts

Both the Celts and Saxons undoubtedly took prisoners who were made into slaves. Given time, these slaves may prove themselves through work and loyalty to their new masters and so gain their freedom and the chance to live as equals (more or less) in a new culture. Players can choose to be of Saxon origin, raised in, and loyal to, their new Celtic tribe – or vice-versa. In such a case, the player creates the character according to the new, adopted culture, but also gains the language of their old culture and the Passion Loyalty (Saxon or Celt) at two thirds of the Loyalty to Community score. The character is considered to have spent a considerable amount of time with their adoptive culture, learned their ways and language, and adopted their loyalties. However, if they have the opportunity to re-join their original culture, then it could make for an interesting moral and cultural struggle.

Homeland and Tribe

The Homeland and Tribe of a character are determined together, along with Native Tongue and Religion.

The following table splits Britain into four regions, which correspond with the arrangement of detailed descriptions in the Kingdoms of Mythic Britain chapter. Each region has a kingdom associated with it, and this then has a corresponding tribe and language spoken. It is perfectly possible for characters to have originated in a different part of Britain and found themselves in another before play begins.

All these regions and kingdoms are described in the Kingdoms of Mythic Britain chapter, and each player should be allowed to read the appropriate description for more information on their background (or current home). The detail included may also provide some valuable background ideas when considering various Passions and the character's Background Event.

All Saxons come from Logres and belong to either the Angles or Jutes, the two main tribes originating from the Saxon homelands.

It is recommended that all characters are located in the same place and be part of the same community. This can be agreed with the Games Master or be at the Games Master's discretion.

Homeland and Tribe					
Region	Kingdom	Tribe	Language	Christian	Pagan
North	Dal Riada	Scotii	Goidelic	01-70	71-00
	Caledonia	Caledonii	Goidelic	01-04	05-00
	Circind/Gododdin	Votadini	Goidelic	01-02	03-00
Middle	Carvetia	Carvetii	Brythonic	01-90	91-00
	Parisii	Parisii	Brythonic	01-10	11-00
	Brigantia	Brigantes	Brythonic	01-85	86-00
	Cornovia	Cornovii	Brythonic	01-20	21-00
South	Dumnonia	Dumnonii	Brythonic	01-50	51-00
	Kernow	Dumnonii	Brythonic	01-30	31-00
West	Powys	Ordovices	Brythonic	01-80	81-00
	Gwent	Ordovices	Brythonic	01-90	91-00
	Gwynedd	Votadini*	Brythonic & Goidelic*	01-40	41-00
	Siluria	Silures	Brythonic	01-02	03-00

**Gwynedd's Celts are descendants of Cunedda and are part of the Votadini tribe. They have adopted the Brythonic dialect, but speak Goidelic equally well.*

Homeland and Tribe - Celts - Random Roll					
1d100	Kingdom	Tribe	Language	Christian	Pagan
01-20	Brigantia	Brigantes	Brythonic	01-85	86-00
21-27	Caledonia	Caledonii	Goidelic	01-04	05-00
28-31	Carvetia	Carvetii	Brythonic	01-90	91-00
32-38	Cornovia	Cornovii	Brythonic	01-20	21-00
39-42	Dal Riada	Scotii	Goidelic	01-70	71-00
43-56	Dumnonia	Dumnonii	Brythonic	01-50	51-00
57-61	Gwent	Ordovices	Brythonic	01-90	91-00
62-65	Gwynedd	Votadini*	Brythonic & Goidelic*	01-40	41-00
66-69	Kernow	Dumnonii	Brythonic	01-30	31-00
70-73	Parisii	Parisii	Brythonic	01-10	11-00
74-76	Circind/Gododdin	Votadini	Goidelic	01-02	03-00
77-97	Powys	Ordovices	Brythonic	01-80	81-00
98-00	Siluria	Silures	Brythonic	01-02	03-00

However, if something more random is preferred or needed, a random table is provided.

Language

Brythonic and Goidelic are dialects of the Celtic language. They have developed along different phonetic lines, with Brythonic resembling the Welsh and Breton languages of contemporary Europe, while Goidelic closely resembles Irish. For simplicity, they are treated as different dialects. Someone fluent in Brythonic can understand the Goidelic dialect (and vice-versa) but using a Hard Native Tongue skill roll. The one exception is the kingdom of Gwynedd, where both Goidelic and Brythonic are spoken together.

This same rule of thumb should be used for the three Saxon languages: Jutish, Angle, and Saxon.

Religion can either be chosen, assigned or the character can roll 1d100, the result determining the religion followed according to the predominant religion of the tribe and/or kingdom.

Class and Rank

Celts have five Social Classes. Mobility is high: individuals can move from the lowest to the highest without impediment (and, of course, go the other way), with advancement being based on the service to the entire tribe – be this through domestic means, or through battle and warfare. However, bravery on the battlefield alone is not guarantee of social advancement: every Celt is expected to fight, or serve the warbands in some way, and so courage with arms does not supersede courage with the ploughshare.

Classes, Lowest to Highest

- Non-Freemen (Outcasts/Slaves)
- Churls
- Freemen
- Aes
- Nobles

Outcasts

This is the lowest Social Class, comprising lawbreakers, outcasts, and exiles who have lost their rights within the tribe and are prohibited from benefiting from the tribe's largesse. Celtic custom demands that lawbreakers repay their debt to the tribe through hard work. Thus, non-freemen are usually forced to live away from their family and undertake the most arduous chores until that debt is paid. This is a considerable humiliation for the proud Celt, and it is the way that deserters, cravens, and prisoners-of-war are treated. Although Celts do not, traditionally, keep slaves, the life of the non-freemen is only partially removed from slavery: it differs insomuch that freedom can be earned and it need not be a life-long sentence. However, some crimes cannot be punished through forced labour. Such criminals are frequently marked as such through branding, scarring, or other forms of mutilation, making it hard for them to gain acceptance within another tribe no matter how far removed. Non-freemen typically become wandering thieves, outlaws, and mercenaries (although even as warriors, they are still despised).

Slaves are usually those captured through conquest and strife. They toil for their owner but, if they show loyalty and willingness, they can easily become churls and freemen and frequently do. Celts do not, in principle, condone slavery and see it as a short- to medium-term punishment that is then commuted to freedom if the slave is deserving of it. Thus, there are many Saxon churls and freemen amongst the Britons, and they have sworn loyalty to their clan. Indeed, the children of Saxon slaves are considered Celts rather than Saxons and are assimilated into society easily. Of course, this is not to say that Saxons who are now part of the Celtic way of life will not revert to their original culture given the chance, but, for now, they are accepting of where they are and who they are with.

Churls

Churls are itinerant peasants. They have chosen not to remain in a single tribe, but to wander from tribe to tribe, hiring themselves as herders and field workers and as levies for the tribal armies. Because churls remain only as long as there is work, trust and appreciation of their efforts is low, and there is always the suspicion that a churl is a non-freeman who has been banished and escaped the marking that shows them to be a criminal. The exceptions to these itinerants are the druids and bards, both of whom occupy their own social strata, as will be discussed.

Freemen

The vast bulk of Celtic society consists of freemen – those who own and work their land. Freemen are the bedrock of the tribe; the group that pays the taxes, elects the officials, and forms the warbands. Although Freemen are typically farmers, the class also includes craftsmen of all kinds, from smiths to weavers, to traders.

Aes

The Aes consists of three separate roles: the public officials (tax collectors, bureaucrats, surveyors, assessors, healers and so forth); the druids, and the bards.

The officials typically serve the nobles directly and have duties concerned almost solely with administrating the life and work of the tribe as a whole. They have the same rights and privileges as freemen, but are likely to have property granted to them by a noble in return for a specific service or knowledge. Aside from this, the officials are expected to pay taxes and contribute to the good of the tribe in the same way as the freemen.

The druids are not simply the priests of the old Celtic gods: they are historians, philosophers, physicians, magistrates, and counsellors. Some remain with a tribe for life; others are itinerant, coming and going as they please. Like nobles – although they are not of the Noble class – druids can hold lands, dispense land rights, collect rents, and so forth. As experts on Celtic law and customs, they frequently act as intermediaries in tribal affairs and even exert control over the process of government. In many respects, the druids out-strip the nobles in terms of authority because their knowledge and powers extend beyond the local tribe and concern the whole of the cultural and religious identity of the Celts.

The bards are the minstrels, storytellers, musicians, and news-carriers of the Celts. Although not religious, they occupy the same strata as the druids because their training is almost as extensive and arduous as druidic training. The Celtic tradition is mostly oral, requiring the memorisation of countless songs, tales, and stories. Bards are expected to be word perfect, and their memories are trained to this level of perfection. This also makes bards essential as carriers of news and important messages. To harm a bard is a crime equal to that of harming a druid or chieftain.

Nobles

The nobles consist of the chieftains and the household of the monarch. Chieftains are elected by the tribe in general, and they are expected to be experts in administration and in war. Chieftains can be male or female and have usually demonstrated their expertise in multiple disciplines and in multiple ways. Chieftains have the right to be called 'Lord' (or 'Lady'), may allocate lands to freemen and Aes, pass sentence to make someone a non-freeman, and benefit from a proportion of taxes so that they can perform their duties and gain reward for their status. Chieftains are expected to use their position and wealth to protect their people and tend to be the heads of clans. It is their responsibility to create fortifications; ensure the smooth running of settlements; raise, train, and equip warbands; and act as counsellors and supporters of the King.

There is no general concept of primogeniture amongst the Celts. When a chieftain dies, his or her title and assets do not automatically pass to the next of kin. The chieftains and monarch are likely to gather in council and decide what to do. This may result

in a relative taking the old chieftain's place, or the freemen may be called on to elect a new chieftain. The monarch may also create a chieftain solely if he or she has good reason, but the appointment can be challenged by the council of chieftains and by the freemen if it is controversial or unpopular. Usually, a druid will be called upon to ratify any unilateral decision, and a druid's support is therefore an important political tool amongst the nobility.

Monarchs are somewhat at odds with the Celtic social structure. Unelected, largely ceremonial, and symbolic, but still expected to represent the tribe, especially in the leadership of war, kings and queens are at the apex of the class structure in Celtic society. They occupy this position because, in the myths and legends of the Celtic peoples, the first kings were gods and demigods – and so it goes that existing kings and queens trace their lineage to divine beings and great spirits and so represent the link between the noble houses of the mortal realm and the noble houses of the immortal realm. The druids have a heavy hand in determining lineage and so in deciding who maintains the symbolic link, much diluted, with the Other World nobility.

Thus, the royal family is an hereditary institution in Celtic society and, really, the only one. Chieftains and Aes change; lords come and go. But the lineage of the kings can be traced and, unless something happens to change a dynastic line completely (which can, and does happen throughout Celtic history), the Celtic monarchy passes from one generation to the next.

The Celts hold kings and queens in equal esteem. If a king begets only daughters, they inherit and become queens. The existing monarch can name his or her successor, meaning that rulership is never guaranteed to pass to the eldest – although, by and large, the tradition is to pass the line to the eldest child, regardless of sex. Kings tend to favour boys, of course. Celts are proud, and boys make for the best warriors, so it is believed, although there is a fine tradition of equally proud and fierce warrior queens.

The monarch represents the entire tribe and all its holdings and assets. The nobles are expected to swear oaths of allegiance to the monarch, thereby swearing the same allegiance to the tribe. The monarch has the right to dispense patronage, to name new chieftains and raise individuals through the social hierarchy – although always with the advice and consent of the chieftains and druids. Any king or queen who attempts to rule solely and without the support and recognition of the nobles and druids treads a precarious road.

Saxon Classes and Ranks

The Saxon Social Class system is more complex than that of the Celts and has, for *Mythic Britain* purposes, been simplified so that it fits the same five-rank model as the Celts.

The lowest rank is that of *Gebur* and slave. The Gebur are native Saxon peasants, a little more privileged than slaves, but wholly dependent on, and beholden to, a landowner such as a Thane or Ealdorman. Geburs own no land, cannot own land, and work the lands allotted by their lord, paying over a substantial amount of the produce to the lord while keeping enough to live by. Gebur and slaves have minimal wergeld.

Social Class Table

1d100	Celt	Saxon	Weregeld (Saxons)	Money Modifier
01-05	Outcast/Slave	Gebur/Slave	50	0.25
06-15	Churl	Carl	600	0.5
16-80	Freeman	Thane	1,200	1
81-95	Aes	Ealdorman	5,000	3
96-00	Noble	High Noble	10,000 - 100,000	5

Carls are free men who can own land and while expected to pay fealty to a lord, such as a Thane or Ealdorman, are allowed to take part in decision-making, which Gebur cannot do. Carls, along with Gebur, make up a substantial amount of the citizen army, known as the fyrd, although Carls, having the right to bear arms, often serve a Thane as professional soldiers.

Thanes are landowners of major standing and they form the backbone of Saxon war bands. Thanes serve an Ealdormen and are considered high-ranking advisers. They command Carls, Gebur, and slaves, and can attract their own oaths of fealty.

Ealdormen are nobles, responsible for entire communities and substantial landholdings. They owe fealty only to the king and dispense justice in his name. Eoldermen have the power to raise the fyrd and serve as a king's generals and advisers.

The high nobility is, essentially, the king and his immediate family. Amongst Saxons, high noble titles are hereditary, and so the son of a king is expected to inherit his father's crown, with the title passing through the male line. Kings can name their heirs if they so wish so being the eldest is not a guarantee of gaining power, although it is the most accepted way.

In 5th and 6th Century Britain any ambitious and successful Ealdorman can carve out some territory for himself and declare himself king, creating his own Ealdormen, Thanes, and so on from his followers. Many Saxon Ealdormen come to Britain to do precisely this. However, amongst Saxons there is not the same social mobility as amongst the Celts. Thanes can be raised to Ealdermen, and Carls can be raised to Thanes, but the process is slow and dependent on the mood of the King, who has final say in such matters.

Wergeld

Wergeld is the price that can be demanded if someone is killed by the victim's family. It increases substantially with rank and its precise value depends on the individual, reputation, usefulness, and what a King thinks is fair. The figure given in the Social Class table indicates the minimum wergeld that be expected: it may be more depending on the circumstances. If a king or Ealdorman declares that wergeld is payable for a death, then the accused must pay it or risk being made a slave, with his possessions being turned over to the victim's family as partial recompense.

High Kings and the Pendragon

Throughout Celtic history there have been High Kings – those who united many tribes under one banner. In the era of Mythic Britain, there have been two such High Kings.

First is Vortigern who brought together all the kingdoms of southern Britain in a union that created much wealth and prosperity. But Vortigern, ever ambitious, grew too greedy and believed he could succeed even where the Romans had not: subjugating the Pictish kingdoms north of the Great Wall. Many of the kingdoms he had united counselled against this folly, and chief amongst them was Uther, Vortigern's friend and chief counsellor. When Vortigern refused Uther's counsel, Uther was forced to cede his position. He led the kingdoms of the west away from Vortigern's alliance and, in time, became their own High King, known as the Pendragon, or 'Dragon's Head' for daring to defy the mighty and charismatic Vortigern.

The two chieftains also carried banners depicting dragons. Vortigern's was the white dragon and Uther's the red. The druid Merlin had, many years before, prophesied that the Land of Britain would become unstable as a result of the battle between the White and Red Dragons. He was correct: Britain split into east, west, and north. Uther consolidated the eastern kingdoms under his own High Kingship, and Vortigern struggled to retain control of the west in the face of the increasing presence of the Saxons.

Two High Kings. Two Dragons. One Land. No Winners.

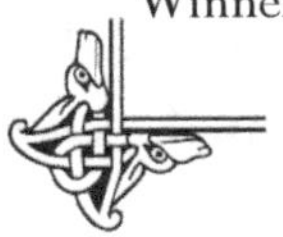

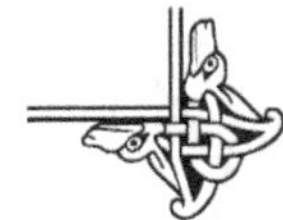

Background Events

The following table serves for both Celt and Saxon characters.

Background Events	
1d100	Event
01	You are an outcast from your previous tribe and have been forced to make a new home in a new land. How did you become an outcast? What was the crime? Who accused you and why?
02	You were abandoned in the forests or woodlands by your parents and raised by the local druid or (if Saxon, shaman). You can choose the druid, shaman, bard, or skald profession if you wish. Why did your parents abandon you? Do they still live? How do you feel about them?
03	You accidentally killed or injured a childhood friend. Gain an enemy – either the injured child or one of their siblings. They intend to cause you harm in the future.
04	You are Saxon by birth (or a Celt, if in a Saxon-based game) and saved by the people you now call your family. You speak the Saxon tongue and have the Saxon looks, but consider yourself a Briton (or a Saxon). You hold no feelings for your old people - or do you?
05	A priceless object (sword, armour or jewelry) owned or protected by your family was stolen by enemies. You have sworn to retrieve it from the thieves.
06	You are afflicted with wanderlust and have never remained for more than a year in any one place. You are therefore well-travelled, but you have no real family and no roots: this makes some people distrust you.
07	A sibling has been betrothed to someone from your childhood that you consider an enemy. You are forced to make a sullen peace with this new in-law but your hatred still burns beneath. What is worse is that you fear your sibling is being turned against you. What can you do to set matters to rights?
08	You believe yourself to be suffering a divine or magical curse. Moan, groan and whinge at every opportunity, or remain completely stoic at every misfortune that befalls you in the future. Who cursed you? Why? Christian or Pagan?
09	You have sworn an oath to complete a task for a dying family member. What is the task? Is it simple or complicated, safe or dangerous? Will it take years to complete or a matter of weeks? What help might you need? What happens if you fail?
10	A bard/skald, priest, or druid visits your community and demonstrates almost supernatural wisdom. You are fascinated by what you see but the individual does not remain long enough for you to learn more. You do, however, receive dreams that show you meeting up with this person again and learning from him. When, where, and how will form a future part of your story.
11	As is common among Celts, you were sent to live with a foster family in a different village. Your foster family was cold and distant towards you: sometimes very cruel. On returning to your true family, they had also become distant with you. What is at the root of this strangeness? Why have you been caught in the middle?
12	Fate has closely watched over you as you grew to adulthood. Siblings have drowned, friends died from plague, parents disgraced, but you have emerged unscathed from everything. Are you truly blessed by the gods (or by God)?
13	You were born with a prominent and distinguishing feature that now provides you with either a life-long nickname (Owain Big-Nose, for example; or Erik the Wide).
14	The spirits have favoured you - even if you are Christian and do not believe in them. You can see them and they can see you. You cannot command them, but you can communicate with them. Whether they lie or not depends on whether you make a successful Superstition roll... is this power something you should keep secret or share?
15	You were viciously bullied when growing up. Now you are mature, it is time for revenge. But who were the bullies, and what form will that revenge take?
16	You were a hostage or ransomed when young - a pawn used by others in some family feud. Your heart tells you to hate those who held you hostage, but, in truth, they were kind to you and you grew to love them, When the obligation was fulfilled, you did not want to leave. Did you leave? If you you returned to your family, how do you feel about them now?

Background Events	
1d100	Event
17	Somehow you have picked up a loyal companion or retainer. Maybe a childhood friend; perhaps a hanger-on from some chance encounter. This does not necessarily make your companion a welcome presence, but the relationship has somehow endured over the years.
18	Your village was raided by the enemy. You watched your family's slaughter. You were too young to do anything. The druid or priest who led the vile sacrifices that followed saw you, laughed, but let you live as the sole survivor of the carnage to tell others of what you saw. You will find that magician one day – and kill them.
19	You have been marked as special by the gods or God. You carry with you a symbol or marking that is of great reverence your religion. This may be a religious treasure or a Holy Relic. Whatever it is, others (druids, priests, sorcerers, shamans) want it and will stop at nothing to get it. What is it? How do you protect it? Why do they want it?
20	You have a favoured and beloved pet which follows you everywhere. It has no abilities or special powers, but offers comfort and companionship.
21	You are considered a hero in your local community – or are regarded with special reverence. What did you do? How did you do it? Are you worthy of all this attention?
22	Blinded in one eye either by an accident or by an act of cruelty. You may use the soubriquet 'One-Eye' although your blindness does not impact on your general daily life.
23	Someone in your family was a thief and lost a hand for it. The reputation has, unfortunately stuck, and whenever anything goes missing all eyes turn to you, even though you are completely innocent. How do you deal with this stigma?
24	You have an uncanny resemblance to someone rich, famous or powerful: a lord perhaps, a hero, warband leader, or even a druid, priest, or enemy of your tribe. Is this a blessing or a curse? Can you use it to your advantage in some way?
25	Your family is engaged in a Blood Feud with a family from a rival clan in the same tribe. For several years no action has been taken by either side, but just recently your enemies have been provocative, trying to rekindle the bloodshed. What started the feud? What revenge should you take? Would it not be better to settle the quarrel before more blood is spilt?
26	Following a drinking contest you discovered that you never suffer from hangovers, no matter what you drink, how much, or how quickly. You always awake the next day as fresh as ever – much to your friends' amazement and annoyance.
27	As a child you were witness to a crime of some form. You were unable to give witness and the criminal got away with their crime. Who was the criminal? What was their crime? They still watch you, and now you are grown there is a chance they may attempt to silence you completely. What do you do?
28	Every member of your family has failed to live beyond the age of 30. The causes of death are many and varied, but everyone thinks your bloodline is cursed. This means you do not make for a good marriage prospect. How can the curse be lifted? Who cursed your family? How long do you have left?
29	When you were a child you nearly died from a fatal disease, but since then you have never, ever been ill. Are you simply paranoid about any type of infection or do you believe you are immune to any form of contagion?
30	A relative who had embraced Christianity, and was an ardent follower of Christ, has suddenly recanted his (or her) views and embraced paganism with renewed fervour. Why is this? Is it a sign that the Christian religion has no real power in Britain? If you are a Christian, how do you feel about this sudden conversion?
31	Several relatives have embraced Christianity and undergone bBaptism. They are now urging you to do the same. If you are Christian already, they are urging you to donate all your worldly possessions to the Church, because God loves paupers and those who think more of others than themselves. How do you feel about this? Will you do as they want?
32	You have made an enemy of the local priest or druid, regardless of what your religion is. What did you do to offend him? How can you make amends? Do you want to? The priest or druid can make a lot of trouble for you – how are you going to deal with that?

Background Events	
1d100	Event
33	You grew up or were born mute, but still able to communicate with sign language or grunts – use the Dance skill to carry across complex ideas
34	Your family was hunted by powerful foes. Why was this? Why did your family need to keep moving and hiding? What do the pursuers want? Are they still following you? Should you confront them? You are sick and tired of being on the run.
35	You are a bastard-born. Your mother swears your father was a man of note and station, but she herself is of low status and you are considered even lower than she is. Where your father is, no one knows, but you would love to meet him some day and discover the truth about him. Perhaps, if reunited with your father, the stigma of your birth might be erased.
36	You have a grotesque physical deformity of a random location – no ill effects, as you have learned to adapt, but you must keep the deformity hidden to prevent causing horror or disgust. However, your deformity is considered a blessing by a local druid – a mark of the gods. How do you react to this? Does it make you special – or more wretched? Much depends on your religion.
37	As a child, you stumbled on a hoard of coins buried by the Romans and forgotten when they fled Britain. There is enough silver there to keep you in luxury for many years. By rights, it should be declared to your tribe and become communal wealth, but you have been reluctant to do this. You also haven't been able to spend the money because it will raise questions. What will you do? Who can you trust?
38	You are hopelessly in love with someone in your immediate community. He or she will only accept your love if you prove yourself worthy. This could be valour in battle, undertaking a hazardous expedition or quest, or obtaining something the object of your love wants and desires. There is much competition for his or her affections. How will you live-up to the expectations?
39	In a fit of anger you cursed someone you were temporarily angry with. Two days later, that person died in tragic circumstances. Everyone blames you for the death and you even blame yourself. You feel you must atone for the curse: how do you do it? What is expected of you?
40	You are a twin. Your brother or sister has similar characteristics and skills to yourself but you are clearly different people. Are you close, as twins usually are, or estranged? You always seem to know where your sibling is, even if relations between you are not good.
41	Inadvertent comments resulted in a fight, battle, or war – the remark or action was innocent but the repercussions tragic. What were the comments? Are you still at fault?
42	You met a great hero (or villain) at a time when he or she was unknown. You suspected, perhaps, that this person was destined for greatness (or infamy), but you still became friends before you parted. Will they remember you? Will you still be friends?
43	Someone of power and influence in your community has taken a shine to you. They automatically become an Ally and will speak in your defence or offer help if its is needed. From time to time you are expected to repay these favours, but you do not mind. It is good to have friends in high places.
44	Your mother disappeared immediately after you were born. You have learned from a relative that she was not a human at all, but a demigod, visiting the Mortal World out of curiosity. If you are a pagan, this is astounding news, if it is true. If you are a Christian, it is terrible, terrible news and means you must seek divine help to rid you of the taint and bring you closer to Christ. Is what you have been told true? Do you have a hidden destiny? Can you accept the news?
45	You are utterly terrified of insects. You can face a horde of the enemy, but spiders and creepy-crawlies drive you to a cold sweat.
46	Your family has a reputation for luck. Everything your family does turns out splendidly; it has wealth it has never seemed to work for; it has a strong reputation; no ill has ever befallen it. You have, however, heard something that makes you suspicious of this charmed life you've led. How did your family come by this luck? Was a much higher price – perhaps a darker price – paid for it?
47	Your clan captured either Saxon or Celtic warriors who were made into slaves. One was gifted to your family and you found that this warrior was not the demon everyone had made-out, but a good, kind man who just speaks a different language and believes in different things. You became friendly and he was grateful for little kindnesses. Somehow he managed to escape and he came to your hut. 'I will remember you, little one', he said, 'and will be your friend for as long as I live. If you are ever amongst my people, give them the name Red Mane – everyone knows me – and that will give you safe passage.'

Background Events	
1d100	Event
48	Your family was ever cruel to you. Why, you do not know, but your siblings always seemed to receive better treatment and more favour. You have always been denied. That is why, at the first opportunity, you left them behind, forgetting them, and seeking the life of an adventurer.
49	The local wise woman claims you are a changeling – an inhuman creature swapped for a real baby shortly after birth. No one believes her, she is quite, quite mad; but you have always thought there was something different about you. You find it difficult to fit-in, and sometimes you have a feeling you are being watched – especially at night. Could the wise woman have been right?
50	Your family was involved in some community event that has made them either famous or infamous. The legacy of what they did follows you everywhere. What did your family do? Can you shake the reputation? Do you want to?
51	Your family was wealthy once, but is now reduced to poverty. How did it lose its fortune? Was it due to circumstance or the actions of others? If others, how did they ruin you – and how will you make them pay?
52	Your family, previously poor and beggared, has ever struggled to survive. Yet when you were a lad somehow your father attained great wealth. How did he come by this money? What effect did it have on the family? Will somebody arrive to reclaim or perhaps terminate the mysterious fortune?
53	Savaged by a wolf as a child, you gain a fearsome facial scar but now wear its skin as a cloak
54	You accidentally killed a close friend or sibling when playing together. The horror of the situation caused you to flee, remaining silent about the tragedy. When the adults finally went out to search for the missing adolescent no trace could be found, although they searched the area where you left the body. You have lived with the guilt ever since, but whatever became of your compatriot? Did they escape death or did something unspeakable happen to the body?
55	You recently experienced a supernatural epiphany, which shook you. Whilst out alone a god personally came to speak with you, or perhaps a host of spirits manifested and danced about you. The event, whatever it was, may be seen as a blessing by the local community or conversely deemed blasphemous.
56	You survived a terrible plague that ravaged your community. Many died, and those who lived have formed a special bond. You are also immune to this strain of the plague – something others see as a gift of the gods (or of God).
57	You inherited your uncle's Throw-Board and dice. There is nothing remarkable about the gaming pieces, but whenever you use them, you always seem to win. Is it good fortune, some kind of magic, or had your uncle found a fool-proof way of cheating?
59	A female relative is the most beautiful creature for many, many miles. As the two of you are great friends, you also become the focus of attention from those who desire her. Are you jealous? Are you pleased? Is the attention annoying? Can you make use of it?
60	You and a group of friends formed a warband as children, fighting imaginary Saxons (or Celts). As grown-ups you have gone your separate ways, but you feel sure that you are destined to fight together, for real, as brothers (or sisters) in arms. Where are your friends now? How can you bring them back together?
61	Near your community is a ring of stones raised either by the gods or the Old People who once lived all across Britain. The stones fascinate you, and you feel drawn to them constantly. What relationship do you have with the stones? What do they mean to you? Are you the only one who feels this way?
62	The older children used to tease you that the nearby forests contained terrible monsters: dwarves, goblins, trolls, vicious soul-eating spirits, and the like. When you grew up you started to dismiss these tales as stupid stories – that is, until several local people disappeared while in the woods. They were never found and now the people believe that the tales of monsters are not stories but the truth. How can you prove them wrong – or prove them right? Can you find the missing people of your community?
63	Your settlement was attacked by Saxons (or Celts) and although you tried to hide, you were dragged kicking and screaming from safety and forced to entertain a drunken group of warriors who stank of blood, sweat, and piss. You must've entertained them well, because they let you live. However, you have never forgotten the smell, the sound of their laughter or the humiliation: you have vowed to make one of those bastards entertain you if ever you get the chance.

Background Events	
1d100	Event
64	A druid insisted that someone close to you be sacrificed to ensure a good harvest following several poor and failed harvest years. Although your relative went willingly to the wicker man, you have not forgotten the screams that followed. The harvest was no better that year. You now hate all druids and abhor any human sacrifice.
65	Priests came to your community seeking donations for the church they were building not far away. Money was given both to please God but also to make the priests go away. However they keep returning and still the church is not built. Where does the money go? When will the church be finished? Can the priests be trusted?
66	You were born, or have become, profoundly deaf. You can communicate by reading the shapes people's lips make and your senses of sight and smell have deepened to compensate for the loss of hearing.
67	You accompanied a trading mission from your community to a place across the seas. While most in the delegation spent the sea voyage vomiting over the side of the boat, you revelled in the sway of the waves, the roll of the sea, the spray on your face, and sheer freedom of sailing. You have never lost that love and you yearn for the sea.
68	Your grandfather and father have always been obsessed with all things Roman. The Romans were great inventors, builders, soldiers, and governors, and what they did for Britain can never be dismissed or forgotten. Although they were invaders, they enforced peace and many Britons chose to become Roman – just as some Celts choose to become Saxons, and vice-versa. You have grown up with an appreciation of, and wonder for, all things Roman and seek them out when you can. You like to dress in Roman styles and hope, someday, to visit Rome or Constantinople.
69	To unite either feuding clans or feuding tribes, it has been decided that you will marry the daughter/son of the enemy. You met for the first time at the betrothal ceremony and, to your astonishment, found you really liked your intended wife/husband. Regrettably, the relations broke down badly and the intended alliance will not take place – but you have fallen in love. You loyalties are torn between your people and the one you love. What will you do? Who will you choose?
70	Your community was afflicted by pestilence. The Christian priests said it was because God was angry because there were so many sinners in the community and they had to be driven out. Strangely, all these sinners were pagans and they were hounded from their homes, their possessions stolen, and the clothes ripped from their backs. Did you take part? Were you one of the fugitives? Was the priest right? Was the pestilence lifted?
71	A very close relative or childhood friend betrays you, leading to loss of reputation, castigation, and shame for you and your family. Why did your relative or friend do this? Was it part of a larger plan? You cannot rid yourself of the need for vengeance and so this person is now your Enemy.
72	You have a recurring dream about a prominent landmark (a river, hill, gorge, forest, or similar). In the dream you are lord of the area where this landmark is located and have great pride in your territories. You know this is your destiny: you must find this place, visit it, and engineer your life so that your fate is manifest.
73	You discovered an animal cub or bird egg and raised it by hand – you gain a fully grown wild animal or bird of prey as a loyal pet, but must feed and control the creature.
74	You are polydactyl – an extra finger on either one or both hands. You don't gain any special benefit from this curious feature, but it certainly ensures your are talked about. Pagans see it is a favourable mark of the gods: Christians see it as a mark of the The Devil. You see it as a bloody nuisance because it is difficult to get gloves that fit.
75	You have eyes of quite different colours. This may be the result of a childhood accident, illness, or simply a quirk of nature. It makes you easy to identify, but is also viewed as a mark of suspicion by both pagans and Christians. Pagans think you can see into the Spirit World with one of your eyes, while Christians believe it is the Mark of Cain.
76	You have an unusually strong stomach and palate for foods that others find repulsive. The smell and taste do not bother you, and you find unusual textures interesting. You are not immune to the possible effects of eating diseased food or drink, but the sight, smell, and taste do not put you off trying them.

Background Events	
1d100	Event
77	One particular foodstuff is simply unpalatable to you. The merest smell or taste has you retching or gagging: cheese, eggs, ale, bacon, game; it doesn't make you ill per se, but you just have no tolerance for it.
78	Your father claims your family is descended from the original line of kings who founded the land: if there was ever an entitlement to High Kingship, it is your family! The proof of this claim was lost long ago — destroyed by the enemy usurpers who set your family on its present course. You should reclaim your birthright. Find the proof needed to show that you and your family are the rightful rulers.
79	A bag of old bones has been in your family for generations. It is claimed that the bones belong to a great hero or Saint of your religion. As such the bones are sacred relics and must always be treated with reverence. Occasionally, your grandmother would set the bones in a line and chant prayers over them. You always thought she was a bit strange. Then, a few years ago, a druid or priests came to your home and demanded to see the bag of bones. Your grandmother brought them forth and the holy man gazed into the bag. He let out a terrified scream, dropped the bag, and fled from your home. When you looked in there, the bones appeared to be quite normal. Now the bag is in your possession. What caused the druid or priest to flee? What do the bones mean? Who did they belong to?
80	A poor traveller came to your village seeking help and shelter. You fed him, clothed him, and tended his wounds. He claimed to be just a lowly wanderer who had been robbed on the road. The next day, he had gone, taking all your family's wealth. Recently you attended a feast with lots of rich and important people. There, at the high table, laughing and joking, was the 'poor' traveller who robbed you. You did nothing at the time because you could not be completely certain, but now you are sure it is same man. What will you do? How will you gain justice for your family? Will anyone believe you?
81	When you were a child, you had a group of close friends. Playing together near some old Roman ruins you found a hidden pit that contained a bag of money and jewels: silver, gold, and precious stones. You agreed to keep your treasure a secret and, when you older, to return together and divide it amongst you equally. You hid the treasure well, so that only the four of you could find it. The day came and you went to retrieve your spoils and found the treasure had gone. It was well hidden and only the four of you could've known about it. Did any of you tell anyone else? Has one of you taken the money and is pretending innocence? Were you watched? You are now all suspicious and resentful of each other. You want to discover the truth. More to the point, you want the money.
82	Members of your clan are traders. You went on a long trip with them north (or south) of the Great Wall built by the Romans. You spent several months among these strange people, learning their customs, and observing their strange ways. You now feel a certain kinship with them, despite the differences between your tribes and ways of life.
83	After an especially spectacular drinking contest you awoke to find that, not only did you have the hangover from hell, you had also acquired a peculiar, swirling tattoo across your shoulder and upper arm. You don't remember having it done, and it looks like it should have taken many hours to do. Your companions were just as drunk, and none of them remember how you got the tattoo — none of them have one. Despite not knowing where it came from, you like it. It is different — much different to the tattoos of your tribe. You also suspect that, one day, you will discover how you got it.
84	You survived a fire that destroyed part of your settlement. Roll 1d20 twice to discover which Hit Locations were badly scarred by the flames. You are now terrified of large fires: anything larger than a camp or cooking fire causes you to retreat to a very safe distance, no matter how cold it might be.
85	As a child you nearly drowned when you fell into a fast-moving river. The water is now a terrifying place for you: you can only cross a river via a sturdy bridge or a very shallow ford. The open sea is just too terrifying to contemplate.
86	Dared by other children, you climbed the highest tree in the local forest and almost reached the top when you lost your footing and fell. You broke several bones in the fall and, although you fully recovered, you are now terrified of heights. Climbing anything higher than 10 feet requires you to make a Willpower roll to carry on and, if you can avoid a climb, you will.
87	You are terrified of confined spaces. Houses and huts are fine, but anything that restricts your movement is terrifying to you and requires a Willpower roll for you to even contemplate entering it. If you are forced into a confined space you need to succeed in a Hard Willpower roll to avoid being paralysed with fear.

Background Events	
1d100	Event
88	Your hair is turning prematurely grey, making you look about 10 years older than you are, but also rather distinguished and mature. You've tried staining your hair with a variety of herbal dyes, but all too soon the grey shows-through again. Do you continue trying to hide it, or embrace the silver mane?
89	On a hunting expedition, you somehow became separated from the main party and were lost in the woods. You came into a secluded dell where a beautiful woman, with golden hair and white robes, was waiting. She knew your name, knew you were lost, and asked you to stay and talk with her. You do not remember what you spoke about, but when you realised it was getting dark you said you had to go. She smiled, kissed you on the forehead, and told you how to find your way to get back to your settlement. When you got home, you found that a whole week had gone by: your family had thought you killed or taken as a slave. When you told them of the Woman with the Golden Hair, they never mentioned your absence again. You sense there's more to all of this. What could it mean?
90	You made an important discovery that needed to be reported to your lord. It was necessary for you to confide in someone else so that you would be able to gain the lord's attention, but the confidante went behind your back and claimed the credit for what you had discovered (and was rewarded accordingly). You feel cheated and driven to expose the treachery you've suffered. How will you go about it?
91	You were made a slave as a child by Saxons (or by Celts, if a Saxon). You were branded on the left cheek with one of the Saxon's strange, angular runes indicating you were someone's property. How did you escape from slavery? Did someone save you? Nevertheless the scar is still there as a reminder. You can try to disguise it with face paints such as woad, or a covering tattoo, but you know, first hand, what it is to be a slave.
92	You either were bequeathed, or found, a scraped deerskin that has been painted with an outline of Britain. It clearly shows the Great Wall, the great rivers, and the hills. It also has a number of deliberate markings made across the map, thirteen in total, which are both north and south of the Great Wall. What do these markings signify? Are they the locations of the Thirteen Treasures of Britain? Perhaps they mark Roman cities? Maybe they mean something else. The map fascinates you and you intend to find out what it represents.
93	Near your village is a long, humped burial mound. It has been sealed for centuries and everyone says that it contains the remains of a chieftain of the Old People. As a dare, you ventured into it, squeezing between the collapsed stones of the blocked entrance. Inside it was cold and damp. You found no body, but you did find a strange stone, the size of a man's fist, carved with many strange marks and sigils. You brought it out of the barrow and hid it. A week later, a wolf killed most of the village's sheep. A month later all the chickens were killed by foxes. A year later all the cows grew sick with fever and died. You never returned the stone – something prevents you from doing so. What will die next?.
94	Your father was a boastful man who claimed that, when you reached adulthood, you would accomplish something very special – something no one else had ever managed. What did he promise? Can you fulfil his boasts? Do you want to? Why did he make the boast in the first place?
95	One of your relatives killed a druid: this means your family is now cursed by the Gods (even if you are Christian and do not worship them). What form does the curse take? How does it affect you? What must you do to lift it?
96	Your brother was someone you loved very much and you got along famously. He was sent for fostering to a distant clan. When he returned, he had changed beyond the belief: the kind, loving brother had become a cruel, snide, arrogant boor. You love him still, but hate what he has become. Who is to blame? The clan or your brother? How does this affect your relationship? He seems to loathe and despise you.

Background Events	
1d100	Event
97	As a child you were chosen to be the focus of a great and intense religious ritual. The experience had a profound effect on you, and you now have no doubt that the gods (or God) exist, shape everything in this world, and have a destiny for everyone. You especially have a destiny to fulfill. What was revealed to you during that ritual? How does it now guide your life?
98	Just before you became an adult, you were seduced by the wife of the chieftain. She did it in secret and what she showed you and what you experienced was so pleasurable that you cannot get her out of your mind – even though you cannot, and should not, think about her in that way. She mostly ignores you these days, but every so often she offers a sly smile and you are filled with lust. What will you do? Can you control your urges?
99	You murdered someone. Why? Was it revenge? Self-defence? Who did you kill? Was it a stranger or someone you knew? You've hidden the body and – so far – it has never been discovered, but you live in fear that someone will find it and start asking questions. If they ask the right questions, then the clues might point back to you.
100	Roll twice more on this table, re-rolling if you get a result of 00, and apply both results.

Families, Allies, Contacts, Rivals and Enemies

These are all determined as per pages 21 to 22 of the MYTHRAS rules.

Careers

Mythic Britain characters are handled slightly differently in terms of their career choice. To maximise the adventuring opportunities, but also to represent the fact that many Celts are warriors with a broad range of skills, Mythic Britain characters have two careers: Warrior, plus one career that acts as a 'down-time' profession – something the character has trained in and practices when not required to fight or directly serve his or her lord. This means that Skill Points for both career and Bonus Skill Points are adjusted in their distribution, as follows:

Career Skill Points	
Career	Points to Distribute
Warrior	100
Secondary Career	75
Bonus Skills Points	75

The rules governing distribution (number of Professional Skills, Hobby Skills, limitations on points placed into a single skill) are the same as for the MYTHRAS core rules.

The Warrior/Secondary Career structure is the same for Celts and Saxons.

Bards and Druids

If the character is playing a Bard or Druid, then the Warrior/Secondary Career structure does not apply: Bards and Druids are specialists focused on their careers. However, the skill distribution is slightly different to reflect the intense, specialist training. Bards and Druids have 175 points to distribute amongst their Career skills, and 75 points for Bonus Skill Points.

The Bard and Druid careers (Skald and Læce being the Saxon equivalents) are outlined below. They are based on the Entertainer and Shaman careers but with necessary modifications to reflect the setting.

Bard/Skald

Standard Skills

Athletics, Brawn, Deceit, Influence, Insight, Sing, Willpower

Professional Skills

Acting, Art (Poetry), Lore (Britain/Saxon), Lore (Myths), Oratory, Musicianship (Harp), Sleight

Druid/Læce

(Læce being the Saxon equivalent, and pronounced 'leech')

Standard Skills

Customs, Dance, Deceit, Influence, Insight, Locale, Willpower

Professional Skills

Binding (Druidic or Norse Tradition), Healing, Lore (Britain), Lore (Pagan), Oratory, Sleight, Trance

Secondary Career List

- Beast Handler
- Courtesan
- Crafter
- Entertainer
- Farmer
- Fisher
- Herder
- Hunter
- Merchant
- Miner
- Priest*
- Sailor
- Shaman
- Thief

*Christian characters only

Superstition

Superstition measures the reliance individuals place on supernatural causality – that is, one event influencing another without the two events being in any way connected. A good example of this are omens, signs and talismans: an owl's screech at a particular time constituting a bad omen for a very recent event or decision; or habitually touching a religious symbol or spitting to ward away the presence of evil. The higher the Superstition score, the more superstitious the character is (and the more willing to accept supernatural events or supernatural interpretations of natural events).

Superstition is rated like any other skill: it can be improved using Experience Rolls if the character so wishes, but it also increases whenever a character witnesses, or is the subject of, supernatural events or effects. Witnessing a supernatural event of any kind – be it a spirit summoning or the working of a Miracle – automatically increases the Superstition score by 1 point. The character can try to resist this increase if he wishes by attempting to roll higher than his Superstition on 1d100 (and adding his INT to the roll). This represents a character's ability to rationalise what he has just witnessed and thus protect against his superstition deepening. Characters who are the victims/subjects of magic gain 1d3 points of Superstition – unless they can rationalise the experience as already described.

Superstition has a direct effect on Willpower when Willpower is used to resist magic or the supernatural.

Superstition Table

Superstition %	Willpower Grade Becomes Harder by...
01-25	0
26-50	1 step
51-75	2 steps
76-100	3 steps
100+	4 steps

Thus, a character with Superstition 74% and Willpower 60% would find his Willpower rolls reduced by 2 grades, taking a normal roll to Formidable (i.e., reduced by half, or 30%) for the purposes of resisting magic.

Druids are exempt from Superstition: they are trained to deal with the supernatural as a matter of course and are unaffected by the usual supernatural fears that grip most people. However, druids can actively use Superstition in their dealings with others. By spending a Magic Point, a druid can invoke an opponent's Superstition, resulting in a reduction to Willpower, during mundane dealings. The druid does this by dropping ominous hints

of what will happen if someone does not do as instructed, or use their sheer force of rank and personality to gain their own way. For example, a druid, trying to convince one of the characters to sacrifice a prisoner as part of a ritual, must succeed in an Influence roll opposed by the character's Willpower. By spending a Magic Point, the druid intimates that, if the character does not carry out the sacrificial killing, one of his loved ones will die instead. The character's Superstition is 45%, and so his Willpower roll becomes Hard. He fails in the opposed test and meekly carries out the druid's command, terrified of the consequences.

Starting Superstition Score

The starting Superstition score is: (21-INT)+POW.

More intelligent characters are better able to rationalise the world around them; or, in the case of Christians, explain supernatural events in terms of God's work.

Pagan Characters add a further 20% to their Superstition score.

Superstition can be used as a skill to recognise omens, signs, and portents. A successful roll lets the character know the right meaning of such a thing, and the right sounds, actions or gestures to make (touching a piece of iron, spitting, praying, invoking a god's or spirit's name, and so on) to help avert any impending misfortune. Those with high Superstition scores – 76 and above – tend to have a constant wariness, forever on the look-out for signs, portents and heralds of misfortune, and constantly make the necessary symbols to protect themselves. Even Christians can have high Superstition scores, manifesting as constantly invoking the name of God, Jesus, Saints, or the Virgin Mary, and touching a crucifix or making the sign of the cross.

Money and Equipment

Barter and trade is the most common form of exchange in Mythic Britain. What coins exist stem from the Roman age or those minted elsewhere in Europe and brought into Britain by merchants and traders. Neither the Celts nor Saxons mint their own coins.

Nevertheless, silver remains the de-facto currency and is the most common precious metal circulating in Britain. Calculate the amount of Silver Pieces a character has according to Cultural Background, Social Class, and Career as per normal. However, only 1d20+5% of that amount is represented by coinage. The rest is jewelry (such as finger and arm rings, brooches, and the like), physical possessions, or property. It is common for jewelry to be used as payment – either in part or whole. Both Celts and Saxons will hack apart items of silver or gold into smaller pieces to pay for what they need.

Armour and Weapons

Metal armour is a rarity in Mythic Britain. It exists, generally in the form of a mail coat, but is expensive to manufacture (and beyond the capabilities of many smiths), expensive to maintain (iron rusts: it needs frequent polishing), and heavy to wear. A coat of mail, and corresponding full helmet, is only going to be found in the possession of the richest and most successful warlords. Most warriors – Celts and Saxons – rely on leather, hides, and furs for protection. Helmets, when worn, tend to be leather and iron caps, although some iron helmets from Rome's occupation have survived, being passed down from father to son.

The weapons of choice are the spear and shield. A spear is a good, all-round weapon that can be thrown as well as used as a melee weapon, and is cheap to make and easy to learn. Most Celtic warriors rely on nothing else and treat their spear as an extension of their being. Shields, too, are essential. Celts use a large, lozenge-shaped shield that is something between a kite and Roman scutum. Saxons tend to favour round shields, similar to the Viking Round of the MYTHRAS rules. For weapons, Saxons use spears too, but supplement their arsenal with a long, thin-bladed weapon called a seax: to intents and purposes, a seax is somewhere between a dagger and a shortsword: very useful in a shield wall for stabbing under and between shields.

Other Equipment

The equipment and prices found on pages 59 to 61 of MYTHRAS are available in *Mythic Britain*. Larger settlements clearly have more items available than smaller communities, and it is very often likely that, in a small settlement, something someone needs already belongs to someone else. Nevertheless, there are shops in medium- and large-sized settlements and, where

there are no shops or manufacturers available, most people are prepared to trade even important possessions if the price is right.

The one exception where price and availability is concerned is swords. Sword making is a skilled business and quality comes at a price. The range of swords is limited, too: see the Weapons Table overleaf.

Weapon Descriptions

Seax

This is the short, single-edged stabbing weapon favoured by Saxons in a shield wall. It is not a common weapon amongst the Britons and is only likely to be used by Saxons.

Short Sword

Remarkably similar to the Roman gladius, the Short Sword has quite a wide blade for its short length and is a stabbing weapon used in the shield wall. It generally has a heavy pommel that can be used as a blunt weapon to stun an opponent.

Long Sword

This is not the equivalent of the Long Sword described in the MYTHRAS rules. It is shorter in length, thinner and lighter, but longer than either a Short Sword or Seax. Like the Short Sword a thick, heavy pommel allows for it to be used as blunt, stunning weapon.

Celtic Shield

Not dissimilar to the Roman scutum, the Celtic Shield is long and lozenge shaped with a heavy central boss and a nailed iron rim. The Shield is made with a slight curve across its face to help deflect blows.

Saxon Round

Almost identical to the Viking Round Shield, the Saxon Shield is reinforced with leather and iron and has a central iron boss.

Armour

Use the Armour Table opposite for armouring options. Note that the Suit ENC/Cost/Armour Penalty column (found on the MYTHRAS Armour Table on page 86 of the core rules) has been removed: this is because full suits of armour, covering all seven Hit Locations are simply not available. Most armour focuses on the head and torso allowing the mobility of the limbs. Legs (and, more precisely, ankles) are likely to be protected by rigid strips of metal sewn into boots or worn above sandals, but full leg and arm protection is rare.

Weapons

Melee Weapon	Damage	Size	Reach	Special Effects	ENC	AP/HP	Traits	Cost
Axe	1d6	M	M	Bleed, Sunder	1	4/8	-	100 SP
Dagger	1d4+1	S	S	Bleed, Impale	1	4/8	Thrown	60 SP
Hatchet	1d6	S	S	Bleed	1	3/6	Thrown	
Seax	1d4+2	M	S	Bleed, Impale	1	6/8	-	100 SP
Short Sword	1d6	M	S	Bleed, Impale, Stun Location	1	6/8	-	200 SP
Long Sword	1d6+2	M	M	Bleed, Impale, Stun Location	1	6/10	-	600 SP
Shortspear	1d8+1	M	L	Impale	2	4/5	Set, Thrown	25 SP

Shields

Celtic	1d3+1	H	S	Bash, Stun Location	3	4/15	Ranged Parry; Passive Blocks 4 locations	150 SP
Saxon Round	1d4	L	S	Bash, Stun Location	3	4/12	Ranged Parry; Passive Blocks 4 locations	150 SP

Armour

Construction	Example	AP	ENC	Cost per Location	Locations Available
Natural/Cured	Furs, Hides	1	2	20	All
Padded/Quilted	Leather Tunic	2	1	80	Chest, Abdomen
Reinforced Leather	Helmet, Reinforced boots/ sandals	3	2	160	Head, Legs
Scale*	Bronze or iron scales over a leather coat	4	3	1200	Chest, Abdomen
Mail*	Close-knit links of iron over a leather coat	5	4	2000	Chest, Abdomen
Plate	Open Helmet with nose and cheek guards	5	4	600	Head

**Scale and Mail come as a single coat covering both chest and abdomen*

Names

The final stage — although some consider it the first — is to name the character. The following pages have copious examples of authentic names for male and female Britons and Saxons, and these can be used freely or as inspiration for an invented name.

Note that surnames do not exist; a character's name, if a Celtic Briton, is the name given by his father or mother, followed by 'ap' or 'an' which means 'son of' or 'daughter of'. So, in choosing an authentic name for a Briton, then you will also be naming the character's father or mother. Saxons follow a similar pattern, with the conjunctive 'ap' being replaced by 'son' or 'dotter' (daughter) appended to the parent's given name. So, a couple of Celtic and Saxon examples are the following:

Bryce ap Eoin (BRY-kee ap OH-in)
Iola an Saith (EYE-OH-la an SAYTH)

Osric Torson (OZ-rick TOR-son)
Lora Kendradotter (LAW-ra KENdru-DOTTER)

In both Celt and Saxon communities, sons are named for their fathers and daughters for their mothers. As characters adventure and gain status, they main gain a soubriquet describing their feats, traits, or appearance: Emrys the Strong, for example; or Beorn Ironside — but such titles are earned, rather than being given.

Celtic Names

The following names are traditional, Brythonic names for both males and females. Brythonic is the precursor to Welsh, and so the Welsh pronunciation needs to be understood to articulate some of the less straightforward vowel and consonant combinations.

There are no silent letters in Brythonic; every letter has a sound, and the sound is vocalised. The letters B, C, D, G, and K are hard sounds: *bad, cat, get, dog, kite*, for example. A single *F* is pronounced with a 'v' sound - so Derfel is Der-vel; however the 'ff' combination is is the traditional f sound - so Ffodor is 'Fodor' rather than 'Vodor' (which it would be if a single f was used). The letter Y is pronounced as the short 'i', 'in' for instance. Where the 'dd' combination is found, it is pronounced as 'th' - so *Gryfydd* is pronounced Griv-ith. The 'wr' combination is pronounced 'ear' - so *Albanwr* is pronounced Alban-eer. Perhaps the most tricky, the 'll' combination, is roughly pronounced as a a rolled 'cloo' sound; so *Llwch* is pronounced Cloo-wuk. The 'ae' combination is pronounced 'Aye'.

In the following lists, female names are italicised.

Names

A

Adair, Ahern, Ahearn, Ailbe, Ailill, Airell, Alan, Allen, Allan, Allyn, Alanson, Angus, Anghus, Aengus, Aonghus, Anna, Anant, Ansgar, Anwell, Anwyl, Anyon, Aod, Ap Owen, Arawn, Argyle, Arlen, Arlin, Arlyn, Arlan, Arthur, Artur, Art, Atty, Attie, Arturo

Aberfa, Abertha, Adain, Adara, Addfwyn, Addiena, Adyna, Aelwyd, Aeron, Amser, Angharad, Anna, Annwyl, Argel, Arglwyddes, Argoel, Argraff, Arial, Ariana, Arianell, Ariene, Aranrhod, Arianrhod, Arianwen, Arlais, Armes, Arthes, Arwydd, Asgre, Auron, Avenable

B

Baird, Barry, Bairrfhionn, Barra, Bearach, Bearchan, Beacan, Becan, Bedwyr, Bendigeidfran, Bevan, Bevin, Bevyn, Blaine, Blayne, Blane, Blainey, Blayney, Blair, Boadhagh, Bowden, Bowdyn, Boden, Bodyn, Boyden, Boyd, Bowen, Bowyn, Boynton, Bran, Brann, Brasil, Breasal, Basil, Breanainn, Breandan, Bredon, Brandan, Brendan, Bran, Bram, Broin, Brennan, Brett, Bret, Brian, Bryan, Bryant, Briant, Brice, Bryce, Bricriu, Britomartus, Burgess

Banon, Berth, Berthog, Bethan, Blanchfleur, Blodeuwedd, Blodwen, Braith, Brandgaine, Branwen, Bregus, Briallen, Brisen, Bronwen, Buddug, Brynn

C

Cachamwri, Cadell, Cadman, Calder, Calum, Cameron, Camero, Camey, Caoimhghin, Caradoc, Cardew, Carew, Carey, Cary, Carney, Car, Carr, Cathaoir, Cathair, Carrol, Carroll, Casey, Cassivellaunus, Caswallan, Cathal, Cahal, Conall, Connell, Cathbad, Cedric, Celyddon, Chad, Clust, Clustfeinad, Cocidius, Coinneach, Conall, Conall Cernach, Conan, Conant, Con, Conn, Cuinn, Conchobar, Condan, Condon, Conlaoch, Conn, Connla, Conroy,

Conway, Corann, Cormac, Cairbre, Carbry, Cradawg, Cuchulain, Culain, Culann, Culhwch, Cullen, Custennin, Cynyr

Cadwyn, Caethes, Cafell, Canaid, Cari, Caron, Carys, Cate, Cath, Catrin, Ceinwyn, Ceri, Ceridwen, Cerwen, Cigfa, Clarisant, Cordelia, Corsen, Cragen, Creiddylad, Creirwy, Cymreiges

D

Dallas, Daman, Darcy, Dearg, Dermot, Desmond, Devin, Devyn, Dillion, Dinsmore, Doane, Donald, Don, Doyle, Doy, Dughall, Dougal, Doughal, Donat, Donal, Domhnall, Donall, Doran, Dorran, Donnally, Donnelly, Donnchadh, Donogh, Doughlas, Douglas, Drem, Driscoll, Druce, Drudwyn, Drummond, Duane, Dewain, Dwayne, Duer, Duff, Dubv, Duffy, Duncan, Dunham, Dyfed

Daron, Dee, Del, Dera, Derwen, Deryn, Deverell, Dicra, Dierdre, Difyr, Dilys, Don, Druantia, Drysi, Dwyn, Dylis

E

Ea, Edan, Eburacon, Efnisien, Egan, Eghan, Egomas, Einion, Elidor, Emrys, Erim, Evan, Evnissyen, Ewen, Ewan, Ewyn, Eoghann, Eoin

Ebrill, Efa, Eheubryd, Eira, Eirianwen, Eiriol, Elaine, Elen, Eleri, Ellylw, Eluned, Eneuawy, Enfys, Enid, Enrhydreg, Epona, Erdudvyl, Eres, Essyllt, Eurneid, Eurolwyn, Eyslk

F

Farrel, Farrell, Ferchar, Ferdiad, Ferghus, Fergus, Fearghus, Ferris, Fiacre, Fiacra, Fiallan, Fiamain, Finbar, Finnbar, Fynbar, Finnobarr, Finian, Finn, Fingal, Floyd, , Forsa

Fiona, Ffanci, Ffion, Fflur, Ffraid

G

Gall, Galvin, Galvyn, Gawain, Gelban, Gildas, Gilmore, Gilroy, Girard, Glen, Glyn, Glenn, Glifieu, Gorsedd, Gruddieu, Guy, Gwalchmai, Gwawl, Gwefl, Gwern, Gwernach, Gwri, Gwynham

Gaenor, Ganieda, Garan, Genevieve, Gladys, Glenna, Glenys, Glynis, Goewin, Goleuddydd, Gorawen, Guinevere, Gwaeddan, Gwanwyn, Gwawr, Gwen, Gwenda, Gwendolyn, Gwener, Gweneth, Gwenhwyfar, Gwenledyr, Gwenith, Gwenllian, Gwenn Alarch, Gwenno, Gwerfyl, Gwladys, Gwyneira, Gwyneth

H

Hafgan, Halwn, Hefeydd, Heilyn, Henbeddestr, Henwas, Herne, Hoel, Huarwar, Hueil, Huon

Hafgan, Hafren, Heledd, Hellawes, Heuldys, Heulwen, Heulyn, Hywela

I

Iden, Innis, Inness, Irvin, Irven, Irvyn, Irving

Idelle, Igerna, Iola, Isolde

K

Kalen, Kailen, Kalan, Kallan, Kheelan, Kellen, Kane, Kayne, Karney, Kearney, Keane, Keene, Kegan, Keegan, Keaghan, Keir, Kelvin, Kelvyn, Kelwin, Kelwyn, Kendall, Kendal, Kendhal, Kenneth, Kent, Kentigern, Kermit, Kermode, Kerry, Keary, Kerwin, Kerwyn, Kirwin, Kirwyn, Kieran, Kevin, Kevyn, Kevan, Killian, Kilian, Kunagnos, Kynthelig

Kelemon, Kigva

L

Lairgnen, Lee, Leigh, Leith, Lesley, Leslie, Lincoln, Lir, Llewelyn, Lloyd, Llyr

Ladwys, Leanne, Linette, Llinos, Llio, Lowri, Lysanor

M

Mabon, Mac, Mack, Maccus, Macklin, Macklyn, Maddox, Maddock, Malcolm, Malvin, Malvyn, Melvin, Melvyn, Melville, Matholwch, Medr, Medredydd, Menw, Merlin, Merlyn, Morfran, Morgan, Morven, Morvyn, Mariner, Marvin, Marvyn, Moryn, Murray, Murry, Murdoch, Murtagh, Mynogan

Mabd, Mair, Maledisant, Mali, Marged, Meghan, Melangell, Meleri, Meredith, Meriel, Modlen, Modron, Mon, Morfudd, Morgan, Morgana, Morgause, Morvudd, Morwen, Myfanwy

N

Naois, Neal, Neil, Nealon, Nell, Neale, Niall, Neill, Niallan, Nyle, Nels, Nelson, Nemausus, Newlin, Newlyn, Niece, Neese, Nisien, Nolan, Noland

Nerys, Nesta, Neued, Nia, Niamh, Nimue, Nona

O

Orin, Oran, Oscar, Oskar, Osker, Osckar, Ossian, Oisin, Owen, Owin, Owyn

Olwen, Oonagh, Owena

P

Pendaran, Perth, Pert, Phelan, Powell, Pryderi, Pwyll

Penarddun, Petra

Q

Quin, Quinn

R

Regan, Reghan, Reagan, Reaghan, Rivalin, Ronan, Roy

Ragnell, Rathtyen, Rhan, Rhawn, Rhedyn, Rhiamon, Rhian, Rhiannon, Rhianwen, Rhodd, Rhonda, Rhonwen, Rhosyn, Rowena

S

Sativola, Sawyer, Scilti, Setanta, , Sheridan, Sidwell, Sloan, Sloane, Sugn

Sabrinna, Saeth, Saffir, Sarff, Seren, Sian, Sioned, Siwan

T

Tadhg, Taliesin, Tanguy, Taran, Teague, Teaghue, Teirtu, Teithi, Tegid, Teyrnon, Tiernan, Tiernay, Torrey, Tory, Trahern, Tremayne, Tremaine, Trevor, Tuireann, Turi, Twrch, Trwyth

Talaith, Talar, Tanwen, Tarian, Tarran, Tegan, Tegau, Tegeirian, Tegwen, Teleri, Telyn, Terrwyn, Toreth, Torlan, Torri, Trevina, Tristana

U

Uchdryd, Uisnech, Usenech

V

Varden, Vardon, Varney, Vaughn, Vortigern

Vala, Vanora, Vivian

W

Weylin, Weylyn, Wynne

Wenda, Winnifred, Wynne

Y

Yspaddaden

Ygraine, Ysbail, Yseult, Yvayne

Saxon Names

Germanic in origin, Saxon names are easier for modern tongues to pronounce than Brythonic names. The 'ae' combination is pronounced 'Ah', so Aethelred is pronounced AHthul-red. The 'eo' combination is pronounced as a long 'ay' (as in hay) - so Beowulf is pronounced Bay-wolf. The letters C, D, G and K are all hard consonants, and the letter Y is the long 'i' sound of 'wine' rather than the short 'i' of wind - so, Aldwyn is pronounced Auld-wine.

Names

A

Aart, Ablenden, Abrecan, Acwellen, Acwel, Aethelbald, Aethelbert, Aethelfrith, Aethelhere, Aethelred, Aethelstan, Aethelwulf, Alden, Aldin, Alwin, Aldwyn, Aldred, Alger, Algar, Almund, Anbidian, Ancenned, Andsaca, Anfeald, Anhaga, Ann, Ane, Anna, Anson, Archard, Archerd, Archibald, Arlice, Arlyss, Arlys, Arwyroe, Atelic, Attor, Ator, Audley, Awiergan

Aedre, Aefentid, Aefre, Aelflas, Aelfles, Aelfrith, Aerlene, Alodia, Alodie, Andsware, Andswaru, Anna, Annis, Ar, Ardith, Arianrod, Ashley, Aisley, Aisly, Audrey

B

Baldlice, Bana, Banan, Bar, Bawdewyn, Bawdewyne, Beaduring, Beadurof, Bearn, Beorn, Beowulf, Berkeley, Barclay, Bestanden, Betlic, Borden, Bordan, Bowden, Boden, Boyden, Bowdyn, Brice, Bryce, Broga, Brogan, Bron

Beornia, Bernia, Bletsung, Bliss, Blythe, Bysen

C

Caedmon, Cadman, Caflice, Camden, Camdene, Ceolfrith, Ceolwulf, Cerdic, Chad, Colby, Corey, Courtland, Courtney, Courtnay, Cuthbert, Cynegils, Cyneheard, Cynewulf, Cynn, Cynric, Cyneric

Catherine, Cate, Catheryn, Cathryn, Cearo, Claennis, Coventina, Cwen, Cwene, Cyst

D

Daegal, Dougal, Douglas, Deman, Denby, Denisc, Deogol, Desmond, Drefan, Dreng, Dreogan, Drew, Durwin, Durwyn

Daedbot, Daira, Daisy, Darla, Darlene, Darel, Darelene, Darelle, Darline, Daryl, Devona, Dohtor

E

Eadig, Ealdian, Edgar, Edgard, Eadgard, Edlin, Edlyn, Eadlyn, Edmund, Edmond, Eamon, Edric, Edward, Eadward, Edwin, Edwyn, Eadwyn, Egesa, Egeslic, Eldred, Eldrid, Eldwyn, Eldwin, Ellen, Elne, Elmer, Erian

Eacnung, Eadnignes, Eda, Edina, Edith, Edit, Edita, Editha, Edyt, Edyth, Edlyn, Eadlin, Edla, Edlin, Edlynn, Edlynne, Edmunda, Edmee, Edmonda, Edris, Edrys, Eldrida, Elga, Ellen-weorc, Ellette, Elswyth, Elva, Elvia, Elvina, Engel, Erlina, Erline, Erlene, Esma, Esme

F

Farmon, Firmon

Fara, Flaes, Fion, Freda, Freya, Frida, Frigga, Frith

G

Gaderian, Galan, Gar, Garr, Garberend, Garrett, Gareth, Geoffrey, Geoff, Gifre, Godric, Godwine, Graham, Grahem, Graeme, Gram, Germian, Grimbold, Grim, Grimme, Grindan

H

Halig, Halwende, Ham, Hengist, Heolstor, Heorot, Hererinc, Heretoga, Hilderinc, Hlaford, Hlisa, Holt, Hrypa

Hilda, Hild

I

Iden, Irenbend, Irwin, Irwyn, Isen, Iuwine

Idris, Ifield

K

Kendric, Kendrick, Kendryck, Kent, Kenway, Kimball

Kendra, Kym

L

Landry, Lang, Leng, Lange, Lar, Larcwide, Leanian, Leof, Lidmann, List, Lufian

Linette, Lynet, Lynette, Lora, Loretta, Lorette, Lyn, Lynn, Linn, Lynna, Lynne

M

Magan, Mann, Modig

Mae, May, Maida, Mayda, Megan, Meghan, Mercia, Mildred, Moira, Moire

N

Nerian, Norville, Norvel

Nelda, Nida

O

Odell, Odel, Odon, Odin, Odi, Ody, Offa, Ord, Ordway, Ormod, Orvin, Orvyn, Osric, Oswald, Oswine, Oswiu, Oswy, Oxa

Odelia, Odelina, Odelinda, Odella, Odelyn, Odelyna, Odette, Odilia, Otha, Othilia, Ottilie, Ora, Orva

P

Piers, Pierce, Pearce, Pleoh, Putnam

R

Raedan, Raedbora, Raedwald, Ramm, Rand, Recene, Renweard, Rice, Ryce, Rinan, Rinc, Rodor, Rowe, Roe, Ro, Row, Russell, Rypan

Raethla, Rosha, Rowenna

S

Scand, Sceotend, Scur, Selwyn, Selwin, Seward, Sherard, Sherwin, Sherwyn, Sibley, Sigebert, Sihtric, Slegc, Snell, Stearc, Stedman, Steadman, Stepan, Stewert, Steward, Stuart, Stillman, Strang

Sibley, Siggi, Sirri, Sunniva, Synne, Synnove, Sunn

T

Tedman, Tedmund, Theomund, Tilian, Tobrecan, Tolucan, Toland, Tolan, Torht, Torhte, Torr, Tracy, Tracey, Trace, Tredan, Treddian, Trymman

Taethle, Tait, Tressy, Trimona

U

Uhtred, Ulric

Udela, Udele

W

Wacian, Wade, Waelfwulf, Wallace, Wallis, Wann, Ware, Warian, Werian, Wigga, Wiglaf, Wilbur, Willan, Winchell, Wynchell, Wine, Wyne, Wirt, Wurt, Wissian, Wregan, Wulf, Wulfgar, Wyman

Wilda, Willa, Wilona, Wilone, Winona

Gods, Religion and Magic

This chapter explores the beliefs and magic of Mythic Britain. Perhaps the first thing to state is that magic *exists*; even if one is a Christian, magic is a very real force and the supernatural impinges on life constantly. Whether one is favourable towards the Old Gods and spirits , or a devout believer in the power of God the Father, the Son and the Holy Ghost, magic, spells and miracles can and do happen. The universe is vast, complex, mysterious and unknowable: supernatural beings are never far from the mortal world and whether they are gods, spirits, saints, demons or monsters, they exist and exert an influence, even though one may not be able to see them.

From a rules perspective, Mythic Britain represents Pagan Magic through Animism (with some additional powers) being available through certain spirits. Theism represents God's (and the Saints') power through Miracles. Sorcery and Mysticism are unknown in Britain — although they could certainly be introduced by travellers from exotic lands far to the east, if Games Masters wish it.

Christianity, the Saints, and Miracles

Although we may feel familiar with the Christian God, Jesus, and the Saints, in Mythic Britain, Christianity is raw, unforgiving, vengeful, and determined to depose the pagan gods of the old Celtic world.

Although Christianity is the religion that the Roman Empire has followed for a hundred and fifty years, on the far reaches of the empire it has been a slow process for it to gain acceptance. There have been missionaries in Britain for more than a century, and, in that time, many have converted to the new faith, but Christianity still has to work hard to survive. It is, like Judaism, a faith that is utterly certain that only one god, the god of all creation, can exist. All other gods are false: either creations of superstitious, misguided minds, or temptations created by the Devil to lure mankind into sin and depravity. The Council of Nicaea, in 325, solidified the doctrines of orthodoxy that have guided all Christians since, and

it is this orthodoxy that proves the divinity of Jesus and, therefore, acts as the foundation for the opposition to pagan religions.

To Britain's Christians, there can be no other faith across the island. The druids are false priests, the pagan gods are false gods, and the spirits are servants of Satan. The rites of sacrifice are blasphemies, and the old Celtic festivals are perversions of ceremonies that have their roots in Jesus and the Disciples.

To prove God's power, there are the Saints: individuals who, having devoted themselves to God and Jesus Christ, have demonstrated God's power through Miracles. Christians venerate and revere the Saints, but they worship God the Father, God the Son, and God the Holy Ghost. In this way, they are separate from, and superior to, the pagans. God is in their thoughts every day — and not only when needed. God does not require sacrifices of blood or life; He requires only love, faith, discipline, and repentance. There is no need to know which god is responsible for what part of the universe: there is only one God — and he made all things.

But God is strict. To protect man from the temptations of evil, he established rules that the Lord Jesus Christ explained carefully. If those rules are followed, if sin is avoided and repented; if men resist temptation and are prepared to accept denial rather than indulgence, then they will be rewarded a thousand-fold in Heaven. This is the promise Christians hold dear: suffering in this life results in glory in the next. Redemption is found through following God's rules and the teachings of the Gospel. There is no place for myth and multiple deities, each with conflicting stories; there is only a singular, divine truth, and only those who embrace God will find that truth.

Structure of the Church

Rome embraced Christianity over a hundred and fifty years ago, when the Emperor Constantine proclaimed it to be Rome's official religion. Rome's power has dwindled significantly in this period, and the true seat of Roman Imperial power is now Constantinople, the heart of the Byzantine Empire, and the seat of Emperor Anastasius. Despite the imperial power being wielded from Constantinople, religious power still rests with the Pope — Pope Symmachus, a living saint, rules from the Vatican district of Rome, installed in a newly built palace.

Bishops are appointed by the Pope and only the Pope can do so. The aim of a bishop is to effectively administrate an area or region, known as a diocese, on behalf of both the Church and Empire. Indeed, ever since Rome left Britain, all residual administration has been left in the hands of its few bishops, which gives them a great deal of local power and influence. Although bishops answer to the Pope, opportunities to do so are few and far between. Travelling to Rome is a long and dangerous business. The protection the Roman legions used to provide in western Europe has almost disappeared. So, unless summoned to a synod by the Pope, communication and governance is scant. The bishops are wholly responsible for their own diocese, the raising of money through taxes, appointing priests, and attending to both the spiritual and administrative affairs of the region.

Priests

There is no official structure of priests below a bishop. Bishops appoint priests according to need, favour and as a way of maintaining loyalty and control. No special orders are required to become a priest; no special training, over and above a love of God, a dedication to Christianity, and, perhaps, an ability to quote from the scriptures.

There are also few moral restrictions on what priests can and cannot do. Priests are free to marry and consume alcohol, and there are few, if any, notions of pious behaviour. Priests can therefore be as cruel, base, and crude as anyone else; indeed, some use the name of God and Jesus Christ as an excuse for such behaviour. But, just as equally, many priests are sound, just men who want to serve Christ through example and strive to live good, wholesome, diligent lives. Bishops rarely care: they have their own worries and responsibilities. Once a priest is ordained, he is expected to serve the bishop diligently, do as he is told, ensure taxes and tribute are collected, and the Word of God ministered, but aside from these duties, a priest may behave as he wishes.

Most priests are attached to a chapel (or, in larger settlements, a church), where they conduct regular ceremonies and lead daily worship. The chapel is the property of the diocese (and therefore belongs to the bishop), but the priest is responsible for its upkeep and maintenance, raising funds through donations and small taxes, under the umbrella of the bishopric. Raising money is a

constant struggle; few have any disposable income, for one thing, and few want to part with what they have. Clever priests know that raising the money needed to keep a chapel in good repair requires clever strategies — things and events that will attract the pious, who will then make donations or gifts. So it is that many priests are on the look-out for relics, holy objects, and anything that might connect their chapel or church with a saint, some Miracle, or other holy deed.

Prayers are held daily, at dawn and dusk, and mass is held several times during the week and always on the Sabbath. Loyal Christians are expected to attend prayers and mass, and priests have the power to question those who lapse in their attendance, demanding that reparations be made. Because Christianity teaches that God's grace is given to those who participate in worship and take mass regularly, priests are able to argue convincingly that regular attendance at prayers and mass is essential if God's good grace is to be maintained. As Christians believe that grace is essential to entering God's kingdom, priests can therefore command a great deal of power and obligation, even at a local level.

The priesthood is forbidden to women. Women are not allowed to preach, although if they wish to dedicate themselves to God's service they can join a convent — one of the new, female equivalents of a monastic order.

Monks and Monasteries

Although hermetic priests have existed for a long time in Britain, monasteries and monasticism are relatively new. The first monastery — a discrete community wholly dedicated to God's service — was founded on the north coast of Kernow, in an abandoned fort, overlooking the fierce ocean, called Dun Tagell, only a decade or so ago. The idea of creating pious, insular communities has become more and more popular, especially in Powys and Gwent, and is steadily spreading across Britain's Christian community. Those who truly want to dedicate their lives to God, gain grace, and enter Heaven are those who are prepared to turn their backs on conventional life and family, and enter a brotherhood where there is nothing but dedication to God.

Bishops can allocate lands to monastic orders, and, in return, expect that the order will pay some form of tribute, usually in produce, to the diocese. The monasteries have many uses: free from outside distractions the bishops can use them for administrative services, for religious ones, and, because monastic orders are wholly separate from the control of a local warlord or chieftain, they can operate almost like a personal fiefdom for a bishop — if he so chooses.

Monasteries are male-only. However, female orders are also beginning to establish themselves, in buildings known as convents. Convents perform similar purposes to monasteries but are reserved for women who want to serve God directly. As the priesthood is denied to them, convents are the only way for women to actively participate in direct religious duty. The bishops have welcomed them; women are useful allies to have in many ways, and so the convents pay tribute to the diocese, just as the monasteries do.

The Saints

Men and women who were so blessed by God, so filled with his grace that they were either willing to die for their faith and/or work Miracles to demonstrate God's power and glory. For Britain's Christians, Saints are the holiest of men and women; those God personally selected to do his work directly on the earth. It is forbidden to worship anyone but God, but Christians can venerate the Saints, remembering their deeds, honouring their names, and using their lives as an example of true Christian devotion.

Even in these early years of Christianity, there are many, many Saints. Most are in Europe and Britain has only a few. These British Saints are known to all Christians, figuring large in sermons and prayers, their stories being recounted time and again. It is believed by all Christians that the Saints can still perform Miracles, even though they are in God's Kingdom, to help their earthly kin in times of great stress and need.

A list of the most well-known Saints follows, along with the kinds of Miracles they can provide to the faithful. See the section on Christian Miracles, beginning on page 149.

Saint Alban

A soldier in the army of Rome, stationed at the city of Verulamium, Alban gave shelter to a renegade priest being hunted as part of a Roman persecution of Christians. Alban refused to give up the priest to his pursuers and was sentenced to execution following a lengthy period of torture. On the way to his place of execution,

Alban was forced to cross a road flooded by a fast-moving stream. Alban called on God, and the stream was parted, allowing Alban to be taken to the execution point all the faster, proving his devotion to God, having previously been a pagan.

Alban was buried in Verulamium, a city that is now occupied by the Saxons, although the small church that was built has survived. The Christians know that this is because Saint Alban is one of the most beloved and powerful of all Britain's Saints, and this is yet another of many miracles attributed to him.

Miracles: Dismiss Magic, Fortify, Perseverance, Shield

Saint Aaron

A martyr of the Roman persecutions, Aaron was executed in the west of Britain along with Saint Julius. Little is known of him, save that he was pious and brave, refusing to recant his faith even under extreme torture.

Miracles: Dismiss Magic, Heal Mind, Lay to Rest, Pacify

Saint Amphibalus

A priest of Isca who, fleeing Roman persecution, was sheltered by Alban. Alban's martyrdom allowed Amphibalus to escape to Western Britain where he made many more converts to Christianity. He was still captured by the Romans and returned to Verulamium where he was, eventually, martyred.

Miracles: Heal Mind, Heal Wound, Pacify, Steadfast

Saint Brighid

Patron Saint of the Brigantes, Brighid was originally from Ireland where she was enslaved by a druid, raped, and brought to Britain as a slave. On the voyage across the Irish Sea the Virgin Mary appeared to her and told her she would be safe if she embraced God. Brighid did so, and the druid who had captured her fell from the boat and was drowned. When Brighid reached shore, she was rescued by a local chieftain who had nineteen daughters and no sons. Brighid, blessed by the Virgin Mother, kissed the chieftain's wife and she then went on to bear nineteen sons. The nineteen daughters of the chieftain became the handmaidens of Brighid and, in time, took husbands and bore children. So was created the tribe known as the Brigantes.

Miracles: Bless Crops, Cure Malady, Fecundity, Ripen

Saint Brychan

Brychan was a warrior-king of Western Britain. As a young man, he was a hostage to the ruler of Powys and fell in love with the king's daughter, Banhadlwedd. Some stories say he raped her while others claim their love was simply frowned upon by Banhadlwedd's father. Either way, Brychan left Powys and returned to his homeland near Gwynedd where he led a pious life thereafter, dedicating himself to the church and God. Married three times, all his many children were pious servants of God and founded chapels and churches, some travelling to Rome and becoming bishops. Brychan, for all his piety, was still a warrior and led his warbands against several warlords who tried to take his lands.

In old age, Brychan became a hermit, devoting himself entirely to God. His example as a saintly warrior of God makes him a patron of Christian warriors.

Miracles: Aegis, Fear, Perseverance, Sacred Band

Christianity to the west coast of Britain, helping to found ministries as far north as the Carvetii lands.

Miracles: Clear Skies, Consecrate, Lay to Rest, Steadfast

Saint Julius

Martyred by the Romans at the same time as Saint Aaron, little is known of Julius save for his piety and devotion to God.

Miracles: Dismiss Magic, Heal Mind, Lay to Rest, Pacify

Saint Patrick

A Briton sold as a slave to the Irish, there are countless stories of Saint Patrick's life, and he is regarded as the founder of Christianity amongst the pagan Irish, and a key figure in helping Christianity flourish in Britain. His is, first and foremost, an Irish Saint, but his name is well known among Britons as are his stories. He performed many miracles, most famous being the expulsion of serpents from Ireland, but he also delivered people from hunger and brought the dead back to life.

Miracles: Consecrate, Dismiss Magic, Resurrect, Ripen

Saint Socrates and Saint Stephanus

Disciples of Saint Amphibalus, Socrates and Stephanus were both persecuted by the Romans and martyred in 304, in what is now the kingdom of Gwent. Socrates was tortured extensively but never cried out in pain and forgave his persecutors even as he was put to the sword.

Miracles: Cure Malady, Heal Body, Pacify, Rejuvenate

Saint Cadgyfarch

Cadgyfarch was a pious man of southern Powys who helped enshrine Christianity in Powys and Gwent shortly after the Romans left the island. He established the Church of St Mary Magdalene and was the first Bishop of Powys, appointed by Pope Celestine.

Miracles: Consecrate, Dismiss Magic, Fortify, Steadfast

Saint Declan

Declan of Ardmore is an Irish Saint who, on a pilgrimage to Rome, met with Saint Patrick and returned with him to Ireland, where the two of them founded several churches. Later, Declan came to Britain (some say with Saint Patrick) and helped bring

Saint Tudful

One of the most recent Saints, Tudful was a daughter of Brychan and a most devout woman, helping to found the first convent in Gwent. She was murdered in a raid by the Silures in 480, along with twenty other members of her order (and including two sisters). The place where she died, by the banks of the river Usk, has become a place of pilgrimage.

Miracles: Consecrate, Dismiss Magic, Growth, Perseverance

Saint Wenna

Another of Saint Brychan's daughters, and a recent, living Saint, Wenna founded the first convent in Kernow, shortly after the founding of the first monastery. It is said that the Virgin Mary has given her the power of healing, and there are several recent reports of how she has cured all manner of afflictions and wounds.

Miracles: Cure Malady, Heal Body, Heal Mind, Heal Wound.

Christian Miracles

Christians believe that only God is capable of performing magic, and such magic is demonstrated in the form of Miracles. In the case of Jesus and certain prophets and Saints, God worked Miracles through them; in others, God worked Miracles directly to either prove His power or to prove the piety of an individual who was loyal unto Him. Those so chosen to be a channel for, or a recipient of, a Miracle, are venerated as Saints – those who have attained the holiest state in God's eyes and are guaranteed a place in Heaven.

Christian priests can call for God's help and, if God is listening and believes the supplicant is worthy, He may work a Miracle on behalf of the supplicant or through them directly. This works as per the MYTHRAS rules for Divine Intervention (MYTHRAS, page 201), with the following exceptions.

- No Devotional Pool is required. Christian priests do not maintain a Devotional Pool anyway.
- The Devotion Roll is *always* Herculean, regardless of the Priest's rank.

A Miracle can take one of three forms. It can either be an immediate, divine effect that directly answers the supplicant's prayer or alleviates a particular situation. The Miracle might be subtle or unmistakably ostentatious, leaving no one in doubt of God's power. *For example, a priest, being threatened by a warband of rabid Saxons, might appeal directly for God's help. His Divine Intervention roll is a success. If the Games Master wants to portray a subtle Miracle, then it just so happens that a warband of Christian Celts are in the vicinity and are guided by God's hand to where the Saxons are, and send them running for their lives. If the Games Master wants to be more overt, then the heavens open and lightning streaks down smiting the heathen warband with Holy Fire.*

The second form is a permanent Gift. Here, the supplicant receives a Gift, such as one from the list of sample Gifts on page 202 of MYTHRAS, which is designed to demonstrate God's love for, and faith in, the supplicant on a permanent basis. The granting of such a divine gift is not to be taken lightly and the Gift should fit (reasonably) with the circumstances of its granting. Our Saxon-threatened priest, for instance, might be granted the Invulnerability Gift, making him immune to the wounds of Saxon spears (but *only* Saxon spears).

The expectation is that the supplicant will remain utterly faithful to God and lead a sin-free and dutiful life from that moment on. If the supplicant does something that makes him unworthy in God's eyes, then the Gift can be revoked as easily with which it was given.

The third form is to invoke the name of a Saint through prayer. This works as per Divine Intervention, but the Miracle is one of the Miracles attributed to the Saint in question. If the Miracle occurs, its Magnitude and Intensity is equal to character's Devotion or Christian Passion, whichever is higher. Invoking the help of a Saint is the only way a non-priest can gain divine help – and it is worked by the Saint through the individual.

Witnessing a Miracle

Any character who witnesses a Miracle, including the recipient of the Miracle, immediately gains a 1d4+1 increase in the Christianity Passion. If the Miracle is particularly incredible, then this increase might be 1d6+1 or even 1d8+1 – the size of the increase is at the Games Master's discretion and should reflect the Miracle's enormity.

Pagan characters who witness a Miracle can make a roll against their Pagan passion. The result depends on the level of success:

- Critical: The character is unmoved by the display of God's power. Gods are meant to display power: that's why they're gods.
- Success: Quite impressed by God's power. Gain the Christianity Passion at a level equal to POW or CHA (whichever is higher).
- Failure: The character truly believes in God's power: Gain the Christianity Passion at a level equal to POW+CHA.
- Fumble: The character is awed by God's power and becomes a convert to Christianity there and then. Gain the Christianity Passion at a level equal to POW+CHA+ half the value of the current Pagan Passion. The Pagan passion is lost as the Old Gods are abandoned.

Becoming a Saint

Any character that works a Miracle or is the recipient of a Miracle may become a Saint, in time. In Britain, only a bishop can recognise someone as a Saint — and that person may even still be alive at the time of their canonisation.

The general requirements for canonisation are as follows:

- The individual has worked one or more Miracles, or been blessed by one or more Miracles.
- The individual has been subject to persecution, severe punishment or has been martyred.
- At least three Christian witnesses of good character can attest to the circumstances that lead to consideration of canonisation.
- The individual's Devotion or Christian Passion is at least 90%.

The final decision rests with the bishop, although he is likely to discuss the matter with his priests, local chieftains and their priests. In rare circumstances he might send to Rome for the Pope's guidance, but usually he sends notification to the Pope that a new Saint has been identified. It is, after all, accepted that the designation of Sainthood only recognises what God has already done: the title of Saint merely confirms God's eternal glory and love.

Celtic Pagan Gods and Magic

The druids of Britain know that there are four worlds existing in parallel. In order of importance for mortals these are:

The Mortal World

This is the living world. It is separated from the Other World and the Home of the Gods but maintains certain sacred connections with both. In the case of the Other World, these connections are the Bridge of Swords, the Bridge of Sighs, the Gate of Horn, and the Gate of Ivory. The Bridges are the connections mortal souls use to cross from the Mortal World into the Other World. The first is the Bridge used by those who fall in battle, and the Bridge of Sighs is used when death comes through other means.

The Gate of Horn is used by the spirits to commune with the Mortal World, usually in the shape of true dreams that are sent to those who can perceive and entreat with spirits: the druids. The Gate of Ivory is similar, but is used by malicious spirits to spread falsehoods, misleading dreams, and lies.

The Mortal and Other Worlds intersect frequently, generally in places of great beauty or age, such as the many sacred groves, sacred trees, sacred pools, and the standing stones found all across Britain. Here, spirits maintain a discernible presence and are easy to communicate with. Magical powers can regenerate and dreams sent through either the Gate of Horn or Ivory.

The Other World: Annwn

Annwn is the realm within the Spirit World reserved for the souls of those born in the Mortal World. It is an idealised version of Britain, unsullied by invasion or new gods; a place where magic is common-place, where heroes can be heroes for eternity, where there is no hunger, thirst, want, or pain. In the Other World, it is always spring and summer. The world appears as each individual wants it to appear, and Ancestors, friends, family, and loved ones mingle freely, if that is what is desired. The Other World is the reward for being part of the community, defending it, contributing to it, killing its enemies, and leading a true and just life. Those who do not are not denied access to the Other World, but for them, eternity is perpetual winter, hunger, thirst, pain, and

hardship. They are forever denied peace, or what they truly desire, in punishment for selfish actions in the Mortal World.

As the Other World is a realm within the Spirit World, souls and spirits mingle as much or as little as they want. Many secrets are revealed and, if a mortal soul wishes it, they can become an Ancestor if their deeds in mortal life were great enough to grant them that power. They cannot, though, become spirits, because the true spirits of the Spirit World are distinct creatures very different to mortal souls. In the Other World, spirits and souls coexist in the ways the gods intended.

The Spirit World

The Spirit World consists of three realms: the Other World, as has been discussed, and the realms of the Great Red Dragon and the Great White Dragon. Both of these are the Great Spirits – the most powerful spirits in all of creation, and together, are the very soul of Britain. Usually, they rest together and sleep. When they do, the world, and Britain, is at peace. If the Great White Dragon stirs alone, then the Gate of Ivory is opened and Britain is vulnerable to its enemies, be they invading warriors or invading gods. If the Great Red Dragon stirs alone, then the Gate of Horn is opened and the underlying truths of Britain's strength are unleashed, making it the most powerful land in the whole of the Mortal World.

The spirits of the Spirit World are the children, dreams, and needs of either the Red Dragon or the White Dragon. Those of the Red Dragon are benevolent and friendly to Britain. Those of the White Dragon are malevolent, deceitful, and cruel. When both dragons sleep together, the spirits are at peace. But when one awakens, its spirit grows in power.

Currently, the White Dragon is awake. Vortigern awoke it by inviting the Saxons to share Britain's lands. The invader god of the Christians keeps the White Dragon awake. The Red Dragon's power is weakened and it must be revived if the White Dragon is to be returned to sleep.

The Spirit World is therefore a manifestation of the Red and White Dragons. It resembles the Mortal World exactly, even down to geography, but has many subtle differences. First, the presence of the Red and White Dragons is tangible: their breath can be felt as the wind; the ground shifts as their bodies shift; the sun is the eye of whichever dragon is dominant. Currently, the sun is a white sun. When the Red Dragon awakes and defeats the White Dragon, it will turn to red. When both sleep, the world will be in twilight. Second, colours are richer, deeper, and more vibrant. Smells and sounds are sharper, clearer, and more distinct. Spirits abound and manifest in countless shapes, ways, and forms. Sometimes they are human and sometimes animals, plants, or natural features, according to their types and true natures. Manifestations of the gods can be found in the Spirit World. These are not the gods themselves, but the dreams of the gods, manifesting in the Spirit World in a similar way to how spirits manifest in the Mortal World. There is no Time. Everything happens as it should, not in any particular order that can be understood by mortal minds.

Mortals cannot remain in the Spirit World for long without becoming insane. The druids have conditioned their minds to accept and understand the Spirit World, but even they do not linger. The Other World is where mortal souls can reside – here they can coexist with the spirit world without risking their sanity and enjoy its rewards as they are meant to enjoy them.

The World of the Gods

The gods of the Celts are many and varied. They made the universe and everything within, including the dragons, spirits, and mortals. But for all their powers of creation, they are remote from mortals and unable to interact with them directly. The gods occupy their own cycles of myth and legend, constantly replaying their mythic roles and archetypes for infinity. The gods dream: and these dreams appear as spirits in the Spirit World, but are always aloof, difficult to comprehend, and driven by needs and desires mortals have trouble understanding. The stories of the gods shape the world. Their constant replaying and retelling keeps creation whole. This means the gods must be remembered and revered constantly. If they are forgotten, the White Dragon awakes and doom is brought to the Spirit World and Mortal World. All Tales Will Cease. Heroes Will Lose. Lovers Will Be Sundered. Battles Will Fail. The universe itself will be lost to whatever replaces it – and that is unknowable.

Mortals can only enter the World of the Gods if taken there by certain, very powerful spirits or by the dreams of gods wandering the Spirit World. Such an experience is life-changing. Merlin claims he was taken to the World of the Gods by an aspect of Macha upon her pure white stallion. There it was revealed to him the whole of destiny, including his own life and that of Arthur. On his return to the Mortal World, he found he had been granted extraordinary long life: Merlin claims he will live for as long as it takes for the Red Dragon to be awoken and then he will be taken into the Spirit World and allowed to sleep.

Thus, passing into the World of the Gods is not something mortals can command or control, through magic or ritual. The gods choose who makes the journey, and the journey always has profound consequences – not all of them welcome or pleasant. The World of the Gods is a world of cyclical myth, with stories well known to all being continually replayed and re-enacted, often simultaneously and frequently out of accepted sequence. From their actions all things are created and come into being, with the very enactment of myths perpetuating the existence of all things. Mortals are a consequence of these actions and are not intended to be their instigators. This is why the gods and mortals are separated by the Spirit World, so that each can fulfil their necessary roles unhindered.

Pagan Beliefs and Rites

The Celts recognise over 300 gods. Many are potent spirits; some are local gods, attached firmly to a tribe, place or particular myth; and a small number are universal, being recognised throughout the Celtic kingdoms of Britain, Ireland, Armorica, and so on. Many gods are mentioned and described in the Kingdoms of Britain chapter, and they are also outlined here, too, and placed into a more formal pantheistic context.

The relationship between mortals and gods is surprisingly straightforward. The Celts do not worship their gods directly: instead, they venerate and respect their names, roles, and deeds,

but stop short of continual ritual propitiation. In stark contrast to Christianity, which demands constant worship of God, Celtic custom dictates that ritual observance need only be carried out with any solemnity at the four major feasts – and, even then, worship is a very loose description. The pagan gods do not demand churches, temples, or shrines. They do not object when such things are built – and the Romans built many temples honouring the Celtic gods – but they do not take notice of such things. The gods have their own agendas and are largely aloof from mortals.

Instead, people partake in small, often unconscious, acts of propitiation that remember and venerate the gods, but do not reach out to them with prayers or cries for help. The same is true for the veneration of the countless spirits of Britain, and here the relationship is much closer because the druids can move between the Mortal and Spirit Worlds and therefore conduct propitiation on a personal level when it is needed. Propitiation demonstrates to the gods and spirits that mortals value the ongoing relationship, respect their power, and hope that the gods will provide a favourable influence upon the world at important times (mainly concerning the fertility of humans, animals, plants, and crops, but also including war, love, marriage, and so on).

Common Rituals

Although Celts do not take part in constant ritual worship, rituals are important to maintain and demonstrate respect for the gods, spirits, and Ancestors. Druids look after the formal rituals of the four major feasts, but there are other, smaller rituals that are observed by many Celts, particularly when wanting to secure the blessings of the gods and spirits.

Sacrifice

Sacrifice, of animals, is common. Human sacrifice also takes place, but is rare and reserved for especially important events. A sacrifice of animal blood is considered a standard offering whenever anyone seeks a favour from a god, or, more likely, a spirit. By sacrificing an animal of appropriate size and type, its soul is sent into the Spirit World to nourish the spirits and live amongst them. The greater the favour (or intensity of spirit), the greater the size of the sacrifice. Birds, cats, dogs, squirrels, rats – all are considered appropriate sacrifices to be made to most spirits. The Great Spirits (those of Intensity 4 or higher) require something more substantial: a pig, sheep, goat, or cow. Very important spirits require a bull or a horse.

The animal is killed quickly by slitting its throat and letting the blood drain into the earth. In some rituals, a druid might collect the blood in a suitable vessel for use in further rituals that do not necessarily require a life to be shed. Once dead, short prayers are said, speeding the animal's soul to the Spirit World, and the carcass is either left as a visible offering, for the elements (and predators) to take or, if it is a domestic animal, such as a pig, goat, sheep, or cow, it is butchered and eaten. Nothing is wasted, and Celts believe a sacrificial death to be a good death, because it is made in a common cause.

Human sacrifices are reserved for the most important rituals where the attention of the gods, or the service of a very great and powerful spirit, needs to be assured. Humans are not sacrificed lightly, and great care is taken in choosing the sacrifice. Prisoners are the most common choices: those captured in battle, or

imprisoned for crimes so terrible that there is no other course of action. Sacrificing a human soul to the gods or spirits is the most potent message possible: it demands their attention and, when made by a druid of high authority, it cannot be ignored. Even the gods, usually aloof from mortal affairs, pay attention when a human sacrifice is made.

As with an animal, a human sacrifice is generally made by slicing open the throat, although the victim may be stabbed from behind, from the front through the heart, or be disembowelled, if the druid believes there is a need to examine the living viscera of the victim (which may be necessary for certain divinations). The act of sacrificing speeds the soul of the victim to the Other World where they will reside with the Ancestors. Any crimes the victim was guilty of in the mortal world are immediately absolved: the sacrifice cleanses and purifies the victim – even if the victim was a hated enemy. The corpse is honoured with either burial or cremation, according to local customs. Frequently bodies are weighted and submerged in pools, ponds, or marshes, which are the traditional gates to the Other World. Amongst the northern Celts deep, narrow pits are dug and the body dropped into it, head-first, ensuring that the head of the soul is the first thing to enter the Other World rather than the feet. The burial pit is then filled with rocks, and then soil, to prevent malevolent spirits from seizing and possessing the corpse and coming back to the mortal world to wreak mischief.

Both animal and human sacrifices are sometimes burned. The traditional time for burning, rather than bleeding, is the feast of Beltane. Beltane honours Beltinus, the God of Fire. It marks the official beginning of summer and it consists of two elements: the driving of animals (usually bulls) through two pyres and the mass sacrifice of domestic animals (and sometimes humans) in a Wicker Man. The driving of animals between burning pyres signifies the transition from spring to summer. If the animals shy away and have to be hauled between the pyres, summer will be short and wet, and the harvest poor. If the animals go willingly, the summer will be long, warm, and just right for a bountiful harvest. Humans also parade between the pyres and some warriors jump straight through the flames. Those who emerge unscathed are believed to be blessed by Beltinus and will come to no harm in the raids and battles of the year to come.

The Wicker Man is the ultimate sacrifice to Beltinus. It is not an annual event; rather, it is staged when the druids believe that the gods must be made to listen and exert a direct influence. Thus, a Wicker Man is made and burned after harvests have failed, or there has been a long string of defeats, or if a tribe has suffered particularly poor fortunes. The Wicker Man is a huge, humanoid effigy, often 20 or 30 feet tall, woven from rushes, reeds, staves, and sticks. It is hollow, and the head and chest cavities are filled with animals for sacrifice: chickens, cats, dogs, sheep, and pigs, for example. One or more humans may also be interred in the Wicker Man, tied into the body, and surrounded by the animals. The limbs are filled with dry hay, rushes, and kindling. As the sun sets, the Wicker Man is set alight and the contents immolated. A well-built, well-stocked Wicker Man can take all night to burn and smoulder for many days after. The sound of the sacrifices is terrible: the screams and petrified wails reach directly into the deepest parts of the World of the Gods and cannot fail to be heard. A Wicker Man ritual is not a joyous affair: it is sombre and grave. Sacrifice on this scale is for the worst of times, and Celts know that a ritual such as this has no place for levity.

Head Taking

The brain, even when the body is dead, contains a huge amount of knowledge and experience. The druids of the Votadini, Cornovii, and Silures believe that keeping the head of an enemy slain in battle allows access to the knowledge held inside. Thus, these tribes are noted head takers, either keeping the heads as trophies to be displayed prominently or to be used by the druids. In this latter case, the druids call upon a Predator Spirit to enter the brain, capture the knowledge held within, and bring it back to the propitiating druid. How this works in game terms is explained in the nearby boxed text.

Eating Knowledge

Only the druids of the Votadini, Cornovii, and Silures still practise Knowledge Eating as a way of gaining memories, experience, secrets, or knowledge from a dead brain. First, a Predator Spirit of at least Intensity 2 needs to be convinced to hunt down the knowledge wanted by the druid. The druid must be specific: he cannot be vague, because the Predator Spirit will not know what to hunt for. Once this is done, the Predator Spirit waits close

by in the Spirit World while the druid cracks open the skull and consumes the brain, raw. As he eats, he enters a trance. When in trance, the psyche of the victim is available as a hunting ground for the Predator Spirit and it can range through this hunting ground of the mind to find what the druid has specified.

The Predator Spirit needs to make a successful Track roll, opposed by the Willpower of the victim (if unknown, then the default Willpower is considered to be 55%). If the Predator Spirit wins the contest, it returns with the information or knowledge the druid sought. The information's clarity is determined by the Intensity of the Predator Spirit, as follows:

Eating Knowledge	
Intensity	Clarity of Knowledge
2	Vague. The druid can establish generalities only.
3	Lucid. The druid can establish specifics: times, places, feelings, and so on
4	Insightful. The druid can understand the emotions and deeper intentions
5+	Revelatory. The druid can see into the deepest plans and secrets: nothing is hidden

If the Predator Spirit wins the Tracking contest with a Critical Success, the Intensity of the knowledge is increased by 1. Thus, an Intensity 3 Predator usually returns with Lucid information. If scoring a Critical Success, the information it returns with is Insightful.

If the knowledge is Revelatory, the druid gains the additional benefit of one extra Experience Roll when Experience Rolls are allocated. This roll must be used to improve a skill or Passion associated with the knowledge that was gained – it cannot be used for general skill improvement.

The Old Gods

Although there are hundreds of gods, the core pantheon is based around two major gods: Don and Bel. Don is the Mother Goddess (known as Danu in Ireland) and Bel is the chief god of the Britons. Each sires several children who have their own myths, sire their own children, and contribute to a huge, complicated and contradictory extended pantheon of gods, goddesses, demigod heroes, and spirits. Only the druids and bards understand the full extent of all the relationships; most don't try to make sense of the many, many tales, names, relationships, children, and so on. Many myths are based around local stories, customs, and traditions, and therefore vary considerably from place to place and tribe to tribe. Also, because all Celtic learning is based on the oral tradition, subtle differences, interpretations, and beliefs creep into a myth over time. Although the bards learn hundreds of myths by rote, every bard embellishes, alters a little, or creates a certain emphasis depending on the audience and the client.

The major, most highly revered, gods are outlined in the following pages. This is not an exhaustive list, and many more (from Ireland and Gaul, for example) exist but are not mentioned because they are not necessarily central to Britain.

Abandinus

A god of war and battle, Abandinus is the Romanised name for a much older soldiers' god who is thought to watch-over those preparing for battle or fighting in the shield wall. Rank and file warriors invoke his name and offer blunt prayers (and a sacrifice of mead or wine, poured onto their spear-blade and shield) for Abandinus to either keep them safe, or bless them with a fast and honourable death.

Abellio

A god of orchards and apples. He blesses the apple crops of early autumn and, if not honoured in the spring and summer months, may either cause crops to be sparse or blight crops with spirits of disease.

Agrona

Goddess of carnage and slaughter. Her name is invoked along with that of Abandinus, as a way of guaranteeing victory before and during a battle; but she is also a goddess of retribution, extracting bloody and cruel revenge on those enemies most deserving of it.

Albia

An enemy goddess, said to be the eldest of the fifty cruel daughters of the King of Syria (a mythical land filled with heroes). Each

daughter was married on the same day and each murdered their husband on their wedding night, in defiance of their father's wishes. The King of Syria placed all fifty into a ship and cast them adrift on the ocean. Eventually, they came to an island which was inhabited by a race of demons who had enslaved the spirits of the island. Albia and her sisters took a demon for a husband and begat a race of giants that ruled the island, known as Albion, until they were driven out by the heroes summoned by the Great Red Dragon. Chief of the giants was Alchendic, Albia's son, and he was slain by the hero Dair, although Dair also died.

Andraste

The goddess of victory. Andraste called together the Heroes to defeat the giants who ruled Albion (as Britain was known then), and led them into glorious and victorious battle. Her name is only ever invoked by the druids, for she is a Queen amongst goddesses. Before a battle, druids call upon Andraste and Coel to bring swift victory, while the spearmen call upon Abandinus and Agrona.

Anextiomarus

A god of light and protection, he founded one of the first tribes after the giants were defeated in the Time of the Heroes. His shield is made from the sun's rays and causes blindness in all who are caught in its glare. No spear, sword, or arrow can pierce Anextiomarus' shield and his light guards Britain from the giants' return.

Ankou

A god of death, Ankou is the ghostly, white-haired driver of the chariot who collects the stranded souls of those denied an honourable death in battle and takes them to Annwn, the Other World.

He is a servant of Arawn, King of the Other World, and is a highly potent spirit who roams Britain in the Spirit World. To see Ankou about his business is to die after precisely a year and a day.

Arawn

King of the Other World, Annwn, is the son of Andraste and the Great Red Dragon. All who cross into the Other World must give Arawn their oath and, upon so doing, they lead lives of eternal youth, health, and joy doing whatever they most treasured during mortal life. Arawn is the King of the Ancestors and the King of all spirits. Occasionally, he adopts physical form and wanders the Mortal World. In such a form, he leads a hunt with hounds of bright, white coats and large, scarlet ears.

Atepomarus

The god of horses. Horses are his creatures, and he appears as a great, silver war horse with a golden mane.

Artio

The goddess of bears. All bears are her creatures and when she sleeps, which is through the entire winter, so do the bears.

Avaloc

Consort of Sabrinna, Avaloc is the protector god of Ynys Wydryn and and the surrounding marshlands. He is little known outside of druidic circles, but a highly important god to the druids and, of course, Merlin. Sabrinna and Avaloc's daughter is Modron, the marsh goddess, and she controls all the spirits of the marshlands throughout Britain.

Aywell

A god of the Picts, Aywell is revered by the Votadini and Caledonii as the protector god of the north. The druids of the Picts believe that Aywell is a brother of Bel, whilst the southern Celts believe he is one of the children of Bel and Don. Aywell is a fierce warrior and his consort is the goddess Mm. His sacred animal is the eagle and the Pictish druids consider all eagle feathers to be gifts from Aywell that have magical powers of strength and protection. Pictish warriors invoke Aywell's name just as other Celts involve that of Abandinus.

Bel

Also known as Beltinus, Beli-Mawr, and Belatucadros. Bel is a god of light and fire, a god of war (and father of all the tribes of Britain), but also a god of healing and fertility. Bel married Don and together they had many children, each of whom was a hero and established a tribe that came to be one of the tribes of Britain. Every tribe is able, often through convoluted myths and stories, to trace their roots to Bel and so prove they are, rightfully, Britons.

His feast is Beltane, and it marks the first day of spring. Before the Romans came, it was the custom for a human sacrifice to be made to Bel, usually through immolation in a huge effigy made of wicker and reeds, and amongst some tribes (such as the Votadini and Silures) the sacrifice is still offered. The traditional way for Bel's sacrifice to be chosen is through the baking of an oat cake, a portion of which is allowed to char on the stones. The oat cake is broken into many pieces and all members of the community choose a piece from a goatskin bag, held by the druid. Whoever chooses a blackened and burnt piece is the Carline — the sacrifice — and is much feted in the hours before their death. The Carline's soul is received by Bel himself, who brings him or her into the Other World to reside in the Great Hall of Bel and Don and become one of the wisest and most honoured ancestors. It is the Carline who guarantees that the year's crops will flourish and the harvest will be bountiful — but only if the Carline meets his or her fate bravely, willingly, and with joy.

Belisama

A goddess of the largest of the Great Lakes of northern Britain, in the lands of the Carvetii. She is no longer revered by that tribe, but she is powerful nonetheless. She is a daughter of Bel and her sister is Yvayne, who is the goddess of the second largest of the lakes, known as the Wolf's Lake. Although the Carvetii do not propitiate Belisama in any formal sense (as they no longer propitiate Belisama's father, Belatucadros), those who live close to the Great Lakes still make occasional offerings to her, to show that she has not been completely forgotten.

Brigantia

Eldest daughter of Bel and Don, Brigantia created the Brigantes as her warband, making warriors from mud and the water of the sea. She and many other heroes drove the giants from the island,

which was, at that time, named Albion after the mother of the giants. Such was Brigantia's bravery, her mother, Don, renamed the island Britain in her honour.

Even the Romans recognised Brigantia's power and named her Dea Caelistis, establishing shrines to her in Eboracum. When the Christian missionaries brought the singular word of God to the Brigantes, it was shown than Brigantia was, truly, Brighid, a Saint from Ireland. Still, in some quarters of the Brigantes' lands, Brigantia is still honoured and referred to, quietly, discreetly, in her real form: the warrior daughter of Bel and Don.

Coel

A war god from the Time of Heroes and husband to Andraste, Coel is a son of Bel and Don, brother to Brigantia, Belisama, Yvayne, and many others. He rides in a chariot of fire, pulled by Atepomarus, and throws spears of thunder. The Romans admired Coel's power and bravery and gave him the name Camulos, a name by which he is sometimes known. Coel is revered by horsemen and cavalry, and they invoke his name before battle, as spearmen invoke Abandinus.

Cernunnos

The God of the Hunt, Cernunnos sometimes manifests in the Mortal World as a man with the head or antlers of a great, twelve-point stag. Deer and boar are his creatures, and while he allows mortals to hunt them for sport and food, he expects reverence and propitiation. Those who fail to make the proper prayers and offerings to Cernunnos may find themselves the subjects of the Wild Hunt in the Spirit World, where Arawn and Cernunnos hunt, mercilessly, Britain's enemies through the immense forests of Annwn, joined by Arawn's hell-hounds and predator spirits led by Cernunnos.

Cisson

The god of traders and crafters, Cisson invented bargaining to avoid being beaten by a local giant who was terrorising the region. The giant threatened to pull Cisson's head from his shoulders, and would have done, if Cisson had not struck a deal with the giant. In return for keeping his head, Cisson would bring the giant a hundred goats – a delicacy the giant found difficult to capture. Cisson did as he promised and kept his head. When the giant came again to pull off his head, Cisson this time offered to capture fifty goats: the giant wanted more, but Cisson explained that now the goats were terrified and would be tougher to catch. The next time, Cisson offered twenty goats, and so this continued until the giant became impatient and demanded to be taken to wherever the goats were hiding. Cisson had guessed this would one-day come, and had made a trap for the giant: a huge pit, deep in the ground, hidden by turf. Cisson led the giant to the hillside where hundreds of goats frolicked and the giant, realising he had been tricked, chased Cisson. He did not see the trap, fell straight in, and starved to death.

Clota

The goddess of the river Clud in the lands of the Caledonii, north of the Great Wall. She is a daughter of Don, but, along with her sister, Coventina, was not born of a union with Bel. Both river daughters were conceived via parthenogenesis, much to Don's surprise, and she hid them in the north of Britain, suspecting that Bel would be jealous of their presence.

Coventina

The goddess of the great river Tin of Britain's north-east, just south of the Great Wall, Coventina is a powerful spirit still revered by the Votadini and Parisii. She is the sister of Clota, the river goddess of the Caledonii.

Cunomaglos

Revered by the Cornovii, Cunomaglos is both a god of the hunt and of healing. Some consider him an aspect of Cernunnos while others, such as the Cornovii, believe him a quite separate god altogether. Cunomaglos' sons and daughters are wolf spirits, and as his sacred animals, they become spirit allies with the druids who recognise and propitiate their father. This results in the ability of certain druids to become wolf-like in form. See page 35.

Don

The mother goddess of Britain, she is Queen of the Island, its spirits, and is the one who tamed the Great Red Dragon, so bringing Britain to life. When she slept, demons crept out of the shadows and stole the island from her. When Albia and her sisters arrived, they took some of the demons as husbands and so begat the giants that enslaved the land, confining the gods to Annwn. When the

giants were defeated, Albia gave her oath to Don and was allowed to remain as a goddess, although her powers were broken.

Don is married to Bel, the god of light. Her brother is Manawydan. Between them, Don and Bel have created most of the gods and heroes revered throughout Britain. As the Queen of the Spirits, Don is the ruler of the Spirit World and may, sometimes, be encountered there by those who she specially favours. Her beauty is unrivalled, as is her kindness and warmth: but, like all mothers, she can be quick to scold and desires love and respect above all things.

Few dare to worship Don directly or even invoke her name. Her reverence is reserved by the druids.

Esus

The god of agriculture, Esus' sacred animal is the bull, and it is traditional for a bull to be sacrificed to Esus as part of the Beltane rituals to ensure good crops, a healthy harvest, and strong livestock. As Esus is also a god of male fertility, some tribes still hold that drinking the fresh blood of the sacrificial bull will guarantee that a man is both fertile and will produce only sons.

Esus is credited with inventing the plough and so is an important and revered god across Britain, but especially so amongst farmers.

Gorfannon

The god of smiths, Gorfannon's Forge is a mighty and gigantic affair that blazes day and night while Gorfannon himself makes the weapons the gods and heroes use in their eternal battles against various enemies. Anything made by Gorfannon is guaranteed to never grow dull or break, and one strike of his hammer is the equivalent of a hundred such strikes by any mortal smith. Gorfannon made the sword Caledfwlch, which is carried by Arthur.

Lenus

The god of healing, and especially revered amongst the pagans of Western Britain. Lenus can heal any wound, cure any disease, and lift any curse. He has the powers of resurrection and to grant eternal life, but the druids maintain that no mortal has yet proved worthy of the former power. Of eternal life, Merlin claims that his extraordinary long life is a gift from Lenus – although he has, at times, also claimed Lenus to be his father.

Lud

Son of Bel and Bon, Lud is a great hero and founded the city known as Lundene, defending it from many perils. Lud is handsome and wise, and the consort of the river goddess Tamesis. A great warrior, he lost his right hand in battle and replaced it with one made of silver, designed for him by Tamesis and forged by Gorfannon.

Lugh

Also known as Lug, Lugg, and Llew, Lugh is the god of the light, the sky, and the sun. His chariot is the sun itself, carrying him over the sky before he descends over the edge of the earth and returns to his golden hall in Annwn. His feast is Lughnasa, as summer

reaches its height, and marks when the first fruits of the harvest to come appear. Lughnasa is the time of a high feast, celebrating the height of Lugh's powers and the strength of the harvest to come. It is common for druids to lead the devout to a high place to watch Lugh rise out of Annwn in the west and begin his journey across the sky.

As the sky is Lugh's domain, so all the creatures of the air are considered sacred to him. Lugh commands the air and fire spirits, which cannot exist without each other.

Manawydan

God of the sea, he is the brother of Don and rules the oceans that surround Britain. Every sailor – including some Christians – revere and invoke Manawydan's name before making a voyage. Manawydan commands everything within the sea and the weather around it: he raises great storms and huge waves, but also controls the trade winds and calms waters that all sailors pray for. Those who drown at sea are taken to the Other World by Manawydan himself, who carries them through the underwater halls of his kingdom and into Annwn. There are many tales and stories relating to Manawydan. He is often depicted as riding the magnificent horse formed of the white-topped waves, who is named Aonbar. In battle, he carries the sword named Answerer, forged for him, like all such swords, by the smith Gorfannon.

Mithras

A god brought to Britain by the Romans, Mithras is a bull-god revered by certain warriors who are chosen to join Mithras' cult, which has seven stages, or trials, that must be passed before one is accepted into the order. The druids do not recognise Mithras's power, but there is no doubt that he is now an important god amongst warriors and so he is considered to be one of the heroes who came to free Britain in the Time of Heroes. He is little known beyond those initiated into his cult.

Mm

The consort of Aywell, Mm is a Pictish goddess associated with fertility, healing, and childbirth. Mm is petitioned whenever a woman enters labour, in the hope that both mother and child will remain healthy and strong, both during and after birth. South of the Great Wall, Mm is relatively unknown, although midwives and wet nurses all know of Mm and call upon her when a birth is imminent.

Modron

The marsh goddess and daughter of Avaloc and Sabrinna. She can sometimes be glimpsed in the waters of marshlands and inland pools where she protects the gateways to the Other World. It is said that Modron can deny any soul entry into Annwn, causing them to serve her as a wandering, tormented marsh spirit instead. If a druid wants to deliver a truly chilling curse upon an enemy, he invokes Modron's name, thereby marking the victim for her attention at the time of death.

Morholt

A god of Kernow, Morholt is a son of Bel and Don and challenged the giant Taulurd who terrorised Kernow at that time. He slew Taulurd and the giant's treasure horde became Kernow's wealth. Morholt is revered amongst Kernow's pagans and all kings of Kernow can trace their ancestry back to Morholt.

Nantsolvelta

Goddess of the hearth, but also a river goddess, Nantsolvelta watches over the home and is a patroness of domestic life. Her name is invoked to ensure a fire does not go out, that milk does not curdle, that thread does not break on the distaff, and that the loom always weaves straight. Her consort is Sucellus, the Thunder God.

Nemetone

Goddess of the Groves, all woodlands and forests are sacred to her. She is deeply revered by the druids and is considered second only to Don in importance as a goddess. She is the Green Lady of the Woods, Queen of Leaves, and the Whisper in the Branches. Cernunnos is both her brother and lover, but even he has given his oath to Nemetone, such is her wisdom and beauty. Once, the whole of Britain was Nemetone's kingdom, Broceliande, lush with forest, but mortals have consistently cleared the woodlands, reducing her power with each passing year. Her symbol is the oak tree, and druids hold the oak most sacred of all Britain's mighty trees. The rustling of oak leaves and branches is Nemetone's voice, echoing from the Land of the Gods.

Nodens

The god of hounds and the chase. All hounds are sacred to Nodens, and it was he who bred the snow-white, scarlet-eared hounds of Arawn. In some stories, he is one of Nemetone's sons; in others, he is the son of Bel and Don.

Ogma

One of Lugh's brothers, Ogma is the god of eloquence and poetry, revered by all bards. Ogma invented language, then created song, and then created the many ways of making language, song, and music work together so that great deeds and important news could be remembered and communicated.

Although a god of communication and music, there are many stories of how Ogma aided the gods and heroes in battle, both inspiring the warriors of the shield walls to fight bravely, and in fighting himself with the spear Orna, which sang as it killed and drank the souls of the Britain's enemies. When Ogma was cut down in battle, Manawydan took Orna and defended Ogma's body, killing entire armies with single sweeps of the spear head. Ogma is therefore a god of warriors and those seeking courage, although he is, chiefly, the god of bards.

Rosmerta

As Nemetone is the mother of all woodlands, so Rosmerta, a daughter of Bel and Don, is mother of all rivers. She is mother of all things green and growing, and mated with the Great Red Dragon so that the plants of the Mortal World might be fed with the magical blood of the Dragon, making the island strong. She gave birth to many silvery, slithering daughters who were the Rivers of Britain, and they went out to sustain the plants and forests. In the south, Tamesis, Ancasta, and Sabrinna (Spirit of the River Severn), were, and still are, the most powerful of her daughters.

Sabrinna

A very powerful goddess of Britain, Sabrinna manifests as the river Severn and also as the marshes known as the Summerlands. Although she is a true goddess, she loves Britain and its mortals and has chosen to remain partially in the mortal world and partially in the Spirit World, so that she can see all that goes on. The druids of Dumnonia have always revered her, but it is Merlin who loves and reveres her most of all. In turn, Sabrinna has taught Merlin much, and he owes his knowledge and power to her. She is a benevolent goddess, but to offend her is to anger her, risking floods and bad weather as she summons the tempestuous spirits of the rain and winds to batter those who displease her. Her daughter is the marsh goddess Modron, and her consort Avaloc.

Sulis/Sulevia

Goddess of the hot springs at Aquae Sulis, she is also known as Sulevia, which is the name given to her by the Romans. A daughter of Don, Sulis is one of Britain's guardians and Great Spirits. Her hot springs are a sacred link between the Other World and the Mortal World, and it is believed that much of Britain's strength comes from these sacred, magically powerful waters. If Sulis should ever leave Britain, these waters will grow cold, the Mortal World will be sundered from Annwn, and Britain will be wholly vulnerable

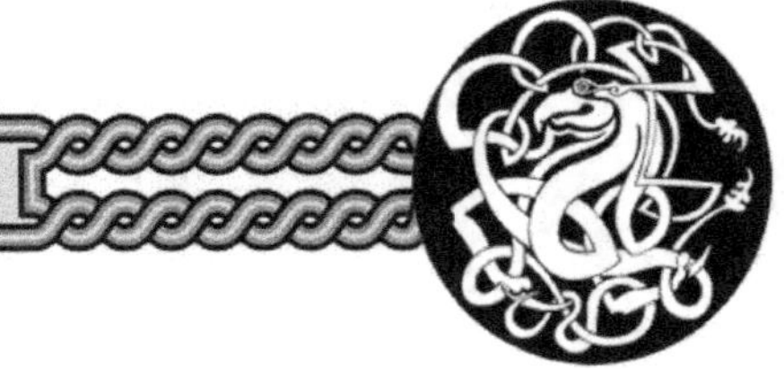

to its enemies. Sulis was one of the first spirits to be restored to Britain in the Time of Heroes, when the giants were driven from Britain's shores, and so she is an important and powerful foundation goddess. Even the Romans recognised her power, providing their own reverence and building a large and richly appointed temple to her.

Sucellus

God of thunder, Sucellus is renowned for three things: his hammer, which, when struck on the ground created both thunder and caused crops to grow; his huge, three-headed dog, bred for him by Nodens; and his raven, which causes storms when it beats its wings. Sucellus is also the god of mercy, who uses his hammer to give a swift to release to those who are wounded and dying in battle.

His consort is the river goddess Nantsolvelta, both a river goddess and a goddess of the hearth. Together they form the household guardians who protect the hearth, home, and crops.

Taran

Goddess of storms and thunder, she is the mother of Sucellus and gifted him with the mighty hammer that he uses to strike the earth. Taran lives in the sky, between the Mortal World and the lands where Lugh rides his chariot. She protects the earth with her clouds and brings-forth life-giving rain, and so is also revered as a nurturer by farmers. Yet Taran is temperamental: when angered she brings forth unceasing rains and driving winds that can scourge crops and bring misery to all mortals.

Verbeia

A goddess worshipped by the pagan Brigantes and the Parisii, she is a local fertility goddess and a daughter of Nemetone.

Celtic Magic

Only supernatural creatures have the ability to manipulate and alter reality in the Mortal World, which means that no mortal can directly cast spells or perform other supernatural feats. Any form of magic is a product of working with supernatural entities, such as gods and spirits, and only the druids have the necessary knowledge and training to enter the Spirit World and contract with the spirits and Ancestors. Druids are therefore animists and their magic is almost exactly the same as Animism as described in the Mythras rules.

There are one or two subtle differences. First of all, some spirits have the ability to work Folk Magic, which, when channelled through a druid, gives the appearance of the druid casting a spell directly. Secondly, no druid ever binds a spirit into a fetish. Such a practice is anathema to druids — spirits epitomise freedom and to entrap them in fetishes is to insult both them and the gods. This is the chief way in which animism of the druids differs to the animism of Saxon shamans — who have no qualms in binding spirits into fetishes.

Druidic Animism

All druids are trained to the level of Shaman (Mythras, page 131) which means they are able to converse and negotiate with spirits, and travel to the Spirit World if they so wish. Attaining the rank of High Druid (which confers the abilities of High Shaman, as per the Mythras rules) requires the following:

- Trance 90% or higher
- Binding 90% or higher
- Customs 90% or higher
- Lore (Pagan) or Pagan Passion 90% or higher

There is no equivalent of a Spirit Lord (Mythras, page 197) although all the High Druids — and there are only ever 13 at any one time — nominate one of their rank to be known as the High Druid of Britain. This has been Merlin for as long as anyone can remember, and no one has seen fit to challenge his status as Britain's High Druid (although, if the High Druids could be brought together in conclave and one amongst them issued a challenge, then Merlin could be replaced).

The High Druid of Britain undertakes a very special quest in the Other World, led by the god Arawn himself, into the lair of the Great Red Dragon — which is to say, the High Druid is taken into the very fabric of Britain itself — and there learns its secrets. He emerges as something more than human: a creature with extended life and incredible insight, who is one with both the Great Red Dragon and, therefore, Britain. The High Druid of Britain is guaranteed a place among the gods when he retires from the Mortal World; and, unless killed, that point of retirement is at

either the choosing of the High Druid or death resulting from a successful challenge.

Spirits of Britain

Druids are taught, as part of their lengthy training, how to recognise and call upon all the myriad spirits of Britain. Almost all the different spirit types listed in MYTHRAS exist in Britain's Spirit World. The exceptions are bane spirits, fetches and medicine spirits; which do not exist in the Spirit World of Britain, although they are available to Saxon shamans.

As mentioned, druids never bind spirits: they only ever negotiate with them and, when the need arises, battle them in spirit combat. Of course, many druids build up alliances and friendships with particular spirits over many years, and such alliances are encouraged as part of druidic training; but binding a spirit to the Mortal Plane is strictly taboo within druidism and any druid who attempts a binding will face the wrath of the High Druids and even the High Druid of Britain – Merlin himself.

Neither do druids locate and awaken a fetch. This is simply not a concept and power that exists among Britain's druids – although it is something Saxon shamans practise.

Spirit Powers

By and large, spirits have the same powers as described in MYTHRAS. If a spirit agrees to aid a druid, either as a result of negotiation or of being defeated in spirit combat, the druid can channel the spirit's powers directly, allowing his body to become the means through which the Spirit World changes or influences the Mortal World.

Some spirits possess spells. Folk Magic spells are the most common, but some great spirits – those of Intensity 4 and higher – can work the equivalent of Sorcery spells and Miracles. The Spirit Magic table shows which spirit types are capable of offering spell-based magic.

If a spirit has Yes in the Folk Magic column, it has a number of Folk Magic spells equal to its Intensity and casts the spell at its Spirit Combat percentage.

If a spirit has Yes in the Miracles column, it knows 1 Miracle for every point of Intensity above 4 (thus an Intensity 6 Ancestor would know 2 Miracles). The Miracles known are appropriate to the spirit's type. The Magnitude and Intensity of the Miracle is equal to the spirit's Intensity. It casts the Miracle using its Willpower percentage but at a Hard grade of difficulty.

If a spirit has a Yes in the Sorcery column, it knows 1 spell for every 2 points of Intensity above 4. Thus, only spirits of Intensity 6 or higher know any Sorcery spells. The spirit can apply a number of Manipulations equal to half its Intensity and casts the spell using its Willpower percentage but at a Formidable grade of difficulty.

Spirit Magic

Spirit Type	Folk Magic	Miracles	Sorcery
Ancestor	Yes	Yes	Yes
Curse	No	No	No
Death	No	No	No
Elemental	Yes	Yes	No
Guardian	Yes	Yes	Yes
Haunt	No	No	No
Nature	Yes	Yes	No
Predator	Yes	Yes	No
Shape Shifter	No	No	No
Sickness	No	No	No
Undeath	No	No	No
Wraith	Yes	Yes	Yes

In all cases of channelling this kind of magic, it is the druid's Magic Points, and not the spirit's, that are used to power the spell. Remember that the druid is acting as a channel between the Spirit and Mortal Worlds and for a spell to have any kind of effect, mortal Magic Points are essential.

The spells available to spirits depend on their nature. The table on page 164 lists available spells by spirit type.

Use of Magic and Magic Point Recovery

Druids never call upon the spirits lightly. Although they are aware of their presence at all times, druids consider the ability to commune with and gain the help of spirits to be a privilege and not a right. Too frequent a use of spirits or too frequent an intrusion into the Spirit World risks offending the gods, especially Lord

Spirit Spells			
Spirit Type	Folk Magic	Miracles	Sorcery
Ancestor	Any, but must reflect the ancestor's deeds in his or her mortal life.	Berserk, Consecrate, Cure Malady, Cure Sense, Enthrall, Heal (Body, Mind and Wound), Lay to Rest, Perseverance	Abjure, Banish, Hinder, Protective Ward, Telepathy
Elemental	Air: Breath, Calm, Chill, Deflect, Dry, Extinguish, Perfume Earth: Bladesharp, Bludgeon, Dullblade, Find Minerals, Ironhand, Shove, Slow Fire: Cleanse, Cool, Firearrow, Fireblade, Ignite, Light, Warmth Water: Cleanse, Cool, Co-ordination, Extinguish, Find Water, Mobility, Polish	Air: Call Winds, Clear Skies, Cloud Call, Lightning, Thunderclap Earth: Bless Crops, Earthquake, Entangle, Growth, Shield Fire: Aegis, Backlash, Illusion, Rain of Fire, Sunspear Water: Breathe Water, Harmonise, Leeching, Rain of Water, Reflection	None
Guardian	Alarm, Avert, Bypass, Darkness, Deflect, Glamour, Protection	Absorption, Aegis, Dismiss Magic, Entangle, Fear, Harmonise, Pacify, Steadfast	Attract (Specify Threat), Damage Resistance, Hinder, Repulse (Specify Creature)
Nature	Any, appropriate to the Nature Spirit's type.	Any, appropriate to the Nature Spirit's type	None
Predator	Beastcall, Bladesharp, Demoralise, Fanaticism, Find Prey, Might, Pathway	Beast Form, Berserk, Fear, Perseverance, Steadfast, True (Natural Weapon)	None
Wraith	Avert, Befuddle, Bludgeon, Chill, Curse, Demoralise, Dishevel, Disruption, Frostbite, Pierce, Repugnance, Shock, Sleep, Slow	Absorption, Backlash, Bind Ghost, Dismiss Magic, Fear, Madness, Mindblast	Dominate (Creature), Intuition, Palsy, Smother, Wrack

Arawn, and incurring a god's wrath is not something any druid wishes to risk.

There is also the issue of Magic Point recovery. To replenish Magic Points, a druid must return to a Sacred Site (see below) and spend time there: Magic Points cannot be replenished in any other way.

Sacred Sites

Britain is filled with ancient, mystical, magical sites that are held sacred either for what they represent or for their inherent magical power. Several of these sites are mentioned and described in the Kingdoms of Mythic Britain chapter; this chapter expands on those entries and summarises more places of sacred wonder. Regrettably space precludes a full listing of all sites found throughout Britain and its islands, but sites of major interest are detailed.

Magical Strength

Each site is given a Magical Strength. This represents the percentage of spent Magic Points that can be recouped from that site, as per Mythras page 116. To benefit from a site's Magical Strength a character must remain there for at least 4 hours per Magic Point regenerated. Thus, a druid with 16 Magic Points visiting a site with a Magical Strength of 25% would be able to replenish up to 4 used Magic Points and would need to spend at least 16 hours at the site to do so.

The site's Magical Strength also provides a positive modifier to a druid's attempts to enter the Spirit World using trance:

Thus, a site with a 75% Magical Strength would make a Standard Trance roll into a Very Easy Trance roll.

The Magical Strength also influences the potential Intensity of spirits found in the site's immediate vicinity – if spirits are, indeed, present. The Spirit Intensity of the Magical Site table can be used to randomly determine the Intensity of a spirit a druid might encounter in the Spirit World while in Trance at that site.

Sacred Groves and Pools

Sacred Site Magical Strength			
Magical Strength	Skill Grade Modifier	Spirit Intensity	Sacrifice Level
25%	0	1d2	Food or Drink
50%	1	1d3	Treasure
75%	2	1d4	Blood Sacrifice – Small Creature
100%	3	1d6	Blood Sacrifice – Large Creature

Ponds, lakes, bogs, and natural forest clearings are places of magical power because they offer connections to the Other World. Druids can find or identify such places, and their Magical Strength, using a successful Locale roll. The Magical Strength is based on the strength of the connection the place has with the Other World and not on its physical size: a small, dark pool in a secluded forest may have a much higher Magical Strength than one of Northern Britain's Great Lakes. To randomly determine the place's Magical Strength, roll 3d6 and consult the following table:

Sacred Groves & Pools Magical Strength	
3-8	25%
9-14	50%
15-17	75%
18	100%

Sacred Site Protocol

Whenever a druid visits a sacred site, be it simply to regain Magic Points or visit the Spirit World, protocol dictates that an offering is left or a sacrifice made. The nature of the sacrifice is up to the druid, but the minimum that should left is dependent on the site's Magic Strength, as indicated in the Magical Site table.

Food or Drink: A small offering of food or drink is expected. This may be a loaf of bread, some cheese, mead poured into the pool, a flask of wine, or whatever can be spared. It is the making of the offering that is important, rather than the amount.

Treasure: Silver is expected, but anything can be left, and if it has personal value, then it has greater meaning. Treasure is usually buried so that it can be found in the Spirit World (or tossed into a body of water if one is present). Anyone who attempts to remove treasure from a Sacred Site can expect to be attacked by the local spirits.

Blood Sacrifice: Either a small (something cat-sized or smaller) or large (cat sized or larger, including humans) animal is ritually slaughtered as a potent offering to the spirits. The sacrifice is usually killed by slitting the throat, which is a fast and efficient death and allows for maximum blood-flow. The killing can be performed by anyone, but a druid officiates at the ceremony with the right prayers and incantations using a Binding roll.

Failing to leave or make a sacrifice diminishes the benefits of the site for the druid. Games Masters should adjudicate as necessary.

Stone Circles

There are over 1,300 stone circles across Britain, stretching the length and breadth of the country, from the islands of the far north down to the end of Kernow. The Celts did not build these monuments, and nor do they claim to have. They also do not claim them to be the work of the gods or spirits. No; these circles of stone were the work of the Old People, those who occupied Britain before it was known by that name; before the Romans and before the Time of Heroes, before even when the land was known as Albia.

The Old People worshipped very different gods. The druids do not know who these gods were, nor do they care. It is probable that they were the sun, moon, and stars, because many of the stone circles align with the movement of these things in the night sky, often with great precision. These temples of stone were clearly

made to impress the gods of the Old People, meaning that their gods were clearly vengeful and insecure, requiring constant propitiation. Sacrifices were made at these circular temples – some in such vast numbers that the remains were buried close by and the spirits of those dead remain close to the stones.

For the Celts, the stone circles are places to be wary of, to be admired, to be used for rituals occasionally, but, mostly, to be left alone. These were places sacred to other gods, other peoples. It does not do to interfere in what went before.

Sacred Sites of Britain

This is a short list of well-known sacred sites found across Britain. It is not exhaustive, and it should be used as an example of the capabilities that can be given to other sacred sites, either real or of the Games Master's invention. Each site has the name used in *Mythic Britain*, along with its contemporary name, for ease of location.

Tartadun Stones (Avebury)

Magical Strength 75%

Tartadun is the name of the Dumnonian hill and small settlement that overlooks the huge stone circle on the plain below. The circle is far wider than The Stones and more intricate in design. The circle comprises of a large bank and a ditch, known as a henge, with a large outer stone circle and two separate smaller stone circles situated inside the centre of the henge. Two avenues of paired stones lead from the south-eastern and western portions of the henge, connecting the Tartadun Stones with the Cenet barrow, an ancient burial mound, and the Sanctuary, a circle of wooden monoliths. The druids believe that Tartadun, Cenet and the Sanctuary formed a single, immense temple that the gods of the sky could see. Processions along and around the network of stones, henges, and wooden uprights formed a ritual dance that appeased the gods.

Tartadun, Cenet and the Sanctuary are highly magical places. Ancestor spirits can be found here, as can nature and guardian spirits. As with The Stones, Tartadun, Cenet, and the Sanctuary fall under the protection of Natanleod and Caer Gradawc. Caedmon and Birkita are authorities on both Tartadun and The Stones: anyone wanting to spend time at either place must seek their permission before doing so. Both Caedmon and Birkita can help prepare visitors and act as guides – important if the unwary are not to be assailed by spirits who take exception to intruders.

Great Lakes of the North (Lake District, Cumbria)

Magic Strength 75%

In the lands of the Carvetii are the Great Lakes of Britain. Merlin believes he was born in this region but cannot truly remember. Still, the Lakes region is a place of great reverence for druids and, although the Carvetii are staunchly Christian, it remains a place of pilgrimage for many pagans, and a place of dismal abhorrence for those who worship the Christian God.

The countryside here is sparsely inhabited fell and moorland, with deep valleys, secluded glades, deep woods in the lower stretches and, of course, the lakes. The druids hold that each lake is a goddess, or the home of a goddess, and there are 19 in total. The three most important are the Wolf Lake (Ullswater), Queen's Water (Coniston), and Winlaye's Lake (Windermere).

All the Great Lakes have the same Magic Strength, but they are very different in character and nature. The three most important are described here.

Wolf Lake

Home to the goddess Yvayne, she is a daughter of Don and her palace is below the lake's waters, protected by wolf spirits. Yvayne is the Keeper of Caledfwlch, and given into her care by Gorfannon the Smith after it was used by many champions in the Time of Heroes. Yvayne gifted the sword to Merlin many years ago, and he gifted it to Arthur, on the condition that Caledfwlch be returned to Wolf Lake when its work was done, and that Merlin find Yvayne a champion who would live with her in her palace and become her husband and lover. Yvayne is said to be one of the most beautiful of all the goddesses – more beautiful than Don herself – but is also the most melancholy because she has never found true love.

Queen's Water

A long, narrow lake, Queen's Water is the domain of Madb, a goddess from Ireland who was once one of the goddess queens of that place, but was killed and forced to live elsewhere. She chose this lake for her palace and she surrounds herself with many

Sacred Places
1. Tartadun Stones
2. Great Lakes of the North
3. The Maiden's Ring
4. The Stones
5. Nectan's Falls
6. The High Druid's Ring
7. Karrek Loos yn Koos
8. Lugh's Gorge
9. The White Horse
0
50
100 mi
0
50
100 km
1
2
3
4
5
6
7
8
9

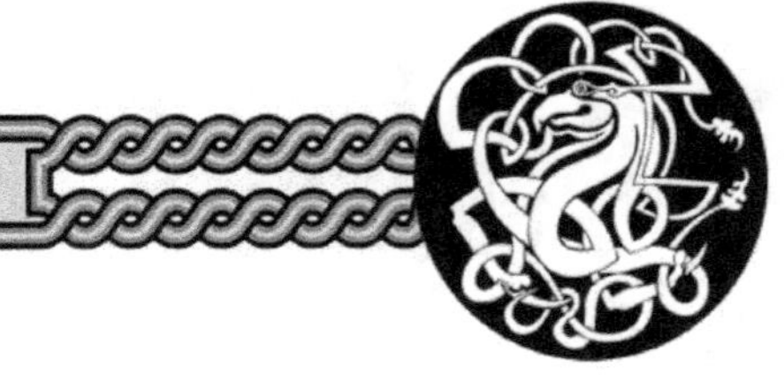

strange, fearsome, vengeful spirits to protect her from her enemies. Queen Madb is duplicitous and covetous, so the druids believe, and she delights in making mischief and causing torment.

Winlaye's Lake

Winlaye is another daughter of Don and she is the opposite of Yvayne. Where Yvayne is beautiful and kind, Winlaye is twisted and selfish. Where Yvayne has been denied love, Winlaye took it by trickery and by stealing the lovers and husbands of others. Winlaye craves company and the spirits that live in and around her lake are under orders to bring mortals, particularly males, into her realm so that she may lie with them, lie to them, and keep them with her until they inevitably die. Many have reported that the forests along the edge of the lake are filled with the laughter of young women, and that lithesome figures can be seen dashing through the trees, enticing, beckoning, and promising all manner of favours. At night, strange lights dance through the woods, causing the weak-minded to follow. All these are lures sent by Winlaye to bring visitors to her hall beneath the lake's surface. There she both loves and torments, as only a goddess can, changing her favours between lovers frequently, sometimes causing them to fight. Others – those she has tired of – are locked away and forgotten. Winlaye always seeks new lovers and companions, initially finding something within them that fascinates her, but soon growing bored and needing a new distraction.

The Maiden's Ring and Wyl Barrow (North Yorkshire)

Magical Strength 100%

The Maiden's Ring is a circle of stones located in the Parisii lands, close to the Gwyr River. The Ring consists of thirty stones, none of them more than 4 feet high, formed into a circle 300 feet in diameter. The stones form the torque of the Maiden, a fertility spirit who was pursued by the giants and almost ravaged at this place. The Maiden is a part of the torque now, and she watches over the lands and ensures the good health and fertility of both people and animals. Her saviour was the great hero Dair, who slew the giant, Alchendic, who was preparing to rape the Maiden but Dair was also mortally wounded in the process. The Maiden could not save Dair's life, but in those final hours as she cradled him, they were deeply in love and the Maiden pledged to remain close to his burial site for eternity. The Maiden then placed Dair in the Wyl Barrow, along with his spears, shield, and helmet. She placed her own torque nearby and then went to sleep, waiting for the Spirit World to embrace both of them as the Time of Heroes came to an end.

More detail can be found on page 39.

The Stones (Stonehenge)

Magical Strength 100%

Even Merlin does not know who built The Stones. It was not the Druids, certainly; and not the race of giants that were driven from Britain before mortals came. The druids believe that The Stones, which align perfectly with the stars, sun, and moon, allowing the solstices and equinox to be predicted, is one of the eyes of the Great Dragon, allowing it to observe the universe. It is close to a further ring of stones, so the druids know that the lands around the plain are of great magical importance, and The Stones are thick with spirits – many of them Ancestors, some malevolent predators and curses, and some mere haunts – the sad remains of ancient sacrifices.

In general, the druids do not use The Stones as a place of worship, because they did not create the place. However, they do conduct some rituals there. It is useful for seeking Spirit Allies, Spirit Knowledge, or simply to replenish magical energy. The Stones do not hold peaceful or benign spirits: the spirits who congregate here have a sinister purpose, a tendency towards mischief, malevolence, and harm, or seek some form of callous revenge on the Mortal World. This henge, then, is a dark and fearful place: frequented by only the strongest-willed mortals, and druids with specific needs; it broods on its wide, flat, desolate plain, alone and pitiless.

Nectan's Falls (Saint Nectan's Kieve, Cornwall)

Magical Strength 50%

At the head of a densely wooded glen in north Kernow, not far from the monastery at Dun Tagell, is Nectan's Falls. This 60-foot waterfall cascades into a circular rock basin, known as the *kieve*, foaming and bubbling with the water then gushing through a hole in the surrounding rock and into a pool below.

Nectan is a water spirit and this place is sacred to him. To commune with Nectan (an Intensity 5 Nature Spirit), one must first

climb into the kieve and then follow the flow of the water, climbing through the hole in the rock and down into the lower pool. Nectan himself appears as a warrior made of silvery water and he commands all the local Nature spirits of both water and land. He is friendliest to those who need the advice and guidance of a warrior, and, in the Time of Heroes, he was a chieftain of Bran, one of the heroes of Britain.

Recently, the power of the Christian God has begun to reduce Nectan's influence. The construction of the monastery at Dun Tagell has brought many powerful followers to the region and the monks have even come to perform their own rites and ceremonies (baptisms, mostly, but exorcisms have been tried) which have started to diminish Nectan's local power. He is still a potent spirit, but Nectan fears for the future. If the monks are questioned, they admit to attempting to create a Saint from Nectan, installing one of their brothers close to the falls and using the peace of this place as a way of coming closer to God.

The High Druid's Ring (Rollright Stones, Oxfordshire)

Magical Strength 100%

The High Druid's Ring is a collection of three separate sacred monuments: the stone circle, known as The Whisperers, the Warband, and the High Druid's Tomb.

The Whisperers is a group of four stones capped by a fifth roof stone, creating a chamber around 6 feet square in area. It marks the burial place of a king of the Old People and each of the four stones contains a powerful Ancestor spirit that guards the dead king's tomb. The Ancestor spirits are Intensity 4 Guardians and anyone disturbing the burial site is subjected to their vicious, incessant whispering (in an unintelligible tongue) that drives mortals mad. These spirits discorporate their targets as soon as the threshold is crossed and engage them in Spirit Combat (Whisper 95%) in the bleak, grey Spirit Plane of the Old People. A victim beaten in Spirit Combat returns to the Mortal World and flees from the place, his

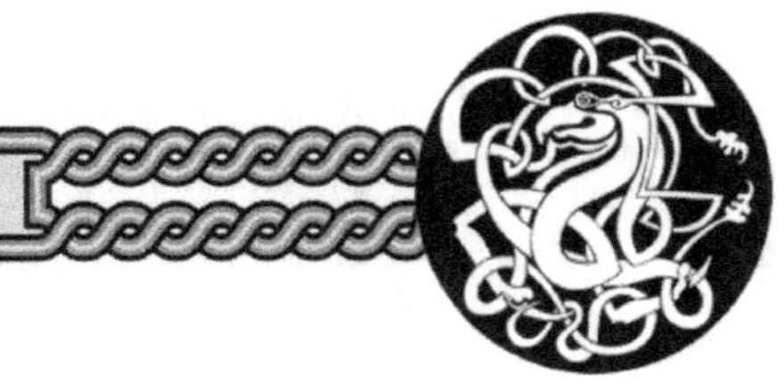

mind broken. In game terms, the character is rendered permanently insane – a terrified, gibbering wreck who can do little but babble, drool, and beg for forgiveness.

The Warband is an almost perfect circle of standing stones, 99 feet in diameter, composed of seventy-seven closely spaced pillars. Although the Old People built this circle, the druids know that it has now become a Ghost Fence to protect the High Druid's Tomb, 210 feet (the same number of feet as the number of stones in the Warband) to the north. A single Intensity 6 Guardian Spirit is bound into the Warband – one of the very, very few examples of a spirit being deliberately bound to the Mortal World. In this case, the spirit inhabits the stones willingly, as it has vowed to protect the High Druid's resting place just as the Whisperers defend the Old People king. The Warband's function is to defend the High Druid's tomb from hostile magic and spirits: it does not affect Mortals and it has no discorporation powers. However, the spiritual emanations of the stone are still disturbing to anyone within a dozen yards, possessing the equivalent of the Intimidate ability (MYTHRAS, page 216) with the target matching his Willpower against the Warband's Willpower of 108%.

The High Druid's Tomb is precisely that. The very first High Druid of Britain, Mug Ruith, is said to be buried here, along with his thirteen disciples, thirteen wives, thirteen children, and thirteen hounds. Mug Ruith brought the Thirteen Treasures of Britain to the island, giving one to each of his disciples for safe keeping. When Mug Ruith finally decided to go to the Other World, his disciples, wives, and children decided to accompany him, and so the Thirteen Treasures were given into the keeping of the druids who were now spread across Britain.

This is a very sacred place for all druids. It was a very sacred place for the Old People and this is why Mug Ruith chose it for his place of burial: it is at the heart of Britain, above the heart of the Great Red Dragon and all magic is potent and powerful here.

Karrek Loos yn Koos (Saint Michael's Mount, Cornwall)

Magic Strength 75%

Karrek Loos yn Koos means 'Grey Rock in the Woods', and is a tidal island 1200 or so feet off the south coast of Kernow. Completely cut off from the mainland at high tide, it can be reached at low tide by a narrow causeway of shingle that leads to the steep-sided, heavily wooded, conical hill, dominating the isle. Before the Romans came, this was home to several druids and is still home to many nature spirits, including the Great Spirit that gives the island its name. The Grey Rock in the Woods is a massive outcrop of grey-green granite and inhabited by an Intensity 6 Nature Spirit – the ruler of the island, its protector, and a mentor to druids, bards, and those who come here in search of knowledge. The Grey Rock in the Woods, or Karrek, sometimes manifests in the Mortal World as an old man with grey and green skin, bent at the shoulder, and with a beard of moss and lichen. He is generally neutral towards visitors and if he is to offer counsel or knowledge (and Karrek knows the entire history of Britain, Ireland, and Armorica, since the Time of Heroes and right through until the present day), he must be carefully persuaded. This persuasion usually requires the telling of a story, reciting of a poem, or construction of a riddle. In

game terms, the persuader must win in a Social Conflict contest, using an appropriate skill, with Karrek using his own Willpower of 116% to critique the performance, solve the riddle, and so forth.

Karrek likes to be amused and if a persuader loses the contest, he may offer knowledge or counsel anyway as long as his opponent was spirited and creative.

Karrek Loos yn Koos has hundreds of local nature spirits, including spirits of healing, animal spirits, plant spirits, and so on. Karrek's three daughters, Oak, Ash, and Elm are the spirits of these respective trees, and they like to manifest as attractive, mischievous maidens who good-naturedly tease visitors before introducing them to their father.

Lugh's Gorge (Cresswell Crags, Worksop)

Magical Strength 50%

Lugh's Gorge is detailed in the scenario Bran Galed's Horn, beginning on page 234. A long, narrow, river gorge, it is peppered with caves and was once a hunting place for the Old People before the druids made use of it as a sanctuary and place of hiding. It has its own spirit protector, as detailed in the scenario.

The White Horse (Uffington White Horse, Oxfordshire)

Magical Strength 75%

Cut from the chalk hills and 330 feet long, the White Horse of Dumnonia is a representation of Atepomarus, god of horses. Those who care for horses or rely upon them in war, such as Dumnonia's cavalry, make offerings to the White Horse to ensure the safety and courage of their mounts.

The Thirteen Treasures of Britain

Assembled by Mug Ruith, first of Britain's High Druids, the Thirteen Treasures of Britain are items and weapons forged during the Time of Heroes either for the gods or by the gods. After Britain was reclaimed from the giants, the Thirteen Treasures were given to Mug Ruith who gave one to each of his thirteen disciples so that they might be kept safe. Most were kept across Middle and Northern Britain and, when Mug Ruith's disciples followed him to the Other World, the treasures were handed to other druids who took them further afield. When the Romans came, the treasures were much sought, because whoever holds all thirteen holds power over Britain itself. Thus, the druids made every attempt to keep the treasures out of Roman hands.

Merlin has dedicated himself to reassembling the treasures. Some he has already found and others elude him. He intends to drive the Saxons and the Christian God out of Britain using the Thirteen Treasures and to fully awaken the Great Red Dragon, bringing in a new Time of Heroes.

The Thirteen Treasures are:

White-Hilt, the Sword of Rhydderch Hael

Forged for the hero Rhydderch by Lugh, this sword burns with the brightness of the sun when drawn from its scabbard.

The Hamper of Garanhir

Placing enough food for one person into the hamper transforms it into food enough to feed a hundred.

The Horn of Bran Galed

Whatever drink the owner desires appears in the horn. Every sip taken from the horn heals the mind, body, and spirit and it can, some believe, bring the dead back to life.

The Chariot of Mywnfawr

This war chariot rides over any terrain, including water, without jolting the driver. No enemy missile can pierce its sides.

The Halter of Eiddyn

Any horse wearing the halter is obedient, brave, and has the strength and speed of twenty horses.

The Knife of Farchog

This knife, with one cut, can serve twenty people at a feasting table.

The Cauldron of Dyrnwch

With this cauldron The Maiden caught the blood of the hero Dair, placing it in Dair's burial mound. It can heal all wounds and restore the dead to life, Dair's final gift to the Mortal World.

The Whetstone of Tudwal

Any brave man who uses the whetstone to sharpen his blade finds that the blade will never grow blunt, never chip, never rust, and never bend. If the whetstone is used by a coward, then the blade will never draw blood, chip at the slightest knock, rust within a year, and bend to the point of uselessness.

The Coat of Beisrydd

A coat of mail that will fit any man, no matter what his size or girth. It will never rust and can never be damaged by mortal weapons.

Caledfwlch

Forged by Gorfannon, whoever carries Caledfwlch is known as a leader of men, inspires loyalty in all, and never shirks in the face of battle. The sword is unbreakable and never needs to be sharpened.

The Throw-board of Ceidio

A gaming board that ensures a just and brave man will always win, and the unjust craven will always lose.

The Mantle of Don

This cloak transforms the wearer into the semblance of whomever the wearer wishes. It is said Merlin let Uther use it to seduce Ygraine, causing him to appear as King Mark.

Eluned's Ring

This ring of stone allows the wearer to cross into the Spirit Plane and observe the Mortal World as though he was there, yet remain unobserved in the Mortal World.

With the exceptions of Caledfwlch, the Throw-board of Ceidio, Eluned's Ring, and the Mantle of Don, all of which Merlin protects, no one knows what the remaining treasures look like or precisely where they have been hidden. They might be miraculous and wonderful works of beauty, or as mundane and unremarkable as everyday items. A druid though, instinctively recognises the power and significance of a treasure — although only a High Druid has the ability to ensure its powers can be awoken and used.

Saxon Gods and Magic

The Saxons have their own pantheon of gods and their own mythology which, while bearing a certain resemblance to that of the Celts differs considerably in its gods and beliefs. The Saxons worship the same gods as the northmen of Scandinavia (and who will, in time, attempt to supplant the Saxons, just as the Saxons attempt to supplant the Celts), and have very similar myths.

The Saxon mythology is very detailed, with many, many stories and legends surrounding their key gods, and space precludes a detailed treatment of the Germanic and Norse pantheons. However, an overview is provided to help establish Saxon belief in relation to Christianity and Celtic paganism.

Æsir, Landvaettir and Wyrd

The Saxons, like the Celts, believe that there is a separation between the gods, known as the Æsir, and the spirits of the land, known as the Landvættir.

They also hold that everything, mortals especially, possess a *wyrd*, or fate. Wyrd is inexorable and cannot be changed. Every aspect of life from the moment of birth through to the moment of death is pre-ordained and immutable: one cannot change one's wyrd and the best one can hope to do is understand it and accept it bravely and pragmatically. If something bad happens, it is wyrd; the same is true of good fortune. These things are destined to happen, and nothing can be done, or could have been done, to change it. A person's wyrd is woven by the three Norns, or Fates, who sit at the base of the World Tree, Yggdrasil, spinning the destinies of mankind.

Where the Æsir are concerned, Saxons believe in all the gods and grant them equal respect, if not necessarily reverence. Thus, throughout a year, folk participate in communal ceremonies to all the Æsir, excluding none out of fear of giving offence. Everyone knows about the gods, as the skalds frequently sing of their tales and deeds, and a Saxon is free to give worship to any of the Æsir he desires, at any time.

Like the Celts, Saxons are also animists. They understand the existence of the spirits and the need to show them respect (or else face petty, but vindictive tricks when an angered landvættir takes revenge for some slight). Spirits are everywhere: they live on the

farmsteads, reside in forests, and live in waterfalls and deep pools where the malicious spirits are ready to drown foolish folk. Dark, wild places are to be avoided so that the less civilised landvættir and the malignant sceadugenga will not be disturbed. The inhabitants of a stead often perform small rituals to placate the spirits, offering small gifts and places at their dining table to keep them happy.

Saxons do not pray to the gods and spirits as a way of requesting miracles; like the Celts they propitiate the Æsir and landvættir in order to ward off possible tribulation and again afterwards, in thanks for withholding calamity. Wyrd is inexorable, but mortals can always try to massage it a little.

Saxons do not have any professional priests. The chieftain or head of the household is responsible for leading ceremonies, with the guidance of the shaman, if one is present, and all members of the community know the required rituals. All ceremonies are held outdoors, and just about all require some form of sacrifice, be it food, drink or livestock.

The major communal sacrifices of the year are the following:

- Yuletide, when darkness is at its deepest and everyone offers food and drink to the gods to ensure the return of spring.
- Spring, when Woden receives sacrifices to avert disaster in forthcoming raids, battles, and wars.
- Autumn, after the harvest has been gathered, to thank the gods (especially Frigga, for protecting the crops).

Smaller, more personal sacrifices are common, usually to request good fortune or the blessing of the gods, and then to thank them if everything appears to go to plan. There are no hard and fast rules for these ceremonies and sacrifices, but it is generally recognised that the more one sacrifices, the more likely it is that the gods will pay attention. Human sacrifice is, of course, the ultimate gift, and Saxons have been known to volunteer themselves as a sacrifice for the good of the community. But, like Celts, Saxons will sacrifice slaves, criminals, and the dishonoured from time to time, if the ceremony warrants it.

The Æsir

The Saxon gods are not particularly willing to intercede in the affairs of mortals. In Saxon legends, the gods have been known to respond personally to a mortal supplicant, where they appear in person and use their own tricks and guile to try and solve a problem, but this is recognised as being incredibly rare. Neither do the Saxons believe that the Æsir are all powerful, all knowing forces of nature: instead they view the gods as great heroes capable of amazing, but still very personal, feats. In fact, the gods are often powerless to intercede for a mortal, simply because the fate of all men is predetermined by the Norns, to whom even the Æsir must bend knee. A warrior may pray for victory on the battlefield, but whether or not he survives has little to do with Woden: the All-Father has no power to change the wyrd of any mortal. If he meddles in the battle, driving fear into his worshipper's foes, then it is because of Woden's own hidden machinations. He will do nothing to directly help his faithful, but he will certainly punish those who fail to show him the correct respect.

Thus Saxon faith is a grim one. Saxons propitiate because they must, since failing to do so brings misfortune. Yet even the most generous of sacrifices will not result in observable aid. Men must achieve their own Miracles by wit and skill, not rely on the Æsir to nursemaid them. This fatalistic attitude, combined with their informal polytheistic habits, means that there are no cults dedicated to the Saxon gods – at least none which offer any sort of reward for spiritual devotion.

As noted there are many Saxon gods, and space precludes a detailed treatment of each. However, the major gods are as follows:

Balder

The son of Woden and Frigga, best-loved of all the gods, and fated to be accidentally killed by his brother Hoder. Balder is known as a gentle and wise god, for which he is fated to return after Ragnarok.

Bragi

The god of poetry and eloquence, patron of skalds. He is a son of Woden and Gunnlod, and husband to Idun. Bragi greets the new arrivals in Valhalla with songs of their heroic deeds.

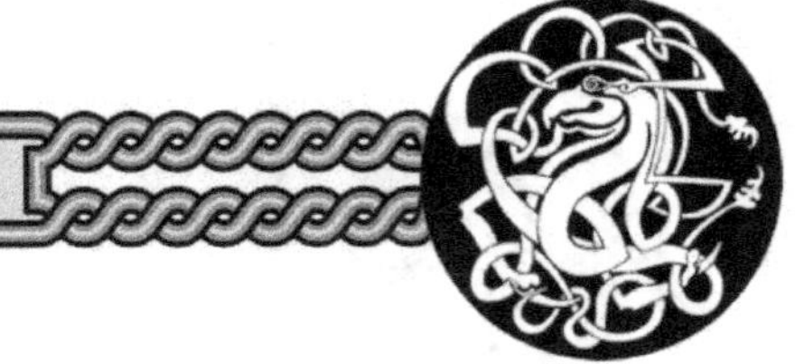

Eir

Goddess of healing and mercy, a handmaiden to Frigga.

Eostre

Goddess of fertility, both of people and crops, with her rites celebrated in the spring.

Frigga (The Loving)

The goddess of prophetic magic and childbirth, she can see the fate of all, but chooses not to prophesy. She is the wife of Woden and mother of six sons and one daughter, including Balder and Hoder.

Gefjun

The goddess of fertility, who married a giant and had four sons. She is the guardian of all those who died unwedded, granting them a life of eternal happiness.

Gullveig

A goddess who is the patroness of evil women. She came to live with the Æsir as a handmaiden but her delight in practising evil magic caused the gods to cast her onto a fire three times to be burned. She survived each attempt so the Æsir magically bound her to the Ironwood in Jotunheimr. There she slept with Loki and bore him three monstrous offspring, Hel, Fenrir, and Jormungand.

Hel (Death)

The goddess of death and daughter of Loki, Hel rules over Niflhel where the dead who do not journey to Asgard come. By Woden's will she commands the dead of all nine worlds in exchange for her oath that those sent to her are granted the hospitality of her hall, which has huge gates and a very high wall. Her appearance is half black (the colour of long dead flesh) and half normal. Whilst her realm is cold, it is not a terrible place, but a hall of restful peace for those who die of old age or misfortune. She punishes evil doers by sending them to Nastrond.

Hermod (Speed)

The god of swift travelling, messengers and bravery. Hermod is a son of Woden and Frigga. He alone volunteers to take the terrifying journey down to Hel to ask for the return of his brother Balder.

Hoder

The god of war and a son of Woden and Frigga. Driven by an evil potion which filled his heart with love for Nanna, Balder's betrothed, he joined a warband of giants, in revolt against Asgard. Blinded in the battle, they were defeated and the repentant Hoder returned to Asgard with his brother Balder. Tricked by Loki into firing an arrow of mistletoe at Balder, he unwittingly killed his brother.

Jord

The daughter of Nott and Annar. She is the goddess of the earth and the mother of Thunor.

Loki

Originally the god of fire, his sly nature changed him to become a trickster god, capable of great cunning, but flawed with a sadistic and cowardly nature. He is the son of giants Farbauti and Laufrey. He married three times producing many children. Loki is a famous shape-shifter, able to turn into a salmon, a fly, a horse, and many other creatures. Responsible for the death of Balder, he is bound by the entrails of his son, Narfi, until Ragnarok, whilst a serpent drips venom into his eyes.

Magni

The god of strength, Magni is a son of Thunor and the giantess Jarnsaxa. He will slay the great wyrm Nidhogg at Ragnarok. With his brother Modi he will inherit Thunor's hammer Mjolnir.

Modi (The Brave)

God of courage and son of Thunor and the giantess Jarnsaxa. He is fated to survive Ragnarok with his brother Magni.

Norns

The three norns are Urd 'that which became', Verandi 'that which is happening', and Skuld 'that which must be'. They respectively represent the past, present, and future. They are the guardians of Urdarbrunnr, the Well of Fate, and they decide the wyrd of all men and gods.

Sif

The goddess of summer and grain. She is the second wife of Thunor with whom she bore Magni and Modi. Sif and shape-shift into the form of a swan. She once had her golden hair cut off by

Loki, but the dwarfs forged her new hair from pure gold which magically bound itself to her scalp.

Skadi

The bringer of snow and goddess of wintertime destruction. The daughter of the giant Thjatsi, she sought revenge for her father's death by the gods. Falling in love with Balder, she accepts a settlement of marrying one of the Æsir based on his feet, but mistakenly chooses the most beautiful pair, which belonged to Njord. Their marriage did not last and she married Ullr instead. With her scathing nature, she leads the Wild Hunt.

Sol (Sun)

Daughter of Mundilfari and sister of Mani, she guides the chariot of the sun, bearing the magical shield Svalin (Cool) to protect herself from the heat. She is eternally chased by the wolf Skoll who will consume her before Ragnarok.

Thunor the Thunderer

God of lightning, thunder, craftsmanship, fertility, defence, and strength. Thunor is the son of Woden and Jord, and married to Sif. He protects Asgard from the giants by the threat of his wondrous hammer Mjolnir and owns a magical belt called Megingjardar ('Strength Increaser') and a flying chariot pulled by two enormous goats. Hot-headed he often slays giants out of pique and is doomed to face the great serpent Jormungand several times before he final slays it, and is slain himself at Ragnarok.

Tyr, the One-Handed

The god of war and honour, he grants victory against the odds to those who deserve it. He presides over contracts, law cases, and assembly votes at the Thing. An older god from before Woden, no one knows where he came from. Tyr bravely agreed to place his hand in the mouth of Fenrir, when the gods were trying to bind the monstrous wolf, as a guarantee that Fenrir would be released if he could not break free; Tyr fully understanding that he was sacrificing his limb. When the gods betrayed their side of the bargain, Tyr had his hand bitten off, but considered it a worthy exchange in order to keep the evil wolf bound.

Weland, the Smith

Weland is the god of smiths and crafters of all kinds. He was married to Hervor the Swan Maiden but she left him for another. Later, he was captured by King Nithad who had Weland hamstrung and imprisoned. There he was forced to forge items for Nithad. The ring Weland made for Hervor, and which she left behind, was given to the king's daughter, Bodvild, and Nithad took Weland's sword. In revenge, Weland slew the king's sons when they visited him in secret, and then fashioned drinking bowls from their skulls, jewels from their eyes, and a brooch from their teeth. He sent the goblets to the king, the jewels to the queen and the brooch to Bodvild. When Bodvild brought the brooch to Weland to be mended, he took it and raped her, fathering a son and escaping on wings he had made from swan's feathers.

Woden, The All Father

The god of runes, shamanistic magic, battle, and death. Woden is the chief of all the Æsir. He has many names and many disguises, which he uses when travelling the nine realms. His most common kennings are the 'all-father', the 'terrible one', 'one-eyed', and 'father of battle'. Woden helped form the cosmos and was the first to discover the runes, after sacrificing himself of the world tree, hanging upside-down for nine days and nights, without food or drink, with his spear impaled into him. He is the bringer of terror on the battlefield, casting his 'battle-fetter' on foes. He drank from Mimir's Well in exchange for an eye. He stole the Mead of Poetry and quaffed deeply of its power. He owns two ravens, Hugin (Thought) and Munin (Memory), which fly across the worlds bringing him news of what occurs. He also has two wolves, Geri (Greedy) and Freki (Ravenous), which accompany him everywhere and eat the meat from his plate as he only drinks wine. The magical spear Gungnir is his.

Woden has had many wives and many sons. With Jord he had Thunor, with Frigga he had Hermod, Hoder, and Balder, with Rinda he gained Vali, with Grid was born Vidar, with the giantess Gunnlod (with whom he slept to gain the Mead of Poetry) came Bragi, and with the nine daughters of Ran was produced Heimdallr. As if this was not enough, he often meets with Saga in the crystal hall of Sokvabek, and sometimes sleeps with Skadi, his mistress of the Wild Hunt.

Saxon Animism

Saxon animists are known as Læce (pronounced as 'leech', but unrelated to the bloodsucking worms) which means, in the Saxon tongue, 'healer' or 'cunning person'. Like druids, they interact with the Spirit World, negotiating with and binding spirits to work their magic. The Saxon view is that most spirits are harmful towards mortals – mischievous at best – and so must be treated with caution. Many spirits cause diseases and curses of some kind, particularly those spirits known as ælfar, and so are not to be trusted.

Saxon læce therefore operate in a similar way to druids and use the Animism rules from Mythras. The Saxon spirits have travelled with the colonists and established their own Spirit World in Britain, which is distinct from that of the Celts. These two Spirit Worlds do not interact, but spirits controlled by a druid can oppose spirits controlled by a læce, and vice-versa, using their respective animist as the conduit for conflict.

Læce, unlike druids, have no qualms about binding spirits and awakening a fetch: indeed, given the hostile nature of so many Saxon spirits, it is often the only way to control them. Saxon spirits also differ from Celtic spirits in three other ways. First, there are no Ancestor spirits in the Saxon Spirit World. When someone dies, they go to Valhalla, there to feast and battle with Woden, fallen comrades and old enemies; they do not interact with the Mortal World any longer.

Secondly, Saxon spirits do not offer any form of spells in the shape of Folk Magic, Miracles, or Sorcery spells: their powers are as described in Mythras.

Thirdly, all Saxon spirits are considered either Neutral or Hostile in attitude. It is exceedingly rare for a spirit to want to help a læce and usually they are exceedingly reluctant. Læce have to work hard to gain a spirit's trust and cooperation.

Saxon Use of Magic

Saxon læce are as reluctant to call on the spirits as druids, but for different reasons. The main reason is simply the antagonistic nature of Saxon spirits. They do not particularly like mortals, and neither do they want to serve them. Læce often find dealing with spirits a trial, and one that should only be undertaken when the circumstances absolutely warrant it.

The other reason is the rate of Magic Point recovery. Læce do not need to travel to a sacred place to recover Magic Points; instead, their Magic Points are recovered at their Healing Rate every week (thus, a læce who spends 4 Magic Points and has a Healing Rate of 2 will take two weeks to return to full strength). This slowrate of recovery is down to two things: the distance from the Saxon homelands, where there are many sacred places to aid recovery; and the natural resistance of Britain itself to Saxon magic.

Britain at War

Combat is a staple of most campaigns, yet attempting to recreate even minor skirmishes, with several dozen troops, using the personal combat rules is likely to lead to prolonged and frustrating melees. The Rabble and Underlings rules (see MYTHRAS page 111) can offset the problem to a degree, but running an entire battle at the unit level is still beyond the scope of the core game.

The following rules have been created to permit characters to participate in full scale battles, whether they are mere line troops or the leader of an entire army. When running such an event during a gaming session, players must accept that the role of their characters is going to be limited, and their fate probably beyond their personal control, unless they, themselves, are acting as commanders.

Realities of Battle

Perhaps the most important concept to understand is that battlefield combat is not the same as single combat. A character might be a feared champion of your city, or the greatest spearman in the kingdom, but still die like a dog in a shield wall. Whilst a duel or brawl allows freedom to attempt feints, and the luxury to focus on a sole opponent, on the battlefield such individual prowess is secondary to formation, morale and above all *teamwork*. In a battle, warriors are subject to different dynamics than regular hand-to-hand combat, much of which is dictated by the limited space to wield a weapon, the inability to use footwork, and attacks that can come from any direction; to either side, or, indeed, from above or below. No matter how hard you try, there is little hope of doing more than occasionally wounding an enemy when a chance opening occurs, then watching in frustration as they are shifted to the side by the constant jockeying of formations, or drop to the ground, beyond reach. Worse still, the chances of suffering a terrible wound are high, and when this happens warriors may be utterly unable to retreat due to the surrounding press of combatants.

Even if one is fortunate enough to take out a foe or two, unless warriors work together protecting their compatriots to either side, they may be injured instead, or lose faith in the ability to ward them. Once morale starts to fray, the formation begins breaking apart, leaving everyone exposed to several attackers simultaneously and, in a matter of moments, the shield wall is overrun.

Melee between shield walls is therefore like no other combat environment: a crushing hell of pinned shields, trapped weapons, sweat, blood, tears, fear and helplessness in the face of approaching death.

Battle Components

MYTHRAS uses a number of specific terms to explain the core concepts of battles. They are further explained in later sections, but in overview these are:

Force

The combined body of troops sent to fight a battle, which can scale from a warband up to an entire army. A force is nominally made up of one or more units.

Unit

A discrete unit of coordinated warriors under control of a commander. Each unit possesses a number of attributes depending on the type and training of its troops.

Formation

A formation is the disposition a unit adopts upon the battlefield. Some units are trained in several different formations which they may select, depending on the tactical situation.

Commander

The character in charge of what a unit does. The actual title depends on the game setting and the number of troops under their authority.

Command Skill

The skill used by commanders to control their troops. Usually this is the Lore (Strategy and Tactics) skill, but Influence or Oratory, at a more difficult skill grade, can be substituted if a commander does not have Lore (Strategy and Tactics). The foundation skill can also be augmented by a suitable Passion to arrive at the overall Command skill roll.

Phases of Battle

Battles have several distinct phases, from the selection of the battlefield, to the retirement of one side or the other, once the main battle has concluded.

Battle Rounds

Length of time, usually about 15 seconds, during which casualties are inflicted upon either side, and, if superiority is gained,

a commander can potentially order one or more Battle Actions.

Battle Actions

Special orders which can be issued by a commander if and when their unit gains a tactical advantage. The equivalent of Special Effects from personal combat.

Forces, Units and Formations

Each side involved in a battle is referred to as a force. This is an abstract term because the nature and scale of a battle can vary wildly. A force can comprise of one or more units, and each unit can be something as small as a bodyguard or warband, or as large as a legion. The scale is up to the Games Master to decide.

In small scale engagements each force is likely to be a single unit, fighting under the control of a sole commander – say a warband under the command of its warleader, or a company of city militia led by its sergeant. Battles involving forces of a single unit are relatively swift to conclude and require very little use of tactical maps and markers to resolve.

For larger battles, forces can reach the scale of armies, which are themselves usually broken down into three parts: a strong centre, and two 'wings'. In most cases the centre and wings are treated as individual units, each under its own commander, with the overall battle plan predetermined by the leading, or superior, of the three. However, some battles are so large that each deployed element is formed from multiple units.

Formation Types

A formation is the tactical disposition a unit of warriors forms, provided that they possess the relevant Combat Style Trait, and have trained in that particular formation. Without the correct trait, it is impossible to coordinate individual unit members as an effective team and ensure they apply the correct tactics.

Some elite, professional units may train their warriors in several formations to grant them more flexibility. For instance, despite learning the Shield Wall trait a Saxon warband may only know how to form a line formation, whereas an elite Celtic warband, with the same trait, could adopt line, block and wedge.

The following list offers guidance as to which Combat Style Traits are applicable for particular formations, and their benefits.

Broken Formation

Trait: None

Move: Up to sprinting speed

Effects: Cannot engage any other formation, but can be engaged – in which case it inflicts no damage on the enemy unit.

Skirmish Formation

Trait: Skirmishing, Mounted Combat or Trained Beast

Move: Up to running speed

Effects: Allows the unit to fight and move through broken terrain with no undue effects. They also suffer only half damage from ranged weapons. Conversely, a skirmishing unit only inflicts half damage when engaged in hand to hand combat with close order infantry formations. Most skirmishing units offset this disadvantage with a higher movement rate and by use of ranged weaponry.

The Shield Wall

The shield wall is the most common, and effective, tactical formation amongst Dark Ages troops.

Each warrior overlaps his shield with the shield of his comrade to the right. The rank behind does the same and raises their shields to protect the heads and shoulders of the front rank. In this way, a solid wall of wood, leather and iron is presented to the enemy, limiting the opportunities for a clean strike and reducing the chances of all but the slimmest weapons to squeeze through gaps (which makes the spear and the shortsword the preferred weapons in such a confining space).

Shield walls are tough to break. Not only is there a wall of shields, but the more ranks of warriors there are available, the greater the ability of the unit to withstand attempts to break the wall, and the greater its own ability to try to break the wall of the enemy.

Most clashes between shield walls are contests of shoving, stabbing and screaming - until, at some stage, one of the walls breaks and the fighting becomes a hellish and desperate chaos as the broken side fights for its survival...

The Saga of the Circle of Britain

For the purpose of illustrating the application and use of these battle rules, we'll look at a battle between Arthur and Aelle.

Arthur has three main troop types. His cavalry is a mounted unit consisting of veteran warriors riding heavy warhorses bred in Armorica. His spearmen, on the other hand, are close order infantry trained in the Line and Phalanx formations and form the majority of the army. Last, but by no means least, are the elite warriors of the Circle of Britain who are skilled in Line, Phalanx and Wedge formations, being particularly adept in counter-charging enemy cavalry.

The Circle of Britain is a highly honoured unit of disciplined veteran warriors dedicated to protecting Britain from the Saxons. At full muster, they have the following ratings: Strength 120, Morale 75%, and Competence 80%. Saxon warbands, on the other hand, are a varied lot, depending on who leads them. Most have ratings averaging: Strength 100, Morale 95% and Competence 70%, some being insubordinate fanatics with a short lifespan.

Line Formation

Trait: Formation Fighting, Shield Wall, Mounted Combat or Chariot Fighting

Move: Maximum of walking speed

Effects: A close order formation that grants advantages over skirmishing units, but retains tactical flexibility. There is no limit to the frontage, or, for that matter, depth, but additional ranks only count as half when engaging phalanxes. Line formation grants the ability to overlap enemy units or split off part of its own strength to create a flanking element.

Phalanx Formation

Trait: Formation Fighting or Shield Wall

Move: Maximum of half walking speed

Effects: A block of close order troops at least 8 ranks deep, which can push back or break through other units. The frontage of a phalanx, once engaged, cannot be changed even by use of a Battle Action (page 194), leaving it vulnerable to being overlapped or flanked. If armed with long or very long weapons, it cannot be frontally engaged by cavalry or chariots.

Circle/Square Formation

Trait: Formation Fighting or Shield Wall

Move: Immobile

Effects: A highly defensive, close order disposition, which can protect other troop types, or non-combatants, on the inside of the formation. This prevents the unit from being flanked or overlapped in exchange for tactical immobility. Like a phalanx, if armed with long or very long weapons, it cannot be engaged by cavalry or chariots.

Wedge Formation

Trait: Formation Fighting, Shield Wall, Beast-Back Lancer, Mounted Combat or Chariot Fighting

Move: Maximum of walking speed

Effects: Used against line or phalanx formations, this close order wedge relies on its shape to penetrate an enemy unit, doubling damage on the first round it engages. If this fails to disrupt or break the foe, it will itself fall apart on the following round, disintegrating into skirmish formation. The 'frontage' of a wedge is based upon its rear width and cannot exceed twice its depth (page 21).

Unit Attributes

Irrespective of its overall size, every unit possesses a key number of attributes which are used during the engagement.

Unit Strength

This is the number of warriors comprising the unit: in effect, its Hit Points, with one warrior equalling one point of Strength. As a unit suffers casualties this number drops, until it reaches a critical level whereupon the formation breaks. At this point, the remaining warriors are considered 'broken' and must flee the battle or be utterly exterminated. When formed up, only warriors trained in a Combat Style which includes that formation trait can be counted towards the unit's strength, otherwise they become a hindrance, or even a weak point.

Unit Morale

The average Willpower skill of the entire unit's warriors. Note that this value can drop if a unit receives less experienced replacements to restore it to full strength, taking time to build back up again.

Unit Competence

The average Combat Style skill of the unit's warriors. This acts as a cap to the unit commander's Command skill (i.e., the Command skill cannot exceed the Unit's Competence). The better trained the unit, the better the commander's ability to get the very best performance in battle.

Unit Morale	
Skill	Temperament
1-30%	Terrified
31-50%	Erratic
51-70%	Steady
71-90%	Disciplined
91-110%	Unwavering
> 110%	Fanatical

Unit Competence	
Skill	Expertise
1-30%	Cannon Fodder
31-50%	Green
51-70%	Seasoned
71-90%	Veteran
91-110%	Elite
> 110%	Heroic

Unit Frontage and Depth

Whilst the number of participants is vital to determine the strength of a unit, its frontage and depth are also very important. The precise disposition depends on the type of formation the unit adopts.

Frontage determines how many combatants are engaged at any one time and thus the potential damage the formation can inflict each round.

Depth, on the other hand, provides stability to the unit, so that it is more difficult to push around or break through. Depth is measured in ranks, with each rank containing a number of men equal to the frontage. Surplus numbers, insufficient to form an entire rank, do not count towards its depth.

Unit Damage

The damage a unit inflicts is normally dependent upon its Frontage. This assumes rough parity in the weapons and armour used on both sides of the combat, between enemies that are used to each other's tactics. The dice roll defines how many casualties are inflicted on the opposing unit during that round, reducing its Unit Strength.

Actual weapons and armour being used are less important than the teamwork employed to protect one another, and overwhelm their opponents.

Troop *types* are important, with cavalry, chariots, and even belligerent creatures (such as packs of hounds) granted a multiple to their frontage value for the purpose of calculating hand-to-hand damage. No benefit is granted for ranged damage.

Unit Damage	
Unit Frontage	Damage
<15	1d2
16-30	1d4
31-45	1d6
46-60	1d8
61-75	1d10
76-90	1d12
91-105	2d6
106-120	1d8+1d6
121-135	2d8
136-150	1d10+1d8
151-165	2d10
166-180	2d10+1d2
181-195	2d10+1d4
196-210	2d10+1d6
Every 15	Continue Progression

The Saga of the Circle of Britain

The commander of the Circle of Britain is Eowald the Ill-Omened, a famed warrior who lost one of his hands battling Saxons in his youth. His personal prowess has faded but his grasp of strategy and powerful voice have only grown with age.

With a Command skill of 103%, he is more than able to draw out the best from the Circle of Britain. In recent years however, the unit's Competence has dropped to 80%, a result of Arthur bringing in relatively unseasoned warriors in order to secure alliances with Powys and Gwent.

This watering down means that Eowald's Command skill is capped to the same value. Whilst his battle knowledge is excellent, the Circle of Britain is simply not good enough to enact his tactically astute orders.

The Saga of the Circle of Britain

At full strength the 120 warriors of the Circle of Britain can be formed into line formation (a shield wall) with a frontage of 30 and a depth of 4, which is more than sufficient deal with most Saxon raiding bands.

During the suppression of several recent raids by Aelle's warbands, casualties start to accrue, dropping its strength to 107. This reduces its depth to 3 since it can only provide three full ranks of men, leaving 17 stragglers in its back row. In terms of game mechanics these excess warriors are considered surplus to the formation's requirements, although they will likely play their own part by watching the flanks and acting as replacements as their comrades are injured.

The limited frontage means that the Circle of Britain can only inflict 1d4 casualties upon the Saxons per round. If they expanded the line to a frontage of 60, they would cause 1d8 casualties per round - however this would risk the formation breaking as it would only be a single rank deep in some places.

Unit Commander

The commander of a unit is the character placed in charge of it – usually someone who holds the highest level of authority, whether from social rank, political office or tactical knowledge. It is the commander who gives orders, using their Command skill, to direct the unit's troops during the ebb and flow of battle. Authority only passes onto a sub-commander if the current commander is killed, severely injured, flees in terror, or proves so incompetent that a subordinate will risk censure to depose control.

The scale at which the focus of the battle takes place depends entirely on the campaign and setting, allowing a Games Master, if they desire, to place all the player characters as low ranking sub-commanders and divide up their unit into smaller files or warbands.

For example, the characters could play sergeants in a small mercenary unit of 100 warriors, allowing the company at times to be sub-divided into teams of 20 men under the direct control of each player character. In this way all the players will assume a degree of agency, despite the overall result of the overall battle being beyond their notice or ability to influence.

Unit Type

Troop Type	Multiplier	Example
Infantry	x1	Warband
Cavalry	x2	Horse Mounted
Chariots	x2	Horse Drawn
Carnivores	x3	Animal handlers paired with hounds
Scythed Chariots	x5	As per normal chariots, but armed with long scything blades

Phases of Battle

A battle is normally broken down into a series of discrete phases, which follow one another in order. These are:

1. Choosing Ground
2. Personal Challenges
3. Stirring Speech
4. Engagement
5. Retiring from the Field
6. Aftermath

Each phase is explained over the next few pages. Depending on the circumstances of the battle, it may not be necessary to use every phase. For example the *Choosing the Ground, Personal Challenges* and *Stirring Speech* phases would be ignored if a unit was ambushed.

Choosing Ground

Before any battle can happen, at least one of the participating forces must decide where the combat will take place. For most battles the selection of the battlefield will be contested, the overall commander of each side making an opposed roll of their Locale skills, or Lore (Specific Region) if not native to the area. The commander who wins the test selects where the battle will be fought.

In certain circumstances, one side might be able to pre-select the battleground, such as laying an undetected ambush or withdrawing to a prepared fortification in advance of an enemy force arriving in the region. Although this may provide a significant tactical benefit to the prepared force, since they automatically choose the ground best suited to them, they may suffer detrimental strategic effects. For instance the enemy refusing to engage in battle, due to scouts detecting the ambush or judging the fortifications too severe, and, instead, ravaging the

Terrain Effect	Example	Effects
Choke Point	Narrow pass or strip of land between disrupting terrain	A choke point limits the maximum frontage of units and prevents units from being outflanked.
Disrupting	Woods, marsh or broken ground	Disrupting terrain prevents the passage of troops unless they disperse into skirmish formation.
Elevated	Hill or mountain slope	Elevation allows the higher positioned troops to double the troop damage inflicted by a charge, but they cannot be charged themselves. Moderate slopes (more than 20o) prevent cavalry charges downhill, whereas steep slopes (more than 40o) prevent foot charges downhill.
Fortified	Ditches, palisades or walls	Until the defenders are pushed back, attacking troops suffer one or more Difficulty Grades to their attacking roll depending on the fortification. Ditches or embedded stakes make attacks Hard, palisades and low walls make it Formidable, high walls make it Herculean and towering walls Hopeless.
Impassable	Rivers, bogs, sheer cliffs	Impassable terrain provides a secure barrier, preventing enemy troops from attacking across it. However, troops adjacent to such terrain are vulnerable if pushed back into the feature.
Open	Fields or plains	Open terrain has no detrimental effect or advantage. Permits the use of chariots.
Precipitous	Steep slope or atop gorge	Prevents direct contact between opposing units, but may allow the higher elevated troops to use ranged weapons unopposed.

undefended countryside or building siege works about the defensive position.

The above table provides the benefits and detriments of each type of terrain. Before the battle starts each participating unit must also decide what type of formation their unit assumes (see Formation Types).

Personal Challenges

Assuming the battle is not an ambush, or that one side is not defending from behind fortifications, there is the possibility for personal challenges prior to both sides engaging. Some cultures use challenges as a way for up and coming warriors to win renown for themselves, settle long-standing scores, or to shame specific enemies with charges of cowardliness if the challenge is not accepted.

From the perspective of a Games Master, such challenges not only allow player characters the chance to perform some individual combat prior to the more abstracted battle, but it can also be a way of introducing drama into their game, since foes are likely to be of high calibre, and any wounds taken by the character will reduce their chances of surviving the forthcoming melee.

A personal challenge need not end with death. A foe might flee their challenger in fear, or be rescued from the field by supernatural intervention. On the other hand, if they are disarmed or rendered otherwise helpless, there is no shame in allowing them to leave the field in honour, perhaps to return the favour at some other time.

As a commander, permitting personal challenges can be a risk. Whichever side loses the greater number of these heroic single combats is in danger of suffering a psychological disadvantage. This requires that any unit from which a loser originated makes an unopposed test of a relevant Passion, for example Love (Commander), Protect (City), Destroy (Enemy) and so on. The results of this check are potentially crucial according to the roll:

- Critical Success: The unit is angered by the defeat of its champion, vowing revenge.

The Saga of the Circle of Britain

When a horde of Aelle's Saxon warbands erupts over the border between Dumnonia and Ceint, sacking villages to the west, Arthur rides out with his own army to drive Aelle away.

After several days of scouting the Saxons are finally spotted and both armies begin to search for a place to battle.

Arthur rolls against his Locale skill of 69% and gets a 31. Aelle, with a Locale skill of only 55% also succeeds, but manages to roll higher with a 48.

Thus it is Aelle who chooses where the fight will be, deciding on a low hill near the River Tamesis where the Saxons will hold the high ground.

The Saga of the Circle of Britain

From their hilltop, several drunken Saxon champions emerge from the gathered warbands to perform lewd war-dances whilst proclaiming their lineage and victories.

One dances down the slope towards the Circle of Britain and cries out a demand for personal combat. Without a second thought, Cullwch (as reckless and foolhardy as they come) steps out of line and accepts the challenge. The fight is intense, but over quickly. When Cullwch finally disarms the Saxon champion, he decides to show how ruthless Celts can be and, transfixes him with his spear, then spits on the fallen Saxon's body.

On the summit, the gathered enemy groans in despair. The Games Master rolls 1d100 for the fallen warrior's unit against their Loyalty (Aelle) passion of 64%, to see if they remain on the battlefield. The roll is a 04, a critical success! Not only does the unit stand firm, but it also begins howling for vengeance. Unfortunately for Cullwch, it seems the man he just killed was Aelle's beloved nephew...

Cullwch returns to the line, expecting some form of praise for killing the enemy champion. Regrettably for him, Bishop Gerhaint, the priest of the Church of the Holy Thorn, has attached himself to the Circle of Britain, hoping to make converts, and launches into an inspirational, yet pious, speech.

Morale checks over the course of the battle are one grade easier.

- Success: The unit laughs-off the loss, claiming the enemy cheated or it was the god's will. Beyond becoming resolute to engage in battle, there is no additional effect.
- Failure: The unit takes the loss as a superstitious sign, or a sign that their foes are superior to them. Although they will stand to fight in the battle, morale checks over its course are one grade harder.
- Fumble: The unit is so overwhelmed by its loss that it withdraws from the battlefield to mourn. Its morale is utterly sapped and they will not participate in any further fighting.

Note that some personal challenges can be used to avoid further phases in the overall battle. For instance, if the fight occurs between the two overall commanders, forcing one side to depart entirely.

Stirring Speech

Commanders may attempt to rouse their unit with a stirring speech, bolstering its morale in the face of imminent combat. Such speeches are risky, however, with a chance of back-firing upon the commander if the oration is lacklustre.

To represent a motivational speech, the commander must make an unopposed roll against their Oratory skill. Influence, at a Hard Difficulty Grade, can be used if the commander does not have Oratory. The results of the roll are as follows:

- Critical Success: The unit is so inspired by the stirring speech that it is immune to morale checks until it has taken 30% casualties.
- Success: The unit gains a temporary boost to its morale checks for the first 1d3+3 Battle Rounds, making them one Difficulty Grade easier.
- Failure: The unit is so underwhelmed it suffers a temporary reduction to its morale checks for the first 1d3+3 Battle Rounds, making them one Difficulty Grade harder.
- Fumble: The unit is so upset or horrified by the speech that it will automatically break as soon as it is forced to make a morale check.

If present, druids and læce can replace the Stirring Speech with their own rituals, sacrifices and chants. Druids, for example, might parade, cavort and dance before the ranked enemies invoking the gods of death and spirits of the ancestors. Animals, prisoners or slaves might also be sacrificed to guarantee the summoning, the blood being daubed on the faces and weapons of the front rank of the shield wall.

Engagement

The next phase of a battle is manoeuvring and exchange of blows. Hand to hand combat requires the units to be in contact, whereas ranged combat does not. Each battle round, both commanders must make a roll against their Command skill. The base Command skill is either Lore (Strategy and Tactics) or Oratory (Hard) or Influence (Formidable). The commander can augment the skill being used with an appropriate Passion (Hate Saxons), for example.

Just as with personal combat, each commander makes a Differential skill roll against their

Command Roll. The level of success determines the effect, and results are applied simultaneously.

- If neither side succeeds, there is no damage that Battle Round
- If both sides succeed, both sides inflict and sustain damage.
- If one side scores one or more levels of success higher than the opposing unit, one (or more) Battle Actions can be chosen and applied to the combat.

This procedure is repeated every round until one unit retires, surrenders or is wiped out. Player characters who are part of a unit risk being seriously injured whenever it suffers casualties. Morale, Character Injuries and Battle Actions are described later (see Running a Battle).

Retiring from the Field

Once fortune turns against a unit, it will usually depart from the battlefield. There are two methods of performing this. First is that a commander can voluntarily order his troops to fall back in good order, maintaining cohesion so that they can protect themselves and prevent further loss. The second occurs when a unit fails a crucial morale check and routs.

A rout spells doom for the routing troops. No longer in formation the warriors scatter, discard heavy weapons such as shields, and run headlong for cover. Although this permits them to outpace the immediate enemy, they can still be caught by other units previously positioned to cut them off, or by cavalry or creatures which have a higher movement rate. If this happens, the routing troops

The Saga of the Circle of Britain

Rather than lauding acts of bravery Gerhaint bombastically preaches the importance of restraint, mercy and trusting in God's Will. The Games Master rolls to see what affect the speech has and Bishop Gerhaint fails his Oratory skill. Instead of inspiring them to work better as a team, he manages to alienate the Circle of Britain, who actually favour Cullwch's no-nonsense victory. Their morale bruised for the first four Battle Rounds, Bishop Gerhaint successfully implores Arthur to hold the unit in reserve, behind the main battle line.

The Saga of the Circle of Britain

Positioned to hold the centre of the Dumnonian line, Arthur's infantry finds itself facing Aelle's personal warband. The Saxons, furious and seeking blood, start the battle by charging down the hill in wedge formation, taking advantage of the slope to increase their impact. As the units engage, both Aelle and Efford, the Dumnonian captain, roll against their Command skill and succeed.

Since neither gained a level of success over his foe, there are no Battle Actions. The Dumnonians, however, still roll 2d6 damage, inflicting 9 casualties on the Saxons. Whereas the less numerous Saxons only do 1d10 damage getting an 8, but double the roll for being in wedge formation, a second time for charging and a third for the charge travelling downhill. Thus the Saxons inflict a horrific 64 casualties as they smash into the Dumnonian shield wall.

Due to suffering so many casualties Efford's infantry has to make a Hard morale check, which it promptly fails and becomes Shaken. Despite this, they continue fighting as they remain engaged. Aelle's warband, on the other hand, failed to disrupt the well trained Dumnonian troops, resulting in the Wedge bogging down and falling apart. Thus, on the second round, Efford's warriors remain in Line formation whereas the Saxon warband is in Skirmish formation.

can be engaged by the new unit, without fear of taking any casualties in return. In this case the likely result will be the total annihilation of the routing troops.

In certain circumstances, the commander in charge of a unit which has just broken its enemy, will want to pursue the routing warriors. This is permitted, but entails the unit devolving into skirmish formation to be able to keep up, at the risk of following the routers into a prepared trap or leaving other units on their side unsupported.

A rout has the added bonus in that it permits player characters a final chance of single combat. If desired, a character may attempt to spot a high value target, such as an enemy banner bearer, or commander, amongst the fleeing foes. Spotting such a prize first requires a successful Perception roll at Formidable difficulty, after which an opposed Athletics test between the pursuer and the foe is needed to capture them before they rout from the field; or, if the enemy is cut off from escape, a group opposed Athletics test between all those attempting to reach the target first.

Aftermath

A battle is won by whichever side maintains control of the battlefield once the fighting has concluded. Since the majority of casualties are still living, albeit incapacitated by their wounds, the victors are not only able to recover a significant number of their own warriors, but have the tough decision of whether to ignore, capture or kill those foes still lying upon the field.

Assume one fifth of casualties die outright during the battle, with the remainder too injured to fight again for weeks or months, assuming they get some form of medical treatment.

Of course, some battles conclude with no clear victor on either side; at which point opposing commanders generally come to terms in order to recover their own wounded and bury the dead before they become a health hazard.

Running a Battle

When preparing a battle, Games Masters should first consider the objectives of the enemy force and then listen to their players' plans, before deciding which battle phases will be utilised. The most detailed and time intensive phase is Engagement.

As described previously, each commander makes a Command skill check and compares them as per a differential roll. Rolling equal to, or under, the skill value means the unit inflicts a number of casualties equal to its Unit Damage rating, remembering to apply any modifiers due to its current formation. Rolling over the skill value results in no additional casualties that round. If both units fail to inflict damage then nothing happens if they are exchanging ranged weapons; or both sides briefly draw apart, breaking contact, if engaged in hand-to-hand combat.

If a commander manages to both inflict casualties and achieve one or more levels of success over their opponent, then they may select an equivalent number of Battle Actions, granting the unit a tactical advantage over the enemy unit, if successful.

In the circumstance when one unit armed with ranged weapons engages an opposing unit without, the targeted unit obviously cannot inflict any damage on its attacker. Its commander can however, still roll against their Command skill to in an attempt to win some Battle Actions, or at least, prevent any being used on his unit.

Units which are not under direct attack may freely move, redeploy, retreat, charge or flank as they desire, provided there is clear space for their formation to manoeuvre. Once engaged they must rely upon a Battle Action to do anything more.

Winning A Battle

Individual units continue to fight until they are ordered off the field by their commander, fail their morale, either surrendering or breaking, or are surrounded and cut down to the last man. The battle is won when one side is left in possession of the field.

Not all battles need end with a clear victor. Some engagements might be so vicious that the commanders of both sides voluntarily call a cessation to combat before their forces are mutually annihilated. In such cases the battle can be either called a draw or a Pyrrhic victory.

Unit Condition

To keep track of what is happening to units engaged in battle, a number of terms specific to their status and condition are defined as follows:

Broken

A unit which has lost all morale or cohesion becomes a Broken Formation and must flee the battlefield.

Contact

Units are in contact when they are engaged in *hand-to-hand* combat with one another. Contact can be broken, for instance if the leaders of both units fail Command rolls causing their troops to draw naturally apart.

Disrupted

When a close order formation is disrupted, it temporarily loses its cohesion and is thereafter treated as a skirmish formation. If a skirmish formation is disrupted, it becomes broken.

Engaged

The circumstance when a unit is in combat against an enemy formation. A unit can be engaged, even if it cannot initiate the encounter itself. For example if it is Shaken or is under attack by ranged weapons and lacks the same.

Enveloped

An enveloped unit is one which has been overlapped by an enemy with a larger frontage. This continues until the unit can retire, redeploy or push through.

Shaken

Being shaken prevents the unit from initiating any engagement. If an already shaky formation is shaken for a second time, it becomes Broken.

Morale Checks

Morale checks test the confidence a unit has in both its commander, and its own members, to stand and fight. They are required whenever a unit loses a certain proportion of its warriors, but can also be triggered by particular Battle Actions. As a battle continues, morale checks often start to suffer increasing penalties due to adverse events and conditions.

When a unit's casualties reach a particular level, a morale check is required. This happens provided that no other morale check was rolled for as part of a Battle Action that round. The listed values illustrate the base difficulty of any and all morale checks for a unit, once it has suffered that many casualties.

Failing a morale check usually results in the unit becoming Shaken, and if it subsequently fails a second time it is Broken. Thus, a commander who suspects their troops are on the verge of breaking should pro-actively initiate an ordered withdrawal from the field to ensure no rout occurs.

The situational modifiers should be made, as applicable, to morale checks by the unit. As per the Mythras core rules, only the largest penalty and bonus should be applied. They do not stack.

Both leaders roll Command skills, this time Aelle gaining a critical and a level of success over his opponent. Damage is exchanged, but Aelle chooses Shake as his Battle Action, driving his screaming Saxons onwards with reckless abandon. This is too much for the Dumnonian shield wall which promptly fails another morale check (Hard difficulty for its current casualty level, increased to Formidable), changing its status from Shaken to Broken. Fearing for their lives the spearmen rout from the field, leaving the way open for Aelle to attack the hated Circle of Britain.

Pausing only to redeploy his disrupted unit into a shield wall, Aelle charges the Circle of Britain in the hope of repeating his previous success. This time, however, it is Eowald who is opposing him, having joined the front rank of the Circle of Britain's shield wall.

They both roll against their Command skills, but this time Aelle fails. For his Battle Action (unbeknownst to the Saxon) Eowald detaches the rear ranks to form a flanking unit.

Over the next four rounds both units grind together, the Saxons proving themselves tenacious foes inflicting 5, 7, 3 and 8 casualties before they are broken and routed, when the detachment hits their flank.

The Saga of the Circle of Britain

As a member of the Circle of Britain, Cullwch must roll each round in which his unit suffers damage, to see if he, himself, is injured. Losses in the first round are 5 in 120, or 5% (4.16% rounded up), so Cullwch rolls 1d100 and gets 56. He survives first contact, although five of his comrades drop. On the second round his chance of becoming a casualty rises to 7 in 115 (9%); on the third round 3 in 108 (3%); and, on the last round, 8 in 105 (9%). Fortunately for Cullwch, he continues to roll over the loss percentage and survives intact, but, if the battle had lasted much longer, the risk of being injured would have risen considerably.

With Aelle fleeing from the field, the remaining Saxon units also turn tail and rout. Cullwch emerges from the battle with no significant injuries save those he received from his single combat. Having no orders to pursue, he stays behind to help deal with the dead and dying.

1 Modifier may be ignored if the unit is in favourable terrain, such as plugging a choke point or behind fortifications.

2 Applies in situations when the unit possesses arms and armour significantly superior to those of its opponents. The bonus can be increased in cases where there is a technological disparity.

3 If the unit knows that it will not be offered mercy, its remaining warriors will fight to the last man instead.

Character Injuries

When player characters join a unit in battle, they face the risk of being injured whenever that unit suffers casualties. Becoming a casualty does not necessarily imply death, but can result in a terrible wound; most likely preventing the character continuing as an effective member of the formation or retreating from the battlefield without aid.

There are several ways of determining whether a player character becomes a casualty, depending on how abstract the Games Master wishes to make the threat. The simplest method is to work out what percentage of the unit was lost that round, and force every participating character to roll 1d100. If the roll is equal to, or less than, the loss percentage, then they have been wounded that round – perhaps because they were attacked more often than they could parry, faced someone better than them, or simply didn't see the blow coming.

Players are permitted to use a Luck Point to re-roll becoming a casualty. On the rare chance that more player characters become casualties that round than the unit actually suffered in damage, the Games Master should either roll randomly to see who suffers, or allow the potential casualties to roll against their Combat Style and declare those who rolled worst as the injured.

Whatever the reason, the character automatically suffers a Serious Wound to a random Hit Location, or if previously damaged in that area, a Major Wound instead. They must make an opposed Endurance test versus the enemy's Command roll to remain functional, conscious or alive.

Morale Checks

Casualties	Base Morale Check
5%	Standard
15%	Hard
30%	Formidable
50%	Herculean
75%	Automatically Broken
> 110%	Fanatical

Situational Modifiers

Situation	Difficulty Modifier
Nearby allied unit leaves the field	1 grade harder
Unit is starving or thirsty	1 grade harder
Unit commander is a casualty	2 grades harder
Outnumbered 2:1[1]	1 grade harder
Outnumbered 3:1[1]	2 grades harder
Outnumbered 5:1[1]	3 grades harder
Unit possesses superior arms[2]	1 grade easier
Unit possesses superior magic	1-2 grades easier
Unit fighting to defend homeland	1-3 grades easier
Unit has no means of escape[3]	Surrenders

1. Modifier may be ignored if the unit is in favourable terrain, such as defending a choke point or behind fortifications.

2. Applies in situations when the unit possesses arms and armour significantly superior to those of its opponents.

3. If the unit knows it will not be offered mercy, its remaining warriors will fight to the last man instead.

Character Rewards

Although the risks of battle are very high, and fate can be distinctly capricious, characters can gain recognition for their efforts in battle. Rewards can range from war spoils, or plunder given in thanks for their noticeable efforts, to honours such as medals or even social promotion.

The chance of being rewarded depends on a number of factors which can be seen in the Reward Points table. Once the battle concludes, each character totals these accumulated points then rolls against that value on 1d100.

- Critical Success: The character is either promoted (in military rank or social class) or, instead, granted a valuable medal, wreath or other badge displaying the honour they have won. Such an award will boost their status and grant a bonus to skills used in the right social situation.
- Success: The character is rewarded with some form of trophy; either an item of armour or weaponry of quality, which they can personally use, or an item (or items) of conspicuous value which can later be traded for wealth.
- Failure: The character falls beneath the notice of their commander.
- Fumble: The character manages to perform an act so crass that they alienate their commander or fellow warriors, such as boasting of a kill which wasn't theirs, or being first to retreat before the enemy. Instead of receiving a reward, they are, instead, punished, or even blamed for some failure.

Character Rewards

Action	Points
Every round of active battle participation	1 point
Fighting on after becoming a casualty	+10 points
Fighting courageously (doubling character casualty chance)	+1 point per round
Fighting cautiously (halving character casualty chance)	-1 point per round
Winning a Personal Challenge	+1/5 of the opponent's Combat Style
Capturing an enemy standard or unit commander	+50 points
Capturing or killing the commander of the entire enemy force	+100 points

Battle Actions

Battle Actions are the equivalent of Special Effects used in personal combat. Each round of battle, a commander who successfully passes their Command skill and gains one, or more, levels of success over their opponent receives the chance to order an equal number of Battle Actions. This can be viewed as taking advantage of an opportunity — perhaps one leader is briefly distracted, his men falter, or a momentary gap opens up in the formation — at which point, the opposing commander can seize the moment to perform a tactical manoeuvre and take advantage of the situation.

Just as with Special Effects, some of the Battle Actions are restricted due to the quality of the initial Command roll, require pre-prepared troop dispositions, or can only be applied by particular formations.

The table of Battle Actions can be found on pages 194 and 195.

The Saga of the Circle of Britain

On the following day, Arthur musters the army and rewards are given out. Since he won a very public personal challenge, and performed well during the fighting, Cullwch expects to gain some form of recognition.

The Games Master tallies up the points: 18 for accepting and winning the challenge, but only 5 from the five rounds of combat against Aelle's warband, since he did not fight particularly courageously. This gives a total of 23. The dice are rolled and Cullwch gets a 47. Although Cullwch sulks and Eowald petitions Arthur, he is granted no special honours, leading both Cullwch and Eowald to suspect that Bishop Gerhaint has influenced Arthur's decision to snub Cullwch's initial bravery.

Cullwch spits, farts in Bishop's Gerhaint's general direction, and decides that he will, from now on, watch the Christian priest closely...

Spot Rules

Some addition spot rules have been included to cover unusual circumstances.

Ambushes and Ruses

Similar in format to flanking, an ambush or ruse relies more on pre-preparing the battlefield to take advantage of its natural features, or by concealing the true nature of a unit so that foes misjudge its purpose.

Ambushes are triggered if an enemy blithely wanders past terrain in which an allied unit has been hidden prior to the battle starting, or is tricked into approaching the area via the Feigned Retreat Battle Action. This normally requires an opposed test of the ambushing commander's Stealth skill vs. the enemy commander's Perception skill.

If the ambush fails to be discovered, then the enemy formation suffers a surprise attack, during which the commander is assumed to have automatically failed his Command roll on the first round, and suffers a difficulty grade of Formidable on the second. If the enemy unit is still intact, there are no further penalties from the third round onwards.

A ruse occurs when a unit is disguised to appear as a completely different body of warriors, either luring the enemy to attack an apparently ill-trained formation or intimidating the enemy from engaging with what seems to be an infamous crack unit. To pull off the ruse requires the deceitful commander to win an opposed test of his Conceal skill vs. the enemy commander's Insight skill.

Changing Formation

Provided that it has trained in the formation being adopted, a unit may freely change formation, provided it is not currently engaged in combat. If it is in contact with the enemy or under fire, it may only change formation by use of a Battle Action.

Charging

A unit not currently in contact may freely charge the enemy, provided they are not blocked by terrain, or, intercepted by the enemy. Charging over a long distance breaks up the cohesion of a close order unit. Thus, most charges occur at short range, often when two formations briefly draw away from each other after both commanders fail to inflict casualties. In this latter case specifically, assume that the re-engaging charge and Command roll for inflicting damage occur in the same Battle Round.

Fatigue

Each Battle Round represents Medium activity in terms of Fatigue. If Games Masters want to add Fatigue into the equation – especially if it appears to be taking several rounds to resolve a shield wall clash – then Endurance rolls should be made at the end of each round to see if the effects of Fatigue should be applied. The Endurance for the unit is the average Endurance for its members. If Fatigue is accrued, follow the scale provided on page 79 of MYTHRAS, but only applying the Skill Grade modifier. When combat moves into standard Combat Rounds, characters should check for Fatigue again, applying the effects as accrued.

Flanking

A flanking attack occurs when an enemy formation, currently engaged in combat to its front, is hit from a second direction. Being unable to turn freely to face the new unit, it suffers a terrible disadvantage in the Differential Roll to determine the effects of the attack; requiring a Hard Command check if struck in the flank or a Formidable Command check if attacked from the rear. If the target formation is a phalanx, make the difficulty grades one step worse.

To perform such an attack, the flanking unit must be out of contact with other units and have sufficient space to manoeuvre so that it can reach the sides or rear of the enemy formation. As flanking can be so devastating, the commander of the targeted formation should be permitted a Perception check to notice the approaching unit. If successful, they gain 1d3 rounds warning to try to protect themselves, either via winning a Battle Action or by calling upon an allied unit to intercept on their behalf.

Ganging Up

The commander of a unit, simultaneously engaged with two or more enemy formations, is permitted to attempt a Command roll against each one that round. This can be done even if some of the enemy units are using ranged attacks, to help avoid negative Battle Actions. No penalty is applied to multiple Command checks,

provided the unit is engaged frontally. Otherwise treat attacks from the side or rear as per Flanking.

Missile Fire

Units which launch ranged attacks inflict the same damage as indicated by their frontage. Whilst it may seem that, logically, the entire unit could loose their weapons together, lack of accuracy over distance and limited rates of fire make it less effective than hand to hand combat. Additionally, some weapons such as slings or crossbows preclude the ability to repeatedly fire in ranks.

Movement & Retreat

All unit movement is treated as occurring simultaneously each round. Therefore units which are not currently in contact are free to move away from the enemy, and cannot be re-engaged in hand to hand combat unless the pursuers have a higher movement rate.

For instance, if two units in Line formation naturally break contact due to both failing Command rolls, one could take the opportunity to retreat off the field safely, whilst the other follows but unable to re-initiate contact.

Units which end up in contact after moving may attack each other in hand to hand combat on the following round.

Final Note

Remember that the battle rules are highly abstracted to greatly simplify the running of large scale engagements. They are *not* intended to be comprehensive, but merely offers a solid framework to fit the core tactics of Dark Ages warfare.

Battle Actions

Battle Action	Restriction	Effect
Charge	Charging unit must start out of contact	Assuming it is currently out of contact with opposing formations, the unit can charge an enemy formation, hitting home on a subsequent round as decided by the Games Master, based upon the distance it must travel. Close order formations which charge for more than one Battle Round automatically disintegrate into Skirmish formation. Charging, however, will double the damage dice on impact.
Combine	Units must share the same Combat Style trait	Units from the same force may combine together, reinforcing one another, providing they share a common Combat Style trait. Thereafter, they are treated as a single, larger formation, potentially offsetting morale penalties and permitting the ranking commander to apply (hopefully) better skills.
Detach	Unavailable to Phalanx or Tortoise formations	Permits a formation to hive off part of its strength to form a smaller subsidiary unit, which can then be used as a flanking or reserve unit, at the expense of reducing the original unit's frontage or depth. The detached unit must be led by a new commander and is treated as an independent entity for the remainder of the battle.
Divide	None	Allows close order troops to briefly split apart, permitting less manoeuvrable, or unstoppable charging units (rampaging elephants or scythed chariots for instance), to pass through without the receiving formation suffering casualties or becoming Disrupted.
Engulf	Skirmish, Line or Circle formations	Assuming it has equal or greater strength, the unit opens up a killing pocket into which the enemy falls unless they win an opposed test of their Competence vs. the original Command roll. Thereafter the enemy cannot Redeploy and are trapped, unable to escape unless they Push free.
Envelop	Line formation only	If the unit has a larger frontage than its engaged opposing formation, its commander may overlap the spare troops around the flanks of the enemy, thus increasing the damage dice rolled each Battle Round to the full amount permitted to its frontage. The enemy unit, however, is still limited to its lesser frontage until it can redeploy.
Feigned Retreat	None	Sets up the enemy formation, luring it into a vulnerable position or pre-prepared ambush. The enemy unit must win an opposed test of their Competence vs. the original Command roll, otherwise, starting on the following round, they chase down the fleeing troops and suffer the detrimental effects of the ruse (see Additional Rules). Once the trap is sprung, the falsely retreating troops must, themselves, pass a morale check to reform, or else the rout becomes genuine.
Guard	None	Reduces the casualty losses of the defending unit by half that round. If the Command roll was a critical success, then no losses are incurred.
Harass	Skirmishers only	Using a combination of false charges or ranged attacks, the skirmishing unit causes an enemy unit to suffer a penalty of one additional Difficulty Grade to any morale checks until the skirmisher ceases engagement.
Push	Unavailable to Circle or Wedge formations	If the unit has an equal, or greater, depth than the enemy, it pushes them backwards. In this case phalanx formations halve the depth of non phalanxes. It can be used to shove an enemy formation from elevated positions, back away from fortifications, through a choke point, or to break free from being engulfed. In confining spaces, such as being pinned against a cliff or river, the enemy must win an opposed test of their Competence vs. the original Command roll, or else become Broken.

Battle Actions

Battle Action	Restriction	Effect
Rally	Shaken units only	Commander may attempt an unopposed Oratory check, which if passed, removes the Shaken condition from their unit.
Redeploy	None	The unit may change its existing formation to another type permitted by its Combat Style trait, whether or not it is currently engaged.
Reform	None	Permits a Disrupted unit to pull itself back into formation.
Repulse	Units receiving charges only	On receiving a charge, whether from foot troops, cavalry or chariots, the unit repulses the enemy, causing them to become Disrupted (if not so already).
Retire	None	Allows the unit to disentangle itself from close combat and withdraw out of contact. Whilst it may then retreat from battle in good order, it remains vulnerable to ranged weapons or being charged by higher movement rate troops until it has left the field entirely.
Savage	None	The unit rolls its damage dice twice, taking the best result and applying it to the enemy formation that round. If the Command roll was a critical success, then maximum damage is inflicted.
Shake	Critical only	Requires the enemy formation to pass an unopposed morale check at one Difficulty Grade harder than it is currently suffering, or become Shaken. If already shaken the enemy breaks.
Shatter	Phalanx or Wedge formation only	Enemy unit must win an opposed test of their Competence vs. the original Command roll, or else become Disrupted. If already in Skirmish formation, they are Broken instead. The enemy roll gains a bonus of one Difficulty Grade easier for each point of depth that they have in superiority to the attacking unit, and vice versa if they have fewer ranks. For this calculation, the depth of Line formations is halved. If the modifier reduces the enemy roll to Hopeless, the formation is automatically Broken and the attacking unit breaks through to the other side.
Shock	Charging units only	Charged unit must win an opposed test of their Morale vs. the original Command roll, or else be reduced to Skirmish formation. If they were already in Skirmish formation, they are Broken instead.
Take Cover	Units under ranged attack only	Assuming it is not engaged in melee, the unit seeks cover, preventing it from taking any more casualties from ranged weapons. In the process, however, it becomes pinned down, unable to move unless the unit wishes to lose its protection.
Target Character	Critical only	The unit focuses on taking out a specific member of the enemy unit, whether a hated foe, a traitor or the unit's commander. The target must win an opposed test of their Combat Style vs. the original Command roll, or else they become a casualty.

YTHIC RITONS

In this chapter you will find extended descriptions and game statistics for some of the major characters mentioned throughout the previous chapters, along with game statistics for generic non-player characters such as typical Celtic warriors, Saxon warband members, and so on.

More descriptions and game values are to be found amongst the scenarios that comprise the latter part of this book so, between this chapter and those, *Mythic Britain* Games Masters should have no shortage of examples of characters and character types for ad -hoc use.

In designing the major characters featured in this chapter, the character creation rules from MYTHRAS and this book have been adhered to as far as possible; however there are one or two characters (Merlin being an obvious example) where we have used some license to be able to fully reflect their peculiar nature.

It is also possible to use these characters in a variety of different ways. The statistics can be used to represent different warlords, chieftains, commanders and so forth, either by using the statistics unchanged or with a few slight amendments here and there. They can also be used as player characters too, just as written. There is no reason why the *Mythic Britain* campaign cannot be played with Arthur, Gawain and Derec as the protagonists, supported by loyal warriors and warbands. Morgana's statistics can be used for any druid and Father Samsun's for any priest — or they can also be used precisely as they are.

It is recommended that Merlin be reserved solely as a non-player character. He is the perfect patron and instigator of adventure for the player characters and his peculiar nature (quasi-immortal, half-in, half-out of the spirit world) makes him somewhat unique when compared with the rest of these Mythic Britons.

Arthur

Bastard son of Uther Pendragon and Ygraine of Kernow, Arthur ap Uther is a warlord entering the prime of his life and on the verge of becoming a legend. Taken from Ygraine by Merlin shortly after his birth (because King Mark sought to murder the child), Arthur was placed into the care of the warlord Cai at Caer Wynd in Elmet. Merlin called spirits to safeguard the infant but had already seen in him a greatness that would, if nurtured, unite Britain against its enemies.

Cai was always honest with Arthur about his ancestry. He grew up in Elmet knowing that his father was the Pendragon and his mother (now dead, killed, presumably by a vengeful Mark) the queen of Kernow. Yet Arthur never showed resentment or rancour. Cai trained him in the arts of war alongside his own son, Derec, and, in time, Arthur proved himself to be an adept leader of men; so much so that, by the time he was 16, he had fought in his first shield wall against Saxons who came north from Mierce and threatened Elmet's border. Soon after this Arthur was commanding men of his own, and Cai found that he had a natural way of gaining their confidence and inspiring them to do their best, no matter what the undertaking.

In time, and after Mordred's death, Arthur moved to Dumnonia, bringing with him his warband and heavy horse cavalry. Uther made use of him against the ambitious Aelle but never once recognised Arthur as his son. Arthur made his name in these battles: clever, cunning, brave and as tactically brilliant as Uther.

In the years since Uther's death Arthur has remained in Dumnonia and made Caer Cadbryg his home and operational base. The other warlords of Dumnonia recognise his intelligence and natural leadership ability, welcoming him into their fold.

Personality

Arthur is instantly likeable. Tall, strong and good-looking, he is able to make easy small-talk and engage with people whatever their background and status in life. He takes a keen interest in everything and has a way of putting people at their ease. When he takes charge, his voice is loud, assured and commanding: he radiates authority and confidence in that infectious way common to all great leaders. He attempts to see the good in all people and this can lead him to be too forgiving and too accepting of weakness. He loves to be liked: Arthur has trouble dealing with rejection, perhaps because he was forcibly removed from one parent and ignored by the other. He is a passionate, loving man and, again, this is a weakness. He is prepared to surrender his usual level-headedness for love (and, sometimes, lust) meaning that he can be manipulated all the more easily.

For all that, people — especially his warriors — genuinely love him and are utterly loyal to him. Merlin's suspicions were right: if anyone can unite Britain, then it is Arthur. But, might he also have the power, as did his father, to sunder it?

Caledfwlch

One of the Thirteen Treasures of Britain, Arthur attained Caledfwlch after fighting in his first shield wall and distinguishing himself in the battle. Merlin took Arthur north, into the land of the Great Lakes, and to the Wolf Lake where its guardian spirit, Yvayne, brought the sword to Arthur on the understanding that Caledfwlch would be one day returned to her, and that Arthur would find a champion to reside with Yvayne for eternity. Caledfwlch cannot be broken, never needs to be sharpened, and inspires in men loyalty and courage. This is represented by Caledfwlch having its own Inspire Loyalty and Courage Passion of 100%. When Arthur calls upon the sword this Passion augments the 100 men closest to Arthur, adding 20% to these warrior's combat styles (or other appropriate skills being used). To look at, Caledfwlch is an unremarkable Celtic longsword — but then, so many of Gorfannon's treasures are unostentatious and workmanlike; such is the way of the Smith of the Gods. When viewed in the Spirit World Caledfwlch gleams and sparkles, its blade like a shimmering razor in the first rays of a golden summer sun.

Arthur-ap-Uther

Characteristics	Attributes	1d20	Location	AP/HP
STR: 15	Action Points: 3	1–3	Right Leg	3/6
CON: 15	Damage Modifier: +1d2	4–6	Left Leg	3/6
SIZ: 14	Magic Points: 14	7–9	Abdomen	5/7
DEX: 16	Movement: 6 metres	10–12	Chest	5/8
INT: 18	Initiative Bonus: 17/11	13–15	Right Arm	0/5
POW: 14	Armour: Leather, Mail, Plate Helm	16–18	Left Arm	0/5
CHA: 18		19–20	Head	5/6

Skills: *Athletics 60%, Brawn 55%, Customs (Celt) 90%, Endurance 63%, Evade 65%, Influence 85%, Insight 74%, Language (Brythonic) 100%, Language (Goidelic) 35%, Lore (Strategy and Tactics) 112%, Oratory 95%, Perception 58%, Ride 95%, Superstition 40%, Survival 59%, Unarmed 63%, Willpower 42%*

Love Guinevere 90%, Loyalty to Britain 100%, Loyalty to Merlin 80%, Pagan 46%

Combat Style: Noble (Spear, Sword, and Shield. Trait, Mounted Combat) 120%; Shield Wall (Spear, Sword, and Shield. Trait, Shield Wall) 112%. Arthur uses his Noble style when fighting from horseback, which is his preferred method of fighting these days. When on foot he opts for the shield wall style when he has comrades close, as this provides greater overall protection and security.

Weapon	Size/Force	Reach	Damage	AP/HP
Shortspear	*M*	*L*	*1d8+1d2*	*4/5*
Longsword (Caledfwlch)	*M*	*M*	*1d6+2+1d2*	*Unbreakable*
Celtic Shield	*H*	*S*	*1d3+1+1d4*	*4/15*

Arthur

Bastard son of Uther Pendragon and Ygraine of Kernow, Arthur ap Uther is a warlord entering the prime of his life and on the verge of becoming a legend. Taken from Ygraine by Merlin shortly after his birth (because King Mark sought to murder the child), Arthur was placed into the care of the warlord Cai at Caer Wynd in Elmet. Merlin called spirits to safeguard the infant but had already seen in him a greatness that would, if nurtured, unite Britain against its enemies.

Cai was always honest with Arthur about his ancestry. He grew up in Elmet knowing that his father was the Pendragon and his mother (now dead, killed, presumably by a vengeful Mark) the queen of Kernow. Yet Arthur never showed resentment or rancour. Cai trained him in the arts of war alongside his own son, Derec, and, in time, Arthur proved himself to be an adept leader of men; so much so that, by the time he was 16, he had fought in his first shield wall against Saxons who came north from Mierce and threatened Elmet's border. Soon after this Arthur was commanding men of his own, and Cai found that he had a natural way of gaining their confidence and inspiring them to do their best, no matter what the undertaking.

In time, and after Mordred's death, Arthur moved to Dumnonia, bringing with him his warband and heavy horse cavalry. Uther made use of him against the ambitious Aelle but never once recognised Arthur as his son. Arthur made his name in these battles: clever, cunning, brave and as tactically brilliant as Uther.

In the years since Uther's death Arthur has remained in Dumnonia and made Caer Cadbryg his home and operational base. The other warlords of Dumnonia recognise his intelligence and natural leadership ability, welcoming him into their fold.

Personality

Arthur is instantly likeable. Tall, strong and good-looking, he is able to make easy small-talk and engage with people whatever their background and status in life. He takes a keen interest in everything and has a way of putting people at their ease. When he takes charge, his voice is loud, assured and commanding: he radiates authority and confidence in that infectious way common to all great leaders. He attempts to see the good in all people and this can lead him to be too forgiving and too accepting of weakness. He loves to be liked: Arthur has trouble dealing with rejection, perhaps because he was forcibly removed from one parent and ignored by the other. He is a passionate, loving man and, again,

this is a weakness. He is prepared to surrender his usual level-headedness for love (and, sometimes, lust) meaning that he can be manipulated all the more easily.

For all that, people — especially his warriors — genuinely love him and are utterly loyal to him. Merlin's suspicions were right: if anyone can unite Britain, then it is Arthur. But, might he also have the power, as did his father, to sunder it?

Caledfwlch

One of the Thirteen Treasures of Britain, Arthur attained Caledfwlch after fighting in his first shield wall and distinguishing himself in the battle. Merlin took Arthur north, into the land of the Great Lakes, and to the Wolf Lake where its guardian spirit, Yvayne, brought the sword to Arthur on the understanding that Caledfwlch would be one day returned to her, and that Arthur would find a champion to reside with Yvayne for eternity. Caledfwlch cannot be broken, never needs to be sharpened, and inspires in men loyalty and courage. This is represented by Caledfwlch having its own Inspire Loyalty and Courage Passion of 100%. When Arthur calls upon the sword this Passion augments the 100 men closest to Arthur, adding 20% to these warrior's combat styles (or other appropriate skills being used). To look at, Caledfwlch is an unremarkable Celtic longsword — but then, so many of Gorfannon's treasures are unostentatious and workmanlike; such is the way of the Smith of the Gods. When viewed in the Spirit World Caledfwlch gleams and sparkles, its blade like a shimmering razor in the first rays of a golden summer sun.

Arthur-ap-Uther

Characteristics	Attributes	1d20	Location	AP/HP
STR: 15	Action Points: 3	1–3	Right Leg	3/6
CON: 15	Damage Modifier: +1d2	4–6	Left Leg	3/6
SIZ: 14	Magic Points: 14	7–9	Abdomen	5/7
DEX: 16	Movement: 6 metres	10–12	Chest	5/8
INT: 18	Initiative Bonus: 17/11	13–15	Right Arm	0/5
POW: 14	Armour: Leather, Mail, Plate Helm	16–18	Left Arm	0/5
CHA: 18		19–20	Head	5/6

Skills: *Athletics 60%, Brawn 55%, Customs (Celt) 90%, Endurance 63%, Evade 65%, Influence 85%, Insight 74%, Language (Brythonic) 100%, Language (Goidelic) 35%, Lore (Strategy and Tactics) 112%, Oratory 95%, Perception 58%, Ride 95%, Superstition 40%, Survival 59%, Unarmed 63%, Willpower 42%*

Love Guinevere 90%, Loyalty to Britain 100%, Loyalty to Merlin 80%, Pagan 46%

Combat Style: Noble (Spear, Sword, and Shield. Trait, Mounted Combat) 120%; Shield Wall (Spear, Sword, and Shield. Trait, Shield Wall) 112%. Arthur uses his Noble style when fighting from horseback, which is his preferred method of fighting these days. When on foot he opts for the shield wall style when he has comrades close, as this provides greater overall protection and security.

Weapon	Size/Force	Reach	Damage	AP/HP
Shortspear	*M*	*L*	*1d8+1d2*	*4/5*
Longsword (Caledfwlch)	*M*	*M*	*1d6+2+1d2*	*Unbreakable*
Celtic Shield	*H*	*S*	*1d3+1+1d4*	*4/15*

Merlin

Merlin is the arch druid of Britain. Chosen by the river goddess Sabrinna when he was a child, he has been blessed – or cursed – with semi-immortality and the ability permenantly to see into the Spirit World. His left eye has no pupil, and it is this eye that is fixed in the Spirit World, meaning that he has no need to enter a trance to locate spirits and can perceive reality from two very different vantage points.

Merlin has advised most of Britain's most illustrious leaders: Boudica, Caractacus, Vortigern and Uther; but his advice and counsel has not always been heeded. As a young man, advising Boudica, he cautioned her against taking revenge on Rome when she and her daughters were raped. He advised she bide her time and raise a united army that could meet the Roman legions as equals. She ignored him and, instead, rampaged. Although Boudica met with some success the Icenii were destroyed and Merlin was forced to flee to the north of Britain, spending many, many years in the Caledonia wilds, honing his skills and deepening his knowledge, before returning to southern Britain in secret.

Merlin is far more than 400 years old. He appears to be in his early 70s but his eyes betray his incredible age. There is little he has not experienced, few mistakes he has not made, few terrors he has not beheld. He has witnessed the massacre of armies, the passage of gods and spirits, the fall of empires. He has travelled the length and breadth of Britain, Ireland and Gaul many times. The older he gets, the more committed he becomes to returning Britain to the Time of Heroes, when demigods walked the land and magic was as common as water. To do this he needs to eradicate all Britain's enemies: the Saxons and the Christians, and those who would see the country sundered. His mind is bent to this goal and nothing can change it. He is prepared to sacrifice anyone who stands in his way — even Arthur — if needs be.

This makes Merlin difficult to trust and difficult to interpret. He can be the friendliest, most charming person in the world one minute and then be hurling evocative insults and threats the next. Sometimes he forgets he inhabits the mortal world and treats everywhere as the Spirit World or as Annwn. He can sleep for weeks and months on end, forgetting what it was that he had been doing. He has little time for minutiae and does not suffer fools, gladly or otherwise. Christians he views with withering contempt and Saxons as worthless as insects. Yet he is fascinated by all things and can take a sudden and almost childish interest and delight in the most mundane subjects if they are, to him, new experiences or concepts.

Nothing can be hidden from Merlin. His Perception and Insight skills, coupled with his ability to view a person's entire history — past and future — from the Spirit World means that there are very few secrets he cannot soon uncover, if he wishes. Yet he is not infallible. Not all the spirits like Merlin and he has many enemies, both gods and spirits, who either keep things shadowed or aid those who would oppose Merlin and his plans.

Magic

Such is Merlin's age and experience, he is the foremost animist in Britain and, perhaps, the world. All the Great Spirits of the island answer his summons when he succeeds on a Binding roll, and most will offer him a favour if he requests it. Merlin never abuses this

power: he only calls on the Great Spirits when there is an absolute need and he never calls upon them simply because someone demands it. Such abuse would quickly find Merlin's spirit allies deserting him and so Merlin is frugal with his power — although when he calls upon it, he has the shocking power of the Great Spirits at his disposal.

Merlin is also able to work certain Theism miracles through his deep relationship with Sabrinna, his spiritual mother. He can work the following miracles at Intensity 10 on a successful Willpower roll: *Awaken, Behold, Bless Crops, Cloud Call, Dismiss Magic, Exorcism, Illusion, Lay to Rest, Resurrect* and *Sacred Band.*

Merlin's real power lies in his incredible knowledge and ability to intimidate and persuade: his incredible longevity is apparent to all and there are very few who are not awed by his name and presence. Merlin uses his infamy and reputation to its fullest effect and often has little need to rely on magic to get his way. There are many who do his bidding out of sheer fear, respect, love, or because the druid has either beguiled or shamed them into doing what he wants them to do.

Attitude to Christianity

Merlin epitomises the Pagan tradition and he certainly wants Christianity banished from Britain's shores — but he does not *hate* the new religion. He has lived long enough to see that all religions have common roots, common goals and common themes. To him, Christianity cannot be trusted because, unlike the Roman gods — and even the Saxon ones — Christianity is unprepared to cooperate and tolerate other gods. It is selfish, destructive, and presumptious of its innate superiority. Other than that, Merlin understands Christian rites very well, has read the scriptures (he quite likes the Book of Revelations) and even likes some Christians that he has met over the years (some of them even became Saints). Merlin believes that Christianity is fine, in its own place, but that place is *not* Britain.

Merlin, High Druid of Britain

Characteristics	Attributes	1d20	Location	AP/HP
STR: 11	Action Points: 3	1–3	Right Leg	0/5
CON: 9	Damage Modifier: +1d2	4–6	Left Leg	0/5
SIZ: 16	Magic Points: 21	7–9	Abdomen	0/6
DEX: 9	Movement: 4 metres	10–12	Chest	0/7
INT: 21	Initiative Bonus: 15	13–15	Right Arm	0/4
POW: 21	Armour: None	16–18	Left Arm	0/4
CHA: 16		19–20	Head	0/5

Skills: *Athletics 25%, Brawn 23%, Culture (Pictish) 90%, Culture (Roman) 80%, Customs (Celt) 130%, Endurance 60%, Evade 32%, First Aid 95%, Healing 90%, Influence 98%, Insight 130%, Language (Brythonic) 100%, Language (Goidelic) 100%, Language (Latin) 100%, Locale 90%, Lore (Herbs) 115%, Lore (Christianity) 85%, Lore (History) 130%, Lore (Pagan) 130%, Oratory 99%, Perception 115%, Ride 25%, Survival 68%, Teach 90%, Unarmed 25%, Willpower 115%*

Magical Skills: Binding 130%, Trance 130%

Love Britain 130%, Love Arthur 90%, Love Sabrinna 115%, Pagan 130%, Distrust Christians 90%, Hate Saxons 100%

Combat Style: Self Defence (Staff, Knife) 75%

Weapon	Size/Force	Reach	Damage	AP/HP
Staff	*M*	*L*	*1d8+1d2*	*4/8*
Knife	*S*	*S*	*1d4+1d2*	*6/6*

Guinevere

Guinevere is young, beautiful, headstrong, flirtatious and good-natured. She is also well aware of her charms and how these can be used to gain an advantage, and this sometimes makes her self-centred. Although she doesn't always need to be the focus of attention, if a situation arises where she feels she *should* be, and *isn't*, Guinevere will use every trick in the book to make sure that situation changes. This fault aside, she is a kind soul, wants nothing more than to love and be loved and, if possible, to help restore her family's fortunes.

Guinevere's family held territory in Gwynnedd but lost it a decade ago in the feud that has riven the kingdom. Although of the noble class, Guinevere's father, Cywryd, is effectively penniless and has had to prevail on the charity of relatives in Gwent to avoid starvation. The only hope is to marry Guinevere and her sister, Gwenhyfach, to wealthy, successful men of means. Guinevere understands her role very well, and intends to fulfil it, but also knows that the right marriage is not just about the power held now, but the power that can be held in the future. Achaius, as sweet and noble as he is, will always be the lowly king of a client kingdom. Arthur though: equally handsome, equally noble, is no one's client. Guinevere sees in Arthur the same greatness Merlin sees and it therefore makes perfect sense for the two of them to be together.

Others do not agree. Guinevere's beauty, charm and the easy way with which she transferred her affections from Achaius to Arthur make a her a target for the wrath of Ladwys, Uther Pendragon's widow. Ladwys sees Ygraine of Kernow reincarnated: a young and beautiful creature that toys with the affections of weak men and lures them into acts that bring treachery and humiliation. Morgana, Arthur's half-sister, also loathes Guinevere, but for different reasons: her beloved brother Mordred knew of Guinevere's beauty and had intended to seek marriage to her. Mordred died too soon and Morgana blames Arthur for that loss; now her half-brother is intent on stealing a woman who should have been Mordred's. Guinevere's presence and betrothal to Arthur reminds Morgana of Mordred's loss each and every day, and reinforces her simmering hatred of Arthur.

For most though, Guinevere is a good and loyal friend. Her ready laugh, playful wit and ability to make most people feel special is endearing and genuine. She is fiercely loyal to those she loves: her father Cywryd and her sister Gwenhyfach especially. Anyone who harms them, or threatens them with harm, earns Guinevere's enmity, and that enmity is devious, cunning and calculated. Indeed, she defends anyone she has any deep affection for with the same calculation, drawing on whatever reserves and resources she can to extract vengeance.

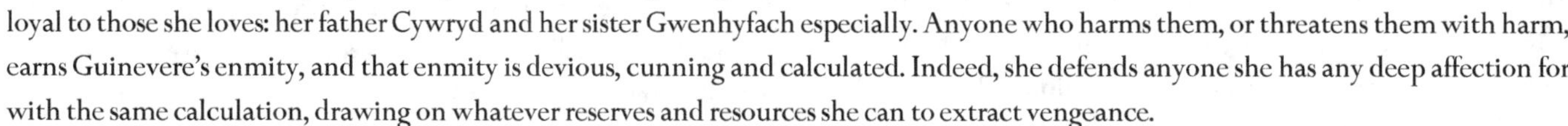

There is one thing neither Guinevere nor Arthur know or suspect (but Merlin knows, and chooses to keep it a close, personal secret): Guinevere is infertile and will never bear Arthur an heir. In time this will become a burden for the couple; Arthur wants children and Guinevere desperately wants to give them to him. For now though, in these first days of their great love affair, such troubles are far away. Conceiving a child does not come easily for many women and Guinevere will not feel herself exceptional for some time to come.

Guinevere

Characteristics	Attributes	1d20	Location	AP/HP
STR: 11	Action Points: 3	1–3	Right Leg	0/4
CON: 10	Damage Modifier: 0	4–6	Left Leg	0/4
SIZ: 10	Magic Points: 13	7–9	Abdomen	0/5
DEX: 15	Movement: 6 metres	10–12	Chest	0/6
INT: 15	Initiative Bonus: 15	13–15	Right Arm	0/3
POW: 13	Armour: None	16–18	Left Arm	0/3
CHA: 18		19–20	Head	0/4

Skills: *Athletics 44%, Brawn 25%, Craft (Embroidery) 78%, Craft (Spinning) 66%, Customs (Celt) 75%, Endurance 38%, Evade 30%, First Aid 45%, Influence 75%, Insight 48%, Language (Brythonic) 90%, Language (Goidelic) 33%, Locale 45%, Perception 55%, Ride 49%, Superstition 60%, Teach 70%, Unarmed 25%, Willpower 75%*

Love Cywyr 90%, Love Arthur 90%, Love Gwenhyfach 90%, Loyalty to Britain 75%, Pagan 51%, Hate Being Ignored 75%

Combat Style: Self Defence (Knife) 36%

Weapon	Size/Force	Reach	Damage	AP/HP
Knife	*S*	*S*	*1d4*	*6/6*

Morgana

Daughter of Uther Pendragon and Ladwys, Morgana is the only surviving child from that union, her brother Mordred having died fighting the Saxons some years ago. Morgana and Mordred were close; intensely so, and there were (unfounded) rumours of an incestuous relationship. Morgana and Mordred were, quite simply, as close as twins can be, sharing that peculiar, symbiotic bond that begins in the womb and cannot be sundered, even by death.

Morgana's sole wish is to bring Mordred back to the Mortal World. As devout a pagan as her mother is a Christian, Morgana knows that, sometimes, souls can be brought out of Annwn and returned to life. For many years she has petitioned Merlin for his help in this, and each time he has refused. She has a natural talent for the druidic ways and finds it easy to lapse into the trances needed to navigate the Spirit World, but Merlin's reluctance to either help her petition Lord Arawn — or even use his own magic (she has seen Merlin work his Resurrect miracle) — increases her bitterness and hatred for the world.

Morgana needs Merlin and so must obey his wishes, but she loathes Arthur and Guinevere. It should have been Arthur, the unwanted bastard, who died fighting the Saxons. Mordred would have been the Pendragon now, and Britain would have the king it deserves with Morgana and Merlin guiding him, making Britain unbeatable, bringing death to the Saxons and scourging Christianity. Instead, there is Arthur — a non-king; an effective warlord, that much is evident, but he is not the man Mordred would have been. That Merlin loves Arthur is anathaema to Morgana; that Arthur has claimed the woman Mordred would have made queen is further insult to her dead brother's memory. Arthur has stolen eveything that should have been Mordred's, and Morgana is determined to bring Mordred back to reclaim what has been lost.

Poor, twisted Morgana is an insular figure. Living in Caer Cadbryg and, sometimes, staying at Ynys Wydryn, she is wild-haired, wild-eyed and a somewhat formidable creature that the Christians of Caer Cadbryg fear and even pagans are wary of. She knows that she is feared and enjoys the power this brings, revelling in her infamy. Christians are treated with contempt: theirs is a religion of weakness, but the myth of their prophet's resurrection intrigues her; what did this Jesus do to rise from the dead? Could there not be some similar power to resurrect dear Mordred? These questions prey on her mind and conflict with her unswerving belief that Christianity is Britain's enemy.

Her relationship with her mother, Ladwys, is complicated. Until Uther slept with Ygraine of Kernow, they were happy. Ladwys was a pagan then, but seeing how Merlin used magic to help satisfy Uther's betrayal helped turn her towards the Christian faith. When Mordred died, the conversion was complete. From then on, Ladwys and Morgana became estranged. It was only their mutual hatred of Arthur that provided any common ground and even then, they vehemently disagree over how Arthur should be punished.

Magic

Morgana is a natural animist — something twins tend to be. Merlin spotted this innate talent at an early age and helped develop it, little knowing that Morgana would one day wish to turn against him. In the early days of her training Morgana found affinity with the traditional nature spirits of Dumnonia but has, since Mordred's death, been drawn to the darker, more malign creatures of the Spirit World. The spirits of darkness — Curse, Disease and Undeath — fascinate her. Her chief goal is to find Mordred in the Other World and return him to life, but entering the Other World is difficult for mortals and so she seeks the help of ancestor spirits, calling on malevolent forces to help her get her way.

One of the ancestor spirits Morgana has allied herself with is a woman called Elois who was tortured to death by the Romans and craves vengeance against the druids who refused to help her. One of these druids was Merlin, although Elois keeps this secret from Morgana. Elois is an Intensity 3 Ancestor and allows Morgana to channel the Theism miracles of Enthrall and Fear, as per the rules on page 149, and to cast the Folk Magic spells of Demoralise and Fanaticism as per page 163.

Morgana

Characteristics	Attributes	1d20	Location	AP/HP
STR: 9	Action Points: 3	1–3	Right Leg	0/4
CON: 13	Damage Modifier: -1d2	4–6	Left Leg	0/4
SIZ: 10	Magic Points: 16	7–9	Abdomen	0/5
DEX: 17	Movement: 6 metres	10–12	Chest	0/6
INT: 17	Initiative Bonus: 17	13–15	Right Arm	0/3
POW: 16	Armour: None	16–18	Left Arm	0/3
CHA: 12		19–20	Head	0/4

Skills: *Athletics 59%, Brawn 31%, Craft (Spinning) 74%, Customs (Celt) 90%, Endurance 46%, Evade 29%, First Aid 68%, Influence 77%, Insight 63%, Language (Brythonic) 100%, Language (Goidelic) 48%, Locale 95%, Perception 48%, Unarmed 41%, Willpower 77%*

Magical Skills: Binding 75%, Trance 79%

Love Mordred 115%, Hate Arthur 90%, Hate Guinevere 90%, Hate Christians 75%, Loyalty to Britain 45%, Pagan 90%, Despise Merlin 65%

Combat Style: Self Defence (Knife) 36%

Weapon	Size/Force	Reach	Damage	AP/HP
Knife	*S*	*S*	*1d4-1d2*	*6/6*

Derec ap Cai

Arthur's foster brother, Derec is the son of Cai, one of the warlords of Elmet and part of the Brigantes tribe. Derec and Arthur are of a similar age and a similar disposition: both are good, keen warriors, both want to see a united Britain and both command loyalty from among their peers and followers.

Derec is less ambitious than Arthur and, of the two, Arthur is clearly the leader, but Derec is his own man. Now that Cai is ailing in health, Derec is the warlord of Elmet: an expert horseman leading his own cavalry band, but also an experienced foot soldier who has fought in shield walls against Saxons and Picts.

He is also a typical Celt: dark haired, passionate, fond of food, drink, songs, stories and games. Derec is at home amongst his shield brothers and the nobility of the Elmet hearth. His loyalty is to his community, his tribe and his country and he is typical of young warlords across Britain: a good man to know and a terrible enemy to face in battle.

As a member of the Brigantes Derec is a Christian. He is not especially devout but he believes sincerely in God and his standard is a leaping salmon which is also a nod to the Christian symbol of the fish. He wears a bronze crucifix around his neck but generally tucks it away when not at prayers.

Use Derec as the template for any young chieftain that might be encountered by the characters duirng play. He makes a good patron and Lord to serve and his deep friendship with Arthur means that service with Derec ensures the characters and Arthur's paths will cross.

Derec-ap-Cai (Typical Young Chieftain of the Britons)

Characteristics	Attributes	1d20	Location	AP/HP
STR: 15	Action Points: 3	1–3	Right Leg	3/6
CON: 14	Damage Modifier: +1d2	4–6	Left Leg	3/6
SIZ: 15	Magic Points: 12	7–9	Abdomen	5/7
DEX: 15	Movement: 6 metres	10–12	Chest	5/8
INT: 15	Initiative Bonus: 15/9	13–15	Right Arm	0/5
POW: 12	Armour: Leather, Mail, Plate Helm	16–18	Left Arm	0/5
CHA: 13		19–20	Head	5/6

Skills: *Athletics 55%, Brawn 55%, Customs (Celt) 85%, Endurance 60%, Evade 60%, Influence 75%, Insight 60%, Language (Brythonic) 100%, Lore (Strategy and Tactics) 75%, Oratory 60%, Perception 50%, Ride 80%, Superstition 40%, Survival 55%, Unarmed 60%, Willpower 40%,*

Loyalty to Warband 90%, Loyalty to Britain 90%, Hate Saxons 70%, Christian 60%

Combat Style: Noble (Spear, Sword, and Shield. Trait, Mounted Combat) 90%; Shield Wall (Spear, Sword, and Shield. Trait, Shield Wall) 90%. Derec uses his Noble style when fighting from horseback. When on foot he opts for the shield wall style when he has comrades close, as this provides greater overall protection and security.

Weapon	Size/Force	Reach	Damage	AP/HP
Shortspear	*M*	*L*	*1d8+1d2*	*4/5*
Longsword	*M*	*M*	*1d6+2+1d2*	*6/8*
Celtic Shield	*H*	*S*	*1d3+1+1d2*	*4/15*

King Mark, Tristan and Iseult

Mark is the ageing and bitter ruler of Kernow, the most westerly part of southern Britain and a distant extension of the Dumnonii. The people of Kernow have long considered themselves a breed apart from the main tribe: Rome never conquered Kernow and this is a source of much pride and arrogance for the doughty kingdom.

Kernow has a long history of trading with the Irish: tin, silver, copper, wood. Mark maintains this tradition and his relations with several Irish warlords have ensured Kernow remains free from Irish raiding parties who instead prey upon the coasts further north. Mark also sought to trade and bargain with the Saxons following Vortigern's death and this caused him to be viewed as a traitor by many other Britons — including Uther. A growing rivalry and bitterness led to war and, finally, a peace that was shattered by Uther's betrayal with Ygraine, Mark's beautiful wife at the time.

Mark's bitterness persists. He hates Arthur, hates Merlin, hates Dumnonia and hates the fact that he is growing old, fat and weak. He comforts himself with a succession of young wives and mistresses, Iseult being the latest. He lacks the ability to act as a husband in the truest sense and, miserable, amuses himself by tormenting his unfortunate bride, even to the point of physical abuse. Iseult is a beautiful chattel. Mark parades her in public but treats his dogs better in private. His anger and violent mood swings

are legendary: many still fear the old man, even though he is now bloated and almost permenantly drunk.

Iseult is very young, very frightened and living in a hell not of her own making. Traded by her father, she was told that King Mark was young and brave; for the past three years her life has been a complete misery as Mark treats her with contempt and disdain. His son, Tristan, has become her confidant. Even though he is as scared of Mark as everyone else he does his best to protect his very young step-mother. She regards him as an older brother. Tristan regards Iseult as someone he will protect until his father dies and then marry and treat as a proper queen of Kernow. The two share a love that has not yet developed into something truly romantic, but it soon will. As Iseult gets older her dark Irish beauty intensifies and Tristan's view of her subtly shifts from brotherly feelings to those of a lover.

Mark is a pagan, although not an especially fervent one. Iseult and Tristan are Christians, with Tristan being a recent convert following long conversations with Iseult in which he learned much about Jesus, the Saints and the Scriptures.

Mark, King of Kernow

Characteristics	Attributes	1d20	Location	AP/HP
STR: 12	Action Points: 2	1–3	Right Leg	3/5
CON: 12	Damage Modifier: 0	4–6	Left Leg	3/5
SIZ: 17	Magic Points: 10	7–9	Abdomen	3/6
DEX: 9	Movement: 4 metres	10–12	Chest	3/7
INT: 15	Initiative Bonus: 12	13–15	Right Arm	3/4
POW: 10	Armour: Leather, Plate Helm	16–18	Left Arm	3/4
CHA: 10		19–20	Head	5/5

Skills: *Athletics 28%, Brawn 30%, Customs (Celt) 100%, Endurance 45%, Evade 30%, Influence 80%, Insight 40%, Language (Brythonic) 100%, Lore (Strategy and Tactics) 80%, Oratory 58%, Perception 44%, Ride 30%, Superstition 75%, Unarmed 40%, Willpower 65%,*

Hate Uther 100%, Hate Merlin 100%, Hate Arthur 85%, Lust for Young Women 80%

Combat Style: Noble (Spear, Sword, and Shield. Trait, Mounted Combat) 60%; Shield Wall (Spear, Sword, and Shield. Trait, Shield Wall) 60%. Mark is in poor health and all his skills reflect his frailty brought about by age, obesity and alcoholism. No weapons arte listed for him: he does not engage in personal combat any more having a champion, Clwyd, who fights on his behalf.

Tristan-ap-Mark

Characteristics	Attributes	1d20	Location	AP/HP
STR: 14	Action Points: 2	1–3	Right Leg	3/6
CON: 14	Damage Modifier: +1d2	4–6	Left Leg	3/6
SIZ: 15	Magic Points: 14	7–9	Abdomen	3/7
DEX: 13	Movement: 6 metres	10–12	Chest	3/8
INT: 13	Initiative Bonus: 13/10	13–15	Right Arm	3/5
POW: 14	Armour: Leather	16–18	Left Arm	3/5
CHA: 13		19–20	Head	3/6

Skills: *Athletics 48%, Brawn 47%, Customs (Celt) 80%, Endurance 52%, Evade 60%, Influence 55%, Insight 51%, Language (Brythonic) 100%, Lore (Strategy and Tactics) 65%, Oratory 44%, Perception 56%, Ride 82%, Superstition 45%, Survival 52%, Unarmed 53%, Willpower 36%,*

Loyalty to Kernow 70%, Fear Mark 80%, Love Iseult 70%, Christian 55%

Combat Style: Noble (Spear, Sword, and Shield. Trait, Mounted Combat) 66%; Shield Wall (Spear, Sword, and Shield. Trait, Shield Wall) 60%.

Weapon	Size/Force	Reach	Damage	AP/HP
Shortspear	*M*	*L*	*1d8+1d2*	*4/5*
Longsword	*M*	*M*	*1d6+2+1d2*	*6/8*
Celtic Shield	*H*	*S*	*1d3+1+1d4*	*4/15*

Iseult, Queen of Kernow

Characteristics	Attributes	1d20	Location	AP/HP
STR: 8	Action Points: 2	1–3	Right Leg	0/4
CON: 11	Damage Modifier: -1d2	4–6	Left Leg	0/4
SIZ: 9	Magic Points: 13	7–9	Abdomen	0/5
DEX: 14	Movement: 6 metres	10–12	Chest	0/6
INT: 12	Initiative Bonus: 13	13–15	Right Arm	0/3
POW: 13	Armour: None	16–18	Left Arm	0/3
CHA: 16		19–20	Head	0/4

Skills: *Art (Poetry) 49%, Athletics 44%, Brawn 18%, Customs (Celt) 31%, Customs (Irish) 75%, Endurance 33%, Evade 32%, First Aid 31%, Influence 32%, Insight 39%, Language (Brythonic) 31%, Language (Goidelic) 90%, Locale 25%, Perception 56%, Superstition 78%, Unarmed 25%, Willpower 31%*

Fear Mark 100%, Hate Mark 90%, Homesick 90%, Love Tristan 60%, Christian 75%

Combat Style: Self Defence (Knife) 25%

Weapon	Size/Force	Reach	Damage	AP/HP
Knife	*S*	*S*	*1d4-1d2*	*6/6*

Custennin

Uther had two brothers: Ambrosius (his twin) and Custennin, his younger sibling. Both Ambrosius and Uther went on to rule; Custennin never got that opportunity and is bitter because of it. Although he believes himself clever and competent enough to be a king, Custennin is lacking in both departments. Dull and unimaginative, he was outstanding at nothing and mediocre in everything. Several years younger than Ambrosius and Uther, he was neglected for much of his childhood, fostered to a noble family of Powys who accepted him only to curry greater favour in the future.

When Uther died Custennin believed he would inherit the family mantle and, indeed, it was discussed: but neither Natanleod nor Havgan had faith in his abilities and Merlin actively advised against it. This was partly because of Custennin's limited capabilities but also because of his enthusiastic adoption of the Christian faith.

Custennin was granted Caer Sulis, the old family seat, as his dominion, and guardianships of all lands in the region of the old Roman city of Aqua Sulis. This, Custennin believes, is an insult and he still sees himself as being able to rule all Dumnonia if Natanleod, Havgan and Arthur can somehow be removed as obstacles. He dislikes the former two warlords but loathes Arthur — a bastard who should have been flung into the sea and not nurtured by a heathen druid and Brigantes chancers. Custennin covets power and intends to have it, even briefly, no matter what the cost.

Custennin, Lord of Dumnonia

Characteristics	Attributes	1d20	Location	AP/HP
STR: 12	Action Points: 2	1–3	Right Leg	0/5
CON: 11	Damage Modifier: 0	4–6	Left Leg	0/5
SIZ: 11	Magic Points: 10	7–9	Abdomen	0/6
DEX: 10	Movement: 6 metres	10–12	Chest	0/7
INT: 13	Initiative Bonus: 12	13–15	Right Arm	0/4
POW: 12	Armour: None	16–18	Left Arm	0/4
CHA: 9		19–20	Head	0/5

Skills: *Athletics 30%, Brawn 30%, Customs (Celt) 100%, Deceit 75%, Endurance 36%, Evade 28%, Influence 77%, Insight 61%, Language (Brythonic) 100%, Lore (Politics) 80%, Perception 52%, Superstition 37%, Unarmed 35%, Willpower 70%,*

Hate Arthur 85%, Love Power 90%, Loyalty to Britain 60%, Loyalty to Self 100%, Christian 95%

Combat Style: Noble (Spear, Sword, and Shield. Trait, Mounted Combat) 35%

No weapons arte listed for him: he does not engage in personal combat any longer having a champion, Gulhed, who fights on his behalf.

Ladwys

As Custennin is bitter for his lack of power, Ladwys is bitter for the way power betrayed her. Uther's loving wife and proud mother of Mordred and Morgana, the Pendragon's seduction of Ygraine left her humiliated and scorned. She turned from loving Uther to hating him. Her revenge was slow and continues even beyond his funeral pyre: when Uther was injured in battle, she ensured his wounds festered so that disease finally took him. She hired a poisoner to find Ygraine of Kernow and murder her. Told by priests that confessing her sins would absolve her of guilt, she has embraced this philosophy wholeheartedly, pouring her hatred into taking vengeance against those who represent the wrongs she suffered. Father Samsun is her confessor, but there have been several others, and by confessing her sins with well-wept tears of contrition she is convinced she is doing what the Lord requires and what those who have wronged her deserve.

Ladwys is cold, calculating and cunning. She has infinite patience and zero mercy. Most people, men especially, prove to be a disappointment to her. Uther, the man she loved and admired, was as unfaithful as any common spearman. Mordred, although brave, was never a match for his father and died in a battle he should have won. Morgana grieves for her dead brother and follows the heathen ways of Merlin. Arthur is forever there to taunt her, Uther's infidelity made flesh.

She can be charming and seemingly kind, but the years and life have not returned such favours and so Ladwys views the world through barbed and jaded eyes and schemes against it. She has not long to live and death will be welcome. Each confession brings her closer to God and heaven is open to those most miserable sinners as long as they confess, repent and go to God with a willing heart. When Arthur's happiness is broken, when Merlin is turned into a slave, Ladwys will finally be content and happy to sip from the hemlock preparation the poisoner Curwan has prepared for her, going to her God knowing that everyone who wronged her has been punished as fully as she could manage.

Ladwys, Widow of Uther

Characteristics	Attributes	1d20	Location	AP/HP
STR: 7	Action Points: 3	1–3	Right Leg	0/4
CON: 11	Damage Modifier: -1d4	4–6	Left Leg	0/4
SIZ: 8	Magic Points: 14	7–9	Abdomen	0/5
DEX: 11	Movement: 5 metres	10–12	Chest	0/6
INT: 17	Initiative Bonus: 14	13–15	Right Arm	0/3
POW: 14	Armour: None	16–18	Left Arm	0/3
CHA: 10		19–20	Head	0/4

Skills: *Athletics 18%, Brawn 15%, Customs (Celt) 100%, Deceit 90%, Endurance 33%, Evade 22%, Influence 78%, Insight 85%, Language (Brythonic) 100%, Lore (Politics) 85%, Perception 60%, Superstition 80%, Unarmed 14%, Willpower 90%,*

Hate Arthur 110%, Hate Uther 120%, Hate Guinevere 90%, Christian 100%

Combat Style: None

In her personal possessions Ladwys has a small earthenware flask stoppered with a piece of carved marble and sealed with beeswax. It contains a potion derived from hemlock made for her by the poisoner Curwan — the man she employed to murder Ygraine and will also employ to murder Guinevere (see *Suppose Your Time Were Come To Die*, starting on page 334). If ever her wickedness is threatened to be exposed she wastes no time in drinking the flask's contents, which will kill her within 3d6 minutes.

Gawain

The son of King Lot of Gododdin, Gawain fled his father's kingdom with his sister Teneu after Lot tried, in a murderous rage, to have Teneu killed. The pair found sanctuary with the Brigantes and Queen Elliw agreed to hide Teneu as long as she and her brother converted to Christianity.

Since then Gawain has wandered Britain as a mercenary, serving whichever warlord needs his skills in battle. While serving with Arthur's warband Gawain was recognised by another mercenary who had served King Lot. Gawain would have been exposed and Teneu endangered had Merlin not intervened. The warrior who threatened Gawain went mad overnight and cut out his own tongue. Gawain continues to be safe but remains in Merlin's debt.

Gawain is strong, brooding and haunted. He believes deeply in both the pagan god and the Christian one and is conflicted by his new faith. Hugely courageous in battle, his prowess with sword and spear makes him a feared opponent — although he hates the constant killing and longs for a life of peace. Merlin told him that the Great Red Dragon had singled out certain people to help decide Britain's fate. Arthur was one, Gawain another, and others would emerge in time, with Merlin bringing them together. That time is at hand and Gawain, whether he likes it or not, is a pagan who has become a Christian who will serve a druid.

Gawain is the archetypal Celt Champion. Strong, fearless and imposing, use Gawain's statistics (or a modification of them) whenever a Champion is required.

More information on Gawain can be found on page 56 and in the scenario *Caves of the Circind*, beginning on page 296.

Gawain-ap-Lot, Exile of Gododdin

Characteristics	Attributes	1d20	Location	AP/HP
STR: 17	Action Points: 3	1–3	Right Leg	3/7
CON: 14	Damage Modifier: +1d4	4–6	Left Leg	3/7
SIZ: 15	Magic Points: 10	7–9	Abdomen	2/8
DEX: 16	Movement: 6 metres	10–12	Chest	2/9
INT: 14	Initiative Bonus: 15/10	13–15	Right Arm	0/6
POW: 10	Armour: Leather. In the shield wall he wears a plate helm for 5 points	16–18	Left Arm	0/6
CHA: 12		19–20	Head	(5)/7

Skills: *Athletics 68%, Brawn 60%, Boating 80%, Customs (Celt) 90%, Endurance 65%, Evade 65%, Influence 55%, Insight 45%, Language (Brythonic) 60%, Language (Goidelic) 100%, Lore (Strategy and Tactics) 66%, Perception 58%, Ride 45%, Seamanship 70%, Superstition 75%, Survival 80%, Unarmed 70%, Willpower 40%,*

Hate Lot 70%, Love Teneu 90%, Loyalty to Merlin 45%, Mistrust Merlin 80%, Loyalty to Elliw 55%, Love Freedom 80%, Hate Killing 60% Christian 55%

Combat Style: Noble (Spear, Sword, and Shield. Trait, Mounted Combat) 88%; Shield Wall (Spear, Sword, and Shield. Trait, Shield Wall) 88%

Weapon	Size/Force	Reach	Damage	AP/HP
Shortspear	*M*	*L*	*1d8+1d4*	*4/5*
Longsword	*M*	*M*	*1d6+2+1d4*	*6/8*
Celtic Shield	*H*	*S*	*1d3+1+1d4*	*4/15*

Aelle

Hailing from the land of the Angles, Aelle is an ambitious, ruthless warlord who has successfully carved out a kingdom in southern Britain that includes the old Roman cities of Anderidda and Londinium. With his sons Aelle is intent on conquering the whole of Britain, in time. It is his belief that the Celts have had their day, that their gods have deserted them and that this Britain is now the rightful inheritance of the Saxon tribes and he shall be the first Saxon king, the Bretwalda, of these new dominions.

Aelle is known for his ferocity and ruthlessness as a warlord. When Anderidda defied him, after he had offered reasonable terms, he massacred every Celt in its walls to make an example of what happens to those who defy him. He has continually pressed the borders of Dumnonia, battling Uther, Arthur, ands the other warlords who protect it; and he has sent his sons to press the northern Britons by strengthening the wild midlands known as Mierce.

Aelle is not the only warlord present in Britain. North of Aelle's kingdom of Ceint is a rival Bretwalda: Guercha, another Angle who claims kinship with Hengest and Horsa and challenges Aelle for rulership of Mierce. Coming across the sea is Cerdic, another warlord intent on making Britain his. These three Saxon chieftains are destined to clash. If they are not stopped they will found new kingdoms, in time, which will come to truly shape Britain's destiny: Ceint, Wessex, Mercia and Anglia and others. Aelle is not the first, but he is one of the most dangerous.

Aelle is the archetypal Saxon warlord. Use these statistics for any powerful Saxon in command of a large body of loyal warriors.

Aelle of Ceint, The Bretwalda

Characteristics	Attributes	1d20	Location	AP/HP
STR: 17	Action Points: 3	1–3	Right Leg	3/7
CON: 15	Damage Modifier: +1d4	4–6	Left Leg	3/7
SIZ: 14	Magic Points: 12	7–9	Abdomen	5/8
DEX: 15	Movement: 6 metres	10–12	Chest	5/9
INT: 16	Initiative Bonus: 15/10	13–15	Right Arm	3/6
POW: 12	Armour: Leather, Mail and Plate	16–18	Left Arm	3/6
CHA: 13		19–20	Head	5/7

Skills: *Athletics 60%, Brawn 68%, Boating 75%, Customs (Saxon) 100%, Endurance 70%, Evade 63%, Influence 80%, Insight 43%, Language (Saxon) 100%, Language (Brythonic) 16%, Lore (Strategy and Tactics) 99%, Perception 63%, Ride 80%, Seamanship 85%, Superstition 90%, Survival 77%, Unarmed 70%, Willpower 66%,*

Love Battle 99%, Loyalty to Warband 90%, Ruthless 90%, Love Power 90%, Saxon Gods 60%

Combat Style: Saxon Noble (Spear, Sword, Seax, and Shield. Trait, Mounted Combat) 110%

Weapon	Size/Force	Reach	Damage	AP/HP
Seax	*M*	*S*	*1d4+2+1d4*	*6/8*
Sword	*M*	*M*	*1d6+1+1d4*	*4/8*
Spear	*M*	*L*	*1d8+1+1d2*	*4/5*
Saxon Round Shield	*L*	*S*	*1d4+1d2*	*4/12*

Father Samsun

As pious as any man can be, Father Samsun has been chosen by God to be his earthly servant. Unworthy of the task but utterly willing, Samsun intends to spread the word of the Lord as far as he can and is quite prepared to do whatever it takes to ensure Christianity's survival and his own.

Samsun is physically weak: thin, malnourished, balding and blessed with the bulbous features only a certain kind of mother could love, but mentally a powerhouse. He understands the nature of political power and, although he does not have the kind of character or presence to wield it himself, he knows how valuable he can be to those who do. So it is that Samsun seeks out people like Bishop Dyfrig, Ladwys, Bishop Gerhaint and anyone who can offer him protection, room to scheme and, of course, room to advance his own agenda.

You see, Samsun does not want to be merely a bishop. No. Samsun wants to be a Saint: nothing less. He wants to ascend to Heaven and know that his name will be spoken in hushed tones and his likeness painted onto the triptychs of the great churches. He wants children (good, Christian children) named after him. He wants cathedrals of stone and slate raised in his honour. He wants to perform miracles; he wants miracles to be performed on him. He wants it all so much.

There is only one, slight, troubling problem with what Samsun wants: suffering. All the Saints suffered. Some were tortured and broken in the most hideous ways; others died in agony, calling God's name as flames lapped over their bodies or spears were driven through their hearts. Samsun wants none of that. He wants to be a Saint without the suffering. It's perfectly possible. He's sure of it. All Samsun needs to do is remain invaluable to people of power, believers like himself, and prove his continued devotion by his usefulness in whatever ways are most expedient.

Samsun has grown close to Ladwys in recent years and is her personal priest, kneeling with her daily in prayer and taking her confession. He *knows* things. Of course, he could never possibly reveal them because Confession is a sacred act that it is sinful beyond measure to betray. But he knows, you know, and knowledge is power.

Father Samsun's characteristics can be used for any Christian priest who embraces the pious, passive approach to life and faith.

Samsun, Priest of Gwent

Characteristics	Attributes	1d20	Location	AP/HP
STR: 7	Action Points: 3	1–3	Right Leg	0/4
CON: 10	Damage Modifier: -1d2	4–6	Left Leg	0/4
SIZ: 9	Magic Points: 15	7–9	Abdomen	0/5
DEX: 11	Movement: 6 metres	10–12	Chest	0/6
INT: 16	Initiative Bonus: 14	13–15	Right Arm	0/3
POW: 15	Armour: None	16–18	Left Arm	0/3
CHA: 10		19–20	Head	0/4

Skills: *Athletics 22%, Brawn 21%, Deceit 79%, Endurance 45%, Evade 33%, Insight 75%, Locale 50%, Lore (Scripture) 88%, Perception 53%, Survival 61%, Unarmed 20%, Willpower 89%*

Loyalty to God 90%, Loyalty to Self 110%, Christian 90%, Loyalty to Ladwys 40%, Love Thy Neighbour (Expect When A Pagan) 45%, Hate Pagans 110%

Combat Style: Grovel for Mercy (Knees) 115%. This Combat Style relies not on weaponry but on guilt. It comes with the Pious Wail Trait which works in exactly the same way as the Intimidating Scream trait found on page 89 of the MYTHRAS rules.

Typical Warrior (Celt Spearman or Saxon Fyrdman)

Attributes	1d20	Location	AP/HP
Action Points: 2	1–3	Right Leg	2/6
Damage Modifier: +1d2	4–6	Left Leg	2/6
Magic Points: 11	7–9	Abdomen	2/7
Movement: 6 metres	10-12	Chest	2/8
Initiative Bonus: 10	13–15	Right Arm	2/5
Armour: Leather	16–18	Left Arm	2/5
	19–20	Head	2/6

Skills: Athletics 59%, Brawn 62%, Endurance 62%, Evade 56%, Locale 66%, Perception 64%, Ride 85%, Survival 67%, Unarmed 59%, Willpower 62%

Passions: Loyalty to Lord 80%, Love Battle 70%

Combat Style: Shield Wall (Spear, Sword, and Shield. Trait, Shield Wall) 75% or Fyrdman (Sword, Spear, Seax, Shield) 75%

Weapons	Size/Force	Reach	Damage	AP/HP
Shortspear	*M*	*L*	*1d8+1d4*	*4/5*
Longsword	*M*	*M*	*1d6+2+1d4*	*6/8*
Celtic Shield	*H*	*S*	*1d3+1+1d4*	*4/15*
Seax (Saxons Only)	*M*	*S*	*1d4+2+1d2*	*6/8*
Saxon Round Shield	*L*	*S*	*1d4+1d2*	*4/12*

Typical Bard or Skald

Attributes	1d20	Location	AP/HP
Action Points: 3	1–3	Right Leg	2/6
Damage Modifier: 0	4–6	Left Leg	2/6
Magic Points: 14	7–9	Abdomen	2/7
Movement: 6 metres	10-12	Chest	2/8
Initiative Bonus: 14	13–15	Right Arm	2/5
Armour: None	16–18	Left Arm	2/5
	19–20	Head	2/6

Skills: Art (Poetry) 99%, Athletics 44%, Brawn 31%, Customs (Own) 100%, Customs (Other) 75%, Dance 60%, Cedeit 75%, Endurance 51%, Evade 44%, Insight 80%, Locale 90%, Lore (History and Myth) 100%, Lore (Gossip) 80%, Musicianship (Harp, Pipes, Drums) 90%, Perception 85%, Sleight 65%, Unarmed 45%, Willpower 85%

Passions: Loyalty to Lord 70%, Love Information 80%

Combat Style: Self Defence (Dagger) 48%

HE YTHIC RITAIN AMPAIGN

From here on is for Games Masters only. The rest of the book comprises seven linked scenarios that form the *Mythic Britain Campaign*. All the scenarios are self-contained, but each follows on from the last with certain events, themes and non-player characters recurring.

The adventures take the characters the length and breadth of Britain: from its heartlands to Dumnonia and the southerly Ynys Wyt; to the northerly kingdom of the Circind and into the deep woods of Powys. For some of the time the characters will act as Merlin's agents, helping him to find and retrieve several of the Thirteen Treasures of Britain. At other times they will be drawn into interpersonal conflicts that require them to choose sides, swear oaths and make certain moral choices that may be at odds with their faith and even other oaths they have sworn.

What is certain is that the characters will be swept into some momentous events. Britain is changing. The Saxons are growing in strength and, unless checked, will force the Britons into an ever-growing retreat, surrendering land as they go. Merlin clearly has an agenda to save Britain, as does Arthur; but will their personal desires make it *more* divided? The characters may well be the ones who help decide Britain's fate.

Games Master Notes

It is recommended that Games Masters give some thought to where the characters come from and who they initially serve before play begins. Having all the characters come from the same region and community will be a distinct advantage because it will be easier to keep them together and give them an automatic reason for adventuring. It would also be helpful if they serve a lord who is sympathetic towards Arthur, or can easily become so, because this will make it easier to have the characters serve Merlin and others as the scenarios progress.

Pacing the Scenarios

It is perfectly possible to play through the scenarios one after the other, with a few weeks of down-time (where the characters can rest, improve their skills, train, and catch up with daily lives) in between. However we recommend that Games Masters intersperse the campaign scenarios with their own adventures, perhaps elaborating on what has gone before or being completely new escapades for the characters to become involved with. This lengthens the campaign but also makes it more fulfilling as both

the characters and Games Master get to make their own mark on Mythic Britain and are not simply agents for one person or another. The Kingdoms of Mythic Britain chapter contains countless scenario ideas and many, many intrigues that could easily form parallel campaigns of their own.

The key is to pace the scenarios of the *Mythic Britain Campaign* offering either downtime or side adventures (or a mixture of the two) to allow for character development. If run consecutively there is a chance that the characters become a little inured to the great events they're becoming part of. Instead, good pacing helps them invest in the setting and actually to help drive the way the campaign unfolds instead of continually being reactive to it. Consider the *Mythic Britain Campaign* to be part of an epic novel: it is not to be rushed and should be allowed to grow and mature with the telling. Careful pacing will help achieve this.

Use the NPCs

Many interesting non-player characters are introduced throughout the campaign and there are scores of opportunities for interacting with them. Use these opportunities wisely but do not shy away from letting the characters interact with legendary figures such as Arthur, Merlin and Guinevere. With the exception of Merlin these are all *people*; many are highly approachable, sociable and keen forge friendships and alliances. The Briton are a closely knit people; news travels with surprising alacrity and it will not be uncommon for the characters' actions and deeds to arrive somewhere ahead of them. The likes of Arthur and Merlin will soon remember the characters' names; they will find uses for them and bring them into their circles. Let the characters enjoy the attention, let them develop the relationships and let them become part of the world.

But, as well as making use of the major non-player characters, do not hesitate to introduce and develop relationships with minor non-player characters too; those incidental people that might not be movers-and-shakers in the characters' world, but may nevertheless be significant. Some of these people may become trusted friends, mortal enemies and even lovers, husbands or wives. Do not be afraid to allow such relationships to blossom - and introduce Passions that reflect the depths of feeling.

Use Passions

Throughout the playtesting of Mythic Britain we continually found that Passions and relationships became the driving force for much of the intrigue, excitement and character development. Whether used as measures for depth of feeling, as augmentations to other skills, or even as skills in their own right, Passions were the engine for the campaign. Great enmities, leading to great deeds, battles, recriminations and even murder arose through the presence and use of passions. At least three great love affairs were forged and at least two sundered. The Passions the characters have are indications of how they both feel and will act. Passions lead to conflicted hearts and minds: sometimes they produce clarity of thought and purpose. However they are used, they are important tools for creating, driving and telling great stories. Do not be afraid to develop and use them. And, if a Passion is used to wonderful effect during game play, do not hesitate to either increase it or decrease it there and then — do not necessarily wait for downtime. Simmering feuds and deep loves are better developed and nurtured during play rather than outside it.

Be Sparing With Magic

Although there is a fair amount of magic to be found throughout the scenarios, it is often subtle and usually involves the Spirit World. Few magicians are reckless with magical power: instead they rely on their reputations and the threat of what their power can do, rather than on demonstrations of it. Magic should be something that is feared and respected. When it happens, it should be momentous and awe-inspiring. Unless there is a druid or læce in the party, magic will be beyond the characters and they will be witnesses to it rather than be practitioners of it. Indeed, is what the characters see really magic? People believe in magic, but is this merely superstition and willingness to see the supernatural at work when, really, it is mere artifice, misdirection and clever psychology? Magic can, quite easily, be nothing more than such tricks and hallucinations. In the ancient world everyone believed in something, where it in one god or several; and many natural (yet inexplicable) events were ascribed to magic, miracles or the work of the spirits or saints. In your Mythic Britain campaign magic need not work at all: but people will think it does, to greater or lesser

degrees, and this is why the Superstition skill has been included in the game, to reflect that capacity for humans to believe in the supernatural and allow it to influence their lives.

Whatever the way in which magic is treated though, it should be a rare event — something wondrous or miraculous, malevolent or shocking. Something that can change one's view of the world.

Mythic Britain Campaign Synopsis

There are seven scenarios of varying lengths, although each should take between six and twelve hours to complete. The scenarios are as follows:

The Winter Council

The characters journey to Elmet and witness Arthur's call to arms for the tribes of Britain. They have the opportunity to encounter many different people who will loom large later in the campaign, and also to come to Merlin's attention.

Bran Galed's Horn

The quest for the Thirteen Treasures begins with the characters having to journey to the occupied city of Ratae to find and retrieve the titular drinking horn. They encounter two feuding Saxon chieftains, stumble across a mystical landscape, and may find themselves rescuing an enslaved noblewoman.

Of Promises Broken

Returning to Dumnonia the characters find themselves in the middle of a conspiracy to shame two major figures and must make some decisions that will shape the destiny of the Alliance of Britain.

Logres Burning

Arthur takes the war to the Saxons who have seized and occupied Ratae and the lands close by. This scenario uses the battle rules found in Britain At War to involve the characters in massed conflicts where shield walls clash and the Saxons find themselves on the receving end of Britain's wrath.

Caves of the Circind

Merlin sends the characters north to retrive another of the Treasures. This time they must seek a man known as Gawain, the only person who knows where the mythical coat of Beisrydd is located, deep within the territory of fearsome Circind. The characters must travel north and may find themselves face to face with a druid even Merlin is wary of: Mawgaus.

Gullveig's Children

The Saxon warlord Cerdic lands on Dumnonia's southern coast and seizes Ynys Wyt, a strategically important island that controls access to Dumnonia's heartland. The characters are sent to Ynys Wyt to gather information on Cerdic's strength and also to discover the fate of an isolated monastery. What they find there may prove divisive in the war against the invaders.

Suppose Your Time Were Come to Die

With a major Saxon attack imminent, Dumnonia sends some of its people to the safety of Powys. But, for one, the village of Builth is far from safe. The characters must uncover a conspiracy - or risk seeing Britain's strength weakened at a time when it needs it most.

HE INTER OUNCIL

So begins the *Mythic Britain Campaign*, this adventure introducing the characters to certain of the key non-player characters integral to the forthcoming story and establishing the characters as essential parts of historic events. It also establishes Caer Wynd as a potential base of operations – although it is likely that the characters will not spend a vast amount of adventuring time here.

The Call to Council

It is the four-hundredth and ninety-fifth year, as the Christian scribes reckon it, since the birth of the infant known as Jesus Christ.

Bards and messengers from Dumnonia have ridden the length and breadth of Britain, visiting each and every hall of the kings, queens and chieftains of the land. The message is the same: A High Council and Feast is to be held at Caer Wynd, in the region known as Elmet in the lands of the Brigantes. All are welcome and under the Old Laws safety is guaranteed. This shall not be a time for feuds or rivalries, but a time for settlement and decision.

A High Council has not been called since Uther was alive – and the last High Council included only the rulers and chieftains of the Western and Southern Kingdoms. This proposed High Council is different: someone is at great pains to invite all the important men and women of Britain, both south and north of the Great Wall. Can the invitation be trusted?

The bards and messengers delivering the invitation are duly questioned and are told that Merlin, High Druid of Britain, Servant of the Great Spirits, has called for the council to be convened. This causes consternation to Christian nobles, but the messengers have answers prepared: "This is not a matter of religion or gods. It is a matter of survival."

Elmet is a good choice for a High Council. It is roughly central to Celtic Britain, meaning that most will have to travel an equitable distance. The Brigantes also have decent relations with most of the kingdoms and can be relied upon to guarantee the safety of even the fiercest rivals – an important consideration when so many powerful egos are to be assembled in one place.

Travelling to Elmet

The High Council is timed for the celebration of Imbolc, which is one of the four feast days and falls between the winter solstice and spring equinox. It is also known as Saint Brighid's Day, and, again, this is a carefully chosen time, designed to appeal to both Christian and pagan sensibilities. It does mean travelling towards the end of winter, which is in itself unusual: most remain at their steads and strongholds at such a time. This must be an important Council if winter travel is being requested.

Of course, some rulers and chieftains refuse to go — because they do not want to travel at such a time of year, because they hate and distrust Merlin, or because they hate and distrust High Councils. The latter remember that both Vortigern and Uther held them, and no good ever came of them, so why bother? But, for the sake of sheer expediency, the rulers or leaders of the characters' tribes have decided to attend. Preparations have been made and retinues assembled. The characters have been chosen to attend this High Council for any number of reasons:

- As punishment for certain misdemeanours (travelling near the time of Imbolc is unpleasant, cold and wet)
- Because they are trusted advisers or warriors
- Because they have never attended such an important event before (and need experience)
- Because they can be spared (the best warriors remain to defend the home settlement)

Whatever the reason, the characters find themselves travelling to Caer Wynd in the company of their lord. It might be a long trudge or a short one. Whatever the circumstances, it is indeed cold, blustery, and testing. The snow is thick on the ground and the winds blow hard from the east, driving these last winter snows across the lands of Elmet and turning the twin hills of Caer Wynd into great mounds of ermine. The earthworks and palisade of the fortress are a welcome sight after so much time on the road — and

retinues from other areas can be seen also making their way to the great stone and wooden gates.

The characters arrive one full day before Imbolc. The High Council is set to convene the next morning, breaking in the afternoon to allow for the Imbolc preparations and feast, and then continuing on the day after Imbolc.

Caer Wynd

The hillfort of Caer Wynd spans two hills in the centre of the small region known as Elmet. It is located between a network of streams and brooks and has a plentiful water supply of its own, accessed by wells dug into the hillside. The surrounding area is relatively flat and open, although a stretch of woodland to the north of the hills provides some shelter. Otherwise, Caer Wynd is exposed, but commands an excellent vantage point across the countryside.

Caer Wynd has two main gates at the east and west, with tracks worn into the countryside and cut into ditches and earthworks forming the first line of defence. Both gates are of similar construction: square stone and wooden towers are set into the wall, with a sturdy gate made of oak planks set beneath the guard platform of the tower. Sentries watch everyone entering Caer Wynd, but there are no challenges: so many warbands and retinues are arriving that it is pointless to try to monitor each and every visitor.

The characters arrive early enough to find room within Caer Wynd's walls, but soon enough the main fortress is filled to capacity and some retinues and warbands are forced to make camp outside Caer Wynd, at the foot of the hills. By the time people have stopped arriving, a reasonable-sized shanty community of tents, lean-tos, and other makeshift coverings has formed around Caer Wynd's base. Campfires create an eerie glow in the low, winter sun, and the sounds of warriors — coughing, arguing, singing, and drinking — can be heard across quite a distance.

Inside Caer Wynd, roundhouses have been made available to each of the nobles specifically invited to the High Council. Their retinues must make their own shelter arrangements as close to the roundhouse assigned to their lord as possible, but at least, within the palisade, the characters are sheltered to some extent from the biting winds that threaten to bring fresh snows for Imbolc.

The first priority for the characters is to find, or make, shelter. Each character should make either a Survival, Streetwise, or Mechanisms roll. If none of these skills are available amongst the characters, then each should make a Hard Endurance roll instead. The result of the roll dictates the quality of shelter for the duration of the council.

- Critical Success: The character finds space in a warm, cosy roundhouse close to his or her lord. The accommodation is shared, naturally, with others, but as warm accommodation is in short supply, this is a lucky break. This character can, if he or she wishes, invite one other character to share the space (but no more).
- Success: The character finds accommodation in a storehouse, or engineers a reasonable personal bivouac that offers fair to middling protection from the elements. A campfire must be lit outside, and each night the character must make a successful Endurance roll or suffer one level of fatigue for half of the following day due to the cold and discomfort.
- Failure: The character struggles to find space for a personal bivouac and is forced to share, an uncomfortable arrangement. One level of fatigue for half the next day is automatically incurred.
- Fumble: As above, but the ground is especially lumpy and hard and the shelter is next to useless, letting in the cold and damp. The character suffers a level of fatigue for the duration of his or her stay at Caer Wynd — unless better accommodation can be begged, borrowed, won, or stolen.

Getting the Bearings

Caer Wynd is packed to bursting. The characters are unlikely to have ever experienced a gathering like this: so many different clans and tribes with so many different accents, unfamiliar dialects, styles of dress, and modes of behaviour. There are nobles, warriors, lords, ladies, rich, and poor. Caer Wynd plays host to Christians, pagans, and those who care little for either faith. The Christians are notable for displaying the sign of the Cross prominently, and several priests have established small congregations where they

Plans Within Plans

The High Council is not Merlin's idea, but a plan put together by Arthur of Dumnonia and Derec of Elmet. Although both of them are leaders, neither of them has (yet) the weight of authority to guarantee a High Council — but Merlin does, so the old druid agreed to put his name to their plan.

Arthur and Derec are foster brothers: Caer Wynd is where Merlin brought Arthur after his birth, placing him in the family of Derec's father, Cai. The two men therefore have very strong ties and are hoping that this friendship between Dumnonian and Brigantian warband leaders will set an example to the others.

What Arthur wants is to gain a commitment from each tribe and kingdom to field warbands to launch an early assault on the Saxons, striking them hard from the northern and western flanks and reclaiming lands lost to the Britons in the last bout of Saxon raids, including reclaiming the town of Ratae.

Merlin though, unknown to the foster brothers, has plans of his own, which will become clear as the Council progresses. His plans are complex and devious: they do not all involve kings, queens, or chieftains directly, but concern the freemen of Britain: freemen like the characters. Those of his plans that do involve Britain's rulers are subtle and cunning, and have much wider, deeper implications. Once set in motion, they will change the course of Britain's history.

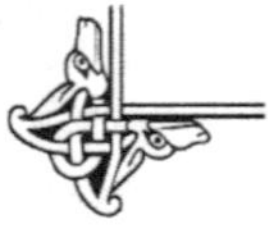
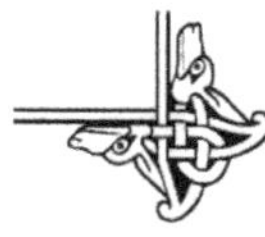

lead prayers, tell stories of the gospel, berate the pagans, and call on their god to deliver them from the sins and temptations that the heathen, godless pagans represent.

The Rumour Mill

The characters have a full day to arrange shelter and then either spend the time keeping to themselves or wandering around Caer Wynd. Despite the cold and snow, there is a certain, special atmosphere holding this place — as though something big is about to start. Most people are in good humour, willing to share mead, ale, wine (occasionally), food, and, of course, gossip. Those characters who choose to socialise should make an Influence or Easy Streetwise roll. The outcome determines what they can learn from those gathered in Caer Wynd.

- Critical Success: 3 pieces of information
- Success: 2 pieces of information
- Failure: 1 piece of information
- Fumble: Nothing; for some reason, no one wants to talk to the character

Either choose one of the following or roll randomly from the Caer Wynd Gossip table.

Encounters in Caer Wynd

The Rumour Mill mentions several important, rich, and/or influential people. The following are Incidental Scenes designed to allow the characters to interact with some of these people, and perhaps, create sub-plots and complications that can be played out as separate chapters in the Mythic Britain campaign.

Brother Niall

Have pagan characters make a roll against their Pagan Devotion passion. If the roll fails, the character or characters are targeted by Brother Niall, a Carvetii proselytiser who sees an opportunity to make some converts to the Christian faith.

Brother Niall is busy preaching to a small group of his faithful, but suddenly stops, points out the character(s) and declares, loudly: 'Join us! The Lord has shone his light on you, showing you to be lost and weary souls in need of the Lord Jesus Christ's salvation! Come, come and feel his warmth!'

Caer Wynd Gossip (F= False, T= True, P= Partially True)	
1d20	Rumour
1 (F)	Word has it that Arthur, Uther Pendragon's bastard, has convened this Council in a bid to have himself named Uther's successor and become High King of Britain.
2 (F)	Lord Derec, chief of Caer Wynd, has summoned this Council in a bid to challenge Queen Elliw of the Brigantes. Queen Elliw is angry that the Council was convened without her permission. If this backfires, Lord Derec could be exiled from Elmet.
3 (F)	The Council is a Brigantes ploy to consolidate power. Queen Elliw wants to be named Queen of All Britons. Word has it that Saint Brighid herself appeared to the queen and told her to summon this meeting – and hold it on Saint Brighid's Day.
4 (P)	Someone wants the tribes united. The Saxons are planning to attack the north en masse. They already sacked Ratae; Elmet and Dumnonia are next.
5 (F)	Word has it that Merlin convened this Council so that he can work a mighty spell to convert all the Christians back to the Old Gods.
6 (F)	This is a trap, like the High Council Vortigern convened to make peace with the Saxons. The Saxons slaughtered every Celt there. Someone means to do the same with one of the other tribes – Cornovii or Silures, most likely.
7 (F)	The Saxons are already marching on Caer Wynd. They'll attack the day after Imbolc. This is why the Council was called – so that there'll be no option but to fight and beat the Saxons.
8 (T)	Did anyone else see that red-headed woman? The one in the jade green dress? Most beautiful girl ever! Her name's Guinevere, apparently, Cywryd of Gwent's daughter, last of the Deceangli tribe. Old Cywryd must be looking for a husband for her. Word is he's desperate to marry her and her sister to anyone of noble blood. Anyone seen the sister? No? Thought not.
9 (T)	Arthur's here, with Merlin and Morgana, Arthur's strange half-sister. She has the look of a druid about her, that Morgana. Some say she's trying to bring her brother, Mordred, back from the Other World. Strange.
10 (T)	There's trouble brewing between Powys and Siluria. They'd made a truce after years of fighting, but word is that the Silures raided Gwent last year and Gwent's an ally of Powys. War will follow. The whole point of the Council is to stop it from happening, because the Cornovii will attack Powys too, leaving the whole of the west exposed to Saxon attack. Bloody Silures. Bloody Cornovii. Bloody Saxons.
11 (P)	Have you ever seen so many Christians packed into one place? They're out to convert every last pagan to that god who got himself nailed to a tree by the Romans. Can't have been much of a god, if the Romans drove nails into him. Anyway, the priests of Gwent, the Carvetii, and the Brigantes are going to so some mass ceremony and then everyone will worship this Jesus. Even Merlin.
12 (P)	Word has it that the druids are planning to bring together all the Treasures of Britain. The cauldron, the chariot, the sword – all of them. That will unite the tribes and scare the shite out of the Saxons. Word is they've already found the Treasures and brought them here. They'll be revealed at the Feast of Imbolc. This is it. The days of the Saxons are numbered.
13 (F)	Who invited the bloody Picts? They're all troublemakers – you mark my words. They wouldn't come all this way if they weren't planning some kind of villainy. They're cannibals and sorcerers, you know. That Roman Legion that vanished? The Ninth? Eaten.
14 (P)	King Mark of Kernow's arrived. He's brought his latest wife. Fifteen, if she's a day. Gorgeous too, a Princess of Ireland. That means Mark's paid the Irish to attack someone else instead of Kernow. Still, that Iseult - she's a beauty all right. That Mark's a lucky old bastard. Good job Uther's not around.
15 (P)	Seen that young King of the Parisii? Has he started shaving yet? People say he wants to marry some Brigantian woman, and this is the best place to find one. Me, I think he's just tired of sheep.
16 (P)	This Council is just another attempt by Dumnonia to get everyone else to fight their battles for them. Why should we care about the Saxons? They're nowhere near us, and when they come, we'll show the bastards what it's like to fight proper Celts.
17 (T)	Apparently the Feast of Imbolc is going to be something special. They've slaughtered about a dozen cows and who knows how many pigs. The Council might be as tedious as all get-out, but at least we'll get a good feed out of it.
18 (F)	Word is that King Lend of the Cornovii plans to challenge Arthur over some argument. We'll see if Arthur's as good a fighter as everyone says.
19 (F)	Derec, Caer Wynd's chief, is a good man – strong warrior, capable leader – but he's blind where Arthur's concerned. The two of them are behind this High Council, but it was Arthur's idea. He wants Derec to get everyone to fight the Saxons, but we have to accept that they're here to stay. They've got enough land. They haven't attacked the north and they don't intend to. The Saxons just wanted to punish the west, because that's where Vortigern came from. This fight with the Saxons – it's not our problem.
20 (F)	A friend of mine has a friend who knows one of the small clans just south of here. He says the Saxons are advancing. They know there's a High Council here and they're going to attack. Keep your spears and shields handy, lads. We'll be drenched in Saxon blood before Imbolc is through.

The devious Brother Niall has a roundhouse of his own, shared with eight of his faithful followers. He uses this to entice any character who is looking tired and weary from a poor night's sleep due to poor accommodation. Match Niall's Oratory of 83% against the targeted characters' Willpower (Pagan Devotion can augment the resistance). If Brother Niall succeeds, his hectoring rhetoric and promises of a warm fire, hot food, and mulled mead prove irresistible and the characters willingly join Niall's little throng, spending the rest of the time at Caer Wynd in the company of the priest and their "new sons and daughters of Christ." The characters cannot escape: if they try, Niall and several of his more devout followers track the characters down and draw them back to the roundhouse, continuing their conversion.

Characters ensnared in this way are allowed to make an Insight roll. If this is successful, they see through Niall's attempts and successfully resist any form of conversion — although they can opt to play along, since listening to Niall guarantees certain luxuries. If the Insight roll is failed, Niall attempts to convert the characters over the course of the High Council. This is treated as a Social Conflict Task (see MYTHRAS, page 287). Niall uses his Christian Devotion of 90%; the characters can resist with the higher of their Pagan Devotion or Willpower (using the other to augment the primary roll). Niall is looking to score a complete conversion (i.e., reach 100%) over the course of the next four days. If he succeeds, the characters adjust their passions as follows:

- Reduce the Pagan Devotion Passion to half its current value.
- Gain the Christian Devotion Passion at 35%+ the character's POW. This represents Brother Niall's Charisma, the strength of indoctrination, and the character's own natural affinity with faith and superstition.

If the Christian Devotion score is now higher than the Pagan Devotion score, the character considers himself or herself a Christian and will, when the opportunity presents itself, want to attend Christian ceremonies such as prayers and communion. The character may try to oppose this desire by pitting his or her Pagan Devotion against Christian Devotion in an oppose roll. To rebuild the Pagan Devotion score, the character will need to use Experience Rolls to do so.

Reversing the Faiths

This scene can be played in reverse, with Christian characters converting to paganism. Simply replace Brother Niall with the druid Glandwyr (see page 27). If Games Masters really want to increase the chances of a pagan conversion, then replace Brother Niall with Merlin, using the statistics provided on page 200.

Guinevere

Cywryd is an impoverished noble living in the Western kingdom of Gwent. He claims to be the last of the Deceangli tribe, dispersed and almost destroyed by Rome and their Cornovii auxiliaries, and there is no doubt some truth lies in this. He and his wife, Gwynedd, have two daughters: Guinevere and Gwenhyfach, and it is Cywryd's hope to marry both daughters to wealthy nobles — kings, if possible — in order to improve his own standing and personal finances.

The daughters couldn't be more dissimilar. Gwenhyfach is plain, homely, and uncomplicated. Guinevere is tall, red-haired, beautiful, and as ambitious as her father. Her real name is, in fact, *Gwynhafhyr*, but she has Romanised it to make it sound softer, more feminine, and more romantic — so Guinevere it is.

Guinevere, her sister, and father are housed with the Gwent contingent and have a small roundhouse close to that of King Tewdric of Gwent. Mostly they have kept themselves to themselves, but being curious girls away from Gwent for the first time in their lives, they are keen to experience the sights and sounds of Caer Wynd in all its cold, chaotic glory. In the evening of the day before the High Council, Guinevere and Gwenhyfach sneak out of their roundhouse and explore the settlement, wandering between the encampments without any real clue as to where they are going. Naturally, they get lost. There are so many retinues making camp that it is easy to lose one's bearings, and this is how the characters (or one particular character, if the Games Master wishes) come to meet them.

The two girls are arguing about which way to go to get back to their roundhouse. A few nearby warriors are grinning, enjoying the squabble and jeering when Gwenhyfach throws them icy looks and snaps at them to be quiet. Guinevere, all poise and charm, reaches out and takes the arm of one of the characters, saying, 'Oh, please help us! We're dreadfully lost!'

Guinevere is one of the most beautiful women in the whole of Britain. Her mother has told her she is Rhiannon born again, and so Guinevere, who, although young, knows exactly how to use her looks, turns her charm full onto the character she has just caused to pause. Guinevere's Influence skill is 75%; match this against the character's Willpower in an opposed roll. If Guinevere wins, the character is awed by her beauty and charm, and has no option but to place him or herself at Guinevere's disposal. If Guinevere wins by a significant degree (i.e., she wins with a Critical success or her degree of success is substantially better than the character's), then the seeds of infatuation are sown. The character immediately gains the passion Love Guinevere at 48% (30% + her Charisma of 18). This applies even if the smitten character is female. Guinevere's beauty and charm work on both sexes, and although Guinevere would never entertain physical relations with another woman, she would certainly make the fullest use of a loving relationship.

The character or characters need to guide the two girls back to the Gwent contingent. A successful Influence, Perception, or Locale roll is enough for them to get their bearings through asking for additional help or simply working out where the different kingdoms have been billeted. As Guinevere, Gwenhyfach, and the characters make their way through the throng, Guinevere links arms with her Chosen One; makes plenty of idle conversation, littered with personal compliments; squeezes the character's arm from time to time; and generally flirts outrageously whilst still managing to conduct herself in a demure manner. Gwenhyfach trails behind in sullen silence. She has seen Guinevere pull this trick many times before and she finds it tedious.

As the group nears the roundhouse where Guinevere and her family have been billeted, another two figures enter the scene. Two men emerge from the roundhouse accorded the high nobles of Gwent. One of the men is tall, broad-shouldered, with thick black hair worn to his shoulders, clean shaven, and dressed in the clothes of a noble-born warlord. This is unmistakably Arthur. With him is a young man of no more than 15 years. His hair is mousey brown, worn in a rough crop, and he wears clothes that were once of fine

quality, but have clearly seen better days. This is King Achaius of the Parisii, and he has sought out Arthur to pay his respects. The young King clearly hero worships Arthur: an Insight roll instantly reads the younger man's adoring body language.

The two men see the characters. The two men see Guinevere. This is what happens.

- There is instant, mutual attraction between Arthur and Guinevere.
- King Achaius is smitten with Guinevere – although she has eyes only for Arthur.
- The characters are forgotten momentarily; although they – and certainly any character who has just developed the Love Guinevere passion – are completely aware of the strange, passionate triangle that has just been established.

Guinevere thanks the characters for their assistance and, head held high, strides to her own roundhouse. Arthur, Achaius, and the characters watch her disappear inside, all dumbstruck. A few seconds later, Cywryd emerges. He is a tall, thin man with the same red hair as Guinevere. He ignores the characters and addresses himself to Arthur and Achaius.

"My lords! How fortunate! I see you have met my daughters? Please, I would be honoured to offer you mead and good, Gwentish cheese. I have plenty within. Come! Come!"

Arthur politely declines, having business elsewhere, but Achaius wastes no time in accepting and he accompanies Cywryd inside, leaving Arthur and the characters outside, perhaps quietly seething with jealousy, perhaps not. This is, however, a chance for the characters and Arthur to become acquainted.

'Who was that?' Arthur asks the characters, and it is obvious he does not mean Cywryd. He listens intently to the characters if they tell the story of the past few minutes. He asks for their names, their lords, and then thanks them before taking his leave. The characters should not be in any doubt that Arthur has been struck by the thunderbolt that is the Lady Guinevere.

What happens after depends entirely on how the characters choose to react and how any Love Guinevere Passion is used. However, the Guinevere/Arthur/Achaius triangle is far from over, and the characters may yet have a part to play in it.

Iseult

King Mark of Kernow has been married no less than eight times. His first wife, Ygraine, was seduced by Uther and fled Kernow with Merlin's help. His next six wives have died either as a result of disease or unfortunate accidents. He is now onto his eighth wife and, as rumours have it, she is a Princess of Ireland, the youngest daughter of the King of Connacht. Her name is Iseult.

She is little more than a child: small, frail, and pretty, with dark hair and large, round, brown eyes. Mark, by contrast, is old, bent, scarred, and hirsute, with the manners of a semi-civilised pig. Iseult is a possession: no more. He agreed to marry her because no one else in Ireland wanted her, and he is in debt to King Oengus of Connacht. In return, Oengus sees his last daughter married to royalty and gains a vital toehold in the kingdom of Kernow.

Iseult is terrified of her old husband. He is rough and uncaring. She has had enough of Mark and this miserable country. She means to escape. She doesn't care where to or what will happen: anything to be free of Mark and his demands. To this end, Iseult intends to use the hustle and bustle of Caer Wynd to try to get away, either stealing out through the gates or even climbing the palisade and taking her chances with the treacherous drop on the far side. She intends to escape at night. Mark is a heavy drinker and usually comatose within a couple of hours of nightfall. She is banking on the duties of the High Council taking precedence over a full-scale search, meaning she'll stand a better chance of making a clean escape now than waiting until the Council is in progress.

So at the dead of night, while her husband snores and farts, the tiny, dark-cloaked figure of Iseult steals from the roundhouse and moves quietly through Caer Wynd, trying to thread through the tents, bivouacs, and lean-tos, and the morass of warriors sleeping rough.

This is how the characters come across Iseult. Answering the call of nature, taking the night air, or simply unable to sleep due to the cold, hard ground, they should make a Hard Perception roll. If successful, a slight figure – a child, perhaps – is seen threading his or her way cautiously through the camp and making towards one of the gates. Why would a child be up so late and trying to leave the fort? Could this be a Saxon spy? There have been rumours, after all.

If a general alarm is raised, Iseult panics and takes flight, trying to evade the tumult of people who rouse themselves to try to catch this (likely) spy. She ducks, dodges, and weaves, screaming and crying with frustration. Someone seizes her around her abdomen and then immediately release her as she bites deep into his arm: she runs once more.

If the characters give chase, an opposed roll to her Evade against the characters' Athletics skill determines the outcome. If no alarm is called and the characters want to follow her and be stealthy about it, their Athletics skills should be capped at the level of their Stealth. If she wins with a Critical success, she manages to get away, either escaping through the gate, or clambering nimbly up the palisade and dropping down into the deep ditch on the far side. If she wins with a straight success, she realises her escape attempt is, for now, futile, and makes it back to the roundhouse she shares with King Mark.

If Iseult is caught – either by the characters alone or the characters and others if a general alarm has been raised – she hurls insults, claws, scratches, spits, curses, and bites at those holding her. Her accent is clearly Irish and anyone making a Hard Insight roll may recall the rumours of King Mark having taken a very young Irish bride. The characters hold here not a Saxon spy, but the current Queen of Kernow.

The dilemma is what to do. Loyalty to Lord or Tribe dictates that Iseult should be returned to her husband. A Passion roll, either straight or opposed against Willpower, could help determine what to do. Iseult, if calmed (it requires a Hard Influence roll), pleads with the characters to help her get away, if no one else is involved. She offers silver and shows them three coins she has taken from Mark's purse as proof she can pay (she would pay up to two of these). She does not tell the characters who she really is or why she wants to escape, but it is evident that, underneath the hell-cat, wildling attitude is a frightened, beaten child far from home.

The characters have two options. Return her to King Mark or help her escape.

Taking Iseult back to King Mark does not result in praise, thanks, or gratitude. Mark's guards wake the old, corpulent King and he is furious at having his sleep disturbed. He is incandescent with rage when Iseult's escape attempt is made known. He demands the girl be tethered like a dog outside the roundhouse for the night and watched over by his guards: he will decide what to do with her in the morning. The characters are dismissed without any further recognition, although the head of Mark's retinue flashes the characters a sympathetic glance, perhaps. For now until the end of the Council, Iseult is held under guard, unable to make good on her escape plans. On return to Kernow, her punishment will begin properly. She will escape, in time, and with the help of one of Mark's sons, Tristan. But that is another story.

If the characters help her escape, all they need to do is ensure she can get away from the fort without being seen. She is small, fast, and with her dark hair and dark clothing, tough to spot if she stays within the shadows, so getting away is not that difficult. She thanks the characters and then slips into the night, perhaps never to be seen again.

In the morning, when Iseult's escape is discovered, King Mark's wrath is felt throughout Caer Wynd and the characters become aware of what they have helped do. Mark blames Merlin and Arthur – this is not the first time a wife of King Mark's has been spirited away – and the King of Kernow uproots his entire retinue to search for Iseult and then return immediately to Kernow. His part in the High Council is finished and he will forever be the enemy of those who place their trust in either Arthur or Merlin.

Using Mark and Iseult Further

There is ample scope for introducing Iseult again in future scenarios. There is also scope for generating a supporting Passion with the characters: Love/Loyalty Iseult, perhaps, and, to balance it, Hate King Mark. If either or both Passions are generated, then they are established at 42% and can be improved as with any other Passion.

Arthur

In the time immediately before the High Council, Arthur spends much of his time going from roundhouse to roundhouse, chieftain to chieftain, and ruler to ruler, thanking each for coming and vaguely outlining the reason for the council. This requires moving around Caer Wynd a great deal, and he is rarely alone. Usually he is in the company of Derec, and on the occasion mentioned earlier, he is in King Achaius's company. Encountering him alone is unlikely.

One of Arthur's qualities is an ability to put people at ease and gain their trust. He has the kind of face and manner that give people confidence and make them feel special — especially commoners. He rarely forgets a face or a name, and he always has time to pause and talk with anyone, regardless of their station. As he makes his way around Caer Wynd, he stops to exchange a few words with the many different warbands, greeting warriors he knows, has fought with, or met briefly before. The effect is obvious: those he speaks with are invariably left smiling and happy, as though a brief chat with Arthur is the highlight of their day. There is no reason why the characters cannot also make his acquaintance.

If the Guinevere scene has been used, then the characters have already had such an opportunity. But otherwise Arthur can simply stroll past where they are camped, pause, remark on the weather, introduce himself ('Arthur-ap-Uther of Dumnonia. Well met'.), and ask after names, home lands, and so on. His stock remark is to tell people that the Imbolc Feast will be spectacular and lavish: 'A dozen cattle slaughtered I hear and countless pigs'. He will make a little small talk before moving on.

In an encounter like this, match Arthur's Influence 85% against the characters' Willpower. If successful, then establish a Passion of Loyalty to Arthur at 36% (20%, plus Arthur's 16 Charisma). If Arthur wins with a Critical success, double this to 72% — such is the impression Arthur makes. If the roll is a failure or fumble, the character is simply impervious to the natural charm offensive. Arthur is affable, but nothing special.

Morgana

Uther Pendragon had two legitimate children: the twins Mordred and Morgana. The two were incredibly close and Merlin always maintained that the spirits were strong with both children. There were rumours of an incestuous relationship, but nothing was proven.

When Mordred was killed battling the Saxons, Morgana was inconsolable. A confirmed pagan anyway and favoured by Merlin, she began to explore ways of travelling to the Other World to find Mordred and bring him back to the mortal world. Merlin refused to teach her what she wanted to learn. Her grief and bitterness has led to an erosion of her sanity. Morgana is now a half-crazed creature, bereft at the loss of her twin and furious with Merlin for denying her the magical help and knowledge she is convinced will help her. She is also hateful towards Arthur. Why could the Saxons not have killed him, instead? Arthur now seems to reap the glories that should have been Mordred's. And, Merlin clearly favours him over her. This maddens her even further. Morgana is determined to have her revenge on both Arthur and Merlin.

As a student of Merlin and a member of Uther's clan, Morgana has come to Caer Wynd to observe the High Council, even though she can play no part in it.

Morgana finds the characters. Each character, at some stage during the day before the High Council, gets a sense of being watched or followed. A successful Perception roll pinpoints a woman, staring intently at the character, from only a few feet away. When it is obvious the character is aware of being watched, Morgana approaches.

She is a tall, thin woman in her early 30s. Her hair is a light brown but filthy, bedraggled, and visibly crawling with lice: it is shaved at the forehead in the style of the druids. Her eyes are narrow, green, and piercing in their intensity. Her mouth is a thin line across her face. She wears a filthy shift of linen that was, long ago, brilliant white. A cloak of quite fine cloth holds the cold at bay, secured at her shoulder by an ornate brooch of silver and bronze. Her feet are bare. She leans in close to the character and hisses in his or her ear: 'He will choose you. You are marked by the spirits to serve the Great Dragon. I can see them. Only I can help you. One day, in time, you will want my help, and I shall want yours.'

Morgana does not wait for a reply or engage in any conversation. She does not give her name, but a successful Hard Locale or Easy Streetwise roll reveals her identity.

The character should make a roll against their Pagan Devotion or Christian Devotion Passion. If Pagan Devotion, the roll is standard. A success indicates that Morgana probably tells the truth and, because she is a druid, can see into the Spirit World. The character most likely feels a little troubled, but this is simply the way of the druids: they often speak cryptically. If the roll fails, then the character is able to dismiss Morgana as a mad woman who probably affects the habits of a druid to impress the foolish and gullible.

If the character is a Christian, and the Christian Devotion Passion roll is successful, the character is forced to drop to his or her knees and pray hard for Christ's salvation, which, after an hour or so of praying, feels like it has been granted. The character can go about his or her business as normal. If the Christian Devotion roll fails, the character knows that this pagan witch has created an obscene curse. The character must seek out a priest who can perform communion. Even then, all skill rolls for the next day will be one grade harder owing to the sheer worry and anxiety Morgana's approach has caused.

This cryptic comment will become clearer later in the scenario. For now, it is enough for the characters to know that Morgana knows who they are and something of their fates...

The High Council

The High Council's purpose is to bring together as many Celtic leaders as possible to forge an alliance against the Saxons. This is not an attempt to unite kings under a single banner, as Vortigern and Uther both tried to do, but to establish a common ground and a common enemy. Arthur, Merlin, Derec, and several Dumnonian warlords believe that either this year or the next, the Saxons will stage a major push both west and north, threatening the South, West and Middle kingdoms. But before this can be addressed, there is more mundane business to attend to.

This mundane business is summarised below. None of it concerns the characters directly and none of it requires any more than a cursory reference (if that). The general structure and etiquette of the High Council is also summarised, although this need only be described to the characters if they decide to actively watch proceedings, which is something they do not need to do.

Council Structure

The High Council is held between the leaders — chiefs, warlords, kings, and queens. Each has one adviser: Arthur has Merlin. The group forms a wide circle in Caer Wynd's Great Hall. Supporters and observers gather around this circle but must observe a distance of a spear length from the seats of the leaders. Derec of Elmet assumes the chairmanship of the High Council, Under Celtic etiquette, he must allow each Council member time to speak, inviting each to do so if they wish. Etiquette demands that leaders be given reasonable time to state their case, but must relent when the chairman calls for it or calls someone else to speak. Interruptions are only allowed if the chairman permits them.

The Order of Business

Derec, having met with each Council member beforehand, has a list of issues to be addressed. He moves through these in turn. Most are concerned with tribal disputes and it is up to the Council to suggest a resolution, which, if accepted by both parties, becomes binding. This round of business takes up most of the morning, beginning shortly after dawn. It is as follows.

- Powys seeks reparations from King Lend of the Cornovii for raids made against them. King Lend dismisses the request but grudgingly agrees to a price of 200 cattle, to be delivered by the summer solstice.
- Siluria is accused by the kingdom of Gwent of hiring Irish mercenaries to raid its coasts. Siluria denies the charge but agrees to expel a group of Irish fisherman who have taken up home close to Gwent's borders. No one expects the Silures to keep their word.
- King Mark of Kernow (if Iseult has not escaped), still drunk from the night before, accuses Merlin of helping his young wife to flee Caer Wynd and brings up the whole, sorry tale of Ygraine's seduction by Uther. Merlin simply smiles, spits,

and points his staff at Mark, who falls silent, then throws up. Nothing more is said.

- The Carvetii demand that the Caledonii cease renewed raids against them. Otherwise, they demand protection from the Caledonii. The Silures, to much amusement, offer to place King Eanraig in touch with some Irish mercenaries they just happen to know.

Eventually, the real reason for the Council is reached. Arthur is invited to take the floor, and he makes an impassioned speech.

'My Lords. Cerdic, yet another Saxon warlord, has his eyes set on our lands. More and more Saxons land on the eastern shores; some are loyal to Aelle, some have leaders of their own. The Saxons grow stronger and bolder. Last year, the old town of Ratae, only a few days ride from Elmet, fell to the Saxons. Each year more farms of Dumnonia are sacked, their owners enslaved, murdered, or raped. The Saxons grow stronger and their greed grows with their strength. They are turning their eyes north. The Saxons do not just want the lands they have — they want the whole of Britain, from the very mountains of the north to the very sounds and cliffs of Kernow. They will not rest until every Celt is a slave or a corpse.

"These Saxons are not the kind for bargains and truces. King Vortigern made that mistake and paid with his life. The Saxons know, and want, only slaughter. Up until now, we have been lucky. But our luck will not hold.

"The arrival of this Cerdic heralds, we believe, a fresh wave of attacks on our lands and way of life. Ratae was just a foretaste. Elmet, Sulis, Caer Ysc, the brochs of the Caledonii... all will be vulnerable unless we act to stop them. Dumnonia, with some help from Elmet and Powys, has fought alone for years: we cannot continue to do so. If Dumnonia falls, then so will Powys, Gwent, the Cornovii, and Elmet. If Elmet falls, so will the lands of the Brigantes and the Carvetii. If they fall, the Great Wall will be next, and then the lands of the Caledonii and the Northern kingdoms. This is a fact. It is what the Saxons want. And what they want, they take.

"I ask of this High Council to form a single alliance, pledging warbands and supplies, to form a defensive line around the lands

the Saxons have taken. We will hold them: we shall break their shield walls. As our resolve strengthens, we will reclaim our land foot by foot, farm by farm, town by town. We shall force Aelle, Cerdic, and the others to form against us as an army. We Britons outnumber these invaders by three to one or more! If we come together, we can beat them bloody and drive them into the sea.

"But if we remain divided. If we continue to fratch, squabble, and fight each other. If we continue to lay blame for ancient arguments that few truly care about, then Britain shall fall. We need Celts to act as Celts. Christians and Pagans must stand shoulder to shoulder. The Romans acted as one and look what they achieved. We must take their example and defend our island.

"We do not have much time. If we do not come together as brothers, if we continue to fight the Saxons battle by battle, but only one by one, our kingdoms will fall, and in five years, or ten, Britain will cease to exist".

Arthur resumes his seat. For a while, there is silence. Eventually, there are murmurings of discontent mixed with voices of agreement. The voices rise, and before long, the Council is in uproar: shouting, accusations of cowardice, betrayal, doom, and even being in league with the Saxons. Derec does his best to take control, but the leaders of the Celtic tribes have reverted to kind: fractious, hot-headed, and unwilling to be reasonable.

It takes Merlin to restore order. The old druid pushes his way into the circle of squabbling leaders. From within his robes he produces a short-sword, Roman by its design and length. With a mighty downward thrust, of the kind one would not have thought possible in one so old, he drives the sword point-down into the floor, between the joints of the stone flags. He turns to each of the leaders, leering, one leg raised and bent at the knee, in the kind of hopping motion the druids use when taunting an enemy.

'You all think you're right, don't you? All think you're smart and clever. All think your way is the right way. There is only One Way. And that is the way of the Red Dragon. Here's a way to prove it.'

He turns on one of the lesser chieftains. 'You! Are you with Arthur or against him?' The chieftain glares at Merlin and tells him he is against what Arthur wants. Merlin grunts, 'Then draw this blade from the stone and strike Arthur down!' The warlord hesitates and Arthur's loyal men come to order, reaching for weapons to defend him. The warlord then reaches out, grasps the sword, and tries to pull it free from the ground. It refuses to move. The warlord strains and heaves, but the sword is firmly stuck. Merlin points his staff at Derec. 'You, Derec-ap-Cai, are you with Arthur? Draw the sword and prove the Red Dragon's plan!'

Derec steps forward and takes the sword. He prepares to strain, but the blade shoots out of the stone causing Derec to fall backwards onto his arse. The Council breaks into laughter. Merlin takes the sword and drives it back into the earth. He then calls on another dissenter to take up the blade and strike Arthur down. Once more, the blade remains stuck.

The process is repeated several times. Only those who pledge their loyalty to Arthur and Derec are able to draw the sword from the stone. Those who want nothing to do with an alliance cannot shift it.

Merlin is accused of trickery and witchcraft, but it is clear that this demonstration has had a profound effect. Several of those who were against Arthur begin to change their minds. Queen Elliw, who had expressed scepticism, steps forward and takes the sword: it comes free easily. 'I, Elliw of the Brigantes, Daughter of our beloved Saint Brighid, believe that this is a sign not of any dragon, but a sign from God that he wants us to act as one. Britain is God's beloved country, and these Saxons are heathen invaders. This is God's Will. And so it is my will. The Brigantes will stand with Arthur.'

There is a profound shift in the mood of the Council following Elliw's declaration. The council forms into two sides – those who are now part of Arthur's alliance, and those who are opposed to it. The sides are composed as follows:

Allied with Arthur	Opposed to Arthur
Brigantes	Gododdin
Cornovii	Gwent
Dal Riada	Kernow
Dumnonia	Siluria
Powys	Caledonii
Carvetii	
Parisii	

Gwent's opposition is based on the troubles it is having with the Irish raiders who harry its coasts and its long-standing feud with

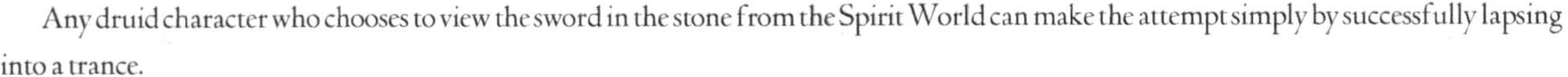

A View from the Spirit World

Any druid character who chooses to view the sword in the stone from the Spirit World can make the attempt simply by successfully lapsing into a trance.

The Great Hall becomes hazy and semi-distant, its sounds rough echoes as the Mortal World always appears when viewed from the Spirit World. The gladius Merlin has driven into the ground is visible and, standing over it, holding it, and keeping it firmly lodged, is the Spirit Presence of a large, stocky, dark-haired man wearing a bear skin around his shoulders and with a complex, stark black tattoo of a dragon curling around and up his right arm. It requires a successful Insight roll to understand that this spirit is Uther Pendragon in his Ancestor form, and he is clearly being channelled by Merlin, who must have struck this bargain with the dead High King. Uther laughs as those who oppose Arthur try to drag the sword from the stone, and he holds it firmly in place. When one of Arthur's allies steps forward, Uther releases his grip and roars with laughter as the sword slips free.

There is a 30% chance that Uther notices any druid watching him on the Spirit Plane. If so, he winks at the druid's spirit form, presses a finger to his lips, and makes a 'shhh' sound. It is obvious that Uther is a powerful ancestor spirit; trying to stop him from this obvious trickery does not result in Spirit Combat: instead, Uther calls out to Merlin, who himself trances into the Spirit World and commands the druid character to leave at once. As Merlin is the High Druid of Britain, defying him is an unconscionable act, but if the druid character wants to make the attempt, Merlin uses his Binding 120% against the character's own Binding — which is subject to the Hard difficulty grade, as well as being reduced by Merlin's own high skill. Merlin aims to eject the druid from the Spirit Plane and strike the fear of the Gods into the druid for such insolence — which he does without difficulty if his Binding roll is one level of success higher than that of the character.

Back in the Mortal World, Merlin, if he had to deal with any disruptive characters, waits until some time after the Council and seeks out the character. He makes it plain in calm, chilling, murderous tones that if the character ever interferes in his plans again, Merlin will have no hesitation in summoning the most malevolent spirits that can be found to torment the character at every waking and sleeping moment: no rest, no mercy, just lasting torment on the Mortal World that will then continue in the Other World too. Merlin will call on the massed ancestor spirits of the druids slain at Ynys Mon to enact this punishment — and this is no idle threat

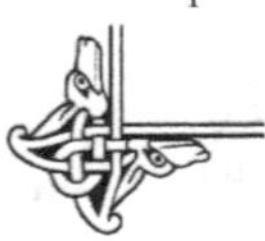

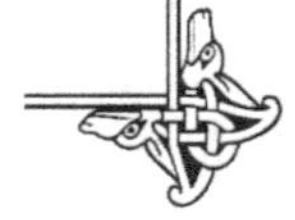

Cornovii. The Silures are naturally belligerent, and the Gododdin are simply unsympathetic to all affairs south of the wall. Kernow has either stormed off from the Council, or King Mark simply refuses to ally himself with the druid who wrecked his first marriage and the bastard of Uther that was the product of Merlin's deceptions.

It does not matter if characters come from a tribe or kingdom that is opposed to Arthur. Merlin has plans for them — as the next Scene details.

Merlin's Plan

With the alliance established, the High Council breaks. It is late in the day and the Feast of Imbolc is highly anticipated. The leaders and chieftains separate in their pro/anti Arthur groups, drifting out of the Great Hall to allow the servants to prepare the place for the feast. All those who attended drift out too, to start drinking and discuss what they have witnessed.

Merlin remains behind, leaning on his staff, watching people depart. The sword is still there, in the stone, where he placed it. As the characters prepare to leave, Merlin calls to them, one by one, name by name. He uses full names, too, including two generations. The characters cannot ignore Merlin's summons: one does

not ignore a druid. If a character is Christian, let that character match his or her Christian Devotion against his or her Willpower. If Christian Devotion wins, then the character can walk away (although the outcome does not change: they simply do not take part in what follows); if Willpower wins, the character feels compelled to remain and listen to what Merlin wants.

Even though the characters do not know Merlin, it is clear he knows them — or at least, a lot about them. He begins by inviting each character to pull the sword from the stone. Each succeeds. Brawn rolls can be called for, merely for general effect, but the sword comes free for each character. Merlin leans on his staff watching each character remove the sword. His face is impassive. When each has finished, he finally speaks.

'The Great Dragon that is Britain chooses those who must work on its behalf. I was chosen five hundred years ago, and I work for it still. Arthur was chosen at birth. Others have been chosen, such as those who also pulled the sword from the stone. And now you each know that you have been chosen....'

What the characters have been chosen to do is twofold. First, they are to serve the Alliance that Arthur is creating. It does not matter what tribe or kingdom they are from. It does not matter if they are pagan or Christian. They have been chosen to serve against the Saxons. "The Saxons have a word for it: the word is "Wyrd". This is your wyrd, your destiny. The Great Dragon knew it the day you were born and your lives have led up to this moment. You cannot deny your destiny. If you try, the Great Dragon will abandon you, and you will wither and die like so many who live their lives without consequence.

"You will serve Arthur through me. It may be that you will serve Arthur directly, but for now, I will be your Lord. Those to whom you already hold allegiance will be told of this. They will not deny me. No one denies Merlin."

The second purpose is more clandestine: "To defeat the Saxons, Britain needs the magic of the Old Gods. In the Time of Heroes, there were thirteen Treasures that formed the centre of all magic and power. These have been lost a scattered. Some I have spent my lifetime finding and reclaiming. The rest, I know where they are and the Great Dragon has chosen you to retrieve them. In time, I will reveal to you what they are and you must bring them back to me. Fail, and Arthur and Britain will fail. Succeed, and the Saxons shall be bathed in their own blood."

Merlin tells the characters that they should remain together. From this point on, they should consider themselves a warband. He will, in time, call them and he will expect them to come when summoned.

And, with that, Merlin turns and leaves the roundhouse. He does not answer questions and he does not say anything more to the characters....

Each character gains a new Passion: Loyalty to Britain at 20% plus their own POW x 3. This Passion applies to dealings with Merlin, Arthur, the Alliance, and the duty the characters now have to saving Britain from the Saxons. As each scenario of the Mythic Britain campaign is completed, Loyalty to Britain will, hopefully, grow, but there are things that may reduce it. Of course, this new Loyalty may very well find itself at odds with other loyalties and oaths. But then, such is the way of things.

The Feast of Imbolc

Christians and pagans celebrate Imbolc differently. For Christians, it is a quiet affair celebrating winter's end and the forthcoming fertility of livestock, and receiving Saint Brighid's blessing. Christians eat and drink, reserving some of their food for Saint Brighid, and then pray until late, when a final communion is taken and then the faithful retire to bed, leaving small wicker or rush crosses affixed to their hearths or thresholds in Brighid's memory.

For pagans, this is a full feast to mark the end of winter and thank the gods and spirits for helping them come through the darkest days of the year. Many gods and spirits are praised; much is drunk, songs are sung at full voice; couples make time for each other; and a generally riotous time is had by all.

The feasting begins in the Great Hall, where the nobles are served directly. Outside, firepits have been prepared and great carcasses have been roasting all day, and these serve the rank and file. The mead and ale is plentiful, deep, and strong. People are served good portions of beef and pork from the spits, taking the food on trenchers to find wherever is comfortable to sit. Serving staff, all from Caer Wynd, make their way through the assembled camps

filling mugs and bowls with mead or wine. The singing starts while the music plays. So does the fighting: squabbles break out over the smallest things and subside as quickly as they began, as a few heads are knocked soundly.

Eventually, the Christians get up and march to the eastern end of the fort, where a Brigantes priest leads the praying, leaving the pagans to continue their party.

The characters are probably still bewildered from their encounter with Merlin. But as the feast progresses, and regardless of where they are, a messenger finds each one of them and tells them they are invited into the Great Hall. This is a rare honour. Only the nobles and their named followers are there, but tonight the characters can join them.

At the far end of the Great Hall, Derec, Arthur, Elliw, and the other nobles who compose the alliance are seated in sheep skins, taking their food and wine and talking amongst themselves. Moving out towards the door are the rows of others entitled to be here, and the characters are given space, food, and drink. As they eat and drink, Perception rolls should be made. Roll 1d3 (or choose) what the characters see from the following list.

1. Guinevere, her father, and sister are present. Guinevere has been positioned next to King Achaius and the young king is clearly besotted with Guinevere's beauty. He gazes at her with a mixture of awe and lust. She flirts with him, laughs at his comments, and brushes his hand with hers. The signals are obvious. Her father, Cywryd, watches approvingly.
2. Arthur is deep in conversation with Queen Elliw and King Lend. There seems to be some mild disagreement between them, although it does not appear serious. Arthur keeps shaking his head before explaining a particular point. King Lend is more forceful. Queen Elliw appears to have the upper hand. From time to time Arthur and Guinevere's eyes meet. Smiles are exchanged despite Guinevere being deep in conversation with young King Achaius, who, with more and more wine, is growing bolder in his approach to Guinevere. His body language could not be more blatant.
3. Merlin is present, but he neither eats nor drinks. He stands in the shadows at the far end of the hall watching everything but remaining aloof. He catches the eye of the characters, but merely to acknowledge their presence.

As the night wears on, the bards recount rousing poems of the deeds of gods and heroes; lead the revellers in a mixture of stirring, raucous, and bawdy songs; and ensure that the feast is as enjoyable as it should be. Here is an opportunity for drinking contests, boasting contests, and the like. If characters are reluctant to involve themselves in such games, then they should be coerced into it by others. At a feast such as this, everyone is expected to eat too much, drink too much, and make fools of themselves.

Part of the feast involves dancing. The Imbolc dances are a mixture of formal, ritual dances and impromptu dances to the pipes and harps of the bards. Everyone in the Great Hall is expected to dance: it is bad form to refuse and could result in a challenge from someone drunk enough to take true offence. This is time to test Dance skills. A success or failure is deemed good enough: there are plenty of people with more enthusiasm with talent, and the flow of mead and ale accounts for the number of left feet in the hall. A Critical success gains whoops, cheers, and applause and a Fumble results ins someone falling flat on their arse or treading on someone's toes.

During a formal dance, to well-known patterns and steps, all the characters have the opportunity to be paired briefly with Guinevere and her sister (as well as any other attractive women that male characters may have noticed during the evening – and vice versa). If a character met Guinevere earlier in the scenario, acting as her escort and flirting with her, she remembers the exchange and begins flirting once again. She is enjoying herself and is probably a little drunk. 'I have a secret!' she whispers as she and the character link arms and twirl. 'I'm to be married!' she confides with a beaming smile as they press together and then part. She winks as the dance takes her to another partner.

When the dancing has finished and people had a little time to relax, Derec slams his drinking horn on the table to attract everyone's attention. 'Lord Cywryd of Gwent has something to say! Silence you rabble, so that our good friend from Gwent can speak!'

Cywryd rises. He is flushed but beaming happily. He thanks Derec for the opportunity to address the hall, thanks Arthur and Derec for their hospitality, and thanks the gods for watching over

such a fine feast. 'I am delighted that Bel and Don watch over us this Imbolc,' Cywryd says, 'because they have smiled on myself and my family. With great gladness I can announce that my daughter, Guinevere, shall be married to King Achaius of the Parisii, thereby uniting our great families and tribes!'

The hall erupts with cheers and applause, especially amongst King Achaius's followers. Arthur leads the toast and heartily congratulates the (deliriously happy) Achaius and makes room at the table so that he can sit next to Guinevere. If the feast was flagging, it is reenergised with this news.

The formal betrothal will take place at Caer Pedwyr, Achaius's home, with Cywryd, Guinevere and Gwenhyfach travelling back together. Achaius, making a nervous speech, invites all present to the betrothal feast, to be held in seven days' time. Arthur and Derec immediately accept, as do so many others.

Any character succeeding in either a Hard Insight or a Formidable Perception roll notices the glances that are exchanged between Arthur and Guinevere. They are surreptitious and (almost) well hidden; but their meaning is clear: Guinevere might be promised to Achaius – a good, solid, political marriage to a young king – but there is chemistry between Arthur and Guinevere, and the two of them are trying to control it – not as successfully as they might wish.

The End of the Council

The Council ends with the conclusion of the feast. Those too drunk to move sleep where they are, but eventually all drift off to their quarters. The characters may or may not be tempted to do something about what they have witnessed between Arthur, Guinevere, and Achaius, but for now, they should not be given the opportunity. Merlin provides the convenient interruption, finding the characters, kicking them awake if he has to, or waylaying them at just the right moment.

"The gods play their games and we must be their pieces," he half whispers. "On this Imbolc night, what you see and what you can do are beyond your control. I have spoken. I have another use for you. You will meet me in the grove in the woods to the north of here at sunset tomorrow. Before then, you will not interfere in the lives of others, and will hold your tongues, no matter what the temptation." He gives each of them a warning look. "Do not disappoint me. You wouldn't like to see me when I am disappointed."

And, with that, he takes his leave. This also brings the first scenario to an end. If the characters want to involve themselves in the affairs of Arthur, Achaius, and Guinevere, then they can, but the Games Master will need to take charge of the consequences. Merlin will not intervene again, but when he next sees the characters, he will make his displeasure acutely known.

The characters will find themselves embroiled in this love triangle again in the third scenario.

Non-Player Character Statistics

The statistics for the bulk of the important non-players characters in this scenario can be found in the *Mythic Britons* chapter, beginning on page 196. For the various warlords, chieftains, warriors and other, nameless, rude mechanicals, use the 'Typical...' statistics also found in the *Mythic Britons* chapter.

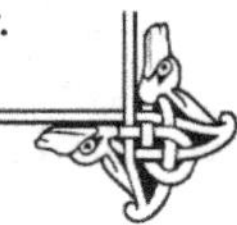

Bran Galed's Horn

Bran Galed's Horn continues on from *The Winter Council.* Merlin commands the characters to travel into Saxon lands in a bid to retrieve the fabled Horn of Bran Galed, one of the Thirteen Treasures of Britain. This also represents an opportunity for Arthur's Council to learn more of the strength of the Saxons in the northern stretches of Logres, so the characters are acting both as spies and questers. In the course of their task, the characters come across the strange and sacred Lugh's Gorge, a sorrowing village close by, and the old Roman settlement at Ratae, now occupied by the Saxons.

Merlin's Orders

The druid summons the characters to meet him at a grove in the woods north of Caer Wynd. They are to come at sunset and tell no one of their purpose. The grove is deep in the woods and located at the bottom of a steep slope that the characters have to scramble down. A natural clearing, with a shallow stream flowing through it, marks the grove; the most curious thing is that the trees surrounding the clearing's edge display summer foliage, despite it being winter. This is the work of the local Nature Spirits: Merlin has asked them to display their trees' greenery to impress the characters, which it surely must.

Merlin has lit several oil lanterns, contained in animal skulls, which are positioned around the edge of the clearing. The evening is crisp and clear: the light cast by the lanterns creates a strange, welcoming, ethereal feel to the glade, as though stepping into another world. Merlin waits in the glade's centre, sitting on a log, watching with wry amusement as the characters struggle down into the clearing. 'I brought Arthur here once,' he says. 'The idiot slipped and fell, rolling arse over tit before landing in that stream.'

Once the characters are assembled, he tells them to listen carefully, because nothing will be repeated and he has no time for questions.

'The Romans made it their business to steal Britain's Treasures,' he begins. 'They knew that to break Britain, they had to control its power. So they found and stole the Thirteen Treasures and hid them carefully. Some I have found. Some I still have to locate, and

some I know where they are and they need fetching. You will do the fetching.'

The Horn of Bran Galed, Merlin says, was in the keeping of the druids of the Corieltauvi tribe. The Romans destroyed the Corieltauvi and hid the Horn somewhere in the town of Coritanorum, which is known as Ratae to the Celts. 'I don't know where, precisely, but I do know that Bran Galed's Horn is still there. With any luck it's where the Romans hid it. If not, then the Saxons have it — and that is no good at all. You will travel to Ratae, find the Horn, and bring it to me.

'The druids of Ratae fled when the Romans arrived with their legions,' Merlin says. 'Their most sacred site was at Lugh's Gorge, two days' walk north of Ratae. Go there first. There may be help to be found in the caves.'

What form that help will take, Merlin doesn't say, but his instructions are clear.

'And while you're about it, make a note of what the Saxons are up to. Who's in charge, how many, where they've camped, all that sort of thing. There were quite a few Britons in Ratae before the Saxons came, and the Saxons captured Ratae quite recently: it's possible there are some of our people there who haven't yet been made into slaves or corpses. Find out what you can, but the Horn of Bran Galed is the priority. And no, I won't tell you what it does; and yes, you'll know it when you see it.'

Merlin tells them that when — if — they recover the Horn of Bran Galed, they are to bring it to him at his tower on Ynys Wydryn in Dumnonia. He intends to return there now that the Council has concluded. If they fail to retrieve the Horn, then they should come to Dumnonia anyway: if the characters ask why,

Merlin mutters something about doing as they're bloody well told, the folly of asking foolish questions, and potentially being cursed for all eternity.

Travel and Encounters

It is ten days' walk, or six days by horse, from Caer Wynd to Lugh's Gorge. The fastest way is for the characters to follow Ermine Strate, the Roman road that leads eventually to Ratae; however, Merlin suggests that the characters follow the River Aire, keeping it to their left as they travel south, and then follow the River Trente. The Roman Road is likely under Saxon watch, so best avoided. The terrain undulates: the characters will travel through valleys, across hills, and have to backtrack in some places. However, much of the countryside is forested, which makes it easy to hide and easy to forage for food. There is good hunting in that huge expanse of forest, but that will also attract Saxons — although no one knows how far north they have ventured.

By the evening of the second day, the characters have left Celt-controlled Britain behind and entered Logres — the territory of the enemy.

The characters can travel lightly. As they make their way towards Lugh's Gorge, have them make a number of skill rolls to assess their progress. Once every three days, there is the chance of a random encounter — roll on the Encounter Table to discover what, or choose something appropriate. The skill rolls to be made are as follows:

- Navigate or Hard Locale to guard against getting lost or waylaid. If the roll is failed, add 1 day to the journey time.
- Track or Hard Perception to pick up on local hunting trails and to secure provisions for the day. If the roll is failed, then characters gain a level of Fatigue for that day.
- Survival or Hard Stealth to remain alert for possible threats and enemies, and to keep their signs of passing to a minimum. There are no consequences if this roll is failed, but Games Masters might wish to make the characters think

Encounters	
1d100	Encounter
01-50	No Encounter
51-60	Charcoal Makers/Woodsmen
61-70	Hunting Party
71-80	Fishermen
81-90	Traders
91-95	*Sceadugenga*
90-00	Saxon Warband

they are running into trouble, just to keep them on their toes.

Charcoal Makers/Woodsmen

These peasant people are scattered throughout the Great Forest and make their living felling timber and trading it, and making charcoal in the special, turf-covered pits that enable wood to burn in the right way to produce good quality charcoal for smithing. There is a 60% chance that the peasants are Britons and 40% that they are Saxons who have wandered north and will soon make their way back south. Either way, they are fearful of warriors, show deference and respect, and attempt to ensure they survive the encounter. If Britons, the charcoal makers/woodsmen can, on a successful Easy Influence roll, tell the characters that the Saxons increase in numbers the closer one gets to Ratae. There are several Saxon warlords in the region, the most feared being Hengwulf, an Angle recently arrived and an enemy of Wiglaf, the warlord who controls Ratae. Once they were allies serving King Guercha, but a dispute over a woman has made them enemies, as the characters may discover.

If the peasants are Saxons, then language is a problem. There is a 25% chance that one of the peasants speaks Brythonic, but only at 22%. The peasants will talk because they want their lives to be spared: but there is always the risk that they will alert any Saxon warbands in the area to the characters' presence. The characters will need to get the peasant to secure oaths that they won't say anything or take more drastic steps. If kindness and mercy are shown, the Saxon peasants keep silent. If the characters are hostile, cruel, or violent, then Hengwulf's warbands near Lugh's Gorge will be alerted.

Hunting Party

These are peasant hunters looking to trap and shoot game. As they are mobile, they will keep their distance from the characters and attempt to flee or hide if they can. They are fearful of warriors who tend to steal any game already caught. To this end, the hunters try to defend themselves with spears and bows if they feel threatened. As with the Charcoal Makers/Woodmen, there is a chance of 60/40 for them being Briton or Saxon. Unlike the previous encounter, the hunters do not stick around to provide help or advice.

Fishers

These fishermen string long nets across stretches of the river in order to catch a wide range of fish and eel. They hide if they hear people coming and only emerge at either dawn or dusk to set nets or haul in a catch. The fishers are reasonably static and so do not know much about the wider world, although they do know that, if one follows the Trente, it is easy to find Lugh's Gorge and there is a village on the southern bend of the river near the gorge itself. The villagers are Celts and fish that stretch of the Trente – if they still live. Hengwulf's men haunt the area, and they are as ruthless as they come.

Traders

These are Saxon traders who have bought charcoal and skins from the scattered Saxon villages in the Great Forest and are making their way south to Ratae to trade these things for commodities that can then be sold elsewhere. The traders travel in skin and wicker canoes, two men to a canoe, their trade goods stashed in the middle. There are two canoes and four traders. They are wary of warriors and do not stop to talk. They are travelled enough to know Celts when they see them and if they can make their escape (successful Boating rolls, 80% or less), they will report what they see – and where they saw it – to Wiglaf in Ratae.

Sceadugenga

The word (pronounced SHAD-oo-GEN-ger) means 'Shadow Walker'. Sceadugenga are spirit creatures capable of physical manifestation whenever there are shadows or an absence of sunlight.

They are a Saxon spirit and have come to Britain in the dark holds of Saxon ships, escaping to dark places to watch, steal secrets, and hunt. They physically manifest as humanoid-shaped darkness: as though a man or woman has been dipped in pitch. They are featureless, save for a massive mouth filling half the head that is filled with needle-like sharp teeth. Sceadugenga they can hide themselves very effectively, but they do require darkness and shadows: if caught in sunlight or bright light, they are forced to flee back to the Spirit World, their physical bodies dissipating.

Sceadugenga feed on warmth. Their preferred method is to creep close to someone sleeping and wrap themselves around the victim. For each round of such contact, the Sceadugenga draws heat from the grasped body and, unless the victim can defend against the heat-drain with an Endurance roll (opposed by the Sceadugenga's Willpower), he or she gains a level of Fatigue as the body heat is transferred. Armour offers no protection. A successful resistance against the attack allows the victim to retaliate: but the Sceadugenga's embrace counts as a Grip Special Effect, meaning it must be broken first. Sceadugenga usually require body heat for 1d4+1 rounds, releasing the victim once satiated. It is rare that they kill outright, although it can happen if the victim is already weakened in some way. People killed as the result of a Sceadugenga attack become Sceadugenga themselves, their souls rising to join the shadow world seven nights after their death.

The creatures usually flee if their Grip is broken: they are cowardly and do not enjoy confrontation.

Non-magical weapons do not harm Sceadugenga: magical ones inflict only the magical portion of their damage. The best way to harm a Sceadugenga is expose it to bright light: a fire of Intensity 2 inflicts 1d4 damage; Intensity 3, 1d6; and Intensity 4, 2d6. Daylight cannot be resisted.

Sceadugenga are wonderful spies. Saxon shamans use them to gather secrets. It is a habit of a Sceadugenga to whisper secrets it knows to the victim, almost as payment for the heat it steals. For every two levels of Fatigue a Sceadugenga inflicts on its victim, it whispers one secret that the victim can try to remember later, on a successful Insight roll to recall the dreamlike mutterings that accompanied the icy embrace.

Treat Sceadugenga as an Undeath Spirit (MYTHRAS, page 153) that animates darkness.

The Sceadugenga encountered in this scenario whisper secrets they have learned from roaming the massive forests of eastern Britain. Choose something from any of scenarios – or even background information elsewhere in this book – to form the basis of the secret given to a victim.

Saxon Warband

This is a small warband that has 1d3 more members than the size of the characters' party. Use the statistics for Saxon Warriors on page 213. Unless the characters have failed to remain alert or have blundered around on their journey, there is no reason why they cannot either hide from the Saxons or retain the element of surprise and launch their own attack. These Saxons are not necessarily hunting for the characters: they are simply ensuring the territories they hold are secured, checking snares, hunting, and so on. A battle between the Saxons and the characters should only occur if there is a dramatic need.

The Saxons fight hard and fight well, but they are as interested in taking slaves as much in killing their foes. They will use Compel Surrender, Disarm, and other tactics to neutralise the characters, and then haul them back to their settlement for humiliation and enslavement. This could provide a dramatic twist for the scenario, requiring a daring escape – especially if taken to Hengwulf's encampment.

Lugh's Gorge

This limestone gorge is 600 yards long and runs east to west, roughly, across the landscape, with the river known as Lugh's Tongue running between the cliff faces. The cliffs are 45 feet high on both the north and south banks, and the foliage – grass, bushes, trees, bracken, and gorse – is a relatively thick, offering a great deal of cover and shelter.

The cliffs are threaded with many caves and tunnels, carved through natural erosion over the millennia. The druids believe this is a crack in the scales of the Great Red Dragon and hold the gorge to be very sacred: there are certainly many Nature Spirits to be found here (all small – Intensity 1 and 2) and in a large cave of the north cliff, about 200 yards from the western end of the gorge, is a tunnel that leads directly into the Other World, Mannwn. Most of

the caves that have been used as habitation are on the south bank and easily accessible from the ground or by a short climb up the rock, which is peppered with hand and foot holds.

The druids used Lugh's Gorge constantly until the Romans drove them from the area in the First Century AD. The High Druid of Lugh's Gorge, Judoc, refused to leave and so the Romans murdered him. Judoc's spirit is still here, watching from the north cave that leads to the Other World: he refuses to leave Lugh's Gorge and so his spirit acts as a haunt for the gorge, keeping-out hostile spirits and especially keeping Hengwulf's Saxons at bay. The people of the village at the western end of the gorge are Celts; they know of Judoc's spirit and fear it, but leave regular offerings of food and drink which Judoc appreciates.

Judoc

Intensity 4 Haunt

INT 17, POW 28, CHA 12

Skills: Deceit 85%, Insight 106%, Influence 88%, Pagan Lore 126%, Willpower 106%

Abilities: Telekinesis, Miasma, Wither, Glamour

Judoc protects the gorge with his abilities. He begins by watching anyone intruding into the gorge and assessing them with an Insight roll. If Judoc is confident the intruders offer no threat, they can pass peaceably and can even spend the night in one of the caves. If they linger, he becomes irritated and uses Miasma to instil feelings of dread and foreboding, which is usually enough. If the intruders are hostile – to Britain, to druids, or to the villagers (and this includes Christians, especially Christian priests), Judoc uses his Wraith Form and Telekinesis to attack the intruders, manifesting as a ghostly, tall, thin man, clad in dark grey tattered robes and wielding a wheat sickle as a weapon. Judoc accompanies this attack with a Glamour recreation of the Roman soldiers who drove the druids from the gorge marching upstream from the village, swords drawn, shields raised. This is usually enough to cause even the toughest warriors to flee.

Recalling Merlin's advice, the characters should remember that help of some kind is available at Lugh's Gorge. This advice is in the shape of what Judoc knows and is prepared to reveal. Having his spirit manifest to torment or interrogate the characters is a good way of establishing a dialogue or leading into one being established. Judoc does need to be placated and persuaded that the characters are deserving of his help: this can be achieved in several ways.

- A druid enters the Spirit World and somehow persuades him that the characters are allies and sent by Merlin. Judoc obviously knows Merlin and therefore knows that anyone the High Druid has sent can be trusted.
- The Ghost Fence separating the gorge from the village (see page 240) is destroyed and the bodies used in its construction are burned according to Celtic funereal customs, thus releasing the souls to cross into the Other World via the northern cave of the gorge.
- A Saxon prisoner is sacrificed to the god, Lugh, in view of the northern cave.

If placated or persuaded, Judoc reveals that the Horn of Bran Galed was hidden in the Roman Temple at Ratae, beneath the statue the Romans erected to their goddess, Minerva. It was the Romans that did this, not the druids, which is why Merlin could not be sure where it was hidden, because the Romans' magic is still powerful in their old temple. The Horn had been held in Lugh's Gorge for centuries, but the Romans took it when they drove out the druids and used it as a wedding gift to marry Lugh, the God of Light, to Minerva, the Roman goddess of Knowledge. 'It is one of the Thirteen Treasures of Britain,' Judoc says. 'And the Romans knew it. They believed if they took all thirteen they could marry their gods to ours and so have full control over the island. That they didn't succeed meant that they would one day be broken and have to leave.'

Judoc can tell the characters little of Hengwulf. The Ghost Fence they have made prevents Judoc from seeing what happens west of the gorge, so he does not know what the Saxons have done, who rules, or how many there are.

The Caves

There are a dozen or so caves along the southern crag with different levels of depth and accessibility. Some channel south for some way into the limestone and many of the caves were used as

N
50ft
VILLAGE
GHOST
FENCE
LAKE POOL

homes and for shelter by the Old People of Britain. They have left their marks in here: a Formidable Perception roll reveals etchings of animals made on the walls and ceilings of some of these caves: deer, bison, and aurochs can be discerned and the bison etching provides a spirit focus to the Great Bison spirit that still remains within Lugh's Gorge. The Great Bison Spirit can be commanded by a druid if it is beaten in a Spirit Race from one end of the gorge to the other (an opposed test of Athletics and the Bison's Spectral Combat) or wrestling (Brawn or Unarmed against the Bison's Spectral Combat). To engage with the spirit, the druid must lapse into a trance in this cave while concentrating on the bison carving.

Great Bison Spirit

Intensity 3 Nature Spirit

INS 11, POW 22, CHA 11

Skills: Spectral Combat (Hooves and Horns) 83%, Damage = 1d10.

Abilities: Bless Damage Modifier (2 steps), Bless Skill (Brawn by one skill grade), Endowment (Bash Special Effect)

The Village

At the western end of the Gorge is a village consisting of twelve huts and small roundhouses, clustered on the southern bank of the river. The village is about a hundred yards from the opening to Lugh's Gorge and standing between it and the Gorge's opening is a Ghost Fence erected by Hengwulf's shaman.

The Ghost Fence

Each part of the Ghost Fence consists of logs, formed into an X, and staked firmly into the ground. Lashed across the X, spread-eagle, is a body. Each body is naked and decayed quite badly. These sacrifices were lashed to the gibbet frame first, and then sliced across the belly in such a way that death took a long time. The fastenings are so tight that the wrists and ankles have been broken, so these sacrifices died in a great amount of pain. All of them are male: those menfolk of the village who resisted Hengwulf's warband when he came to conquer the area. Their souls are fastened to the gibbets still and cannot go to the Other World until their bodies have been cremated according to Celtic customs. If viewed from the Spirit World the victims, lashed to their gibbets, writhe and scream in agony, their howls creating a great barrier across Lugh's Gorge keeping the spirits of the Gorge trapped within their domain. They scream insults at the Celtic gods for not helping them, lash out at the spirits of the Gorge for allowing their sacrifice, and raise verbal hell for their torment. If the bodies are cut down (a grisly business that requires Hard Endurance rolls to prevent from vomiting) and then cremated on a pyre, the sacrificial souls are released from torment and led into the Other World by Judoc himself. Judoc and the Great Bison Spirit recognise this service in their dealings with the characters.

Unless the characters have dealt with the villagers, they will be resisted in trying to destroy the Ghost Fence. Moreover, tampering with it alerts the Saxon shaman, Moust, to the characters' presence in the region. It guarantees that Hengwulf's warbands will be looking for them, and guarantees reprisals against the villagers.

The Villagers

The villagers raised a few cattle on the nearby pastures, cut wood from the forest, caught fish and eels in the river, and generally lived a peaceful, subsistence life. The village was called Lugh's Mouth, given its proximity to the Gorge, and the villagers are all pagans. There are nine families, numbering forty people. All the menfolk have gone: either slaughtered by Hengwulf's men, or, as is the case with the majority, forced to labour at Hengwulf's stead, building his new hall and labouring in the forest. The women and children were spared to maintain the crops and livestock, half of which Hengwulf takes as tribute. He intends to slaughter the remaining inhabitants of the village when other families arrive from across the sea, but until then he wants the land worked and prefers to have compliant labourers to do it rather than slaves. Hengwulf also fears Lugh's Gorge. His shaman, Moust, has told him it contains great and powerful spirits, and so Hengwulf fears what curses might befall his people if he slaughters the villagers outright: this way, a Ghost Fence keeps the spirits at bay and the villagers can continue propitiating Judoc.

The villagers are an abused, terrified, fearful mess. They cower in their homes when the characters are first spotted (there is always someone watching for Hengwulf's warbands). Once they recognise that the characters are Celts, they watch cautiously and

need to be cajoled from their dwellings (Formidable Influence roll) along with assurances that the characters mean no harm.

If the characters start to dismantle the Ghost Fence before negotiating with the villagers, then villagers are brought screaming from the village, imploring the characters to leave it intact. They are more frightened of Hengwulf and Moust's punishment than their menfolk's souls and they have to be fended off while the Ghost Fence is taken down. Drawing weapons causes the women to back away, but it also ends any chance of dialogue.

If dialogue occurs, the villagers are obviously reticent. The spokeswoman is called Dalla, a haggard-looking woman whose husband is one of the souls lashed to the Ghost Fence. She tells how, months ago, Hengwulf's warband had come to the area. 'Before then the Saxons had not ventured far from Ratae, but Hengwulf wants a kingdom for himself,' she says. 'He builds a hall about half a day to the east, and that's where he took all those strong enough to work. He left us here to tend the land, give him half our food and make sure the Ghost Fence doesn't fall down.'

Insight rolls tell the characters that Dalla and the rest of the villagers are so terrified of Hengwulf's retribution that they will do anything to preserve their lives – including selling out the characters. They are too weak to flee, too scared to fight, and so traumatised by their experiences (every woman has been raped) that they are in Hengwulf's thrall.

They do not believe that the characters can help them, although, if the Ghost Fence is broken, and Judoc and the Great Bison Spirit persuaded to help, the village of Lugh's Mouth can be given some magical protection. Judoc can summon forth apparitions to scare away the Saxons, and the Bison Spirit can lead local nature and predator spirits to harry the warbands. A druid amongst the characters might be able to convince the villagers of this.

Dalla tells the characters that they still send small offerings to the spirits of Lugh's Gorge as they always have, but that the offerings are meagre because they have so little food left. They do not know Judoc's name, but a couple of the older woman believe that the Gorge is guarded by a druid's spirit, one that the Romans killed.

If the characters choose to bypass the village and leave the Ghost Fence intact, there are no consequences: the villagers say nothing when Hengwulf comes for his tribute. However, it will be harder for the characters to gain Judoc's help.

With the Ghost Fence destroyed and the villagers vulnerable, they readily tell Hengwulf, when he comes with a full warband, all about the characters, in a bid to save themselves. Hengwulf, eager for some sport – and to take revenge on those who broke Moust's Ghost Fence goes hunting for the characters, dragging Dalla with him.

Hengwulf

Hengwulf was one of the chieftains who helped Wiglaf take Ratae. The two had a falling out and so Hengwulf took his retinue (50 warriors, plus their families) and his shaman, Moust, and came north, eventually reaching Lugh's Gorge. He had found an area a day's ride to the east where had decided to build a permanent settlement, and Hengwulf decided that all land between the river, the Gorge, his hall, and a day north of Ratae would be his kingdom. He wants to extend his kingdom to include Ratae if he can, but Wiglaf is too strong for him to tackle single-handedly. He must therefore content himself with the lands he has.

Any Saxon warbands or peasants encountered before the characters reach Lugh's Gorge can alert Hengwulf to the characters' presence in northern Logres. Similarly, disturbing the Ghost Fence alerts Moust to the presence of intruders. Hengwulf can therefore be used as a very serious complication for the characters in their mission to get into Ratae. There is, however, something that may work in the characters' favour. Hengwulf hates Celts, for certain, but currently he hates Wiglaf more. The characters may be useful to him – and he can use the village of Lugh's Mouth as leverage.

Leading a warband to find the characters, he brings with him Dalla as a hostage. The warband is twenty warriors strong, and they track the characters with their large, shaggy-haired hunting hounds. The characters might, if they are lucky (and the Games Master lenient), evade Hengwulf's pursuit. Otherwise, they are going to be easily overwhelmed and captured. Hengwulf certainly aims to inflict injury – serious if necessary, and maybe even one or two fatalities – but he wants the characters alive for a couple of reasons.

First, he wants to know about Celtic forces to the north and west of this region. The characters can tell him. This information will be valuable in attracting men away from Wiglaf's garrison at Ratae and prove that Hengwulf is the lord they should be following.

Second, Hengwulf will allow the characters to steal into Ratae to do whatever it is they want to do, if they perform a service for Hengwulf in return for their lives and the lives of every villager in Lugh's Mouth. Wiglaf and Hengwulf fell out over a woman: a beautiful Celt Hengwulf captured in Ratae, but who was demanded by Wiglaf – as was his right. Hengwulf wants this beauty, with whom he is completely smitten, brought to him at his new hall.

If Hengwulf captures the characters, he drags them to his camp where they can see the construction work under way on a massive Great Hall being constructed in a wide clearing of the forest. It is being built by slaves, and these are the menfolk of Lugh's Mouth, along with others Hengwulf has captured along the way. The hall is a status symbol as well as a base, and Hengwulf knows it will attract other men to his ranks.

The characters are brought to the temporary roundhouse Hengwulf occupies while the hut is being built. He speaks only a little Brythonic, but Moust, his shaman, is reasonably fluent. Moust is a stocky, intense individual who claims to understand Hengwulf's wyrd and his fate, and knows that his own is entwined with that of his master. Moust translates the plan for the characters, which is thus:

'These are Hengwulf's lands now. You have trespassed in them, and the penalty for trespass is death. But Lord Hengwulf is merciful and generous! He will let you live on these terms.

'You will tell us of the tribes and lords within five days ride of the Gorge. Who they are, how many spears, and their wealth.

'Next, you will go to Ratae. I know this is your destination. The spirits tell me all, and I can see your wyrd. This is good. Lord Hengwulf wants you to go to Ratae because there is something there he wants you to fetch. Her name is Ydwina the Golden, a beauty so fair that Woden has decreed she shall belong to Lord Hengwulf.

'Do these things and you shall live. You shall be allowed to leave Lord Hengwulf's lands. Refuse, and a new Ghost Fence will be made. This Ghost Fence will be made of every woman and child still in the village near the Gorge. Lord Hengwulf will have his men enjoy each of them three times before they are lashed to their posts and then bled. You will be forced to watch their dying and then you will be added to the Ghost Fence. Do as Lord Hengwulf wants, and the villagers remain in peace to serve Lord Hengwulf.

'You have until dawn tomorrow to decide.'

If the characters need further persuasion or refuse, Dalla, who the characters may very well have met at Lugh's Mouth, is dragged before them, sobbing and pleading for her life. Moust calmly steps behind her, draws a dagger, and prepares to slit her throat. He stays

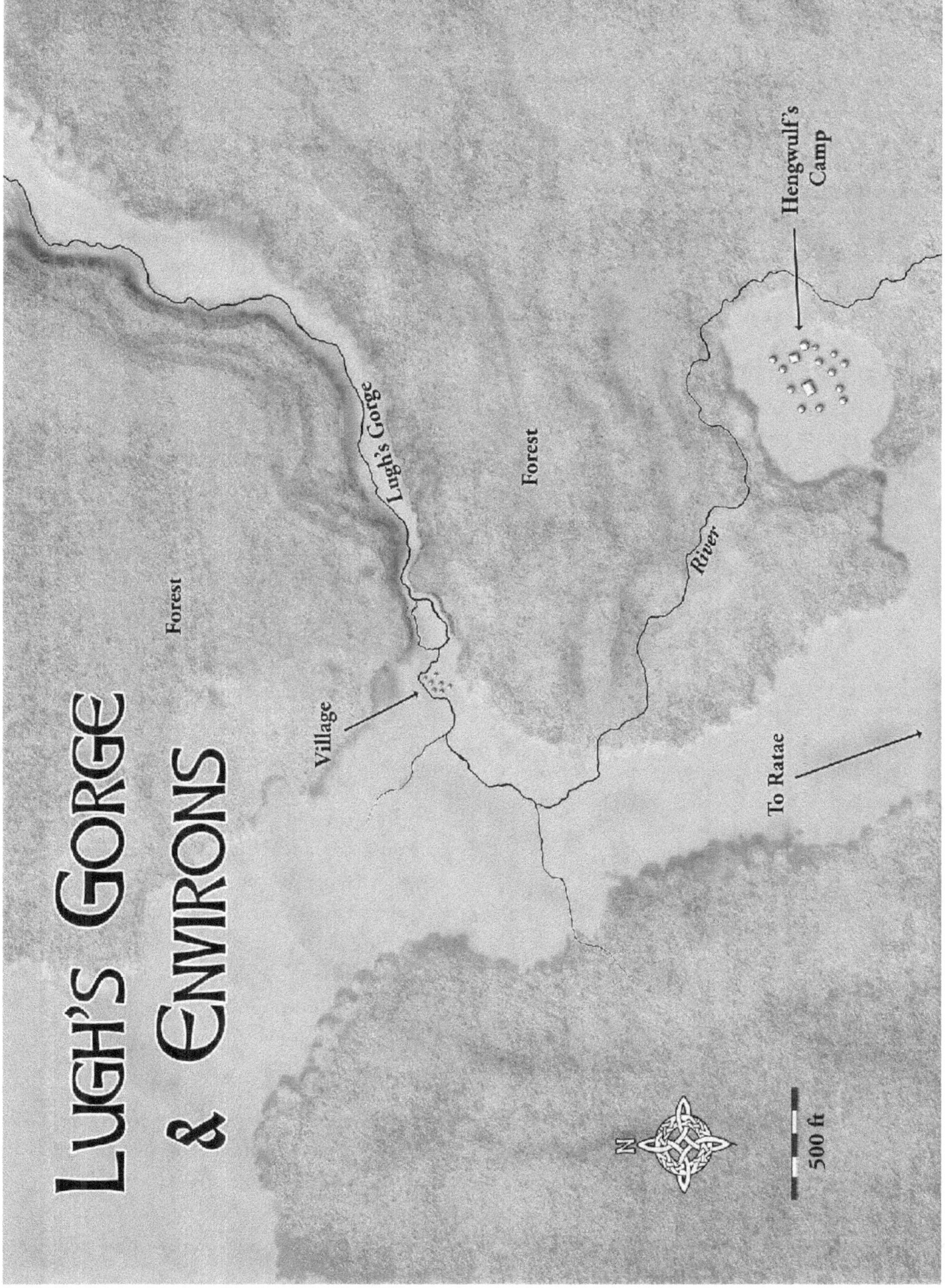

Lugh's Gorge & Environs

Forest

Village

Lugh's Gorge

Forest

River

To Ratae

Hengwulf's Camp

N

500 ft

his hand if the characters agree to the deal. If not, she dies. 'Let us go and make a new Ghost Fence,' he says.

There is the chance for the characters to escape Hengwulf's clutches. They are given a whole night to ruminate on the offer. Possibilities for a daring escape include the following:

- Characters can use their skills and wits, but they will need to bypass the camp's sentries who are vigilant. Also, the characters have been stripped of weapons and armour: fighting will be difficult.
- Depending on what they have done in Lugh's Gorge, then spirits of Judoc and the Great Bison can be called upon to help, if the characters have a druid. Although Moust has established charms around the hut where the characters are held, these two powerful spirits can still come to the characters' aid, helping to cause diversions that terrify Hengwulf's men, cause confusion, and allow the characters to escape.
- If they have created a bond with Dalla, she manages to escape from where she is held and comes to free the characters. She has an antler knife that she uses to cut their bonds, helping them to get away, but begs them to leave.

The Camp

Hengwulf's camp is in a natural, elevated clearing that has been widened further by felling surrounding trees to construct the Great Hall that Hengwulf has demanded. This heavy labour is being undertaken by about thirty slaves who are worked relentlessly throughout the day cutting, shaping, and fixing timbers.

Meanwhile, the rest of Hengwulf's followers – about a hundred or so – have formed a sprawling makeshift camp of wattle, daub, and bracken-thatched huts around the clearing's edge. Half the followers are warriors; the rest are women and children. Most are Anglians and speak no Brythonic, although there are one or two women who have taken Saxon husbands willingly: these women may help the characters if they are imprisoned.

Although Hengwulf has fifty warriors loyal to him, he only has twenty-five horses (these are corralled in a make-shift pen on the southern edge of the camp). They are, currently, his most valuable commodity and he wants more: if the characters are captured and have horses, they are considered a great prize and added to his collection. It also means that the mobility of half his warband is compromised, so Hengwulf is always careful about how he uses his forces and his horses.

By day the camp is a hive of activity with constant building. Hengwulf spends a lot of time hunting and the Great Forest provides rich game for the community. The rest of his warriors patrol the area: they know Wiglaf may decide to attack at any time, and they also want more slaves for the building work.

At night, the Saxons drink and carouse, with most being too drunk to function once it has become truly dark. However, Hengwulf has twelve sentries at all times watching the perimeter. They are forbidden drink, are armed and armoured, and expected to guard against intruders and escapees.

When the hall is finished it will be an impressive place. Hengwulf believes that if you act like a king people will see you as a king and pledge their oath. It is important for him to have kingly trappings, and the hall is the start. Next, he wants Ydwina the Golden to become his queen (conveniently ignoring the wife he has across the seas in his homeland), and then he intends to raid to extend his lands, driving the Celts of Elmet and northern Dumnonia further back so his lands can grow.

About Hengwulf

In his early twenties Hengwulf is a blond, broad, and round-eyed Anglian. He is ambitious and sees the opportunity for making himself as powerful as Aelle or Guercha. The shaman, Moust, has been with Hengwulf many years and has told him that the Norns – the three spinners of Fate – have shown him Hengwulf's tapestry, which is one of conquest, riches, and kingly colours. Hengwulf has therefore followed Moust's direction, which involved following Wiglaf to begin with, and now involves stealing away the beautiful Celt even though Wiglaf is smitten with her too. Hengwulf is a man of ambition and destiny, but he is also superstitious and trusting of Moust.

About Moust

Moust is a Jutish shaman who has been with Hengwulf for many years. He is an unassuming-looking man with a clean-shaven face, long hair worn loose, and wide, quite intense, brooding eyes. He speaks very quietly and very deliberately, as though weighing the meaning and value of each word before uttering it.

He is cold and calculating. Every choice he makes, he believes, is fated to be made: he is therefore without remorse or regret. Despite this cold assurance, he is suspicious and nervous of Britain's magic: although the Saxons are conquering, he knows the magic of the druids is still strong and Saxon magic is weak. He fears the spirits of Lugh's Gorge, but would never admit this to Hengwulf or anyone else.

About Ydwina

When Wiglaf and his warbands sacked Ratae, they took many prisoners as slaves. Ydwina was the daughter of a warlord who opposed the Saxons and died in the shield wall defending Ratae from the attack. She is a remarkable beauty: golden haired, slender, blue-eyed – more Saxon or Norse-looking than Celt. She also displayed little fear of Wiglaf when he had her brought to him to decide her fate. She looked him in the eye, stood firm, and even answered some of his questions in halting Anglian. Hengwulf was the one who found her, and he was smitten from the moment he set eyes on her: but it was Wiglaf who took her, when she stood before him and refused to cower even when threatened with rape and blinding. Wiglaf did neither: he intends to make her his wife and so gain a certain legitimacy over the surviving Celts now in his territory.

Hengwulf simmers with resentment. Wiglaf could not have taken Ratae without him. Moust has already read the rune sticks and determined that Ydwina is destined to be with him. Hengwulf had no choice but to leave Ratae and make his own settlement, fully intent on returning to claim Ydwina when the time is right.

Ratae

Ratae consists of two settlements: the Roman town, known as Coritanorum, and the hillfort on the east bank of the River Soar, known as Caer Leonis. This was the stronghold of the Corieltauvi tribe, which the Romans subsumed into Coritanorum over the course of their presence in the region. Caer Leonis was abandoned as the populace moved into the Roman town and remained there. The town remained vibrant until the Saxons came: for a long time, the Saxons ignored Ratae (which is Brythonic for 'ramparts') while they gathered their strength and conquered the surrounding lands, but eventually they came and attacked. The Celts of Ratae, a mixture of pagans and Christians, split into two forces: those defending the Coritanorum and those defending Caer Leonis, where women and children had fled on seeing the Saxon advance. This was a mistake. Even with Caer Leonis' impressive earthworks, the determined Saxons easily overwhelmed the outnumbered Celts and seized the hillfort. Coritanorum lasted a while longer, but Wiglaf and Hengwulf broke the defences and took the city too.

The Saxons do not feel comfortable in Coritanorum and so Wiglaf has set up his camp at Caer Leonis, which has commanding views of the countryside. He has a garrison stationed in Coritanorum, and slaves are busy dismantling some of the old Roman buildings for use in new walls, roundhouses, and halls in Caer Leonis. The slaves are held in Coritanorum; Wiglaf and his chiefs occupy the hillfort, and Ydwina is with them. The object of the character's mission though, the Horn of Bran Galed, is in Coritanorum. The Roman temple is still reasonably intact, although the Saxons have defiled the statues of the Roman gods to ensure their power is broken and no Roman magic can be worked. They have not found the Horn and, indeed, do not know of its existence (or its importance as one of the Thirteen Treasures).

The characters then may well have two objectives, depending on previous events: retrieve the Horn of Bran Galed and steal Ydwina away from Caer Leonis. How they achieve this is up to them, and it will require some careful planning. The details of Caer Leonis, Coritanorum, and the movements of Wiglaf, the slaves, the Saxon garrison, and Ydwina will all prove to be essential.

Coritanorum

The Roman town is located on the western bank of the River Soar where it bifurcates to form an island within the river network. It is walled with three gates, and the streets within the walls form a grid pattern very much in the traditional Roman style. Coritanorum contains a number of large villas, many smaller dwellings and workshops, plus small warehouses and storehouses. It has two bathhouses, one large and one small, but neither has been used since the Romans left and the hypocausts in both have collapsed and been choked with rubble. Many buildings and parts of the wall are being dismantled with the stones being carted out

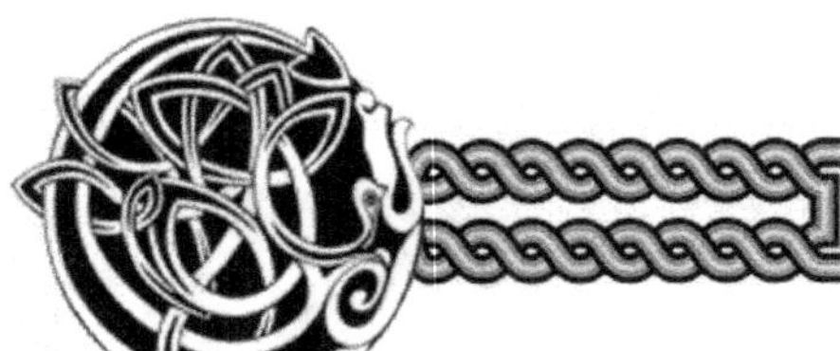

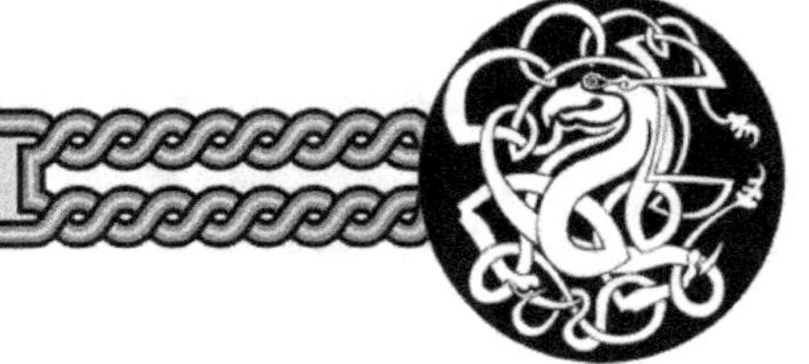

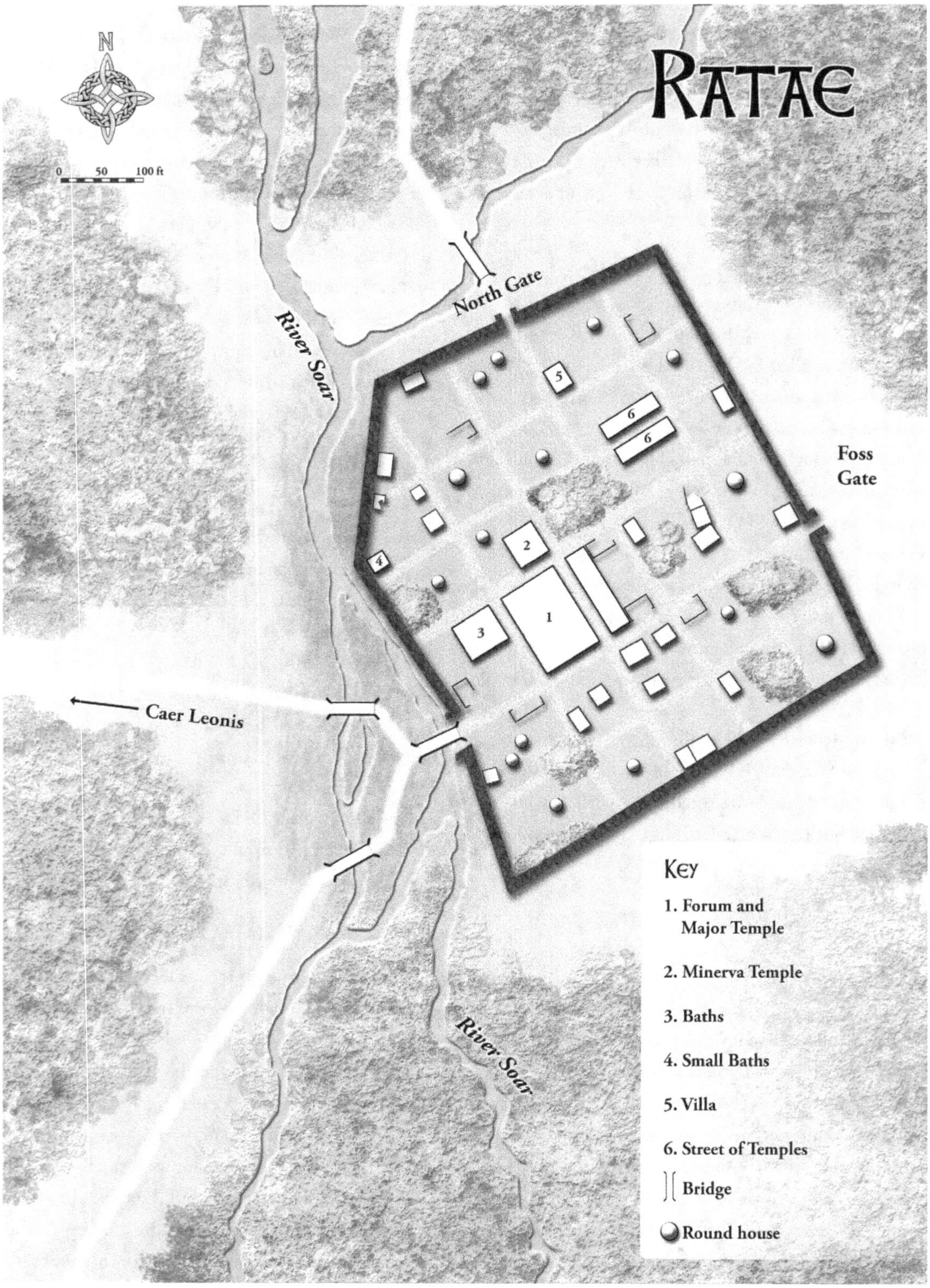
Ratae
N
0 50 100 ft
North Gate
River Soar
Foss Gate
Caer Leonis
River Soar
1
2
3
4
5
6
6
Key
1. Forum and Major Temple
2. Minerva Temple
3. Baths
4. Small Baths
5. Villa
6. Street of Temples
Bridge
Round house

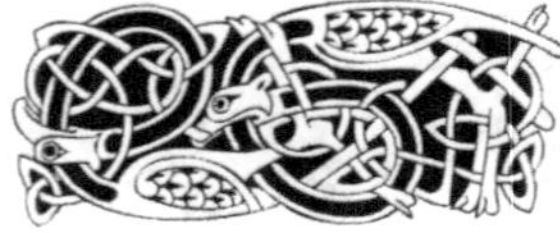

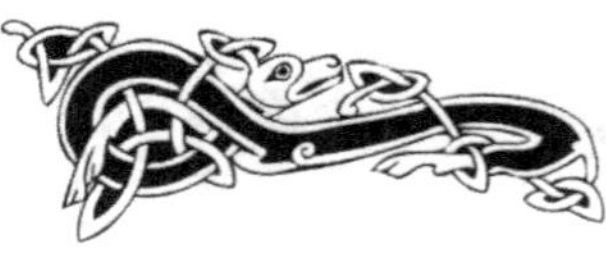

through the East Gate, across the Fossway, to Caer Leonis where the stone is being used to build up Wiglaf's defences at the hill-fort. The slaves responsible for this work are housed, at night, in the large bathhouse near the Forum. This is also near to the temple where the Horn of Bran Galed is hidden.

Sentries and Patrols

The three gates are watched by a pair of Saxon sentries, day and night. During the day the East Gate is very busy with slaves and building traffic, so the sentries have a tough time observing everything and therefore lack a certain vigilance. At night they are more cautious, but because Ratae is considered secure and the nearby Celts have been thoroughly subjugated, attacks and assaults are not expected, so vigilance is wanting. None of the gateways have functioning gates and are merely squared entry points through the walls. The sentries watch over each gate from the ramparts on either side, but spend as much time talking and drinking as they do watching.

There are three night-time patrols of three Saxon spearmen apiece through the settlement, going north/south, east/west, and around the perimeter. Again the patrols are not especially vigilant and are more concerned with potential slave escape attempts than daring break-ins.

The most heavily guarded area is the bathhouse where the slaves are held. Six sentries watch the doors and interior, making sure the slaves remain in the compound – which is the huge bathing area itself. The slaves are fastened together in groups of three with iron slave collars and thick rope; all are forced to sleep with only a thin woollen blanket on the bare tiles of the sunken bath. Conditions are cramped and unsanitary. There are a hundred slaves of all ages and sexes, and their task is to dismantle the masonry of Coritanorum and haul it to Caer Leonis to build Wiglaf's fortress, mirroring exactly what Hengwulf is doing north of the city.

The sentries guarding the slaves have little to do. To amuse themselves, they sometimes take one of the women and haul her to one of the alcoves surrounding the bathing area where she is tormented and raped. A lot of time is spent drinking and taunting the slaves. If the interior guards can be overwhelmed, the slaves will have no trouble rising up to take care of the rest of the sentries and patrols in the city.

The Bathhouse

A large, tile-roofed building, the Bathhouse has not seen water or bathing for almost eighty years. The building is in reasonable condition, but the stucco peels away from the brick, the roof leaks and has tiles missing, and the courtyard outside is choked with grass, moss, and weeds. This is where the slaves are held. These slaves are what are left of Coritanorum's residents and defenders, now made into Wiglaf's property and forced labour.

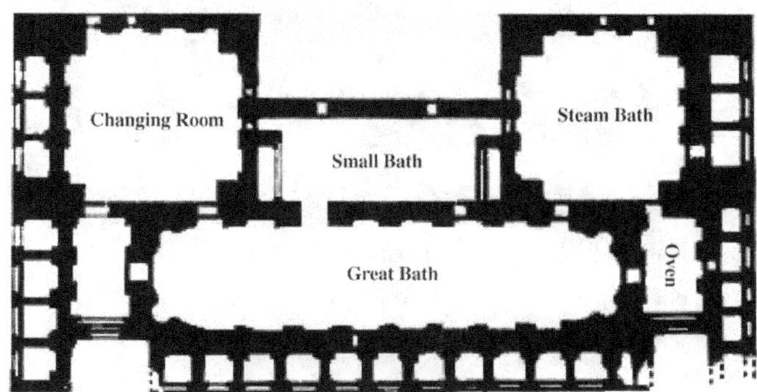

By day, the baths are empty but, at dusk, the slaves are forced to return here where they huddle into the Great Bath and spend a miserable night, chained together. Food is thrown in from the side by the jeering Saxon sentries: stale bread, hard cheese, the occasional lump of greasy meat. By day, the slaves are fed a thin, oatmeal gruel at noon: at night, they almost starve.

The baths are divided into five areas. The Changing Room, which is where the sentries gather to warm themselves, gamble, and drink; the Small Bath, which is where Roman bathers would first wash and prepare; the Steam Bath, which maintained sauna-like conditions; the Great Bath, which is where the slaves are held; and finally the Oven Room, which is where the fires for the hypocausts were maintained.

Only the Changing Room and Great Bath are constantly in use. The other areas are seldom or never used. The Small Bath and Steam Bath can be accessed through open windows set into the wall almost at ceiling height: this involves a 3-metre climb but is the easiest way of getting into the baths unseen.

There are six sentries within. One watches the main entrance, three watch the Great Bath and a couple are usually to be found in

the Changing Room or perhaps one of the alcoves surrounding the Great Bath tormenting one (or more) of the female slaves. None of the sentries are especially vigilant.

The Temple

Adjacent to the Bath House is the Temple. It is a large, roofed, semi-enclosed, and colonnaded structure. Outside are statues to Jupiter and Juno, both of which have been pulled over and shattered, their remains scattered over the weed-lined stairs leading into the main temple area.

The temple is divided into three. The first area is the common temple and is open to the air. Here, local deities, family gods, and ancestors were propitiated, along with animal sacrifices. The sacrificial altar still stands and the Saxons have hastily carved a hammer symbol into the marble, sanctifying it to their thunder god, Thunor.

Beyond is the Inner Temple. Around the walls are niches that held statues to Janus, Vesta, and Ceres – gods of the door, hearth, and crops. Again, the shrines have been desecrated by pulling down and smashing the statues, although whether Celts or Saxons have done this it is impossible to tell. Searching the Inner Temple thoroughly takes a good hour of time and uncovers nothing useful. There are no hidden caches and certainly no Horn of Bran Galed – although one might mistake the statue of Vesta for that of Minerva.

The third section, reached via a narrow passage leading from the Inner Temple, is the Sacred Temple. It is long and narrow. On either side are pillars that hold shrines and rooms for the Roman priests. There are six shrines in all, three to each side, and these held statues of Mars, Apollo, Diana, Venus, Mercury, and Minerva. At the far end, the largest alcoves held statues to Jupiter and Juno.

All the statues have been pulled down and destroyed. Their parts and fragments – some quite large – are strewn across the sanctum floor and it is impossible to tell which god belongs with which alcove.

There are eight alcoves in total and Games Masters should roll 1d8 to decide which was that dedicated to Minerva. It requires a Hard Perception roll to locate the hidden edges of the plinth that can be moved out into the sanctum revealing the pit beneath. Rubble and statue fragments need to be cleared first to allow the plinth to shift forward enough so that one can see into the pit below.

The Horn of Bran Galed

The Horn was hidden in a deep, narrow pit beneath Minerva's statue. The pit is 7 feet deep and about a foot wide. The Horn rests at the bottom: it is a curved auroch's horn, a metre and a half in length, as wide as a man's head at its widest point, and a beautiful, elegant, curved horn with gradated colouring ranging from amber at the open end down to deepest black at the horn's tip. The rim of the open end is clad in silver and bronze, the metal chased with tiny interwoven animals and plants. It is a very fine drinking horn, of the kind used at special feasts, but to the characters it seems unremarkable. Valuable, certainly; but perhaps, as a Treasure of Britain, the characters were expecting more. If a druid enters a trance while holding the Horn he can perceive the spirit of the aurochs who gave the Horn and sense the Horn's power. When used at the right rituals, and when the correct words of power are spoken, the Horn provides a never-ending supply of whatever drink is so desired. This might be a fine wine, the best mead, the sweetest ale, a potion of courage or healing, or even of poison. No druid character can hope to command this magic, but Merlin can, and so this is an item of great and wonderful power.

Threats in Coritanorum

The city itself is not patrolled. The Saxons are secure enough here that they do not feel any need to maintain tight security inside the city. But this does not mean the characters can move around without risking a challenge. A Group Stealth or Deception roll should be made to see if a group of Saxon warriors spots the characters as they steal through the city streets (failure of the Group roll meaning that they are noticed). A small warband, equal or perhaps slightly greater in number, threatens the characters, gives chase, or otherwise provides a threat. As slaves are useful and any intruders ought to be questioned by Wiglaf, the Saxons are likely to incapacitate or force a surrender rather than kill outright.

A further threat comes from Wiglaf's own læce, Isen, who lives in Coritanorum and has allied spirits watching from the Spirit World. Isen's watchers take the form of ravens, the bird sacred to Woden, and only the most observant notice the number of ravens perched in high places around the city. These keen-eyed spirit guardians, from their Spirit World vantage, see into the hearts of those they observe and swiftly alert Isen to anything peculiar.

Isen himself is blind: he gave one of his eyes to obtain Woden's wisdom, which is what grants him the control over the ravens via the Spirit World. The other eye simply became diseased and so Isen plucked it out: he wears it still in a small leather purse around his neck. If he spots the characters retrieving the Horn, he watches what they do and then despatches a group of warriors to intercept and capture them, bringing them to the villa he has taken for his own, and conducts a brief interrogation before having them sent to Caer Leonis.

The læce, Isen, is a middle-aged man, clean-shaven, with his hair severely cut away from his narrow scalp around the sides but worn long at the front so that it falls over his empty eye sockets. His face is hard and stern; his mouth full but unsmiling. To make his appearance to others even more disturbing, Isen has allowed his nails to grow for many, many years so that they are now horrible, thick, extensions of his fingers. Isen has had the nails filed into the semblance of bony talons - almost like those of some dreadful raven. Despite being blind he has two sets of surrogate eyes: his ravens, in the Spirit World, and Frenz, his human slave. Frenz is devoted to Isen – a mixture of love, awe, and fear – and describes everything to him in detail. He leads the way for Isen when the læce goes out, clearing the way for the shaman and telling him what is happening around. Frenz is seedy, unctuous, and patronising: he hates to deliver bad news to his master and so tells him precisely what he might want to hear.

It will not take Isen long to understand that the Horn, if the characters have retrieved it, is of magical importance: naturally he wants it for himself, but he is oath-bound to Wiglaf and so must let his lord make the final decision. He taunts the characters with their fate: he speaks passable Brythonic. 'Lord Wiglaf is less understanding and lenient than I. If you are lucky, you will be made into slaves. Perhaps he will have you serve me. More likely is that you will be killed and have your heads displayed on spikes outside the city. Come, let us make the journey to Wiglaf's Hall and decide your fate''

Caer Leonis

Caer Leonis was established by the Corieltauvi long before the Romans came, but was abandoned more than a hundred and fifty years ago as the tribe was subsumed into Roman society, based

around Coritanorum. The hillfort has fallen into wrack and ruin over the century and a half, its wooden palisades rotting away and only its earthworks remaining to mark its existence. However, it gives a commanding view over the surrounding countryside and Wiglaf, feeling uncomfortable in the old Roman city, has decided to rebuild Caer Leonis using stone from Coritanorum. He calls his fortress Laegre, after a place in his native lands, and it is being steadily developed into a substantial fortress with a stream of stone coming from the Roman city, hauled up the hill by slaves.

The wall surrounding Caer Leonis is incomplete. It will be almost circular in shape when done, following the earthen ramparts, but there are large gaps in its structure that Wiglaf has not bothered to fill or protect. It is therefore vulnerable to a large-scale attack, and anyone wanting to sneak into Laegre has no trouble in doing so by creeping around the ditch and then scaling the rampart where there is a gap in the wall. There are no sentries, but plenty of warriors loyal to Wiglaf who are building their own houses within sight of Wiglaf's long house, roughly in the centre of the fortress. Use the Saxon Warrior statistics elsewhere in the scenario whenever one of Wiglaf's warbands might be encountered.

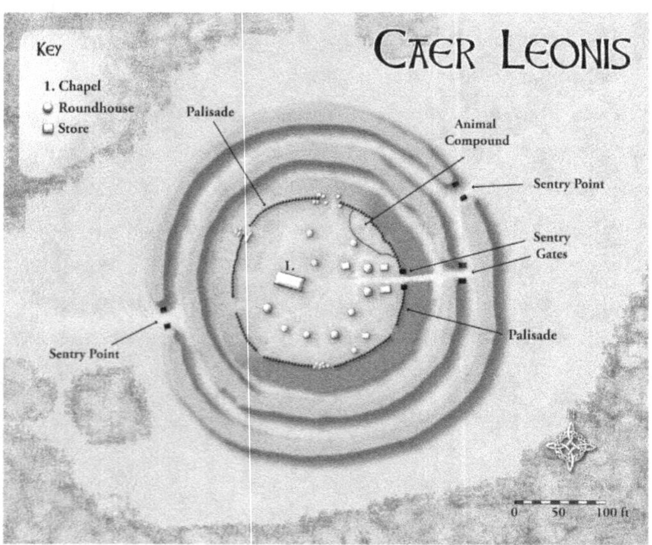

The Long House

Wiglaf's hall is just about complete. It is a rectangular long house in the Angle style, with steep eaves, a steep roof made of thatch, a stone foundation wall, and stout wooden logs that form its walls, covered in local mud and clay. Wiglaf lives here with his immediate personal warband and with his mistress, Ydwina. Wiglaf has a wife back in the old country, but he has not sent for her and has no intention of doing so, not while he has the youth and beauty of Ydwina to warm his bed. He is smitten with this blonde Celtic beauty; she is everything his wife is not: tall, lithe, intelligent, fearless, and passionate. Although Ydwina is technically a slave, Wiglaf intends to free her and make her his Bretwif (Briton-Wife).

The Long House is divided into three areas. The Feast Hall is the largest ares and is where all communal activities take place. The wooden dais where the long table is located acts the division between the Feast Hall and other areas.

Behind the long table, defined by wooden walls, are Wiglaf's quarters: a bed chamber and a chamber for his clothes, armour, and weapons. Ydwina shares his bed and room has been found in the clothing chamber for her own garments. Wiglaf and Ydwina only ever come in here to sleep and have sex; most of their time is spent in the Feast Hall or around the fortress or in the old city. Ydwina is forced to accompany Wiglaf everywhere. He knows how desirable she is and can see the wanting amongst his own men. He does not trust anyone else to be alone with Ydwina and so she is forced to go everywhere he goes. She seems to embrace this role; she looks content and dutiful, even though she wears a slave collar. To show she is Wiglaf's, her slave collar is not iron, which is what all other slaves wear, but a strip of Wiglaf's cloak, tied around her throat, indicating possession.

Adjacent to Wiglaf's quarters are the household slaves' quarters. The six slaves who tend the Long Hall sleep here on rushes. They are three men and three women, all cowed into submission, all forced to wear iron slave collars. They hate and fear their Saxon captors, but also hate and loathe Ydwina and her privileged position. Ydwina, though, does not hate them. They are Celts and therefore her kith. She uses the power she has over Wiglaf to ensure that these slaves are well treated, well fed, and given a lot

more leeway than many others. If she can be freed, Ydwina will try to free these slaves also.

Ydwina

Her father was Cailte, chief of this area of Britain and loosely allied with Dumnonia. His warbands held Ratae for years: Guercha's Saxons did not seem especially keen on capturing either Caer Leonis or Coritanorum and so he was unprepared when Wiglaf and Hengwulf arrived and decided to carve out territories for themselves with Ratae as the starting point.

Ydwina is Cailte's only child. He spoiled her and allowed others to spoil her, so that she grew into a wilful young woman who expects and gets the best. She learned early on to use her undoubted beauty to get her own way, and Cailte taught her never to fear anyone. These talents have served her well. When Wiglaf and Hengwulf defeated Cailte and made slaves out of his people (Cailte died in battle, honourably), Ydwina knew that securing the eye of one of these chieftains was crucial to her survival. Hengwulf found her first and was just as awestruck as Wiglaf: but Wiglaf took her for himself while Hengwulf spent too much time consulting his druid, Moust, over the right course of action. Wiglaf knows what he wants and takes it. He took Ydwina, and it broke Wiglaf and Hengwulf's friendship and alliance.

Ydwina knows this and intends to use it to her advantage. She hates the Saxons and wants to be returned to Celt-owned lands, but she also enjoys the attention and adoration Wiglaf gives her. Hengwulf is the kinder of the two men, and more easily manipulated than Wiglaf, so if it is her fate to be taken to Hengwulf, then so be it: but ultimately she wants to escape to Dumnonia or Powys – somewhere as far away from the Saxons as she can.

Although Ydwina uses her beauty to get her own way, she is not brazen or flirtatious. She is proud, confident, and clever: she does not need to resort to such tactics to have men do things for her. She does not promise her affections or her body to anyone. Wiglaf has taken her, of course, and has proved to be a satisfying if rough lover, but Ydwina allows this only to keep in his good graces. She knows Wiglaf would throw her to his warbands to be brutalised if she denied him what he wants or tried to tease him with unfulfilled promises.

Buildings

The settlement inside the walls is growing. Most of the small huts and roundhouses belong to Wiglaf's warriors and their families. There are pens for livestock, a corral for horses, and the usual accoutrements found in any hillfort, be it Celt or Saxon.

Only those warriors named by Wiglaf are allowed to make a home for themselves in Caer Leonis; the rest must find shelter in the old Roman city, so Wiglaf's fort is nowhere near full strength and there are, at present, only about thirty or forty families, most clustered around the Long House, living inside the walls. More are invited from time to time, but Wiglaf uses such invitations as rewards for loyalty and good service. Saxons do not feel comfortable in the Roman city and are keen to be amongst surroundings they have built in the styles of their homeland, rather than amongst Roman and Celt ghosts.

The Walls

During the day the walls are the focus of most of Caer Leonis' activity. Slaves are constantly hauling blocks up the slopes, using rollers, sleds, and their own backs to get masonry from the city to the fortress. Saxon warriors act as overseers, supervising the activity, punishing laziness, preventing any escape attempts (very, very few), and ensuring the work continues at an acceptable pace. Wiglaf rarely gets involved in the construction although he takes a tour of the walls from time to time to ensure things are going well.

Slave Revolt

At night, the slaves are led back to Coritanorum where they are taken to the old bath house, fed, and bedded down. Morale is low; the work is back-breaking. With the right encouragement and opportunities, the slaves will happily rise up against their persecutors. They are roughly equal in numbers to the Saxons (around 200 slaves and Saxon warriors; there are more civilians – wives, children, and the elderly) and many were warriors before being captured. Given an incentive and some leadership, they would fight back. Some would prefer an honourable death in battle to the living hell of slavery. If the characters decide to try this tactic, in a bid to create a diversion to rescue Ydwina or simply to escape, it requires a series of four Influence, Oratory, or a similar leadership skill, phased as a Social Conflict task, over several hours, to convince the slaves to rise up. The slaves could resist with their Accept

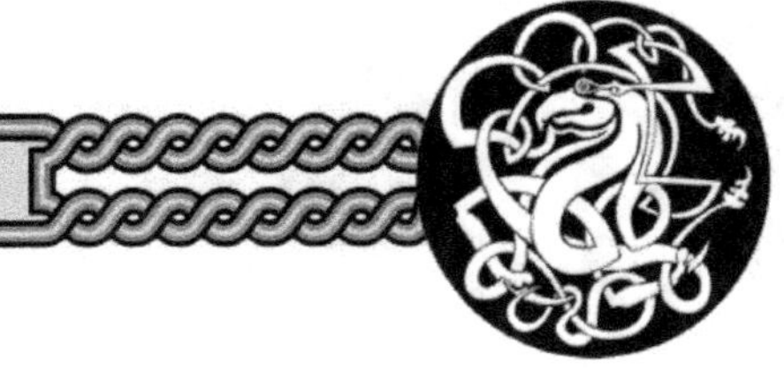

Slavery Passion 60%, but if the characters win the task, they would have a two-hundred-strong army of slaves at their command. Although unarmed, it will not take them long to overwhelm a small warband, and seize spears and seaxes.

Captured?

If the characters have been captured, either by Saxons in Coritanorum or by Isen, they are brought up to Caer Leonis for an audience with Wiglaf. If they have the Horn of Bran Galed, it is confiscated along with other possessions, but only Isen has any true inkling that it is an item of magical power – and this information he keeps to himself; he does not inform Wiglaf.

Wiglaf accuses them of being Dumnonian spies, which is almost true, and wonders aloud if he should have them gutted, blinded, and then beheaded. The characters can make pleas and he listens, eventually deciding on slavery. The characters are then taken to the smith not far from the Long House, where they are fitted with iron slave collars and, to begin with, iron shackles around their legs to prevent them from fleeing. They are beaten by Wiglaf's warriors (have the characters make Hard Endurance rolls. If they succeed, then they sustain 1d3 points of damage to 1d3+1 locations. If they fail, they received 1d6 points of damage to 1d6+1 locations from the sustained kicking).

During their beating Wiglaf watches unenthusiastically. He is used to making an example of Celts and he takes no real pleasure in the violence: it is simply something that has to be done as part of breaking a slave's will. Ydwina watches, though, and any character who makes a Hard Influence roll catches her eye and seems to elicit some expressions of sympathy. After their beating, the characters are chained to large, heavy lumps of wood, ensuring they cannot run anywhere, outside the Long House, to spend a freezing night exposed to the stars before being taken to Coritanorum the next day.

Ydwina can help the characters get free, sneaking out to them in the dead of night after exhausting Wiglaf with a night of unbridled passion – which the characters may be forced to hear. She can bring a little food and water, and also a small, broad-bladed knife that can be used to help work the shackles from the wooden stump. She can also help in causing a diversion in and around the Long House, if needed.

Should the characters tell her that they intend to take her back to Hengwulf, it requires a Formidable Influence roll to persuade her to come with them. This can be reduced to Hard, if the characters promise to help her then escape from Hengwulf somehow and take her to Dumnonia. She makes them swear an oath to help her reach Dumnonia safely, which should be treated as a Passion equal to 30% plus half the characters' Willpower. As a daughter of Cailte, a warlord of Britain, she has prestige among the Celts and her knowledge of the Saxons, gained from Wiglaf, will be of enormous use to Arthur and the Alliance of Britain.

Ydwina can also help the characters retrieve the Horn of Bran Galed, if it has been confiscated. If Isen hasn't taken it, she convinces Wiglaf it was her father's drinking horn and she would like it as a reminder of him. If Isen has the Horn, then it will be up to the characters to work out how to retrieve it – with or without Ydwina's aid.

Conclusion

The key objective is for the characters to retrieve the Horn of Bran Galed, learn more of the Saxons, fight some of them, and perhaps become involved in the complications between the two rival Saxon warlords. Games Masters should decide in advance how complicated and difficult they want to make the characters' lives, and use those sections of the scenario and complications accordingly. It is perfectly possible to run the scenario as a straightforward quest for the Horn, with few complications save those required to evade the Saxons of Coritanorum and escape with the treasure.

If the characters agreed to capture Ydwina for Hengwulf, and also have the Horn, there is nothing to prevent them from reneging on their promise to him and Moust and heading for Dumnonia and Ynys Wydryn, as instructed. However, two things will happen. First, Hengwulf slaughters the inhabitants of Lugh's Mouth and Moust creates a new Ghost Fence from their remains. Then, Hengwulf swears an oath to Thunor to catch and kill the characters for their treachery. Hengwulf and Moust become hated enemies and Moust uses his powers to find the characters, helping Hengwulf extract revenge.

If the characters take Ydwina back to Hengwulf, keeping their bargain, he keeps his and lets them go free. He has what he wants and does not care much about a small band of Celts abroad in Saxon lands. If the characters meet Hengwulf again in the future, he treats them with a certain degree of respect. If they aid him in any way against Wiglaf, then he may even come to treat them as friends.

In the matter of stealing Ydwina away from Hengwulf, just as they stole her from Wiglaf, Games Masters should run and adjudicate such circumstances as they see fit.

Reaching Dumnonia should be as easy or difficult as the Games Master wants to make it for the characters. Wiglaf will certainly give pursuit, as might Hengwulf. Ratae is only a day from the Dumnonia's northern border, and the territories controlled by Natanleod. Crossing into Dumnonia attracts Natanleod's scouts' attention and warbands are sent to engage any Saxons pursuers and provide help to Celts being pursued. The characters, if they need help, shelter, and aid, can request Natanleod's sanctuary and will be given it at Caer Gradawc. Natanleod will be keen to hear about Hengwulf, Wiglaf, and what is happening in Ratae, and then provide horses and an escort to get the characters safely to Ynys Wydryn.

If the characters have Ydwina, taking her with them to Caer Cadbryg is a sound and astute move – as the next scenario, 'Of Promises Broken', makes clear.

Non-Player Characters

Typical Saxon Fyrdman

Attributes	1d20	Location	AP/HP
Action Points: 2	1–3	Right Leg	2/6
Damage Modifier: +1d2	4–6	Left Leg	2/6
Magic Points: 11	7–9	Abdomen	2/7
Movement: 6 metres	10-12	Chest	2/8
Initiative Bonus: 10	13–15	Right Arm	2/5
Armour: Leather	16–18	Left Arm	2/5
Abilities: None	19–20	Head	2/6

Skills: Athletics 59%, Brawn 62%, Endurance 62%, Evade 56%, Locale 66%, Perception 64%, Ride 85%, Survival 67%, Unarmed 59%, Willpower 62%

Passions: Loyalty to Lord 80%, Love Battle 70%

Combat Style: Fyrdman (Sword, Spear, Seax, Shield) 75%

Weapon	Size/Force	Reach	Damage	AP/HP
Seax	*M*	*S*	*1d4+2+1d2*	*6/8*
Sword	*M*	*M*	*1d6+1+1d2*	*4/8*
Spear	*M*	*L*	*1d8+1+1d2*	*4/5*
Saxon Round Shield	*L*	*S*	*1d4+1d2*	*4/12*

Hengwulf

A relatively young and ambitious man, Hengwulf has only been in Britain two years, having come across the sea at Guercha's behest to aid Wiglaf in the taking of Ratae. Hengwulf distinguished himself and has gained many followers, but he does not believe his success has been fully recognised by either Guercha or Wiglaf and this makes him bitter. He has decided to make his own lands now, and this has led to the split from Wiglaf, but Hengwulf is still obsessed with Ydwina and does not intend letting the older, uglier Wiglaf keep her.

Hengwulf does not consider the indigenous Britons to be outright enemies: he is quite prepared to live and let live, as long as he gets what he wants. He'll take what he needs, use force to do it, and if he needs to make a few examples, well, he had Moust to help him.

Characteristics	Attributes	1d20	Location	AP/HP
STR: 15	Action Points: 2	1–3	Right Leg	0/6
CON: 14	Damage Modifier: +1d2	4–6	Left Leg	0/6
SIZ: 13	Magic Points: 12	7–9	Abdomen	3/7
DEX: 10	Movement: 6 metres	10–12	Chest	3/8
INT: 12	Initiative Bonus: 7	13–15	Right Arm	0/5
POW: 12	Armour: Furs	16–18	Left Arm	0/5
CHA: 13		19–20	Head	0/6

Skills: *Athletics 37%, Brawn 58%, Customs (Saxon) 70%, Endurance 62%, Evade 55%, Insight 29%, Language (Saxon) 80%, Lore (Strategy and Tactics) 79%, Perception 40%, Survival 65%, Unarmed 70%, Willpower 38%, Stealth 63%*

Loyalty to Guercha 63%, Loyalty to War Band 70%, Love Ydwina 80%, Distrust Wiglaf 80%, Norse Gods 60%

Combat Style: Fyrdman (Sword, Spear, Seax and Shield. Trait, Shield Wall) 81%

Weapon	Size/Force	Reach	Damage	AP/HP
Seax	*M*	*S*	*1d4+2+1d2*	*6/8*
Sword	*M*	*M*	*1d6+1+1d2*	*4/8*
Spear	*M*	*L*	*1d8+1+1d2*	*4/5*
Saxon Round Shield	*L*	*S*	*1d4+1d2*	*4/12*

Moust

An Anglian læce who came across with Guercha, Moust is striving to extend Saxon influence by banishing the gods and spirits of Britain. In truth he has no hope of succeeding: his skill and knowledge is simply not strong enough; but what he lacks in capability he compensates for in brutality. Moust is charismatically sadistic. He enjoys watching all forms of pain, be it physical, psychological or emotional. His favourite form of torture is to make ghost fences, breaking the bones of the flayed and disembowelled, confining their spirits to a living hell, denied their own afterlife. Moust has been in Britain for a decade and speaks the Brythonic language reasonably well. In truth he is terrified of the power of the druids and these strange Christians, and his cruelty is a vain attempt to protect himself from their power.

Characteristics	Attributes	1d20	Location	AP/HP
STR: 12	Action Points: 2	1–3	Right Leg	0/6
CON: 12	Damage Modifier: +1d2	4–6	Left Leg	0/6
SIZ: 14	Magic Points: 14	7–9	Abdomen	0/7
DEX: 9	Movement: 6 metres	10–12	Chest	0/8
INT: 14	Initiative Bonus: 12	13–15	Right Arm	0/5
POW: 14	Armour: None	16–18	Left Arm	0/5
CHA: 14		19–20	Head	0/6

Skills: *Athletics 45%, Brawn 36%, Customs (Saxon) 90%, Endurance 44%, Evade 32%, Insight 48%, Language (Saxon) 90%, Lore (Torture) 75%, Perception 56%, Unarmed 35%, Willpower 66%*

Magical Skills: Binding 36%, Trance 55%

Loyalty to Guercha 75%, Loyalty to Hengwulf 48%, Fear Britain's Gods 80%, Norse Gods 85%

Combat Style: Self Defence (Seax) 47%

Weapon	Size/Force	Reach	Damage	AP/HP
Seax	*M*	*S*	*1d4+2+1d2*	*6/8*

Wiglaf

Middle-aged now, and knowing that this is his last chance to truly make himself great, Wiglaf is a chieftain loyal to the Angle King Guercha and is married to one of Guercha's sisters. His wife is in the homeland, waiting to be summoned to Britain, but now that Wiglaf has found Ydwina and fallen for her, he is not so sure that he wants his wife around. Wiglaf is a stern, battle-hardened man, but not an uncompassionate one. The slaves he has made of the local Britons are a necessary example and he does not feel they are badly treated. Nevertheless, he is busy making a land for Saxon men and women. If the Britons will not accept that they have new neighbours, then they will die in battle or be turned into slaves. The choice is a simple one.

For now though, it could be that Wiglaf is the real slave. Although she wears a slave collar, Ydwina is clearly favoured and many have noted this apparent weakness in their chieftain.

Characteristics	Attributes	1d20	Location	AP/HP
STR: 13	Action Points: 2	1–3	Right Leg	2/6
CON: 13	Damage Modifier: +1d2	4–6	Left Leg	2/6
SIZ: 15	Magic Points: 10	7–9	Abdomen	4/7
DEX: 9	Movement: 6 metres	10–12	Chest	4/8
INT: 10	Initiative Bonus: 8	13–15	Right Arm	0/5
POW: 10	Armour: Scale and Padding	16–18	Left Arm	0/5
CHA: 12		19–20	Head	4/6

Skills: *Athletics 33%, Brawn 58%, Customs (Saxon) 80%, Endurance 48%, Evade 59%, Insight 40%, Language (Saxon) 80%, Lore (Strategy and Tactics) 81%, Perception 49%, Survival 52%, Unarmed 66%, Willpower 41%*

Loyalty to Guercha 90%, Loyalty to War Band 90%, Love Ydwina 85%, Distrust Hengwulf 80%, Norse Gods 60%

Combat Style: Fyrdman (Sword, Spear, Seax and Shield. Trait, Shield Wall) 80%

Weapon	Size/Force	Reach	Damage	AP/HP
Seax	*M*	*S*	*1d4+2+1d2*	*6/8*
Sword	*M*	*M*	*1d6+1+1d2*	*4/8*
Spear	*M*	*L*	*1d8+1+1d2*	*4/5*
Saxon Round Shield	*L*	*S*	*1d4+1d2*	*4/12*

Isen

This eccentric læce believes he is Woden's voice in the middle world and it is his duty to bring the Saxon gods to this strange land that worships many different kinds of spirit. It is Isen's wyrd to gain the same wisdom as Woden and so he has plucked out one of his eyes, just as Woden did, and traded it for knowledge. When his remaining eye failed, Isen was left in darkness and so his eyes are a spirit raven that acts as Isen's fetch, and the simpering slave known as Frenz. Isen does not think much of Wiglaf or Hengwulf: both are weak-willed and do not have the true strength to conquer these Britons. Isen believes the task will be one of defeating all their gods first, not slaughtering their warriors.

Isen has begun this task in Ratae. He has ensured that all the old Roman temples are defiled, their gods humiliated and the images of Thunor, Woden, Hoder and Frigga replacing them. He sacrifices regularly for Woden's wisdom and is eager to learn how these lesser gods of the Britons can be vanquished.

Characteristics	Attributes	1d20	Location	AP/HP
STR: 9	Action Points: 2	1–3	Right Leg	0/5
CON: 9	Damage Modifier: 0	4–6	Left Leg	0/5
SIZ: 12	Magic Points: 12	7–9	Abdomen	0/6
DEX: 9	Movement: 6 metres	10–12	Chest	0/7
INT: 14	Initiative Bonus: 13	13–15	Right Arm	0/4
POW: 12	Armour: None	16–18	Left Arm	0/4
CHA: 7		19–20	Head	0/5

Skills: *Athletics 20%, Brawn 18%, Customs (Saxon) 100%, Endurance 31%, Evade 28%, Insight 90%, Language (Saxon) 100%, Lore (Norse) 90%, Perception 30%, Unarmed 44%, Willpower 78%*

Magical Skills: Binding 60%, Trance 80%

Loyalty to Wiglaf 40%, Hate Britons 75%, Norse Gods 90%

Combat Style: Woden's Talons (Fingernails) 44%

Weapon	Size/Force	Reach	Damage	AP/HP
Fingernails	*S*	*S*	*1d3+1*	*As for Arm*

Isen's allied fetch is a spirit raven that once belonged to Woden. It is named Rægg and is completely loyal to Isen having fully appreciated the way the man gave his sight in exchange for true wisdom and power. Rægg's details are thus:

INT: 14, POW 17, CHA 9

Skills: Spectral Claws and Beak 76%, Lore (Woden's Wisdom) 134%, Willpower 84%

Abilities: Autonomy, Comprehension, Domination, Manifestation, Perceptive

Rægg can manifest for short periods in the mortal world and Isen uses Rægg to act as his spy abroad in Ratae. Through the Domination ability Isen gains command over all crows and ravens in the Ratae vicinity, meaning that there is little that happens he is unaware of, and if he needs to call for defence, he can summon a flock of crows to descend and drive off (or even peck to death) any who dare challenge him.

In addition to Rægg, Isen has Frenz. A slave that Isen brought with him, Frenz is broken to the point of abject devotion to the læce. He goes everywhere with his master, constantly whispering what is happening around, guiding him, and acting as a physical protector. Frenz will gladly lay down his life for Isen, firmly believing that, in the afterlife, he will become one of Woden's advisers and a man of repute, wealth and status.

If statistics are needed for Frenz, treat him as a Typical Saxon Fyrdman but with a Combat Style of Self Defence (Seax and Unarmed) of 52%.

Ydwina

Daughter of Cailte, Ratae's now-dead chieftain, Ydwina is a blonde haired, blue-eyed goddess made flesh. She knows men desire her and this gives her confidence. As a chieftain's daughter she knows how to read people and manipulate them. She is adept at getting her own way.

The rivalry between Hengwulf and Wiglaf amuses her. She is content to be with either man if that is what brings her power and status eventually, but she would rather be back amongst Britons and treated as a princess, as is her right. If the opportunity to escape arises, she takes it.

Ydwina sees herself married to someone of status. She has heard stories of Arthur and the other warlords of the west and can picture herself as the wife of a powerful chieftain, adored by the war bands, feted by the bards, envied by the other wives. She is patient though, and has faith that God (for she is a good Christian) will deliver her to her destiny. It is merely a matter of time.

Characteristics	Attributes	1d20	Location	AP/HP
STR: 9	Action Points: 3	1–3	Right Leg	0/5
CON: 15	Damage Modifier: -1d2	4–6	Left Leg	0/5
SIZ: 8	Magic Points: 10	7–9	Abdomen	0/6
DEX: 15	Movement: 6 metres	10–12	Chest	0/7
INT: 15	Initiative Bonus: 15	13–15	Right Arm	0/4
POW: 10	Armour: None	16–18	Left Arm	0/4
CHA: 17		19–20	Head	0/5

Skills: *Athletics 30%, Brawn 20%, Customs (Celt) 80%, Culture (Saxon) 38%, Dance 70%. Endurance 45%, Evade 45%, Insight 56%, Language (Brythonic) 80%, Language (Saxon) 36%, Lore (Scripture) 44%, Perception 45%, Superstition 65%, Unarmed 27%, Willpower 60%*

Love Status 90%, Despise Saxons 70%, Christian 75%

Combat Style: Self Defence (Dagger, Unarmed) 27%

Weapon	Size/Force	Reach	Damage	AP/HP
Dagger	*M*	*S*	*1d4+1-1d2*	*6/8*

Of Promises Broken

Of Promises Broken focuses on Caer Cadbryg and the unfolding events concerning Arthur, Guinevere, and Achaius, the young King of the Parisii tribe of Britain's north-east. It continues from *Bran Galed's Horn* and two separate ways of introducing the characters are provided. Games Masters can create their own ways of bringing the characters to Caer Cadbryg if they wish.

The scenario is based on intrigue, plots, schemes, and blackmail. It is complex, has many moving parts and many potential outcomes. Games Masters should read the scenario carefully, familiarising themselves with its structure and, crucially, the motivations of the various non-player characters. When running the scenario, let the characters discuss, argue, plan, and re-plan as much as they need to. Their allegiances will be tested and the choices they make will influence Britain's future. If a particular outcome needs to be secured, Games Masters have a number of ways of ensuring it without necessarily railroading the characters, but ultimately the characters should be given agency to significantly influence events – and reap appropriate rewards.

Introduction

When the characters last encountered Guinevere, she was publicly promised to King Achaius of the Parisii at the High Council. The characters may or may not have witnessed the way she flirted with Arthur, but in this scenario, they will learn more about the problems this attraction has caused.

Guinevere and Arthur have fallen in love, despite Guinevere's impending betrothal to Achaius. Guinevere's father's ambition is to marry his daughter to a king, gaining land and patronage and seeing out his days in comfort. Achaius was the best avenue to this comfort at the time, hence the public announcement at the Council, but now that he knows he can aim higher; Achaius is no match when compared with Arthur. Faced with a choice between the windswept and remote lands of the Parisii or the warmer, more fertile Dumnonia with its old Roman towns and the safety of Caer Cadbryg, both Guinevere and her father choose Arthur.

While the characters are engaged on their business for Merlin, Guinevere and her family have contrived to leave Achaius behind and travel to Dumnonia. Cywryd sent a message to King Achaius

annulling the betrothal prior to the ceremony in Caer Pedwyr, as it is his right, leaving Arthur and Guinevere free to marry — which they will do. This scenario concerns the events of the new betrothal and marriage, scheming within Caer Cadbryg's halls, and what Achaius decides to do about the situation.

Reaching Dumnonia

If this scenario follows on directly from Bran Galed's Horn, then the characters should head for Ynys Wydryn to meet with Merlin, as instructed by the druid. Even if the characters have failed to secure the Horn, they are still expected to explain themselves to Merlin and report on the situation regarding the Saxons in northern Logres. This is the ideal starting point for the scenario.

If the characters have gone elsewhere, news soon reaches them that Guinevere and Arthur are to be married. The news is surprising and, given Arthur's general reputation, of huge interest. All lord and chieftains who are part of Arthur's Alliance are expected to travel to Dumnonia for the celebrations or send representatives: thus, the characters will find themselves heading for Dumnonia in one way or another.

Setting the Stage

The following are opening encounters or situations to help frame the scenario and provide the characters with the opportunity for some inside knowledge and intrigue. Use whichever is appropriate.

Rhiannon and Pwyll

Naturally enough, Merlin knows all about the betrayal of poor King Achaius and the developing love between Arthur and Guinevere. 'Achaius is young, he's not ugly, and he's a king. He'll find someone to warm his bed and whelp his children, but it was never going to be Guinevere,' he says. 'This is all part of the Great Red Dragon's plan: it is in its dreams, its memories. Just as Pwyll and Rhiannon were meant to be together, so are Arthur and Guinevere. And just like Pwyll and Rhiannon, there will be much strife too — but that can't be helped. It's all part of the Plan.'

The druid is, of course, referring to the legend of Pwyll and Rhiannon, which every Celt knows. Rhiannon, a fabled beauty, was wooed by King Pwyll, but had been promised to another king, Gwawl. Pwyll uses tricks and dishonour to win Rhiannon, but later, when Rhiannon gives birth to a son, the child disappears and Rhiannon's midwives contrive to blame their mistress for the disappearance, accusing her of infanticide and cannibalism. Rhiannon is forced into a dreadful penance until her son, Pryderi, is returned to her safe and well as a full-grown man, named Gwll (meaning 'Of Golden Hair') by his foster parents. Rhiannon is exonerated for the crimes, and Pryderi goes on to become one of the legendary kings of Britain. If the characters mention the story or question him on it, Merlin grows tetchy and impatient.

"No, I am NOT suggesting Guinevere is Rhiannon, and neither is Arthur Pwyll. I am not suggesting Guinevere is a cannibal and neither am I suggesting that this is a replaying of that story. All I am doing is drawing an analogy! If you cannot see that and understand it, then you truly are the cretins I always thought you were. Mind you, history does have a habit of repeating itself..."

Merlin then, believes all this is predestined and part of a much larger scheme. What that scheme is, he will not say, but he does insist on the characters accompanying him to Caer Cadbryg ahead of the betrothal so that they can report to Arthur and his Council. "Arthur might be love-struck, but he'll still want to know about what's happening in Ratae, so I dare say you'll prove to be of some use again."

As they travel from Ynys Wydryn to Caer Cadbryg, Merlin offers the characters some advice. 'There is bad blood in Caer Cadbryg. Uther's widow despises Arthur and she loathes me. That's fine; the feelings are mutual. There are other enemies too — those who feel Arthur has no right to command in Dumnonia. Keep your eyes open, your ears unclogged, and your wits about you. I want to know of any schemes you might hear about. You're unknown in Caer Cadbryg and you'll have the opportunity to learn things others might not.'

A King's Grief

As an alternative opening to the scenario, the characters might encounter King Achaius en route to Caer Cadbryg.

Achaius is grief-stricken but trying to put a brave face on things. First of all, he hero-worshipped Arthur, wanting to become just like him: a feared warlord and a leader commanding the loyalty of his warriors. He is having a great deal of trouble reconciling the Arthur of his imagination with the man who has stolen away his intended wife. Second, he was beguiled by Guinevere's beauty, charm, and wit: he would have readily given her all she and her family wanted, and so the insult shown is too much to bear.

Any other king and chieftain might declare a blood-feud with Arthur. Indeed, Achaius still might. But right now, he is trying to see reason, trying to find a way through the insult, and trying not to give in to hatred and vengeance. His counsellors are divided: they know that the Alliance is important as the Saxons grow stronger, but they also tell Achaius that he cannot allow this insult to go unpunished. Therefore, Achaius is travelling to Caer Cadbryg to attend the betrothal. He will offer his respects, but also demand a public apology from Arthur. He is, however, vulnerable, and an easy tool for Arthur's enemies, as is later revealed in this scenario.

The characters encounter Achaius and his entourage as they ride south-west into Dumnonia, skirting Saxon-held lands. If the characters met Achaius at Caer Wynd in the first scenario, he remembers them: they are invited to accompany him to the betrothal. Although this expands his retinue, a few more spears will not go amiss as they skirt lands claimed by the Saxons. Indeed, the party might already have had to fend off or evade Saxon patrols, heightening the characters' importance.

Achaius, or advisers close to him, explain what happened with Guinevere. "We were to be married. All agreed. I was happy. And then, on the day of the betrothal, A message from Guinevere's father. A change of plan, he said. Arthur, he said, had fallen in love with his daughter and she him. a better alliance he said, for the good of Dumnonia and Gwent. They left together. Who can blame her, eh? I have a draughty fortress on a hill facing the sea, and Arthur has Dumnonia and the line of the Pendragons behind him. I'm sure they will be happy together. I am still Arthur's man; he is still the one to lead us against the Saxons."

Timeline of Events

A timeline of key events is provided. Games Masters should consider this a loose approximation and change the timeline (and events) to suit the unfolding nature of the scenario. Each event is expanded upon later.

1. Characters arrive at Caer Cadbryg. Make their report to Arthur on the situation in Ratae.
2. Ladwys, Custennin and Samsun begin their scheming.
3. Father Samsun takes an interest in the characters.
4. King Achaius arrives. Tensions grow.
5. The Betrothal ceremony takes place.
6. The characters have opportunities to save the day.
7. Decisions are made; schemes succeed or fail.
8. The Alliance of Britain is made or broken.

Insight rolls easily indicate that Achaius is trying to put a brave spin on things. Young, unsure of himself, and scorned, he does not know how to act or how to feel. He is open to counsel from those outside his usual circle and he looks to the characters for their advice.

If any of the characters have developed a Passion with Guinevere and commiserate with Achaius, he readily bonds with that character, finding a kindred spirit, wounded by a beautiful woman, that he can relate to. Achaius is young, needs role models and is painfully naive in matters of the heart. This is an opportunity for the characters to become deep friends with the Parisii king, if they are not friends already.

Enemies Within

Arthur has three enemies – the Three Schemers – within Caer Cadbryg, who will soon be joined by a potential fourth when Achaius arrives. The Three Schemers are Ladwys, Uther's widow; Custennin, Uther's youngest brother; and Father Samsun, the leading priest at Caer Cadbryg. All three are Christians: Ladwys and Custennin have their own reasons for hating Arthur while Father Samsun is simply seeking greater power for himself and Christianity. Morgana, Ladwys' daughter, knows of their plots and watches from the periphery, but has her own agenda.

The three of them know that the best way to hurt Arthur is to injure his pride: the current source of his pride is the beautiful Guinevere. The way that Arthur and Guinevere have treated the young Parisii King is, in itself, a terrible betrayal of trust and friendship, and provides grist to the mill of Arthur's enemies. However, Arthur and Guinevere fell in love and left Caer Pedwyr, Achaius's home, before the betrothal took place. Technically, if not morally, there was no real relationship between Guinevere and Achaius: Guinevere's father, Cywryd, was quite at liberty to change his mind over whom his daughter would marry. It is bad form, but it quite within Cywryd's rights.

None of this matters to Ladwys, Father Samsun, and Custennin. Together they scheme to ruin Guinevere's reputation and damage Arthur's pride. They will pretend to side with Achaius, befriend him, and offer sympathy: it is a charade – Achaius is nothing but a tool of their spite and vengeance. Father Samsun also sees an opportunity to garner further favour with Ladwys, intending to convert Achaius to Christianity.

Arthur's Gambit

Having just forged a shaky alliance of Britain's kingdoms, Arthur knows full well that his rash romantic actions now jeopardise it. The Parisii are a client kingdom of the Brigantes and an insult to Achaius risks insulting the Brigantes and the Carvetii, perhaps turning them into detractors. However, romance aside, a marriage to Guinevere, who has been sheltered by Gwent, could help bring Gwent into the Alliance. This is brinksmanship. Arthur needs as many kingdoms as possible to make his Alliance strong. He has one important gambit left to him: if it seems that the Brigantes and Carvetii – both Christian kingdoms – might break from the Alliance of Britain, he will convert to Christianity and agree to be baptised. Arthur has never declared for one religion or another, but the ever-present counsel of Merlin has always marked him as pagan, as has his possession of Caledfwlch; but Arthur is quite prepared to become a Christian if it cements the current Alliance, brings Gwentish spears, and gives him Guinevere.

Whether or not Arthur puts this plan into action depends very much on the outcome of this scenario – and the characters play a key part in the results.

The Three Schemers' Plan

The Three hate Arthur and want to see his power broken, each for very personal reasons. For Ladwys, Arthur is a reminder of Uther's treachery with Ygraine. Custennin has always been jealous of Arthur's rise to power following Uther's death: he wants to take Caer Cadbryg for himself. Father Samsun hates pagans and wants to consolidate Christian power within Caer Cadbryg with himself at its head. Working together the Three have the following plan:

- Manipulate Achaius into denouncing Arthur and Guinevere's union and breaking away from the Alliance.
- Persuade Achaius to have the Brigantes and Carvetii also break from the Alliance.
- Have Achaius denounce Guinevere as a seductress and whore (and provide trumped-up or real proof).
- Position Custennin as the man to save the Alliance of Britain.
- Convince Arthur to leave Caer Cadbryg – with a sullied Guinevere if he wishes – and cede his command to Custennin.
- Have Achaius convert to Christianity and pledge loyalty to Custennin.

For their plan to work, popular support is needed. The Christians of Caer Cadbryg and surrounding settlements can help sway opinion against Arthur. It is up to Father Samsun, the wily priest, who has the favour of both Ladwys and Custennin to spread lies about Arthur and Guinevere's sinfulness and secure the support of Christians — even those who are normally favourable towards Arthur.

Their plan could work — if no one intervenes. Also, this would force Arthur into announcing his intention to become a Christian (something none of the Three Schemers anticipate and would be seen as a severe wedge between Arthur and Merlin). The characters' actions will make all the difference.

The Characters' Dilemma

In the opening scenario, *The Winter Council*, the characters were given several opportunities to meet Arthur, Guinevere, and Achaius, and develop some form of relationship with each of them. This scenario is going to test these relationships and place the characters in a position where they need to make a number of difficult choices. Although it is impossible to predict what the characters will do, who they will support, and how they will act, they will be key to the outcome and Britain's future. Some possibilities are outlined.

Achieve Reconciliation

Helping Achaius, Arthur, and Guinevere reconcile with one another over what has happened, with Achaius giving the Betrothal and eventual wedding his blessing, and supporting Arthur, is the ideal outcome for all concerned. The characters can do this by thwarting the Three Schemers and convincing Achaius to accept what has happened, or even by helping him find another focus for his broken heart.

Side with the Schemers

It could be that the characters believe that Arthur and Guinevere deserve to be punished for their treachery, and support the Schemers. This would ultimately wreck the Alliance of Britain and significantly weaken Dumnonia. Custennin is a weak and vain man who cannot command the loyalty of the other Dumnonian leaders, Havgan and Natanleod. But this could win them a greater role in leading Britain, if their ambitions run that way.

Prove a Point

Achaius has been hurt. Perhaps Arthur and Guinevere need to be rebuked somehow and make amends or a sacrifice so that Achaius' honour is restored. However, it need not be that the Three Schemers triumph and the Alliance is broken. The characters may be able to engineer a way for Arthur to retain his position and marriage, make significant amends to Achaius, and for the Three Schemers' plan to be thwarted. This would revolve around probing more deeply what Achaius truly wants (what are his ambitions; does he want to more prominent role in the upcoming

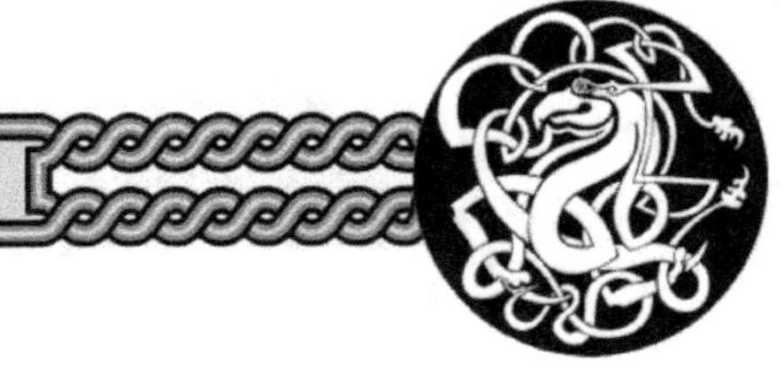

conflict?) or breaking Achaius' infatuation with Guinevere (either through showing him her true perfidious nature, without making him angrier; or redirecting his affections to a better choice) so he can dismiss the loss and re-forge a love for Arthur.

Some Other Outcomes

There are many possible outcomes. Games Masters are advised to provide the characters with as much time and room as needed to wrestle with their Passions, their oaths, personal feelings, moral feelings, and considerations of what is the best for Britain. This may be a lengthy and fraught process, but it will help decide the ultimate outcome of the scenario and guide Games Masters in how they run things. The intended solution, as written, is for Reconciliation, but Games Masters should not feel tempted to overtly railroad the characters towards it. It may be more fun – and even desirable – for the Three Schemers to win and for a deposed Arthur to have to live with his choice of Guinevere, fighting for Britain from exile or a more humbled position.

Merlin can, of course, intervene if Games Masters want to secure a particular outcome and everything seems to be stacked against it. However, having Merlin expose the Three Schemers or take action against them should be an absolute last resort. Merlin has his own agenda and considers this nothing more than a petty squabble over a pretty young woman. If Arthur opts to become a Christian, Merlin is angry but does not divert from his plan to unite the Treasures of Britain and increase the power of the Old Gods. Even Arthur will not be allowed to stand in Merlin's way.

Events

Arrival at Caer Cadbryg

Caer Cadbryg's layout and key is provided on page 267

It is assumed that the characters have come to Dumnonia from Ratae and are accompanied by Merlin. Their first duty is make a report to Arthur and his Council. Merlin escorts them to the Great Hall of Emrys; sentries melt out of the way as Merlin leads the characters through the settlement and a few devout Christians make the sign of the Cross as he passes, fearful of the druid's ancient magic. Merlin says nothing and takes the characters into the Great Hall; word has already been sent ahead, so the characters are expected.

In the feast hall, where all major meetings of the Caer Cadbryg council are held, Arthur is present with Derec, Bors, Lord Custennin of Caer Sulis, Lord Natanleod of Caer Gradawc, and Lord Havgan of Caer Uisc. There are other advisers and retainers also present, but these six form the High Council of Dumnonia. Arthur welcomes the characters: if he met them at the Council at Caer Wynd, he greets them as old friends. Mead, ale, bread, cheese, and seasonal fruits are brought and the characters invited to eat, make themselves comfortable, and then tell of their exploits in Ratae. The Council wants to know about warrior numbers, locations, divisions of loyalty, shamans – everything possible about the Saxons' capabilities, strengths, and weaknesses. Arthur listens patiently. Havgan and Natanleod interrupt every now and again with shrewd, sometimes challenging, questions, but are clearly just ensuring they understand everything correctly.

Custennin seems bored. He snorts with derision if the characters recount a failure or error on their part and contributes little to the discussion. He makes a number of disdainful comments about the Horn of Bran Galed and makes the sign of the Cross (Merlin feigns not to notice). He flashes Arthur several glances as the characters tell their story and a successful Insight roll indicates that there is certainly either a tension between the two men, distrust, or something else: Custennin is definitely not according Arthur much respect.

When the characters are through, a few more questions are asked, but Arthur, Havgan, and Natanleod appear to be satisfied with what they have heard. 'We will discuss more, later,' Arthur says. 'But you, my friends, have done well. It was a brave act to venture so deeply into Saxon lands and return with such a detailed report. Dumnonia is grateful.' He, Derec, Bors, Havgan, and Natanleod remove an arm ring, finger ring or some other form of jewelry and present them to the characters as a reward. Custennin does not and both Havgan and Natanleod are visibly irked at this, but Arthur seems unconcerned. 'Silver is such an obvious – though much deserved – reward. Is there something else this Council might offer as a gift?'

Successful Customs rolls mean the characters can ask to serve one or other of the Lords directly, ask for a modest, non-material favour, or something else that would not create problems or issues of protocol. Any outrageous requests or demands are met with wry smiles or even chastisement. If any character raises the issue of Arthur, Guinevere, and Achaius, Arthur scowls and simply tells the characters that this is something they should not be concerned with. He is not angry, but he makes his displeasure known and dismisses the characters.

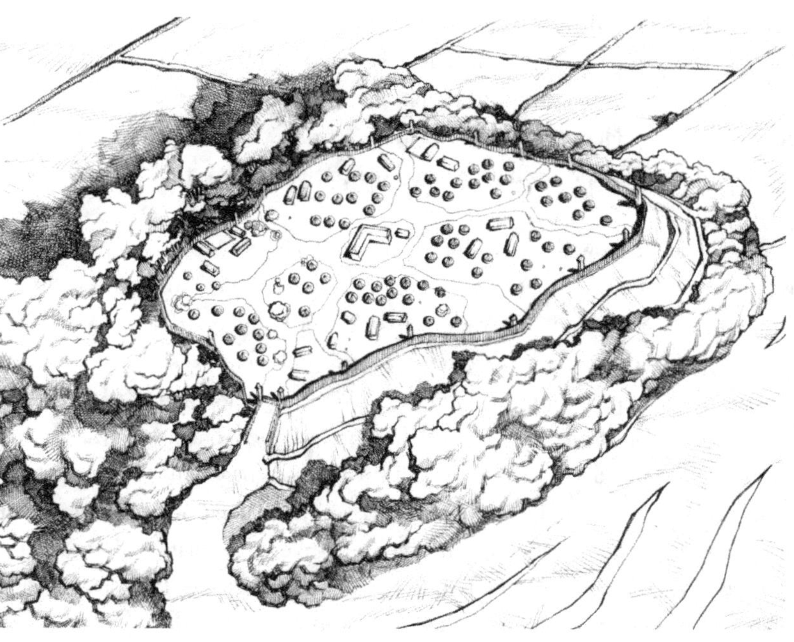

Merlin is generally pleased with how this audience went, unless the characters went too far in their reward requests, in which case, he gives them a blunt warning about upsetting powerful and bloodthirsty warlords and, he adds, 'ancient and vengeful druids'. He tells the characters that he intends to return to Ynys Wydryn but reminds the characters that he needs them to be his eyes and ears over the next few days. 'I have things to do: also it would not be prudent for me to remain in Caer Cadbryg while the Lord Custennin is present. We do not agree on certain things.'

Merlin takes his leave and waiting attendants show the characters to a round house on the western side of the hill fort that has been reserved for their use for as long as they need it. This is also a good opportunity for the characters to notice, although not necessarily interact with, the Three Schemers. Custennin they have already seen in the Great Hall of Emrys and he does not reappear soon, having a chamber within one of the Great Hall's wings. Ladwys, however, can be spotted, with a successful Perception roll, returning from prayers in the Christian chapel, not far from the Great Hall. She is an ageing, sharp-faced woman with greying hair worn in a long plait. Her woollen dress is also grey, but she wears a dark blue cloak over it and takes care to avoid puddles and mud patches as she threads her way back to the Great Hall. She pays no attention to the characters; they are just more warriors in Caer Cadbryg. Following her is a small, scrawny, beady-eyed priest clad in stained robes that were presumably once white, but have now adopted some other, unnameable colour entirely. This is Father Samsun and he follows in the wake of Ladwys having spent the past few hours in devout prayer with her. She has promised him cheese and mead in her chambers as a reward. Samsun does notice the characters, even if they do not notice him. He also sees Merlin, even if the druid is leaving, and immediately makes an association. The characters will be seeing more of Father Samsun later.

Just as Father Samsun notices the characters, so does Morgana. The characters may have met Morgana at Caer Wynd and, if so, she approaches them. If they haven't met before, they notice her, Arthur's bedraggled half-sister, skulking in the eaves of the Great Hall, eyeing them intently. If anyone approaches her, she turns and quickly disappears: she has seen them with Merlin, knows Arthur favours them, and that is enough, for now. If, however, they have met before, Morgana walks towards them confidently, but scowling heavily. 'Did I not tell you that you now serve the Great Dragon? Can I not see the future? My spirits are as powerful as his,' she spits. Suddenly her attitude changes: she focuses on the character with the lowest Willpower score, smiling, seductive, encouraging (even if the character is female), 'There are great things happening, things you are part of. You will need my help. Let me offer it.' The character needs to match Willpower versus Morgana's Seduction or Influence (the latter for female characters) in an opposed roll, with Morgana using her magic to invoke the character's Superstition. If Morgana wins the contest, the

character is convinced of Morgana's desire to help the characters — that this is fate or destiny. That character gains the Passion Loyalty to Morgana at 48%. Once this is accomplished, or if Morgana loses the contest, she smiles to herself, stares at each character in turn, and then rotates sharply on her heel and disappears towards the Great Hall.

The characters now have time on their hands. Unless Arthur or the Council summon them, they can do as they wish until the Betrothal celebrations. They can explore Caer Cadbryg and one thing they do notice is that rumours are rife and speculation intense concerning Arthur and Guinevere. It seems that some support the union (though agreeing that disappointing Achaius is regrettable); an equal number oppose it ('Arthur was beguiled'; 'Achaius has been betrayed'; 'The devil's work') and an equal third cannot decide ('It is only bad if Achaius chooses to make issue of it'; 'I can see what Arthur's doing but I'm not sure it's the right thing.'). Opinion amongst warriors and civilians, men and women, Christians and Pagans, is divided: there is no clear consensus, but everyone is talking of these recent events.

If the characters look for Guinevere, or ask after her, it transpires she is sequestered on the far side of Caer Cadbryg, well away from the Great Hall and protected by appointed servants. No male is permitted to see her before the Betrothal and any attempts to gain access to her are repulsed by the female servants who stand guard at the roundhouse Guinevere has been allocated. If the characters are overly insistent, or try to break in, their attempts will be noticed and armed guards summoned. The characters will find themselves hauled in front of Lord Bors and having to explain themselves. Irrespective of their standing with Arthur or anyone else, breaking the Betrothal Observances is a serious matter and Bors may banish the characters to outside Caer Cadbryg until after the Betrothal ceremony.

Schemers Scheme

It is three days before the Betrothal and Ladwys, Custennin, and Father Samsun meet to put their plan into practice.

Custennin and Ladwys try to worm their way into Achaius' favour when he arrives, making lavish displays of sympathy and understanding, trying to convince him to denounce Arthur and Guinevere and renounce the Parisii's part in the Alliance of Britain, along with the Brigantes and Carvetii. Both will use the characters to help in this if they possibly can.

Father Samsun is beginning to spread rumours in Caer Cadbryg concerning Guinevere's wanton (and sinful) nature: her willingness to lie with men and women for money; how she resembles the Whore of Babylon and represents the Apocalypse; how she has beguiled and ensorcelled Arthur — a scheming witch who will lead Britain to destruction, and so on. Father Samsun is sneaky and clever. He works first on the Christians, using daily prayers to bolster these falsehoods via general sermons on feminine virtue and the danger of wantonness and inconstancy. He also works his way through Caer Cadbryg dropping hints about the couple's premarital activities, spurring aggressive debate about loyalty vs. lust, and encouraging those who already oppose the marriage (pushing whatever point leads to the greatest discord). He uses every trick possible to fan the flames against Arthur and Guinevere; some the characters will notice if they decide to follow him or happen to be nearby when he begins his whispering campaign. Father Samsun is devious and duplicitous — the characters will need to decide whether to support or oppose his campaign to discredit Arthur and his lady.

Custennin focuses his effort on those who have come from other tribes and kingdoms: there are representatives from the Cornovii, Powys, Gwent, the Brigantes, and the Carvetii. He goes to pay his respects to each delegate in turn, seemingly as a general act of welcome, from one chieftain of Dumnonia to another honoured guest, but during each visit, he slyly poses questions regarding Arthur's decision: what will this means for the Alliance of Britain, can someone who wilfully dishonours a young, impressionable king like Achaius truly be fit to lead Dumnonia, is this not the rash actions of a boy, not a man who would lead us, is he really ready and the most able to carry such an important Alliance of its Kingdoms?

'I recall how my brother Uther almost plunged us into war with King Mark. The want of women can lead to mad acts even in grown men,' Custennin might be overheard saying. 'Can we afford to have that happening once more: do we really want history to repeat itself?' Games Masters should make five Hard Influence rolls for Custennin, representing his discussions with the Cornovii, Powys, Gwent, the Brigantes, and the Carvetii delegates.

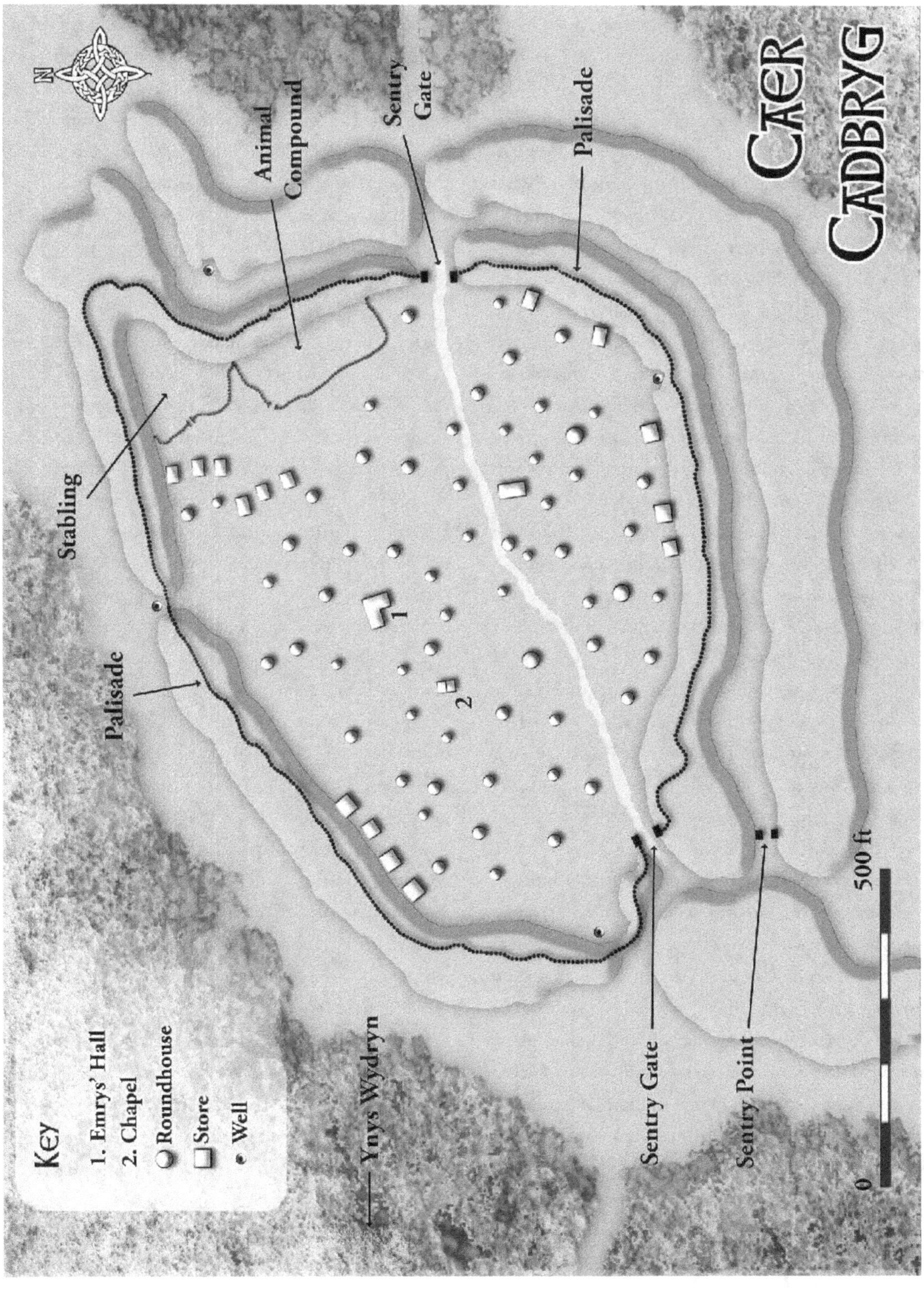

Caer Cadbryg

Key
1. Emrys' Hall
2. Chapel
Roundhouse
Store
Well

N
Animal Compound
Sentry Gate
Palisade
Stabling
Palisade
Ynys Wydryn
Sentry Gate
Sentry Point
0
500 ft

Each success represents the turning of that delegate to supporting Custennin's position – and turning against Arthur. The characters may or may not have opportunities to counter or bolster Custennin's influence, depending on their social rank, their tribe, and other allegiances. Otherwise, they can, on a successful Hard Perception roll or Standard Streetwise roll, at least learn of what Custennin is doing and who he's reached through others. The information may come in useful later.

Ladwys, meanwhile, is working directly on Bors, Havgan, and Natanleod. She knows all of them well, and they all served Uther. It is a harder task for her, so make for her three Hard Influence rolls with each success indicating that the Dumnonian Council member grudgingly comes round to thinking that, perhaps, Arthur has caused more harm than good and has, through his actions, proven unfit or at least uncertain for continued leadership. If Ladwys fails or fumbles a roll, then that councillor sees through her words and instead is moved to support Arthur more fervently: each knows on some level that Ladwys and Custennin act together, and that Ladwys hates Arthur due to Uther. They say nothing to her, because doing so would be an insult to Ladwys, but they become stronger allies for Arthur, rather than detractors.

This scheming takes place over the three days prior to the Betrothal ceremony – not all at once or all in one day. The characters may, therefore, have ample opportunities to learn of what is happening, overhear it, or witness it for themselves.

Enter Samsun

All Christians are wary of pagans, but some, like Father Samsun, loathe them with a passion. Father Samsun wants to drive paganism from Britain with the same fervour that Merlin wants to drive out Christianity. Over the past two to three years, Father Samsun has inveigled his way into Caer Cadbryg, gaining the confidence and support of Ladwys, and installing himself as the chief priest of the community. Father Samsun operates with Bishop Dyfrig of Gwent's blessing: Bishop Dyfrig is highly influential among all Christians in the south and west, and, with the Bishop and Ladwys' support, Father Samsun is able to extend his influence and consolidate his position in Dumnonia.

Father Samsun constantly, loudly, and unrelentingly rails against the evils of paganism, pagans, druids, the Old Gods, and all who still cling to the old ways. Every pagan who converts to Christianity is a triumph to be celebrated with hymns and prayers. Every pagan who refuses to repent and convert is to be harangued and bullied – and those who openly consort with druids, especially a druid like Merlin, are to be targeted by Father Samsun and those loyal to him. He has developed a small following of ardent Christians who hang on his every word, intimidate, insult, and then fall to their knees in prayer, begging forgiveness and the Lord's deliverance.

This is what Father Samsun has in mind for the characters. Having seen them with Merlin, he begins to ask questions about them. When he establishes that they are working for Merlin, he sets his followers to work, trailing the characters, haranguing them to turn away from the Old Gods or forever rot in Hell. If any of the characters are Christians, they are singled out by Father Samsun personally and he demands that they repent, beg the Lord's forgiveness, and leave Merlin's service. If a Christian refuses, Father Samsun takes a different tactic. 'Then prove to the Almighty Lord that you still serve God's glory!' The priest demands. 'Guinevere is a whore of Satan, sent to tempt our beloved Arthur, and destroy Dumnonia.' The character must resist Father Samsun's commands, which come with, and are couched in, religious authority, with his or her Christianity Passion roll. This is a standard roll against the Passion: if the character rolls equal to or less than the Christianity Passion, he or she feels compelled to obey Father Samsun; if the roll is failed, Father Samsun can be safely ignored.

Anyone brought into Father Samsun's service is implored to convince Achaius to denounce Arthur and Guinevere's union, and show Achaius that it is God's will that he should do so. 'Thou shalt not covet thy neighbour's wife,' Father Samsun reminds. 'If King Achaius comes to the Lord God, as have the Brigantes and Carvetii, with whom he shares so much and owes to so much, he will be rewarded and shall know peace.'

If Father Samsun has no Christians amongst the characters to work with he uses another tactic. If he is threatened, cornered or subjected to questioning, after a substantial amount of grovelling and pleading he carefully makes it known that, if the characters were to help convince Achaius to denounce Arthur and Guinevere's union, there will be rewards made: rewards of status. He does not say by whom and makes no reply if the characters mention

Ladwys or Custennin —allow the priest a Deceit roll to convince the characters that it is someone else (Bishop Dyfrig, perhaps) that would become their benefactor. Father Samsun can be persuasive, and Deceit or Influence rolls can be used to help convince the characters that they should help poor, wronged Achaius.

Father Samsun's attempts to enlist the characters are less about his succeeding and more about drawing them further into Caer Cadbryg's machinations — creating, or perhaps easing, the moral dilemmas they face.

King Achaius Arrives

Achaius has decided to demand a public apology from Arthur. His closest advisers think he should be demanding more: gold, warbands, favours. An apology is easy to make and it is expected that Arthur will make the most gracious apology possible. Any other tribe — any other King — might have declared war on Arthur, but Achaius wants very much to be like Arthur, to be liked by Arthur, and to become Arthur. Even if he could face fighting his idol, the Parisii do not have the warbands to challenge Dumnonia. Further, as a pagan king, Achaius cannot easily persuade the Brigantes to support him. In truth, Achaius has very little leverage to force anything from Arthur — but appearances are important. Socially, it is agreed that Arthur must acknowledge there is now a substantial debt owed to Achaius personally and to the Parisii as a whole for this impulsive gaffe.

In his heart, Achaius sees himself as warrior, the equal of Arthur if Arthur would but rely on him. Achaius wants to play a leading part in the war against the Saxons. He wants to lead warbands from the north and crush the Saxons heroically, and he wants Arthur to supply horses and spears for that task. He also very much wants a wife, and, if he cannot have Guinevere, he feels that Arthur should find him someone suitable.

For all this, Achaius is vulnerable. His advisers counsel him not to appear weak, to lever the situation as far as he can, and to extract a specific punishment or reparation from Arthur. Arthur's enemies, the Three Schemers, intend to side with Achaius, offer him the leverage and means with which to truly humiliate Arthur, and weaken Arthur's position in Dumnonia. It is all a question of who gets to Achaius first.

The Ydwina Gambit

It might occur to the characters — and it will certainly occur to Arthur — that (if she has been rescued and brought to Dumnonia) Ydwina of Ratae, a beautiful chieftain's daughter, would be the ideal match. If characters did not rescue Ydwina, and she is with Hengwulf, Arthur may very well suggest that King Achaius should mount a quest to rescue her. Arthur would provide resources for such a quest and ask the characters to take part — after all, they know the area. If she is still with Wiglaf, then the next scenario, *Logres Burning*, provides another way of rescuing Ydwina.

The young king takes his time arriving at Caer Cadbryg. Riders are sent ahead to announce his approach, so Caer Cadbryg has time to prepare and knows of his impending arrival. There is time for everyone, schemer and character, to prepare.

Arthur wants to go out to greet Achaius, but is persuaded otherwise by Bors, Havgan, and Natanleod: they advocate that to do so would be to look like he had tried to unduly influence the young king before Achaius gets to make any requests or say what he wants to say. Arthur accedes. But this does not prevent Custennin, Father Samsun, or the characters from riding out to meet him and his entourage, and Custennin intends to do precisely that. His intention is to gain spread some falsehoods before Achaius arrives, namely, the following:

- Arthur and Guinevere have shown no contrition for what they have done.
- There is a great deal of support for Achaius in Caer Cadbryg: the king has friends who will support him, especially the lady Ladwys, widow of the Pendragon.
- Arthur has always been wilful — nay, arrogant — and Achaius has now witnessed this for himself. Unless this

arrogance is exposed and challenged, it will grow worse, which spells doom for Dumnonia.

- Arthur is not a king: he is the bastard son of a king. Achaius outranks him and should not allow himself to be humiliated by someone who has forced his way into rank and station.

Custennin is persuasive. Achaius is vulnerable and impressionable. The Games Master should roll to see how much of an impression Custennin makes on him with an Influence roll opposed by Achaius's Willpower. If he gets to Achaius first, then Custennin's Influence roll is Easy. If he gets to Achaius after the characters have been able to reach him and, perhaps, provide the opposite counsel, then it could be Hard or Formidable. Custennin will try to persuade Achaius regardless, and he also conveys an invitation from the ladies Ladwys and Morgana to meet with him privately before the betrothal of Arthur and Guinevere – another opportunity for more pressure to be exerted, veiled under the guise of correct courtesy to honour a man of such rank and stature.

The characters find Achaius in a conflicted mood. He is drinking heavily – mead is never far from hand – and if Custennin has managed to get to him before the characters, Achaius is showing doubts over his preferred strategy of simply putting a brave face on things and accepting what has happened. 'I have been wronged. I have been dishonoured. Arthur has insulted me!'

The longer he is left, and if nothing is done to alter his mood, the more vulnerable he is and the more likely he is to accuse Arthur openly of treachery and fall prey to the Three Schemers. Ladwys and Morgana, if given the opportunity, simply reinforce everything Custennin has told him and feed him more alcohol, fanning Achaius' immature passions.

If Father Samsun gets to Achaius, he sympathises with the young king. 'Jesus himself was frequently wronged in this way,' he explains. 'The Devil spreads hate and temptation before us. This is a test and you lack the strength to face it alone. If you embrace Christ, take his baptism, and then the sacrament, leaving behind those useless, pagan gods, you will find strength!'

How all this plays out is dependent on successfully influencing Achaius. Treat it as a Social Conflict task (see page 287 of MYTHRAS) that plays-out over the two days before the Betrothal.

- Appropriate Character Skills: Customs, Influence, Insight, and Passions (If either Custennin or Father Samsun have reached Achaius first, the character's Skill is at the Formidable grade.)
- Achaius's Resisting Skills: Willpower
- Objective: Convince Achaius to come to terms with Arthur and Guinevere.

If the characters succeed – and it should not be easy for them – then Achaius agrees to preserve the status quo. Achaius, if brought to his senses, may request a private audience with Arthur, and Arthur will agree – although he will not force an issue. The characters can also be present, acting as the young king's supporters and friends, if deemed appropriate. During the audience Arthur does the following:

- Apologises with utmost sincerity for what he has done. He acknowledges the hurt and insult caused, and says that neither he nor Guinevere could help themselves. He begs Achaius not to blame Guinevere: 'This was my doing. I pursued her. I brought her here. She is blameless.'
- Agrees, without reservation, to make a full apology to Achaius at the Betrothal feast. 'But I need you to accept that apology, publicly, for the good of the Alliance of Britain.'
- Includes Achaius in the decision making of the Alliance: 'Indeed, we are planning a strike against the Saxons and you are a key part of the strategy. I would welcome your thoughts in the planning.
- Promise Achaius a wife: 'You should be married. I have some ideas for a suitable bride – please let me help you with this.'

The planned strike against the Saxons is a two-pronged attack against Hengwulf and Wiglaf. The bride Arthur has in mind for Achaius is Ydwina – and if the characters have not managed to bring her to Caer Cadbryg already, then her rescue from either Hengwulf or Wiglaf forms part of the battle plan.

Given the opportunity Arthur plays to Achaius's youth, vanity, and aspirations. Achaius wants to be a warlord, and Arthur is giving him that chance. Achaius wants a wife, and Arthur is giving him that, too. Achaius wants more than anything to be like Arthur, and Arthur is bringing him into his confidence. It's a masterstroke that the Three Schemers will struggle to beat.

Sluagh

The Betrothal formalises and celebrates Arthur and Guinevere's intention to marry. They will not be formally married for several months yet, but the Betrothal binds them together and is the first stage of the marriage contract. Even if their betrothal was not complicated in the way it has been, there is still tension over how the ceremony will be conducted.

Both Arthur and Guinevere are pagan, and so the Betrothal rites should follow the pagan tradition with Merlin leading the ritual. Yet such is the strengthening of Christianity in Caer Cadbryg – and the hatred towards Merlin – that the Three Schemers, instigated by Father Samsun, are pressuring for a Christian ceremony. Both Christian and pagan ceremonies allow for the union to be challenged on any of the following grounds:

- Revelation of a prior commitment or marriage
- Evidence of infidelity

Although neither Achaius nor the Three Schemers can mount a truly successful challenge on any of these grounds, Arthur and Guinevere's reputations can still be wrecked if any of these reasons is raised as a serious objection.

If Achaius has been successfully persuaded against denouncing Arthur at the Betrothal, the Three Schemers become more insistent on this being a Christian, rather than pagan, ceremony. To avoid acrimony and further hostility, Arthur is prepared to agree to a Christian ceremony. Father Samsun grumbles that the betrothed should be baptised first and he is insistent that Arthur and Guinevere become Christians so that they may gain God's forgiveness for the wrong done to Achaius.

Morgana's Fury

Although she hates Arthur, blaming him for her beloved Mordred's death, Morgana is no lover of Christianity. It has divided her and her mother for years, and Morgana is desperate for Merlin to show her the deeper secrets of the spirits and Old Gods so that, one day, she can use this power to gain her revenge on Arthur.

Right now though, the thought of a pagan Betrothal ceremony being turned into a Christian ritual with prayers and grovelling for forgiveness fills Morgana with anger. She sees countering that as a way for her to gain Merlin's love. If she can ensure that the Betrothal stays pagan, Merlin will thank her, she is certain of it. For this, she needs the characters.

Morgana wants to disrupt this aspect of Three Schemers' plans by summoning a particular type of Death Spirit to seize control of Ladwys, Custennin, and Father Samsun, and force them into recanting their insistence on a Christian ceremony, allowing Merlin to conduct a pagan Betrothal. She has ventured to the Spirit Plane and made contact with a Death Spirit that has lingered for many, many years in the vicinity of Caer Cadbryg. The spirit was created when the Old People, who originally made Caer Cadbryg, fought amongst themselves and committed hideous atrocities. This spirit, a sluagh, is a creation of doomed, corrupted souls and it thrives on bringing corruption to the Mortal World.

Yet the sluagh does not serve lightly: it requires a sacrifice; a fresh soul for it to feast on the Spirit World. In return, it will do Morgana's bidding for one day and one night. Morgana needs the characters to bring the sacrifice she has chosen to the appropriate place on the night before the Betrothal.

She does not, of course, reveal the true nature of her plan to the characters. She tries to gain the characters' help by pretending she is working in Merlin's name. 'The Betrothal between my brother and his woman should be a pagan affair,' Morgana says, when she has the characters alone. 'I have been entrusted with making it so.' She does not mention Merlin's name directly and will avoid doing so if pressed, demurring by smiling mysteriously. Merlin has no knowledge of what Morgana is planning.

If the characters refuse to help her, Morgana becomes their enemy immediately and will, in time, have revenge on them, too. If they agree to help her, she tells them what they have to do.

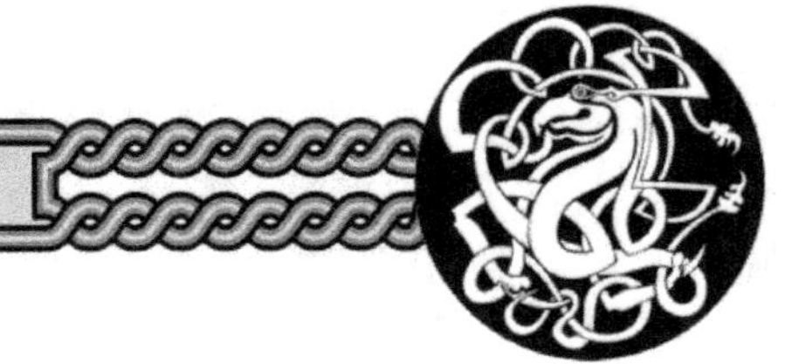

'Samsun favours a young Christian man here in Caer Cadbryg,' she says. 'I hear this Ioan is being taught how to grovel to God, but once he was a pagan and loyal to my brother, Mordred and I. I think he was once in love with me. He turned into a Christian after Mordred died, but Ioan owes me and Mordred a debt. I need his help in something and, if he agrees, the debt is paid. But he looks at me with disdain these days. When I try to talk with him, he crosses himself and flees, eager to be as far away from a pagan as he can.'

She tells the characters that they are to find a way to get Ioan to the hill immediately north-west of Caer Cadbryg – she points it out to them specifically – on the night before the Betrothal. They are not to be seen and Father Samsun must not know. The hill is a couple of hours' walk from the hillfort, but there are paths and these are only lightly travelled. At the hill's summit is a standing stone, a remnant of the Old People who once ruled these lands. Morgana is evasive if the characters ask if this will harm Ioan. If they press, she will lie, but only a last resort – she would much prefer to say something like 'I have no desire to harm him' (she doesn't want to harm him, but the Death Spirit requires it, a fine point). Even if she does lie, she will do so with such conviction that any character looking for a lie in what she says must defeat Morgana's Easy Deceit roll with an Insight roll in an opposed contest.

Morgana admits she is intending to perform a druidic ritual, and the ritual requires someone indebted to another. There is never any mention of sacrifice or harm befalling Ioan.

Ioan the Priest

What Morgana says is true. Ioan served Mordred thirteen years ago and was being groomed for Mordred's warband. As a boy of only 11 or 12 he was besotted with the beautiful Morgana and pledged his service to both twins. When Mordred was killed, he was mourned by many and Ioan was one of several who were convinced to convert to Christianity in the wake of Mordred's death. He broke his vow to Morgana, just as she claims, and has grown fearful of pagans over the years. When Father Samsun arrived at Caer Cadbryg, he took Ioan under his wing, promising to train him in the ways of the priesthood, and this has deepened his fear of Morgana. But Ioan still loves her in his heart, even though she now represents a faith that he abhors.

Ioan has been kept out of Father Samsun's schemes. His time has been spent running general errands for Father Samsun and attending to other matters of business while Father Samsun plots. Ioan can be found at, or close to, the chapel where most of the services are held. He's tall, thin, and nervous looking, with a shock of red hair and a face young with freckles. How the characters convince him to come with them to the hill is for them to devise, but any mention of Morgana immediately makes any rolls used to persuade him Formidable. A successful Insight roll though, may uncover that poor Ioan still holds some love for Morgana – or at least still feels some guilt over breaking his oath to her. This can be used to persuade him to come to the hill. Another tack might be to convince Ioan that his new faith could be used to turn Morgana from her pagan ways – that his love could redeem her.

While Father Samsun is likely to be busy scheming, there is a chance that he senses the characters have an interest in Ioan (a successful Insight or Perception roll for him) and he either confronts the characters, warns Ioan not to have anything to do with them (going so far as physically beating Ioan with a birch cane), or has them followed by some of his disciples to learn the characters' intentions. If Father Samsun grows too suspicious, he is not above asking either Ladwys or Custennin to send warriors to prevent Ioan leaving the Caer, or have some of his followers rough up the characters to warn them off Ioan. Physical threats result in beatings but not death: that would bring down too much on Father Samsun. He may even tail the characters to the hill himself and intervene at the ritual. Morgana can also intervene in any intimidation of the characters at the Caer – her skills with magic are feared by the Christians and threats of curses are enough to scare the timid and superstitious ones, but she will make no displays in front of Ioan, lest his fear increase and keep him from her.

The View from the Hill

Assuming the characters persuade Ioan to come to the hill (abduction is also a valid if difficult and noticeable plan), the characters have to make the walk to its summit. The hill is covered in thick grass, gorse, and heather, making the climbing slow going (slower if Ioan is under duress). At the summit, where Morgana waits, there are splendid views back to Caer Cadbryg and across almost to the Summerlands and Merlin's home, Ynys Wydryn.

The summit is perhaps 60 feet in diameter and is dominated by a single upright stone, 7 feet tall, and with a circular hole, wide enough for someone of SIZ 16 or less to squeeze through, at roughly waist height. This is known as an Adder Stone, or Glain Neidr, and is intensely magical, creating a portal between Worlds.

Morgana is dressed in a white robe and has woven buttercups into her tangled mass of black hair. She has applied plant dyes to her lips and eyelids, and looks eerily beautiful as she waits for the characters and Ioan to arrive. Ioan is very nervous, more so once he sees Morgana, but she coos to him softly, telling him not to be afraid. 'I won't hurt you,' she says. 'But you were close to both of us – me and Mordred – and tonight I need someone who was close to us.'

Unless the characters intervene, and unless Ioan fumbles a Willpower roll, Ioan (reluctantly) takes part in the ceremony. The ceremony is designed to create a bridge between the Mortal World and the Spirit World: the hill temporarily becomes a place where the sluagh can manifest and receive the sacrifice Morgana has planned. Morgana has prepared the summit of the hill in advance. The upright stone is circled with mistletoe, dried blood, various fired herbs, and other, specialised ingredients any druid recognises with a Locale roll. She bids the characters and Ioan to form a circle within this prepared circle, so that the upright stone is at the centre. Then she begins to chant, lapsing into a trance. Her chanting is hypnotic and the characters must succeed in Willpower rolls, modified by Superstition, to resist lapsing into a trance too. Ioan falls readily into a trance, but each character should make the test.

Those who fail in the Willpower roll find that they can see the Spirit World as clearly as they see the Mortal World and experience The Coming of the Sluagh, as described below: they are powerless to act. Those who succeed in the Willpower roll are unaffected and can act freely.

The Coming of the Sluagh

The area outside the circle formed by the characters, Ioan, and Morgana is plunged into deep shadow. More shadow begins to pour through the hole of the Glain Neidr, forming a pool of darkness akin to a pool of water that spreads slowly across the diameter of the circle, coming to a fluid halt before the feet of each character. Morgana walks across the pool, her feet not breaking its surface, and up to Ioan. She circles him slowly, caressing him, whispering to him. On the third encirclement, she draws a knife from within her robes and slices his throat swiftly and neatly, from ear to ear. His blood floods down to meet the pool of shadow and his body crumples to the ground. Morgana then tosses the dagger into the pool of blood and darkness, and calls a single name: Sluagh. From her robes, she takes a pouch of linen and empties it onto the pool. The pouch contains hair taken from Custennin, Ladwys, and Father Samsun. It sizzles as it hits the shadow pool, filling the air with an acrid scent. Then, a figure begins to rise from the pool – a creature made of liquid darkness – that grows in size until it towers over everyone present on the hill. It is a hunched, writhing, barely humanoid form, but devoid of features save for what ripples across its surface: the faces of countless souls, the damned

The Sluagh

The sluagh (pronounced slop-ah) forms where many souls have been slaughtered and denied proper funeral rites. They lie dormant and brooding until summoned, and require the soul of a loved one as a sacrifice if they are to provide magical aid. If given something of the body of a potential victim — hair, nail clippings, or tears, for example — the sluagh can remotely possess the victim and compel it to act as the druid demands. The sluagh can influence one person for each point of Intensity, and Morgana's sluagh is an Intensity 3 spirit.

The possessed victim must succeed in an opposed roll of Willpower versus the sluagh's Spirit Combat roll to resist being influenced. Unless they do as commanded, every thought they have for the duration of the possession is filled with the screams, moans, pleas, and wails of the doomed souls that form the sluagh's fabric. The possessed must do as commanded or succumb to a terrible, crippling depression that inflicts one level of Fatigue for each point of the sluagh's Intensity.

In all other respects a sluagh has the characteristics of a Death Spirit (see MYTHRAS, page 148). At the end of the period negotiated by the druid, the sluagh departs, leaving the victim to regain its senses.

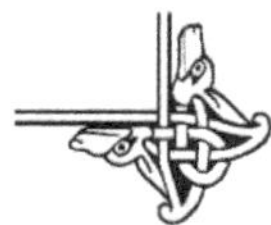

and doomed souls from which the sluagh is made. Morgana commands it: 'I have given you the life of a loved one. I have given you the scents of those I wish controlled. For one day and one night, you will obey me.'

The sluagh seems to sway and from the place where one might expect a head comes a single nod of agreement. And, so engaged to do Morgana's bidding, the sluagh sinks back into the pool of darkness and the darkness begins to retreat through the hole of the Glain Neidr. As it retreats, it pulls with it Ioan's body, and as the corpse of the priest and the foul darkness disappear through the hole, Morgana's trance ends and the characters return to the Mortal World.

Anyone not part of the trance sees only the participants swaying in time to Morgana's chanting. No one moves, but suddenly Ioan gasps, reaches for his throat, and then crumples to the ground. His body bears no marks, no wounds, and it is as though he has suffered some form of seizure. The characters not under the trance can, at any point, disrupt the ritual by attacking Morgana, causing her to drop the trance, but she will visit upon them the sluagh's curse at a later time.

After the ritual Morgana has an almost triumphant air about her: she has worked powerful magic and this is the first sacrifice she has made. That she is sending pagan spirits to torment Christians is a joy to her, and she can barely conceal her feelings. 'I will guarantee Arthur and Guinevere's marriage,' she declares. 'No one now shall stand in their way, and I have shown the power of the Old Gods in a way that even Merlin must admire!'

She forces each character to swear that they will say nothing of what they have witnessed tonight. She tells the characters that arrangements will be made for Ioan's body, but if any of them breathe a word of the sacrifice, the sluagh will be summoned again, but this time for the characters. Of the priest's body, Morgana simply says that it will be dealt with and they should not worry. 'Father Samsun will not come looking for him: the sluagh will see to that. Father Samsun can make Ioan a saint if he wants; Ioan might like that.'

The result of helping Morgana is as she has said. The sluagh compels the Three Schemers, through a mixture of nightmarish and depressive thoughts, coupled with the compulsion to follow Morgana's direction, to leave Arthur and Guinevere to their betrothal, to drop all insistence on Christian trappings, and, in the case of Father Samsun, to believe that Ioan has left Caer Cadbryg to pilgrimage to Rome following a vision from God. Games Masters may wish to allow each the Schemers a chance to resist the sluagh (or just decide to have one, either Ladwys or Custennin, of the three resist), making division among them possible and adding to the confusion.

The Betrothal

The day of the Betrothal arrives. Caer Cadbryg is alive with preparations. More guests pout into the fort, including representatives from the tribes allied with Arthur following the Winter Council. Animals are being slaughtered and prepared for the feast, and there is much gossip — both good and bad — of how Arthur and Guinevere have come to be together.

The Three Schemers (or most of them) may have been silenced if Morgana has summoned the sluagh. Father Samsun has been gripped by visions, his faithful followers report, and refuses to leave his bed; Ladwys and Custennin are sombre and strangely reluctant to say anything bad or damning about Arthur and Guinevere (if one fought off the sluagh, they still know a great force attacked them and proceed with caution since who did is unknown). If King Achaius has been persuaded to accept the situation, he shows signs of beginning to enjoy the forthcoming celebrations.

Much, of course, depends on how the characters have acted up until this point. If nothing has been done, then the Three Schemers can easily derail the Betrothal, forcing Arthur to accept that the only way for it to go ahead is to convert to Christianity, humiliate himself before Achaius, or risk having the Alliance of Britain broken before it has begun. Otherwise, the characters' actions may have ruined the Three Schemers' careful plans and ensured that Arthur and Guinevere's Betrothal continues unmarred.

The ceremony takes place in the early evening in the feast hall of the Great Hall of Emrys. The place is packed with supporters and guests. The characters will have to struggle to gain a good vantage point. Anyone who is anyone is present: the characters will see Merlin, Morgana, Achaius, and others in different parts of the crowd. Eventually, drummers and harpists begin the music signalling the ceremony's start, and Arthur, accompanied by Derec and others of his warband, proceed into the hall. Arthur is resplendent in his mail, which has been sand-polished to a high shine. His cloak is white and embroidered with his symbol the Bear, and he carries his helmet under his left arm, his right hand on Caledfwlch's pommel. Merlin presides over the Betrothal, if this is a pagan ritual; Father Samsun if it is Christian (and Morgana's plans to raise the sluagh have failed). Merlin has made no concessions to ceremony: he is clad in the eclectic and grubby robes he usually wears — and it would be a brave soul who complained otherwise. Arthur kneels and waits for his Guinevere to be brought to him.

Guinevere enters next, and her beauty causes a hush to fall over the entire gathering. Her red hair is unbound and has been washed and brushed so that it glows like the sun. Her dress of brilliant white linen is offset with a simple belt of gold and silver, and her green, mischievous eyes are filled with happiness. She is barefoot at her father walks her towards where Arthur waits and then she kneels. Her father kneels too, so that Guinevere is between her father and intended husband.

Whoever is presiding offers blessings and prayers in the names of the Gods and Spirits, or the Father, Son, and Holy Spirit, and then calls on anyone who objects to this Betrothal to state their case plainly and with evidence. A hush remains over the gathering, and this is the point at which the entire ceremony can be undone.

Does anyone challenge? All the previous events in this scenario dictate the moment, but, assuming efforts have been made to prevent the Betrothal from becoming a farce, no words are uttered. Custennin and Ladwys may be seen, dark-eyed and sorrow-filled as the moment passes. Achaius might be seen casting his eyes to the ground and sighing deeply, resigning himself to silence. Morgana might be witnessed smiling, triumphant that this day has been preserved for the Old Gods. Perhaps Merlin looks at the characters with the kind of expression that says, 'Well?'

But, if no challenge comes, Cywryd, Guinevere's father, hands a bridle to whoever presides. The bridle represents the ownership of Guinevere, and the bridle is then passed to Arthur, representing the transfer of Guinevere's care into her future husband's hands. Arthur wraps the bridle around Guinevere's hands, and then about his own, and the two kiss. Insight rolls at this point show the characters that there is true and deep love between these two: this is a partnership that was meant to be — fated to be, even. Arthur and Guinevere complete each other as Pwyll and Rhiannon completed each other, in the old myths.

The congregation applauds. Warriors hammer spears and sword hilts against shields, and together Arthur and Guinevere walk back through the hall and then separate, being taken to their respective roundhouses. Remember, they are not married yet; but now they are betrothed, they are, in all but title, husband and wife.

Hefeydd's Challenge

An *optional* complication to introduce.

Hefeydd, a known womaniser, is a warrior in one of Custennin's warbands. He was at the Winter Council and is at Caer Cadbryg now. At the betrothal, when challengers are called for, he comes forward and claims he has slept with Guinevere several times: at the Winter Council and since she arrived in Caer Cadbryg. This is a lie, of course: Hefeydd has been paid handsomely in silver by Custennin to besmirch Guinevere's reputation, and it is true that he and Guinevere have met and been seen together at Caer Cadbryg. Hefeydd has become deliberately friendly with Gwenhyfach so that he can be seen in Guinevere's company. His claims are met with gasps of horror. Guinevere faints. Arthur is grim-faced and so angered that he almost draws Caledfwlch.

Customs rolls indicate that the characters know Arthur, as a wronged party in this challenge, cannot defend Guinevere. The onus is on her to prove her own innocence. When she recovers she denies the charges vehemently through her tears of rage, but Hefeydd calmly and confidently stands his ground, recounting the times when they made love — all carefully thought through to concide with times when Guinevere was alone. Guinevere's innocence can only be proved in one of two ways: Hefeydd's claims are proved to be false (and Custennin has loyal people planted to support every word Hefeydd says) or for someone to act as Guinevere's champion and challenge Hefeydd in the Court of Swords - a dual to the death. If Hefeydd wins, Guinevere will be expelled and Arthur broken. If he is defeated, Guinevere's innocence will be proven. Arthur cannot act as her champion; Achaius could, although he too is a wronged party and he also knows he would lose against a warrior like Hefeydd. Here is a chance for one of the characters - perhaps the one with the highest Passion for Guinevere, or Loyalty to Arthur, to step forward and challenge Hefeydd's word in the Court of Swords.

Hefeydd is a big, burly warrior. Use the statistics for Typical Celt Spearman found on page 213, but his Combat Style is 70%. and he has 3 Action Points. He accepts the challenge: if he did not, he would automatically lose. Besides, he has an armful of warrior rings showing how many Saxons he has slain: why would he fear a challenge from one of the characters?

The duel takes place at dawn the next morning. Before then, Gwenhyfach comes to the characters. She is distraught for her sister, who she knows to be innocent. "This Hefeydd has tried to bed me several times," she says truthfully. "I know now that he was using me so that he could invent this story about him and Guinevere. It is true I left the two of them alone when Hefeydd sent me to get things for him." But Gwenhyfach also knows Hefeydd's weakness, something he revealed to her in a drunken moment: "His left leg was badly hurt by a Saxon spear. He can walk on it well enough, but he wraps his knee and ankle in heavy bandages to give him support. He cannot run and he soon tires if forced to favour his left leg. The character fighting Hefeydd can use this information in several ways:

- The left leg has never healed properly after a bad fracture. Hefeydd only has 3 Hit Points in that leg: it will not take much to disable it.
- He reacts badly if taunted about his injury - especially if called a cripple. If he fails an opposed roll of his Willpower against the character's Influence, he flies into a rage, slashing wildly with his sword. This increases Hefeydd's Damage Modifier to +1d4 but it reduces his Combat Style rolls to 47%.
- If forced into an Overextend Special Effect, Hefeydd must make an Endurance roll. If the roll fails to beat the character's Combat Style roll in an opposed contest, his left leg goes into a painful spasm and Hefeydd immediately loses one of his Action Points for the next 1d4 rounds.

The Court of Swords is a serious business. The combatants are allowed a shield and weapon of their choice (Hefeydd chooses his sword), but armour is forbidden. The whole of Caer Cadbryg comes to watch with the exception of Guinevere. Arthur is there and speaks with the character just before the fight. "I am in your debt for this," he says. "Fight well and ward as much as you can with your shield. I do not know this Hefeydd, but I suspect he loses his temper easily. That will help you if you keep your own. Win this thing for Guinevere. Win it for Britain."

Havgan presides over the Court of Swords. He calls the combatants into the circle formed by the onlookers and asks Hefeydd if he stands by his accusations - which he does. He eyes the character

disdainfully and spits. His breath reeks of ale from the night before. Havgan reminds the two that the Court of Swords is a fight to the death unless one man yields and either recants his accusation or, in the case of the character, calls for mercy and agrees that the accusation is true.

Hefeydd fights like a demon and shows no mercy unless compromised as suggested earlier. If forced into a Compel Surrender Special Effect he stops short of revealing the truth of the deception he has woven, but declares that Guinevere is innocent. It is up to the character if they show clemency - if the character catches Arthur's eye, he indicates that Hefeydd should be allowed to live, but it is the character's choice. There are plenty who bay for his death, but others who remain silent.

If allowed to live Hefeydd is forced to leave Caer Cadbryg in disgrace. He also becomes the sworn enemy of the characters and Games Masters can use him in later adventures as a recurring adversary. If killed, Hefeydd's friends, all loyal Custennin men, want vengeance and will take their time in meting it out to the characters.

The Feast

The hall is cleared and the feast prepared. There is a sense of relief in Caer Cadbryg, and people go about their business while anticipating the festivities. After an hour or so, while Guinevere and Arthur change from their Betrothal garb, the feast begins, with Arthur, Guinevere, Cywryd, Merlin, and other dignitaries seated at the high table. Achaius is positioned there too, on Arthur's right-hand side, as a guest of honour. There is music, song, story, and much drinking.

Arthur, Guinevere, and Achaius spend a lot of time in discussion. Achaius has a serious expression that, from time to time, breaks into smiles. Eventually, he stands, calls for silence, and leads the toast to Arthur and Guinevere. It is the sign that all is well between the three of them. As the raucous cheering and applause subsides, Arthur also rises. He thanks Achaius for his blessing, and says, publicly, that he is sorry for any slight caused. 'It is something when men such as us can come together and be friends in this way,' he says. 'This is the alliance I had wished for, and to show our commitment to that alliance, let me share with this hall the news that, soon, we will take our fight to the Saxons! The efforts of a small group of our fine warriors,' — and here he acknowledges the characters with a raised goblet — 'have secured intelligence we can use to strike a blow against Aelle, the so-called Bretwalda, and show him that Britain belongs to the Britons. Are you with us?'

Achaius, Derec, Havgan, Natanleod, and the other assembled alliance leaders climb to their feet and shout their confirmations. Warriors pound the tables with fists, knife hilts, goblets, and drinking horns. There is whooping and cheering, and the entire hall is brought together in a fervency that takes many minutes to subside, and is rapidly replaced with songs of battle and glory, led by the bards.

And here the scenario can conclude — or be continued if needed, to deal with any further scheming or plot developments that simply cannot be anticipated in a scenario as potentially complex as this. However, in the next scenario, Arthur makes good on his promise to take the war to the Saxons.

Non-Player Character Statistics

The statistics for the bulk of the important non-player characters in this scenario can be found in the *Mythic Britons* chapter, beginning on page 196.

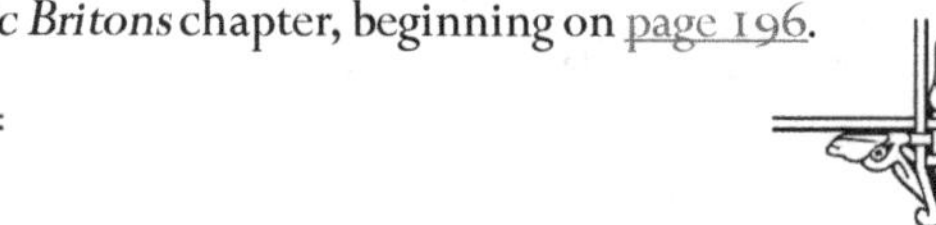

Logres Burning

Logres Burning draws extensively on the battle rules, found in the *Britain at War* chapter. It offers two separate opportunities for the characters to fight the Saxons in pitched battles, either as spearmen in the shield wall or taking the role of commanders (using either their own skills or temporarily adopting the roles of the commanders described in the appropriate sections). Of course, if the players do not feel comfortable taking part in a large battle – either as commanders or participants in a shield wall – the scenario can be treated simply as a rescue mission with the battle as a backdrop.

Prelude to War

The first act of the Alliance of Britain is to strike fast and hard at the Saxons. Following the characters' exploits in Ratae, Arthur calls for a meeting of the Alliance and proposes that raids should be made on the settlements of both Hengwulf and Wiglaf. He proposes a two-pronged attack: Dumnonia and Powys will strike at Ratae from the east, while the Parisii and Brigantes strike at Hengwulf from the north. Both men are vulnerable, but these raids are intended not to necessarily recapture these lands, but to send a message to Aelle and his sons that Britain will not tolerate Saxon incursions any longer.

The plan is to raid and burn Saxon settlements east of Ratae, luring Wiglaf out of Coritanorum and Caer Leonis, defeat him, and then retreat back to Dumnonia. At the same time, the Parisii and Brigantes will outflank Hengwulf's camp, strike fast and hard, breaking his forces, freeing slaves, and then retreating north.

If Ydwina is still with either Wiglaf or Hengwulf, an objective for the characters is to rescue her. If she was rescued by the characters in *Bran Galed's Horn*, then, between the events of *Of Promises Broken* and this scenario, she has been betrothed to King Achaius. Achaius is much taken with Ydwina's beauty and self-confidence, and she with the prospect of being named Queen of the Parisii.

Preparations for War

A month has passed since Arthur and Guinevere's Betrothal. In that time, the Alliance of Britain has used the intelligence gathered by the characters to prepare a plan for launching an ambitious attack against both Hengwulf and Wiglaf. Natanleod has sent spies deep into Logres to confirm what the characters have reported and survey the overall strength of the Saxon forces between Ratae and Dumnonia's border. Both warlords are concentrating on building their fortifications: Hengwulf is clearing lands north of Ratae while Wiglaf strengthens the hillfort of Caer Leonis.

There are several meetings of the Alliance leaders and the characters are invited to some of these to once again share their experiences, recount what they saw, and contribute to the strategy being developed. Natanleod says that he believes Caer Leonis is being strengthened not for Wiglaf's sole use, but for someone else.

'The Saxons call the lands north of the Tamesis River "Anglia". A warlord called Guercha controls it, and he's a rival to King Aelle, who controls Ceint south of the Tamesis. I think Wiglaf is preparing Caer Leonis and Ratae for Guercha to use as a permanent stronghold. From there he can attack Dumnonia, Elmet and, if he needs to, Aelle's lands in the south. If we can capture Caer Leonis, we'll be denying the Saxons an important staging post for conquest.'

The Alliance agrees, but it is also agreed that Hengwulf must also be defeated. As he grows in strength, he can raid deeper and deeper into the lands of the Brigantes, and both Queen Elliw and Derec of Elmet are keen to prevent that from happening.

The plan the Alliance draws-up is as follows.

Several small warbands drawn from Powys, the Cornovii, and Dumnonia will scour the many small settlements the fan-out from Ratae, destroying homes and burning crops. As Wiglaf grows in strength, he will rely more and more on the harvests of these small farming communities. Striking now, before the harvest, denies Wiglaf vital winter stores: it is also a challenge to lure Wiglaf out of Caer Leonis – which, like most hillforts, is very difficult to assault head-on. If he does not respond, then the Britons will continue ravaging the countryside, just the Saxons have done countless times, denying Wiglaf more and more food, and sending more and more refugees in Ratae's direction. Once lured out, Arthur will command the forces of Dumnonia Powys and the Cornovii and destroy Wiglaf once and for all.

At the same time, the Brigantes, Carvetii, and Parisii (with Achaius leading his warbands) will strike at Hengwulf from the north. Hengwulf has nowhere to flee and he does not have the strength and reserves Wiglaf has amassed, so defeating him should be an easier task. King Achaius is given a leading role in this assault on Hengwulf, with Derec providing key support and counsel, and with auxiliary warbands coming from the Brigantes and Carvetii. All the lands north of Ratae are promised to Queen Elliw and the Brigantes, and she, in turn, has promised Achaius substantial territories to add to the Parisii's holdings if they are successful.

The Characters' Role

If Ydwina is held by one or other of the Saxon leaders, an objective of either battle is to free her – something the characters can take as a personal mission while the main forces are fighting, or in the aftermath of the main battles.

The characters can choose which assault they will join or the Games Master can assign them to whichever part of the Alliance best suits their role in the events. If they fight with the southern forces attacking Wiglaf, then they are assigned to warbands under the overall command of Natanleod (Arthur will command the Dumnonian cavalry). If they fight with the northern forces attacking Hengwulf, then they are assigned to warbands under Achaius's command.

If the group contains a character with Lore (Strategy and Tactics) or 70% or higher, then that character can act as the leader for the warband he or she is attached to. A warband consists of thirty warriors who typically fight in a shield wall with a frontage of ten warriors, three ranks deep. It is common for warbands to form together to give greater frontage, so the characters can be assigned to separate warbands, yet still come together to fight as one unit.

If none of the characters have a high enough Lore (Strategy and Tactics), then use one of the Non-Player Character commanders provided in the Forces section of this chapter. However, each player should be given the chance to make rolls for the commander, and

decisions regarding tactics can be made as a group effort so that everyone has a role to play in these battles.

The intention is for both the battles to happen more or less simultaneously (or close enough together to prevent Hengwulf from reinforcing Wiglaf and vice versa). The idea is that the characters participate in one battle while the other rages miles away – but if Games Masters want to, they can certainly run both battles as separate events and have enough time between the two for the characters to span the distances between battle fields. If the characters only take part in one battle, then the off-stage battle should result in a victory for the Britons while the battle of focus is gamed-through. If things look desperate for the Britons, reinforcements can be rapidly brought in from other tribes in the Alliance to help secure victory.

The Battle of Lugh's Gorge

The bards will sing songs of the Battle of Lugh's Gorge, where the warriors of the north met Hengwulf's Saxons. The battle's focus is in the fields close to the village at the western end of the gorge. The army comes from the north, sweeping through the gorge and ignoring the ancient history of this place and its sacred nature to the druids. Christian priests of the Brigantes, supported by Christian warriors, march ahead of the main force, chanting prayers and calling for God to cleanse the place of evil. The warbands teardown the Ghost Fence, which alerts the shaman, Moust (see 'Bran Galed's Horn') to the Britons' arrival. The village is garrisoned and is the rallying point for the main warbands.

Brigantes and Carvetii warbands scout the surrounding forests, ensuring that Hengwulf's Saxons cannot spread out through the trees to outflank the main forces. King Achaius sends emissaries to Hengwulf's camp – and this could be the characters – offering the following terms:

- Surrender now and live.
- Release Ydwina into the care of the Britons (if she is there) and know mercy.
- Fight and die.

Hengwulf spits in scorn on all these terms. This is his wyrd: to meet the enemy in battle and either defeat them or be defeated. The norns have woven this tapestry, and it is now up to him to bring the final threads together. Hengwulf will fight. He has, by now, one hundred and fifty warriors he can deploy and he has no intention of surrendering to the Britons. If Non-Player Character emissaries have been sent, their headless bodies are returned to the Britons, tied onto their horses, delivering the message that Hengwulf will stand and fight.

The Terrain

The battle will be fought in the wide fields directly south of the village and the important terrain features are shown on the Battle Map.

Hengwulf's Tactics

Hengwulf has one hundred and fifty warriors of Seasoned and Veteran levels of competence, plus he also has thirty hunting hounds that he intends to unleash on the Britons' ranks when the time is right. He splits his army into two wings of sixty warriors (20 frontage by 3 ranks) and a unit of thirty hound handlers formed into a single rank that are held in reserve behind the tree line.

The battleground is already chosen and Hengwulf has the trees behind him: if routed or forced to retire, his warriors can creak into skirmish formation and use the paths and trails they know well to retreat to the camp. Hengwulf then intends to unleash the hounds on any warriors who pursue across the field and into the forest.

Hengwulf's champion is a huge Anglian called Steppor and he challenges the champion of the Britons to single combat in the Personal Challenges phase of the battle. Steppor's statistics are on page 282.

Steppor uses brute force to toy with an opponent, using his shield to attempt to stun or render a limb useless, before slicing with his seax and causing bleeds. He fights partially sky-clad, with only a leather kilt to protect his lower body, his upper body is a mass of scars and tattoos, and his right arm is thick with bronze and iron warrior rings forged from the spears of his previous victims. As he wears minimal armour, Steppor uses his shield to Ward his Head, Chest, Abdomen, and Left Arm if he runs out of Action Points before his opponent. He uses his Fyrdman combat style

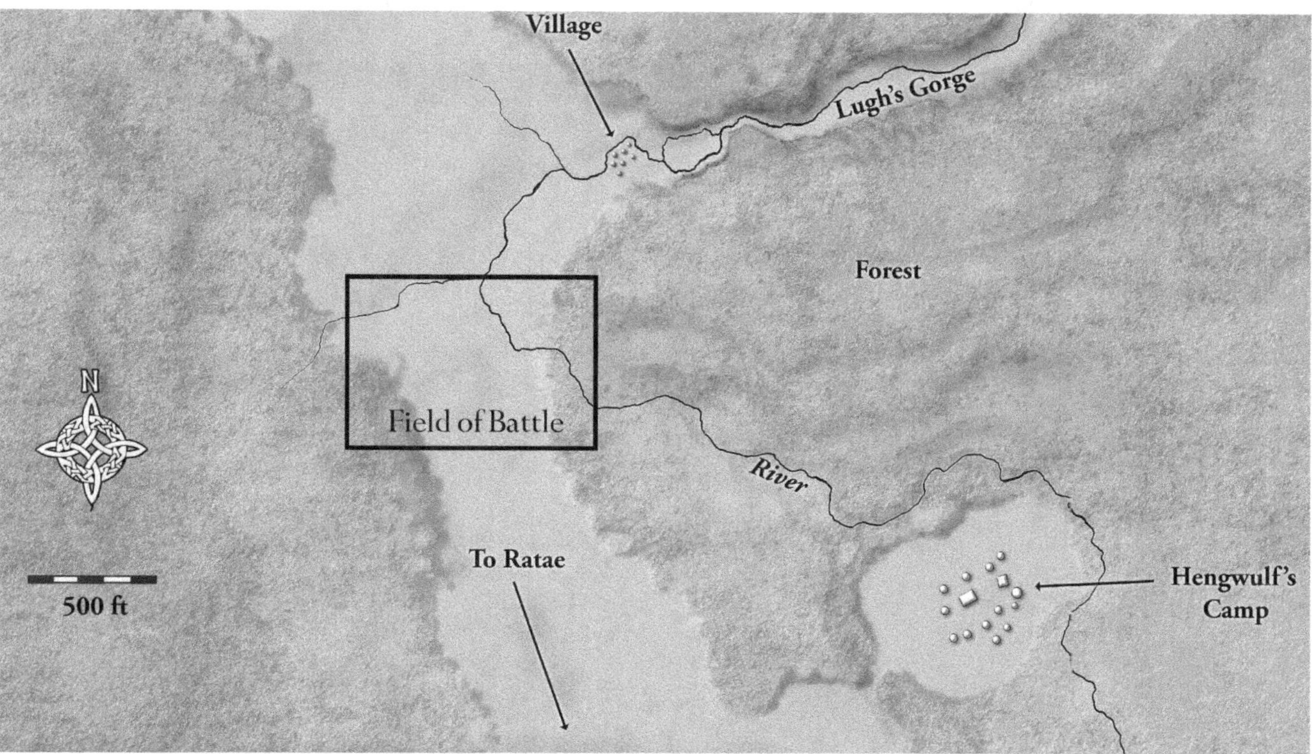

in personal challenges and he always tries to wear an opponent down, toying with them, before unleashing brute force stabs with his other weapons. He shows no mercy against Britons.

If Steppor loses the personal challenge, roll against the units' Loyalty to Hengwulf Passion of 85% to assess the effect of the loss on their Morale checks (see page 189 of the Battle rules).

In the Stirring Speech phase, the Saxons do not bother with their commanders using words to rouse their troops to battle: instead, Moust the Læce leads ten slaves out of the lines and proceeds to cut the throat of each one, dedicating the sacrifices to Hoder, the Saxon war god. He makes the dedications in halting Brythonic so that the Britons can understand that these Celts are being sacrificed to foreign gods and so will be denied access to the Other World. When the last sacrifice is made the Saxon shield walls begin to strike spears and seaxes against their shields and scream taunts at their foes, encouraging them to come and meet their deaths. For Moust's sacrifice, roll against his Norse Gods Passion of 80% to determine the Stirring Speech morale modifier (see page 186 of the Battle rules).

For the Engagement phase, the two main wings advance confidently, hammering weapons against shields, until they are within 15 feet of the Britons' line(s). They then wait, taunting and cursing the enemy, challenging them to come forward and fight. The Saxons are the defenders here, so the onus is on the Britons to make the first charge into engagement and if the Britons dither or delay, the taunts and jeers become more and more ferocious.

Once the engagement begins, Hengwulf, who fights in the front line of Unit A, orders his Saxons to hold their ground for one round and then, for subsequent rounds, to fall back in formation, still remaining engaged, but drawing the Britons closer to the tree line. Once the Saxon shield walls are within a few yards of the trees, he orders the hound handlers to move out of the tree line and move into a position to outflank one of the Britons' shield walls, engaging them with the frenzied dogs. As the hounds and handlers crash into one enemy unit, Units A and B of the Saxons draw together and concentrate their energies on one of the Celtic units, aiming to cause either complete destruction or a rout.

Steppor

Characteristics	Attributes	1d20	Location	AP/HP
STR: 17	Action Points: 2	1–3	Right Leg	0/7
CON: 14	Damage Modifier: +1d4	4–6	Left Leg	0/7
SIZ: 18	Magic Points: 10	7–9	Abdomen	2/8
DEX: 11	Movement: 6 metres	10–12	Chest	0/9
INT: 10	Initiative Bonus: 10	13–15	Right Arm	0/6
POW: 10	Armour: Leather Kilt. In the shield wall he wears a plate helm for 5 points	16–18	Left Arm	0/6
CHA: 8		19–20	Head	(5)/7

Skills: *Athletics 37%, Brawn 78%, Endurance 75%, Evade 70%, Superstition 80%, Unarmed 76%, Willpower 59%*

Hate Celts 70%, Loyalty to Hengwulf 84%, Love Battle 100%

Combat Style: Fyrdman (Battleaxe, Seax and Shield. Trait, Formation Fighting) 90%; Shield Wall (Spear, Seax and Shield. Trait, Shield Wall) 95%

Weapon	Size/Force	Reach	Damage	AP/HP
Seax	*M*	*S*	*1d4+2+1d4*	*6/8*
Battleaxe	*M*	*M*	*1d6+1d4*	*4/8*
Spear	*M*	*L*	*1d8+1+1d4*	*4/5*
Saxon Round Shield	*L*	*S*	*1d4+1d4*	*4/12*

If Hengwulf's Saxons are defeated or broken, survivors scatter into the tree line and make for the encampment. Hengwulf, if he still lives, can command the hounds to be loosed as a last-ditch attempt to inflict casualties on the Britons. Saxons caught in individual combats, once the shield walls break, fight to the death, welcoming the chance to go to Woden's Feast Hall in the afterlife. Hengwulf and Moust fight side-by-side, looking to challenge the leaders of the Britons. If taken alive, Hengwulf is defiant to the last and demands a clean death with a sword in his hand, so he might also join his comrades at Woden's side. Moust is more pragmatic and attempts to escape. He may even offer to provide information about Wiglaf and/or trade his life for Ydwina's.

Battle Actions

Hengwulf likes to maintain order among his units, keeping them in tight formation. For his first Battle Action, no matter when it comes, he orders a Feigned Retreat, luring the enemy closer to the treelike where the hounds are waiting.

For his second Battle Action, Hengwulf uses Guard to mitigate any casualties while the hounds are prepared.

The third Battle Action is to Feign Retreat again, this time reaching the trigger point for the hounds.

When the Hound Handlers engage, the Battle Action for Units A and B is to Combine and attack the stronger of the enemy units.

The Hound Handlers use the Savage Battle Action to increase their damage each round.

The Camp

Hengwulf doesn't have enough warriors to face the Britons and defend the camp. He therefore has to gamble on defeating the Britons while leaving the camp undefended. If his shield walls are broken and warriors flee back to the camp, there still won't be enough spears to defend it and the occupants will, eventually, be forced to surrender to the Celts.

If Ydwina is with Hengwulf, then she is kept with other women and children in a roundhouse guarded by three older warriors who

have volunteered to remain behind. They are loyal to Hengwulf and prepared to die in defence of the women. The women are prepared to kill themselves rather than be raped or made into slaves, and have knives for these purposes. However, if the sentries are defeated and the women shown compassion (and Queen Elliw demands that innocents, even though they are Saxons, should not be mistreated), then they surrender with a vocal struggle but not much else.

Hengwulf himself does not intend to flee his people and fights with the intention of dying on the battlefield if he cannot defeat the Britons. If mortally wounded, he asks only for a swift death with his sword in his hand. However, he will not betray either Wiglaf or Guercha with information that the Alliance of Britain can use.

Defeating Hengwulf

Defeating Hengwulf's fledgling community does two things: it removes a threat to the Brigantes borders and also removes a challenge to Wiglaf's growing power in Ratae. The Brigantes and Parisii, using Elmet as a base, can begin to reclaim territories lost to the Saxons between Caer Wynd and Ratae. However, the real prize is Ratae itself – the subject of the next battle.

If Hengwulf Defeats the Britons

This would be a major catastrophe. It also gives Hengwulf the confidence to start expanding his range deeper into Brigantes lands, focusing on Elmet and Caer Wynd. More Saxons will join Hengwulf, some defecting from Wiglaf's warbands, and King Guercha starts to look favourably on the way Hengwulf is expanding the borders of Anglia into the contested realms of Mierce.

Hengwulf's Forces

Unit A: Hengwulf's Fyrdmen

Unit Name: Hengwulf's Fyrdmen	UnitType: Seasoned and Veteran Fyrdmen
Unit Traits: Formation Fighting	
Commander: Hengwulf	Command Skill: 79%
Strength: 60	Current Damage: 1d4
Competency: 70%	Morale: 65% (Steady)
Current Formation: Line	Frontage: 20 x 3 ranks

Hengwulf commands this unit and he fights from the front rank, flanked by solid, disciplined warriors, barking orders and encouragement at those around and behind him. The unit carries his standard of a deer's skull, with prominent antlers, raised on a pole of iron-shod yew. He maintains a Line Formation and is not afraid to adjust the frontage and reduce the depth if there's a chance of overlapping the enemy.

Unit B: Aeselle's Fyrdmen

Unit Name: Aeselle's Fyrdmen	UnitType: Seasoned and Veteran Fyrdmen
Unit Traits: Formation Fighting	
Commander: Aeselle	Command Skill: 65%
Strength: 60	Current Damage: 1d4
Competency: 72%	Morale: 68% (Steady)
Current Formation: Line	Frontage: 20 x 3 ranks

Aeselle is a trusted lieutenant and the brother of Steppor. He is a less experienced commander but his men are loyal to him. His orders are to lure the Britons back towards the tree line so that the hounds can be unleashed at their ranks. His standard is simply a hide banner depicting Thunor's Hammer.

Unit C: Hound Handlers

Unit Name: Hounds of Woden	UnitType: Seasoned Warriors with Hunting Hounds
Unit Traits: Trained Beasts (Hounds)	
Commander: Wigga	Command Skill: 70%
Strength: 30	Current Damage: 1d12
Competency: 70%	Morale: 70% (Disciplined)
Current Formation: Line	Frontage: 30 x 1 rank

The hunting hounds are bred for bringing down deer and rooting out boar. They are huge, shaggy-haired, long-limbed animals that are kept hungry to exacerbate their aggression. They are trained to attack limbs and are not afraid of shield walls. The unit's tactics are to wait for the command and then loose the hounds, with the warriors rushing in behind the animals, a mixture of brute force and howling ferocity to tear at the enemy, hoping to break their formation. The hounds fight until killed: once their blood-lust is up, only their handlers can call them off.

The Britons

Unit 1: The Parisii

Unit Name: Parisii Warband	UnitType: Seasoned Spearmen
Unit Traits: Formation Fighting	
Commander: Achaius*	Command Skill: 60%
Strength: 120	Current Damage: 1d4
Competency: 60%	Morale: 65% (Steady)
Current Formation: Line	Frontage: 20 x 6 ranks

**Nominally, Achaius, but Derec of Elmet assists providing an Augment to the Command roll*

Achaius fights in the shield wall with his men, keen to prove his mettle. His strategy is to inflict damage and then start to expand his line so that he can quickly overlap the Saxon shield wall and outflank it. If morale begins to falter, Derec has told Achaius to order a retreat in good order so that men can regroup and the shield wall be reformed, rather than rushing forward to try to slaughter the Saxons outright. The Parisii can be split into two wings of sixty warriors, with Achaius forming one wing and the second wing being placed under the command of a player character. The character's responsibility will be to hold the Saxons so that Achaius can outflank.

Unit 2: Brigantes Cavalry

Unit Name: Elmet Heavy Horse	UnitType: Seasoned Horsemen
Unit Traits: Mounted Combat	
Commander: Derec of Elmet	Command Skill: 75 %
Strength: 30	Current Damage: 1d8
Competency: 75%	Morale: 70% (Disciplined)
Current Formation: Skirmish	Frontage: 1 rank of 30 horsemen

Derec is the leader of Elmet's cavalry. The aim is for the Brigantes to act as reserves and charge only if Achaius runs into serious trouble. If the Saxons are routed, the cavalry aims to pursue beyond the tree line and mop up survivors. If the Saxons release their hounds, the morale roll for the cavalry becomes one grade of difficulty harder. The mounts are troubled by the dogs and become difficult to control. If any of the characters are good horsemen, then they can join this cavalry unit.

Unit 3: Carvetii Skirmishers

Unit Name: Carvetii Warband	UnitType: Seasoned Hill Warriors
Unit Traits: Skirmishing	
Commander: Bryce	Command Skill: 70 %
Strength: 50	Current Damage: 1d4
Competency: 70%	Morale: 70% (Disciplined)
Current Formation: Skirmish	Frontage: 25 x 2 ranks

These are Carvetii skirmishers who are used to fighting raids across the border from the Caledonii Picts. They are armed with a pair of light throwing spears, shields, and shortswords. Their primary aim is to make the best use of broken terrain and cover to inflict fast, ranged damage on the enemy. The Carvetii are hidden in the tree line and will focus on the Hound Handlers in a bid to protect the cavalry and the Parisii units..

The Battle of the Wreake

Arthur's plan is to draw Wiglaf out from Ratae and Caer Leonis by laying waste to the outlying farms and villages, forcing Wiglaf to send out his warbands to stop the destruction. By razing crops, livestock and stores, people will be driven to Ratae, overburdening both the city and the hillfort, while, at the same time, driving down its resources. If Wiglaf does not fight, he faces potential starvation and a much-increased population.

Warbands from Dumnonia, Powys, and Cornovia fan across Logres. They move quickly and brutally, killing herds, burning buildings, and forcing villagers to move east in a steady stream. The few warbands protecting these outlying settlements are no match for Arthur's heavy horse cavalry, King Lend's vicious skirmishers, and Natanleod's efficient shield walls. The Alliance of Britain takes no prisoners and makes no slaves. Defeated Saxon warriors have their right hand amputated so they cannot raise a spear against Britain again, but their lives, for the most part, are spared and they are sent back to Ratae and Caer Leonis with a simple message for Wiglaf: Arthur is waiting.

Wiglaf has no choice. He sends his own warbands out to try drive off the Celts, but they are soon overwhelmed. Finally, with his best three hundred men, Wiglaf himself must ride out from Caer Leonis in a bid to defeat Arthur.

The armies of the Alliance of Britain and Wiglaf's Saxons have their first clash west of the river Wreake. Wiglaf's five warbands converge on an area where King Lend's Cornovii have made camp, on the west side of a wood, and attack. This is a carefully laid ambush: Arthur's cavalry waits to the north and charges into the fray as two of Wiglaf's shield walls meet three of Lend's. Wiglaf sounds an ordered retreat and his Saxons fall back through the woods managing to hold to a skirmish formation, which forces Arthur's cavalry to become strung out, reducing its effectiveness.

Wiglaf now seeks to get all his warriors across a narrow ford on the Wreake so they can fall-back in safe order towards Caer Leonis. Arthur knows of another ford several miles to the north and leads his cavalry towards it, intending to circle Wiglaf and attack his flank as he completes his retreat. Meanwhile the Cornovii and some Dumnonian units are attempting to prevent Wiglaf's warbands from even making it across the ford. If Wiglaf succeeds, he stands a chance of getting back to Caer Leonis before Arthur catches him. If he loses two or more of his warbands without getting them across the river, he will have no way of being able to properly defend either Ratae or Caer Leonis, making it easy for Arthur to take both back from the Saxons, with the aid of Powys' spearmen (who are already across the Wreake, much further to the north and coming south at a rapid march).

This scenario begins with Wiglaf's Saxons close to the ford. Fighting has already been heavy. At the start of the Battle Rounds, the first of Wiglaf's warbands is attempting to cross the river, protected by the others (see the diagram on page 295).

Wiglaf's Tactics

The Ratae Saxons are arranged into five warbands of sixty warriors. The warbands are fighting a tactical retreat towards the ford where one warband at a time can safely cross. Wiglaf wants to assemble all five warbands on the eastern side of the river so that he has a strong, coherent force – a three-hundred-strong army, in effect.

Each warband has been ordered to move across the ford in turn, starting with Warband A and ending with Warband E. The remaining warbands are instructed to maintain formation, offer protection for the cross warband, and prevent the Celts from overlapping or outflanking.

It takes one full Battle Round for a unit to cross the ford. While it crosses, the unit is in Skirmish Formation.

The Saxons are in Line Formation (a shield wall). The court defending warbands are arranged into three ranks of twenty, each under its own commander. Wiglaf is on horseback just at the edge of the ford, with a small retinue of mounted spearmen, helping to marshal the retreating warriors.

There are no Personal Challenges at the beginning of this battle. Wiglaf does attempt a stirring speech, reminding his Saxons that the Celts have been burning innocent farms and have been too cowardly to try to assault Ratae. The Saxons have taught the Celts lessons in bravery and Wiglaf aims to have this Arthur flayed so that his skin can become a new Saxon standard. Wiglaf's statistics can be found on page 256.

Battle Actions

Each Battle Round, one unit makes the crossing and if not damaged through outflanking actions, will cross successfully. The protective units attempt to maintain cohesion until it is their turn to retreat, where they change to Skirmish Formation.

The first Battle Action any of Wiglaf's commanders use is Combine, so that the remaining warbands can close together to form a larger array.

The next Battle Action a Combined warband uses is Engulf, if it has greater strength than its opposition, or Guard, if it does not. The aim here is to try to suck in the Britons, wherever possible, or mitigate damage if there are insufficient numbers.

The warbands then, use a combination of Guard and Redeploy to allow each group of sixty warriors time to escape across the ford.

Isen

Wiglaf's læce, Isen, is present at this battle. He has been preparing harmful Raven Spirits to attack the Britons. Each Battle Round Isen can make a Binding roll which can be opposed by the Command roll of the enemy force he targets. If Isen wins the opposed

contest, roll 1d6 to determine the effect. If he loses, there is no supernatural aid this round.

1. Ravens attack a Commander. The Commander of the Celts becomes a Casualty, as though suffering the Target Character Battle Effect.
2. Ravens flood from the skies and plunge into a unit. The unit is treated as Disrupted until it can Reform.
3. Ravens Harass a unit. The enemy unit's Morale roll is one grade more difficult.
4. The Saxon warband engaged with the targeted unit gains the Savage Battle Effect for that round (and in addition to any other Battle Effects).
5. The unit under attack by Ravens must Take Cover (see Battle Effects) and is pinned until it can be helped.
6. The Ravens inflict 1d3 damage on the enemy unit.

The battle continues until either Wiglaf has managed to get four of the five units across the river, or his warriors are forced into a rout before the second unit has managed to make the crossing.

If Wiglaf can make it across the river, his men can safely begin a controlled retreat towards Ratae.

The Cornovii and Dumnonian Plan

King Lend has two warbands of eighty warriors apiece, and Natanleod has two warbands of fifty, plus a cavalry unit of fifteen horsemen. The Britons are therefore outnumbered here, as Arthur has taken his forces to try to circle around Wiglaf using a ford further to the north.

Lend's tactics are to Charge and then inflict as much damage on the assembled Saxons as possible, while Natanleod attempts to flank them on one side with his warbands and sends his cavalry to try to outflank on the other side. The Britons are going for an all-out assault here. If Wiglaf crosses the ford, he can escape, so the intention is simply to do as much damage as possible, giving Arthur time to cross the river to the north, and then charge into Wiglaf's ranks in a massive rear assault.

The characters can be part of either the Cornovii or Dumnonians and may, of course, act as Commanders on a unit. King Lend leads his men in the front rank of the shield wall. Natanleod devolves tactical command to his shield wall commanders while he leads the cavalry unit to try to circle round Wiglaf's lines.

Isen is with Wiglaf and can only be reached by Natanleod's cavalry, if they can outflank the Saxon shield walls.

The forces for both Britons and Saxons start on page 290.

Aftermath

If Wiglaf is beaten, Caer Leonis can be retaken by the Britons. Ratae is quickly evacuated, but the Saxons do not travel very far to the east. Word will be sent to the Angle King, Guercha, who will want to retake both Ratae and Caer Leonis. He can assemble a 1,000 strong army and call on favours from Aelle to gain more spearmen. Arthur can liberate Caer Leonis and Ratae for a time, but he will need a substantial garrison to keep it.

This is not really his aim. He wants to provoke Guercha and Aelle to come further west, so that he can meet them head-on with troops from Gwent, Powys, Cornovia, and Dumnonia. These battles are taunts – skirmishes to humiliate the Saxons and hopefully provoke them into a rash retaliation.

If Wiglaf survives, he is taken hostage to be held by Havgan at Isca. Isen, if he survives, is given to Merlin to be held at Ynys Wydryn. Both Havgan and Merlin will use their considerable persuasive skills to learn what they can about the Saxons, although neither are to be killed. Havgan grows to like Wiglaf. Merlin loathes Isen, although he is fascinated at the læce's command of the Saxon Spirit World and devotion to attaining Woden's wisdom.

All told, this scenario is designed to give the characters and players experience of shield wall fighting and chance to seriously injure the Saxon holdings not far from Dumnonian and Brigantes borders. Give the characters a chance to command and, certainly, to fight, emerging with honour and glory where they can.

Wiglaf's Forces

Unit A: Horath's Shield Wall	
Unit Name: Horath's Fyrdmen	UnitType: Seasoned and Veteran Fyrdmen
Unit Traits: Formation Fighting	
Commander: Horath	Command Skill: 78 %
Strength: 60	Current Damage: 1d4
Competency: 78%	Morale: 75% (Disciplined)
Current Formation: Line	Frontage: 20 x 3 ranks
Horath's warband will be the last to try to make it across the ford. This means they will fight the longest and may not survive. Horath cares not: to die defending others is a privilege few are given and he intends to take as many Britons with him as he can. Isen's magic is used to support Horath the most..	

Unit B: Gaelle's Shield Wall	
Unit Name: Gaelle's Fyrdmen	UnitType: Seasoned and Veteran Fyrdmen
Unit Traits: Formation Fighting	
Commander: Gaelle	Command Skill: 70 %
Strength: 60	Current Damage: 1d4
Competency: 80%	Morale: 75% (Disciplined)
Current Formation: Line	Frontage: 20 x 3 ranks
Gaelle is a worthy commander. Solid and strong, his Saxons are the lynchpin of the army, fighting hard and long. They throw support to Horath where possible.	

Unit C: Caellthe's Fyrdmen

Unit Name: Caellthe's Fyrdmen	UnitType: Seasoned and Veteran Fyrdmen, but battered and bruised
Unit Traits: Formation Fighting	
Commander: Caellthe	Command Skill: 70%
Strength: 80	Current Damage: 1d4
Competency: 80%	Morale: 58% (Steady)
Current Formation: Line	Frontage: 20 x 4 ranks

While competent, Caellthe's force suffered heavy losses earlier and morale is lower as a result. The retreat has bolstered them a little, but morale is still fragile. Caellthe is aware of this and will not do anything rash to injure morale further.

Unit D: Aemon's Shield Wall

Unit Name: Aemon's Fyrdmen	UnitType: Seasoned and Veteran Fyrdmen
Unit Traits: Formation Fighting	
Commander: Aemon	Command Skill: 65%
Strength: 60	Current Damage: 1d4
Competency: 72%	Morale: 60% (Steady)
Current Formation: Line	Frontage: 20 x 3 ranks

Aemon is a young commander eager to prove himself. He has fought well in this campaign, but the retreat requires a precision that may be beyond his experience. His men sense this, and morale is lower as a result.

Unit E: Brecca's Fyrdmen

Unit Name: Brecca's Fyrdmen	UnitType: Seasoned and Veteran Fyrdmen
Unit Traits: Formation Fighting	
Commander: Brecca	Command Skill: 72%
Strength: 60	Current Damage: 1d4
Competency: 72%	Morale: 60% (Steady)
Current Formation: Skirmish	Frontage: 20 x 3 ranks

Brecca's warband is retreating across the ford in Skirmish Formation. They are intent on getting to the other side but can retaliate should the Britons manage to break through.

The Britons

Unit 1: King Lend's Shield Wall

Unit Name: Cornovii Warband	UnitType: Seasoned and Veteran Warriors
Unit Traits: Formation Fighting	
Commander: King Lend	Command Skill: 85 %
Strength: 80	Current Damage: 1d4
Competency: 85%	Morale: 70% (Disciplined)
Current Formation: Line	Frontage: 20 x 4 ranks
Lend is a ferocious commander who leads from the front and is unafraid to die. His tactics are simple: break the Saxon shield wall and slaughter as many as possible.	

Unit 2: Cornovii Shield Wall

Unit Name: Cornovii Warband	UnitType: Seasoned and Veteran Warriors
Unit Traits: Formation Fighting	
Commander: Uffa	Command Skill: 76 %
Strength: 80	Current Damage: 1d4
Competency: 79%	Morale: 85% (Disciplined)
Current Formation: Line	Frontage: 20 x 4 ranks
Uffa's role is to work with Lend to break the Saxon shield wall down. His favoured tactic is Savage, using this as his preferred Battle Action.	

Unit 3: Dumnonian Spearmen

Unit Name: Dumnonian Warband	UnitType: Seasoned and Veteran Warriors
Unit Traits: Formation Fighting	
Commander: Nerys	Command Skill: 80%
Strength: 50	Current Damage: 1d2
Competency: 79%	Morale: 75% (Disciplined)
Current Formation: Wedge	Frontage: 10 x 5 ranks

Nerys is one of Natanleod's Shield Maiden commanders. Her role is to drive a wedge into one of the Saxon flanks, breaking it open, then switching to Skirmish formation when through the Saxon lines to tackle the fleeing warbands.

Unit 4: Merdyn's Warband

Unit Name: Dumnonian Warband	UnitType: Seasoned and Veteran Warriors
Unit Traits: Formation Fighting	
Commander: Merdyn	Command Skill: 74%
Strength: 50	Current Damage: 1d4
Competency: 74%	Morale: 75% (Disciplined)
Current Formation: Line	Frontage: 25 x 2 ranks

Merdyn's orders are to try to Envelop the Saxon flank, but also to join with (and support) Nerys if her warband fails to drive through the Saxon lines. His favoured Battle Action is Guard.

Unit 5: Natanleod's Cavalry

Unit Name: Dumnonian Heavy Horse	UnitType: Seasoned and Veteran Horsemen
Unit Traits: Mounted Combat	
Commander: Natanleod	Command Skill: 85%
Strength: 15	Current Damage: 1d4
Competency: 85%	Morale: 85% (Disciplined)
Current Formation: Line	Frontage: 1 rank of 15 riders

Small in number, Natanleod is, nevertheless, leading an excellent force. Their tactic is to hit an unprotected flank and try to break through or ride around. Natanleod intends to hit both Wiglaf and Isen if he can, using the Target Battle Action, while Nerys and Merdyn smash through the other flank.

Battle of Lugh's Gorge

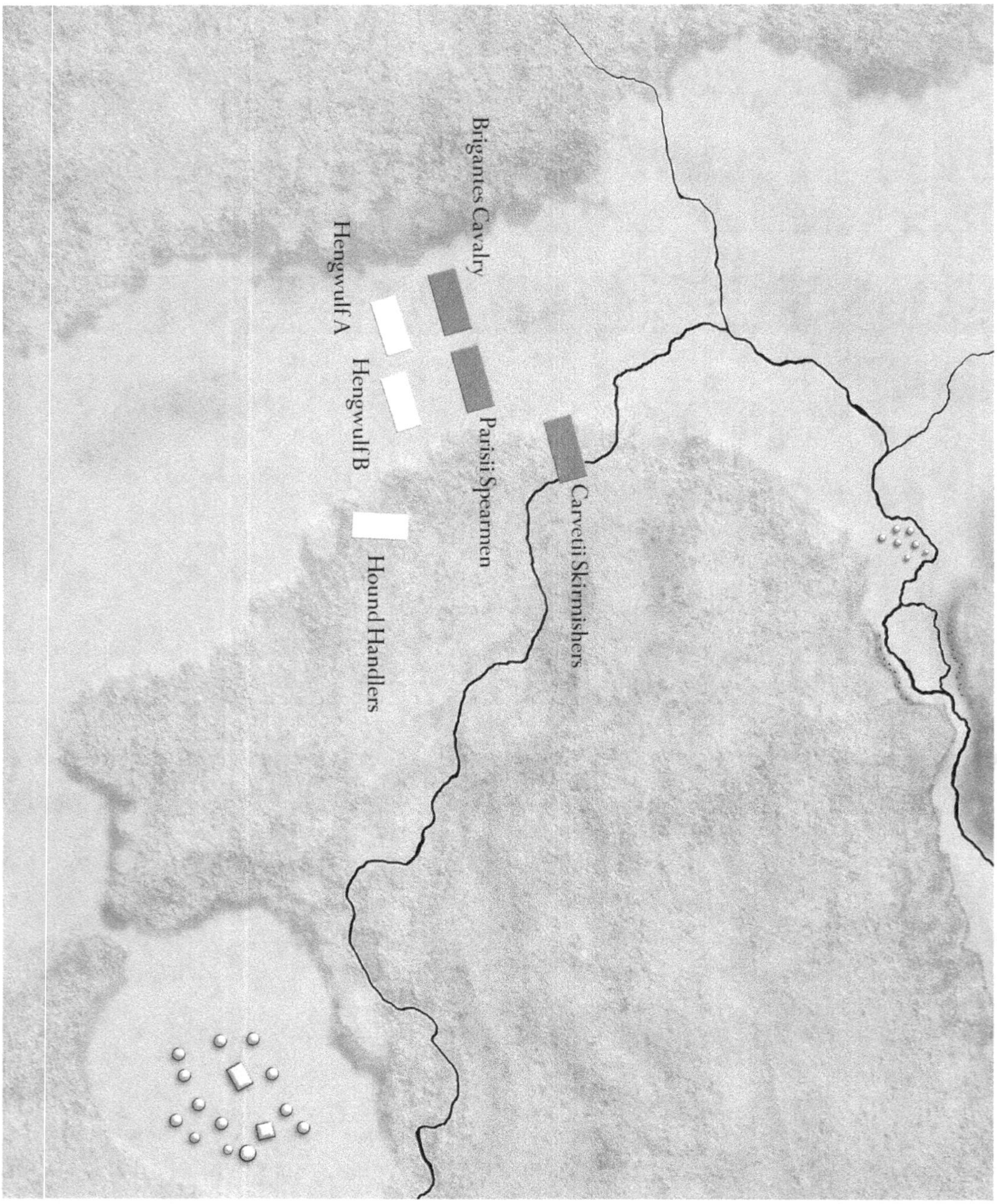

Battle of the Wreake

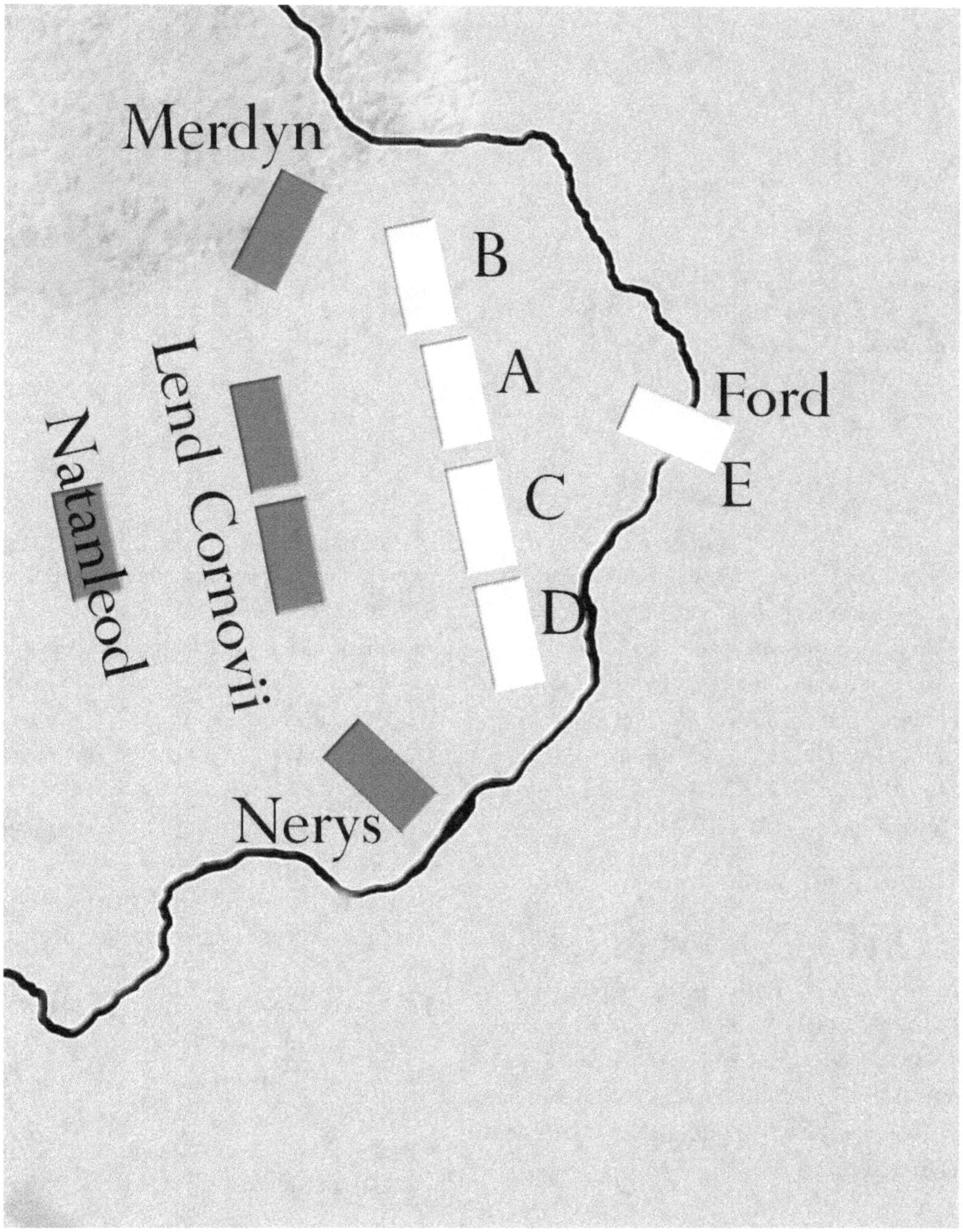

Merdyn
B
A
Ford
Lend Cornovii
Natanleod
C
E
D
Nerys

Caves of the Circind

The search for the Treasures of Britain continues as Merlin sends the characters into the Pictish lands in a bid to retrieve the Coat of Beisrydd. Here they will encounter the Druid-King Mawgaus and his brutal Pictish tribe, the Circind. They also gain an ally in the form of Gawain, son of King Lot, the Votadini ruler of the Gododdin kingdom. Gawain knows where Mawgaus has hidden the Coat of Beisrydd and, being a northerner himself, knows the wild country of Circind.

The Coat of Beisrydd

The full name of Beisrydd is *Padarn Beisrydd ap Tegid*. The name translates as Paternus of the Scarlet Robe, son of Tegid, and the name Tegid is a Goidelic pronunciation of the name Roman name *Tacitus*. Beisrydd hails from a Roman family that was among the first to come to Britain, settle, and learn the way of the Celts rather than subjugate them, as was the general way. Beisrydd's ancestors learned the ways of the Old Gods, married into the local clans and, although they remained Roman, were accepted as Britons and became very much like them. Beisrydd lived two hundred years ago and, accompanied by a druid of the north, went in to the Other World where he performed a great service for Arawn, the King of the Other World. Beisrydd was noted for the scarlet cloak and tunic of his family, and was known as the Prince in Scarlet: such was his service to Arawn that he was rewarded with a coat of armour impervious to rust, mortal weapons, and which will fit any person, of any size, who is deemed suitable to wear it. The Coat passed into the hands of the Votadini tribe and became a treasure in the care of the southern Votadini whose lands would become the kingdom of Gododdin. However, the coat was stolen by the Circind Votadini who claimed it rightly belonged to them. It was hidden by the Druid-Kings and is said to be well-protected. Only a handful of Circind Votadini know the coat's true whereabouts, and they are not going to surrender it to anyone, even someone as powerful and influential as Merlin.

Merlin's Instruction

It is likely that several weeks - if not several months - have passed since the previous scenario, allowing the characters time to rest, heal and catch up with their more routine lives. The High Druid gathers the characters together at wherever is convenient to the campaign. This could be at Ynys Wydryn, but Merlin is prepared to travel to engage the characters in this latest quest for a Treasure of Britain. He recounts the above history of the Coat of Beisrydd to the characters, and concludes by saying "Mawgaus rules the Circind and he and I have always been enemies. He denies Britain this treasure out of hatred for me, so there is no way that I can be involved in its retrieval. I do not expect Mawgaus to be persuaded either: he has a habit of eating those who displease him. No, I rather think you're going to have to steal it..."

The coat's location is protected by certain Votadini ancestor spirits and even Merlin has been unable to determine its precise whereabouts. But, he says, there is one who is willing to help: the warrior known as Gawain. "Gawain is the son of Lot, king of the Gododdin Votadini. Lot's ancestors let the coat be stolen into the keeping of the Circind and, because Gawain has no love for his father, he is prepared to help us steal the Coat of Beisrydd from Mawgaus. It will not be easy, but Gawain claims to know where the coat has been hidden, and he knows the Circind lands. You will travel into Brigantia first and meet with Gawain; he will then be your guide as you go beyond the Great Wall and into the Pictish lands of the north. After that, it is up to you. If you recover the coat, bring it to me at Caer Ysc, capital of the Brigantes lands."

Journeying to Brigantia

The lands of Middle Britain are a mixture of deep forests, rolling hills, sheltered valleys, and wide pasture lands. Merlin tells the characters to go to Caer Ysc to find Gawain; this is the hill fort of Queen Elliw of the Brigantes, the ruler Gawain has chosen to serve as a hired sword. The journey to Caer Ysc should be uneventful and reasonably easy going. At this time of year the weather is more agreeable and may even be warm and sunny for the most part, making travel a pleasure more than a chore. The characters pass to the north west of the old Roman city of Eboracum and must cross several rivers before picking their way through the deep woodlands that make up the northern part of the Brigantes territory. They frequently see the old, pagan markers of the Brigantes: leering and ominous faces carved into both rocks and tree-trunks, often with swirling designs. With a little less frequency the characters encounter hamlets and villages: simple collections of roundhouses with corrals and pens for livestock and peopled with wary, but welcoming, locals who are happy to offer a little food, a little ale or mead, and a dry roof to sleep under. The Christian religion has taken firm root in Brigantia: the signs of the cross are everywhere and some of the villages have crude chapels and a priest or two. These Brigantes Christians do not seem too perturbed by Pagans: clearly something of the Old Gods still lingers in their hearts although the blessed Saint Brigid has replaced the propitiation of the local forest spirits, and there are no druids to be seen.

Eventually the characters reach Caer Ysc, the sprawling hill fort built long ago by the founders of the Brigantes tribe. Caer Ysc encompasses several low hills and is more an enclosed town than a hill fort in its strictest sense. The characters are intercepted by mounted patrols several miles before reaching Caer Ysc's boundary ditches, but once it is established that the characters are coming peacefully, the Brigantes war band patrol provides an escort into Caer Ysc's heart.

Given Ysc's area, there are several small villages, all a part of Caer Ysc, inside the palisade. Lodging and other amenities can be easily found, and the Brigantes prove to be very hospitable people. They are keen for news from the south, and God and Jesus are praised as news of victories over the Saxons is delivered. If anyone asks about Gawain it is clear the name is known - as is that of Teneu, his sister. It transpires that Gawain has travelled much throughout Britain, hiring his sword to Dumnonia, Powys and Gwent in recent years. "He is a good servant of Christ, now," someone tells the characters. "But he still hates the Saxons and the Picts." With a little questioning the characters can learn a little more about Gawain's hatred from his kinsmen - and the way his own father tried to murder his sister.

Gawain has now sworn his service to Queen Elliw and has quarters near her hall. Gaining introductions isn't difficult: successful Customs or Influence rolls are enough to gain the right level of assistance.

Gawain of the Votadini

The man the characters seek can be found chopping firewood outside a modest roundhouse not very far from the Great Hall of Queen Elliw. Gawain is not especially tall or broad; in fact, he is quite unassuming, but, stripped to the waist, his athletic physique is unmistakable: he is muscled, fit and, most likely, fast. His chest, back and arms are coated in swirling black and red tattoos typical of the Votadini tribe. Votadini get their first tattoo at the age of eight, and then one is added every year: many are completely covered in tattoos, and this why the Romans called them 'picts', or 'painted ones'. Gawain's tattoos though, only cover his upper body; elsewhere he is free of them. His hair is dark, coarse, and tied in a severe ponytail. His beard is neatly trimmed though, and his brown eyes have a softness to them. He pauses in his work as the characters approach and nods when they ask if he is the Gawain they seek.

"And you'll be the ones the druid sent," Gawain says. "Whether you are or not, we'll not be idle while we talk; find axes and help me finish this lot." He indicates the pile of logs that need splitting and it is obvious the characters have to assist if they are to earn his trust.

While they work Gawain listens to what the characters say or ask, and replies that he does, indeed, know where the Coat of Beisrydd is located. "I fought with the Circind against the Caledonii for a time," Gawain says. "Several of them bragged about this coat of mail made by the gods and how it was now a Circind prize and treasure. All of them claimed they touched it, or wore it. When drunk, a couple told me where it's meant to be. No reason not to believe them. Many's the truth uttered through drink."

If asked why he wants to help take it from the Votadini, he shrugs. "My father tried to murder my sister. He's tried to murder me. He had Circind help both times. If I can take something of theirs, it's fair compensation for them trying to take my life."

After finishing the wood splitting, Gawain fetches a pail of water, washes, then dons a simple tunic that he fetches from his roundhouse. "I'm going to pray now, before supper. Come, if you want." He then disappears in the direction of the impressive wood and stone chapel where others are going for early evening prayers. Christians, naturally, will join the assembly, but there does not seem to be any admonition for pagans who choose to remain behind.

After prayers Gawain invites the characters into the Great Hall of Queen Elliw. It seems Gawain's status as a warrior grants him the privilege of dining amongst the queen's people and, with Gawain, the characters are made welcome. The food is good, and prayers precede each course. Finally, Gawain is called to the high bench where it is obvious he is explaining who the characters are to Queen Elliw. She talks earnestly with Gawain but does not acknowledge the characters. When he returns, Gawain explains. "I told them I'd agreed to help Arthur. The queen does not like or trust Merlin so, if she asks you, you've come from Arthur and it's because I owe him a service in the south. Do you understand?"

Teneu

If the characters ask Gawain about his sister, Teneu, he remains silent and flashes an angry look. Gawain suspects that King Lot still wants Teneu dead for shaming him: she lives under Queen Elliw's protection now, and has a new name. Gawain is not about to reveal it to anyone. When he leaves with the characters he doesn't even let his sister know that he is going - just in case the characters are spies for his father and try to follow him.

Insight rolls, successfully made, gather that Queen Elliw would disapprove of Gawain leading the characters in search of the Coat of Beisrydd: critical successes go deeper and gather that Queen Elliw would probably want the coat for herself, if she knew the truth of this mission. Despite the Thirteen Treasures being of pagan importance, there is still enough belief in the old magic of Britain for Christians to want these treasures - perhaps to deny the pagans any chance of accruing power.

Journeying to Circind

Gawain tells the characters that, to find the Coat of Beisrydd, they need to travel far north, to the Pictish kingdom of Circind. "We can go overland, but it is long and dangerous. We have to cross the Great Wall the Romans built and then venture through my father's lands of Gododdin. After that we have to head west around the firth, which crosses into the lands of the Caledonii; then we have to travel back east and close to where Mawgaus, king of the Circind, has many scouts. Instead, I suggest we go by boat. Faster, safer." If any characters object to a sea journey, Gawain merely shrugs: "Then good luck in finding what the druid wants. I'm risking my life helping you as it is; I shan't risk it any more than I need to by traipsing through my father's lands." He cannot be swayed and neither will he reveal the coat's location: the characters have to do as he says.

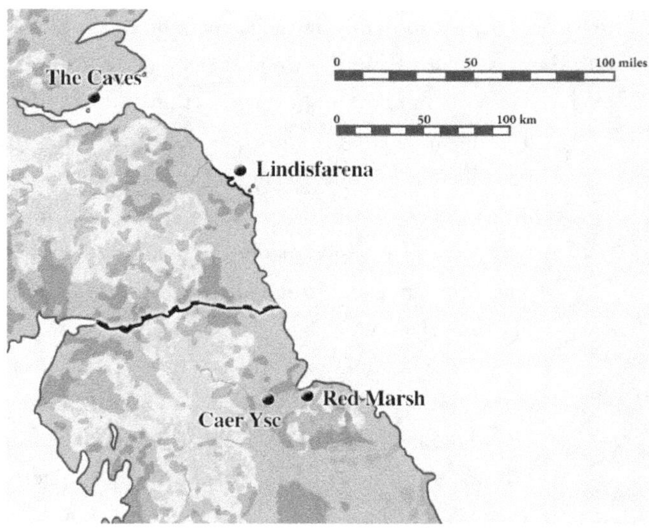

The closest place to obtain a boat is at the fishing village of Red Marsh, a day's ride to the east. From there, it is a 160 mile sea journey around the eastern coast, turning due west into the huge firth, or bay, Gawain referred to. The boats in these parts are simple fishing vessels that are not capable of travelling too far from the shore; but, with a good wind and a decent captain, it should take no more than 2 days to reach wherever it is Gawain has in mind. Once agreement is reached, Gawain recommends leaving at dawn the next day.

Caer Ysc to Red Marsh

The journey to Red Marsh takes around a day on horseback, and mounts from Caer Ysc are provided. It is a gentle journey that follows well defined trails through the surrounding forest, eventually winding into the hills to the east and over them. The hills are sparse moorland and from the summit the characters can see across to the east coast of Britain. Gawain reins his horse and points-out the village of Red Marsh. "Village is too grand a name," he says. "A group of hovels is more like it. If we pay the people in silver, they will be grateful. You do have silver, don't you?"

During the ride the characters have an opportunity to try to get to know Gawain better. He is a very quiet, thoughtful man; he rarely speaks and it requires a Hard Influence roll to get more than

one word answers from him. If the characters do encourage him to talk, they learn 1d6 of the following:

1. The Votadini are split into two factions: north and south. The northern tribe is known as the Circind and that is also the name of their kingdom. The southern tribe, ruled by King Lot, controls Gododdin. There is no love lost between Circind and Gododdin: the Circind are barbarians, murderers and cannibals. The Gododdin are more like the Caledonii.
2. It was the Votadini that conducted most of the raids south of the wall that triggered Vortigern's desire to conquer the Picts once and for all. "The Votadini defeated the Roman 9th Legion," Gawain says. "What hope did Vortigern and a few Saxons have?"
3. King Lot has a fierce temper and hates the Celts of the south, especially the Brigantes. But he hates the Caledonii just as much. "His rule is based on hate," Gawain says. "He even hates himself."
4. Gawain became a Christian only recently. Before that, the Old Gods had been strong with him. "I still feel the presence of the spirits, and I know that the Old Gods exist. But the One God is real also, and this is the time of his power. Does it matter which god we worship as long as we are sincere?"
5. He owes Merlin a debt. "The druid helped me in a time when I needed help the most: "If I help get him the armour, my debt is paid. I look forward to that day." (Merlin helped hide Teneu and Gawain when they fled Gododdin; he created certain spirit charms that ensured King Lot could not easily find them south of the Great Wall).
6. Where they are heading is on the coast. "This is one of the reasons why a ship is better. Along with everything else I told you."

By the late afternoon the party reaches Red Marsh. It is aptly named: the coast land hereabouts is low-lying and waterlogged. Horses have to be led through narrow, raised trails and across makeshift firm ways made of logs and reed mats. The group of reed, wattle and daub and moss-roofed huts stands back from the sandy beach, crouching behind grassy dunes that offer the only shelter from the northerly winds. Three simple boats are pulled onto the shore: long, wide-beamed boats with oars and a single mast - typical fishing vessels: leaky, uncomfortable, but sturdy. The horses will need to be left at Red Marsh, but the boats are large enough to accommodate up to 18 people.

The locals are nervous and wary. Although Brigantes they have little communication with Caer Ysc, they worship both the Christian God and the Celtic God of the sea, Manawydan, just for good measure. They are scared of warriors and do nothing to upset the characters. There are twenty villagers altogether - a mix of ages, but with men dominating. Over a simple meal of fish stew, Gawain tells the villagers a boat is needed. "We will pay 1 piece of silver for each day we keep the boat away from fishing. We pay another silver piece to the people who sail it for us. We pay another silver piece for you to look after the horses while we are gone. We will pay a silver piece for their safe return when we get back. We pay one last silver piece for your silence. We were not here. We never came. That is about 10 pieces of silver you can earn by helping us - more than you would make in a month."

The Red Marsh villagers readily agree. If the characters want to try to barter, Gawain flashes them a dangerous look. On the waves, they will be at the boat captain's mercy; if they are generous now, they are ensured safe passage home. Upset them or insult them, and they might find the boat gone after they have finished their task in Circind.

By the time the arrangements have been made, it is too late to sail, and the owner of the boat nominated to take them north says it will be better to sail at dawn. "We will pass the isle of Lindisfarena," he says. "The currents are strong and the winds tough. Better to sail at dawn and reach Lindisfarena by dusk where we can make shore for the night."

Lindisfarena

The next morning, the sky is overcast and the winds strong. The boat owner, Nubh, is reluctant to sail but conducts a short ritual that involves reading various pebbles thrown onto the sand and claims it is safe enough - although hard work. Supplies are loaded - Gawain says it will take two days to reach where they are going, and take two days to return, with perhaps two days there - and the

ship is dragged down to the sea by the villagers and the characters scramble aboard.

The sea is, indeed, rough. Unless the characters have a previous occupation as fishermen, the chances of sea-sickness are high. The ship sails for six hours before reaching Lindisfarena; each character must make a Hard Endurance roll. If the roll is successful, then sea-sickness is kept at bay. If the roll is failed, then 1d6 hours is spent hanging over the edge of the boat, vomiting and wishing for death. Every 3 hours so afflicted imposes a level of Fatigue on the character. This is recovered after a decent night's sleep. Gawain and Nubh are unaffected: clearly Gawain, who grew up near the sea, has robust sea legs, and Nubh concentrates on guiding the ship. He always keeps land in sight, but the shore is still distant and the waves pummel the small craft as it rises and falls with the sharp swells.

As the light begins to fade, Lindisfarena appears ahead. A small, rocky island, it is separated from the main shoreline by a narrow causeway of sand which is only accessible at low tide. The western end of the island is dominated by a large tor of rock overlooking the sea. Nubh steers the boat north of the island and then tacks hard around to find a sheltered cove not far from where the ground slopes towards the sandbank causeway. The characters and Gawain have to disembark and guide the boat onto the shore, wading waist and knee-deep through the surf, until the ship is secure. Nubh says that island is home to a druid who lives in the caves on the south side of the tor; if they give him some food and ale (which they have brought), he'll be happy enough and may even call on the local spirits to calm the seas the next day.

Camp is made in the shelter of the rocky cove. Within an hour or so, Perception rolls pick up movement coming from the south. A single figure, quite tubby, waddles across the rocks. He is dressed in shabby, threadbare robes that are barely held together, has bare feet, and short hair, shaved at the front in the familiar tonsure of a druid. He waves his arms frantically and, in thick northern accent, calls out in Brythonic, "I'm peaceful! I'm a druid! I'm hungry!"

Ofydd

The druid is called Ofydd and he has lived, alone, on Lindisfarena longer than he can remember. "The island is alive you see, the Great Spirit Lindis is all around and she called to me to be her guardian, so here I am. I cannot leave, not until she tells me to, and I shall most likely die here. Have you any ale?"

Given food and, especially ale, Ofydd becomes effusive company. Occasionally, the Votadini from Gododdin come to Lindisfarena but they haven't been here for several years. Only local fishing vessels make any stops, and then only to shelter for the night and to ask Ofydd to call on Lindis to grant calm seas. "A Christian priest came to drive me out two years ago," Ofydd says, "but Lindis took offence. He slipped on the kelp and dashed his brains out just over there." He points to a small cairn marking the priest's burial site. "There'll be no Christian churches on Lindisfarena, you mark my words!"

It seems customary for Ofydd to repay any small kindness by communing with Lindis and requesting calm seas. One he's eaten and drunk his fill, he sprawls out on his back, arms and legs spread, staring at the sky, and lapses into a trance, calling Lindis's name over and over. His eyes roll back into his head and he passes into the Spirit World. Any druid character can accompany Ofydd if they wish: Lindisfarena is intensely magical and the links with the Spirit World are strong. Attaining a trance is at an Easy grade of success. The passage below describes what happens to Ofydd on the Spirit World: those observing in the Mortal World see the druid start to spasm and fit, his lips foaming, limbs flailing violently: he is under assault in the Spirit World and there is nothing the characters can do to save him. A druid might be able to summon spirit help of his or her own to assist Ofydd - although the spirit attack is very powerful.

The Ancestors

On the spirit world, Lindisfarena is a wide, grassy, peaceful island filled with buttercups and bird-song. Lindis herself appears as a dark-haired maiden sitting by the sea strumming a harp and calming the local natural spirits with her songs. Ofydd, tall and handsome, presents her with gifts of food and drink brought from the Mortal World. Suddenly, from the north, the sky grows dark and rapidly becomes black. Thunderheads roll across the waves, turning the peaceful sea into a roiling storm. Two chariots are born over the waves, bearing down on the small island. Each chariot is driven by a fierce, tattooed, scarred, spiky-haired warrior, eyes blazing with fury. Spears are hurled as the chariots close on the

beach: one strikes Lindis and the second strikes Ofydd. The warriors laugh and spur their chariots forward so that the wheels crush the bodies of Lindis and Ofydd; then they wheel and ride north, back the way they came.

Druid characters can try to attack the charioteers with any spirit allies they might have, but both ancestor spirits are Intensity 5 creatures and likely to shrug off any damage that might be done to them before killing any lesser foes.

These are Votadini ancestor spirits - Cing and Cruithne - who guard the spirit borders of Votadini lands against those who would steal and pillage. The Spirit World is aware that someone is coming to steal the Coat of Beisrydd and this is a warning from the Spirit World that the Circind Votadini will defend what is theirs. The spirit Lindis has the recurring trait and so will eventually recover from her ordeal, but Ofydd perishes on the Mortal World, although, in time, his spirit will come to live with Lindis once the correct burial rites are performed.

If the characters bury Ofydd (Customs rolls help determine the correct rites in this part of the world) correctly - and not merely bury his remains under rocks, as he buried the Christian priest - Lindis herself manifests on the Mortal World as the rites for Ofydd's burial conclude. She appears now as a black-haired young woman, clad in black robes, her feet merging with the substance of the island as though she has grown from it. She manifests high on the rocks, overlooking the place where Ofydd is laid to rest. She calls down to the characters and beckons for one of them to ascend. "Ofydd served me well and he will come to me, in time, in my golden realm. I give this to you with thanks from Lord Arawn: it should be taken to the High Druid, for it is something he has long-sought." She hands over a stone knife. It does not appear to be anything special: a flint blade with a crude bone handle wrapped in old, frayed leather. However, a successful Pagan Lore roll by a druid (or Formidable Pagan Lore roll by an non-druid character) recognises this as the Knife of Farchog, one of the Thirteen Treasures of Britain and a knife that, with one cut, can serve twenty at a feasting table. Even though it is a simple, mundane-looking thing, a Trance roll or Formidable Insight roll picks up on the natural, magical aura it radiates. Viewed in the Spirit World the knife gleams and appears as though newly-made (although is still a simple tool of flint, bone and leather). Once the knife is passed to the characters, Lindis fades from view, returning to the Spirit World.

As an alternative way of handling this whole encounter, the characters could simply find the Knife of Farchog on Ofydd's body, or hidden amongst his possessions if they search his cave. Indeed, they could even arrive in Lindisfarna just after the Ancestor Warriors of the Votadini send their warning against helping the characters, leaving behind Ofydd's corpse for the characters to find.

Gawain understands the ominous events that befall poor, hapless Ofydd: "The spirits of the Votadini ancestors know we are coming. This is a warning to stay away. Mawgaus and his headtakers will be ready for us."

If the characters investigate the cairn where the Christian priest is buried, they find the skeletal remains of a man, his brown robes rotting away, clinging to the bones, and a wooden crucifix around the neck. The skull has been caved in, but a successful First Aid roll indicates that this was no fall: the back of his head is completely crushed - the result of a repeated battering by some blunt object. Ofydd most likely did it using a nearby rock. Gawain insists that the Christian priest should be reburied and a cross placed to mark his grave (there is plenty of driftwood on the beach to fashion a crude cross). Gawain buries the priest himself if no one else will help, and he kneels and prays for the man's soul, begging God to forgive his murderer.

There is also the opportunity to investigate the caves where Ofydd made his home. Across a narrow cave mouth at the base of the southern cliff is a makeshift screen of dried seaweed, grass, reeds and packed mud. Inside the cave (which extends about 20 feet into the cliff) is a stinking bed, made from more rushes, reeds and dried weed, cooking utensils, a hearth close to the cave entrance, and, hidden in a niche, covered by a carefully placed stone, various items of jewelry, some coins, and a few trinkets that have been scrounged or given to the druid over the years. They come to about 30 Silver Pieces in total, and amongst the treasures, if it has not already been given to the characters, is the Knife of Farchog.

Customs rolls remember that stealing from a druid is forbidden, and these items should be either left or interred with his remains. Only the knife, which is clearly magical, can be safely taken, although a Pagan may need to successfully overcome his Pagan passion with Willpower to have the strength of will take the knife.

Nubh, having witnessed these weird and sinister events, is terrified. He is all for turning back to Red Marsh and the characters will need to convince him otherwise by overcoming his Willpower with their own Influence rolls. Offering him an additional 1d4 Silver makes the Influence roll one grade easier.

The Firth

The next day's sailing is as rough as the previous day. The waves roll and rain lashes the deck. There is no shelter from wind or rain, and, as well as feeling sea-sick, characters are cold and miserable. The mood is sombre. Both Nubh and Gawain pray frequently and every lurch of the boat is enough to have Nubh calling to both Jesus and Manawydan for mercy.

Towards dusk the sea begins to grow calmer and Gawain goes to the prow of the boat and squints into the distance. The headland is visible, and before it the sea cuts into the land to the west, forming the wide, jagged bay Gawain calls The Firth. "To the south is Gododdin, my home." He says. "North is Circind. The Firth marks the division between the two clans of the Votadini. We head now to the north shore."

Gawain tells Nubh to head for the northern bay but to keep following it on the seaward side. He wants to find a safe and secluded landing place where Nubh can wait. "We will head west to where we need to be, but there are many hiding places along this coast where Nubh can stay safe."

Gawain is also pleased because they have arrived at their destination at night. He explains that there are Votadini patrols along the various coastal paths to protect against raids from Gododdin. "I doubt they will have seen our little ship approaching, but Mawgaus will know thieves are coming because the ancestor spirits he worships will have told him. Perhaps though, we may be lucky and he won't be expecting our arrival just yet."

The characters have to help row the boat while Nubh steers and Gawain watches for somewhere suitable, squinting into the half light. Eventually, after perhaps an hour, he sees somewhere suitable and guides Nubh towards it. A narrow, gravelly cove has been carved into the landscape. The upper part is covered with undergrowth, obscuring anything below from casual sight. Once more the characters have to wade into the water to guide the boat safely aground, but once this is done, it is clear that the hiding place is good enough. The boat is tough to see from either above or the water.

Gawain suggests a few hours sleep, but that they should leave before dawn, making the most of the darkness to keep out of sight of Votadini. Now, he reveals a little more about where they are headed. "If we follow the northern coast of the firth we come to a beach and cliffs. In the cliffs are several caves. On the land above them is a broch, used by the Circind patrols as shelter and watch tower for the coast. That is where we search for the Coat of Beisrydd, for that is where Mawgaus has hidden it."

The Caves, The Broch and The Coat

From here on, the characters need to plan how they intend to locate and steal the Coat of Beisrydd. Gawain knows the coat is kept here, but he does not know if it is kept in one of the caves (and if so, which one) or on the Broch. In actual fact, the coat is held in a secret cave beneath the broch, and accessible either from the broch or from Cave 1.

About the Area

The Votadini call this area *Aywell Uamh*, which means Aywell's Caves. Aywell is one of the chief gods of the north and these caves, the druids hold, lead into his lands in the Realm of the Gods. For generations the Votadini of Circind have made sacrifices to Aywell in the caves and inscribed many charms, prayers and symbols into the cave walls. Given the sacred nature of the caves, hiding the Coat of Beisrydd here makes sense, although one would never leave it completely unguarded. So, the broch that has been built above one of the caves is a permanent garrison for the war band chosen by the Druid Kings to protect the coat from intruders - not that any intruders have ever come before.

Aywell Uamh

Key

1. Trail
2. Broch
3. Tower Wall
4. The Spring Cave
5. Aywell's Cave
6. Cave of Serpents
7. Beach

Nubh's Ship 1.86 miles to the NW

0 300 600 900 1200ft

The countryside inland from the caves is relatively flat, reasonably well-wooded, and within a day's ride of three Votadini hill forts, to the north-west and west. These hill forts supply the warriors who patrol the border with the Gododdin and also supply the warriors who guard the Coat and watch the coast for potential sea-raids.

The caves are cut from sandstone. The rock is soft and easily worked, and this has allowed the Votadini to carve a secret tunnel and chamber between the broch and the Spring Cave. It is here that the coat is hidden. The caves are close to the beach, which is a wide plateau of wave-cut rock; the Spring Cave is 90 feet from the low-tide mark, whereas the other caves are only 30 feet from the water. The sea no longer reaches into the caves, although it did at one time, and the druids have carved inscriptions to Manawydan - fish - into the caves to act as wards against the sea's intrusion.

No one lives in the caves, but once a year, at high summer, Mawgaus leads a ritual where animal and human sacrifices are made to Aywell in the Cave of Serpents. This perpetuates the magical links between Aywell's realm and the Mortal World and also pleases the ancestor spirits charged by Aywell to protect these caves. These spirits are Cing and Cruithne, the ones sent to kill Ofydd and subdue Lindis. They watch the coasts from the Spirit World constantly and provide Mawgaus with warnings of likely attacks. They can only bring direct harm to those who are in the Spirit World, or passing into Aywell's Realm: but they can forewarn the Votadini, ensuring they are always ready for their enemies - no matter what precautions those enemies might have taken.

The Caves

There are three caves.

The Cave of Serpents

The Cave of Serpents is a long, narrow cave (30 feet in diameter) that penetrates 150 feet into the rock and slopes steeply downward before levelling. It is high-ceilinged; 9 feet overall and 12 feet at its highest point. Halfway into the cave is a hand-dug pit where the ritual sacrifices are carried out. Bones - animal and human - are strewn all around the pit and extend almost to its back wall. Next to the pit are carved two serpents, one above the other, and these represent the rule of the Druid Kings over the Votadini.

The Cave of Serpents stinks of death: ancient blood that has seeped into the earth, old bone, and the fear of the creatures and men who were sacrificed. It is also magical. A druid lapsing into a trance sees that the rear wall of the cave disappears (although it looks, and feels, quite physical to anyone not viewing the cave from the Spirit World) and a long, sloping tunnel replaces it. This tunnel leads into the Realm of the Gods and emerges in the feasting hall of Aywell where the Votadini ancestors celebrate their immortality with song, war, drinking, hunting and tormenting their enemies. To non-Votadini the tunnel represents a terrifying passageway into a ghastly, barbaric and enemy realm: not that non-Votadini can reach it: Cing and Cruithne guard the tunnel - they ride up from Aywell's hall in the chariots and hurl spears at, or ride over, intruders. They can be engaged in Spirit Combat, but they are extremely tough opponents. Their spirit statistics can be found on page 312. Note also that Cing has the Demoralise Folk Magic spell: if he strikes with his spear, the Demoralise spell also takes effect, as well as any Spirit Damage from the weapon itself.

Manawydan's Cave

This cave is a third of the length of the Cave of Serpents and is kept sacred to two gods: Manawydan, God of the Sea, and Mm, the Votadini Goddess of Fertility. Inscriptions of fish, animals, double-circle charms and other carvings are all over the walls of the cave, protecting it from the sea and calling for blessings for the farmland further inland. The Druid Kings do not lead the rituals here; that is left to the female druids and druids-in-training to do. Although Manawydan and Mm are important gods, Aywell is the most important and so requires the attention of the Druid Kings.

Aside from food remains and general detritus, there is nothing else to be found in here.

The Spring Cave

The Spring Cave is 36 feet in diameter and 90 feet long. Like the other two, its walls are etched with Pictish symbols recognising the power of the local water spirit who manifests in this cave as a natural spring of fresh water in the far corner. The water spirit is a daughter of Mm but has no name mortals can pronounce. The general magical nature of all the caves allows her to take shape in the Mortal World, forming from the water into a child-sized, aqueous creature with wide eyes, long, watery hair, and a curious expression. Mortals fascinate her, but they rarely come, save to leave a few offerings of fruit and ale. She is child-like and adores games - especially riddles and guessing games. If a mortal plays a game with her and wins, she provides three truthful answers to three questions relating to the caves, the broch or the nearby countryside. Abstract the games as a Social Conflict test. The water spirit uses her Spectral Riddling skill of 77% while the character chosen (and there can be only one) uses Insight to guess the riddles she sets. If she loses, she disappears into her pool in a petulant tantrum, causing the water to boil and hiss angrily.

On the other side of the cave to the spring is the entrance to the tunnel leading both to the broch and the cavern where Beisrydd's Coat is hidden. The entrance is blocked by a massive slab of sandstone set flush with the cave floor. It requires a successful opposed test of Perception versus the Craft skill of the tunnel's creator (74%) to detect. It then requires three successful Brawn rolls to clear enough dirt and dust away from the edges to gain a reasonable purchase and lever the slab up. Beneath it is a 4 metre drop into the tunnel, which leads deeper into the bedrock. The shaft is only a metre wide and can be climbed down easily enough with Easy Athletics rolls. Once inside the tunnel, it is pitch black.

The tunnel is a metre and a half wide, but high enough for anyone of SIZ 15 or lower to walk upright; SIZ 16 or higher must stoop, and all physical skills undertaken while stooped are one grade harder. The passage runs for 150 feet in a straight line before widening into a man-made chamber. This is where the Coat of

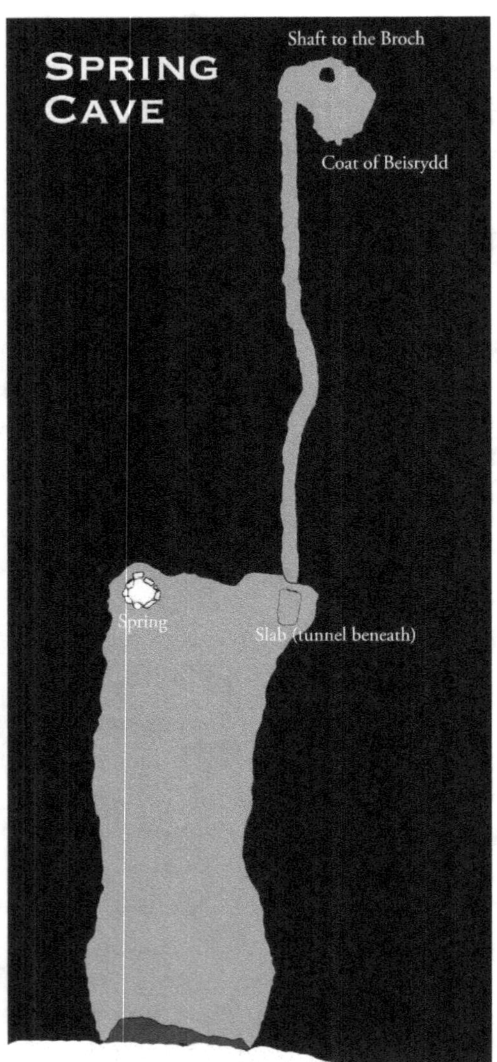

Beisrydd is kept: on the northern wall of the chamber is a hand-dug niche, 1 metre above the floor, 1 metre high, half a metre wide and 1 metre deep.

The Coat of Beisrydd

Inside, wrapped in a bear skin, is a coat of finely woven iron mail that gleams as though newly forged and crafted. It is heavy when lifted, but when donned it fits every size and seems to weigh nothing at all. No mortal weapon can damage the armour and it never rusts and never needs polishing. It protects just as any coat of mail does, providing 5 Armour Points to the Chest and Abdomen; but it does not contribute its ENC to the Initiative penalty. Furthermore, it looks like no other armour anyone has ever seen. Its links are so finely forged and tightly woven that it seems to shimmer and flow, almost like water. Certainly no human smith could make such a wonderful suit of armour and it was, indeed, crafted by Gorfannon the Smith for the Prince Beisrydd in the Scarlet Robe as thanks for his service to Arawn of the Other World.

The Broch

Located atop the sandstone shelf, 60 feet above the Spring Cave, the broch is 27 feet high, 45 feet in diameter, and built with two concentric walls of stone, with a stairway within the gap created by the two walls leading to the upper floors. The roof is made from a cone of trimmed logs with a smoke hole at the apex for the central fire that is kept burning on the broch's ground floor. Slits in the outer wall allow the warriors who garrison this broch to keep watch across the coast and inland. Where the outer wall meets the wooden roof, a sturdy wooden platform has been built around the circumference allowing for proper watch patrols at the broch's summit.

Inside the broch is divided into three levels. The ground floor is the living area; the first floor is the sleeping gallery and the upper floor is storage - mostly for weapons and gear. The broch's warriors hunt for food every week, finding deer in the nearby forests, and there are plentiful fresh water sources, including the spring in Spring Cave.

The ground floor has a vertical tunnel leading down, directly into the secret chamber where the Coat of Beisrydd is held. The warriors are forbidden to enter the chamber unless directly instructed by Mawgaus and, terrified of what the Druid King would do to them if he were disobeyed, they keep to their instructions: however, because the ancestor spirits Cing and Cruithne have warned Mawgaus of enemies approaching the caves, Mawgaus has sent orders for the armour to be protected while he and his war band ride for the broch from the north.

The broch is home to a war band of 20 Circind Votadini, chosen from among the clans of the nearby hill forts. To protect the Coat of Beisrydd they deploy thus:

- Six come down from the broch to the mouth of the Spring Cave and form a small shield wall across the entrance, preventing escape (without a fight) along the coast.
- Four warriors are present in the chamber to directly protect the armour.
- Six more warriors watch the coast from cliffs above the caves, using bows and spears to attack anyone fleeing along the beach.
- Four more warriors remain inside the broch to attack anyone who overcomes the guards in the armour chamber and tries to escape through the broch itself.

All the Votadini warriors are under orders to take these intruders alive. Mawgaus wants them so they can be sacrificed to the ancestors, their flesh eaten by himself and his personal retinue, and their blood used as ink for more tattoos.

Capture!

If the characters are captured they are held in the broch on the ground level until Mawgaus arrives, approximately 8 hours after their capture. The Votadini confiscate weapons and armour, stripping the characters as much to humiliate them as anything else. Their hands and feet are bound with long, strong, leather thongs which are tied tightly enough to cut into the flesh. Four warriors guard the prisoners while the rest go about their usual chores: patrols, hunting and fetching water. This may offer the characters a chance to escape, if they can break their bonds (Herculean Brawn rolls or Herculean Sleight rolls to untie the knots somehow) and overwhelm the guards. Their equipment is thrown into the storage area on the top floor of the broch.

Mawgaus, when he arrives, is a terrifying sight. He comes with his personal retinue of twelve warriors. All of them are heavily tattooed, but Mawgaus stands out. Tall and imposing, his long hair is spiked and bleached white. His body is a mass of red, blue and black swirling designs and it seems that no part of his flesh is unadorned: he truly is a pictii - a painted one. His eyes are dark and piercing and he radiates power. There is no mistaking that he is

a formidable druid — even though he is like no druid any of the characters are likely to have seen before. He hunkers down before the characters, staring at them for a long time. He tells the guards, using Goidelic, to give them food and water, but he does not order their bonds to be released. Then, he changes to flawless Brythonic.

"Merlin sent you to steal the armour. I know this. I am friends with many spirits who watch our borders and our treasures. They told me through dreams and omens. He sent you because he fears my power. He cowers, like a Christian, behind the Great Wall and sends his puppy dogs to do what he is afraid to do. This is why Britain is broken: because Merlin is unfit to mend it.

Here is what I will do. One of you will live and not be harmed. The rest of you shall be sliced open, your blood drained for ink for my tattoos, your bones broken and your heads boiled until your

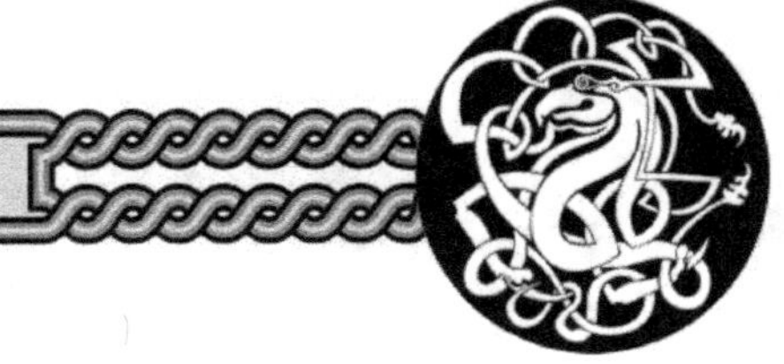

The Broch

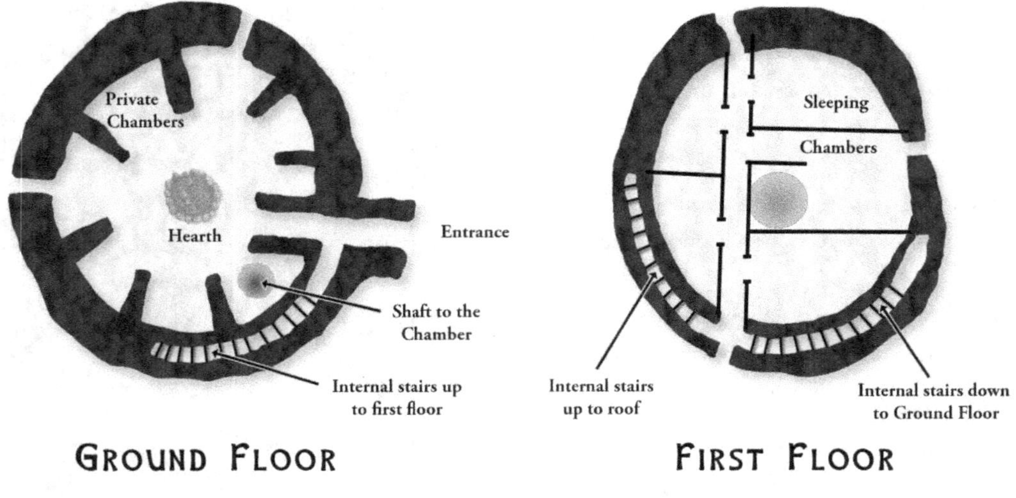

brains shrink and I can swallow them whole. The one who lives will watch all of this. Then he will be given your skulls in a sack to take back to Merlin as message from his friend Mawgaus. This is what we Votadini of Circind do to thieves.

You have until dawn. Choose which of you will live. The rest can prepare for your painful passing into the Other World."

Mawgaus is icily calm as he delivers this speech. There can be no doubting that he means every word, and his retinue of warriors, standing behind him, leer and grin as he describes their fate. Then, he goes to the upper level to sleep, leaving four of his personal warriors to guard the characters and observe as they must make their choice of survivor.

Escaping from Mawgaus and the Votadini will not be easy, but it can be done with some ingenuity and help from the circumstances of the scenario. The following are options and tools that can be used to help the characters survive the fate Mawgaus has promised them.

- *Gawain volunteers himself. Gawain is a noble warrior and he will call on Mawgaus to let the characters survive and take him as a sacrifice instead. Gawain does not fear death. His faith in Christ is all he needs. If this is agreed to, Gawain insists that the characters find his sister, Teneu, at Caer Ysc and tell her what has happened, not to be upset, and that he will wait for her in God's Kingdom. It will require the characters to succeed in a Herculean Influence roll to convince Mawgaus to accept one sacrifice, but when the Druid King learns it is King Lot's son, he is open to persuasion.*
- *Gawain as a rescuer. If the Games Master has decided to let Gawain escape and return later to help the characters, he is able to sneak into the broch, or create a suitable diversion outside, giving the characters the chance to flee Mawgaus*

and his men. Games Masters should improvise the nature of the diversionary tactics.

- *Working a miracle. Christians can call upon God to work a miracle (and if there was any time to call for a miracle, then this might be it). If no priest is present, then the roll is made against the Christian Passion score. Gawain can also help by calling for a miracle too. If successfully called for, God sends an immense storm during the night. Thunder cracks the heavens and lightning lashes the countryside, striking the broch's roof and causing the whole roof to cave in. The characters must make Formidable Athletics or Evade rolls to avoid taking 1d10 damage from falling wood and masonry, but this plunges the broch into chaos as men fall through the broken upper storey and crash to their deaths on the stone floor below. The characters have a chance to make their escape as the Votadini forget their immediate orders and try to save themselves.*
- *Help from the Spirit of the Spring. If the characters encountered, were polite to, charmed, or let the Spirit of the Spring Cave win the riddling contest, she is aware of their predicament and prepared to help. She causes the waters of her spring to build up in the sandstone layers beneath the broch and then explode through the floor and walls in a similar manner to the broch being hit by lightning. The result is enough confusion for the characters to take advantage and make their escape.*
- *The Knife of Farchog. One of the knife's powers is to serve twenty people at a feast: while it is not designed as a weapon, it can be used to help escape. If a character successfully makes a Pagan Passion roll, the knife's power can be activated — with one slice it can sever up to 20 bonds with a single cut. An Insight or appropriate Lore roll might be necessary to work out that the knife can be used in this way. And, although not intended to be as an offensive weapon, it is capable of inflicting 1d2 points of damage and the Bleed Special Effect; if the wielder of the knife successfully inflicts a cut on one enemy, up to 20 enemies also suffer the same cut, in the same place, for the same damage. The character uses a Combat Style involving knife, or uses Unarmed. Resisting the Bleed Special Effect is handled as a Group Sorting Roll (page 52 of MYTHRAS).*

Gawain as the Escape Card

Games Masters might contrive to have Gawain escape if the characters are overwhelmed and taken prisoner. He can be used as a deus-ex-machina to help the characters escape at a later point, appearing at just the right time in the scenario.

The Sacrifice

Escape need not come in the time between Mawgaus's ultimatum and dawn; it can come in the preparation for the promised sacrifice.

The characters, if they have not escaped, are dragged down to the Cave of Serpents. This is where Mawgaus intends to sacrifice them, one-by-one, with the nominated character to be saved watching. The intention is to stake out each character, in a spread-eagle position, on the floor of the cave in a line. Mawgaus then slices the throat of each victim and sets a bowl (made from a human skull) by the neck to collect the blood. As he moves to the next character, one of his warriors slices open the belly of the first and carefully arranges the entrails so that they can be seen by all watching. Once the characters are dead, their heads are severed and plunged into a cauldron of boiling sea water, and left to cook until all the flesh has been cleaned from the bone. The shrunken brains are extracted and served to Mawgaus and his warriors: the remaining skulls are given to the character nominated to return to Merlin.

This is, of course, a ghastly situation for the characters to find themselves in, and, unless a swift (and miserable) end to the campaign is needed, then some last-ditch escape attempt should come at this point.

Fleeing the Caves

The ideal scenario is that the characters retrieve the Coat of Beisrydd, evade capture and hightail it to their hidden ship. Mawgaus and his warriors will give chase, hurling spears and loosing arrows at the characters as they make for the secret cove where Nubh waits for them. Conduct the chase as a desperate flight for survival but an opportunity for combat. Mawgaus's warriors are far more competent than those who garrison the broch, and Mawgaus will not let the characters run off with the Coat of Beisrydd without a strong fight; it is possible the characters will be injured and some may even be killed in attempting to get away, but, once Nubh's boat puts to sea, the Votadini must abandon the pursuit and let the characters go.

Mawgaus though, is not without one last trick. Watching the characters flee, he curses them, howling his curse so loudly that it carries across the waves to the character's ears. He curses their loved ones to die within a year and day, and promises that the lord Aywell, God of the Votadini, will deny them - and the characters — the right to the Other World for all eternity. Have the characters make Willpower rolls modified by their Superstition. If the Willpower roll is failed, then the characters believe the curse. It is up to the Games Master how the curse then manifests (and whether it is, in fact, real); but Mawgaus intends its effects to be long-term, subtle, and a slow retribution for their theft of the Votadini's treasure.

Concluding the Scenario

Gawain is quiet and reflective on the journey back to Red Marsh. The sea is still as rough as before, but this time Nubh avoids Lindisfarena and beaches for the night in a small, secluded cove. Gawain prays, alone, and only speaks if questioned - and then only gives the briefest of answers.

The return to Red Marsh is uneventful. The people of the fishing village have kept their side of the bargain and expect payment as promised, which Gawain ensures the characters pay, if they seem reluctant.

As the characters make their way back to Caer Ysc, a lone figure can be seen on the path ahead, stumping determinedly along. It does not take long to recognise the figure of Merlin, even though he wears a hood over his head and has changed from his usual druid robes into less recognisable travelling garb. He greets the characters and insists they dismount, make camp, and tell him what happened. Naturally he wants to see the Coat of Beisrydd and is delighted when the characters display it. But, if they also bring forth the Knife of Farchog, he is overjoyed. "So Ofydd had it all along, did he? The sly old goat. I suspected as much but couldn't be sure. I thought perhaps Lot had it. But this is splendid! Splendid! I had not expected you to bring back one treasure, let alone two"

Gawain watches Merlin sullenly and, finally, asks the druid if his bargain is now repaid. "To me?" Merlin asks. "Of course. You owe me nothing. Never did. You simply used this 'debt' as an excuse to get back at your tribe. But I'm grateful for your help. Even if you are a Christian these days."

Gawain is angered at this, but Merlin doesn't care. "I can tell you now, though, that Arthur wants you. Or if he doesn't, he soon will. Come to Caer Cadbryg. Bring Teneu and don't leave it any later than when the first leaves fall from the oak trees. But, for now, go home. Go to Caer Ysc and rest. I have work to do"

The characters may, if they wish, return to Caer Ysc with Gawain. Merlin says he needs no accompaniment, but if they want something to do, they should go to Caer Cadbryg without delay. "Arthur will have work for you," he says. "Things are getting interesting"

Non-Player Characters

Queen Elliw of the Brigantes

Characteristics	Attributes	1d20	Location	AP/HP
STR: 10	Action Points: 3	1–3	Right Leg	0/6
CON: 16	Damage Modifier: 0	4–6	Left Leg	0/6
SIZ: 11	Magic Points: 18	7–9	Abdomen	0/7
DEX: 10	Movement: 6 metres	10–12	Chest	0/8
INT: 18	Initiative Bonus: 14	13–15	Right Arm	0/5
POW: 18	Armour: None	16–18	Left Arm	0/5
CHA: 14		19–20	Head	0/6

Skills: *Athletics 28%, Brawn 15%, Customs (Celt) 100%, Deceit 78%, Endurance 33%, Evade 32%, Influence 87%, Insight 85%, Language (Brythonic) 100%, Lore (Politics) 85%, Lore (Strategy and Tactics) 70%, Perception 70%, Superstition 80%, Unarmed 31%, Willpower 90%,*

Loyalty to Brigantes 100%, Loyalty to Britain 60%, Mistrust Pagans 75%, Christian 100%

Combat Style: None.

Typical Circind Votadini Warrior

Attributes	1d20	Location	AP/HP
Action Points: 2	1–3	Right Leg	2/6
Damage Modifier: +1d2	4–6	Left Leg	2/6
Magic Points: 11	7–9	Abdomen	2/7
Movement: 6 metres	10-12	Chest	2/8
Initiative Bonus: 10	13–15	Right Arm	2/5
Armour: Leather	16–18	Left Arm	2/5
Abilities: None	19–20	Head	2/6

Skills: Athletics 59%, Brawn 62%, Endurance 62%, Evade 56%, Locale 66%, Perception 64%, Ride 85%, Survival 67%, Unarmed 59%, Willpower 62%

Passions: Loyalty to Mawgaus 80%, Love Battle 70%

Combat Style: Circind Warrior (Sword, Spear, Sling, Shield. Trait, Skirmishing) 75%

Weapon	Size/Force	Reach	Damage	AP/HP
Shortspear	*M*	*L*	*1d8+1d2*	*4/5*
Shortsword	*M*	*M*	*1d6+1d2*	*6/10*
Celtic Shield	*H*	*S*	*1d3+1+1d2*	*4/15*

Cing and Cruithne: Ancestor Guardians of the Circind

This malign pair are two of the Great Ancestors of the Votadini, heroes from ancient times who have pledged to guard Circind's borders and destroy its enemies.

Both are Intensity 5 Ancestor spirits, and Cing commands Folk Magic spells that can be cast at their enemies in the Spirit World. Cruithne has the Discorporate ability at 70%.

Mawgaus can call upon both spirits to aid him, if needed.

Cing and Cruithne				
Ancestor (Intensity)	INT, POW, CHA	Customs & Lore	Spectral Combat & Willpower	Abilities
Cing (5)	10, 31, 14	120%	95%, 111%	Folk Magic 124% (Bladesharp, Demoralise, Fanaticism)
Cruithne (5)	12, 33, 8	124%	70%, 116%	Insight 120%, Discorporate 70%

Mawgaus, Druid-King of the Circind Votadini

Characteristics	Attributes	1d20	Location	AP/HP
STR: 13	Action Points: 3	1–3	Right Leg	0/6
CON: 14	Damage Modifier: +1d2	4–6	Left Leg	0/6
SIZ: 14	Magic Points: 18	7–9	Abdomen	2/7
DEX: 10	Movement: 6 metres	10–12	Chest	0/8
INT: 18	Initiative Bonus: 14	13–15	Right Arm	0/5
POW: 18	Armour: Leather	16–18	Left Arm	0/5
CHA: 14		19–20	Head	0/6

Skills: *Athletics 37%, Brawn 33%, Customs (Celt) 100%, Endurance 49%, Evade 44%, Insight 95%, Language (Brythonic) 40%, Language (Goidelic) 100%, Lore (Ancestor Spirits) 90%, Perception 84%, Unarmed 46%, Willpower 85%,*

Binding 90%, Trance 95%

Loyalty to Circind 100%, Pagan 100%, Hate Christians 90%

Combat Style: Gododdin Warrior (Spear, Sword and Shield. Trait, Mounted Combat) 81%

Weapon	Size/Force	Reach	Damage	AP/HP
Shortspear	*M*	*L*	*1d8+1d2*	*4/5*
Longsword	*M*	*M*	*1d6+2+1d2*	*6/10*
Celtic Shield	*H*	*S*	*1d3+1+1d2*	*4/15*

Mawgaus is a potent druid. Although he has no bound spirits, he has powerful spirit allies in the form of a High Wing, an eagle Predator Spirit who hunts for knowledge whenever Mawgaus consumes a new brain, and Luithne, his personal Ancestor spirit who grants the druid several spells. Mawgaus can easily enter the Spirit World and command other spirits as he so needs, but High Wing and Luithne are his trusted and most favoured spirit allies.

High Wing (Intensity 4 Predator Spirit)
Spectral Claws and Beak 98%, Stealth 98%, Willpower 88%

Luithne (Intensity 5 Ancestor Spirit)
INT 17, POW 34, CHA 12
Lore (Celt) 134%, Spectral Circind Warrior 96%, Willpower 74%

Luithne knows the Theism miracles Corruption, Fear and Heart Seizure. They are cast at Intensity 5 and on a successful roll of 50% or less. Although Luithne provides the magic, Mawgaus channels it, using his own Magic Points to do so.

Gullveig's Children

The Saxon warlord Cerdic and his son Cynric arrive on Dumnonia's southern coast, intent on capturing Dumnonia. Arthur mobilizes the Alliance of Britain to halt Cerdic's advance and inflict devastating casualties on this new influx of invaders. The characters are required to undertake a daring mission on Ynys Wyt designed to keep the Saxons contained.

Cerdic's Arrival

In the autumn of 495 Cerdic and his son Cynric, with five ships filled with men, land on the south coast of Britain in the kingdom of Dumnonia. The landing takes place in two waves: first, Cynric attacks and captures the island of Ynys Wyt, intending to secure it so that the sea passage known as The Solent is fully under Saxon command, giving them control also over key ports and bays on the Dumnonian coast. Meanwhile Cerdic pushes into the estuary of the River Test, bringing him into Dumnonia proper.

This attack has come sooner than the Alliance of Britain anticipated. Natanleod and Havgan of Dumnonia mobilize their war bands: Havgan's aim is to halt - and destroy, if possible - Cerdic's main force. Havgan is to secure the coast. Meanwhile, war bands from Powys and Gwent march south to help reinforce Dumnonia.

Cerdic's army consists of no more than 350 warriors: however, more are on their way, and this is why securing Ynys Wyt and The Solent is of paramount importance - so that these reserves have a safe port of landing waiting for them when they complete the journey from the Germanian coast. Cerdic has taken the bulk of the warriors, leaving Cynric with 50 to garrison Ynys Wyt.

This scenario concerns itself with an assault on Ynys Wyt and retaking it from Cynric, while Natanleod and war bands from powys engage with Cerdic. Ynys Wyt is home to a small monastery that has been captured and the kingdoms of Powys and Gwent, as is Lord Custennin of Dumnonia, are adamant that it should be freed. The characters are responsible for the task, under the command of Havgan, although both Merlin and Morgana have ideas about how they can help.

War Meeting at Caer Sulis

The Council of War is called with Caer Sulis, the seat of Lord Custennin, as the rallying place. Locale or Lore (Strategy and Tactics) rolls from characters mean they immediately understand that this is a sound strategic and political move. Custennin is a Christian, and Caer Sulis is closest to the Christian kingdoms of Gwent and Powys: if Arthur and the other commanders want to be certain of the support of the Alliance, recognizing Gwent and Powys's importance is crucial.

Caer Sulis overlooks the old Roman town of Sulis, where numerous pagan gods, including the spirit goddess Sulevia, are still worshipped — alongside a hotchpotch of Christian chapels and shrines to the saints. Sulis is a holy place for pagans and Christians, and it is where the characters are billeted when they return from their recent exploits (Caer Ysc, and in Gawain's company, if this scenario is following directly on from *Caves of the Circind*). A walled city, much of the old Roman splendour has fallen to recent ruin, with stones from the walls and buildings being taken for use elsewhere.

Still, Sulis is a marvel: the streets are neatly paved with tightly-packed cobbles and the array of streets converge, from two directions, on the Temples of Minerva and Sulevia: the largest, grandest structures in the city, and located next to the natural hot springs that are a sure sign of a connection to Sulevia's realm in the Spirit World. The sulfurous waters bubble and pop, and the Romans channelled these waters into the large baths that are occasionally used by those who want to cleanse and to propitiate the Great Spirit of Sulevia by being embraced in her breath and blood. It is customary for pagans to come to the Temple, make a small offering or prayer, and then either sip the bubbling waters or bathe in them. There are several areas where one can inscribe a wish, blessing or curse onto a pebble and toss it into the waters. Sulevia, if willing, accepts whatever is written on the stone and ensures it comes to pass.

When the characters arrive, someone is already proselytising on the raised stones by the Pool of Offerings. Morgana, Arthur's wild-haired and wild-eyed sister, is imploring everyone — locals and warriors assembled for the council — to curse the Saxons, Cerdic and his bastard son Cynric. Plenty are taking-up the suggestion, and there is a healthy throng of people scratching onto stones and tossing them into the steaming waters. The characters can use Stealth rolls to avoid being seen by Morgana, but if they do not beat her Perception in an opposed roll, she catches sight of them and starts to harangue them if they do not make their own curses. She smiles, perhaps a little ominously, as the characters complete their curses, and nods her head in gratitude as each stone plops into the pool.

Away from the temples, more proselytising is happening: this time it is Samsun, from Caer Cadbryg, and a tall man with a shock of black hair. Christians who succeed in a Hard Locale or Christian Passion roll recognize the tall man as Bishop Gerhaint, the priest in charge of the famed Chapel of the Thorn near Glestinga. Gerhaint is extolling to a growing crowd of Christians, encouraging them to abandon the pagan practice of cursing and, instead, put their faith in God and Jesus. In what seems to be a carefully rehearsed pattern, Gerhaint makes a declaration and then Samsun, kneeling beside him, screams 'Amen!' or 'Blessed Lord!', leading the crowd to the do the same. Samsun is too enraptured to notice the characters, but clearly there is competition between gods, prophets and priests for the hearts and minds of those who have come to Aqua Sulis. Gerhaint is calling for the 'souls of Ynys Wyt' to be spared and, if any of the characters ask what he means, someone listening to the sermon explains: "The monastery on Ynys Wyt was seized by Cynric. He's turned all the monks into slaves and made the chapels into pagan shrines!' He or she then hastily makes the sign of the cross, cries an 'Amen' in time with Samsun, and shakes a weary, pitying head.

The old city is busy, but there is plenty to keep everyone occupied. Open-fronted houses selling ale, mead, and food, including the superb fish caught from the river outside the city walls, are popular places for warriors and war bands to hang around and kill time. There are dice games, board games, wrestling matches, spear and sword sparring all taking place and the city has more of a festival atmosphere than as a rallying point in the prelude to war. It isn't difficult for the characters to find somewhere to stay and pick-up information and gossip. Call for Perception rolls to learn 1d3 from the following.

The Rumour Mill (1d10)

1. Cerdic has beached his boats on the River Test and is marching inland. Natanleod and his war bands have marched south already and occupied the high ground overlooking the Test.
2. Natanleod's druids, Ceidmon and Birkita, are preparing rituals to call on the Great Spirits of the rivers Ayvon and Test to rise up and drown Cerdic. Some say they have one of the Treasures of Britain, recently found, to help them.
3. All the monks of the Ynys Wyt monastery are dead - butchered by Cynric's Saxons - and the abbey put to the torch. Nothing can be done for them except pray for their souls.
4. The feeling is that Cerdic can be easily contained and most likely beaten by Natanleod, but war bands from Powys will be sent to reinforce. War bands from Gwent are heading towards the western side of the coast where they will join with Havgan and launch an assault on Ynys Wyt.
5. All this excitement in Dumnonia, involving Powys and Gwent, leaves Gwent vulnerable to raids by the Silures. They've been waiting for a chance to raid into Gwent, and here it is - courtesy of the Saxons.
6. The Saxons are not working alone. It's said that the Irish are providing auxiliaries in return for territories such as Gwynedd and Powys.
7. The Saxons are not working alone. King Mark is up to his old tricks and is going to allow Cerdic's supporting ships to land in Kernow and attack from the west — just like he did when Uther, Mordred and Arthur held them off.
8. Cerdic hasn't brought many men because he doesn't need them. The Saxons have strange magic and their priest-sorcerers, the laece, are in league with demons.
9. The Saxons on Ynys Wyt captured the monastery so they can sacrifice the monks to their gods and gain the help of the giants that once ruled Britain. These giants are the size of mountains and made of ice.
10. Arthur was asked to garrison Ynys Wyt but refused. So did Natanleod. That's why they're trying to get Powys and Gwent's help now: because they knew the monks on the island were vulnerable.

Rumours, Rumours

There's a little truth to all the above rumours - with the exceptions of 7 and 8. However, Games Masters may want to embellish this scenario and their Mythic Britain campaign by making some of these rumours far more substantial. What if the Saxons are attempting to summon Ice Giants? What if the Irish are in league with the Saxons? Perhaps the Silures are? These are all tempting possibilities for a truly intriguing *Mythic Britain* campaign.

At the Council

Several bards are sent down to Aqua Sulis to summon the rank and file to hear the decisions of the Council of Britain. Some war bands go in their entirety; others send representatives to listen and report back. The characters can decide what they intend to do, but someone from the group needs to be in attendance.

Custennin's hall is a sombre place. In contrast to other halls the characters have visited, it lacks warmth (Custennin only ever has a fire lit for a coldest days) and hospitality (Custennin is a very frugal man). It is packed with people and, at the far end, Dumnonia's three warlords (Natanleod is already en-route to engage Cerdic) have been joined by King Meurig of Gwent and King Cyngen of Powys. These latter two, being Christians, are seated close to Lord Custennin, and their advisers, Bishops Dyfrig and Frych, are nearby. They are in discussion as Arthur rises and calls for order.

"We knew Cerdic was coming and we know he is just the first of many. Lord Natanleod's war bands are already marching to give him a warm welcome to this green and pleasant land! I shall reinforce him, and so my war bands will march tomorrow to ensure that Cerdic has nowhere to flee to and must face us.

There is another important matter. Cerdic's son, Cynric, holds Ynys Wyt. He must be driven from it so that the passage between

the isle and mainland, the Solent, is not under Saxon control. A small monastery on Ynys Wit has also been seized, and its brothers, all worthy and devout men of Gwent, have been imprisoned. War bands from Powys and Gwent, supported by the spears of Lord Havgan, will approach the isle from the south west and invade it. We shall retake Ynys Wyt and save the good monks from the Saxons!"

A loud cheer echoes through the hall and the Christian contingent appear to be very happy with Arthur's decisions. The different warlords and kings make their own addresses, ensuring all present know their orders; afterwards, Bishops Dyfrig and Frych lead a lengthy prayer for Britain's success against the heathen invaders. At the prayer's conclusion, Arthur leaves the gathering and pushes has way towards the characters. "Walk with me," he says.

As they walk, Arthur talks. "You have performed several errands for Merlin, and this is well and good, but now I would have you perform an errand for me - and one that is not pagan in nature. Your experiences in Ratae showed you have some skill in slipping into the enemy's territory and managing to escape cleanly when you have done what you were sent to do.

"I want you to get close to the monastery on Ynys Wyt. Find out what fate has befallen the monks and, if they live, where they are held and how they are held. Bring this news to Lord Havgan so that it can be given to King Meurig in the most appropriate way and most appropriate time. If the monks are dead, then try to discover how they were killed. We've heard tell that Cynric has some kind of priest or magician with him: we want to know who this is and something of their powers, if possible.

"This is a dangerous task. If you find yourself in a position of having to kill, do not hesitate. If any of the monks can be saved, do so. But your priority is information. Lord Havgan is aware of this part of the plan, but King Meurig and his people should remain ignorant. King Meurig believes that a straightforward assault on the monastery is the best way to retake it: he believes God will preserve the lives of the monks. Lord Havgan and I are more pragmatic. Intelligence is what's needed here, and I feel you are the ones to obtain it."

A direct request like this from someone like Arthur cannot be refused easily. If the characters try to, Arthur expresses grave disappointment and uses a series of arguments to talk them round, implying that the Alliance of Britain commands them. He also mentions that Merlin is well aware of this plan and, in fact, fully supports it. One way or another, he works on persuading them to scout the monastery. There is a chance for great glory, the thanks of King Meurig, and the thanks of the church. On this last point, Arthur adds something that may well compel them. "The monasteries, despite being places of simple living, are wealthy. The monastery on Ynys Wyt has a great deal of silver, along with a lock of the beard of John the Baptist. Bishops Dyfrig and Frych would ensure that anyone who helps the monastery would be well rewarded."

Gawain

Gawain has come south to help Arthur, as Merlin requested he do at the end of the last scenario. He can either accompany the characters - and, indeed, as a devout Christian, but one with an understanding of pagan lore, he may be very useful - or he can form part of either Havgan's main war band, or that of either of the Christian kings (Meurig, Custennin or Cyngen). Remember that Gawain has been a mercenary for some time and is used to working with many different lords. Whatever capacity he is used in, he speaks highly of the characters (unless something went truly and badly awry in the previous scenario).

The Situation on Ynys Wyt

The island is sparsely populated: peasant farmers, fishermen and a few crafters, plus the monks of the monastery. Cynric has managed to subdue the island with no more than 50 men because, although it had a chieftain, Bricce, he was old and did not have the respect of his spearmen. Bricce mounted a half-hearted defence, but the well-trained Saxons of Cynric's war band easily defeated the scant resistance shown. Bricce was thrown into the sea, along with several of his warriors, and the rest told to flee - which is how news of what Cynric has done came to Arthur's ears.

The monks offered no resistance. Their abbot attempted to convince Cynric that the monastery had no gold or silver, but the

monks' trove was quickly unearthed when Cynric sliced open the abbot's throat and threatened to kill one monk every minute until the treasure was produced. Cynric has left a small force of 15 warriors to guard the monastery; he, meanwhile, has been touring the island with his warriors, pillaging what can be pillaged, and reinforcing that this is now Saxon land. He has pairs of mounted warriors patrolling the coastline and keeping a watch-out for likely resistance, but this is stretching his forces too thin and there is no way he can hope to watch every possible beach, bay and port.

With Cynric is the laece, Aelfles. Aelfles claims to channel the spirit of Gullveig, the patron god of witches and evil women. She wants to sacrifice the monks to Gullveig, raze their monastery, and so bring Gullveig's magic to Britain, and with it Gullveig's monstrous children: Hel, Fenrir and Jormungand. Aelfles is an expert at commanding the spirits of fire — the element that three times tried, and three times failed, to kill Gullveig. She is desperate to burn the monks, and Cynric has said that she can, but only if his father approves. However Aelfes is not a patient woman and she has decided to take matters into her own hands. After all, what can Cerdic and Cynric do? They are mortals, but she is inhabited by the spirit of a goddess.

Reaching Ynys Wyt

The characters are instructed to join with Havgan's war band, which is marching due south to the Dumnonian coast, where it will meet with the Gwentish war bands. Havgan is not the sort to wait on anyone else, and he moves quickly, so the characters have to match Havgan's pace. Unlike most warlords he does not ride, preferring to walk with the men, sharing jokes, singing songs and generally being part of the throng.

At a rest point Havgan calls the characters over so he can brief them. "Arthur's told me the job you've been given. Here's my part in it. I've sent word ahead that a boat is to be made ready for you. You'll sail ahead and make land on the north east coast of Ynys Wyt. There's a secluded bay, so I'm told, and you can head into the forest if you follow your noses towards the south. The monastery is built in a clearing. There's a quarry due west of the place, so if you find the quarry and head east, you'll find the monastery.

"I'll be about one day behind you. I'm going to land on the south coast of the island. Meurig will land on the west coast. We'll both push into the centre of the island and hopefully flush out this Saxon bastard, either driving him to the north coast or forcing him to stand and fight wherever he is. When you've found out what's happening with these monks, come and find me. Look towards the centre and the south of the island."

A Christian Perspective

If the characters are predominantly Christian, and the Games Master wishes to give this scenario a more Christian angle (to contrast with the pagan nature of earlier scenarios) then the characters receive the same briefing, but this time by Bishop Dyfrig, King Meurig's chief adviser. Dyfrig gives the same instructions as Havgan, and Havgan provides off-stage back-up.

As the sun sets, the characters reach the coast, finding a wide bay accessed via a steep, winding path that goes to the beach. Several boats, with Dummonian owners and crews, are waiting, and Havgan points-out the smallest of the vessels that the characters will take. There are three crewmen, who row, steer the vessel and manage the single sail. They know this coastline intimately and the captain assures the characters that he can get them safely to the bay closest to the monastery without being seen. "I know every wave, ripple, rock, pebble and reef. Them Saxons won't see us. We sail on this moon-tide, so get aboard."

Even though the sea is relatively calm, there is always the chance of sea-sickness. Games Masters can use the same rules for managing sea-sickness as from the previous scenario (page 301). It only takes about 2.5 hours for the small boat the reach the southerly shore of Ynys Wyt, and then a further half hour of carefully navigating around to the north west stretch of the island, and the secluded bay the characters have been told about. The captain brings the boat as close to the beach as he can, so the characters can wade ashore, but then he turns his boat around and steals back towards the sea, returning the same way he came.

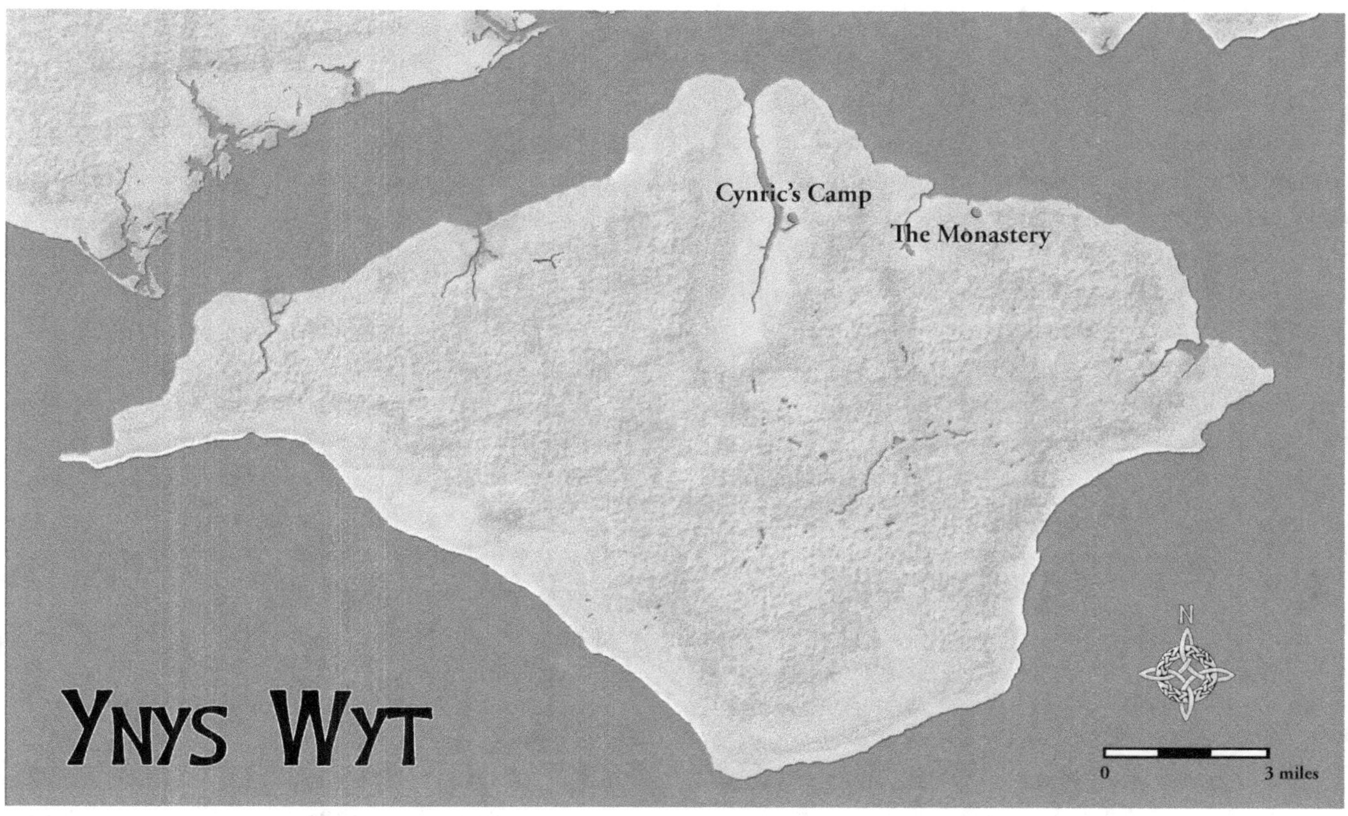

About Ynys Wyt

From here, the characters are on their own and need to find their way to the monastery. The island is roughly diamond shaped, 20 miles wide and 17 miles north to south. At night, there is a 10% chance of the characters experiencing a random encounter (see Ynys Wyt Encounters, below), rising to 25% during daylight.

The island is heavily forested in the north east and down the eastern side, whilst the rest of the island is a mixture of pasture and uncultivated moorland. Most of Ynys Wyt is reasonably flat: the hilliest part is on the western side of the island. Ynys Wyt has been under the control of Bricce's extended clan for as long as anyone can remember. The Romans called the island Vectis and they annexed it from a clan of the Durotriges tribe, known as the Wyt. After the Romans left the Wyt clan found it had outlived the rest of the Durotriges tribe and decided not to involve itself in Dumnonia's affairs, having first sided with Vortigern before, grudgingly, changing allegiance to Uther after Vortigern's murder. The clan converted to Christianity when Gwent sent some of its first missionaries, fifty years ago, and several miracles were performed on the island. The leader of the missionaries, a priest called Selwyn, had ventured to Rome and returned with a lock of the beard of John the Baptist; this brought power to Ynys Wyt, and the stories say that the spirit of John the Baptist appeared to the islanders on numerous occasions, hastening their conversion. The monastery was established by Selwyn at the site where John the Baptist first appeared, not far from the quarry.

Over the years the island became more and more devout. It also became more determined to remain aloof from Dumnonia. Bricce did not attend the Winter Council and had abstained from the Alliance of Britain. Natanleod had warned him, several times, that Ynys Wyt was vulnerable to Saxon attack, but stubborn old Bricce knew better: his swift and undignified demise signalled the end of the Wyt clan's rule.

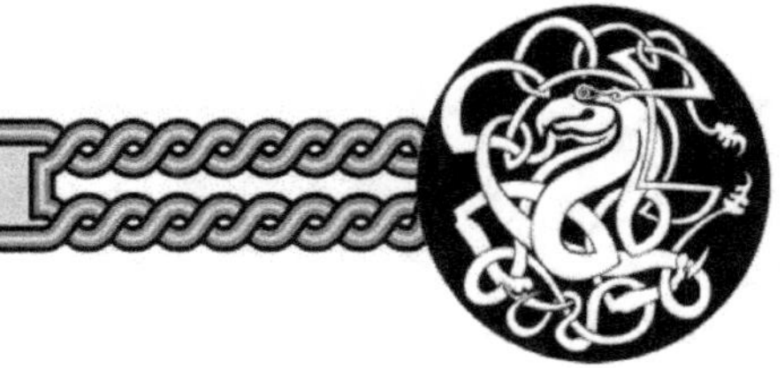

Before the Romans arrived Ynys Wyt had many spirits and the island itself was a very powerful spirit, on a par with the great river spirits such as Sabrinna and Tamesis. However, with the arrival of the Romans the druids lost most of the power and never really reclaimed it; as Christianity grew stronger, so the spirits retired wholly to the Spirit World and Wyt's magical energy dissipated. However, any druid character setting foot on Ynys Wyt can still feel the island's residual energy. Even though the spirits have left Ynys Wyt, something of their presence remains: in time, and with much work, the spirits could be summoned back. Of course, Aelfles has sensed much the same thing, and decided to harness Ynys Wyt's magical energy for her own, dreadful goddess. The battle for Ynys Wyt is therefore more than simply a battle for land: it is a battle for both a magical and religious resource.

Ynys Wyt Encounters

Roll 1d6 (or choose according to situation, location and mood)

1. Large Saxon Patrol. This is a patrol sent by Cynric to maintain a presence in the centre of Ynys Wyt. It consists of four mounted Saxon warriors (use the statistics on page 213) who challenge everyone they meet to prove their identity and role on the island. Anyone bearing obvious arms and armour is challenged in the Saxon tongue with a failure to respond being met with force. These warriors are keen to capture potential Briton spies for (painful) interrogation leading to a slow death.
2. Small Saxon Patrol. A foot patrol of a pair of Saxon warriors who are weary after tramping the coastal path watching for interlopers. If overwhelmed, they make an attempt to flee. If they can, they aim to kill their opponents: they have no interest in taking prisoners — only making examples. They use the statistics on page 213, but treat them as Tired from their long walk.
3. Escaped Monk. Callws is a young monk of the monastery who was out collecting kindling when the Saxons first struck. He managed to evade capture and has continued to do so for several days now — although on a couple of occasions he has come close to being spotted by patrols. Callws is hungry, dirty, cold and frightened. His habit is ripped, his feet cut, and he has a wild, desperate look in his eye. He regards anyone carrying a spear as an enemy - but he is more frightened of Aelfles, the woman he refers to simply as The Witch. He watched her have one of the monks broken and then set ablaze, summoning a fire spirit from his burning remains. Callws is therefore the one person who can confirm Aelfles' powers as a magician and he continually appeals to God and Jesus to deliver all mankind from such evil. Getting him to stay put, let alone talk, requires a successful Formidable Influence roll opposed by his current emotional state of Terrified 80%. If calmed down, has his wounds are treated, is given food and water, and reassured, then he can reveal roughly how many are guarding the monastery, and, of course, Aelfles' presence. He knows that although some of the monks were butchered by the Saxons, including the abbot, at least half of them still live although they are kept under guard. He can lead the characters to the monastery and help point out the best ways of getting in and out.
4. Cynric's Patrol. Occasionally, Cynric leads his own patrol. This is a six-strong, mounted war band led by Cerdic's son himself. There is a 45% chance that Aelfles accompanies the patrol. They behave as for the Large Saxon Patrol described above, save that Cynric is desperate to take prisoners so he can learn more about the Britons. He is intrigued by Christianity: the idea of a single God, rather than many, is a new and fascinating idea. He is keen to learn more and, although he is in no danger of converting to Christianity, he is inclined to question Christians with genuine interest and enthusiasm. In conversing with, or simply observing (Insight rolls) Cynric, it becomes apparent that while he is clearly ambitious and keen to forge a new kingdom in Britain, he is more respectful of the Celts than other Saxons. If he and Arthur could meet and talk, it would, perhaps, be a good thing - and there is something of Arthur's character in Cynric: a curiosity and intelligence that goes beyond the brute defeat of apparent enemies. If Cynric is captured, he makes a fine hostage and even Havgan understands the importance of holding Cerdic's son to terms.
5. Islanders. A group of suspicious Wyt islanders — peasants or similar — mistake the characters for the invading

Saxons. They've gathered their courage and staged an ambush using makeshift spears, stones, knives and fishing nets. There number is equal to the characters' number +2, and their intention is to surprise and take revenge on the Saxons who've come to seize their island. It requires some effort to convince the islanders that they are, instead friends and not the enemy: the islanders fight for two rounds before anyone can attempt to convince them otherwise. If the islanders suffer a beating, they soon surrender (half try to flee) and, once they realise the characters are Britons, then they offer abject apologies and grovel for forgiveness. In return, they can provide some information on patrols, help the characters navigate the island, gain shelter and so on.

6. The Burning Man. When the monastery was attacked, Aelfles decided to demonstrate the power of her goddess, the Thrice Burned Gullveig, to the monks. One of them was seized, tied to a stake and set alight. As he burned, Aelfles bound into the immolating body a Fire Elemental spirit. This is the fire spirit seen by Callws, as mentioned earlier. The poor monk's body has become the fetish for this bound elemental and Aefles has, cruelly, sent it to roamWyt, bringing terror and spreading her fearsome reputation. The elemental is an Intensity 1 (6 cubic feet) Elemental Spirit and it uses its own intellect and characteristics to cause the charred remains of the monk to walk. The body is a hideous black cadaver, smoke rising from its husked skin, the eyes long-since melted and the fury of the elemental's fire is visible as purple flame as the thing opens and closes its mouth in a cruel parody of breathing. The Burning Man has the following characteristics:. The ground where the Burning Man walks is charred and scorched. Anything flammable within 3 feet stands a chance of igniting if the Burning Man remains stationary for more than 1 minute. In time, the fire elemental will completely consume the corpse it animates and be released to the Spirit World but, for now, it is bound to the Mortal World and abhors all life.

The Burning Man

Characteristics	Attributes	1d20	Location	AP/HP
STR: 15	Action Points: 2	1–3	Right Leg	0/2
CON: 3	Damage Modifier: +1d2	4–6	Left Leg	0/2
SIZ: 11	Magic Points: 10	7–9	Abdomen	0/3
DEX: 7	Movement: 3 metres	10–12	Chest	0/4
INS: 11	Initiative Bonus: 9	13–15	Right Arm	0/1
POW: 10	Armour: None. Hit Points reflect the growing fragility of the immolated body.	16–18	Left Arm	0/1
CHA: 0		19–20	Head	0/2

Skills: *Athletics 22%, Brawn 50%, Endurance 12%, Evade 56%, Perception 49%, Unarmed 30%, Willpower 75%*

Combat Style

Burning Man (Unarmed) 30%. The Burning Man can gout Intensity 3 Fire (Mythras, page 79) at targets up to 10 feet away. If the Burning Man makes contact with an opponent, its flesh radiates Intensity 3 fire damage as heat, and it attempts to use the Grip Special Effect to maintain a hold and so cause damage each round. If the body holding the elemental is reduced to 0 or lower hit points in the Abdomen, Chest or Head, it breaks the binding and releases the elemental which rushes back to the Spirit World. However, it has one, last Engulfing attack as it blasts forth from the body. Anyone within 6 feet of the rapidly dissipating elemental sustains 1d6 damage to 1d6+1 Hit Locations unless they can successfully roll against Evade (unopposed) to throw themselves clear.

Weapon	Size/Force	Reach	Damage	AP/HP
Hands	*M*	*T*	*1d2+1d6*	*As for Arm*

The Quarry

Established by the Romans, this quarry produces good-quality limestone although it is many years since the quarry was actively worked. It was last used by the monks and local labourers to build the nearby monastery, using crude and rudimentary cutting and shaping techniques.

The quarry is a wide, semi-circular pit formed by steep shelves where blocks of stone are cut by hand from the earth. There are several natural and man-made caves in the quarry and it offers a good hiding place if one wishes to avoid pursuit. The Saxons believe the witch, Aelfles, when she says the quarry is a gateway to the Underworld, and so they tend to avoid it. However, if desperate and pressed, the Saxons will descend the limestone ledges in pursuit of anyone they are hunting on a successful Hard Willpower roll.

The quarry makes a good place to encounter the Islanders, the Escaped Monk or even The Burning Man. It also forms a good base for reconnoitring the monastery — somewhere to quickly fall back if pursued.

The Monastery

East of the quarry is reasonably dense forest. There are typical game animals and small clearings used by charcoal burners. About two miles from the quarry, the woodland has been substantially cleared to make way for the monastery formed by Selwyn some fifty years ago. Close by is a decent stream and there are two underground streams that the monks have dug into, creating a well.

The clearing is large enough to support forage for pigs - the chief source of protein for the monks - chicken coops and runs and a vegetable garden. Everything is enclosed by a stout wall of local limestone and, even though this is a place of religious contemplation, it is remarkably well fortified. The perimeter wall is high enough to slow down assailants and, if the wall can be adequately defended, only the most determined will get in. The monks were not expecting any form of attack, and the arrival of Cerdic and Cynric took them wholly by surprise: if they had had warning and the support of some of Bricce's war bands, then things might have been different for the Saxons.

The wall surrounding the monastery is seven feet high and a foot and a half thick. It is dry-stone, with limestone blocks and slabs expertly locked together with smaller stones. Even though it uses no mortar, it is very strong and resistant to direct attack. The compound it forms is 260 feet across. Selwyn designed the monastery with the intention that it should have ample room for growth, not doubting for one second that many would want to come and make the place their spiritual home. There is therefore a lot of open space, the plan being that subsequent generations would expand the size of the chapel, or build additional chapels, and that more dormitories would also be required. Selwyn was very much inspired by similar monasteries seen on his travels to and from Rome, and the Ynys Wyt monastery is unlike any other monastery found in Britain.

Before the Saxons arrived, the monastery was home to 35 monks, a mixture of locals and men from Gwent and Powys. The Saxon's raid resulted in the deaths of 6 monks: the abbot, the monk Aelfles sacrificed to Gullveig, and four others who either attempted to resist the warriors or, in the case of old Gethin, died of a heart attack. Callws, the youngest member of the order, escaped. The 28 survivors are kept in the dormitory building until Cerdic and Cynric decide what to do with them. At present, Aelfles is in command and she is very keen to sacrifice more of the monks to her goddess. The monks are forbidden to pray, and Aelfles has ordered the warriors to beat senseless anyone who so much as mutters a prayer or psalm.

The Saxon garrison is 15-strong, including Aelfles. The warriors are bored, waiting for Cerdic to defeat the Britons and return to Wyt (or send news of what to do with the monks), and spend their time drinking and eating their way through the monastery stores, and tormenting the monks simply for something to do. One of their favourite games is to fashion makeshift bridles from rope and then ride the fitter of the monks around the compound, staging races. There are other, more explicit humiliations too — and Aelfles revels in each new indignity heaped on these poor wretches.

N
0
300 ft
Quarry
Path
Inlet
Path
Path
Monastery
Ynys Wyt Monastery
& Surrounds

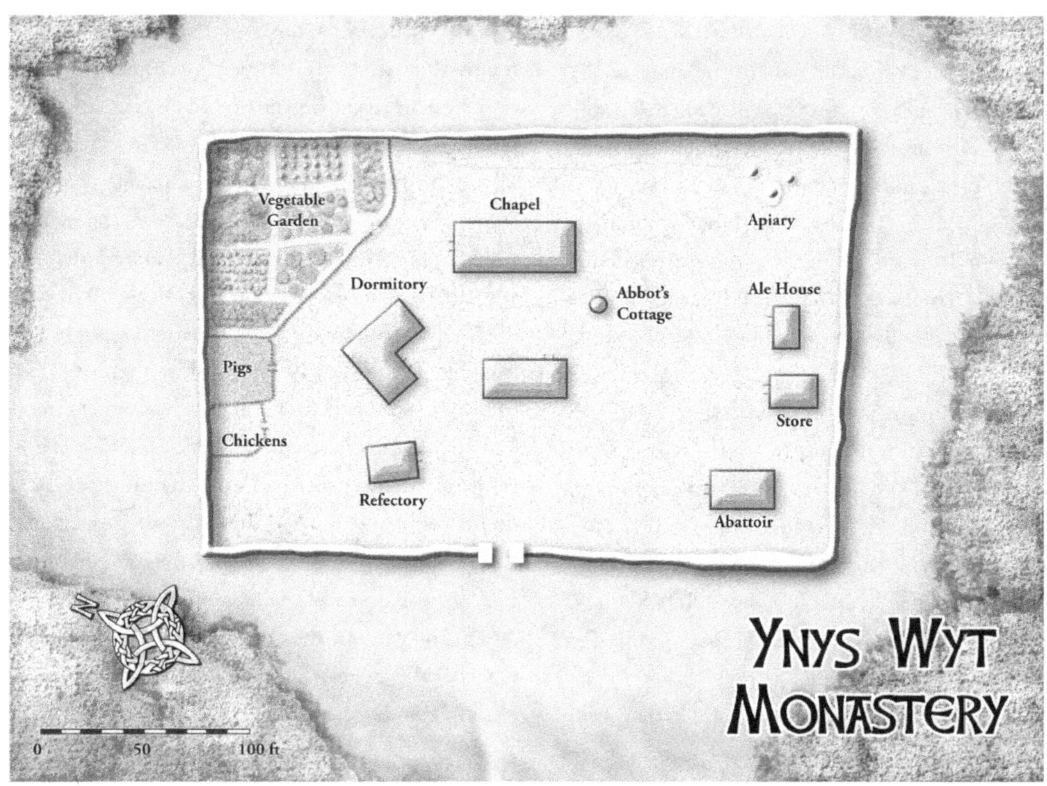
Vegetable Garden
Chapel
Apiary
Dormitory
Abbot's Cottage
Ale House
Pigs
Store
Chickens
Refectory
Abattoir
N
0
50
100 ft
Ynys Wyt
Monastery

Gate

Eight feet wide, the gate was built to this width to easily accommodate carts hauling stones from the quarry. The gate itself is made from local oak staves, lashed together with leather and then bound with very sturdy bronze and iron fittings. It creaks and groans when opened: the monks occasionally lubricate the leather and iron hinges with pig fat, but that hasn't been done in some time. The gate can be barred from the inside with an oak beam (requires two people to lift with Easy Brawn rolls).

Chapel

Built entirely of stone, and in much the same dry-wall style as the wall, the chapel is directly opposite the gate and reached by a path of straw, reeds and bracken. It faces east-west and its steep roof is made from thick thatch. The windows are no more than 1 foot square openings in the wall.

The wooden crucifix that was located above the doors at the eastern end has been torn down and used for the pyre that Aelfles used to create the Burning Man. The simple wooden pews that lined the north and south walls have also been ripped out and burned, along with the altar. The Saxons have turned the chapel into their hall.

Aelfles occupies the eastern quarter (where the altar stood), using a crude wicker screen and a couple of cloaks to form a barrier. She has made a new altar from earth, ashes and stones on which stands a hand-carved representation of her goddess, Gullveig. The carving is 12 inches high, quite crude, but with discernible female features. A hole has been drilled through the stone and a wooden dowel represents the spear thrown at her by the Aesir, according to Saxon myth. The figure is daubed with ash and soot, accentuating the carved features.

This carving is a powerful magical foci and is used by Aelfles to achieve a trance state and communicate with the Saxon Spirit World. It is her most prized possession, travelling with her everywhere, and if it is destroyed, Aelfles's Trance and Binding skills drop to a Formidable grade while she is in the confines of the sanctified grounds of the monastery (Hard, anywhere else). She also flies into a murderous rage because, without it, Gullveig is blind to her when Aelfles enters the Spirit World.

The rest of the chapel has become a makeshift barracks for the Saxons garrisoning the monastery. Bedding areas have been established, along with a crude hearth. There are six Saxons in here at any one time in daylight hours, and ten at night. The rest watch the compound and stand guard over the monks in the dormitory.

If necessary, Aefles releases one of her bound fire elemental spirits to gush through the thatch, setting light to the chapel's roof. The thatch burns easily and falls into the chapel. Within 1d3+1 Combat Rounds after the fire elemental engulfs the thatch, it turns into a blazing raised carpet that steadily drops from the ceiling, dealing 1d8 fire damage on anyone who fails an Evade roll below. After 2d6 minutes, the rafters of the chapel burn through and collapse, causing 1d10+1d8 damage to anyone failing an Evade roll, and foolish enough to have remained inside the building.

Dormitory

This L shaped building is, like the chapel, a mixture of drystone and thatch. Inside are wooden beds (little more than crude wooden frames with straw-filled sacks for mattresses) enough to sleep up to 50 monks. The windows are reasonably large openings in the wall, with woollen curtains to act as shutters. The place stinks of fear, blood, shit and vomit. One of the humiliations was to make the monks defecate on their own beds, but as the stench grew too bad, the Saxons took to letting the monks go outside to relieve themselves (under guard, of course). The monks spend most of their time in the dormitory. The Saxons let them out in groups of three or four to fetch food, ale and run errands — and when certain of the monks are bridled and forced to become mounts for the Saxons, the rest are forced to watch from the windows. Their usual routine of prayers, tending the vegetable garden, the livestock and so forth, have been abandoned for one of miserable imprisonment.

Any Christian witnessing the monks' plight must make a Formidable Willpower roll opposed by their own Christian Passion to keep his or her temper (and rash actions) under control. If the Christian Passion succeeds in this challenge of faith, the character is filled with a murderous desire to visit the most violent revenge on the Saxons. This may lead to certain characters acting without thinking, which runs the risk of jeopardising the mission.

Even pagans must make a Willpower roll to avoid feeling disgust at the way the monks are being treated: these are, at the end of it all, Britons, and the Saxons deserve punishment for what they are doing on Britain's soil.

Abbot's Cottage

This is a traditional roundhouse reserved for the abbot. Buried in the floor was the monastery's stash of silver - coins, jewelry and artworks - that has been taken by Cynric and is safely away from the monastery. The abbot, Tolwyn, is in the cottage - or, rather, his putrefying remains are. His throat was cut when he refused to reveal where the treasure was hidden and, when some of the other brothers revealed its hiding place, Tolwyn's body was dumped into the hole left when the treasure was dug out and simply left to rot. The stench around the cottage is bad, so woollen curtains have been nailed over the window openings and the door is kept shut. Inside, the place is filled with flies and the stench of Tolwyn's decaying corpse.

The one treasure the Saxons have missed is buried separately to the hoard of silver. In a box the size of a man's fist, wrapped in linen and carefully buried in one corner of the roundhouse, is the lock of the hair of John the Baptist. Tied in a small plait, the relic is unassuming and, to a pagan, is meaningless. To Christians though, it is hugely significant: hair from the man who baptised Jesus, and as important to Christians as the Thirteen Treasures of Britain are to pagans. At the Games Master's discretion, the lock of hair has healing properties if one is a Christian, functioning as an automatic Heal Body, Mind or Wound miracle of Intensity 8 (Mythras pages 186-187).

Tolwyn's soul has now become a Haunt, and a vindictive one at that. Tolwyn blames all pagans for his fate and intends to take revenge on them in spirit form, as he is denied that vengeance physically. Tolwyn's statistics are:

Abbot Tolwyn, Intensity 2 Haunt

INT: 16, POW: 18, CHA 10

Skills: Unarmed 78%, Willpower 86%, Hate Pagans 136%

Abilities:

- Miasma. Tolwyn's Miasma only affects pagans and induces thoughts and feelings of suicide. Test Tolwyn's Willpower vs that of pagan targets. If Tolwyn succeeds, the victim is filled with suicidal despair lasting for 18 months or until the character converts to Christianity, at which point the feelings of despair are lifted. Despairing characters have to succeed in a Willpower roll once a month to stave off a suicide attempt. The nature of the suicide, and whether or not it succeeds, is to be decided by the character and Games Master. A successful Insight roll by the character understands that converting to Christianity is the only way to gain hope and salvation. The range of the Miasma effect is confined to the Abbot's Cottage.
- Wraith Form. For 1 Magic Point (18 available), Tolwyn can make a physical attack using Unarmed for 1d8 points of damage, ignoring armour and non-magical parries. Injuries take the form of the victim's flesh becoming necrotic and, if untreated by Holy Water within 3 days, becoming infected, leading to the loss of 1 Hit Point per week. Once infected, and if left untreated, this gradual decay, in the form of gangrene, is irreversible and can only be treated by amputation of the affected limb.

Ale House/Store House

Another reasonable-sized, barn-like building, made of stone, wood and thatch. It is split into two levels with a mezzanine floor reached by a ladder. On the mezzanine the monks store foodstuffs: flour, grain, salt and so forth. On the ground floor are the necessary facilities for brewing and storing ale and mead: vats, tuns and barrels, along with barley and hops. Much of the ale has been drunk by the Saxons already, and only a couple of barrels remain.

Apiary

In the north-east corner of the compound are three beehives. The monks keep bees for honey to eat, trade and make into mead. The hives are filled with bees which, if disturbed, swarm, creating an Insect Swarm as per page 251 of Mythras. Each hive produces a SIZ of 14 capable of inflicting 1d3 Sting damage and with 3 Action Points.

Bee Swarm

SIZ 14, 1d3 damage, Action Points: 3

Athletics 60%, Fly 60%, Willpower 30%, Swarm Attack 60%

The hives can be carried and, if required, thrown (or rolled, or broken open). It requires two people to carry one hive and a Hard Athletics roll, based on the average of the two carriers, to move the hive without causing the bees to swarm prematurely.

Bee stings are generally painful and, in sufficient intensity, can cause the Asphyxiation Condition (MYTHRAS, page 71 and page 75). When the amount of damage caused to a single individual exceeds his or her CON, Asphyxiation begins to take place. Aelfles, unbeknown to her, is highly allergic to bee stings and so suffers from both asphyxiation and anaphylactic shock if she fails an Endurance roll after being stung for the first time (the damage is unimportant). Anaphylactic shock includes the conditions of Asphyxiation and Paralysis.

Any character stung by a bee also has a 10% chance of suffering from anaphylactic shock.

Pig Sty and Shelter

Behind a semicircular wicker barrier is the monastery's pig sty: a large mud patch with a lean-to shelter that is home to the monks' eight pigs (two hogs, six sows). Two of the sows have been butchered recently for the Saxons' consumption but the rest remain in their sty. Since the monks have not been tending the pigs, their routine has been disturbed and they are both agitated and hungry. A starving pig will eat almost anything and can make short work of a human carcass. Anyone falling into the sty, or clambering into it, will be attacked by 2d3 of the pigs intent on eating as much as they can. If released, the pigs run amok and are hungry enough - and agitated enough - to charge, flatten and then try to eat anyone in their path.

Refectory

Close to the abattoir, this stone and wicker structure serves as both kitchen and dining area, with a circular area set aside for meals to be taken cross-legged on the floor. The kitchen contains cooking utensils and a large, stone-encircled hearth. The Saxons use the refectory for their own meals. The monks are being fed scraps and leftovers.

Abattoir

Used to butcher the pigs and chickens, this wooden hut has space for hanging carcasses and an area for preserving meat in salt. There are a couple of fletches of good bacon still remaining, plus hooks, butchering knives and a sturdy wooden block.

Chicken Coop

Next to the pig sty is the chicken coop - again, a wicker enclosure with a raised wooden hen-house for the monastery's twenty or so hens and single cockerel. If disturbed, the fowl raise a terrible alarm. Fox attacks are not uncommon and the slightest noise near the coop sets off the chickens' panic and self-preservation instincts.

Vegetable Garden

Neat furrows grow onions, carrots, turnips, beets and, against the wall, peas and runner beans. The Saxons have corralled their six horses here - local mounts taken from the islanders.

Pyre

The pyre where one of the monks was sacrificed to Gullveig. It still smoulders although there are no remains: they were turned out of the monastery and roam freely as the Burning Man.

Reconnoitring the Monastery

To fully assess what is happening in the monastery, the characters need to be inside the compound, on top of the wall, or find a vantage point from the tree-line, climbing onto sturdy enough branches. Using the trees as a hiding place is fine, but the foliage and distance means that it is impossible to gain a single, clear view of the compound.

To gain a fully accurate idea of how many Saxons there are and how many surviving monks, the characters need to spend a full 8 hours watching the monastery. This can be reduced to a fraction by actually getting inside and performing a survey but is, of course, very risky to do, relying on Stealth rolls opposed by Perception rolls from the Saxon sentries.

During the day there is always some form of activity, be it weapon practice in the open air or humiliating the monks with races or other cruel games. Gaining entry to the compound is possible, but Stealth rolls are at either Hard or Formidable depending on the number of Saxons around and the type of activity. There are always two warriors on gate duty and, at night, two Saxons patrol the perimeter in four-hour shifts, alternating with the gate guards.

Pigs

Characteristics	Attributes	1d20	Location	AP/HP
STR: 16	Action Points: 2	1–3	Right Hind Leg	1/7
CON: 16	Damage Modifier: +1d4	4–6	Left Hind Leg	1/7
SIZ: 17	Magic Points: 7	7–9	Abdomen	1/8
DEX: 11	Movement: 8 metres	10–12	Chest	1/9
INS: 11	Initiative Bonus: 11	13–15	Right Front Leg	1/6
POW: 7	Armour: Hide	16–18	Left Front Leg	1/6
		19–20	Head	1/7

Abilities: Frenzy. The pigs' agitation and hunger makes them automatically behave in the frenzied state

Skills: *Athletics 22%, Brawn 50%, Endurance 12%, Evade 56%, Perception 49%, Unarmed 30%, Willpower 75%*

Combat Style
Hungry Porcine (Teeth) 57%.
The pigs aim to Charge, Bash and Trip their opponents, making it easier for them to attack with their teeth.

Weapon	Size/Force	Reach	Damage	AP/HP
Bite	*M*	*S*	*1d3+1d4*	*As for Head*

If the characters do not go into the compound and watch from the trees, there is still a 15% chance that an observant sentry senses something is wrong and spots the characters, raising the alarm. This prompts eight warriors, accompanied by Aelfles, to give chase. If caught, the characters are dragged back to the monastery for interrogation by Aelfles, with the prospect of at least one of the characters being sacrificed to Gullveig and becoming another Burning Man.

There is also the chance (20%) that Aelfles senses something amiss after communing with the spirits. She casts her rune sticks and the results indicates the monastery is being watched. Quietly and subtly she orders four of the warriors to go beyond the compound and search for spies - these warriors rely on Perception and Stealth rolls to locate the characters and ambush them. While the warriors are hunting, Aelfles decides to give the spies something to watch. She has two monks dragged out into the open air and commands pyres to be built: Saxons fetch firewood and kindling and build two fresh pyres close to the existing one. With the petrified monks tied to stakes, Aelfles strips them, slices out their tongues, gouges out their eyes, and then sets fire to each pyre. As the monks burn, she dances around them, shifting into a trance, and calling forth a fire elemental spirit to inhabit each body, creating new Burning Men. When the flames subside, the magically animated bodies are pulled down from their stakes and turned loose.

Aelfles may perform this ritual anyway out of sheer boredom and spite.

Effecting a Rescue

With cunning, the characters can rescue the monks. There are enough resources in the compound to create a number of diversions:

- Releasing the pigs
- Causing the bees to swarm (and even dumping the hives into the chapel)
- Freeing the horses and causing them to stampede
- Killing the sentries and guards
- Somehow dragging a Saxon into the Abbot's cottage

Let the characters plan and establish their tactics, encouraging creativity and perhaps using Insight, Lore and other skills to understand the potential of the available resources. If it comes to a straight fight, hit and run tactics can be effective against the Saxons, even though they probably outnumber the characters. Much depends on cunning, stealth, and thinking around the challenges, instead of charging in with spears lowered and shields raised. If Callws, the young novice, is with the characters, he can offer helpful suggestions. He knows much about the monastery and the Saxons and has just enough courage to help establish a diversion.

Gullveig's Children

It is enough for the characters to simply reconnoitre and leave, meeting Havgan and then returning with the liberating force. However, Aelfles has other plans. Even though she might burn an individual monk or two, her master plan is to immolate the entire monastery and summon Gullveig's children: Hel, Fenrir and Jormungand. Burning every monk alive and destroying the entire monastery will help her achieve that end and she is impatient to do it. The only way to stop her is to set the monks free, and so one impetus for the characters will be for them to witness the preparations being made for a huge immolation: wood being cut and prepared for a huge pyre, oil being poured over the thatching, and so forth.

Once the pyre is complete, and as the sun sets, Aelfles calls for the monks to be brought out of the dormitory. Saxon warriors comply, dragging the monks out in groups of two or three, while Aelfles watches, impassively. She has brought her carving of Gullveig from her quarters in the chapel and set it on an upturned barrel facing the huge pyre in the centre of the compound. The struggling monks are dragged, screaming and praying, to the pyre where they are herded onto the woodpile and tied together. Perhaps a monk or two tries to escape - and this might be an excellent time to intervene as the Saxons are occupied with trying to subdue the escapees. Aelfles shrieks that they are not to be killed: Gullveig wants to consume their souls herself through fire.

When all the monks are tied onto the pyre, torches are brought and the warriors form a circle about it. Aelfles calls on Gullveig (and remember - this is in Saxon, so the characters may not understand it) to claim these offerings, unbelievers and deniers of the True Gods, and to release her children to destroy all enemies. Aelfles dances and sways as she chants this litany over and over again. The priests moan and pray. The Saxons watch solemnly. When Aelfles halts abruptly and gives a nod of her head, the warriors place their torches to the pyre and let the flames take hold.

As the monks start to burn, Gullveig's name is chanted over and over again by Aelfles and the warriors. Then warriors peel away from the main group and throw burning brands onto the thatch of the buildings in the compound, so that everything is burning. The first screams of dying monks mark the culmination of the ritual to release Gullveig's Children.

If Aelfles is allowed to complete her ritual, Hel, Fenrir and Jormungand are summoned to the Mortal World to support Cerdic's forces. All three manifest as truly immense, terrifying creatures, appearing in the sky to the south of the monastery and thundering across it to Cerdic, who prepares to battle Natanleod.

- Hel manifests as a huge hag, one half of her body coal-black, the other ghastly white, astride a decaying, three-legged horse. She is accompanied by baying hell-hounds the size of aurochs that feed on the souls of the living.
- Fenrir manifests as a gigantic wolf, with eyes of fire and teeth of sword blades. His tail is a huge, writhing serpent and he breathes flame like a dragon.
- Jormungand is a half-mile long, three-headed serpent that slithers through the air as easily as a mortal snake through grass or water. Its venom cause the sea to boil and the earth to char as it drips from each head.

If summoned, these monsters from Saxon nightmares hunt down and lay waste to the forces of Powys and Dumnonia, either as they engage Cerdic or just before they prepare to. They can only be stopped by beings of similar power, which Merlin can summon if he has the time and certain of the Treasures of Britain; but on this occasion he has neither. Of course, Aelfles plans to repeat this summoning with each new battle Cerdic and Cynric fight - Gullveig's children are happy to be summoned if there is slaughter to

be carried out — proving that Saxon magic is stronger than that of the Britons. If she is not stopped, then it brings a new and terrifying dimension to the war with the Saxons and, at this stage, the characters are the only ones who can prevent Aelfles from bringing forth this supernatural wrath.

Freeing the Monks

Managing to free the monks and help them escape thwarts Aelfles' plans completely; it also brings-down her personal wrath. Aelfles tries to find time to enter the Spirit World to summon to her aid the Sons of Fenrir - spectral predator spirits in the form of ravenous, black-coated wolves. Unlike the predator spirits described on page 151 of the MYTHRAS rules, the Sons of Fenrir do not need physical bodies to hunt on the Mortal Plane and as long as Aelfles has a mental image of who they are to hunt, they can take physical form during the hours of darkness and give pursuit. The Sons of Fenrir are uninhibited by terrain, tireless, merciless and cunning. Aelfles can summon 1 Son of Fenrir for every 3 Magic Points she wants to spend, and one spirit wolf tracks one character (or monk). The spectral wolves do not cease in their task until either their quarry, or they, are killed.

If the characters succeed in setting the monks free, they break into several groups and flee for their lives. 2d6 Monks remain with the characters, fearing for their safety with anyone but their rescuers and perhaps even willing to fight alongside the characters in their bid to evade the Saxons. If given weapons half the monks accompanying the characters are prepared to fight - use the statistics for Typical Monk on page 333.

The other alternative for freeing the monks is to quickly join with Havgan and lead him and his war band to the monastery so that the Saxons can be engaged by a full fighting force. Havgan can easily send 30 warriors - more more than enough to engage and defeat the Saxons (using the battle rules, if Games Masters wish) while the characters attempt to capture or kill Aelfles. Havgan, when he learns of the laece, is adamant that she be captured alive to be used for ransom; but if she dies, he sheds no tears and merely grumbles that she might have been a useful hostage.

With the monks and the monastery secured by Havgan's war band, it is really a case of then waiting for King Meurig's troops to cross the island and bring reinforcements.

End Game and Extending the Scenario

There are, of course, opportunities to extend this scenario by having Cynric's remaining warriors engage Havgan's forces before Meurig arrives, or even attempt to engage both Havgan and Meurig. Cynric is hopelessly outnumbered — although, if Aelfles succeeds in raising Gullveig's Children, just about every Briton on Ynys Wyt, including Havgan, is terrified at the sight and flees for safety, effectively allowing Cynric victory on the island while Cerdic attains victory on the mainland.

Games Masters should decide the scope of the ending of the scenario and plan accordingly, bringing to bear whatever elements are required by the characters' success or failure in their main mission (as well as the overall needs of the campaign itself).

If the characters succeed in saving the monks, defeating Aelfles and securing the monastery, they receive the gratitude and thanks of King Meurig and Bishop Dyfrig. Christian characters are much lauded, but even pagan characters are given worthwhile credit and Meurig rewards each character with the equivalent of 20 Silver Pieces each from his own coffers. This takes the form of jewelry, brooches, crucifixes and torques, but is treasure nonetheless. If the hair of John the Baptist is recovered, then Meurig names them as heroes of the church and commissions one of his bards to write a poem in their honour. On their return to the mainland, Meurig insists on them travelling to Gwent where he intends to hold a feast in their honour and, hopefully, convert any pagans in the group to Christianity.

The Saxons

As for Cerdic and Cynric — they should survive in one shape or form. Cerdic may be routed by Natanleod, and forced to retreat to Aelle's lands. Or he might be victorious if Gullveig's Children are summoned, claiming Ynys Wyt and the lands surrounding the River Test and the Solent as a new kingdom he calls West Seax

— or, when spoken quickly, as the Saxons tend to do, 'Wessex'. If he manages to establish this new kingdom for himself, it places greater pressure on the Alliance of Britain to engage the Saxons and attempt to halt their advance into Dumnonia.

Non-Player Characters

Aelfles

In her mid-30s, Aelfles is a slight, thin woman, not unattractive, with her hair dyed crimson with natural pigments (it is usually blond). Her eyes are dark and intense, her mouth unsmiling, and her presence naturally intimidating. Although she appears quite frail, her inner core is like iron and her fervour for the Gods palpable. She revels in cruelty, is impatient, demanding and sinister. Her powers as a shaman have been proved time and time again, which is why she has risen to become one of Cerdic's chief allies (and, occasionally, his lover) and has predicted that he will become Bretwallda, challenging Aelle.

Aelfles is ruthless and cunning. She places her own safety first and is adept at manipulating others, using sex if she needs to, to get her way and secure what she wants. Like Merlin, she wants to see her gods rule Britain - not the Christian god. In many ways she is Merlin's counterpart: single-minded, gifted and resolute.

Cynric

The only legitimate son of Cerdic, Cynric is a young Saxon with a famed and successful warlord as a father who aims to follow in the same footsteps. In his native land there is much talk of the extensive, fertile lands of this island known as Britain, and it is clearly a place where there can be many chieftains, many kings, with everyone prospering. Cynric is youthful and idealistic. He wants to be victorious but also sees that the Britons and Saxons could coexist given the right circumstances. For that to happen, there will be a certain amount of battle, but in time there can be peace.

So Cynric has followed his father on this, his first real campaign. He sees holding Ynys Wyt as his duty but he also wants to learn more about these Britons, including those who are Christians, and not just slaughter them. He therefore contrasts sharply with his father, Cerdic, who seeks to carve-out a kingdom at any cost. Neither does Cynric like or trust Aelfles. The laece scares him but he also sees her as a liability. Her magic might bring victory for Cerdic, but it will surely arouse the wrath of Britain's gods and even the wrath of this Christian god. That cannot be a good thing.

Cynric then, is a reasonable man and an honourable one. He is loyal to his father and his people but he is no blood-thirsty conqueror. He has heard of the Briton called Arthur and thinks that, if they were to meet, they might have much in common. For now, though, that is in the future. Cerdic and Cynric's campaign is beginning and Cynric intends to hold Ynys Wyt as his father has commanded.

Cynric is tall, broad-shouldered and charismatic. His blond hair is long and unkempt, usually worn in an untidy side-braid. His beard is wispy, and this lends to his boyish appearance. His eyes, clear and blue, appear older than their owner and he has many creases around them, a sign of his love of laughter. Cynric is popular with most people he meets: easy-going, interested, casual, but still with an air of authority. He has learned a little Brythonic from Celtic slaves and is keen to practice its use.

Aelfles, Saxon Laece

Characteristics	Attributes	1d20	Location	AP/HP
STR: 7	Action Points: 2	1–3	Right Leg	0/4
CON: 9	Damage Modifier: -1d4	4–6	Left Leg	0/4
SIZ: 8	Magic Points: 16	7–9	Abdomen	0/5
DEX: 9	Movement: 6 metres	10–12	Chest	0/6
INT: 14	Initiative Bonus: 11	13–15	Right Arm	0/3
POW: 16	Armour: None.	16–18	Left Arm	0/3
CHA: 14		19–20	Head	0/4

Skills: *Athletics 35%, Brawn 24%, Endurance 71%, Evade 36%, Lore (Norse Gods) 120%, Lore (Rune Sticks) 95%, Perception 85%, Survival 76%, Unarmed 54%, Willpower 84% Stealth 68%*

Loyalty to Cerdic 85%, Love Gullveig 110%, Hate Christians 88%, Hate Britons 75%, Norse Gods 100%

Magic
Binding 90%, Trance 90%

Aefles has a pair of Intensity 2 Fire Elementals bound to pieces of flint she wears as charms around each wrist. These are for her personal defence but when required she releases the spirits from their fetish completely, ordering them to engulf any immediate foes as they escape back to the spirit world.

Fire Spirits. INT 2, POW 18, CHA 7, Willpower 70%, Spectral Flame 75%, Dam 1d8.

While she has the spirits bound she is completely immune to fire and heat in any form.

Combat Style: Bone Seax 40% (Intimidate)

Aelfles's knife is made from the femur of one of her enemies. Anyone facing her as she wields the knife must make a Superstition roll. If the roll succeeds, the knife seems to writhe and moan in her hand, as though alive. This has the same effect as the Intimidate creature trait as described on page 216 of Mythras. If the Superstition roll is failed then it is simply a knife made of bone.

Weapon	Size/Force	Reach	Damage	AP/HP
Bone Seax	*M*	*S*	*1d4+2-1d4*	*3/3*

Sons of Fenrir

The Sons of Fenrir take the form of spectral wolves that can still inflict grievous wounds on physical foes. They can be damaged by fire, taking normal rolled damage, but mundane weapons inflict only minimum available damage. If enchanted with some form of magic, they inflict normal damage. A Treasure of Britain also inflicts normal damage.

Intensity 3 Predator Spirit

INS 11, POW 22, CHA n/a

Action Points 3, Initiative Bonus 11, Magic Points/Tenacity 22, Movement 10 metres, Spirit Damage 1d10

Skills

Spectral Claws and Teeth 94% (S/T 1d10), Stealth 72%, Track 116%, Willpower 94%

Abilities

Intimidate, Leaping

Cynric

Characteristics	Attributes	1d20	Location	AP/HP
STR: 13	Action Points: 2	1–3	Right Leg	3/6
CON: 11	Damage Modifier: +1d2	4–6	Left Leg	3/6
SIZ: 15	Magic Points: 13	7–9	Abdomen	4/7
DEX: 10	Movement: 6 metres	10–12	Chest	4/7
INT: 11	Initiative Bonus: 7	13–15	Right Arm	0/5
POW: 13	Armour: Scale, Leather, Plate Helm	16–18	Left Arm	0/5
CHA: 16		19–20	Head	5/6

Skills: *Athletics 55%, Brawn 52%, Customs (Saxon) 75%, Endurance 54%, Evade 44%, Insight 52%, Language (Brythonic) 25%, Lore (Strategy and Tactics) 46%, Perception 53%, Survival 65%, Unarmed 57%, Willpower 45%, Stealth 59%*

Loyalty to Cerdic 90%, Loyalty to War Band 70%, Love of Learning 75%, Distrust Aelfles 77%, Norse Gods 59%

Combat Style: Ealdorman (Battleaxe, Seax and Shield. Trait, Mounted Combat) 75%

Weapon	Size/Force	Reach	Damage	AP/HP
Seax	*M*	*S*	*1d4+2+1d2*	*6/8*
Axe	*M*	*M*	*1d6+1+1d2*	*4/8*
Saxon Round Shield	*L*	*S*	*1d4+1d2*	*4/12*

Typical Monk

The brothers of the monastery are a very mixed bunch in terms of ages and personalities. One or two are even ex-fighting men who, if called upon, can still wield a weapon, even though they have taken vows before God to lead peaceful lives.

Attributes	1d20	Location	AP/HP
Action Points: 2	1–3	Right Leg	0/5
Damage Modifier: 0	4–6	Left Leg	0/5
Magic Points: 13	7–9	Abdomen	0/6
Movement: 6 metres	10–12	Chest	0/7
Initiative Bonus: 12	13–15	Right Arm	0/4
Armour: None	16–18	Left Arm	0/4
	19–20	Head	0/5

Skills: *Athletics 52%, Brawn 40%, Endurance 45%, Evade 33%, Locale (Ynys Wyt) 50%, Lore (Scripture) 88%, Perception 53%, Survival 61%, Unarmed 38%, Willpower 89%, Stealth 39%*

Loyalty to God 100%, Christian 90%, Loyalty to Order 90%, Love Thy Neighbour (Expect When A Saxon) 75%, Hate Pagans 60%

Combat Style: Ex-Soldier (Spear, Shield, Shield Wall Trait) 60%

Weapon	Size/Force	Reach	Damage	AP/HP
Hoe	*M*	*L*	*1d4*	*3/8*
Rake	*M*	*L*	*1d6*	*3/8*
Pig Goad	*S*	*S*	*1d4+1*	*3/3*

Suppose Your Time Were Come to Die

"Listen, suppose your time were come to die,
And you were quite alone and very weak;
Yea, laid a dying while very mightily

The wind was ruffling up the narrow streak
Of river through your broad lands running well
Suppose a hush should come, then some one speak:

One of these cloths is heaven, and one is hell,
Now choose one cloth for ever; which they be,
I will not tell you, you must somehow tell..."

From The Defence of Guenevere *by William Morris*

Depending on the outcome of *Gullveig's Children*, the tribes of Britain may have suffered a monumental blow (if the Children have laid waste to the Celtic forces, allowing Cerdic to secure the western bank of the Test, the Solent, Ynys Wyt and parts of eastern Ceint) or have attained a great victory (Cerdic has been defeated and driven out of Ynys Wyt, but still maintains a presence in Britain — a threat to both the Celts and Aelle). Whatever the outcome, the Alliance of Britain faces dark times. The Saxons are gaining strength, are bringing more potent magic, and are now preparing to launch attacks against Dumnonia, the Brigantes, and the Parisii. To make things worse, Guinevere has fallen ill, distracting Arthur. This scenario, the final part of this stage of the Mythic Britain campaign, concerns Guinevere's illness and the part the characters play in finding a cure.

The Truth of It

Arthur is hated by Ladwys, Custennin, and Morgana. All three see him as a usurper even though Arthur makes no claim to Uther's title, estates, or possessions. Surrounded by capable and loyal warlords and followers, Arthur is difficult to harm directly but Ladwys knows that the key to injuring him is to hurt what he loves the most, impairing his judgement, preying on his insecurities, and weakening his position in the eyes of those who look to him for leadership. Since her plan to shame him over his betrothal to Guinevere failed, Ladwys intends to take a more direct and lethal approach: she is steadily poisoning Guinevere.

Since the battle with Cerdic, Arthur has insisted that as many womenfolk as possible leave Caer Cadbryg and travel to Powys where King Cyngen has offered sanctuary in the event that the Saxon amass and manage to overrun Dumnonia. Ladwys has refused to leave Caer Cadbryg but Arthur has sent his beloved Guinevere into hiding. This is a perfect opportunity for Ladwys to set in motion her plan to injure Arthur and kill the one he loves the most. Because Arthur is so far away from Guinevere, there is little he can do directly to help and the worry will torment him precisely as Ladwys wants it to. Ladwys is also distanced from Guinevere and so, naturally, is above suspicion. She is working through an agent, Curwan, to procure poison, which is then being introduced into Guinevere's meals by Rowenna, a handmaiden loyal to Ladwys who sends back secret reports on the plan's progress.

The Poison

The poison is a subtle, herbal concoction: any decent herbalist knows how to make it but only a true expert knows how to make it so that its toxicity builds slowly and steadily. In single doses, spaced apart, the toxin has no outward effects: but introduced consistently, over time, it builds, eventually overwhelming the body until the victim lapses into a coma and dies.

The poisoner is Curwan. Custennin has used him before, although never in such a murderous scheme, and introduced him to Ladwys, although Custennin himself has no involvement in, or knowledge of, Ladwys' plan.

Introduction

A messenger of Caer Cadbryg is sent to find the characters, whether they are at Cadbryg or elsewhere in Britain. The messenger is one of Cadbryg's bards, a jovial man named Cellan who is well travelled and well trusted.

'Arthur sent me to find you. He would have the pleasure of your company in his hall, but you are to tell no one of the meeting.'

If it proves necessary, Cellan travels with the characters and is good company. He can bring news from all around the country and his memory (as with all bards) is exceptional. If questioned more as to why Arthur wants them (Influence rolls contested by Cellan's 64% Willpower) Cellan either shakes his head and says he knows no more, or bites his lip and says, somewhat cryptically, 'All I can tell you is that Arthur seemed troubled.'

On reaching Caer Cadbryg, they are taken to Arthur's private room A fire burns and Arthur us warming himself before it, his two favourite hunting hounds lounging at his feet. Cellan receives a silver coin for his efforts and is dismissed. Arthur offers hot, herbed ale, which he mulls himself using an iron close to the fire.

'Although Cellan said I summoned you, it was really Guinevere,' Arthur says. Insight rolls detect that his voice is somewhat strained, and he looks tired.

'For several weeks my beloved Guinevere has been ill. Her illness has worsened and she desperately needs help. Prayers are being said and wise people who know remedies of various kinds have been consulted, and I am sure they will find the cause of the sickness but she needs someone with her. I cannot leave here, not with Cerdic at our borders, and so I need someone Guinevere knows and cares for to go to Powys and be at her side. She has asked for you. Comfort her, sit with her. If you can, try to help those who are trying to find a cure. Be my ambassadors. If you are loyal to me and love Guinevere, then you will do me this favour.'

This means the characters need to travel to Powys and, in particular, the village of Builth, where Dumnonia's refugees have been given shelter. The journey takes 3 to 4 days and passes through the beautiful hill country of Powys, skirting the southern edge of the Cornovii lands, and then into the pleasant, peaceful, wooded valleys of the region. Builth is in a large clearing, close to

a river, reasonable roads, and a couple of hours ride from Caer Branog, the Powysian capital.

If the characters consult with Merlin or Morgana before leaving for Powys, neither can find any information from the Spirit World that is useful or hints at the cause of the sickness.

'Sometimes these things just are,' Merlin says. 'Not all illness is caused by a malignant spirit: sometimes people fall foul of natural causes. Yet I shall make a sacrifice for Guinevere and you can take these charms to place around her chamber. They will help ward against further evil from invading.'

Merlin (or Morgana) gives the characters a cloth pouch filled with dried mistletoe, cobwebs heaped into a ball, desiccated badger testicles and a pungent, oily substance that burns slightly when touched. He explains how the charms should be arranged (characters should make either an Insight or Pagan Lore/Passion roll to correctly recall the ritual) and wishes the characters, and Guinevere, well.

If the characters consult a priest, such as Father Samsun or Bishop Gerhaint, either man shakes his head and makes the sign of the cross. 'Let us not forget Guinevere wronged a King and further sinned by consorting with Arthur. God has a way of punishing sinners and this is a trial sent by God. If Guinevere survives it, it will be by His grace. Her fate is in the hands of the Blessed Virgin now but we should pray for her. You should bring the Lord's word to her bedside. Have her renounce her sins.' And either priest gives the character a wooden crucifix, inlaid with silver, to place near Guinevere, or even upon her breast, to help her find God.

Curing Guinevere

The only way to cure Guinevere is to stop the poison from entering her food. The poison is being handed to Rowenna, the handmaiden assigned to travel with Guinevere and recommended by Ladwys. Rowenna works to Ladwys' instructions and is happy to do so because she believes Guinevere is a fallen woman who must be brought into God's hands. This is a holy trial, Ladwys has told Rowenna and by putting Guinevere through it, she is doing the Lord's work. Rowenna genuinely believes she is helping Guinevere but she also knows, help or not help, it is better to do as Ladwys bids rather than cross the formidable lady.

Morgana? Help Guinevere?

If the characters approach Morgana for help or insight they find her naturally incredibly reluctant to help her half-brother or his beloved Guinevere. The characters will need to work very hard to convince her to offer even the slightest scrap of assistance, with any rolls they make being at a Herculean grade of difficulty. Nevertheless, any character that might have a positive relationship with Morgana could gain her very grudging assistance although she offers only the bare minimum, as indicated in the main text. She also makes it clear to the character that a favour is now owed and Morgana *always* collects on her debts.

However, Rowenna is not acting alone. Curwan, the poisoner, travels between Caer Cadbryg and Builth regularly as part of the supplies Caer Cadbryg sends to help support its refugees (indeed, he may even travel out to Builth with the characters as part of the supply train and become friendly with them). He gives Ladwys regular updates and if the characters manage to foil the poisoning regime somehow, Curwan is given instructions to find a way to administer a heavier, potentially fatal, dose. The characters therefore need to identify and neutralise Curwan before he can murder Guinevere.

The poison works by breaking down the body's defences. In practice, each dose of the poison reduces Guinevere's Endurance by 1d4+1 points per day. She began by suffering flu-like symptoms, followed by dizzy spells, fainting, and then nausea. Her Endurance has now fallen to half normal and she is suffering from considerable fatigue, unable to leave her bed for more than a few minutes at a time, and suffering fevered sleep and nightmares.

Now, an Insight roll (Very Easy for any female characters) soon equates that the symptoms of Guinevere's ailment could be those of pregnancy and although she is suffering at the moment, it could be joyous news. However, once one takes into account that

Guinevere is gaining no respite from her condition, and is deteriorating, it becomes apparent that this is not pregnancy.

If the poison stops entering Guinevere's system she starts to steadily recover, regaining 3 Endurance points (her Healing Rate) per day until it reaches its normal level. Her strength and health steadily improve and it is noticeable to all. However, if Guinevere starts to improve, Curwan intends, as per Ladwys' orders, to introduce a single dose of the poison which will overwhelm Guinevere's system and cause her to lapse into a coma, with death following in 1d6 days unless a cure can be found.

Journeying to Builth

Although the characters can travel to Builth alone, there is a regular train of supplies – food, ale, and mead – sent from Caer Cadbryg to help pay for the upkeep of the refugees until Dumnonia's warlords deem it safe enough for them to return home. The train consists of several carts pulled by a mixture of donkeys and horses, laden with foodstuffs and other commodities Powys wants from Dumnonia. A small warband travels with the caravan, scouting ahead and watching for potential bandits but the procession is safe enough. Only the very reckless or very desperate would attack a caravan protected by Dumnonian warriors and even Cerdic's Saxons have not yet reached this far across Britain to be a threat. If the characters accompany the caravan, the journey is pleasant and uneventful. The carts are under the command of a master-of-horse who cajoles the donkeys for the length of the journey and the rest of the travellers are simply those being employed to help unload at Builth, or who have paid a silver penny so they can ride in one of the carts rather than walk. At night the caravan pulls off the road at regular and well-used camp spots and the warriors drink, happily sharing mead and stories with those who want to listen.

One of the travellers, Curwan, seems well known to the warriors. He is a Cornovii who has made Builth his home but knows Caer Cadbryg well: a Formidable Locale roll places Curwan around Caer Cadbryg where he is known as something of an entertainer. While certainly no warrior, each evening Curwan entertains with folk songs, stories, and a few acts of legerdemain that amuse, astound, and confound. He is sociable enough but keeps himself to himself outside of communal meals and rest stops. If engaged in conversation, he makes animated and pleasant small talk but never enters into long discussions. It is, however, clear he knows Builth well and, if questioned about Guinevere can say very little: 'I've heard she has not been well,' he says with genuine-sounding concern, 'but then quite a few people have suffered fevers recently; the daughter of a friend of mine died in her sleep not two weeks' past. These things happen.' Curwan seems very plausible. To detect any dishonesty requires a character to succeed in a Herculean Insight roll opposed by Curwan's Very Easy Deceit roll.

Builth is a pleasant village of around two hundred people, reached by a wooden bridge spanning the River Wye. Roundhouse and storage huts cluster around the chapel with the largest roundhouse being where Guinevere has been given lodging. Since falling ill, Guinevere has been moved to a smaller roundhouse nearby so she has seclusion, but also to protect against possible contagion. Surrounding the buildings are corrals for livestock (pigs, chicken, and goats), places for communal vegetables and more storage. Most of the Builth villagers either serve Caer Branog, two hours to the north-east, or make their living from charcoal burning, timber, and fishing the Wye. A Christian settlement for years, the local spirits are long dormant and even the Great Spirit of the Wye knows better than to whisper her songs when flowing past Builth.

The People of Builth

Around half the populace of Builth are the womenfolk and children of Dumnonia's chiefs and warband leaders. They have been here for six weeks now, while Dumnonia is on a war-footing, readying itself for the inevitable battle against Cerdic, Aelle, or both. Although insulated from what might happen in Dumnonia, the refugees are well aware of the dangers and constantly seeking news from their homeland, displaying visible relief when they hear that, so far, the Saxons have not attacked. The other half are Builth natives, with a man named Geheris being their headman. A few are resentful of these Dumnonian interlopers but most are welcoming. Father Dafydd, the priest, and his wife Brenna, have gone out of their way to make the Dumnonians feel at home. The

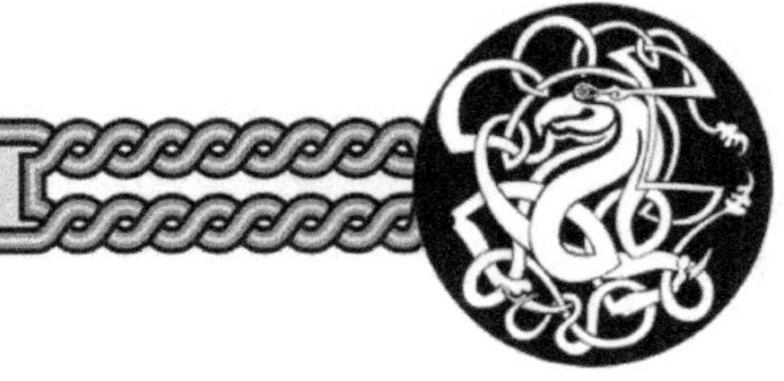

roundhouse where Guinevere rests is Dafydd and Brenna's home: they are living with neighbours, so that Guinevere gets the rest she needs.

As Curwan has said, people know of Guinevere's illness but as a few others have also fallen ill and one girl has died, there is no real suspicion. Some blame a Saxon curse, others blame bad eels fetched up from the river Wye by local fishermen whilst one or two blame evil spirits brought down by pagans. Although there is a mixture of Christians and pagans, Christians dominate and some pagans are being converted, either through fear, necessity or proximity. Most people go about the same duties they would if in Dumnonia and, despite the tension, fear, and strangeness of the situation, life goes on as usual.

The following are people the characters are most likely to interact with, either directly or indirectly, and with varying levels of frequency as their investigations deepen.

Rowenna

Rowenna is seventeen years old, good-looking and a dutiful (if flirtatious) Christian. She was raised at Caer Cadbryg and came into the favour of Ladwys four years ago when Ladwys had need of a new handmaiden. During this time Rowenna and Ladwys became close and Rowenna dotes on the ageing widow of the High King of Britain. Ladwys shows kindness and makes Rowenna feel important and special. As a result, Rowenna has been completely beguiled. There is nothing Rowenna would not do for Ladwys and when Ladwys says Guinevere is a devil-born harlot, Rowenna agrees without reservation.

When it was announced that Guinevere would need a handmaiden of her own, Ladwys was quick to suggest Rowenna. Guinevere agreed, although she was reluctant to do so as she had hoped Gwynhafach would naturally fulfill the role. Arthur convinced Guinevere that accepting Rowenna was a good political move: it would help placate Ladwys. It was therefore decided that both Gwynhafach and Rowenna would serve Guinevere and this made all parties happy. When it was announced that Guinevere would go to safety in Powys, Gwynhafach was meant to go too but as her father had fallen ill and could not travel, Gwynhafach remained at Caer Cadbryg to care for him. This was the perfect trigger for Ladwys' plan and Rowenna received her orders eagerly.

Father Dafydd

Dafydd is in his early 30s, broad, tall, and missing his right arm following a confrontation with a Saxon axe ten years ago. Before becoming a priest he was a spearman in King Cyngen's warbands but after losing the arm retired from the shield wall and took on the duties as Builth's priest, a role his uncle had held until his death eight years ago. Dafydd is therefore worldly and capable, but he is also affable and humble. He was one of the first to offer Builth as a place of refuge for the Dumnonians and he believes in helping his neighbours whoever they might be, just as someone called Samaritan helped a poor traveller who had been robbed by bandits in the Holy Lands where Jesus was born. He is a good, honest man, pious but not a proselytiser, who tries to lead by example.

Guinevere's condition concerns him. He has seen this young, vibrant woman become a shadow of herself with each passing week. He has sent to Caer Branog for healers, including a druid: none have been able to help. Cures and remedies have had some effect but the disease persists. Dafydd visits Guinevere every day, sits with her, occasionally recounting bible stories, but mostly quietly prays for her. An Insight roll when observing Dafydd and Guinevere might infer that the priest is a little bit in love with Guinevere, but he also loves his wife and this is very evident in the way he smiles whenever Brenna is about. After all, who has not fallen to Guinevere's charms?

Dafydd is therefore an ally. He wants Guinevere restored to health and believes that this is a test from God — for the entire village and not just Guinevere. These are concerns he voices privately and never to the general public.

Brenna

Dafydd's wife is dark haired and beautiful in a tired, forlorn way. She and Dafydd have one child, Gryff, now 7 years old, but Brenna has lost three children to miscarriages and is now unable to bear more. This saddens her and she fears she has been cursed by God for something she did before she and Dafydd were married. She is hugely supportive of Dafydd, but has also seen the look in his eye when he sits with Guinevere and is quietly jealous of his obvious regard for her. A successful Insight roll of Brenna when she is near Dafydd and Guinevere, or even when Guinevere's name

is mentioned, intimates a jealousy and fear of their house guest. Nevertheless, Brenna helps to tend to Guinevere and has struck up a friendship with Rowenna, Guinevere's handmaiden. The friendship is growing and now Brenna allows Gryff, her son, to run errands for Rowenna.

Gryff

A shy lad, the 7-year-old Gryff wants to be a warrior like his father once was, or a priest, if he gets injured. He likes to help and although he balks at the chores his father and mother give him, he lives to perform the errands Rowenna asks him to do. She tickles him and tells him funny stories and Gryff wishes Rowenna was his older sister. In fact the two of them have a secret. Every so often Gryff goes into the woods and high up the hill to one of the old huts near an abandoned charcoal pit. There, hidden in the hut, he finds a small pouch with a white powder in it, which Rowenna says is 'spirit dust'. He brings the pouch to Rowenna, telling no one about this special little errand, and she rewards him with a tickle, a hug, or, sometimes, something brought from Caer Cadbryg, like a honeycomb. This is their secret, and it is precious to him. A number of the errands Rowenna has him do, the normal ones, take him into the woods, so it's not unusual for him to venture into them on his own. No-one questions these excursions.

Little does Gryff know that he is collecting the poison that is slowly killing Guinevere. Rowenna has told him the 'spirit dust' is used to help keep Rowenna's skin as clear and rosy as it always looks, and so childishly smitten is Gryff with his new, surrogate, older sister, he believes her. Were he to discover the truth, he would turn on her an instant, his Love Rowenna Passion of 85% becoming Hate Rowenna at the same percentage almost immediately. Gryff loves Rowenna but he loves his father and mother and God more, and he would never do anything to knowingly harm a pretty woman like Guinevere, even if she is a pagan.

Curwan

A sly fellow, Curwan is a failed bard from Gwynedd who has drifted across Britain bringing his particular brand of amorality to those willing to pay for it. Lacking the physique, health, and courage to become a warrior, he was meant to train as a bard but found the requirements too taxing and far less lucrative than he desired. Curwan likes wealth and intrigue; he likes to court the rich and powerful but this is not the bardic calling. Instead he left the bardic pursuit and honed his skills in deceit. In time, he branched into herbalism and became fascinated with poisons. Focusing on their manufacture, he has become an expert. Curwan can, for a price, make poisons that maim, kill, simulate illness, are tasteless, odourless, fast acting, and slow. His knowledge of plants and various natural minerals is, perhaps, unrivalled and he has discreetly made a name for himself amongst those who require the secrecy of his art.

Curwan has lived in Powys for many years. The forests are a ready source of plants, malignant and benign, for the potions and poisons he specialises in. He travels widely through Gwent and Dumnonia too, gathering work in the process. He uses a variety of names, and even Curwan is not the name he was born with; merely the one he uses for his Builth/Caer Cadbryg dealings. In Builth, he is known as a tracker and forester, not as an herbalist, and so he has not been approached to help find aid for Guinevere. He makes his home in the forest about a mile east of Builth, on the other side of the bridge over the Wye in a place unknown to the locals. His roundhouse is well concealed in the forest and unless one knows the trails, very difficult to find. He uses local bracken, branches, and leaves to help conceal its existence and the clearing around the hut is deliberately overgrown to keep it secret. But within is both a poisoner's and healer's paradise: chock-full of dried plants, herbs, weeds, berries, plus solutions of his own devising from all manner of sources that can be combined to achieve all manner of effects.

The poison made for Guinevere is prepared from fifteen different plants, including foxglove and deadly nightshade. He makes only small doses at a time – enough for three meals – which he puts into small cloth pouches and then takes, under cover of night, to the charcoal burners' hut where he leaves it for Gryff to collect. Naturally enough, he has an antidote, or can manufacture one and will do so if severely threatened. However, Curwan operates to one simple rule: if paid for a job, carry it through, and Ladwys has paid in gold for slowly killing Guinevere.

The payment was made in the form of a gold ring and a gold chain Uther gave to Ladwys after his indiscretion with Ygraine. Ladwys was glad to be rid of both and instructed Curwan to melt them down to avoid either piece of jewelry being tracked back to her. Curwan melted down the chain, which is now in the form of a small ingot (worth 6 GP) and hidden in a leather bag, containing coins and jewelry amounting to some 200 SP, secreted beneath the floor of his hut.

But the ring he has kept intact, in case he needs insurance and a way to return any blame to Ladwys. The ring is very carefully hidden in the hollowed-out trunk of an old, dead elm tree close to his hut, in a pouch similar to the one he uses for his poisons, hooked onto a nail pushed into the wood a good arm's-length above the hole appears in the trunk. Unless one knows the pouch is there, stumbling across is nearly impossible and would require a Herculean Perception roll, plus a clue provided by Curwan. The ring is engraved: it shows a dragon intertwined with a fox across its outer face. Anyone who knows Uther and his family knows that the dragon is the Pendragon's symbol, and the fox the name Uther used for Ladwys. Although Ladwys rarely wore the ring, it can be traced back to her without much effort and will act as proof of her complicity in the plot against Guinevere.

If Rowenna is Discovered,

After administering the fatal dose or if discovered himself, Curwan will make a run for it. In the latter case, also abandoning his plan to deliver a fatal dose of poison to Guinevere if it proves necessary. He takes his money and the ring, sets fire to his hut and heads deep into the forest using little-known paths and trails, making for secluded and difficult to reach areas where he can hide, live off the land, and eventually leave by heading north and thence into Cornovia or even into Brigantes lands. Curwan is careful and can change his appearance by shaving his beard, cutting his hair and altering his clothes, accent and even posture. He has no scruples save self-preservation and the pursuit of wealth. All else is secondary. If caught, he bargains, readily surrendering Rowenna and Ladwys in exchange for his own life.

Curwan ventures into Builth occasionally to obtain things he needs, drink mead with some of the locals, and catch up on local news. It's a clever pretence but seems natural enough. He keeps his distance from Guinevere, Rowenna and the Dumnonian refugees but mingles easily with the Builth locals who have known him for a long time and suspect nothing of his true vocation. He's known as a good trailsman and tracker and often acts as a guide for hunters in the woods although he rarely hunts himself. It's likely he'll encounter the characters, especially if he travelled from Caer Cadbryg with them. If so, he's easy-going, inquires politely after Guinevere and offers to help in whatever ways he can. He acts as a concerned Powysian and it takes a Herculean Insight roll (opposed by Curwan's Deceit) to gain even the slightest inkling of his involvement in all of this.

Lucene

Lucene is one of the refugees and also Natanleod's mistress. She travelled down with Guinevere and has been friendly with her ever since she came to Caer Cadbryg with Arthur. On arriving in Builth, she has acted as the leader of the refugees, developing a liaison with both Geheris and Dafydd in a bid to ensure the Dumnonians feel welcome. Lucene is, like Guinevere, flame-haired, but is fifteen years her senior and has a distinct gravitas. While she is not married to Natanleod, her position as one of his counsellors is assured and her reputation in Dumnonia is that of a well-liked consort who has also served time as a spear maiden, fighting alongside her lover.

Natanleod is married to a woman called Yvet, and she is much older than he and in very poor health. It was a political marriage and Yvet has been quite accepting of Natanleod's relationship with Lucene. Neither Natanleod nor Lucene flaunt their love for each other and remain discrete. It is a reasonable arrangement and not uncommon amongst Celts.

Lucene is welcoming to the characters and is the first one to greet them when they arrive. She is deeply concerned for Guinevere and it was she who sent word to Arthur that Guinevere had asked for the characters. 'She fell ill a few days after we arrived here,' she says. 'There seems to have been a general illness in Builth, but Guinevere did not shake it off as others have. I've watched her grow weaker almost by the day. Nothing we've done seems to work and I'm worried that if we don't find a cure soon, Guinevere will die. If she does, it will ruin Arthur. Dumnonia needs him. He needs Guinevere. It is that simple.'

Lucene has her suspicions. Builth is staunchly Christian and because Guinevere is both a pagan and the woman who broke a betrothal vow to King Achaius, many of the Builth locals have taken an immediate dislike to her. They sneer, snipe, and gossip about her, and Lucene has heard the whispered insults and snide looks. 'A curse perhaps? Many of these Christian women were once pagan and remember the old curses and rituals for attracting spirits of disease and weakness. I would not be surprised if some of the Builth women have not colluded into bringing such a thing to pass.'

If poison is suggested, Lucene says she is unsure. 'Rowenna tastes everything Guinevere is given to eat and drink and I, too, have tasted her food at random times. Neither of us has fallen ill. There is nothing in what she is given that indicates a poison. It is possible, of course, but few gain access to Guinevere's chamber: myself, Rowenna, Dafydd, and, on occasion, his wife, Brenna. That is it. Most are unwilling to go near Guinevere in case they contract whatever malady ails her.'

Everything Lucene says is truthful, of course. Her suspicions about Builth women causing the sickness are misguided but not without foundation. The Builth women spit when Guinevere's name is mentioned, whenever they pass the roundhouse where she is interned, and touch their crucifixes in a bid to avert her evil.

Lucene has grown to know people in Builth and most respect her. Although not a Christian herself, Lucene has attended prayers and this has gone some way towards her gaining their trust. She can provide introductions to others in Builth, including Geheris and Dafydd.

Magda and Mebh

Twin sister and brother, Magda and Mebh live on the outskirts of Builth and are the most hostile of the locals to the Dumnonians' presence. Magda maintains Guinevere is a witch and a whore, and Mebh, meek and mild-mannered, agrees with his shrewish sister. Magda leads the gossip against Guinevere and Mebh reinforces it amongst the men-folk. Like several of the Builth men, Mebh is enthralled by Rowenna, who, as a clearly Christian woman, must surely be a saint in the making for tending with such devotion to a fallen women like Guinevere. Whenever he mentions Rowenna's virtues, Magda is quick to slap her brother or twist his nose in a bid to cure him of such thoughts.

If there is anyone in Builth who can detect Curwan's poison, it is Magda and Mebh. They too are herbalists although they specialise in cures for common ailments rather than poisons. Nevertheless, the twins have an acute senses of smell and taste, and the ability to detect even the tiniest traces of something suspicious and herbal contained in a dish or drink. Their hut, like that of most herbalists, hangs with drying herbs, flowers and weeds. They have pestles, mortars, and other equipment for grinding and preparing herbs for poultices, balms, powders, potions, and many other delivery devices. If brought in to sample Guinevere's food or tricked into trying it themselves, either Magda or Mebh immediately detect the presence of foxglove and then express no surprise as to the effects Guinevere is suffering. Of course, they have been unable to make such deductions previously because they have shunned Guinevere (and are sure that her ailment is a curse sent by God, not concocted by man).

And yes, they can create a cure. But they require repentance from Guinevere and acceptance of Christ into her life. To save her body, first one must save her soul....

Cenor

The gruff Cenor is Gerheris' brother and the leader of Builth's small warband. He has never faced the Saxons but he has plenty of experience fighting Silurians in defence of Gwent. He's a tall, grizzled man with shaggy grey hair and a greying beard and he communicates in a series of grunts, snorts, and snapped phrases, perpetuating the image of the hard, taciturn, shield wall veteran. In practice, this is a veneer. Cenor has fought in shield walls but never in the front rank. He has survived dozens of battles against Silures, often by fleeing whenever possible. He gives a very good show of training the small number of Builth spearmen that compose Builth's warband but anyone succeeding in a Lore (Strategy and Tactics) roll can see that his knowledge is rudimentary and flawed. Builth's spearmen, faced with any decent enemy, would crumble sooner than they would stand.

Not that Cenor recognises any of this. If his methods are challenged, he uses his size and ferocious appearance to brow-beat his naysayers. He acts in the manner of the classic bully. No-one in Builth stands-up to him and so he gets away with this posturing; but when faced with a competent warrior, his meagre skill (65% in the Spearman combat style) soon becomes apparent.

Cenor makes it his business to let anyone new in Builth know that he is its muscle. He makes a show of drilling his 20 spearmen (of varying years, but uniformly mediocre competence) in front of any proven warriors and enjoys regaling everyone with his brave exploits against the Silures whenever he has had much to drink — which is most nights. His wife, Oonagh, is a timid Irish woman who finds it easier to agree with what Cenor has to say, thereby avoiding his fists. His sons left Builth years ago, tired of their father's bluster.

Unfulfilled, save by a simmering internal fury, Cenor eyes Rowenna greedily. Some of his men have circled her already like love-sick dogs, but Cenor has made it plain to them that if anyone has Rowenna, it will be him. Some are gathering the courage to tackle him. Cenor has a sharpened dagger in his belt as a response. He does not like the Dumnonians. He does not like anyone who comes to Builth who might see through his pretence. But he does want Rowenna, and he means to have her.

Geheris

The acknowledged headman of the village, Geheris is getting old but still commands respect and loyalty from the villagers. He was never a warriors, always a fisherman and woodsman, but he displays a quiet authority that makes him a natural leader. His younger brother, Cenor, was the hot-head of the family while Geheris was always measured, responsible and homely.

Geheris lives close to the river with his extended family. Although he is not keen on the Dumnonians coming to Builth he knows this is temporary and it is the Christian thing to offer them safe lodgings if their home is under threat. He is loyal to his king, loyal to his God and loyal to his people. If the Dumnonians are to be his people for a while, he will be loyal to them, too.

He does anticipate trouble. The people of Builth are quite insular, and not at all used to outsiders. Guinevere's reputation preceded her and Geheris knows she invites resentment. But, he considers everyone under his protection and will defend Guinevere unless she does something to bring misfortune upon herself. From what he's seen of her, before she fell ill, this has all been fuss over nothing - not that the locals see it the same way.

For this reason he is keeping a careful eye on Cenor. His younger brother is a braggart and a bully. If anyone is going to cause trouble, you can guarantee Cenor will be involved somewhere. Still, he is family, and family comes first. If Cenor crosses the line too drastically, Cenor will not hesitate to do whatever is needed to put things right.

He is full of quiet admiration for Lucene. She is a strong, diplomatic woman and were he not married he would seek her affection. As it is, he is cordial and polite towards her, and has formed a good relationship which should help ease any tensions between the two communities. Secretly he thinks she is the most wonderful woman to have stepped into Builth in many years. If only things were different. He keeps his passions to himself, admiring Lucene from afar, and concentrates on tending his fishing nets and ensuring the Builth community tends to its own affairs.

General Builth Locals

With instruction from Gerheris and guidance from Dafydd, the Builth locals have been made to accept the presence of the Dumnonian refugees. Some are courteous and even friendly; others neutral, and some are hostile – especially to Guinevere. To determine the attitude of a random local (other than the personalities described above), roll 1d100 and consult the Builth Attitude table, below. Their attitude dictates the demeanour and skill grade the characters face whenever employing social skills or interacting with a Builth local.

1d100	Attitude	Skill Grade
01-20	Friendly	Standard
21-60	Neutral	Hard
61-90	Hostile	Formidable
91-00	Hateful	Herculean

Arriving in Builth

If travelling alone, the characters are intercepted before they can cross the bridge by Cenor and ten of his spearmen. They have formed a crude shield wall across the bridge and Cenor stands in front of them, resting on his spear, demanding to know what business the characters have in Builth. Cenor says little. He grunts, spits when he hears something he dislikes, and occasionally glances at his men and sniggers if the characters say something he finds amusing. He only moves if...

- Any character succeeds in a (Formidable) Opposed Influence roll against his own Willpower 63%
- Any character challenges him to direct combat: he swaggers forward as though to commence battle, but relents at the last minute, spitting and grumbling that 'Dumnonians aren't worth the effort.'
- Any female character challenges him, in which case the Opposed Influence/Willpower roll is at Easy for the woman.
- If an impasse occurs, Geheris and Lucene eventually arrive and force Cenor to stand down and return to the village.

Once the characters cross the bridge, they are formally greeted by Geheris and Lucene.

If travelling with the supply train, the characters arrive in Builth without any trouble and are greeted by Geheris and Lucene. Geheris arranges for somewhere for the characters to stay (a barn or storehouse that is hastily cleared). When the characters are rested – or sooner, if they insist – Lucene takes them to see Guinevere.

Guinevere

The roundhouse given over to Guinevere smells of sickness and fatigue: sweet, unpleasant, and cloying. A fire burns in the hearth constantly, tended by Rowenna, but Guinevere's bed is still heaped with furs and skins. Guinevere is very pale, with dark rings beneath her eyes and cracked lips, and her normally lustrous hair tangled and slicked with sweat. She has lost a great deal of weight, even though she tries to eat every day. She coughs frequently and has little strength although she tries to summon some when she sees the characters.

'Ah! You came. I am so glad. I knew Arthur would send you. Have they made you comfortable here? Have you been fed?'

She tries to explain her illness. 'At first I had trouble sleeping and was so tired during the day that I was next to useless. Then it just seemed easier to sleep at day anyway. My bones ache and I feel both hot and cold at the same time. I get headaches sometimes and my bowels feel loose but little happens. I have nightmares too, and times where I wonder if I'm going mad. What's happening to me?'

Rowenna is present during the characters' audience with Guinevere, but she is simply a compliant handmaiden who spends a little time fussing over her mistress and trying to make her comfortable. The characters can easily learn the following...

- All Guinevere's meals are prepared by Rowenna.
- Both Lucene and Rowenna have sampled meals – all seems fine.
- Guinevere started to fall ill a few days after reaching Builth and each day she gets a little weaker.
- Guinevere says she has suffered nightmares where she sees apparitions circling her bed, calling her to cross through the Gate of Ivory to find peace.

After half an hour of talking, Guinevere is too tired to continue and Lucene insists the characters leave her. From here on, it is up to the characters to decide what they do and how they do it. If the cause of Guinevere's illness is not found, she will die and Arthur's devastation will weaken Dumnonia and shake the Alliance of Britain. The characters, if they do not realise it, are pivotal in the battle against the Saxons — and everything hinges on Guinevere's survival.

Investigation

Success in this scenario depends on the characters achieving the following:

- Uncovering Rowenna's poisoning, or putting an end to it somehow.
- Uncovering Curwan's role in the scheme.
- Preventing Curwan from delivering a fatal dose of the poison to Guinevere.
- Tracing the scheme back to Ladwys to prevent future attempts.

Although there are many clues given in the description of the situation in Builth and in the actions/motivations of the different personalities, it can be easy for the characters to miss something vital because a skill roll has been failed, or because they begin to chase a dead-end. The role of the Games Master is to build a compelling story but not to hinder the chances of a successful conclusion simply because the dice happen to be unkind. If, for example, the characters say they keep close watch on Rowenna but the crucial Perception roll fails, allow the characters another chance at a later point in the scenario. Or, reward inventive and cunning investigative ideas with easier skill grades or perhaps use Group Luck points to act as a further pool for changing unlucky rolls.

Uncovering the plot should not be fast or simple but neither should it be impossible. Although Rowenna is involved and uncovering her role helps save Guinevere, Curwan and Ladwys are the real sources of evil in this scheme. Curwan is ruthless and will certainly try to kill Guinevere — and, if necessary, kill the characters too. Curwan can manipulate others, such as Geheris, Cenor, Brenna, Magda, and Mebh, into assisting him — either in poisoning Guinevere on his behalf or attacking the characters if they learn too much and get too close. Therefore, disrupting the scheme is only part of the goal: catching those responsible is the only way to thwart the plan completely.

The characters should be given plenty of chances for interaction with the listed personalities: some help, some hinder, some are a distraction, and some are enemies who could be turned into allies. For example, Brenna is jealous of Dafydd's apparent fondness for Guinevere. Curwan can exploit that and convince her to try to poison Guinevere if Rowenna is caught (or the poisoning via Rowenna's food disrupted). Cenor desires Rowenna greatly and hates the characters, so if Curwan's exploitation of Rowenna can be exposed, Cenor can become a reluctant ally. He could also be made to protect Rowenna if Curwan fans Cenor's lust.

Read the different motivations carefully and assemble an idea of how the personalities may interact with the characters, what use they have, and how they can add intrigue to the time spent in Builth. Use the Builth Events, if necessary, to help build additional tension and add layers of interest. It is, of course, impossible to second-guess what characters will come up with when left to their own devices but there are a few factors that can be used by Games Masters to craft a rewarding scenario.

Players Love a Mystery

There's a tendency to ignore the obvious solution in favour of something more devious. For instance, if the characters decide that Guinevere is under some form of spirit attack, let the idea develop by, perhaps, giving Magda and Mebh a druidic background that might suggest some form of supernatural cause. Later, steer the characters back to the real plot by having them stumble across one of the clues to the real situation.

Passions Are a Powerful Tool

There's plenty of jealousy surrounding Rowenna and Guinevere. Allow these passions to rise and misdirect the characters from the more straightforward revenge plot Rowenna and Curwan are enacting on Ladwys' behalf. As passions and tensions rise, there will be plenty of opportunity for the characters to discover the truth.

Embrace the Obvious

If the characters immediately recognise that Rowenna must be the poisoner, they still need proof. Encourage them to take their time getting it. Also show that Rowenna is a mere pawn in a larger game, one that requires circumspection and discretion to follow. Provide additional action through the various passions, tensions, and side events offered in the scenario. Note Rowenna has defenders in Cenor, Mebh and Gryff.

Turn the Tables

If the characters get too close, too quickly, have the tables turned on them. Curwan somehow plants poison in the characters' belongings and ensures Lucene or Dafydd finds it (or he could plant it on Brenna). Or have Cenor violently intervene. Perhaps Rowenna is murdered and all the signs point to the characters as the culprits. Turning the tables is a drastic, risky thing to do, but can provide an incredibly rewarding way to develop the story. Instead of being the investigators, they are, instead, the investigated.

No Help From Beyond

One thing to avoid is allowing the characters clear access to the Spirit World. Even if they have a druid, gaining access to the truth in that way should prove inconclusive or hazy. Powys is a Christian country and the spirits are very, very weak here. Such examination could also be confounded by a weak curse being wrought by the locals — ineffective but present enough to cause confusion. Note that Merlin has no power in Powys and Morgana will not help. The characters need to rely on their wits, cunning and logic to solve this crime.

Using the Locals

How the various personalities act is going to vary depending on what the characters do, whether they are confrontational with their suspicions, and so on; however, in general, the personalities act as follows:

- Father Dafydd: Helpful, genial, secretly besotted with Guinevere
- Brenna: Slightly resentful, helpful, jealous of Guinevere
- Gryff: Helpful, willing, besotted with Rowenna (sisterly)
- Rowenna: Pious, flirtatious, crafty, malleable
- Curwan: Amoral, clever, deceitful, ruthless; charming, disarming, witty, manipulative
- Lucene: Concerned, protective, guarded, honest, sensible
- Magda: Spiteful, righteous, disdainful, smart, manipulative
- Mebh: Hen-pecked, manipulated, lovelorn over Rowenna
- Cenor: Brash, untrustworthy, craven, bullying, slow, jealous, besotted with Rowenna
- Geheris: Stern, brusque, honest, admiring of Lucene.

Description of Builth and Environs

Builth occupies a naturally raised plain on the south-west side of the Wye river. It is effectively surrounded by woodland with the ground rising to both north and west, and the clearing has been considerably expanded over many years to accommodate the growing community.

A wide path to the north runs through the forest until it reaches Caer Branog. Officially, Builth is part of the wider Branog community; in reality, Branog exercises no administrative control over it and so Builth is left to its own, simple devices. Its residents make their living through timber, charcoal and a small amount of farming. Hunts are frequent and the locals supplement their diets with fish and eels from the river along with other game caught in the woodland. Builth has been Christian for almost fifty years and every Builth-born person follows the Christian faith although a handful still hold to a few, non-contentious, pagan beliefs and small rituals.

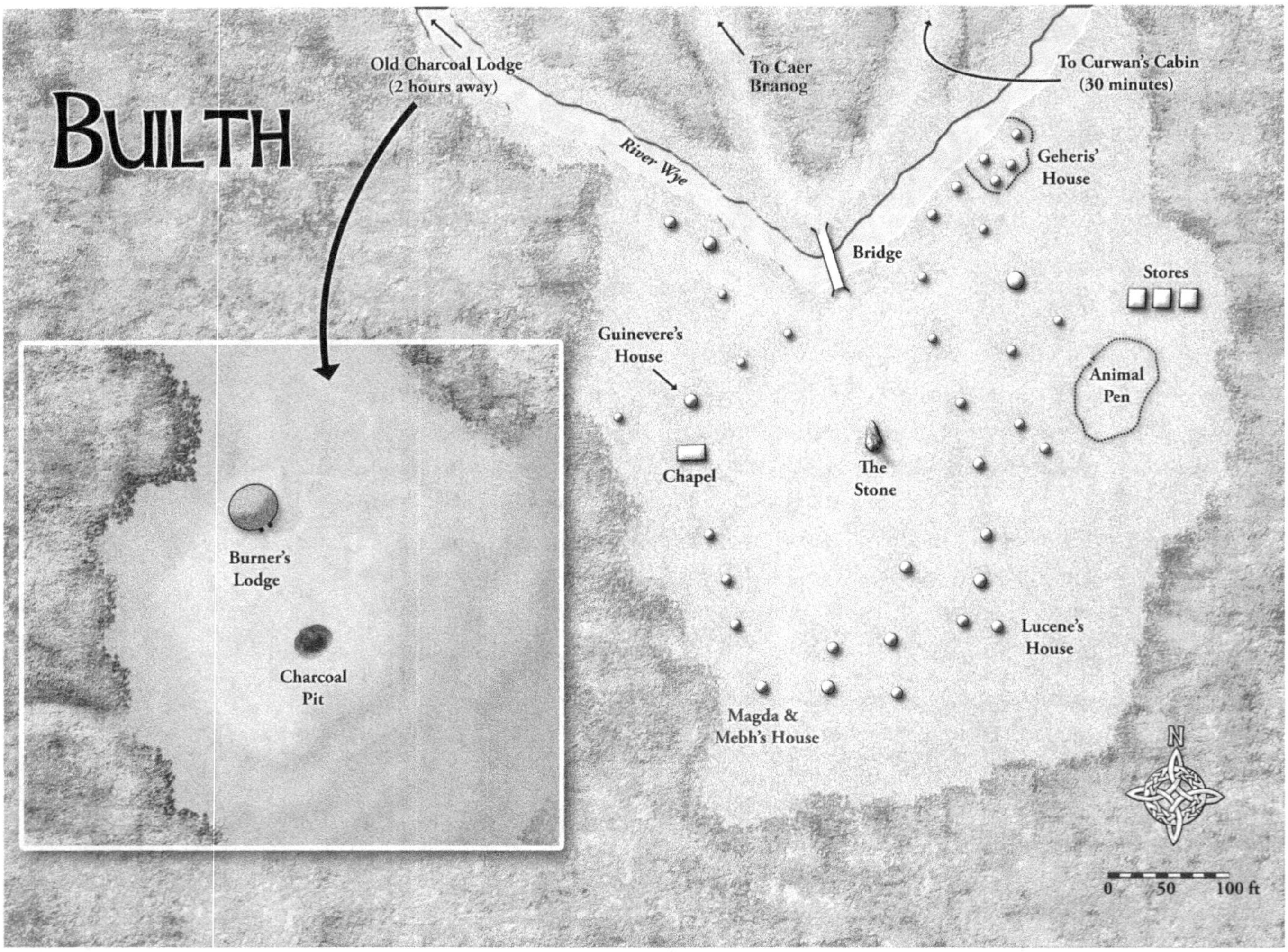

Builth

The Bridge

The bridge over the River Wye was built by the Romans more than two hundred years ago. It is sturdy and strong, made from dressed stone, with piers sunk into the river bed. The bridge arches over the river with a gentle camber and is wide enough for two carts to pass. The eastern bank of the Wye marks the start of Builth and so the river is considered part of the village too.

The Chapel

Built from stone and timber in the traditional rectangular design, the chapel is large enough to accommodate all Builth residents for communal services. With the added Christians from Dumnonia, it is now bursting at the seams. The chapel is simple enough inside: a stone altar, carved by a mason from Caer Branog, forms the impressive centrepiece, and a large crucifix of polished oak, made by Dafydd's father, crowns the altar. Seating is a few wooden trestles reserved for the older members of the congregation while everyone else stands or sits on the floor. Dafydd and Brenna can often be found here, outside of ceremonial times, in quiet personal prayer. On the northern wall is an alcove that acts as a shrine to the Virgin Mary. It contains a crude carving of the Mother and Christ Child, made from alabaster, and brought from some land to the east. Women in general and especially those looking to fall pregnant pray at this shrine. Brenna prays here when no-one else is around, asking the Virgin to send a sign that her husband will not be stolen by the 'red-head whore'.

Stores

This collection of huts and ramshackle stables hold communal winter supplies and house the chickens, geese, and pigs that form part of the community livestock. Some of the huts have been cleared to make way for Dumnonian refugees and this is where the characters can expect to be billeted, uncomfortably close to the pig sty.

The Stone

Opposite the chapel, in the centre of the village, is a lone standing stone, about the height of a man and 3 feet in diameter. It is roughly arrow-head shaped and was erected by the Old People of Britain long, long ago. These days it has been turned into a Christian symbol with an intricate Celtic cross carved into its surface and painted ochre with locally produced pigments. The stone forms a natural focal point for community meetings and it is also where Cenor assembles his spearmen before leading them off for training.

Dafydd's House

This roundhouse belongs to Brenna's sister, her husband, and three children. Dafydd, Brenna and Gryff are staying here while Guinevere occupies their house, so the roundhouse is very cramped at present. Tension is alleviated by Dafydd and Brenna spending most of their time at the chapel while Gryff, when not out playing, runs errands for Rowenna.

Guinevere's House

Close to the chapel and the Stone, this modest roundhouse was built by Dafydd and is now given over to Guinevere. The window holes are covered with hide curtains, and a storage hut just behind the house is where Rowenna sleeps and prepares Guinevere's meals. Supplies are brought to her from the communal stores by Brenna, which may heighten suspicions that Brenna is behind the poisoning. Inside the roundhouse the furnishings are simple and typical: a bed, hearth, cooking utensils (now moved to Rowenna's hut) and somewhere to store clothes.

Guinevere is really too weak to leave the house but every couple of days she insists on trying to walk a little to gain some air. Rowenna helps her, along with whoever else might be on hand: Dafydd, Brenna, Lucene, or the characters. Guinevere tells the characters that Arthur mustn't know how weak she really is. 'He worries too much and he has enough to think about with the Saxons. If you must send him word, tell him I'm no worse and, perhaps, feeling a little stronger. See how much I walked today! I must be improving!'

Lucene's House

Shared with five other Dumnonian women and several young children, the house Lucene occupies is cramped and chaotic but the women are making the best of the conditions. As Natanleod's mistress, Lucene has the de facto role of leader of the Dumnonian refugees and she has risen admirably to the responsibilities, negotiating with the locals, ensuring good relations are established and setting boundaries for the Dumnonians. Lucene has gathered a decent amount of respect amongst the Builth locals and easily commands the same from the Dumnonian women.

As the conditions in her shared house are so cramped, Lucene is often abroad in the village, visiting others (especially Guinevere) or walking in the forests. She helps with the village chores, including laundry, cleaning, tending to livestock, and so on, so Lucene always seems to be busy and occupied. The Builth women like her and even those who loathe Guinevere, are careful not to voice their opinions in Lucene's earshot — not that this stops Lucene from hearing what is truly being said.

Geheris' House

In reality, a close cluster of four roundhouses, for Geheris and his family (which includes Cenor), this is the largest grouping in Builth and stands close to the river. Geheris is a fisherman these days, and always has nets in and out of the water, trawling for eel, trout, and crayfish, within sight of his house. All Geheris' children are grown now, with his three sons serving in Caer Branog's warbands and his daughters married to good husbands. Two of his daughters are in Isca in Dumnonia, but the youngest married

a local man and lives in one of the four roundhouses. She had two children, both girls, but one died of a sudden fever last year, much to everyone's grief. Geheris dotes on his grandchildren and this loss was especially poignant.

Cenor, Geheris' younger brother, lives in the third house with his timid wife. Where Geheris is popular and capable, Cenor lives on a flimsy reputation and in Geheris' shadow. Cenor is bitter, bullying, and a mean drunk. Although he commands the twenty-strong warband of Builth it has never seen action and, most likely, never will. Poorly trained due to Cenor's slipshod ways, the Builth warband is viewed with some disdain by seasoned warriors from Caer Branog.

Geheris' house is always a hive of activity. People come and go frequently, the menfolk who are direct cronies of Geheris gather on the riverbank to drink and gossip while repairing fishing nets and crayfish traps, and there is always an air of business about the place. Only when Cenor is raving drunk do people make themselves scarce, and Geheris occasionally has to intervene, especially when poor Oonagh, Cenor's downtrodden wife, might be in danger of a beating.

The Old Charcoal Lodge

Northwest of the village the ground rises quite steeply until it reaches a broad plateau that offers stunning views across the Wye valley and southern Powys. It takes about an hour to reach the summit from the village. There is a wide clearing at this summit where an abandoned charcoal pit and burner's lodge remains. The lodge is a collapsing structure of wood, wicker, dried mud, moss, thatch and bracken. It is designed to be weather-proof, rather than roomy and comfortable, and was used by the burners who had to tend a charcoal pit for several days. Because the lodge is partially collapse, gaining entry to it requires someone small and lithe, and young Gryff from the village is perfect. Curwan is able to secretly stash a pouch of poison inside the lodge from the outside using a cunningly disguised gap in the structure. When retrieving it, if one does not know about the concealed external access, it is necessary to crawl into the lodge, avoiding the sharp outcrops of twig and fumbling around in the dark (Formidable Perception rolls for anyone over SIZ 10, Hard Perception rolls for SIZ 9 or less).

Curwan hides a fresh batch of poison every three days. Rowenna sends Gryff to retrieve it on the morning after Curwan deposits it. Gryff is told to also collect the moss that clings to the outside of the lodge because this is useful in a variety of poultices Rowenna (and others) can make to help Guinevere but this is really just a cover for retrieving the 'spirit dust' as Gryff knows it. Gryff believes that Rowenna uses the spirit dust to keep her skin soft and hair glossy. She teases him by saying if she doesn't have the dust to rub on her skin she'll turn into an old crone like Magda, and Gryff, not wanting his new, adored big sister to become ugly, is very happy to help.

Gryff never wastes time when he comes to collect the poison. He scrambles up the hillside using one of several paths he knows, darts into the lodge, locates the pouch, gathers some moss, and is on his way back to Builth within 10 to 15 minutes. He also doesn't pay too much attention to whether he is being followed: he's a guileless lad and doesn't consider what he's doing is wrong or suspicious. If befriended, he might be persuaded to show the characters this secret place only he and Rowenna know about, although she has told him to keep the spirit dust itself a secret and only the direst threats would get him to reveal what he really comes for.

Curwan's Cabin

On the eastern side of the river Wye, the forest is thick, dark and not frequently visited by the villagers. This is where Curwan maintains his base of operations: a concealed roundhouse, deep in the woods a mile east of the bridge, and at the bottom of a natural basin in the forest. The roundhouse merges well with its surroundings, with the foliage around being allowed to overgrow and encroach, keep the building concealed.

Curwan knows the locale very, very well. He has several game snares set up to catch a variety of creatures, including a couple of traps that can disable someone of human size. Approaching the cabin and avoiding such precautions requires a Herculean Perception roll, or a Formidable Track/Survival roll. Failing ensures that an ankle or wrist becomes ensnared by strong, sharp wire that cuts into the skin causing 1d4+1 damage. Freeing oneself from a snare is easy enough but Curwan coats the wire with a sticky toxin of his own devising that prevents the wound from healing properly, resulting in an infection 1d8 days later that causes a burning

sensation within the affected limb and results in a further 1d2 points of damage daily. It requires a Healing roll to clean out an infected wound and if not treated properly by the time the limb reaches Major Wound status, if becomes gangrenous and must be amputated to prevent the damage from spreading to an adjacent location.

Curwan's secrets are already described on page 339. He uses the cabin for sleeping and preparing his poisons but prefers to spend time out and about, listening and watching what is going on. Information is something he values and can use in trade. If discovered, he has no issues with fleeing the cabin after first setting light to the place (and trying to retrieve his valuables).

The old elm where the ring is hidden lies on the south side of the cabin, about 20 feet away. Two snares, concealed at ankle height, as previously described, need to be avoided to reach the elm — although the ring within is not protected by any particular traps.

Events in Builth

These events can be used to any degree Games Masters wish, or ignored if necessary. They can be used in any order and help provide additional interaction and encounter opportunities for the characters, along with adding further drama, interest and intrigue.

The Dance

It is decided to hold a small feast and dance to help liven up the mood in Builth. The area around the Stone is cleared, food and alcohol brought out, a pig slaughtered for roasting, and people encouraged to come and dance the evening away. Guinevere insists on coming out of her house to enjoy the evening and she does so, though weak and the object of several spiteful and peevish comments.

At first, the locals and Dumnonians keep to themselves, but Lucene encourages the characters to ask Builth women to dance. She and Geheris lead by example, which soon encourages others to mingle. Within an hour, everyone is dancing and enjoying themselves.

Guinevere encourages Rowenna to join in and she is the focus of many of the Builth men's attentions. She accepts as many dance invitations as she can but still some men glower with resentment — along with some Builth women as their menfolk dance with the pretty handmaiden. Cenor, in particular, grows more and more jealous although he never asks for a dance himself. Eventually, drunk, he rudely barges into a dance where Rowenna is partnered with one of the characters and things may turn ugly. Cenor is ready for a brawl — even though he is too drunk to win one — and has a few of his cronies watching his back and ready to step in. If a fight breaks out, it ruins the night and Geheris, Lucene, and Dafydd are needed to restore order. Cenor is blamed of course, but some Builth locals hold Rowenna responsible. Does she not know the effect she has? She should have stayed indoors with that whore she serves...

Samsun's Arrival

Father Samsun arrives from Caer Cadbryg. Ladwys has sent him to observe Guinevere's sickness and report back but also to report on the characters too. Father Samsun knows nothing of the real plot and is grateful to be away from Caer Cadbryg because of the strong rumours that Cerdic and Aelle have joined forces and are planning an attack on Dumnonia within weeks. Powys is as safe as anywhere.

Father Samsun spends his time praying, watching, and meddling. He takes an instant dislike to Father Dafydd and tries to supplant him as the leader of the Christians while in Builth, insisting on leading services, preaching the sermons loudly and arrogantly from the Stone, and generally undermining Father Dafydd wherever possible. Although Father Samsun's style is not what the Builth locals are used to, it appeals to the more devout. Father Samsun quickly gains a small following, including Magda and Mebh, who believe he is the best thing to happen to Builth in years and is clearly destined to be a Saint. Father Samsun takes every opportunity to slyly insult Guinevere and any other pagans but stops short of direct insults because he wants to curry favour with Arthur as much as with Ladwys.

He is genuinely shocked at Guinevere's illness and believes that only turning to Christ will save her. However, if foul play is uncovered while he is present, Father Samsun can become a useful ally in finding the culprits. Father Samsun sees this as a chance to get

into Arthur's good graces somehow and if Guinevere can become a convert too, so much the better.

Gryff Goes Missing

On one of his errands to retrieve a pouch of poison, Gryff slips on the steep slope of the hill and falls, twisting his ankle and managing to knock himself unconscious. He is not badly hurt but he is missing for an entire day and this requires a search by the concerned villagers and the characters. Finding him is not too difficult although it takes time, because no-one thinks to venture in the direction of the old charcoal burner's lodge – but he is not far away. The Games Master can decide if Gryff has retrieved the poison or not and, if he has, if it is on his person or has fallen nearby can be found. Gryff also has to explain why he's in this area and he says, truthfully, that he was looking for moss for a poultice Rowenna wants to make. He tries to keep quiet about the old lodge, but if pressed (Influence versus a Hard Willpower roll), Gryff tells where he was going to get the moss.

This provides an opportunity for the characters to perhaps find the poison and start piecing together the truth behind the plot.

End Game

In an ideal conclusion, Guinevere will be cured and Rowenna, Curwan, and Ladwys exposed. Arthur's fury is vast: it might be possible for Rowenna to weather the humiliation (although she risks expulsion from Dumnonia) but Curwan will be hunted down (another potential quest for the characters) with a view to execution or sacrifice at druidic hands (Merlin would find Curwan's spirit a very useful thing to torment and pick apart for knowledge). Ladwys though, being who she is, would be forced into exile, voluntary or not, in a Gwentish or Powysian convent, well away from Dumnonia and denied contact with the likes of Custennin or Father Samsun. Arthur could not even bring himself to publicly accuse Uther's widow of attempted murder and may even make excuses for her actions. She would certainly find defenders in Custennin and Father Samsun, although both men, devout as they are, would be privately appalled at the depths Ladwys has plumbed in her bid for revenge.

It is likely that Rowenna will be the scapegoat with Curwan escaping and Ladwys going undetected. Ladwys, of course, has little trouble sacrificing poor Rowenna and, with others, shakes her head sadly and condemns the poor, deluded girl who believed she was doing God's work. Without proof, few would believe Rowenna over Ladwys – although Merlin and Morgana certainly would and Merlin would find it a fascinating exercise to extract some form of elaborate revenge on Uther's wife.

There is the possibility of Guinevere dying. This would be an extreme conclusion and a sad one, but one that would plunge Arthur into a world of pain and sorrow that sees him retreating from his responsibilities and becoming a hate-filled agent of carnage as he takes his bitterness out on the Saxons – and anyone else who might cause him harm. Merlin could tolerate this for a while, but Arthur abandoning leadership renders Caledfwlch useless and jeopardises the unity of Britain. Merlin might therefore send the characters into Annwn, accompanied by Morgana perhaps, to negotiate with Lord Arawn for Guinevere to be returned to the living. This would be a perilous supernatural quest fit only for devout pagans, but one that would rescue Arthur's sanity and bring a truly mythic element to their relationship. How would Guinevere be changed by her experience? Would the carefree, flirtatious young woman be replaced by someone more hard-hearted or less faithful, or perhaps someone utterly devoted to Arthur and a force of power for Britain? This is for Games Masters to decide.

Non-Player Characters

Father Dafydd

Characteristics	Attributes	1d20	Location	AP/HP
STR: 11	Action Points: 2	1–3	Right Leg	0/5
CON: 10	Damage Modifier: 0	4–6	Left Leg	0/5
SIZ:13	Magic Points: 15	7–9	Abdomen	0/6
DEX: 11	Movement: 6 metres	10–12	Chest	0/7
INT: 13	Initiative Bonus: 14	13–15	Right Arm	0/1
POW: 15	Armour: None	16–18	Left Arm	0/4
CHA: 10		19–20	Head	0/5

Skills: *Athletics 42%, Brawn 41%, Endurance 45%, Evade 33%, Insight 75%, Locale 50%, Lore (Scripture) 74%, Perception 53%, Unarmed 50%, Willpower 48%*

Loyalty to God 80%, Love Brenna & Gryff 75%, Christian 90%,

Combat Style: None. If ever challenged and he has to defend himself, Dafydd relies on unarmed.

Brenna & Gryff

Attributes	1d20	Location	AP/HP
Action Points: 2	1–3	Right Leg	0/4
Damage Modifier: 0	4–6	Left Leg	0/4
Magic Points: 9	7–9	Abdomen	0/5
Movement: 6 metres	10–12	Chest	0/6
Initiative Bonus: 11	13–15	Right Arm	0/3
Armour: None	16–18	Left Arm	0/3
	19–20	Head	0/4

Skills: *Athletics 30%, Brawn 25%, Endurance 30%, Evade 25%, Locale (Builth) 70%, Lore (Scripture) 45%, Perception 40%, Willpower 48%*

Christian 75%, Loyalty to Builth 90%, Gryff - Love Rowenna 80%, Brenna and Gryff - Love Dafydd 90%

Combat Style: None.

Rowenna

Characteristics	Attributes	1d20	Location	AP/HP
STR: 10	Action Points: 2	1–3	Right Leg	0/5
CON: 10	Damage Modifier: 0	4–6	Left Leg	0/5
SIZ: 9	Magic Points: 13	7–9	Abdomen	0/6
DEX: 14	Movement: 6 metres	10–12	Chest	0/7
INT: 9	Initiative Bonus: 12	13–15	Right Arm	0/4
POW: 13	Armour: None	16–18	Left Arm	0/4
CHA: 16		19–20	Head	0/5

Skills: *Athletics 28%, Brawn 20%, Craft (Cook) 60%, Dance 80%, Deceit 59%, Endurance 30%, Evade 32%, Insight 45%, Locale 50%, Lore (Scripture) 30%, Perception 55%, Unarmed 25%, Willpower 39%*

Loyalty to Ladwys 80%, Hate Guinevere 60%, Christian 75%,

Combat Style: None.

Lucene

Characteristics	Attributes	1d20	Location	AP/HP
STR: 10	Action Points: 3	1–3	Right Leg	0/5
CON: 10	Damage Modifier: 0	4–6	Left Leg	0/5
SIZ: 10	Magic Points: 13	7–9	Abdomen	0/6
DEX: 14	Movement: 6 metres	10–12	Chest	0/7
INT: 14	Initiative Bonus: 12	13–15	Right Arm	0/4
POW: 13	Armour: None	16–18	Left Arm	0/4
CHA: 16		19–20	Head	0/5

Skills: *Athletics 34%, Brawn 20%, Craft (Spinning) 70%, Dance 74%, Endurance 41%, Evade 32%, Insight 76%, Locale 50%, Perception 59%, Unarmed 35%, Willpower 47%*

Love Natanleod 90%, Loyalty to Dumonian 80%, Love Guinevere 60%, Pagan 51%,

Combat Style: Self Defence (Unarmed and Dagger) 35%

Weapon	Size/Force	Reach	Damage	AP/HP
Dagger	*S*	*S*	*1d4+1*	*6/8*

Curwan

Characteristics	Attributes	1d20	Location	AP/HP
STR: 13	Action Points: 3	1–3	Right Leg	0/6
CON: 11	Damage Modifier: 0	4–6	Left Leg	0/6
SIZ: 12	Magic Points: 13	7–9	Abdomen	0/7
DEX: 17	Movement: 6 metres	10–12	Chest	0/7
INT: 17	Initiative Bonus: 17	13–15	Right Arm	0/5
POW: 13	Armour: None	16–18	Left Arm	0/5
CHA: 16		19–20	Head	0/6

Skills: *Athletics 55%, Brawn 52%, Customs (Celt) 75%, Deceit 90%, Endurance 54%, Evade 58%, Insight 62%, Language (Brythonic) 90%, Local 95%, Lore (Herbs) 96%, Lore (Poisons) 95%, Perception 73%, Sleight 77%, Stealth 65%, Unarmed 57%, Willpower 75%*

Loyalty to Self 90%

Combat Style: Self Defence (Dagger, Quarterstaff) 75%

Weapon	Size/Force	Reach	Damage	AP/HP
Dagger	*S*	*S*	*1d4+1*	*6/8*
Quarterstaff	*M*	*L*	*1d8*	*4/8*

Cenor, Self-Styled Champion of Builth

Characteristics	Attributes	1d20	Location	AP/HP
STR: 15	Action Points: 2	1–3	Right Leg	0/6
CON: 14	Damage Modifier: +1d2	4–6	Left Leg	0/6
SIZ: 15	Magic Points: 12	7–9	Abdomen	2/7
DEX: 12	Movement: 6 metres	10–12	Chest	2/8
INT: 12	Initiative Bonus: 10	13–15	Right Arm	0/5
POW: 12	Armour: Poor-Quality Leather Jerkin	16–18	Left Arm	0/5
CHA: 10		19–20	Head	0/6

Skills: *Athletics 55%, Brawn 55%, Customs (Celt) 85%, Endurance 60%, Evade 60%, Influence 35%, Insight 30%, Language (Brythonic) 100%, Lore (Strategy and Tactics) 40%, Perception 43%, Superstition 70%, Survival 48%, Unarmed 60%, Willpower 40%,*

Loyalty to Builth 60%, Love to Intimidate 75%, Fear Battle 65%, Christian 60%

Combat Style: Shield Wall (Spear, Sword, and Shield. Trait, Shield Wall) 60%.

Weapon	Size/Force	Reach	Damage	AP/HP
Shortspear	*M*	*L*	*1d8+1d2*	*4/5*
Celtic Shield	*H*	*S*	*1d3+1+1d2*	*4/15*

Geheris, Headman of Builth

Characteristics	Attributes	1d20	Location	AP/HP
STR: 14	Action Points: 2	1–3	Right Leg	0/6
CON: 14	Damage Modifier: +1d2	4–6	Left Leg	0/6
SIZ: 15	Magic Points: 9	7–9	Abdomen	2/7
DEX: 13	Movement: 6 metres	10–12	Chest	2/8
INT: 14	Initiative Bonus: 12	13–15	Right Arm	0/5
POW: 9	Armour: Poor-Quality Leather Jerkin	16–18	Left Arm	0/5
CHA: 13		19–20	Head	0/6

Skills: *Athletics 61%, Boating 83%, Brawn 70%, Craft (Fishing) 80%, Craft (Netmaking) 80%, Customs (Celt) 90%, Endurance 66%, Evade 44%, Influence 65%, Insight 44%, Language (Brythonic) 100%, Lore (River Wye) 84%, Perception 51%, Superstition 70%, Unarmed 60%, Willpower 58%,*

Loyalty to Builth 100%, Love Family 90%, Admire Lucene 65%, Christian 80%

Combat Style: Self Defence (Dagger, Net) 63%.

Geheris's net is a half-repaired fishing net - a huge, long weapon with stones sewn into the bottom for ballast. It can't be thrown but it can entangle and the stones inflict only 1d2 damage if he lashes out with it. He can also wrap the net around his left arm to add 4 Armour Points if needed.

Weapon	Size/Force	Reach	Damage	AP/HP
Dagger	*S*	*S*	*1d4+1+1d2*	*6/8*
Fishing Net	*H*	*S*	*1d2+1d2*	*4/15*

Magda and Mebh (Twins - Same Characteristics for Both)

Characteristics	Attributes	1d20	Location	AP/HP
STR: 9	Action Points: 3	1–3	Right Leg	0/4
CON: 11	Damage Modifier: 0	4–6	Left Leg	0/4
SIZ: 9	Magic Points: 14	7–9	Abdomen	0/5
DEX: 14	Movement: 6 metres	10–12	Chest	0/6
INT: 14	Initiative Bonus: 14	13–15	Right Arm	0/3
POW: 12	Armour: None	16–18	Left Arm	0/3
CHA: 9		19–20	Head	0/4

Skills: *Athletics 40%, Brawn 27%, Customs (Celt) 90%, Deceit 52%, Endurance 36%, Evade 42%, Insight 42%, Language (Brythonic) 78%, Locale 90%, Lore (Herbs) 85%, Lore (Poisons) 80%, Perception 36%, Stealth 30%, Unarmed 25%, Willpower 46%*

Loyalty to Self 90%, Loyalty to Builth 55%, Hate Pagans 75%, Christian 85%

Combat Style: None

Magda is the dominant of the two and Mebh comes across as somewhat henpecked. He does, though, manage to sneak out and lead his own life from time to time and, when the two are working together on their herbalism, there is intense and close cooperation and a genuine joy in working closely together. Without each other, they would be bereft.

INDEX

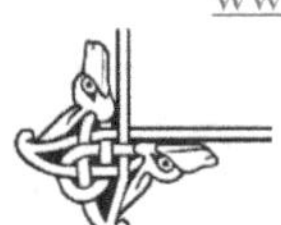

Additional Resources

Space regrettably precluded the inclusion of a character sheet in the print version of the book — although you will find one in the PDF version of Mythic Britain, directly after the Bibliography. You can download a character sheet from: www.thedesignmechanism.com/downloads.

Bibliography

All the works listed here were essential resources for *Mythic Britain* and are highly recommended for anyone wanting to learn more about the Dark Ages, Celts, Arthur and the Anglo Saxons. This is not an exhaustive list; merely the resources most influential for this book.

Of the non-fiction, Chris Gidlow's two exceptional books are especially recommended. They provide a fascinating and scholarly insight into the people and literature of the late Dark Ages and early Medieval periods of British history, but also a thoughtful and compelling analysis of how the Arthurian myth developed.

Of the fiction, Bernard Cornwell's *Warlord Chronicles* are, for me, the best depictions of the Arthurian saga from a historical viewpoint, and a major influence on this book. Huge liberties are taken with known events, and even huger ones with the major characters of the more traditional Arthurian stories (you will never look at Lancelot the same way again); but they are thrilling, visceral, well-told and thoroughly absorbing. I also recommend Robert Holdstock's *Merlin Codex* which creates a truly different, *mythical* Merlin and provides some of the best treatments of animistic magic anywhere in fantasy. In fact, I recommend *anything* by Robert Holdstock, who is one of the most underrated and overlooked fantasy writers of all time.

Where film and TV are concerned, resources are more patchy. I thoroughly recommend the HTV series *Arthur of the Britons*, starring Oliver Tobias and Brian Blessed (as King Mark!); if anything began my fascination with this period, it was this series, which was, for its time and limited budget, a superb attempt at a realistic Arthur. I have also included The History Channel's *Vikings* drama which, although 350 or so years later than Mythic Britain, is still an excellent depiction of the late Dark Ages, warfare, magic and the clash of pagan and Christian faiths. And, of course, John Boorman's glorious *Excalibur* is still the best film version of the traditional Arthurian legend. Two other films are worth mentioning: *First Knight* (with Richard Geere) and *King Arthur* (with Clive Owen): *avoid them both.*

I also want to cite two other roleplaying games as excellent references: Greg Stafford's masterpiece, *King Arthur Pendragon*, and Wordplay Games' *Age of Arthur*, by Graham Spearing and Paul Mitchener. I deliberately refrained from reading *Age of Arthur* while writing *Mythic Britain* because I didn't want to be unduly influenced by what Graham and Paul (both friends of mine!) were doing. But knowing the quality of their work, I have no hesitation in recommending their game here.

Non-Fiction

Arthur and the Anglo Saxon Wars, David Nicolle
Arthur The Dragon King, Howard Reid
Anglo Saxon Chronicle, The (Ann Savage Translation)
Battles of the Dark Ages, Peter Marren
Celts, The, Frank Delaney
Dictionary of Mythology, The, J A Coleman
Elements Encyclopedia of the Celts, The, Rodney Castleden
Encyclopedia of Mythology, The, Arthur Cotterell
Faded Map, The, Alistair Moffat
Gods, Heroes and Kings, Christopher R Fee
History of the Britons, Nennius
Lebor Faesa Runda, The, Steven L Akins
Mabinogion, The, Lady Charlotte Guest
Myths of the Celts, Frank Delaney
Old World Mythology, Dr Alice Mills
Reign of Arthur, The, Christopher Gidlow
Revealing Arthur, Christopher Gidlow

Fiction

Gate of Ivory, Gate of Horn, The, Robert Holdstock
Kingmaking, Helen Horlick
Lavondyss, Robert Holdstock
Le Mort d'Arthur, Sir Thomas Malory
Merlin, Robert Nye
Merlin Codex, The (Celtika, The Iron Grail, The Broken Kings), Robert Holdstock
Mists of Avalon, The, Marion Zimmer Bradley
Mythago Wood, Robert Holdstock
Warlord Chronicles, The (The Winter King, Enemy of God, Excalibur), Bernard Cornwell
Way of the Wyrd, The, Brian Bates

Film and Television

Arthur of the Britons, HTV, 1972-1973
Excalibur, John Boorman, 1981
Vikings (seasons 1 & 2), The History Channel, 2012-2014
Warrior Queen (Alex Kingston), Channel 4/WGBH, 2004

www.ingramcontent.com/pod-product-compliance
Lightning Source LLC
Chambersburg PA
CBHW081141300726
48982CB00006B/1030

* 9 7 8 0 9 8 7 7 2 5 9 5 0 *